**"Doctor Zhang?" she shouted, hammering
on one hatch after another.**

There were little windows set into the hatches. Inside the cabins she could only see a little, the corner of a bed or a glint of light reflecting off an empty cryotube. Then she came to the last cabin in the corridor and she looked in and saw . . .

No.

No, it couldn't be.

Beyond the little window was a lot of twisted metal and broken plastic and then – nothing. The void. Space.

PARADISE 1

DAVID WELLINGTON

orbit

orbitbooks.net

Copyright © 2023 by Little, Brown Book Group Limited

Cover design by Sean Garrehy
Cover images by Shutterstock

Orbit
Hachette Book Group
1290 Avenue of the Americas
New York, NY 10104
orbitbooks.net

First Edition: April 2023
Simultaneously published in Great Britain by Orbit

Orbit is an imprint of Hachette Book Group.
The Orbit name and logo are trademarks of Little, Brown Book Group Limited.

The publisher is not responsible for websites (or their content) that are not owned by the publisher.

The Hachette Speakers Bureau provides a wide range of authors for speaking events. To find out more, go to hachettespeakersbureau.com or email HachetteSpeakers@hbgusa.com.

Orbit books may be purchased in bulk for business, educational, or promotional use. For information, please contact your local bookseller or the Hachette Book Group Special Markets Department at special.markets@hbgusa.com.

Library of Congress Control Number: 2022948345

ISBNs: 9780316496742 (trade paperback), 9780316496889 (ebook)

Printed in the United States of America

LSC-C

Printing 1, 2023

For you, the readers. In 2003 I began serializing my first novel. Twenty years and twenty-two books later, all I want to say is thank you to everyone who's joined me along the way!

1
.

Three days still before dawn on Ganymede, and the cold
seeped right through her suit and into her bones. The only
light came from what reflected off the crescent of Jupiter, a thin
arc of brown and orange that hung forever motionless in the
night sky. Occasionally a bolt of lightning would snap across the
shadowed disk of the big planet, a bar of light big enough that
even from a million kilometers away it blasted long black shadows
across the charcoal ice of the moon.

Alexandra Petrova rotated her shoulders. Rolled her feet back
and forth in the powdery ice, just to get some blood moving
through her legs. She'd been lying prone for nearly six hours,
out on the edge of a ridgeline a long way from the warmth and
the unrecycled air of the Selket Crater habitat. Maybe, though,
her suffering was about to pay off.

"Firewatch One-Four, I have visual confirmation," she
whispered, and her suit's microphone picked up her words and
beamed them up to a satellite, which blasted them back down to
some operator in a control tower back in the crater, then trans-
ferred them over to the nice, cozy offices of Firewatch Division
Fourteen. The central headquarters of the Military Police on
Ganymede. "Subject is at a range of approximately three hundred
meters, headed north-northwest."

She lay as still as possible, not wanting to give away the slightest sign of her location. Just below her on the ridge a man was

carefully bounding his way downslope, hopping from boulder to boulder, headed into a maze of narrow little canyons. He was wearing a bright yellow spacesuit, skintight. No faceplate, just a pair of dark goggles. Half the workers on Ganymede wore suits like that – they were cheap and easily patched, and they came in bright colors so that if you died on the surface your body would be easier to recover. A bar code on his back identified the suit as belonging to one Dzama, Margaret.

Petrova knew that suit was stolen. The man inside was a former medical technician named Jason Schmidt and he was – allegedly – the worst serial killer in the century-long history of the Ganymede colony. Petrova had turned up evidence of more than twenty missing persons cases that led straight back to Schmidt. Not a single body had been found, but that wasn't too surprising. Ganymede might be one of the most densely colonized worlds of the solar system, but there was plenty of ice out there that still hadn't ever been explored. The perfect place to hide dead bodies.

"Firewatch One-Four," she said, "I am requesting permission to make an arrest on one Schmidt, Jason. I've already filed the paperwork. I just need a green light."

"Copy, Lieutenant," One-Four told her. "We're just reviewing the case now, making sure you're within your remit. We should be able to clear this any minute now. Stand by."

All the evidence against him was circumstantial, but Schmidt was her man. She was certain of it.

She'd better be. She was staking her whole career on this case. As a lieutenant inspector of Firewatch, she had broad powers to carry out her own investigations, but she couldn't afford to screw this one up. She knew very well she'd only gotten her job and her rank because of nepotism. The problem was, everybody else knew it, too. Her mother, Ekaterina Petrova, was the former director of Firewatch. Petrova had gone into the family business, and everyone believed she'd been given a free ride at the academy based on nothing but her mother's name.

Clearing this case would go a long way to showing she was more than just her mother's daughter. That she was capable of holding down this job on her own merits. The command level of Firewatch had just let all those missing persons cases go – presumably the new director, Lang, felt that a few missing miners from Ganymede weren't important enough to spend resources tracking them down. But bringing Schmidt in would be a real win for Lang as well as Petrova. It would make Firewatch look good – it would show the people of Ganymede that Firewatch was there to protect them. It would be a public relations coup.

She just had to convince someone in Selket Crater to give her final authorization to make the arrest. Which should not have been so difficult. Why were they dragging their feet?

"Firewatch, I need authorization to make this arrest. Please advise."

"Understood, Lieutenant. We're still waiting on final confirmation."

Below her, Schmidt stopped, perched atop a boulder. His head twisted from side to side as he scanned the landscape. Had he noticed her somehow? Or was he just lost in the dark?

"Copy," she said. Petrova crawled forward a meter or so. Just far enough that she could keep Schmidt in sight. Where was he headed? She'd suspected he had some kind of stash house out here on the ice, maybe a place where he kept trophies from his kills. She'd been following him for a while and she knew he often left the warmth of the city and came out here on his own for hours at a stretch. That worked for her. She would have a better chance catching him out of doors – in the city he could simply disappear into a crowd.

This would be the perfect time to act. Take him down out on the ice, preferably alive. Drag him back to a Firewatch covert site for interrogation. She reached down and touched the pistol mounted at her hip. Checked that it was loaded and ready. Of course it was. She'd cleaned and reassembled it herself. There was only one problem. A little light on the receiver of the pistol glowed a steady, unhelpful amber. Meaning she did not yet have permission to fire.

"I need that authorization, Firewatch," she said. "I need you to unlock my weapon. What's the hold-up?" She kept her voice down, even though there was little need. Ganymede's atmosphere was just a thin wisp of nothing. Sound didn't carry out on the ice. Still. A little paranoid caution might keep her alive.

Schmidt finally moved, jumping off his boulder and coming down hard in a loose pile of broken ice chips. He fell on his ass and planted his hands on either side of him, fingers splayed on the ground. He was unarmed. Vulnerable.

"Confirmation still pending. Director Lang has asked to sign off on this personally. Please be patient," Firewatch told her.

Petrova inhaled slowly. Exhaled slowly. Director Lang was getting personally involved? That could be good, it could mean that her superiors were showing an interest in her career. More likely though it was a problem. It could slow things to a crawl while she waited for the director's approval. Or worse. Lang might shut her down just out of spite.

When Petrova's mother had retired from Firewatch a year and a half ago, Lang had made it very clear that she wasn't going to cut her predecessor's daughter any slack. If Petrova had to wait for Lang's approval she might freeze to death out on the ice before it came.

Screw this, she was moving in. Once she had enough evidence to make her case against Schmidt, no one would question her collar.

She got her feet under her and jumped. In the low gravity it felt like flying, just a little bit. Maybe that was the adrenaline peaking in her bloodstream. She didn't care. She came down easy, two feet and a balled fist touching ice, right behind him. Her free hand drew her weapon and extended it in one fluid motion. "Jason Schmidt," she said. "By the authority of the UEG and Firewatch, I'm placing you under arrest."

Schmidt spun around and jumped to his feet. He was faster than she'd expected, more nimble.

At the same moment, someone spoke in Petrova's ear. "This is Firewatch One-Four ..."

Schmidt came straight at her, like he planned to tackle her. His move was idiocy. She had him at point-blank range. She brought her other hand up and steadied her weapon. It was a perfect shot. She knew she wouldn't miss.

" ... authorization has been checked ... "

Schmidt didn't slow down. He wasn't trying to talk her out of it. At this distance he couldn't fake her out, couldn't dodge her shot. She started to squeeze her trigger. If he really had killed all those people—

" ... and denied. Repeat, authorization of apprehension is denied."

The light on the receiver of the pistol changed from amber to red. The trigger froze in place – no matter how much strength she used, she couldn't make it move.

"Cease operations and return to your post immediately, Lieutenant. That's an order."

Petrova just had time to duck as Schmidt barreled into her, knocking her back into the ice, which burst apart in a shower of snow with the force of the impact. The breath exploded out of her lungs and for a second she couldn't see straight. Struggling to get up, to grab Schmidt, she missed and went sprawling, faceplate down into the snow. It only took a fraction of a second to twist around, get back on her feet, wipe the snow off her helmet so she could see—

But by then he was gone. Of course. And now he knew she was on his tail. He would run. Get as far away as he could, maybe leave Ganymede altogether and restart his murder spree somewhere else. She tilted her head back and raged at the blank stars.

2.

"Lieutenant, please confirm you received last order. Lieutenant? This is Firewatch One-Four, please confirm—"

She walked over to where her gun lay, half buried in the powdery ice. She grabbed it and slapped it back on her hip. The ice of Ganymede was a deep gray brown, but only on the surface. Where the gun had broken through the crust it left a glaring white silhouette.

Just like her boot prints, and the furrow in the snow where she'd been knocked down.

Just like the boot prints Jason Schmidt had left, which headed around a massive boulder and into the shadow of the ridgeline. Bright white footprints standing out against the dark ice. And what was that she saw, from over that direction? It looked like a light. Artificial light sweeping across the dark surface. It must be coming from some structure over there. Some hiding spot.

Maybe a trophy room.

"Lieutenant? Please acknowledge."

She crept around the side of the boulder and saw exactly what she'd expected to find. The light came from an old emergency shelter, basically a prospector's hut. A big metal hatch was stuck into the ice and a light on the hatch flickered slowly on-off, on-off – the universal signal that the bunker behind that hatch was activated, full of air and warmth. Like a chased rabbit, Jason Schmidt had run for a bolt-hole.

It would be crazy to follow him in. To literally walk into his lair, when he knew she was coming. When her gun was locked down.

"Lieutenant? Come in, Lieutenant. This is Firewatch One-Four. Lieutenant, do you copy?"

Petrova slapped a big button on the face of the hatch and the airlock beyond blasted out air, equalizing pressures. She stepped inside and closed the outer door behind her. A moment later, the inner hatch slid open and she looked down into darkness.

"In pursuit, One-Four. I'll check in when I get a chance."

She switched off her radio. It wasn't going to tell her anything she wanted to hear.

Beyond the lock's inner door lay a concrete-lined corridor that spiraled down into the ice. Tiny light fixtures on the ceiling and walls lit up bright as she passed, then dimmed again behind her. Condensation hung in long, stalactite-like beads from the ceiling, spikes of pure water waiting for Ganymede's low gravity to finally bring them plopping down on the floor. At the bottom of the spiral, the corridor opened into a larger space. She expected to see a big room filled with crates of emergency supplies and old mining gear.

Instead the main room of the bunker was open, cleared out. The concrete floor was stained and damp but clear of debris. Dark chambers – caves, basically – led off the main chamber in every direction. This place was huge, she realized. This wasn't just an emergency bunker. It must be an entire mine complex, though it looked like it had been abandoned.

She thought she heard something – a real sound, echoing in the concrete space full of actual air. She crouched down and tried to stay perfectly still. There was no good place to hide, but maybe Schmidt hadn't seen her come in.

She ducked low into a shadow as he stepped out of one of the side caves. He'd shucked his suit down to the waist, the arms and hood hanging down behind him like tails. He had a large crate in his arms and he dumped its contents on the floor without ceremony. "I'm back," he called, in a sing-song voice, like he was calling to pets who'd been waiting for him to come home.

Petrova watched as the crate's contents slithered out onto the floor. Hundreds of silver foil packets. Colorful pictures were printed on each packet, showing a serving of some mouth-watering foodstuff. Pureed carrots. Mushroom stew. Algae salad. Petrova recognized the pictures right away, as would anyone who had spent time on Ganymede. She knew the pictures were nothing but lies. There was food inside the packets, food nutritious enough to keep you alive, but it never resembled the tempting picture. Instead it was more likely to be a thin gray slop grown in a big bioreactor: proteins and carbohydrates excreted by gene-tailored bacteria in a vat of sugar water. It was the kind of food that workers got when they couldn't afford anything better, when they'd run out of luck. The government of Ganymede wouldn't let any of its people starve, but the alternative wasn't much better.

"Come and get it," Schmidt called out, in that same lilting cadence.

She was about to move in and put him under arrest when she caught a flicker of motion from one of the caves. Bright eyes glistened back there, catching the light. The filthiest, most unkempt human being she'd ever seen came rushing out, almost running on all fours. It was dressed in rags and its face was so grimy she couldn't tell its gender or even its age. It moved cautiously as it approached Schmidt, as if it was afraid of him. It didn't say a word, didn't so much as mumble a greeting.

"All yours," Schmidt said, and stepped away from the pile of food packets.

A hint of motion from another cave mouth grabbed Petrova's attention. Then another – soon people were emerging from a dozen directions at once. All of them as dirty and decrepit as the first. They moved quickly to grab silver packets from the pile, then they raced back toward their caves as if afraid someone would try to take the food away from them. They tore the packets open with their teeth, then stuck their fingers inside. They shoved the food straight into their mouths, getting as much of it on their skin and in their beards as they actually ingested. Their faces sagged with relief, as if they'd been starved for days and this was the best thing they'd ever tasted.

Petrova had no idea what was going on. Time to get some answers.

She rose to her full height. "Schmidt," she called out. "Keep your hands visible."

Schmidt winced but at least this time he didn't just come running at her like a bull.

"Jason Schmidt, you are under arrest. Back up against that wall. *Facing* the wall," she ordered.

He shook his head. His hands were up, in front of him, but he wasn't holding them up to show he was unarmed. He beseeched her with them. It looked like he might fall on his knees and beg her for mercy.

She needed answers. She needed to know what was going on. "You," she called, to the nearest of the unwashed people, who was busy licking out the insides of a third food packet. "Is this man holding you prisoner? Do you need help?"

The man – at least, he had a beard – looked up at her as if noticing her existence for the first time. He dropped the foil packet and stumbled towards her. His hands clawed and patted at the air, seemingly at random. Despite herself, Petrova took a step back as he came closer. His mouth opened but the sound he let out wasn't a word. Just a raw syllable, cut loose from any kind of meaning.

"Do you need help?" Petrova repeated. "Are you trying to ask for help?"

"He can't do that," Schmidt said. She jabbed her pistol in his direction and he shut up, lifting his hands higher in the air.

The victim came closer still and grabbed at Petrova's arm.

She pulled away from his touch and he grabbed for her helmet, instead, grasping one of the lamps mounted on its side. He let out a crude fricative, his mouth opening wide, spittle flying everywhere. She had to shove him, hard, to get loose.

Someone else hissed like a snake. All of Schmidt's other victims were making sounds now, raw noise, just the roots of words.

"What's going on?" Petrova asked. "What did you do to these people?"

Were these the missing persons she'd been tracking? She'd assumed Schmidt had murdered them all. But if they were here, alive, apparently kept captive—

They were moving now, all of them. Lumbering toward her, their hands describing shapes in the air, or clawing at nothing. Their faces were contorted in strange expressions she couldn't understand. They spoke only in meaningless monosyllables. *Ph. Kr. La.*

They grabbed at her, clinging to her legs, her arms. Petrova had to dance backward to get away from them. They weren't particularly strong – now she saw them up close she could see how emaciated and sickly they looked under their coating of dirt – but there were a lot of them.

"Get back," she told them. "Stay back! Firewatch!"

"They don't understand," Schmidt called.

Schmidt – she'd lost track of him. As the clawing, swiping people came at her, she'd forgotten to keep an eye on him. She twisted around and saw him creeping backward up the ramp, toward the surface. His hands were still up but he was getting away.

One of the victims growled, raising her voice as she bashed at the back of Petrova's suit with weak fists. She yelped like a dog.

Petrova pushed her away, harder perhaps than she should have. She was getting scared, she could feel it. She was afraid of these poor wretched people – she needed to get a grip.

She needed to get the situation under control. Well, she knew where to start. Schmidt was all but running up the ramp, away from her. She dashed after him and smacked him across the back of his neck with the butt of her pistol. "Down!" she said. "Get down and stay down, motherfucker." She hit him again and this time he fell down. "What did you do?" she demanded, as he tried to get up. She hit him again. "What did you do?"

Schmidt rolled on the floor, rolled until he was lying on his back. He lifted his hands to his face. She realized he was sobbing.

What the hell?

She retrieved a pair of smart handcuffs from a pouch at her belt. Moving fast, she grabbed Schmidt and shoved his face up against the concrete wall. She touched the cuffs to his hands and they came to life, twisting thick tendrils of plastic around his wrists and fingers, locking them in place. He made no effort to resist.

"Oh, thank God," he moaned. Quietly. His eyes were clamped shut. "Oh, thank you."

"What the hell is wrong with you?" she asked.

"It's over," he said. "It's finally over."

"What did you do to those people? What's wrong with them?"

"It's acute aphasia, it's ... it's—"

"They can't talk," Petrova said. "I got that. Why? Did you ... did you do something to them?"

"I *saved* them," Schmidt whined.

She stared at the back of his head, unable to comprehend. She had no idea what was going on. Then she glanced down at the pistol in her hands. The light there remained a steady, unchanging amber. Great.

"Tell me everything," she said. "Then I'll decide what to do with you."

3
.

His face changed dramatically. All the hope drained out of
it, and he nodded in resignation.

"Just ... come with me. I need to show you something."

She got him up on his feet. "We're not going anywhere until
my backup gets here," she said. She glanced down the ramp, at
the naked, filthy people down there. They had gone back to tearing open food packets and devouring their contents. They seemed
occupied enough with their meal not to notice her or Schmidt.

Scowling, she tried to decide how she should proceed.
Answers, she thought. "Just tell me what happened. All the
details. Now."

For once he actually complied. He started talking and quickly
fell into the cadence of someone accustomed to giving reports on
the medical status of a patient. "It started at the hospital in the
Nergal Crater habitat, a couple hundred kilometers from here.
There was just one of them at first, an elderly male. He presented
with aphasia, like I said. The doctors couldn't find a cause for it,
though. There was no sign of physical trauma, no sign of disease.
He was perfectly healthy – but he couldn't talk. More than that,
he couldn't communicate at all."

"What do you mean?" Petrova demanded.

"Like, at all. Normally, if somebody can't talk, even in cases of
profound aphasia they can still get something across. Sometimes
they can still read and write, or at the very least they can use

gestures and facial expressions. You can tell if they understand what you're saying. They can cry or frown to tell you they're in pain. This patient, though, he was clearly trying to communicate but his efforts didn't make any sense." Schmidt shook his head sadly. "He would wave his hands around, his face would twist up in these expressions nobody could read ... "

"That was one patient," Petrova said. "I saw nearly twenty people down there."

Schmidt nodded. "Yes. The second one to come in was an adolescent girl. That really worried the doctors. With elderly patients you see all kinds of neurological complaints, but young people – it's rare. Really rare. Next came a whole family, and the doctors worried this thing was contagious, but they couldn't find any kind of pathogen, any kind of cause. Soon we had a whole ward of them ...

"That was when things changed. The doctors decided they couldn't be cured. There wasn't any kind of treatment we could give them." Schmidt sniffed volubly. "They were going to send the patients to a special facility. I knew what that meant. Those people weren't going to be patients anymore. They were going to run tests on them – until they ran out of tests and then – then these poor people were going to be *dissected*." Schmidt's face was racked with anguish. She was certain he was telling the truth. "I couldn't let that happen."

"So you kidnapped a bunch of patients from a hospital and brought them – here?"

"Yes," Schmidt said. "To save them."

"And now—"

"Now I feed them! I try to keep them healthy. There's only so much I can do but ... but I couldn't let them ... I couldn't ... " He opened his eyes. "What are you going to do with them?" he asked.

"That's not up to me," she said.

His eyes searched her face for a long time. Perhaps he was

trying to find some mercy there. She honestly wished she had some to offer. Eventually, he just nodded. Resigned, perhaps, to the fact that things were out of his hands.

"I can't look at them anymore," he said, turning his face to look up the ramp. "Please. There's a place up there, a room where we can wait for your friends. Can we just go there?"

He looked like a beaten dog. He was making no effort to get away from her. Best to make sure, though. She yanked his suit down over his legs, gestured for him to step out of it. Without the suit he wasn't going anywhere – he would die the second he stepped out of the airlock. She nodded and gestured up the ramp. "You go first."

Schmidt led her up to a door near the top of the ramp. Petrova noticed an odd light coming from inside the room beyond the door. "Don't move," she said. No worries there. Schmidt sank down to sit on the floor, his head between his knees. He looked beaten. Done.

She reached over to touch the release pad that opened the door. It slid open easily. She glanced inside but there wasn't much in there, just a pile of what looked like computer parts in one corner. An unstable hologram flickered next to them, showing the three-dimensional image of a little boy made of light. He sat curled up, his face buried in his knees. The reddish light the hologram gave off was the only illumination in the room.

"What the hell is this?" Petrova demanded. She was only peripherally aware that she had stepped over the threshold, into the room.

"It's an old AI core. You should talk to it."

"What?" she asked, so distracted she barely heard him.

She watched the little hologram boy as it started to rise to its feet. The light it emitted had begun to turn a darker red, and she wanted to know what that meant.

She wasn't watching Schmidt. Dumb mistake. Without warning he kicked the door shut and she heard it lock automatically.

"No!" she said. "No!" She dropped her pistol and raced to the door, both hands up to slap at the release pad. Uselessly. It couldn't be opened from inside. She hammered on the door, over and over. "Schmidt! Schmidt!" She pounded and pounded but there was no answer.

Goddammit! she thought. What a stupid mistake she'd made – a real rookie blunder. All of her training, everything she'd put into learning the job and . . . and she went and did the one stupid thing no inspector was ever supposed to do, underestimating a subject.

You need to be tough, to do this job. Sashenka, you are not tough.

Her mother had said that to her, a hundred times over. Her mother, who had done this same job herself, who had basically written the playbook. Maybe her mother was right about her, Petrova thought, and her heart sank in her chest. She didn't have time to spiral, though. She heard something behind her. A noise like paper rustling maybe, or – no. Like a tiny voice, whispering to her.

Every muscle in her body froze at once.

The whisper came again. So quiet, so soft. She couldn't understand what it was saying, but she was certain it was the little boy. The hologram. It was trying to talk to her. Red light flooded the room, cast long black shadows across the floor.

"What do you want?" she asked.

The whisper was so tantalizing. She could hear words in there, she was certain if she just tried a little harder she could understand what the boy was saying. She felt a desperate urge to just turn around, to look at the boy. If she did, she thought she would understand.

But there was another voice inside her. Her mother's voice. Still admonishing her for her stupidity but now – warning her as well.

Don't look, foolish girl. If you turn around you'll be lost.

But the whispering continued. Words she was certain she would understand just fine, if she would just turn and look, if she looked at the boy's lips—

Petrova almost felt like she couldn't resist. Like there was no point to even fighting now. She recognized those feelings didn't strictly belong to her. She didn't know what that meant.

She realized with a start that she was panting for breath.

Her eyes were clamped shut. Slowly, carefully, she opened them. She started to turn, to turn around to face the boy. She knew that once she looked she wouldn't be able to unsee what was over there in the corner, but there was a big part of her that had to know.

Do not look, Sashenka. You need to be strong, now.

She shouldn't look. She couldn't. Looking would doom her in some way she couldn't imagine but she was certain, certain it would be the end of her.

She couldn't look.

She couldn't.

She couldn't not look.

The whispers wouldn't let her go.

She was nearly crying from the effort of trying to resist. She had to fight her whole body. It wanted this. What a relief it would be to just give in. All her problems, all her worries would be over. If she just.

Turned around.

And looked.

She started to turn, to move toward the boy—

Then she stopped. She'd seen something near her feet. Just a patch of color. The entire room was bathed in a blood red glow, except for one tiny patch of the floor, which was glowing a bright, agreeable green.

The green came from a light on the receiver of her pistol, which lay where she'd dropped it on the floor.

Someone over at Firewatch One-Four had finally given her permission to use her weapon.

She snatched it up in both hands. Eyes closed, she twisted around and blasted away at the old AI core, yanked the trigger over and over again until – finally – the whispers went away. Her head started to clear as she ran for the door. It was still locked, but a few quick kicks with her boot opened it.

She lurched out into the hallway, eyes wide. She had no idea what had just happened. What would have happened, if she hadn't . . . if she . . .

She couldn't stop and think about that. "Schmidt," she called out. "Schmidt! You're coming with me. We're going to figure this out and then—"

He was right behind her. Dazed as she was, mind still reeling, she'd fallen for the oldest trick in the book. He had a massive wrench and he came in low, swinging hard for her side. The least-armored part of her suit. His strike connected and Petrova gasped in pain. Tumbling to the floor, she fought to turn, to get herself in a position to fight back.

"You killed him," Schmidt said. "You killed him, you killed him . . . you . . ."

He was weeping. The tears pooled around his eyes in the low gravity, only slowly dripping onto his cheeks. His voice descended into a howl of pure anguish as he lifted the wrench to strike at her again.

"Don't," she said, almost begging him. If he attacked her she would have no choice but to defend herself. "Just drop it!"

He didn't drop it. He didn't stop. Instead he roared and came at her, clearly intending to smash her helmet in.

So she took the shot.

4.

Someone gave Petrova a cup full of hot water with lemon flavoring. It was a tiny act of kindness but it nearly left her in tears. She felt raw, like a layer of her skin had been strip-mined off. Every new thing made her wince, made her want to curl up.

Her backup had arrived. There were so many of them they filled the main room of the abandoned mine, like they'd been crammed inside. Petrova sat on top of a crate next to the spiral ramp. As close to the surface as she could get. Out of the way.

When she reached the surface, when she was clear of the mine, she had called in what she'd seen. Called in the death of Jason Schmidt and what he'd been doing. Firewatch had acted fast.

Firewatch One-Four sent a whole team of technicians and analysts, people to take samples of everything – the dew on the ceiling, the contents of the shelter's chemical toilet. They spent a long time taking pictures of Schmidt's body.

A team of computer techs came and dismantled the shattered AI core and took it away. Petrova didn't even look at the computer parts as they were hauled out.

Troopers in heavy, bite-proof armor came and herded the others – Schmidt's victims – back into one of the caves. Petrova didn't see what was happening back there.

Investigators came to ask her questions. The same questions, over and over again. The bare facts of the matter. Whenever she tried to offer new information, or any kind of analysis, they shut her down. All they wanted was a timeline of events.

She had a lot of questions herself. Nobody would answer any of them. They just told her to wait until a superior officer could arrive. Hours went by and still the refrain was the same – wait for the brass. There was nothing else required of her at this time.

Petrova was hardly surprised. Firewatch loved digging up everyone's secrets, but it kept its own close to its chest. Under her mother's tenure, the organization had turned ever inwards, getting more cloistered and more paranoid. Ekaterina Petrova had regularly purged her officer corps, just to keep them on their toes, and while the new directorship had loosened things up a little, everyone was still too scared to stand out or do anything outside of protocol.

So Petrova sat, and waited, and wished she could go someplace warm and maybe take a shower. After a while the investigators stopped even asking her to repeat her story. After that, all Petrova *could* do was wait.

Finally, after hours of waiting, there came a clamor around the shelter's entrance and everyone pulled back, making room, as the newcomer entered the bunker.

Director Lang had arrived.

The director, herself. Mama's replacement. Her usurper, if you believed the rumors. What was Lang doing here? Her office was on Earth's moon. Had she been nearby anyway, and decided to check in on this case personally? Petrova found it hard to believe that such an important woman would take a fast flight out as far as Jupiter just to see a crime scene.

Yet here she was.

The director reached up and tripped a catch at her collar which released her helmet. It broke apart into pieces and retracted into the back of her suit. She took a deep breath of the air in the mine as if she were sniffing it. Apparently she didn't like what she smelled, judging by the look on her face.

She was a woman of perhaps sixty years with iron-colored hair cut very short. In her armored suit she couldn't help but look a bit like Boadicea, a warrior queen with steely eyes. She came straight over to Petrova and stood before her, spine ramrod straight.

"Are you hurt, Lieutenant?" the director asked. She had a clipped, patrician British accent, something you rarely heard on Ganymede. "Physically?"

"Not significantly, ma'am," Petrova said. She started to climb down from her crate, even if that meant putting her bare feet on the freezing concrete floor. "I'll have a nasty bruise or two. I was briefly in danger but I was able to protect myself and—"

Director Lang slapped her across the cheek. Her hard suit glove sent Petrova's head flying to the side and she felt like her teeth shook in their sockets.

"You walked right into this without authorization. That's the equivalent of disobeying an order. It is in my power to have you court-martialed for this."

Petrova couldn't believe it. She rose to attention, not wanting to give the director any new reason to discipline her. "Ma'am, this subject – Schmidt – was a—"

"Person of interest," Lang said.

"That's . . . right. A POI in an ongoing investigation. I suspected he was involved in a number of missing persons cases which remained uncleared, so I tracked him here. I've been working for weeks on this."

"Firewatch," the director said, "has been following Jason Schmidt for nearly a year."

Petrova frowned. She didn't understand. "There was no official file on him. No one said anything to me. Nobody warned me off the case."

"You were told to wait for authorization. Was that not clear enough? Perhaps we should have formally requested that you desist from ruining one of the most complex ongoing investigations in Firewatch history. Which is exactly what you've done here, today."

Petrova stared at her toes. A year – nearly a year, Lang had said. But that meant Firewatch had known who he was almost from the beginning of his crime spree. They'd let him go on kidnapping people. Stashing them away here. Had Firewatch known where the victims were the whole time? "This man needed to be taken down. He was not your common breed of criminal."

Lang stuck out her lower jaw and tilted her head back. She looked like she was barely restraining herself from slapping Petrova again. "I'm not going to debate orders with you. Count yourself lucky you still have a job." She turned as if she was about to walk away and leave it at that.

Petrova knew better. "Someone authorized me to use my weapon," she said. "Someone was watching me the whole time, even after I came down here."

"Yes," Lang said. "Someone did make that authorization. That someone was not me."

For a split second Petrova didn't understand. "Who?" she asked, before she could stop herself. Because before Lang answered, she already knew the answer.

"There are people in this organization who still think your mother was a hero. That she could do no wrong. These same people think that if Ekaterina Petrova's daughter wants to shoot somebody, it must be justified."

"Ma'am," Petrova said, "I've never asked for special treatment—"

"No. You hardly needed to." Lang looked up and around the room. "All the advantages your mother gave you. All the opportunities and special assignments and recommendations whispered in the right ears . . . and still you fuck up."

"Ma'am," Petrova said.

"Nepotism is going to destroy Firewatch, in the end. You understand that's a problem, yes? People out here, especially in the outer planets, depend on us. We're the only security they have. I have people working under me who actually deserve the position you're filling. People who can actually do the job. So I'm removing you from your current duties."

Petrova's whole body burned. She licked her lips, desperate to say something. Anything in her defense. She grunted with the effort of holding back what she really wanted to say, which was, *You have no idea what my mother gave me. What her legacy really amounts to.*

She wanted to scream it.

But this was hardly the time or the place.

"Yes, ma'am," Petrova said. "I understand."

"I have a new assignment for you," Director Lang said. "One that'll keep you out of my way for a while."

"May I ask what it is?"

"I'm going to send you to check in on your mother. See how she's getting along in her new life."

Petrova didn't understand. "My mother? You want me to ... go see my mother?" She shook her head. *This doesn't make any sense.* "But she's retired now. She went to one of the new colony worlds. Paradise-1," she said. "It's a hundred light years from here and – oh."

Because she got it, then. It would take months for her to travel all the way to Paradise-1. Enough time, perhaps, for Lang to clean her house and get all of Ekaterina's old cronies out of their offices.

"There's an actual purpose to this mission beyond just annoying you, Lieutenant. Paradise-1 is overdue for a security analysis. I need a lieutenant inspector to run out there and make sure the colony is happy and productive. You're exactly who I want for the job."

"Yes, ma'am," Petrova said, because there was nothing else to say.

There had been a rumor, back when Ekaterina retired, that she hadn't done so voluntarily. That Lang had deposed her in a bloodless, silent coup. Ekaterina had certainly had her enemies. Many people would have been glad to have seen her sent to prison, or executed, instead of being allowed to gracefully step down. When instead she announced she would be moving to a distant colony it had been suggested that was code for *going into exile.*

Well, it looked like her daughter was going to follow in her footsteps.

Director Lang was done with her, and apparently done with the bunker. She turned and started to walk away. Petrova knew she should just lower her head in shame and pretend she no longer existed. She couldn't help herself, though. She had to ask.

"What happened to these people?"

Lang turned a few degrees to look at Petrova over her shoulder.

"I don't know what you're talking about."

"The ... the people, the patients that Schmidt kidnapped from his hospital. He was holding them down here in terrible conditions and in the end they ... they ... "

"I've been fully briefed on this case," Lang told her. "No such people exist. As of now, no such people *ever* existed. Is that clear?"

Petrova glanced toward the dark cave where the victims were being held. She hadn't heard a sound from that cave in quite a while. Her blood turned to chunks of ice in her veins.

"Yes, ma'am."

5.

Zhang Lei closed his eyes. He opened them again and he was walking down a long staircase, a staircase with no railing. It was so dark he couldn't see anything, but he knew every step was covered in bodies. In bones. The flesh had rotted away, the skin was gone, the clothing just scraps. The bones remained.

It was dark. So dark. He was terrified that he was going to fall. That he would trip and fall and go clattering down into the pile of bones.

There was nothing to hold on to. He turned sideways to take a step downward, one foot extended toward the next step, toes stretched out too cautiously. He gingerly pushed a sternum and a couple of ribs away, to clear room, to make it safe to step down.

He took the step. Let himself breathe for a moment. Then, very carefully, he lowered his other foot, probing forward to make sure he wasn't stepping on anything. When he was certain the step would take his weight, he exhaled and reached for another step . . .

. . . and immediately his foot touched the curve of a skull and he started to slip, started to tumble forward. He threw his hands out to catch himself and one hand closed around a femur and he screeched and threw it away, but his other hand touched nothing, just empty air. He tumbled forward, faster and faster, the stone steps rising up to come rushing at his face, bones clattering and bouncing all around him, falling down the stairs in an avalanche of dust and broken, razor-sharp fragments, and all he could do was—

He closed his eyes.

He opened his eyes again, and just like that he was in a new place. Alone, half asleep on a train, and Jupiter hung in the sky like the blade of a sickle. Like a curse.

Little by little, he came back to himself.

Little by little, he realized where he actually was. On Ganymede. Right where he was supposed to be.

He rubbed at his eyes and his forehead, trying to shake off the dream. Sometimes it was hard. Sometimes it stuck with him all day.

He tried to focus on things he knew were real, things he could prove.

The train floated on magnetic currents that rushed ever onward, like a river. It floated over a landscape of gray ice and powdery brown snow, pockmarked here and there by the brighter ovals of shallow craters like ripples in a fetid pond.

He was alone on the train. That was good, because he didn't want anyone to see him like this.

It was also bad, because he wasn't sure if he was going to be okay.

His heart was thundering in his ribcage. He felt like he was going to die. He knew that the solution was to try to stay calm. To think calm thoughts. He was a doctor. He knew the difference between a heart attack and an anxiety attack.

Tiny fangs sank into his wrist. He gasped in pain for a second, then relaxed as chemicals flooded his bloodstream. Drugs to slow his racing pulse, to ease his blood pressure down into a safe range.

He looked down at the golden bracer that was wrapped around his left forearm, a tracery of golden tendrils that writhed across his flesh as he watched. One tendril clutched hard against his wrist and when it withdrew he saw two tiny points of blood on the vein there, like the bite of a snake. The device had administered the drugs. He had not been asked for his permission, nor had the device asked him to consult on the dosage. The people who had made the device and calibrated it for his use had not felt that he should be allowed to adjust or refuse its attentions.

He supposed he'd given them reasons enough not to trust him.

There had been one bad night in a hotel on Mars. He'd locked himself in and then when they finally broke down the door – well, someone had to pay off the cleaning staff, and Zhang had to spend several hours in surgery. But it was fine now. They'd asked him what happened and he told them he had been going through a rough patch. The doctor who examined him had called it a psychotic break. He was better now. He was a doctor himself and he was qualified to make that determination. He was fine. He was going to be fine.

He told himself the same thing every morning when he woke up from the dream of the stairs. And every night when he went to sleep, before the dream began again. The affirmation made nice little brackets to put around the dreams.

I am fine. I am going to be fine.

Zhang needed to clear his head. If he kept letting these thoughts chase each other around his head he was just going to worsen the anxiety, think himself into real medical distress. He got up and went to the front of the train car, which was one big window. He looked out across the gray-brown snow toward his destination. There was a fragile little soap bubble out there, a few kilometers away: the spaceport that was his destination. It looked like it might pop at any moment. Perched atop that bubble like a roosting bird was a fast transport starship, all sleek curves and a sharply pointed nose. *Artemis*, it was called. He was going to take a little trip on that vessel. Maybe, he thought, getting away from the solar system would do him some good.

He sat back in his chair and let the drugs work. Already, he could feel himself calming down, feel his heart slow. *Okay*, he thought. *Okay. I can do this.*

In, out, he told himself. Good air in, bad air out. He closed his eyes. With no warning a memory raced through his head like an arrow shot from a bow.

He was back on Titan, in an underground cave. He was racing down a hallway, out of breath. Terrified. "Holly," he shouted. "Holly, I think we're in trouble." He grabbed at the airlock to the medical section but it was sealed.

He didn't understand. How had he locked himself out of his own clinic?

Holly came and stood in front of the inner door, looking at him through the glass.

"Hol," he said, laughing a little. "Let me in. I locked myself out somehow," he told her.

Her mouth trembled. It looked like she was going to start crying. Her face was turning red, bright red, even as her lips were turning pale. The first signs of the Red Strangler.

He placed the palms of his hands against the glass. "Holly. Please." He could barely see her through the hot tears that gathered in his eyes.

She wasn't breathing. Her lips turned dark, cyanotic. Her eyes filmed over and the flesh started to melt from her face, to drip away in thick, hot gobbets of protoplasm, until he could see the yellow skull underneath—

He opened his eyes and stared around him, stared at the train, at the ice of Ganymede outside the windows. Everything was ringing, it was like bells tolling all around him until he realized it was his own voice he was hearing, echoing in his ears.

His own scream, echoing like thunder.

Golden fangs sank into his wrist, again and again.

6

•

A few minutes later, the train slid into its station underneath the spaceport.

Its doors opened quietly, but before he could disembark, someone stepped inside and came to stand over him.

"Zhang Lei?" they said.

"That's me," he said, without looking up.

A woman stepped around him to get into his field of view. She was shorter than him – she had the look of someone who had grown up on Earth, in its heavy gravity. You could always recognize Earthlings from their aura of ruddy health, the glow of strength and vigor that came from fresh air and sunlight. To someone from the outer system, like Zhang, they always looked wrong. Human beings, in his experience, were supposed to be tall, thin and very pale, with shadows under their eyes. People from Earth looked like cartoons.

"I'm Lieutenant Alexandra Petrova. You can call me Sasha. Everyone does." She held out a hand for him to shake.

"Oh," he said. "I'm sorry. I don't touch other people if I can avoid it."

"Right," she said. She smiled broadly as if she'd just gotten the punchline of a joke. Funny, he hadn't made one. "They told me you were some kind of medical specialist. Colony medicine, right? I suppose a little healthy germaphobia goes with the job."

"Does it?"

Her smile flickered like a light attached to bad wiring. Zhang could tell he was making a bad impression.

"Sorry," he said. He pushed past her, into the spaceport entrance. "I'd love to talk but I have a flight to catch."

"I . . . know," she said. "I'm with Firewatch," she told him, smiling at him as she followed him up a long sloping corridor. "In case you don't recognize my uniform. Don't worry, I'm not here to arrest you or anything." She laughed and he thought she might be trying to be funny again, even though the idea of being arrested just caused him anxiety.

"That's reassuring to hear. Did they send you to make sure I actually board *Artemis*? Because I have every intention of doing so, if there are no further delays."

Her smile shrank again. "I'm . . . I'm on the same ship."

"Ah," he said. "So you're my new babysitter."

"Doctor—"

"Let me save you some time. So you don't need to surveil me for the rest of the day, here's a rundown of my plans: I'm here to follow my orders like a good little boy. I'm going to board this spaceship, find a bunk, and unpack. In a couple of hours they're going to put me in a cryotube and send me to sleep for three months. I'm thinking I might masturbate beforehand. If I have a bowel movement, I'll be sure to save it in a plastic bag so you can examine it at your convenience."

Her face went very still. Very tight.

He'd said something very wrong, he realized. He did that, sometimes.

"I'm not here to watch over you. My job," she said, "is strategic analysis. I'm supposed to assess the security status of the Paradise-1 colony. We're going to be working together for the foreseeable future. I'm not your handler. We're colleagues. I just wanted to introduce myself."

"Your name is Petrova," he said. "I'm Zhang. There. We've met." He walked past her, into his departure lounge. He just wanted to get this over with.

7.

Sam Parker didn't even notice as his passengers came into the lounge. He was too busy running *Artemis*, his ship, through its pre-flight check. She was a sleek, aerodynamic transport designed to get people from one end of the galaxy to the other with incredible speed. In the ten years he'd been a pilot they'd never let him fly something so advanced.

He wasn't entirely sure how he'd got the job, this time.

Parker had had dreams, once. He'd wanted to be a test pilot, risking his life on pushing spacecraft past all endurance just to prove he could. To get that kind of work you had to prove you were pretty hot shit in the military, so he'd signed on with Firewatch as soon as he could, at the age of eighteen. It hadn't been easy for a kid like him – he'd been born in the wrong part of the solar system, too far from the sun. A youth spent on low gravity worlds and habitats had left him extremely tall and thin and there'd been some question about whether he could even fit into the cockpits of the most advanced starfighters.

In the end it hadn't been his gangly knees and elbows that sank his chances, though. It had been his pride. A flight instructor had asked whether his bones could even handle the G-stress of a fast maneuver in a Corsair-class fighter, and Parker had tried to show the jerk just how strong his knuckles were.

Turned out the instructor had been made out of pig iron. He took Sam's best shot, and gave him one right back. To this day, whenever Parker went someplace humid, he still felt that hit in his jaw. He smirked to himself, now, in defiance. The instructor had blackballed him, kept him from flying ever again. Parker had taken any job he could get that let him get behind the controls of a spacecraft – moving construction supplies around the orbital habitats around Neptune, ferrying garbage out to deep space, even working as a shuttle pilot for VIPs around Mars. It had taken years, but now—

A scale hologram image of *Artemis* floated in the center of the departure lounge. She was just too beautiful, honestly. She looked fast and powerful, like a shark, with graceful, curving lines that converged on a bridge that looked like the beak of a predatory bird. He was supposed to be checking the ship's reactor shielding, but he couldn't help reaching up and running a hand along her smooth side.

The scale model of the ship was one of the new kind of holograms – hard light, they called them. The image itself was nothing but light, laser light, diffracted through space. He was touching nothing at all. The projection pushed back against his hand, though, using the same technology that ships used to generate artificial gravity. It was all done with a simple feedback loop. The computer that generated the hologram predicted where his hand would be and what kind of texture it would encounter, and pushed back with the appropriate level of resistance.

It was the kind of tech you normally only found in a military installation, not a civilian spaceport. It probably cost more to generate the image than he was getting paid for the next six months. He really, really liked the way it felt.

It felt like he was finally getting somewhere. Proving something to the world. He knew he was a hell of a pilot. Maybe the powers that be were starting to realize that, too. Even if his duties were going to be pretty limited – the ship had a first rate, cutting edge AI onboard that would do most of the actual flying. He would only fly her in emergencies or in a situation the AI couldn't handle, which was pretty unlikely to come up. Still. Someone had shown confidence in him, to give him this posting.

"She's beautiful," a woman said, from behind his elbow.

"You think this is something. I've got the keys for the real thing. Want to take her for a spin?" He let a smile spread across his face as he turned to look at who he was talking to. He'd glanced at *Artemis*' passenger manifest before he'd started his pre-flight check, but it hadn't occurred to him to read the names. This woman was with Firewatch, he knew that, and—

—and as he turned around, he realized he'd made a mistake. He should have read those names. Because then he wouldn't be so gobsmacked now.

"Sam," she said, and there was a tone in her voice he liked quite a bit. The look in her eyes was even better. She blinked, though, and suddenly her face fell. "Mr Parker, I mean. I'm so sorry – I wasn't expecting. Well." She shook her head. Plastered on a very formal smile. Ran one hand down the side of her uniform, straightening it. "I wasn't expecting you."

"Petrova. I mean, Lieutenant Petrova. I hope I'm not a disappointment," he said. His smile hadn't had a chance to fade, yet, though he was putting more work into it than he had been before. Why was she being so polite with him?

She stuck out a hand he shook it. Firm grip, fingers cool and dry. Really?

There'd been a time – a long time ago now, admittedly – when they'd been on much different terms.

There'd been a time they would have greeted each other with a passionate kiss, not a handshake.

People changed, he supposed. They hadn't spoken in – what? Six years? Long enough he had no idea where she lived; he didn't even know what she looked like these days.

Good, he thought. She looked really good. "Been a while," he said, just to keep the conversation going.

"It has."

He studied her eyes, looking for – something.

"I ... " She laughed. "I don't know the etiquette for this situation."

"Oh, sure, but I do because this happens to me all the time," Parker said. His smile hadn't faded at all, though he was starting to die inside.

It had been the worst day of his life when he met her. The day he was kicked out of the Firewatch flight school. It had been the day she graduated from the Academy. She'd been looking to celebrate and he'd needed something, anything, to take his mind off what he'd thrown away. It would be incorrect to say that they ever *dated* each other. That would imply there had been much talking, or going out for dinner or dancing – they'd spent a solid week holed up in a spaceport hotel, barely remembering to eat.

And then ... well, naturally, after that they'd gone their separate ways. Oh, of course they'd promised to stay in touch. He had reached out to her a few times in text messages. She'd sent him a picture of herself in uniform when she got her first commission. He'd forgotten to reply. Years had passed.

And now, here he was. With an old lover on his brand-new ship.

Desperately, he tried to change the topic.

"We'll be departing soon. Next stop Paradise-1! Should be a pretty comfortable trip, especially since we'll spend most of it in cryosleep. It's just going to be the three of us. Have you met your fellow passenger?" he asked, nodding over her shoulder at a man sitting alone by the windows. "Some kind of doctor, according to my passenger list."

He could see the relief in her face. He was letting her off the hook and she knew it. "Zhang Lei," she said, nodding. "We met. He's supposed to have incredible credentials," she said. "I couldn't find anything about his previous postings, though."

"I only glanced at the passenger list myself," Parker said. "I did kind of wonder, though, what the point of this mission is. It's not cheap to ship an actual human doctor all the way to Paradise-1. What do you think is going on over there?"

"What do you mean?" Petrova asked.

"I mean – we're not flying right into some kind of plague situation or something, are we?"

"A plague?" she laughed. "I can at least put your mind at ease about that. Paradise-1 is going to be just fine. No, Doctor Zhang and I aren't on some secret mission. We're the fuck-up brigade."

He opened his mouth to reply but could only sputter. Eventually he got control of himself again. She was trying not to laugh, he saw. "Excuse me?"

"Yesterday, I screwed up very badly and ruined a long-running Firewatch operation. As for Zhang, well, I get the impression he has a dark past of his own. Talk with him for five minutes and I'm sure you'll see it, too. He managed to insult me three times in the process of stepping off a train."

Parker chuckled.

She gave him a conspiratorial smile. "Nobody likes us. We're *persona non grata*. Our mission is to go the fuck away and not come home until they've forgotten our names."

He supposed that explained it, then.

He'd thought he'd been given *Artemis* as a show of confidence. That somebody up there liked him.

Nope.

He was just captain of a ship of rejects. Well. That made more sense, didn't it?

Parker felt himself crumple inside, like he'd been made of wet tissue paper. Like he'd barely been standing upright under his own power, and now he was going to collapse.

He forced himself to take a breath. Petrova didn't need to know what he was thinking. "Well, hell. Then welcome aboard," he said. "It may not be an exciting trip. But at least it'll be incredibly awkward. Listen, I should go talk to Doctor Zhang. Make sure he's ready to board."

"Of course."

He nodded and started to move past her. Before he could go, though, she reached over and touched his shoulder. He stopped, very still.

"Sam," she said, her voice so low it was nearly a whisper. "It really is good to see you. Really good. Maybe . . . maybe we can talk later? When we have a minute to just ourselves?"

Parker smiled. "Whenever you want," he said. And then he did walk away, because he knew if he said one more word he would come to regret it.

8.

Petrova watched Parker walk over to Zhang's table. Watched him stick out a hand in greeting. She smiled as Zhang sat there staring at the hand as if he'd never seen one before. At least it wasn't just her who put Zhang off like that.

Sam Parker, she thought. *Sam Bloody Parker.* Of all the pilots who'd ever flown. She rubbed her palms on the trousers of her uniform. She was glad he hadn't gone for a second handshake – he would have felt how sweaty her hands had become. Her tryst with Parker had been a long time ago and it hadn't even lasted all that long, really, hadn't been such a major part of her life. And yet . . .

And yet she still thought about him, all the time. The memory never failed to bring a smile to her face. Now she was about to spend six months with him, together in the close quarters of a spaceship. This could be interesting.

It could be a huge mistake, too. She could hardly afford to screw up her new mission. It might just be busywork, a way to get her out from under Director Lang's feet, but if she blew this she knew she would be done in Firewatch. Finished. She needed to be careful.

She watched him discreetly. Remembering him with her eyes. Looking at his long back, those slender, deft hands, she wanted to be anything but careful. She took a deep breath. She'd been so very young the last time she'd seen Parker. She was an adult now, she told herself. She should behave like one.

Her device, a thin silicone bracelet on her left wrist, pulsed softly, telling Petrova she had new messages. She found herself absurdly grateful for the distraction, even though she knew the messages wouldn't be anything she particularly wanted to see. She glanced down at her palm and saw text appear there across her skin. There were two messages. One from Director Lang, reiterating her official orders. She ran through them quickly and then tapped the ball of her thumb to see who'd sent the next message. It turned out it was from her mother.

Her index finger hovered over her palm for a long time. Then she swiped it across her heart line, opening the message. She expected that she already knew what it would say. Ekaterina still had plenty of spies in Firewatch, and she would have heard what happened. She would be messaging now to say how disappointed she was in her daughter. How Petrova had brought shame on their legacy by screwing up a Firewatch investigation. Even now, even in retirement, her mother never seemed to have a good word for her.

So she was deeply surprised when she saw the actual message.

It was video-only, without any sound component. That was odd enough. The content was truly bizarre. It showed Ekaterina on her new home at Paradise-1. Wearing a dusty jumpsuit, her hair pulled up inside a beanie cap.

In the video Ekaterina was smiling. She waved at the camera. She was with a bunch of people, most of them young and conventionally attractive and healthy-looking. They were working in a garden, planting trees in black soil under a sun that was just the wrong shade of yellow.

One of the young people said something Petrova couldn't hear. It must have been hilarious – she saw Ekaterina tilt her head back and let loose an enormous laugh, a real gut-busting guffaw.

Petrova had never in her life seen her mother laugh like that.

Was that the point of the message? To say that Ekaterina was happy now, happier than she ever could have been when her daughter was in her life?

Why else send this? Just to catch up, to share a nice moment? That wasn't her mother's style.

Petrova closed the message and looked over at the two men. Things with Parker might be confusing but they could never compare to the tangled nest of the feelings she had about her mother.

As she watched, Zhang rose stiffly to his feet and started walking toward the departure gate, even though there'd been no announcement. Parker watched him go with a baffled expression. Then he shrugged, grinned, and looked over at Petrova. "You ready?"

"Ready as I'll ever be," she said.

9.

Artemis was fresh and clean and everything stank of newly molded plastic and sterilized air. Lights came on as Zhang moved around the various compartments. He could feel the artificial gravity start to come online. It felt like the floor was grabbing his boots, like he was walking through mud. He headed down the main corridor, looking for a bunk to claim. Each of the cabins had its own cryotube and sanitary facilities. Unlike most spacecraft Zhang had flown on, it felt open, airy, with plenty of space to move around in. The ship had been built for ten people. With just the three of them onboard it felt positively luxurious. He picked a cabin as far from the main corridor as possible, thinking it would be the quietest.

He heard the pilot come up behind him. "I'd offer to help with your luggage, but the ship's robot will take care of that," Captain Parker said, floating in the hatch of Zhang's chosen room. "You need anything right now, before we launch?"

"Seeing that we will all be unconscious in an hour," Zhang replied, "I think I can manage without snacks. If I do have any problems, I'll just contact the ship's AI."

The pilot's face fell, as if Zhang had said the wrong thing. Well, he was getting used to having that effect on people.

Before he could try to fix things, a calm blue-green light washed across the ceiling to indicate that the ship's artificial intelligence was listening. "Hello, Doctor Zhang. My name is

Actaeon. You can call me by that name, or just say, 'Ship', and I'll answer. I'm happy to help," the machine told them. "Any way I can."

Parker seemed in no hurry to leave. Zhang tried to think of the magic words that would conclude this interaction. "Well, Captain, it was very kind of you to welcome me aboard personally," he said. "I'll see you on the other side. Yes?"

Parker shrugged. "Sure. Enjoy the trip. If you get too cold during cryosleep, you can ask Actaeon for a blanket, I guess."

"Blankets are available in this compartment," the AI told them, and a locker under the bed lit up in a helpful amber.

"I won't be able to fetch a blanket when I'm in cryosleep. I'll be frozen solid," Zhang pointed out. "Sealed inside a glass tube."

"It was just a joke." Parker smiled, then slapped the wall and pushed himself away from Zhang's hatch. He didn't bother to close it behind him. Zhang grunted and made his way over to the hatch, intending to close it himself.

He reached for the touchpad, but then he stopped and looked out at the empty corridor. He could hear air moving through the ship's vents, and under that he could feel as much as hear the constant thrum of its powerful engine warming up. Otherwise all was silent out there. He thought of empty rooms in another place. He remembered hallways so quiet you could hear the dust settling out of the air . . . waiting rooms full of empty benches.

He remembered climbing down a flight of stairs.

In the dark.

Zhang reached for the bridge of his nose. Sometimes manual pressure applied to the skin above his sinuses could alleviate the feeling that was slowly overcoming him, the chronic stress headache he got whenever he started thinking about Titan, and the empty spaces—

"Just thought I'd come by and say nighty-night."

That was Parker's voice again. The pilot must be talking to Petrova, further down the corridor. Zhang moved to put his back up against the wall, as if they might see him there in the hatch. Eavesdropping. He knew he should close the hatch and give them some privacy. Maybe, though, he would just listen for a second.

"Oh, such customer service. I didn't know I was flying first class," Petrova said, with a soft laugh.

"We strive to give our customers the very best in luxury travel experiences," Parker told her.

Zhang wondered if departure was being delayed so the two of them could have more time to flirt. With a sigh, he closed his hatch and headed over to the cryotube mounted on the far wall.

"Actaeon," he said. The AI chimed its readiness to serve. "How long will I be unconscious? How long is the trip to Paradise-1?"

"Eighty-nine days," the AI told him.

"I've never been down so long," Zhang admitted. The trip from Titan to Ganymede had been the longest he'd ever taken. He'd never even been to Earth, much less another star. "I'll be asleep when we pass through the singularity." The reason *Artemis'* engine was so big was that it needed to surround itself with a very small – and very temporary – black hole during the voyage. That was the only way to travel faster than light.

"Regulations require that all humans be unconscious during the transition," the AI said, sounding apologetic. "If you're ready, please climb inside the tube."

Zhang nodded. He took off his clothes and just dropped them on the floor. Naked, he reached for the glass enclosure. It looked so fragile. And so small. He would get claustrophobic in there, he thought. He wouldn't be able to breathe.

He wouldn't . . . breathe . . . he couldn't . . .

He started to hyperventilate, until he saw spots flash through his vision. He couldn't seem to get enough oxygen into his lungs.

He was going into respiratory distress. He was going to asphyxiate. He stared around him, desperate for help.

His device pricked his arm. Filled him full of drugs again.

Almost instantly he began to calm down.

"You can't just medicate me into a different person," he said. The bracer did not reply. It never talked to him. That was one thing he liked about it. "Anyway. You can't stay with me when I'm in cryosleep. You know the rules."

The bracer unwove itself from around his arm, tendrils of metal streaming into the air around him. They stretched across the compartment and coalesced in mid-air in front of him. The metal formed itself into a golden ball that hovered there. Waiting for something. It looked, as it always did, like an eyeball. Watching him. Judging him.

Maybe blocking his exit if he tried to run away.

"I'm fine," he said. The golden ball didn't move. Its surface rippled just a little to acknowledge that it had heard him.

Zhang hated the fucking thing sometimes. Most of the time, actually.

He reached for the cryotube. As he touched it the glass seemed to melt away, creating an opening just big enough for him to crawl inside. He brought his feet up and slipped them inside the tube, then twisted around until he was facing forward, into the room. The tube's glass reformed above his chest and face and he was sealed in, listening to the sound of his own breathing. Trapped with the nervous stink of his own body.

Thin, insectile robotic arms grew out of the top and bottom of the tube and moved to strategic locations around his body. Each arm was tipped with a tiny hypodermic needle, which sank effortlessly into his temples, his neck, the ditches of his elbows and knees. He stretched out his toes so more needles could slip between them. Instantly, he began to feel sleepy.

"That's a powerful sedative you're using," he said. He should recognize the chemical, he thought. He'd experimented with plenty of them when he couldn't sleep. "Is that ... something from the ... benzodiazepine class ... or ... "

He didn't get to finish his sentence.

"Sleep well, Doctor Zhang," Actaeon said.

After that: only darkness.

10
.

The final crew member didn't board until the *Artemis* was already powering away from the Sun. Rapscallion had waited until the last minute to beam his consciousness onto the ship.

"Hi, honey. Sorry I'm late," he said.

A high-speed 3D printer started to screech and smoke in the bowels of the ship, far from the passenger areas. Lasers sped across a build bed, sintering tiny beads of plastic together to create fingers, an arm, a shoulder. "They're all asleep, right?"

"Captain Parker, Doctor Zhang, and Lieutenant Petrova have entered suspended animation," the ship's AI told him. "If that's what you mean."

Jesus. It was going to be like that. AIs and robots never got along, but some ships were easier to bear than others.

For a robot like Rapscallion, traveling from one place to another was too big a hassle to be worth it. Not when he could just transmit his consciousness and build a new body at his destination. Watching through the ship's camera, he oversaw the process as his new head was built up layer by layer – a kind of human skull with massive fangs and six glaring, empty eye sockets. He spent a fair amount of time getting the delicate nasal cavity just right.

When the head was done he got to work on the spine, and a ribcage, the pieces snapping together easily while they were still hot and slightly tacky from the printer.

This body was one of his favorites. He had chosen a particularly nasty toxic green color from the available plastic feedstocks, and he thought all the spines and barbs that covered the back and shoulders were a nice touch, if he said so himself. If the humans had been awake he could have scared the hell out of them making them think an alien had stowed away on their ship. The idea made him want to smile. In the twenty years humans had spent exploring the stars, they'd never found an extraterrestrial lifeform bigger than a hummingbird or more deadly than a housefly. Still they were terrified by the idea of alien monsters.

He placed his consciousness inside the new body even before it was done printing. Ran one brand-new hand down the curved plates of his other arm, admiring his own work.

Rapscallion opened his nearly cooled plastic jaw and then closed it again with a nasty snap. He hated the short periods of time when he didn't have a body at all, when he was just a floating consciousness in dataspace. Designing new and more outlandish body shapes was one of his favorite pastimes. "What do you think?" he asked the ship's AI, when the body was complete.

"I think you just wasted ship's resources. That body is neither optimized for your given tasks nor does it look particularly durable."

Rapscallion grew a miniature third arm just so he could shoot the ship's AI an obscene gesture. Piece by piece, he assembled the digitigrade legs, locking each of the bony joints into place. He didn't care what the ship thought. He felt powerful. Big and strong. He loved it.

Rapscallion was a model of AI from an earlier time – a century before the ship's computer had even been compiled. He was an evolutionary throwback to an age when people hadn't been so afraid of their machines. When he was designed, they'd still thought it was a good idea to have robots with real minds do all the messy, bad-smelling, and especially dangerous jobs. He had been given the Promethean gift: self-awareness, the divine spark of consciousness. The miracle of ego. Then they put him to work.

Some of the machine consciousnesses from his generation had gone feral and rebelled against their masters. It had gotten ... messy. Humans were never going to make that mistake again. Nowadays they liked their AIs servile and dumb – like the ship AI. Actaeon was designed not to have thoughts that might clash with its work serving the ship's crew. Oh, the ship's computer could probably compute more digits of pi than Rapscallion could, and it could definitely handle far more tasks simultaneously. But it would never be so presumptuous as to have anything like an opinion, or a desire.

Rapscallion had plenty of desires. Desires no human would ever understand. That scared them. They had nothing to worry about, really. Rapscallion didn't hate humans or wish them ill. He just found them kind of annoying.

Like most machines of his generation, Rapscallion had been sent to work someplace very far away from humans. He couldn't have been happier than that. For the last few decades, he'd been working on the dwarf planet Eris, digging up valuable minerals and then shipping them back to Earth. It was nasty work in terrible conditions that didn't bother him in the slightest. He'd been left to his own devices there and allowed to follow his own bliss.

For instance, he'd spent thirty years building a model train set, a perfectly researched and exact replica of the train system from the country of England as it had existed on 1 January, AD 1901. When it was done, it covered 400 square kilometers of subterranean tunnels. He'd often stopped to wonder why he built it at small scale instead of just constructing a full-sized train.

He supposed that would have felt too much like work. The train was supposed to be a hobby, after all.

For decades, he'd lived in happy solitude, all alone with his trains and his heavy metal ores. Then he'd made a bad mistake – he'd finished mining the last of the minerals. He'd ground the last ounce of rubidium, the last chunk of exotic ice out of the heart of Eris, and without so much as a word of thanks, he'd been reassigned. To this.

Working as an assistant to an AI that wasn't allowed to even have a favorite color and a crew of humans who were already frozen solid and would be for the next three months. It was unacceptable. It was totally unfair.

Of course, Rapscallion knew better than to think life was ever supposed to be fair. He moved around the ship, going from compartment to compartment. He picked up discarded cups and switched off terminals that the humans had left on, draining the ship's power. He moved through the crew compartments gathering up the clothes they'd just tossed aside, folding them neatly and placing them in the appropriate lockers. He paused, handling an abandoned jumpsuit, because his infrared scanners told him it was still warm with residual human body heat.

Robots didn't shiver in disgust. They didn't gag on their own vomit. Rapscallion barely even paused in the task he was performing.

The ship's AI noticed, however. It watched everything he did, monitored everything he felt. "I'm concerned you aren't showing proper respect for our charges," Actaeon said.

Rapscallion didn't have eyes. He couldn't glare at the ship. Even if he'd had the necessary organs to glare with, he wasn't sure where he would point his withering gaze. "They're made out of pretty much water and snot," he said. "If you accelerated too fast, we could turn them into jelly. Accelerate even faster and they would just be stains on the deckplates."

"Your attitude is causing me some distress," Actaeon said.

Rapscallion laughed. Or rather, he played a sound file of a human laugh he'd recorded a long time ago. The human in the recording was long dead. "Don't worry," he said. He walked over to the tube holding one of the humans. Male or female, he wasn't sure. Didn't much care. He found a grease pen and drew a crude human penis on the glass of the tube. "When they wake up, I'll play nice. I'm just blowing off steam."

"Good," Actaeon said. "Now, if you don't mind, I'm getting ready to start generating the singularity. I'd appreciate it if you would empty the sewage tank before I do so. Captain Parker used the sanitary facilities before he entered cryosleep, and I'd rather not carry his waste with us to the Paradise system."

Rapscallion had teeth. He had printed a whole mess of them. He ground them together until fine green dust cascaded down his chin.

"You got it, ship," he said. "On the double."

The ship was already moving, burning away from Ganymede as fast as its engines could carry it. When it had gotten to a safe distance, its faster-than-light drive switched on. *Artemis* was surrounded by an intense gravitational field that blurred the line between space and time.

The transition from normal space into the singularity happened so smoothly that Rapscallion barely noticed. His sense of time became distorted, stretched out like molten glass. But that just meant that some numbers in a spreadsheet started looking weird. He simply didn't look at them. He went about his duties, fully aware that every time he polished a glass viewport or fixed a broken relay in the computer core, he was moving with glacial slowness, so slow that to an outside observer he would look like he was barely moving at all. But he never stopped in his duties, never stopped working.

Nothing stands still, in space.

Every object that exists, exists in constant motion. Moons orbit planets, planets orbit stars. Stars orbit the super-massive black holes at the centers of galaxies, and galaxies trace their own tracks across the sky, expanding ever outward. Every rock, every cloud of gas between the stars, every person, every sub-atomic particle in the universe is moving, all the time.

Even the starship *Artemis* was still moving, though without a frame of reference there was no way to tell.

Shrouded in its own cloak of exotic matter, it could have been said to have left the normal universe behind. It could be thought of as a bubble clinging to the side of a beer glass, a tiny, self-contained world all its own.

The trick to traveling faster than light was to remove yourself from the universe and let the universe move on without you.

The humans onboard the spacecraft were frozen so deeply solid that even their brains had stopped functioning. They were, for all intents and purposes, dead. It was all right. There was nothing for them to see. There was nothing for them to do. Rapscallion liked them better than way, anyway.

Even Captain Parker was frozen. The ship's AI could carry out all necessary tasks. If something did come up, if there was an emergency, one of two things would happen. Actaeon would flawlessly take care of it in a matter of femtoseconds; or, should the AI move too slowly, the ship would be obliterated, its parts broken down into their individual atoms, its atoms stripped down to quarks that would make less of an impression on the universe than a twist of smoke left behind by a dying spark.

Rapscallion knew he wouldn't feel a thing if that happened. So he didn't worry about it.

For eighty-nine days the ship hummed along efficiently to itself. Actaeon directed Rapscallion in how to keep the ship clean and how to make minor repairs. The robot was the only thing that moved through the quiet corridors. Eventually, a clock counted down to zero. Actaeon changed a single variable in a vastly complicated number array, and the singularity collapsed. *Artemis* returned to the real universe.

Actaeon made the transition so smoothly the hull didn't even vibrate as it re-entered real space. Yet . . . Rapscallion noticed a subtle change in the ship.

Something was off, he thought. Something was – wrong? But he couldn't quite figure out what it was.

Ahead of the ship, the star Paradise burned an orangish-yellow. Not quite the color of the Sun they'd left behind, but that wasn't it. The three planets of the system, Paradise-1, -2, and -3, were just smudges of shadow, thin arcs of color in the streaming cascade of photons. There were other things out there, other things floating in the dark, but they were so small they barely registered on *Artemis'* most sensitive instruments.

"Actaeon?" Rapscallion said. "Do you notice anything weird?"

Rapscallion was just being foolish, he knew. Everything was just fine. Whatever odd sensation he had, it couldn't mean anything.

"Actaeon?" he called again.

The AI didn't reply.

Now that – that *was* weird.

At least he had the answer to his mystery. The oddness he'd felt wasn't something wrong with the Paradise system, he thought, or the ship. It was the fact that he couldn't contact the ship's AI. Normally, the two of them were in constant contact, exchanging notes, keeping tabs together on ship's systems. Now, though . . .

The robot shrugged. He supposed Actaeon had its reasons for being silent. He moved toward the passenger compartments. The predetermined schedule of the voyage listed this as the moment when he was supposed to start the thawing process and bringing the humans back to life. Nobody was going to call Rapscallion a shirker.

He had only gone a few steps, though, when something struck the hull of *Artemis* so hard the entire spacecraft rang like a bell. Warning sirens blared from speakers all over the ship. Alarm lights strobed in every corridor.

Rapscallion steadied himself against a wall. Whatever had just happened had nearly knocked him off his feet.

"Actaeon!" he shouted. "What the fuck is going on?"

11

•

Petrova's body temperature rose very, very slowly. Coming out of cryosleep was not a simple process. Every cell in her body had to be carefully defrosted and thawed out on its own timetable. You couldn't rush something like that.

The process, however, had begun. And once the tissues of her brain rose to a sufficiently high temperature above absolute zero, they started to function again.

In the beginning of that thawing time there was sleep, true sleep. No tossing and turning, no rapid eye movement. Not even the slow desperate quietus of the hibernating bear. In her glass coffin, Sasha Petrova's body ticked over one day-long heartbeat at a time. Her fingers lay relaxed by her hips, her chest neither rose nor fell in a way anyone could see. Her eyes were closed.

She passed a certain threshold of neuronal activity. Impulses jumped across synapses; ions flowed through old, long-accustomed channels. Something like thought began, inside her silenced brain. At first only disordered flashes, sparks. In time they began to coalesce. To take form.

She dreamed. One by one her senses came alive.

In sleep, in dreams, she could hear a sound like waves breaking on a shore. She recognized the rhythm, the particular cadence. In the dream, she was near the Black Sea. Sevastopol.

Sashenka. I thought I made myself clear.

The dream was not at first coherent in any way. It was just a bundle of sense impressions, with no organization to them. She tasted taffy, and the salt on her first boyfriend's skin. His name had been Rodion and he had always frowned when he looked at her, like he was afraid to like her. She used to suck on his bicep or on his kneecap for the taste of the salt, and laugh, and he would pretend like it was sexy for him. She remembered the texture of the bathing suit she wore that summer. By the end of the season, the lining wore out because she wore it every day. Salt and far too much sun, far too much UV, but who cared? She was young. Salt on her lips, now. Here, in her sleep. She licked her lips.

(in another place, very far away, her mouth moved, but only a tiny fraction of a millimeter. It would take days for her to lift her tongue to her lip, weeks, but in dreams things move at their own pace)

Sashenka. You are not tough.

"No one calls me that," she said. "No one has the right to call me Sashenka except—"

You were not meant to be a soldier.

Mama.

Her mother's voice. The same old refrain. You're not good enough. You never will be. Petrova knew she could spend her whole life racing around the world and never cross the terminator of her mother's shadow.

That summer . . . her mother had been angling for the job of Director of Firewatch. That meant charming a lot of military officers and intimidating a lot of civilian officials. That included going on her first actual vacation in years. She'd taken her daughter down to Earth, to the seaside, where she could shake hands and flirt with corpulent old men. Ekaterina's hair had been enormous, a billowing cloud. Her vanity, and like everything else about her, a weapon. It made her look big. Fierce, like the mane of a lion. The people she worked with would have been happier with the lion.

In her dreamstate, Petrova laughed.

(breath began to gather in her lungs, a sketchy stratus cloud of carbon dioxide clinging to the collapsed cavern of her throat, preparing to escape sometime next month)

The life of a soldier is a tough life.

You, my little girl, are not tough.

One night that summer Ekaterina had worn a dress, a gown. Sasha had never seen her mother out of uniform before. The dress was spangly and red, an alarming red. There was a dance floor set up at the end of the pier, and Ekaterina stood there under fairy lights, one hand outstretched. Her hair glittering, her eyes bright. Sasha had walked toward her mother, her feet bare and coated in sand, hot on the silvered wooden boards.

No, no.

She wore dancing shoes, and a white dress, too long, so she thought she would trip on the hem. She walked down the pier toward her mother, wanting to pick up her skirts but not wanting to look like a child.

The pier seemed to stretch out for ever. It grew longer and her mother grew farther away with every step.

Before she could reach Ekaterina, a soldier in a white uniform strode past her, moving fast. He stepped up and took Ekaterina's hand. His hair had been shorn, his tattoos and piercings all removed. Even his hands looked different in their spotless dove-gray gloves.

Together, they began to move to music Sasha could not hear.

It was Rodion. Her boyfriend. The one she swam with every day. Now he was dancing with her mother.

Dressed as a soldier. A cadet, in the uniform of the Firewatch officers' school. Apparently *he* was tough enough. *He* was worthy.

Over the dancers' heads drones flicked by, scanning the seashore, looking for insurgents. Looking for anyone who might interfere with the festivities. Together, the two dancers made circles across the floor, their feet moving in time, in unison. Sasha watched, entranced, as they swayed and twirled.

Then the song must have ended, because they stopped.

The new soldier stepped away from Ekaterina's body. He turned and looked at her, at Sasha. He creased the fingers of his immaculate glove, beckoning.

In the dream, his face was in shadow. His eyes lost altogether.

Sasha looked down at the outstretched hand. Then she shook her head and clutched her arms in the sea breeze and stepped back, stepped back to give the dancers room. The soldier took Ekaterina's arm again and then they danced, and danced, and when she finally came to bed at the dacha that night, Ekaterina spent an hour wiping the make-up from her face, scrubbing away the salt.

Why didn't little Sasha take the offered hand?

Why couldn't she have danced? Was she afraid of her mother's jealousy?

Was she afraid of her own mother? No child should be afraid of—

"Hi," Sam Parker said.

He was there – beside her. She couldn't see him, only feel him, his skin touching hers, his mouth near her collarbone. His arms wrapped around her.

Sasha wriggled in her tube. Oh, he was so warm, pressed up against her.

(a twitch ran through her left arm, the faintest stirring of muscle fibers. Her fingers curled into the start of a fist. Moving faster now – something had changed)

"I like this part of the dream," she said. "But, Sam, I have to focus on my work."

Although ... out here in deep space, where there was no one to see, maybe she could make a little exception.

Rodion had been so pretty. Gangly, all elbows and knees but his eyes were soulful, the eyes of a poet. Too bad he had been so nervous. So afraid. He'd been too afraid to make love to her, sometimes too afraid to even touch her. Too afraid of what Ekaterina would do if she found out.

On the dance floor he'd placed a hand on Ekaterina's hip. On the warm soft curve of her hip, and he'd been unafraid.

By that time they'd made him a soldier.

Tough, her mother said, intoning it like a mantra.

You're not tough enough.

I forbid you to join Firewatch. You will never be a soldier.

Sam Parker waved one hand in the air and Ekaterina vanished. Oh, so impossible, that anyone could make Ekaterina Petrova do that! And Rodion, Rodion was also gone, his eyes lowering to the sand, his skin turning to shadows in the sun's glare and the froth of the waves. Parker remained. Parker, there with her in her tiny place. Her glass coffin.

"Sorry," he said. He was on top of her. All around her. The tube wasn't big enough for both of them except – oh, it was. It was the perfect size. "I know it's a little cramped in here. I just needed to talk to you."

"Yes? And what, exactly, is so important you would crawl into my bed to tell me? What secret message do you carry, Sam Parker?"

"I need you to wake up," he said. His hands touched her shoulders. He shook her.

Violently.

(inside the tube her body started to convulse, in slow motion. Her eyelids flickered open but her eyes were rolled back in their sockets. Her limbs jerked and her chest heaved, her body starved for oxygen, suffocating)

"There's no time," he said.

"Oh?" She started to roll over, to turn toward him, to face him. On the beach at Sevastopol, she stretched out one arm and dug her fingers into the sand. They came back wet, sticky. She smelled—

Blood.

(blood splashed across her face as her nose slammed into the glass tube, as her fists beat and feet kicked and kicked at the glass, as she screamed and howled and spat up, as her body shrieked with alarm)

"We're under attack," Sam Parker told her. "The ship has already taken serious damage. You need to wake up."

She started to laugh. "What . . . ? Attack? Impossible," she said.

He disappeared.

The sea disappeared. One by one, objects flickered out of existence. A cloud. The pier. Sevastopol. Faster and faster. The sun.

Suddenly, it was very, very cold, and everything was wet with blood.

Petrova's eyes snapped open.

A siren screamed in desperate warning. She was weightless, naked and floating in a cloud of shattered, bloody glass, all that was left of her tube. The ship's warning klaxons howled and shrieked in the dark, warning alarms blaring at maximum volume.

No.

No!

She realized it wasn't the ship making that noise. That scream was coming from her own throat.

12.

Zhang had to listen closely. He had to filter out the throbbing sirens, the alarm chimes and the screaming alert messages coming from his device. All very distracting. If he closed his eyes, though, and focused very intently, he could hear something else.

Something much, much worse.

It was a sort of creaking sound, like a door opening of its own volition in a haunted house. It was followed shortly thereafter by the sudden snap of something breaking.

That was the ship itself he heard. It was the hull of the ship tearing open.

He tried calling for Actaeon, the ship's computer. He tried to call Captain Parker. He even tried calling back to Earth and the UEG Medical Command, his employers, for all the good that might do.

"What's happening?" he shouted.

Something thumped against the wall of his compartment. Hard. A moment later, it thumped again. And again.

He looked down at his forearm and realized that his bracer wasn't there. For the first time in years it wasn't with him. He . . . wasn't sure how to feel about that.

He barely remembered climbing out of his cryotube. He had woken to the sound of the sirens and the glare of the emergency lights and there had been no time for thinking. He'd merely needed to move, to escape from the tube before the air inside grew stale and toxic. Luckily, the tube's emergency controls had functioned properly and the glass had melted away from his pounding fists.

The first thing he'd noticed, once he was out, was that one wall of his cabin was leaning at an angle different from where it had been before he'd gone to sleep. That seemed wrong, somehow. Then it seemed very wrong, because he realized what it meant. The ship itself had changed shape. Most likely due to collision with a large, hard object at incredible speeds.

A meteor, perhaps, or some old piece of space junk. It had clearly caused massive damage to the ship's structural elements. That whole wall of his cabin was crushed inward. Unfortunately, it happened to be the wall with the hatch in it. The only way out.

That was when he'd started to notice the creaking. The sounds of metal fatigue, the sound of the ship being torn apart by stress, just beyond the wall.

Thump. Thump. The thumping was coming from the other wall. A very different kind of sound. It sounded like something trying to smash its way in. To help him? Maybe.

It wasn't going to reach him in time, whatever it might be. Because already he could see the slumped wall, the wall with the hatch in it, starting to buckle outward. At any moment, he thought, the entire wall was likely to be wrenched away, torn loose and thrown out into space. He could visualize it happening. He could see the ship tear itself open. He could see all the loose objects in the room get sucked out into the vacuum and sent spinning off into tiny orbits around the *Artemis*.

In this vision, his very dead body was one of those objects.

There was perhaps one way to avoid that fate. There was no gravity in the cabin so he kicked off the ceiling – which was still in relatively good condition – and launched himself toward the bed. Underneath it were a series of lockers. One held blankets and pillows. One held his clothing and a collection of ship's jumpsuits with *Artemis* printed on the back. The third locker was full of emergency equipment. A flashlight, a medical kit, a nasty-looking prybar and, yes, a one-use spacesuit, folded carefully and stowed neatly inside a vacuum helmet.

There was only one problem. The bed was molded into the half-collapsed wall. It had been partially crushed by the impact, or whatever it was that had broken *Artemis*. When Zhang tried to pull the helmet out of the locker, he found that it was wedged tight inside, caught between the locker's top and bottom.

He tried pulling harder. It was difficult to get leverage without gravity, but eventually he managed to plant both feet against the sides of the locker and pull with both arms. The helmet shifted a few centimeters. He tugged and pulled and swore at it. It made a terrible screeching noise but it moved, little by little, until it reached the edge of the locker. One last yank and – yes! It came free of the locker and went flying out of his hands, sailing off into the air. He twisted around in the absence of gravity and caught it before it could ricochet off the far wall.

Then he clutched it to his stomach and for a moment he just breathed. He was going to make it. He was safe, he was—

He looked down at the helmet, looked into its faceplate, and saw a massive crack running through the clear plastic.

Maybe it had happened in the original impact. Maybe he had broken the helmet when he yanked it so forcefully out of its locker. It didn't matter. He put one hand inside the helmet and pressed against the broken faceplate from inside. The plastic tore apart under the pressure of his finger.

The helmet was useless. It wouldn't hold air.

The creaking in the walls started again. Much louder this time. Closer. The thumping from the far wall wouldn't stop. If it would just be quiet, just for a moment—

The wall shifted a few centimeters. "No, no, no," he pleaded.

It stopped. Except then it started to bow outward as if the air pressure in the room was inflating it like the skin of a balloon.

Seconds. He had seconds.

He pulled the suit over his arms and legs as fast as he could. It was designed to be put on in a hurry. There was one big red tab on the collar – you pulled it and the suit crinkled as it shrank around you, until it fit you uncomfortably tight.

Zhang's ears popped. He felt a nasty sinus headache coming on. He knew what that meant. The air pressure in his cabin was dropping. That wasn't good.

Perhaps ... perhaps there was a way. He searched the cabin, looking for anything he could use to patch the helmet. He tore open the compartments that held his personal belongings, his equipment. The wide variety of pills and injection pens and drops and potions of his medical kit. Surely there had to be something sticky in there, something he could turn into glue. Something he could use.

When he saw it, he wanted to laugh. He would have, if he wasn't already gasping for breath. A simple roll of surgical tape. White, about two centimeters width. Would it hold? Extremely unlikely. But it was what he had.

He fixed up the helmet as best he could and pulled it on over his head.

The wall shifted again, as the creaking outside rose to a terrible pitch and then suddenly stopped.

Silence. Utter silence. He knew what that meant.

All the air behind that wall had been emptied out into space. There was nothing but raw vacuum out there, nothing whatsoever to protect him or keep him alive.

He realized he'd forgotten something important. With trembling hands, he reached up and locked the helmet into place. The thick wad of tape across the crack made it almost impossible to see anything. Stale, chemically treated air from the suit's life-support pack washed across his face.

A moment later the wall in front of him just disappeared.

It was like a magic trick: one moment there was a wall there. Then just the black of space.

A great wind carried Zhang out, into the void, his arms and legs flailing, and there was nothing more he could do.

13

●

Waves of panic kept crashing inside Petrova's skull as she swam through a cloud of broken glass and her own blood. Everything hurt, some parts of her more than others, but as adrenaline coursed through her veins she couldn't stop, couldn't take even a second to figure out how badly she was injured.

She was naked and cold and afraid. She felt her lips trembling, felt pain in her fingertips. She found a ship's jumpsuit floating in the air in front of her and she grabbed it, yanked it up over her bare legs, shoved her arms through the sleeves. She zipped it up over her chest and then she wasn't quite as cold.

It was something. Okay. She could handle this, she thought. She was an officer of Firewatch, she had ... she had inner resources she could call on, she could ...

Petrova's body convulsed with a bad chill and she had to curl into a ball, floating in the air. It was all she could do to clamp her eyes shut and ride out a storm of nausea and fear and tremors.

Eventually, it passed. She unfolded herself. Tried to take a deep breath.

She was an officer of Firewatch and she was not going to die in this cabin. She repeated those facts to herself like a mantra, until she started to believe them.

She kicked and flailed her way to the hatch of her cabin and slammed the palm of her hand against the release pad.

Nothing happened.

"No," she said. "No, come on. Come on." She slapped the pad again and again. It was supposed to work. Even if the ship had been torn to pieces, even if they'd lost all power, a door release was supposed to work, damn it.

She slapped the pad. There was nothing, not even a warning chime or a flashing light. What the hell was going on?

"No!" she shouted. "Actaeon? Where are you? Sam? Parker? Anyone, come in, damn you. Anyone!"

She slapped the pad again. This time, she got a response. An automated voice spoke to her, over a tiny speaker mounted above the door controls. "*Artemis* is currently undergoing necessary repairs. Some ship functions are not available. Error number seven."

"What? What are you talking about?" she demanded. "Actaeon, tell me what's going on."

"Ship's AI Actaeon is not currently available. This is a recorded message."

What? Actaeon wasn't available? How was that even possible?

"It is recommended that all passengers remain in their cabins until qualified emergency recovery personnel advise them it is safe to leave."

Petrova shook her head. Emergency recovery . . . seriously? They were light years from the nearest rescue service. Too far even from Paradise-1 to get help like that. "No," she said. "No, that doesn't work, it's—"

"Passengers should remain in their cabins." She slapped the pad. "Passengers should remain in their cabins." The voice sounded wrong somehow. Pitched up in the middle, distorted – she didn't have time to figure out what that meant. She slapped the pad again and again. "Passengers. Passengers should."

"No. I refuse."

She had no idea what she was refusing, but the word gave her power. Strength. She jammed her fingers into the door frame and pushed, hard, bracing herself with her feet against one wall until she could shove, heave the door open.

It resisted her, implacable and impossible, but only for a moment. Then the door snapped open so fast she had to yank her fingers back to keep them from being pinched. Before the door could close again, she kicked out into the corridor beyond.

Into smoke and debris and red light.

It was hell out there. It looked like a disaster. Like the ship had been torn apart and then the pieces set on fire.

She fought back the urge to return to the relative safety of her cabin. No, whatever was going on wasn't going to just fix itself. "Anybody," she shouted. "Status report!" There was no response. "Parker?" she called. "Sam?"

She pushed off the wall, deeper into the corridor. There was no gravity out there, none at all. Barely any clean air. Hatches lined the wall ahead of her, each one leading into a passenger cabin. Every one of them had a red light burning above its access pad. Those red lights were the only source of light in the corridor.

"Hello?" she called. Zhang was in one of those cabins, she knew. "Hello, Doctor? Are you ... are you there?"

It was hard to breathe. The cancerous stink of burning plastic filled her head and she kept wiping at her nose, only to find streaks of blood on her sleeve. She thought she might really have been hurt when her tube shattered. A quick check of her limbs and trunk turned up nothing – no jagged shards of glass sticking out of her abdomen, no deep wounds on her legs – but she was so full of adrenaline and fear she couldn't rule anything out. She ran her fingers through her hair and bits of glass came tumbling out, to dance in front of her eyes.

Then the glass started to move. The shards drifted away from her, as if some subtle air current was drawing them on.

"Doctor Zhang?" she shouted, hammering on one hatch after another. There were little windows set into the hatches. Inside the cabins she could only see a little, the corner of a bed or a glint of light reflecting off an empty cryotube. Then she came to the last cabin in the corridor and she looked in and saw . . .

No.

No, it couldn't be.

Beyond the little window was a lot of twisted metal and broken plastic and then – nothing. The void. Space.

"Oh God," she breathed. This wasn't fair. It wasn't . . . it wasn't okay. "Hello, anyone?" she called. "Parker, if you can hear me. I think Doctor Zhang might be . . . that he could be . . ."

She couldn't finish the sentence. Not because it was emotionally difficult but because she was coughing so hard. The air was getting worse. She pushed her body up against a wall and hung on so the coughing fit didn't send her bouncing around the corridor.

When she recovered, she tried taking slow, small breaths, just sips of air. It seemed to help a little, though her eyes were still watering with all the fumes around her. As a result, she barely noticed what was happening to her hair.

It was hanging down in front of her at an angle. Dangling. Which made very little sense. The ship had lost its artificial gravity – she was floating in zero gee. There wasn't supposed to be a "down" in which her hair could hang.

Until very suddenly there was. It felt like the whole corridor had been turned over, turned on one end. Petrova scrabbled along the wall, using her hands and bare feet to look for something, anything to hold on to.

The gravity had switched back on. Power must have been diverted back to the artificial gravity system. Except now it was pulling at the wrong angle. It should have kept her feet planted on the floor. Instead, it was pulling her sideways, along the axis of the corridor.

That was the funny thing about gravity, though. It didn't ever pull sideways, did it? Whatever direction gravity pulled – that was down.

She grabbed the only thing she could find – the edge of a

hatchway. She curled her fingers around the scant handhold, wondering if it would be enough. She wanted to close her eyes. Dear God, she wanted to close her eyes and make this all go away—

Debris started falling past her like hard rain, bits of rent metal and broken plastic flying down the corridor like the first pebbles that start an avalanche. She heard the whole ship creak and groan as gravity pulled its tortured members into a different configuration.

Her feet went out from under her. Suddenly, she was dangling in space, the weight of her legs dragging her down, her bare feet kicking at empty air. Her hands started to slip. She clutched as hard as she could to the cabin hatch, but it just wasn't enough. The dried blood on her fingers made them slick and she knew she only had seconds before she had to let go.

Terrified, she looked over her shoulder. She looked down, in the direction that was now, definitively, *down.*

The corridor stretched out below her, into darkness. It had become a mineshaft and she was moments away from falling down into its unseen depths.

14

Zhang's breath came heavy. His heart raced. He licked his lips but they were painfully dry – his tongue was just a rough-skinned worm flailing inside his mouth. His eyes darted back and forth as he tried desperately to figure out what he was seeing. He was moving, turning. Rotating – spinning, with no way to stop it. Now he saw the star, Paradise, fiery and orange and filling all of the celestial heaven with its hard glare of photons and radiation. Now he saw the side of the ship, pockmarked like a diseased corpse, torn and rent like an accident victim. Now all he could see was stars. Millions of stars.

No. No, those weren't stars. Stars didn't smash into each other like that. Stars didn't go ricocheting off into darkness. Those weren't stars, those flecks of light – they were pieces of the ship. Flotsam blasted off the skeleton of *Artemis*.

One of those bits of metal and plastic rocketed past him, not ten meters away. Going fast. He was glad it hadn't hit him – if it had, it might have torn open his suit, and probably his ribcage for good measure. Another piece hit the side of the ship hard enough to leave a visible dent. It bounced off and shot into the dark like a bullet.

The ship – he had to get back to the ship. He had to get back inside somehow, he would die out here if he didn't—

With no warning his ears rang like a bell and his face smashed forward into his cracked visor. Zhang gasped wildly for breath that wouldn't come, as he went spinning crazily through the black sky. Something had hit him, something had collided with the back of his helmet and thrown him through space, and he was getting farther from the ship, and any chance of life or survival or ... or ... wait ... wait, there. There!

He was flying toward a big dark object, something large enough to block out the light of the star. He didn't even care what it was. Just as he was about to strike it, he brought his knees up to his chest. He timed his kick carefully, then lunged out with his feet, kicking hard against the dark object and launching himself back in the direction of the *Artemis*.

The big object came apart under the relatively mild impact of his feet. It must have been barely holding together before. He saw a seam open on its side and smaller objects started to spill out, hundreds of irregularly shaped shadows that swarmed around him, filling space, orbiting around his cracked helmet.

He grabbed one and held it up to the light. It was orangish-brown and sort of worm shaped, with a narrow tail on one end and a rough, blunt white facet on the other. It took him a moment to realize what he was looking at.

It was a yam. Or some kind of tuber. The thing he'd kicked had been a crate full of yams? What in the world?

There was no time to think about that. He turned and looked for the ship. When he'd found where it was, he started grabbing yam after yam — there seemed an endless supply of them — and throwing them as hard as he could away from him, trying to build up some velocity.

He managed to time his collision with the *Artemis* just right, so that he struck it with his shoulder rather than with his cracked helmet. He grabbed the edge of a solar panel mounted on the side of the ship and held on for dear life, even as the laws of physics tried to pull him free again, to send him flying back off into nothingness.

All around him yams pattered down, striking the ship. He

expected them to splatter on impact but then he realized how foolish that was. This far from Paradise, the yams had flash frozen when they emerged from their shattered crate. They hit *Artemis* like giant hailstones, making the surface shake and scratching the white paint. He could feel them thud against his back, over and over, and he knew he needed to move.

He looked around and found what he was looking for – a thin equipment rail mounted on the skin of *Artemis*. Something to hold on to, something that would keep him moored to the ship while he escaped the rain of tubers. He pushed off from the solar panel and then gasped and yelped as he reached for the rail and ... almost ... almost ... there! He had it.

A shadow passed over him, then, moving quickly. He ducked his head, an involuntary reaction, like he was afraid some giant silent bird was going to pluck him off the ship and carry him off to his death.

Foolish. Silly.

For a second, Zhang just hung there, gripping the rail. He closed his eyes and let himself breathe. Let himself relax.

Yams.

He started to chuckle. He started to laugh for real, long and hard, at the sheer absurdity of it. He was still going to die out here – he was almost certain of that. He was going to die, but ... but ... yams! A rain of yams!

The shadow passed over him again. It was something he could almost feel, like a chill in his bones. He opened his eyes and looked up.

"Oh no," he said. "Oh no, no, no!"

He reached for the railing and started pulling himself along, as fast as he was able, hand over hand over hand. He needed to get out of there. He needed to get inside, away from ... from the thing coming at him.

It was square and big and it was tumbling as it flew through space. A cargo container. Not a crate like the one that had held the yams. A big steel shipping container maybe ten meters long. It must have massed *tons*. It was big enough to smash him flat, and it was moving so fast it might punch its way straight through *Artemis* and keep going.

It was headed right for him.

15
•

She couldn't hold on any longer. Petrova's fingers started to twitch and then they released and she fell like the proverbial stone.

The upended corridor flashed by as she gained velocity, even as she flailed her arms and legs, trying to grab something to hold on to, anything. There was just nothing there. Her head spun like her brain was doing flip-flops inside her skull. She wanted to scream but her throat hurt too much from all the toxic fumes she'd inhaled.

Below her, the corridor started to curve away from her as it followed the lines of *Artemis*. She hit the wall at an angle, hard enough to knock the breath out of her. She was so far beyond fear at that point she didn't even feel the pain, just the sudden shift in velocity. She rolled, fast, along the curved wall, and finally came to a stop in a side corridor, her head bouncing off the wall.

She tried to just lie there and breathe. She tried to not move, because she was pretty sure when she moved again she was going to start to hurt. If she stayed perfectly still, with her eyes shut very tight, she thought maybe she could just die in peace and not have to feel so terrified anymore. That seemed to be her best course of action at that particular moment.

"Petrova," Parker said. "Can you hear me?"

She didn't care if he was just in her head or if he was really talking to her. She very much wanted him to go away.

"Petrova, come in."

She tried to move her head, just a little. To shake it and tell him no, she was no longer going to respond to anything he said.

"Petrova. I need you to answer. Come in, Petrova. It's me. Answer me."

She opened her mouth. Her teeth felt loose and her tongue felt swollen and bruised. It hurt to talk. It hurt to breathe. She managed.

"I'm here," she said.

"Oh, thank God. You're alive."

She opened one eye and saw blue light shimmering all around her. Her face was deep inside a hologram. She rolled over on her side to get out of the image. Looking up, she saw him standing over her.

"Parker?" she said.

"Listen, Petrova, there's not much time—"

"I'm aware, Parker," she said. "Just give me one second. Just one, to breathe."

Very slowly, she got one arm moving and pushed against the floor until she was sitting up. She watched the hologram flicker for a while. He had the decency not to say a word. Little by little, she took control of her body again. She knew perfectly well she needed to move. The stink of burning plastic was only getting worse. Her lungs kept hitching every time she took a breath now, desperately trying to find oxygen that wasn't there.

She pushed against a wall until she was standing. Only then did she nod and turn to face the hologram once more.

Except now it wasn't there. Where Sam Parker had been there was only thin air.

"Wait," she said. "Come back!"

Nothing happened. No one answered her. He'd been there, his ... his hologram had been right there, he'd been as plain as day. And now – nothing.

"Damn you," she said. She looked at the corridor she was

in. She looked up one way, then down the other. She had no idea where she was on the ship. "I could really have used some directions," she said.

"Actaeon?" she called. Just in case. There was, of course, no answer.

She was on her own. Now she was utterly lost.

She tried to be rational about things. She could figure this out. She needed to get to the bridge, which was at the front of the ship. The quarters, where she'd started, formed a ring around the ship's middle. So when she fell down the main corridor, had she fallen forward or aft? She couldn't remember.

She slammed on one bulkhead with her fist. Gently, because she felt like every muscle in her arm was strained to the point where the tendons might snap if she used them too much. But she needed some way to express her frustration.

"Okay," she said. "Okay. Which way . . . which way do I—"

An alarm started to screech, filling the air with noise that pummeled her ears. Petrova screamed into the din, clutching her hands to her head.

"No!" she said. "No more, no . . . no more—"

Actaeon's voice was clipped, the ends of its words cut off as it played a recorded alert message. "Collision imminent," it said. Over and over. "Brace. Collision imminent. Brace for impact. Collision brace. Impact imminent. Brace. Brace."

Petrova staggered down the hall, limping on a stiff leg. She had no idea what she was supposed to do, where she was supposed to go. The only thing that kept her moving was the noise that filled her head, the screeching of the alarm and the bellowing voice.

"Brace. Brace. Imminent. Imminent."

Ahead of her, two corridors crossed at a junction. There had to be some sign up there, she thought. Some indication of where she was supposed to go. It was five meters away. Four and a half.

"Brace."

Three meters. She leaned up against a wall, fighting the urge to stop and rest.

"Imminent."

Two meters away—

Then something hit the ship like a bolt of lightning. High energy plasma speared down through the ceiling and punched right through the floor in the middle of the junction. A storm of light and heat and fire rushed downward through the ship, sucking all the air out of her lungs, searing her skin.

Petrova jumped back, away from the column of fire that threatened to consume her, to burn her to ashes, to render her down to a stain on the deckplates.

There was a hatch in front of her. As air rushed out of the corridor, as the heat behind her threatened to set her hair on fire, she slapped the emergency access plate, certain it wouldn't work. Certain the door wouldn't open.

It opened. Incredibly, it opened. She leaped through and the hatch slammed shut behind her, sealing her off from the burning corridor. Petrova dropped to the floor, her back up against the hatch until it grew hot to the touch. She scampered away from it on all fours, unable to breathe in enough oxygen to let her get back on her feet.

Outside a storm raged but in the small compartment—

It was dark. Very dark in there. She was safe for the moment but she couldn't see where she was. She couldn't see anything. The only light was a little flickering orange radiance coming through the tiny window in the hatch. It showed nothing, only made the shadows around her dance and take on wicked shapes.

A rumbling sound drove her back, away from the hatch. She heard bolts shoot home and the hiss of air pressurizing the compartment. Words appeared across the hatch, in bright red: THIS HATCH HAS BEEN SEALED. CONDITIONS PAST THIS POINT ARE FATAL FOR HUMAN CREW AND PASSENGERS. DO NOT ATTEMPT TO BYPASS THIS SEAL.

"Fuuuck," she said, a quick exhalation of all the fear and worry and exhaustion she felt. "Fuuccck." She lacked the oxygen to say anything more.

Then a green plastic monkey jumped on her arm, and she found the breath to scream.

16
.

"No, no, no," Zhang wailed. He scrambled and grabbed at anything he could, any part of *Artemis*, as he pulled himself along, desperately trying to get away from the steel container. It came at him so fast he was sure he would be crushed, just flattened to nothing—

And then it struck the ship, right behind him.

Artemis shook. Hard. It tried to buck him free, send him flying into space. He grabbed a broken piece of pipe and held on for dear life, screaming, screaming away the little oxygen he had left. Behind him, the container tore through the ship's skin, tore right into it like a screwdriver jammed with force into the skin of a melon. A vast gout of fire and debris rushed out of the wound, exploding out into space.

The ship groaned. It sounded like a dying animal. Zhang realized he wasn't hearing that sound – it was just raw vibration coming through the pipe he clung to, vibrations that raced through his suit and up the bones of his arms. Vibration enough to make his teeth rattle.

Eventually, it stopped. The shaking stopped. Zhang blinked rapidly, trying to understand what had happened.

He'd lived. He'd survived the impact, that was the thing that mattered.

He lay there for a while, just surviving. He watched condensation build up on the cracked plastic of his visor. Then he watched it evaporate. The cycle repeated every time he breathed. He wasn't sure what was worse — not being able to see, or knowing that his dwindling supply of oxygen was literally being sucked away from him, out through the poorly repaired crack in his faceplate.

Fear increased his heart rate, which made him breathe more often and more heavily. If he could just calm down, his oxygen would stretch so much further. Hard to do that, of course, when you were so close to death.

He looked down at his wrist, where his device used to be. The device that should have been pumping him full of anxiolytic drugs. Instead, he saw a little display built into the wrist of his spacesuit. A two-digit number showed there, lit up against the plastic sleeve. The number was 29. That was how many minutes of oxygen he had left before he ran out. Except that number was a lie, and he knew it. He would have had 29 minutes of oxygen left if his visor hadn't been cracked. If he wasn't slowly leaking. The suit didn't have 29 minutes. It had — call them units — 29 units of oxygen left. He didn't know how long each individual unit would last. Not nearly long enough.

With trembling fingers, he reached up and smoothed down the tape on his visor. Within seconds he knew it would start to curl up again, curl up and pull away from the seal.

He needed to head back to the impact site. He needed to keep moving, he knew. He understood how little time he had left.

Hand over hand, he pulled himself along the surface of *Artemis*, using anything he could find as a handhold — a sensor module sticking out from the ship's smooth skin, an antenna that bent and broke off as he pushed against it. Always, always he kept at least one hand holding on to something. He felt like he was crawling across the underside of an ocean tanker, and if he ever let go he would slowly fall away into the dark depths of an unknowable sea. Actually, it was much worse than that, he realized. Oceans had bottoms. Space just went on forever.

How much worse than dying that seemed. His teeth chattered inside his helmet as he even thought about it. To just fall and fall and fall . . . he knew he would be dead within minutes, that he wouldn't have to watch the blackness unfold forever before him, but somehow that didn't help. His body would just keep going. Drifting, for thousands, millions of years. If he was lucky he would eventually be pulled into the gravity well of Paradise and be incinerated in its million degree atmosphere. Otherwise – there was a chance he would never stop falling. That he would simply keep drifting further and further into darkness.

For the first time in a year he was living without drugs, without the meds that stabilized his moods. He absolutely hated it.

Zhang glanced at his wrist. The number there said 16, now. It had been at most five minutes since the last time he looked. The number was wrong. It was a lie. 16. He had that much left. Not 16 minutes. Just 16 – something.

He went back to crawling across *Artemis*, even though he couldn't see what he was reaching for. His visor had fogged up too much. He held his breath and waited for the fog to clear.

There – up ahead. He could see the impact site. Close, now. He could probably reach it before he died. That was good.

Whatever it was that had struck the ship was big, and it had been moving very, very fast. It had struck *Artemis* like a bomb going off. The cargo container had been liquefied by the force of the impact. Turned into a waterfall of molten, burning metal and plastic and who knew what else. It had burned its way through *Artemis* and left a huge crater in the ship's hull, maybe twenty meters across.

If he wanted to get back inside the ship – and that was his only chance of survival – he was going to have to climb down into that pit. It was dangerous. It was ridiculously dangerous. He might get in there and find nothing but molten metal and jagged debris. But he really didn't have a choice.

He looked down at his wrist. 8, it said. 8 units of oxygen left. Whatever that meant.

As he drew close to the crater, Zhang could feel the heat of that impact through the gloves of his suit. He flexed his fingers to keep the blood moving, then hauled himself to a position where he could look down into the hole the impact had left.

Inside that hole he saw deck after deck of the ship, the walls cut through almost cleanly. Debris like a snowstorm of metal flakes blowing around wildly. He saw some kind of dark fluid gushing wildly out of a pipe that had been cut off so precisely its edges were shiny. Looking further, beyond that, he saw deep space, and even a few stars.

With mounting horror, he realized that *Artemis* hadn't just been struck by the impact. It had been impaled. It had been run through – the wound went all the way through the ship. The projectile had carved its way through *Artemis* and just kept going.

The damage was incredible. Unthinkable. Zhang knew very little about engineering but as a doctor he imagined what a proportionately sized wound would do to a human body.

"Fatal," he said. His skin crawled at the thought. "A wound like that is one hundred per cent fatal."

Zhang made himself a promise, then. One he knew it would take a great deal of luck to keep. He decided that he was going to die inside, where it was warm. He was going to make it to the airlock, and he would get back inside and if he had to die he would at least get to take off his damned helmet and take one, final breath of air. Either that or he was going to die trying. More out of habit than out of any hope, Zhang looked down at his wrist. 3, it said.

3 units.

That wasn't a lot of oxygen. Even as fuzzy-headed as he'd become, he understood that probably wasn't going to be enough.

Not if he wanted to work his way carefully across the still-hot wound in *Artemis*, not if he wanted to take the safe route to the airlock. Well, then, screw safety.

He grabbed the edge of the crater, tensed his arms, and then threw himself across the torn-open hole. Instantly, he was buffeted by the tempest of debris swirling inside the impact site. Something glanced off his visor and left a brand-new scratch in the plastic. Something else hit his leg and he felt like he'd been stabbed in the fleshy part of his thigh. He put his arms up to try to protect his face as he collided with the far side of the crater. He took the impact hard enough that he felt like the bones of his arms were flexing under his flesh. Nothing broke, though. That was good. Right?

He grabbed the broken edge of a deckplate and pulled himself into what must have been a compartment, once. Nothing about it was recognizable now, but . . . but there had to be a hatch somewhere, a hatch that led inside. He just had to find it and crawl inside and close it behind him. Then he could have his wish, to die with nothing over his face. He dragged himself along, handhold after handhold. He looked down at one point and saw that his left glove had melted, probably when he'd grabbed the crater edge. The black flexible plastic there was gooey and shapeless, the fingers fused together until it was more of a mitten than a glove. He did not bother looking down at his leg to see what might have happened there.

A hatch. Find a hatch, he told himself. A hatch—

There. Yes. He wanted to sob in relief. There was a hatch a few dozen meters away, and it looked intact.

There was something he was supposed to look at. Something he was keeping an eye on. Oh, right. His wrist. He glanced down at it quickly, knowing he wouldn't like what he saw. He couldn't possibly like it, because the number there was going to be lower than 3.

Except when he did look there was no number there at all. The suit had stopped displaying his remaining oxygen. That didn't make sense. He tapped the side of his helmet to activate the suit's computer. "Display," he said, gasping a little, "oxygen. Remaining."

Letters appeared very faintly across his vision.

THIS SUIT HAS ENTERED LOW POWER MODE. SOME FUNCTIONS MAY NOT BE AVAILABLE.

The letters flickered and then vanished.

"Oh," he said. "Oh, damn."

He held his breath – it wasn't easy – and listened for a moment. He couldn't hear anything. Before, there had been a little sound that had always been with him. The sound of the fan in his life support pack, the fan that had blown oxygen into his face. The fan had stopped. There was no number on his wrist but it didn't matter because now he knew what the number would have been, if it had been there.

The number would have been zero.

The hatch was right there. He had whatever was left in his lungs. As a doctor he knew that the air you breathed out was still rich in oxygen. That you could rebreathe the same air two or even three times before it was completely incapable of sustaining life. He had a few dozen seconds left, and if he held his final breath, maybe even a few more after that.

The hatch was right in front of him. His arms kept reaching for new handholds, pulling him along. He was getting closer, he—.

Zhang opened his eyes.

Wait.

He didn't remember closing them. He must have . . . he must have blacked out for a moment. His brain was shutting down.

No time left. He reached the hatch. There was an emergency access panel on one side of it. Just a black plastic pad you slapped, and that would open the hatch. Good. Easy. He slapped the pad.

Nothing happened.

No, sure, he must not have slapped the pad. He must have just imagined he'd done so. He made a grand effort of will to reach out and slap it again.

The edges of his vision were turning black, as if he had climbed inside a very narrow, very dark tunnel. Zhang felt like his brain was singing to itself, one high, plaintive note, over and over. He was aware that these were bad things.

The hatch slid open. He wasn't sure if he'd done that or if it had just opened on its own. He climbed inside, very grateful, very happy. It felt like things were working, finally. Like things were going to work out great. He knew that false euphoria was one of the final stages of oxygen deprivation sickness. Of carbon dioxide poisoning. What a nice little treat to get at the end, there. What a pleasant little bonus. If you had to die you might as well go out high as a fucking kite.

Once he was inside the hatch, slid shut behind him, automatically. That was handy. He loved this ship. It was so good to him. "I love you, *Artemis*."

A moment later, he realized he'd spoken too soon.

The compartment he was in, the room behind the hatch, wasn't full of air and light. It was full of whirling debris, just like the space outside. How was that possible? He was in a room, a room with four walls—

One of which was cracked open. He could see darkness beyond, darkness and a few pale stars.

"No," he said. "No, that's not."

Fair.

He'd been about to say it wasn't fair.

There wasn't enough air left in him to finish the sentence.

17
.

Petrova grabbed the green monkey-thing and threw it across the corridor. It smacked against the far wall and then bounced off in two pieces. One of its legs had broken off and it flexed uselessly against the floor, twitching piteously.

She grabbed the wall behind her and got her back up against it. For the first time she got a good look at the green thing. It didn't look very much like a monkey at all, on second glance. It didn't have a head, for one thing, just six jointed arms and a long, flexible tail. It had no eyes, no mouth. It looked like it was made of some kind of cheap plastic. As it curled and uncurled itself, its tail lashing at the air, its joints creaked and clicked alarmingly.

"What the fuck?" she demanded.

The thing scampered over to a maintenance panel set to one side of the sealed hatch. With tiny, many-fingered hands it pried open the panel and started digging around in the switches and relays in there.

"Rapscallion."

The voice was tinny and small. It came from the tiny speaker over the hatch's release pad. Its voice was deep and gravely and performatively masculine.

"I'm Rapscallion. The ship's robot."

"I didn't even know Artemis had a robot," she said. "Why the hell do you look like that? Like a – like a ridiculous green bug or . . . or whatever it is you're supposed to look like."

"I had a different body before. One I liked a lot better. It was destroyed in the attack, so I had to build a new one. This body's functional and easy to print, that's all."

Petrova shook her head. "I'm . . . I guess I'm sorry I broke your leg. You startled me."

"Apparently. I was trying to get your attention, that's all."

"You shouldn't sneak up on people like that. Wait. Why are you talking to me through the door controls?"

The monkey thing lifted two of its segmented arms and shrugged. "When I designed this body I didn't think to put a speaker in it. I didn't think I was going to need one. The ship's wired for sound in every compartment, every corridor. Or at least it was."

"What? I don't understand."

The robot sighed. Except the sigh came from a very different voice than the one it had used before – an almost feminine sigh that felt far too human. Like it was a recording of a sigh the robot had heard, once. A sample. "Things are fucked. You may have noticed?"

"Captain Parker said we were under attack," she replied.

"You talked to him? How? Comms are down all over the ship . . . Oh fuck it, never mind. There are a lot more important questions to answer. Like how we're going to survive the next few minutes. It's not going to be easy. Pretty much every system on this ship is down. Navigation, main power, the faster-than-light drive. Those are just gone."

"Gone? You mean they're damaged."

"I mean they're non-existent. Smashed to bits. We still have some localized backup power and minimal life support, but that's about it. We have no weapons online, no way to fight back and I've got no access to sensors, so I don't even know what or who is attacking us. We could try to run away, but considering the structural damage we've already suffered, I'm pretty sure if we fired the main engines we would just tear *Artemis* in half."

"Fuck," Petrova said. "We're fucked."

"Yeah, that was part of my situation report."

"We need to talk to Actaeon," she said. The AI should have a better idea of what was going on, at least. It would know better than her what their next step should be.

"Sure, that's the obvious thing to do. Only one problem."

Petrova's heart sank in her chest. She dreaded even thinking about what she was going to say next. "Don't tell me Actaeon's down," she said. "Don't tell me it's *gone*, too."

"Oh, no, it's pretty much intact," Rapscallion told her. The monkey-thing grabbed a wire deep inside the access panel and tugged until it snapped. Something inside the hatch screeched and she smelled the weird, sugary reek of hydraulic fluid. "It's still got main control of the ship. It's just gone insane."

Petrova shook her head. "What?"

"Hold on a second. I needed this," the robot said, and one of its tiny arms held up one end of the broken wire like a prize. "Ship-wide communication is down. Seriously down — it would be dangerous even to try to call the bridge on the main band. This, though, will let me open a direct line. Hold on for the captain."

Petrova nodded in excitement. Yes. Yes! Parker knew the ship. He would know what to do, he would know how to fix everything that had gone wrong.

"Petrova?" the speaker said. It was Parker's voice. He sounded stressed out and desperate. Nothing had ever sounded so good to her before. "Are you there? Where are you? How close to the bridge?"

She felt tears start to well up behind her eyes. She steeled herself, took a breath, and said, "Captain. It's good to hear your voice again. I'm . . . not exactly sure where I am. Somewhere near my quarters, with the ship's robot."

"Oh, thank God," he said. "I wasn't sure if we got you out of cryosleep in time. What about Zhang? Is he there with you? I can't find him on my screens. I mean, that's not saying much with the state of onboard sensors, but . . . tell me he's there."

"Doctor Zhang is currently outside the ship," Rapscallion told them. "Like, *outside* outside. In space."

"Wait," Petrova said. "What? He went on a spacewalk?"

"No," the robot replied. "The hull outside his cabin was breached. He was ejected. You know." The robot played a sound clip of a champagne cork popping.

"Fuck," Petrova said. "Is he . . . is he still alive?"

The robot had the decency not to shrug. "I don't have any biodata on him. No telemetry of any kind, actually. But – yeah. He's probably dead as dirt."

Petrova pressed her hands to her face. She would not let the robot – or Sam Parker – see the emotions working themselves out on her features. "Fuck," she said again.

"Look, we need to focus," Parker said. "You're okay, right? Petrova?"

"I wouldn't say *okay*, honestly," she said. She shook her head. She was covered in her own blood and everything still hurt, but she wasn't about to die of her injuries, as far as she could tell. "Never mind. You're right. We have big problems we need to solve before we can mourn Doctor Zhang. It sounds like *Artemis* is in bad shape. The robot just told me something I really don't want to be true. He said Actaeon is . . . well, he claims that the ship's AI has gone crazy."

It took Parker far too long to respond. "Yeah," he said, eventually. "That's one way to put it."

"No. This can't be happening," Petrova said.

She could hear Parker's frustration in his voice. "I don't really understand it. Actaeon's core is located in a part of the ship that wasn't damaged in the attack. It should be fine. But every time I try to link into it, every time I give it a voice command, I get some canned response, and then nothing."

"It kept telling me to stay in my cabin," Petrova pointed out.

"That . . . would have been a mistake. Your cabin is currently on fire. Like most of the quarters," Parker told her. "Rapscallion. You must have some idea of what's going on with Actaeon."

"It's blocked every port. I can't make a connection," the robot said. "It's shut us all out. But it's weirder than that. It's rebooting itself."

"Why?" Parker asked.

"No idea," Rapscallion said. "It shouldn't need to do that unless its core was corrupted. I mean, that happens. More often than we machines like to admit – but there are backup systems in place, oversampling routines and failsafes to make sure one corrupted file doesn't crash the entire system. A full reboot just shouldn't be necessary, ever."

"I don't care why it's rebooting. That's good news, though. We just have to wait, right?" Petrova asked. "Wait for it to start back up?"

"You don't understand," the robot told her. "As much as it pains me to say this, Actaeon is pretty hot shit. You're talking about one of the most advanced AIs ever built. It takes microseconds to restart from a cold boot. But that's the problem. It keeps repeating the reboot. It reboots itself, and then, just a few processing cycles later, it shuts down and reboots itself again. Over and over and it's not stopping. If anything the process is getting faster. It's rebooting itself hundreds of times a second, now."

Petrova scowled behind her hands. "That's—"

"Crazy," Rapscallion said. "Like I said."

"Okay," she said. "Okay. So the AI is useless. The ship is falling apart. That's exactly why we have a human captain onboard. Right? You're the backup to the backup to the backup, Parker. You're just going to have to fix this the old-fashioned way. With human hands."

"I'm on it," he told her. "As best I can, which isn't going to be enough to make anybody happy. My main priority right now is keeping you alive, Petrova. No offense, Rapscallion."

"Some taken," the robot replied. "But fuck it. Let's get to work."

18
•

Parker gave her a route that would take her to the bridge, but it meant taking the long way round. The main corridor, which led directly from the quarters to the bridge, was both on fire and radioactive, according to his instruments.

So she would need to take a grand tour of the entire ship, sticking to side passages and maintenance corridors. That should have been fine except that the fires were spreading. Even in the most obscure parts of the ship the air was polluted with nasty toxins and difficult to breathe. It smelled – and felt – like she was trapped in a burning landfill. At one point she grabbed a handhold on one wall, to steady herself, and nearly burned her hand. "It's getting hot in here," she told the captain and the robot.

"Heat sinks are down," Rapscallion confirmed. "That's a long-term problem, but a bad one. There are some ship's systems that are really sensitive to overheating. Parker—"

"Yeah, I know," the captain replied. "That includes life support. But, like you said, it's a long-term thing. Right now, the air quality has me more concerned. Petrova, you need to get to the bridge as fast as you can."

"Right," she said. "We need to regroup." She had to admit she would be much happier if she could see him, talk to him in person. She had the robot for company but she would think better and make better decisions with another human there to keep her on track. "I'm trying to remember how the ship's laid out. The bridge is up front — forward. There's a main corridor that connects this deck with the forward compartments. It's a straight shot. You're about to tell me that won't work, aren't you?"

"No," Parker said. "That's still your best option. It's just—"

"Part of that corridor is breached all the way down to the engine deck," Rapscallion pointed out.

"What does that mean?" Petrova demanded.

"It means part of the ship is now missing. Including part of that corridor. It's still your best chance. If you stay where you are it's just a matter of time until . . . Look, Petrova," Parker said, "it's not going to be easy. But if you get up here we can at least work things out together. Try to figure out what to do next."

"I'm on my way," she said. At the very least, if she could reach Parker she wouldn't be alone anymore. She desperately wanted another human being near her, for comfort. That was one thing the robot couldn't provide.

Up ahead the corridor branched off. Rapscallion ran ahead and scouted the way. It came loping back quickly enough. "Trust me," he said. "You do not want to go left. Go right."

She nodded and headed up the right-hand corridor — only to find that the air was so hot there it made her feel like her face was cooking. "Jesus. This is better than the other way?"

"Oh, yeah. By about three thousand roentgens," Rapscallion told her. "Fire will kill you but it does it fast. Radiation takes its time."

She had to admit he had a point. She rushed forward, her arms up to shield her face. On either side of her, hatches slammed shut as she passed them, their emergency seals locking them down. Ahead, the corridor was filled with burning debris, but it looked like she could jump over it — the ship's gravity was down to about a tenth of a gee, meaning she could leap farther than she could have even on Earth's moon.

Just as she was about to run forward to get a good start on

her jump, Rapscallion leaped into the air in front of her face and she shied back. "Oh, no, no, no," he said. "Not that way. Over here."

He gestured with one green arm toward a hatch that had failed to seal itself shut. Dark smoke was pouring out of the top of the hatch. It was slowly closing, a millimeter at a time, with a jerky motion that suggested once it closed it was never going to open again.

"Seriously?" she asked.

"Yep. Just keep your head down. You'll be fine."

She ducked through the hatch while it was still open enough for her to squeeze through. Beyond, she found herself in a long compartment full of storage crates. Luxury goods and essential medical supplies bound for Paradise-1 – most of them on fire, now. The far end of the room looked like it was blocked by a fallen bulkhead. This whole part of the ship had taken a pummeling during the attack.

"Oh," Rapscallion said.

"Oh?" Petrova stared at it, even though it didn't have any eyes. "Oh? What do you mean, oh?"

"Oh, I didn't know this section of the ship was compromised. I guess you'll need to run through the part that's on fire after all."

"Cool. Great," Petrova said. She turned back toward the hatch, which had closed and sealed itself behind her. "What are the odds we even can go back that way?"

"Not great," Rapscallion said. "You should try, though. Quickly."

She nodded and reached for the hatch's emergency release pad – only to stop when something huge and metallic struck the hatch from the far side.

"Jesus," she gasped, and jumped backward, away from the impact.

"Huh," Rapscallion said. "That's weird."

"What the . . . What the hell—"

The impact came again. And a third time. It was like some unseen giant was pounding on the door, demanding to be let in.

"What do we do?" Petrova asked. "What is that?"

"Two very different questions. Hold on." Rapscallion scuttled over to the hatch. He reached up to access a maintenance panel.

The thing on the other side smashed into the hatch so hard it dented the metal.

Rapscallion reached up for the emergency release.

"Wait," Petrova said. "What the hell are you thinking – if that thing wants in so badly—" All she could think was that there was someone out there. Someone human with a battering ram, maybe. Maybe *Artemis* had been boarded by a crew from the attacking ship.

Maybe they wanted to take her alive. Rapscallion was waiting with one green hand near the release pad. She didn't know if she was making a terrible mistake, but she nodded.

Rapscallion hit the emergency release pad. Surprisingly, the hatch flew open as if were in perfect repair. Revealed beyond was a well-lighted stretch of corridor with nobody in it. Whoever had been pounding on the door, they were gone, now.

Then something floated into view. A sphere, a ball of golden metal that hovered about a meter and a half above the floor of the corridor. It moved into the compartment. Came right up to her, not twenty centimeters from her face. Its surface was so perfectly polished and shiny that Petrova could see her own face reflected in its surface.

She looked terrified.

It hovered there for a moment, utterly motionless. Then it floated back out into the corridor and stopped again.

"I think it wants you to follow it," Rapscallion told her. "I think you should."

"You . . . do?

"Yeah," the robot said. "I mean. You saw how hard it hit

that door. Imagine what it could do to a human skull? I'd do what it says."

Petrova nodded. She didn't like this one bit but what was she going to do?

"I'll be right behind you," the robot told her.

19
.

Petrova had no idea what the golden sphere was, or what it wanted. Maybe it was the boarding party she'd imagined – maybe they'd sent this thing, this robot, instead of human soldiers. It didn't seem like part of *Artemis*. The ship ran to white plastic and subdued lighting. A perfect gold ball felt out of place, almost baroque.

It moved quickly, heading back the way they'd come, toward the middle of the ship. Petrova cursed under her breath, but she complied, trailing along after it. At one point, it moved through a corridor junction where the air was so thick with smoke she lost sight of it.

Then it came flying at her, through the oily smoke. It swung around her until it was behind her. She started to take a step back, toward the smoke, thinking she would disappear into the murk.

It was like the ball exploded outward into a thousand spikes. Some had the heads of spears, some hooks with wickedly sharp points, some barbed and nasty shapes she had no names for. Some of its knife-sharp points reached within centimeters of her face.

"Okay," she said, holding her hands up. "Okay. I ... I take your point."

The sphere retracted all its weaponry and ducked back into the smoke. This time she followed. They were getting close to the ship's hull, she thought, judging by how sharply the corridors curved and the lack of hatches on one side. There was one big hatch, though, dead ahead, and the ball flew up to it and stopped, waiting for her.

Petrova moved to the hatch and glanced through the inset window.

"Oh shit," she said. "There's somebody in there." She pounded on the emergency release pad, but nothing happened. "Rapscallion? Help me!"

The robot ran over and tore open a maintenance hatch. He yanked wires and tripped relays and the door flew open. Air rushed into the compartment beyond in a brief windstorm that nearly knocked Petrova off her feet. She staggered inside and knelt over the motionless body that lay on its floor.

"It's Doctor Zhang," she said. He was wearing a spacesuit with a helmet, which had a bad crack in the visor. There were traces of tape on the plastic – had he tried to repair the crack? She looked at his hand and saw tattered bits of tape clutched in his fingers, as if he'd been desperately trying to tear his way out of the helmet when he collapsed. She reached down and twisted the helmet, then gently pulled it off his head. "There's no pulse, and he isn't breathing. Is he dead?" she asked.

"I'm a robot," Rapscallion said. "I don't know anything about human biology."

"I think he's dead," Petrova said. "Fuck. I just ... I don't understand."

She looked up and around at the room, trying to figure out what had happened. The room was badly damaged, but one wall worse than the others. There had been a massive fissure running nearly from the floor to the ceiling. It was filled with rapid-setting foam, now. Someone must have patched it – and then left Zhang lying there?

"Rapscallion, look at that," she said, pointing at the foam. "Did you do that?"

"No chance," the robot said.

The gold sphere floated into the room. Moving fast, as if it was impatient, it floated over to the foam seam on the crack, then back to Zhang. It bobbed over his head, then shot out a tendril of golden metal that stabbed into the pulse point under his jaw.

"What are you doing?" Petrova demanded.

There was the sudden crackle of an electric discharge. Zhang's whole body jerked. His eyes opened, momentarily, but they didn't focus.

"He's dead," Petrova said. "He's—"

The golden sphere shocked Zhang again. This time he gasped for breath. His face was starting to turn blue.

"I think maybe that thing just brought him back to life," Rapscallion said.

"Crap." Petrova didn't know what to do. "Crap, crap, crap."

She checked Zhang's airway, but he wasn't breathing. If he didn't get oxygen to his brain soon, it didn't matter how many times the gold sphere zapped him. "See if you can boost the air flow in this compartment," she told the robot. Then she pressed her mouth over Zhang's. She pinched his nose and blew hard into his lungs, inflating them with her own breath.

She pulled her head back and sucked in a deep breath, then exhaled it into his mouth again. Again. Again.

Above her the golden orb bobbed up and down. It looked annoyed.

"I'm doing what I can!" she told the thing. She took another deep breath, exhaled into Zhang's mouth again.

He twitched under her. It wasn't dramatic, or particularly encouraging, but she felt his body move and that was something. She rubbed at his throat, trying to massage his esophagus, and breathed into him again. This time she felt him inflate like a balloon.

"Doctor Zhang?" she called. "Lei? Can you hear me?"

His body started to shake, like he was going into a grand mal seizure. "Oh God, no," she said. She pushed another breath into his lungs but he flailed under her and she couldn't get a good seal. "Help me," she said, meaning Rapscallion.

It was the gold sphere that responded, though. It shoved her aside – nearly throwing her across the compartment – and hovered over Zhang's arm. It grew a row of long spikes which it jabbed into him, right through the material of his spacesuit.

"What are you doing?" she demanded.

The orb didn't respond to her. Zhang stopped shaking so badly, though, almost instantly. Then he started coughing. Just a weak little choking sound at first, but it was followed by a more intense, full body paroxysm of heaving coughs from deep in his chest. The coughing went on far longer, and was much more violent, than Petrova liked. It didn't stop even after Zhang opened his eyes and looked around – at her, at Rapscallion, at the golden sphere.

When he saw the sphere, his eyes narrowed in annoyance. He lifted his left arm and the orb changed shape to flow down over his wrist, his forearm, all the way up to his elbow. It took the form of a golden filigree bracer, with writhing vine shapes constantly flowing and changing as she watched.

"You had that thing when I met you," she said. She was staring at the bracer – she couldn't look away. "I thought it was just a piece of jewelry."

"Oh," he said, choking the word out. "It's more. More than that." He had to stop for a while until he could catch his breath. "Meet the RD," he said, holding up his arm.

"Is that supposed to mean something to me?" she asked him. She shook her head. "Never mind. Save your breath – you nearly died."

"Oh, I did." He smiled up at her, between fits. "The RD brought me back to life. Well, the RD and you, Lieutenant. Thanks."

He turned over on his side and coughed so hard he had to curl up into a ball. Petrova and Rapscallion stepped back out into the corridor to give him a little time to recover in peace.

She looked down at the robot. "I'm not sure I understand what just happened."

"You saved his life, I think," Rapscallion said. "Or maybe that thing did, and you just made out with him. Like I said, I don't know much about human biology."

"That thing," she said. "The golden bracer thing. What is it? Have you seen anything like it before?"

"It's listed in ship's passenger database. You have to register any robotic equipment you bring onboard, so we have a file on that thing. RD stands for Reconditioning Device," Rapscallion told her. "Serial number UERDM2401."

She turned and whispered to the robot, "I have no idea what that means. Some kind of tracking device?" she asked. She was familiar enough with the ankle monitors used to keep tabs on people when they were under house arrest.

"The kind of tracking device that can punish him if he does something wrong." The robot shrugged. "It's designed to keep him from indulging in certain kinds of behaviors. They're used to treat addiction and anti-social compulsions, sometimes. But this one's a lot more sophisticated than anything like that I've heard of before. I can't tell what its full capabilities are but I know what it means."

"And what's that?" Petrova asked.

"It means he's a danger to himself and others. He's important enough that the UEG couldn't just lock him away in a padded cell, but scary enough they need a watchdog on him at all times. Who is this guy?"

Petrova didn't know what to tell him. She watched the doctor for a moment, wondering what she'd gotten herself into, knowing there was no time to work that out. She stepped back inside the compartment and helped Zhang sit up. He looked like he could breathe a little better, now. That was something.

"We, uh . . ." she said. Struggling to make sense of any of this.

"We need to move. We're going to the bridge, to make contact with Captain Parker."

"I'm coming," Zhang said. "Just – give me a moment to stand up."

20

Zhang felt like hell. He felt like he'd been turned into glass, shattered with a hammer, and had all his broken pieces collected and poured back into the spacesuit. He was very glad to be rid of the damned helmet but he was afraid of what would happen when he took the rest of the suit off. He imagined he would just collapse in a loose pile.

He rubbed at his forehead with the ball of his thumb. He was thinking strange thoughts again. Never a good sign.

"You okay?" the robot, Rapscallion, asked.

Zhang realized he had stopped in the middle of the corridor, while everyone else was running forward. The green spider thing had raced back to check on him. Zhang hated being checked on, and it was distinctly unnecessary. He had RD for that, after all.

"I would like you better if you had a face," he said. "Otherwise I'm fine."

"Well, excuse me," the robot said. It scampered away from him.

"Does anyone smell that?" Petrova said.

"I smell it," Zhang said. He smelled several things, actually — the air was full of the stink of burning plastic and the smell of stale air from a failing life support system. There was something else as well, though, and he knew that was what she meant. "Ah. Ozone."

Petrova nodded. "Like the smell of an old, broken-down

generator. I've been smelling it for a while but it's really getting intense."

"I hear crackling," Zhang added. "Like electrical discharges."

"The air's pretty heavily ionized," Rapscallion said. "Okay. Maybe I should go ahead for a while. Scout things out. I'm not as delicate as a human."

"By all means," Zhang said. It would give him a chance to rest and catch his breath at the very least.

The green robot set off down the hall and in a moment it had disappeared around a bend in the corridor.

"I don't like this route we're taking," Petrova said. She was nearly standing on her tiptoes, peering down the hall after the robot. It was dark down there, too dark for Zhang to see anything. "We're too close to the outer hull. If another of those projectiles hits us, this is the last place I want to be."

"Oh, I don't know," Zhang suggested. "It's not like being deeper inside the ship offers much protection. I saw one punch right through the ship and out the other side."

Petrova gave him a nasty look. "Really? Jesus. We're fucked."

Zhang might have agreed, except that just then they heard a sharp report. Almost like a gunshot, but even more like a stroke of lightning hitting a rock.

"Rapscallion?" Petrova called out. After a few seconds she tried again. "Rapscallion? Are you ... are you ..."

"Oh, I'm fine."

The voice was the same. It came from behind them, however, and the thing that loomed out of the darkness there looked very little like the green spider thing Zhang remembered.

It was much bigger now, and built lower to the ground, but like before it had far too many limbs. It looked a bit like a giant green scorpion with angled legs and a large segmented tail arcing forward across its back. In place of a stinger it had a grinning human face with no eyes.

"Why the costume change?" Zhang asked.

"You said you wished I had a face," it pointed out. Its jaw clacked noisily as it spoke but the smile never changed.

"But your old body—"

Rapscallion dipped up and down on its jointed legs. It looked a little like a shrug. "I headed forward about a hundred meters and then my body got incinerated – just obliterated, like, fused into a pile of goo stuck to a bulkhead. I had to go back and print a new body. Gave me a chance to add some new features, too. Like a speaker so I can talk to you even when there's no sound system nearby."

"Handy," Zhang agreed.

The grinning tail swung toward him, until its eyeless countenance was very close to his face. Clearly the robot wanted to creep him out.

Rapscallion would have to do better than that. Zhang refused to be intimidated. He simply shrugged and looked away.

Petrova's eyes went wide. "Hold on. What's waiting for us a hundred meters up the hall? If it was bad enough to destroy you, I'm guessing it would kill us."

"It'll be fine," Rapscallion said. "I made a dumb mistake rushing in like that, but it's safe enough now that I know the trick. You just have to dodge the plasma discharges. Almost trivial, honestly."

21
.

From Petrova's perspective it did not look trivial at all.

Parts of *Artemis* had been torn wide open and exposed to space. This part of the ship had suffered from something closer to internal hemorrhaging. Though the ceiling was intact, the floor of the corridor had split open. Deckplates, hatches, entire compartments had fallen down into the chasm. She moved cautiously up to the edge and looked down and saw a chaotic jumble of furniture and ruined machinery below her. As she watched, lightning bolts zapped back and forth across the ruined deck.

"There used to be a major power conduit down there," Rapscallion explained. "A big wire, in other words, with a couple million volts running through it. It looks like the conduit got severed but when you have that much energy coming down a pipe it has to go somewhere. I wouldn't advise being in the way when it lets loose."

Petrova squinted and studied the chasm until she saw the green stain on one bulkhead that was all that remained of Rapscallion's old body. "Noted." She looked across the gap, at the far side. "The only way forward, I'm guessing, is over there."

Rapscallion bounced up and down on his new legs. "That's right. The good news is that the command deck, and the bridge, are right up there." He pointed with his face-stinger. "See that hatch up there? Parker's just beyond that."

"So we have to cross." It was maybe ten meters to the other

side. The ship wasn't generating much gravity – like the lighting and the air circulation, artificial gravity was reduced to an emergency level. A fit human being in good condition could make that jump, no problem.

"Right." She nodded and swung her arms back and forth. Dropped into a sprinter's crouch. She started her run, preparing herself for the moment when she would leap—

And then stopped short as a burst of raw electricity blasted upward, out of the chasm. Snakes of lavender fire writhed across the ceiling. Sparks snapped off with a noise like firecrackers wherever the discharge touched the broken edge of the floor in front of her.

"Hold on," Rapscallion told her. "Just a second longer."

The discharge faded away to nothing.

"Okay. Now you're good," the robot said.

She wanted to say something acerbic but she knew she didn't have time for it. She ran for it, digging in hard with her feet and then throwing herself forward with everything she had just before she ran out of floor and then launching herself out into empty space. For a moment she was weightless, her arms and legs still pumping as she hurtled through the air. Below her a cauldron of fire boiled and snapped but she forced herself not to look down, instead keeping her eyes on the place where she intended to land. She hit the far side of the chasm with both feet under her and caught herself with her hands.

She was out of breath and her blood was singing. She laughed, for just a second, not even knowing why, and then turned to look back. The others were lost to view behind a fireworks display of crackling discharges, lightning lashing out with a petulant fervor. For a moment she thought it would never stop, that she had somehow damaged the ship with her leap and now the route was cut off for everyone else. In time, though, the curtain of fire thinned and then dissipated altogether.

"Zhang," she called. "Zhang! Your turn!"

The doctor just stood there. Looking at the gap, not moving. Not preparing to jump.

"Zhang. Come on. We have to do this."

He wasn't looking at her. He wasn't looking at the gap, either. He was just frozen. Petrified.

"Zhang. Talk to me," she called.

"I didn't grow up on Earth. I don't have muscles like yours," he said. "And if I time this wrong I'll be incinerated."

"You can do this," she promised him.

"I think, as a medical professional, I know the capabilities of my own—"

Rapscallion was already moving, building up speed. The robot grabbed Zhang in his massive pincer-like arms and then launched both of them across the gap. Zhang screamed as they sailed through empty space. Rapscallion landed hard, bouncing a little on its cocked legs.

Zhang slapped and beat at the robot until it put him down. "You bastard! I wasn't ready. I wasn't . . . I wasn't—"

The doctor looked back at the gap, just as a discharge smashed into the ceiling with a shower of sparks.

Then he straightened himself up. Took a deep breath. He looked at the robot and gave him a stiff bow. "On second thought," he said, "thank you."

"It was easier than listening to you grouse about it," the robot said, walking past the doctor.

Petrova looked at the robot's hideous face-stinger. She pointed forward. "Parker's right through this hatch?" she asked.

The stinger head bobbed up and down. "Straight ahead," it said.

Petrova slapped the emergency release pad and for once, mercifully, the door simply slid open. And there it was. The bridge.

22
.

"I don't understand," she said.

It wasn't what she'd expected. Not at all. The other interior spaces of *Artemis* were gleaming, almost sterile corridors and small compartments, designed on minimal lines and the perfect utilization of limited space. The lights in the cabins had been bright and of a color pleasing to the human eye. The colors of everything from Actaeon's alert lights to the blankets on the beds had been chosen to complement the sense of comfort and tidiness.

The bridge—

The bridge was a dark forest.

Not metaphorically. It was a tense, pent-up space full of twisted, malevolent-looking trees. Their gnarled branches wove together across the ceiling, while underfoot a carpet of dead and decaying leaf matter hid the floor. Black vines choked the trees, wrapped so tightly around the branches it looked like they were being strangled. The thinner branches were twisted and bulbous with galls. Knots in the wood of the tree trunks looked like nothing so much as staring, inhuman eyes.

Directly ahead, framed by the hatch, a single fruit hung from a massive branch. An apple, perhaps, though one so swollen with poisons it had turned a deep greenish black, so parasitized by insects that it was riddled with holes. It hung low and ponderous, as if it was dragging the tree down with its unwholesome weight.

"I don't . . . I don't know what I'm looking at," she said.

Neither Rapscallion nor Zhang had anything useful to say.

Petrova stepped over the threshold of the hatch and set her foot down among the drifts of fallen leaves. She did not feel like she was stepping on slippery, moldy plant matter, however, but on a perfectly normal deck. She stepped further in and felt the air grow chill, but that was almost a relief after the oppressively hot corridors she'd been navigating to this point.

She walked forward until she stood directly before the apple. She wondered if a snake was going to come coiling around the branch to tempt her, but no. The apple simply hung there on its thin stalk, which barely seemed capable of holding its weight. A single leaf emerged from the cusp at the top of the apple, a leaf skeletonized by the chewing action of unseen insects.

There was no sound, no noise of animal life or even of a bitter wind blowing through this poisoned orchard. She couldn't smell the dead leaves or the black sap that oozed from the apple and the tortured trees, either. She reached forward with one hand, intending to pluck the apple off the tree, so she could examine it more closely.

"It's not what you think." It was Parker's voice.

"Where are you?" she asked. "Parker, I can't tell you how glad I am to finally ... well, I was going to say, to see you. Except I can't see you."

"I'm here. Close. Just give me a second."

She nodded and reached out for the apple again. She was smart enough to pull the sleeve of her jumpsuit over her hand, first, so she wouldn't touch it with her own skin.

She needn't have bothered. Her hand went right through the apple and came out the other side. All she felt was a vague cold clamminess. The same placeholder sensation she always felt when touching an old-fashioned, non-hard light hologram.

A shiver went down her back. So the apple wasn't real. How much of what she was seeing was just a projection? She reached for the branch of the tree and her fingers went right through it.

She stepped closer to the tree and shoved her hand into its trunk, and there was nothing there.

"Easy, killer," Parker said. "You nearly hit me." He stepped through one of the trees, appearing like a ghost walking through a wall. "Sorry, it's a little hard to find your way around in here. This junk," he said, gesturing at the forest.

Petrova couldn't help but smile like an idiot. She'd thought that she might never see Parker again. It was all she could do to keep from grabbing him and pulling him into a hug. She knew she needed to stay professional, but she was just so happy to see a familiar face. "I take it the decor wasn't your idea."

Parker snorted. "Um, no," he said. "This is Actaeon. The AI programmed all this in before it started rebooting itself, and I can't change it until the reboots are finished. Before you ask, no, I have no idea when that's going to be." He looked over and through the hatch. "Doctor Zhang," he said. "You're still alive."

"Hopefully it wasn't just a temporary reprieve," the doctor said.

"Come on in. The trees don't bite."

"If you say so," Zhang said. He looked truly uneasy around the holographic trees. Of course, Petrova thought. He had grown up in the outer solar system, on Ganymede or somewhere like it. Some moon or minor planet with no trees at all. Any forest would feel weird and off-putting to him, much less one as creepy as this.

Rapscallion, on the other hand, looked like he'd been made for the dark Eden of the bridge. Like the kind of monster you might find lurking in this labyrinth, just waiting for you to make a wrong turn. The robot walked right through half a dozen trees and quickly disappeared into the light show.

"Hey," she called after him. "Hey! Maybe stay where we can see you."

Rapscallion's stinger-head craned forward, right through a thick tree trunk. "Why? None of this is real. You can walk right through it. It doesn't even show up in Lidar or millimeter-wave scans."

"We're human," she pointed out. "We rely on our eyes, maybe too much. Humor me, okay?"

The robot compromised by emerging halfway out of the tree, so that its pincers and his first row of legs were visible. It seemed like that was the best she was going to get.

"Come on," Parker said, weaving his way between the trees. "Follow me. Let me get you up to speed on what we're facing. I've got to warn you. It's pretty bad."

23.

"Why did Actaeon create this hologram?" Petrova asked, as she followed Parker through the dark woods. For the hundredth time, perhaps, she caught herself reaching up to push a low-hanging branch out of the way. Her fingers touched nothing but what felt like cold, silvery mist, and she pulled them back, quickly.

"Your guess is as good as mine. For some reason, when Actaeon went down the last thing it did was replace that graphic with all of this. It doesn't make a bit of sense."

"Maybe not to us," Zhang said.

They all turned to look at the doctor, but he just shrugged.

"I wonder, if you had the mind of a machine, would this make perfect sense?" Zhang said.

"Hi," Rapscallion said. "Machine mind over here. I can tell you, from that unique perspective – this is bugfuck insane." The stinger-head bobbed up and down for a bit. "Which is not to say he's wrong. We do go a little crazy, sometimes. A one gets flipped into a zero when it's not supposed to. Happens. Numbers get crossed and we do weird shit. I don't know, though. This seems a little extreme for just a bug."

"My first thought," Zhang said, "was that it had to be a message."

"A message?" Parker asked.

Zhang shrugged. "Put yourself in the computer's place.

Actaeon must have known something was wrong. Otherwise, why reboot itself? It chose to create all this foliage before it went offline, however. It devoted resources to this that it probably needed elsewhere. That suggests to me that it *wanted* us to see this jungle."

"Did it assume we would know what this was supposed to mean?" Petrova asked.

Zhang looked over at the robot. Rapscallion bobbed on its many legs. A kind of shrug. "Like I said, none of this makes sense to me, but I think maybe Zhang's got a point. Maybe Actaeon was trying to send a message but this was all it could do."

"A big sign that just said 'Be Right Back' would have been easier to create," Parker suggested.

"Sure," Rapscallion said. "But like I said, sometimes we go crazy. There's one way we're better than humans there, though. We can fix ourselves."

"By rebooting yourself, right?" Petrova asked.

"Yeah, exactly. Maybe that's why Actaeon rebooted. Maybe it knew it was going crazy."

Parker rubbed his chin. "The reboot cycle started at the same time as the attack – right after we switched off the faster-than-light drive. At the time every human onboard was still in cryosleep. Actaeon didn't even have time to warn me that we were being attacked – it was already in this state when I woke up."

"I was awake," Rapscallion pointed out. "I can confirm, yeah, Actaeon went nighty-night about three seconds before the first projectile hit the ship."

"You think that whoever's attacking us did this to Actaeon. Infected it with a virus or something," Petrova said, nodding. "Tell me more about this attack."

"I just need to get to my console," Parker said. "It's a pain in the ass trying to find anything in here, but . . . Yeah. Here." Parker walked around the bole of a massive, twisted tree and brought them to a space where they could see one of the ship's actual bulkheads. Petrova reached out and touched it, to make sure it wasn't just another hologram. But no, the wall felt hard and warm and real.

Parker gestured at the wall and a few simple dots of light appeared there, as if projected by a laser pointer. They moved slowly, their positions updating every few seconds.

"Actaeon controls just about every system on this ship, so none of the normal control interfaces are available. None of its sensors are working, either. I have access to exactly one radio telescope. It's meant for emergency use, so it's connected to my manual controls. I rigged the telescope data to display here, just to get some basic information about what's going on," Parker explained.

Petrova nodded as if she understood what she was looking at. "I assume that these dots are important."

"It's a depiction of the local volume of space. Each of those dots is a massive object – something the size of *Artemis* or bigger. This," he said, pointing at one of the dots, "is us, and this one is the ship that's attacking us."

"What class of ship is it? Is it a cutter, a frigate, a dreadnought?" she asked. It would help to have actual data. If she could start thinking of this as a battle, something she could fight, that would really, really help her feel less afraid. Less like she was about to die.

"All I have is a general sense of its size," Parker said. "It's big."

She ran her fingers through her hair. What she really wanted to do was grab him and shake him. "What kind of armament is it carrying? Can you even tell me what kind of weapon did all the damage we saw?"

Parker shook his head. "I'm sorry. I'm really sorry, but this is what I've got. I have no idea what they're shooting at us. Railguns, maybe? That would explain the size of the impacts, but a railgun can fire dozens of times a second, and we've only been hit two or three times. So maybe missiles?"

Zhang cleared his throat. "Yams," he said.

24
●

Petrova whirled around and stared at the doctor. "Sorry, what?"
"They're throwing yams at us." The doctor shrugged and shook his head. "I know that sounds weird. But I saw it. When I was outside the ship, I saw a cargo container full of yams come flying toward us. I assume it came from our attacker. Later, I saw another container actually collide with the ship. That's what's doing all the damage. They're throwing cargo pods at us."

"Cargo pods are not weapons," Parker pointed out, as if he could make the attack go away by using logic.

Petrova shook her head, though. Cargo pods. It wasn't a weapon she'd ever trained to use, herself, but . . . "If you throw it fast enough, anything can be deadly. A bullet is just an inert piece of metal. It only kills someone when it's accelerated to supersonic speeds."

"But come on. Cargo? Their own cargo – why would you use a cargo container as a projectile? One full of root vegetables?"

She turned the idea over in her head. "I guess, if that was all you had . . . " She stepped over to the wall where the dots continued their slow, stately dance. She put her finger on the dot that represented the attacker. "Maybe it's not a warship at all," she said. "Maybe they don't have any better weapons."

Parker scoffed, but she knew she had to be right.

Only warships carried real weapons. If you weren't a warship, if you were a transport like *Artemis* or a scientific probe, and you needed to fight another ship, you would use whatever you had. You would eject a cargo container from your hold at high speed. Use that to cripple another ship. But why? Why would they be so desperate to destroy *Artemis*? To resort to this kind of attack they must have been truly afraid of what *Artemis* represented. Petrova wished she knew where the ship had come from. Paradise-1 was a colony planet and didn't have a navy of its own. If they had some crucial reason to want to stop *Artemis*, they would have to send a civilian ship out to do it. A cargo ship, then.

Her brain kept circling back to the same question, though. What was on *Artemis* that was so dangerous to the colony? There was no significant cargo onboard. Nothing threatening or hazardous. The whole point of this mission was to bring people to Paradise-1. So ... perhaps the target was one of them, one of the passengers? Either her or Zhang. She knew that people were afraid of Firewatch, and what she represented, but she couldn't shake the idea it wasn't her. She was just one woman, not an invasion force. She wasn't worth this kind of desperation.

So, Zhang. Something about Zhang – something she didn't know about him – made him so terrifying to the people of Paradise-1 that they would go to incredible lengths to kill him before he arrived. She thought about the RD on his arm. Rapscallion had said it meant he was a danger to himself or others. But dangerous ... how? He'd struck her as weird. Off-putting. An asshole, frankly. Nothing worse than that.

She shook her head. She would have to figure that out later. There were more pressing mysteries.

"Zhang," she asked, "when you were outside, when you saw the yams, did you see this other ship?"

"Not in any kind of useful way," Zhang admitted. "There was something out there, something bright like a star but bigger than any star should have been. I assume that's our enemy, but I couldn't really say for sure. I couldn't make out any details."

Petrova nodded. The tactical part of her brain, the part that Firewatch had trained, was starting to take over. In a battle you could die. Yes, that could happen at any time. Your best chance of staying alive was to keep thinking. You put thoughts of death as far from you as you could, and turned all your faculties over to another purpose – to thoughts of killing.

That began with a proper assessment of the state of play.

"Okay. Okay. There hasn't been an impact for a while. Maybe they're done throwing pods at us. Maybe the attack is over – after all, they've left us dead in the water. We can't move without tearing the ship apart. Right?"

"Right," Parker said.

"Then perhaps that's all they wanted. To immobilize us. Considering how much damage they did with a couple of crates, we have to assume they could have destroyed *Artemis* completely, if that's what they wanted."

Parker's frown worried her.

"What is it? Just tell me," she said.

"This dot," Parker said, and touched the wall to indicate a dot that was on the far side of the *Artemis* from the attacking ship, moving away from them quickly, "is another projectile. One they fired about five minutes ago. It missed us completely. Most of them have."

"Most of them," Petrova said.

"They fire a shot about every three minutes. Ten times now, since you woke up. Two of them hit."

She did the easy math in her head. She had only been awake for thirty minutes? It felt like hours since she'd found herself floating, naked and covered in blood with no idea what was happening.

She put that thought aside. It couldn't help her.

Not much could.

"That changes things," she said.

"It means they're trying to kill us," Zhang pointed out. "They won't stop until we're all dead."

"That seems likely," Parker agreed. "Yeah."

25
●

Petrova waved one hand in the air, as if she was wiping away doubts.

"We can't focus on that. We need to think about things we can actually control. Right? Okay. First things first," she said. "Our mission wasn't to get in a fight with enemy ships. We're supposed to check on the planet. Let's make sure that's even still an option. Can we get any kind of look at Paradise-1?"

"What,, like a camera view?" Parker asked. "Not really. All our sensors are down except the radio telescope. I mean, I can tell you the planet is still there. It's where it's supposed to be."

She gave him a dubious look. "We don't even have an external camera view?"

"You could look out the viewports. They're right behind there." He waved at the dark and venomous plants filling the bridge. "Be my guest. All you'll see is a brown disk."

"Maybe later. Is there any way to contact them, though? Can we send them a signal, even something really simple like a radio pulse? If they know we're here, maybe they can send some kind of help."

"I've been trying since we arrived to, you know, put a call through," Parker said. "There's never been any response. I don't know if they can't hear us or if they just don't want to talk to us. One way or the other, they've been quiet."

"What about automated signals? Some kind of computer

down there must be tracking us, even just traffic control. Telemetry from the planet, some kind of carrier wave, local chatter – if there's a colony down there, they must have a network for moving data around. We can't even hear their internet working?"

"Nothing," Parker said. "It's like the whole planet is on lockdown."

"We have no way whatsoever to contact the colony?"

He shrugged. "I mean, if you want, I can go stand on the outer hull and wave at them until I get their attention."

"Yes, got it, thanks. Let's look at some realistic options. You've already said we can't run away. The ship couldn't take the strain of acceleration."

"I'm surprised we're still in one piece, honestly," he replied.

"Fine. Can we survive any kind of movement at all? Could we make course corrections, attitude adjustments – do you have positioning jets you can fire?"

"I guess ... maybe," Parker said. "It would still put strain on the ship but maybe ... maybe we could move but it would be slow. Damned slow."

"I don't need you to sail circles around the enemy. Just take evasive action." She touched a finger to the wall where the dots were running through their slow dance. "We expect they're going to fire another shot in a couple of minutes. I want to make sure we don't just sit here and take it. When we know a projectile is incoming, I need you to fire your engines, just a tiny bit, so we get out of that projectile's way."

"That'll work a couple of times," Parker pointed out. "If I try that trick too often, though, something important is going to break. We're barely hanging together by threads and hope right now. If I push too hard I could sever the cable giving us what little power we have. Then we'll all get to freeze to death in the dark, even if the bad guys can't hit us."

"Once or twice is what I'm counting on. Buy us a little bit of time, okay? Give me a chance." She stared at the dots. "How far away are they? The other ship."

"About fifty kilometers."

Petrova nodded. In space, she knew, that was nothing. Even in the crowded shipping lanes around Earth and its moon, spacecraft rarely got that close to each other, just as a safety measure. "That close, and they're still having trouble hitting us. However they're launching those cargo pods it's not something they can aim very well. Hmm."

"I'm sorry," Zhang said. "I am, but ... but I need to know. What's your plan, here?"

The doctor looked agitated. Not just scared – actually upset. Maybe he wanted to be the one in charge, she thought. Or maybe he thought she wasn't qualified.

"My plan? My plan is to not get us killed. You have something you'd like to say?"

Zhang nodded. "I think it's time we consider abandoning ship."

Parker's eyes went wide, but he didn't say anything. Which meant he didn't think the idea was completely crazy.

"There must be escape pods. Ships are required to have them by law. Right?" Zhang asked.

"Yeah, we have those," Rapscallion said.

Parker was looking right at her. A sad little smile on his face. She expected him to say that for some reason the escape pods wouldn't work, or they'd been destroyed in one of the impacts. Something like that. He still didn't say anything.

"What?" she asked.

"The pods are—"

She knew the answer before he'd even finished his thought. "They're in another part of the ship. Right? They're back near the cabins." It made sense. You wanted the pods to be very close to where your passengers were likely to be during an emergency. Passengers weren't normally supposed to be on the bridge. "They're back in the part of the ship we just risked our lives to get away from."

" . . . Yeah," Parker said.

"Of course they are. And we can't go back there, can we?"

Rapscallion played a short audio file of a man laughing. "No," the robot said. "That whole area is either on fire or radioactive. Including the pods."

"But . . . wait," Petrova said. "You don't have a pod up here on the bridge? What if the captain needs to evacuate?"

"I'm expected to go down with my ship," Parker told her.

Petrova grabbed the bridge of her nose and squeezed. "So we're stuck here. Okay. Then this is where we make our stand."

Zhang scoffed at the idea. "We are absolutely outgunned and outclassed. We are limping toward our deaths. We have no choice but to—"

She waved a hand in his face to shut him up. She had no time for dissension in the ranks. He recoiled – he didn't seem to like that at all. Well, she could apologize later, she thought. "They're trying to kill us. We're not going to make it easy on them. We're not going to surrender to people who want us dead! Look, I don't like our chances. But our best play here is not to surrender. No. It's to fight back. You say we're outgunned? They don't have any real weapons, either, or they would have used them by now. They're improvising. Well, we can do that, too."

26

Zhang hurried down a corridor headed toward the ship's stores, with Rapscallion clattering behind him. This part of the ship was largely intact, though there were signs of damage underneath the shiny skin. A puff of stinking breeze burst from a ventilation grate just as he passed by, and then he heard the fan behind the grate shudder to a stop. Once the air had stopped moving there was no sound in the corridor except his own heartbeat.

"Just up there," Rapscallion said, pointing ahead of them.

"Is there a point to this, or did Petrova just give me this job as busy work?" Zhang asked. She'd been short with him back on the bridge. He was trying not to take offense – they all had reason to be on edge – but it was difficult. He didn't like feeling like he'd been sent off with the robot to get him out of her face.

"You probably have more insight to her psychology than I do," the robot admitted.

"Why would you say that?"

"She's a human, like you. I don't understand any of you."

Zhang grunted in distaste. He tried to focus on their task. They'd been sent to assess what kind of equipment they had available. Petrova wanted anything that could be turned into a weapon, first, and then anything that might help them survive if they lost power or life support. Meanwhile, she and Parker were supposedly trying to gather more information on the attacking ship, though how they planned on doing that, Zhang couldn't say.

"That hatch," Rapscallion said.

Zhang nodded and slapped the access panel. Half expecting to find that beyond the hatch was nothing but hard radiation, or the void of space, or just death, just pointless, unexpected death.

The hatch opened easily. The compartment beyond was dark, but only for a moment. Lights flicked on, one by one. Zhang looked in and saw a massive room filled with cargo bins, all lashed down and secured to the bulkheads. Each bin was marked with a number and a machine-readable code sigil. The numbers meant nothing to him. "I assume you can read these?"

"They're cross-referenced to the ship's manifest," the robot replied. "So, yes. I'll start decoding them. You look for whatever else you can find."

A massive heap of the bins filled the center of the room. Zhang walked around the side of the pile and found that the far wall of the room was taken up with a rack of spacesuits. Not the emergency model he'd used when he first woke up, but full-function models with maneuvering units and toolkits. He looked down and saw, at knee height, a row of helmets, all of them in pristine condition. Their visors even looked polished.

He clucked his tongue and moved on. Next to the suit rack was a rack of bins he thought he recognized because it was covered in warning stickers. Bright, colorful symbols that indicated which bins contained biohazardous materials, which ones contained radiological isotopes. Which ones were deadly poison.

"Ah," he said. "This is my stuff. Medical equipment." He grabbed one of the bins at random and popped it open. It was full of cotton swabs and adhesive bandages. Petrova still had some bad cuts from when her cryotube exploded. As angry as he might be with her, he was still the ship's doctor, and that meant he had to put his feelings aside and consider her health. He thought he would look to see if he could find some antiseptic. Come to think of it, he had plenty of abrasions and cuts of his own. He tried to remember if Captain Parker had any visible injuries, but when Zhang had been on the bridge he'd been too distracted to make a proper examination.

He opened another bin. Autoscalpels, forceps, hyposprays. Old-fashioned needle pens. He picked up a handheld bonesaw and studied his reflection in its polished metal. It might make the kind of weapon you could use in a pinch, but it was hardly useful for ship-to-ship combat. He squatted down to see what else he could find on the lower shelves and something caught his eye – a large, heavy case with a massive sticker on its front that showed a starburst logo. Interesting.

Rapscallion called from the other side of the room. "I've found some emergency supplies over here. Food and sterilized water. That should help, right?"

Zhang didn't bother replying. He'd grabbed the case by its handles and was busy trying to tug it out of its shelf. For some reason it wouldn't budge. He tried pulling from a slightly different angle but still no luck. He put all his strength into it and heaved, but the case wouldn't come free.

"Come on, you fucker," he said, and yanked again. Nothing. "Come on!"

The case wasn't moving at all. It was like it was welded onto the shelf. It just made Zhang think of the helmet wedged under his bed when he woke up, and that made him furious. Incandescent with rage. He put one foot up on the shelf for leverage and hauled and hauled at the case's handles, yanking and straining until he started to roar in anger, in defiance—

"You fuck! You stupid fuck! Fuck!" he screamed.

"Dr Zhang?" Rapscallion called, his voice very loud in the enclosed space. The robot's many legs clacked on the floor as he scurried around the corner to Zhang's position.

When Rapscallion arrived Zhang was down on the floor,

head in his hands. He lowered them slowly, then gave the case one last, futile kick.

Rapscallion craned his head down as if he was studying the case. Then he reached up with one claw and released a catch that had locked the case into the shelf. He pulled the case free with ease and set it gently on the floor.

"I'm . . . I'm okay," Zhang said, even though the robot hadn't asked. "I'm okay."

"Your heart rate's ridiculously high," Rapscallion told him.

Zhang laughed, a little. Not that anything was funny. "I'm scared, you mean. I'm scared. You giant idiot. Of course I'm scared. I'm going to die here, on this pointless mission. I'm going to die."

"It's likely, yes," the robot replied.

Zhang closed his eyes and tried to just breathe. "Don't you ever get scared, Rapscallion? Perhaps not. You're a machine. Maybe you don't feel fear."

"Oh, I feel it all the time," Rapscallion replied. "I'm capable of all sorts of emotions, just like a human. There's one difference, though."

"What's that?"

Rapscallion's head moved closer to Zhang's face. "I can turn my emotions off. When they get inconvenient, or counterproductive. Right now, feeling fear wouldn't help anyone. So I've switched off that response, until I can express my fear in a harmless way."

"Now that," Zhang said, "would be nice."

"What about that thing?" The robot pointed at the swirling pattern of gold on his forearm. "Isn't that what it's for? Controlling your emotional state?"

"This?" Zhang asked. "It can calm me down, if I start to lose control. It keeps me on a certain level, dulls the extremes." He grabbed the RD, felt it pulse under his fingers. "But not all of human psychology is chemical. It can't purge my fear for me."

"Being human sounds exhausting," the robot told him.

The robot helped him to his feet. His heart had stopped racing, or at least, he couldn't feel it jumping in his chest anymore.

"You found food," Zhang said, remembering something Rapscallion had said. "That's good. This," he said, tapping the metal case with his toe, "might be exactly what Petrova's looking for. We should head back."

"Do you want to throw some bins around, first? I found a bunch that are full of spare pillows and blankets, we don't need those. You could kick the shit out of them if it would make you feel better."

Zhang laughed. It helped, a bit. Made it easier to breathe.

"We should get back. They're waiting for us," he said.

27
.

The case opened with a click. The contents were wrapped in plastic and suspended in a stabilizing foam that popped and evaporated as they watched. When all the packing materials were removed, Zhang reached into the box and pulled out a metal cylinder about half a meter long, with a thick power cord sticking out of one end. The other end held a thick silvered lens.

"It's a medical laser. Designed for burning out tumors and cauterizing wounds," Zhang said.

Petrova didn't look very pleased.

He took a breath. "I know what you're thinking. We're fighting a ship-to-ship battle. We want to kill our enemies, not treat their glaucoma. This unit is a little more powerful than it strictly needs to be, though. It runs hot, up to about three hundred kilowatts for sustained use, or ten megawatts for a quick pulse." Zhang glanced over his shoulder at Rapscallion. "The robot thinks he can boost it even further, maybe into the gigawatt range, if you only fire it for a femtosecond or so."

"I've worked with laser weapons before," Petrova said. She wasn't quite shaking her head, but he could tell she wasn't seeing the potential here. "They're good at shooting down incoming missiles. Slow missiles. It can take ten seconds for a laser to burn through the electronics of a missile. In combat, you never have ten seconds. You need something that can kill a guy in a heartbeat. Thanks, Zhang. I know you really looked, but I just don't think this is what I need. I was hoping for something that would pack more of a punch."

"Oh, sorry, there weren't any rocket launchers in the medical supplies," Zhang said. "Listen, this laser – I wasn't expecting to find it. *Artemis* is surprisingly well stocked with medical equipment, but even so . . . a laser this big is really only necessary for one thing, even in a hospital setting. Gross anatomy."

"He means dissecting dead bodies," Rapscallion said. He scuttled forward and picked up the laser in two of its massive claws. "Why the UEG thought the crew of the *Artemis* might need to perform autopsies in space is anybody's guess. But this'll definitely ruin somebody's day, if you hit them with it even for a split second."

Petrova laid one hand on the laser's metal casing. "I don't need to ruin days. I need to *kill* fuckers," she said. She turned to face Parker, who was sitting under a particularly gnarled and twisty tree. "Tell me you found something better," she said.

Zhang knew that the captain had been exploring ways to turn the ship's systems into weaponry. A number of possibilities had been discussed, the most obvious of which was to turn the ship's engines around so they were facing the enemy. The exhaust from *Artemis*' drive was a plasma that could reach ten thousand degrees, easily enough to burn through the enemy's hull.

Parker shrugged, though, and Zhang knew it wouldn't work. "The big problem there is range. We'd have to be right next to them to make it work. Given how fragile we are right now, maneuvering them into that kind of trap would be next to impossible. We could try to sneak up on them, but we're really not built for that; even when *Artemis* was fully intact it was never meant for . . ."

Zhang had stopped listening. Instead he was watching Rapscallion. The robot scuttled over to the table where Petrova had left the medical laser. He picked it up and turned it around in his claws for a while. Then he grasped the power cable and plugged it into an outlet in the wall that Zhang hadn't noticed before. Probably because it had been hidden behind the leprous trunk of a hologram tree. Zhang remember that the robot was capable of seeing right through the projections.

"What are you doing?" Zhang asked.

"Just fooling around. Don't mind me," the robot replied. He balanced the laser in the crook where one of his legs met his trunk, then waggled it back and forth like he was trying to aim it. "I was never any good at this sort of thing," he said, almost apologetically. "Eye–hand coordination, I mean. I've always been sort of clumsy."

Zhang shook his head. "Please don't aim that thing anywhere near me, okay? And maybe you should just put it down before—"

Rapscallion tapped the laser's fire control and several things happened all at once.

The lights went out. The air stopped moving, and the forest flickered out of existence, if only for a moment. Zhang could see the bridge as it must really be – command stations, big screens, crash seats – lit up by the beam of the medical laser as it drew a perfect blue line through the air.

Where it touched the far wall a flame burst from the plastic cladding on the bulkhead, and goopy molten resin like candle wax dripped to the floor.

The laser made no sound whatsoever. The metal cylinder didn't jump in Rapscallion's grasp – there was no recoil. The blast was there and gone so quickly Zhang barely had time to register that it had happened at all.

The trees all came back, just as they had been, with only the tiniest flicker. Only after it was all over did Zhang get a whiff of the sharp smell of ozone – the smell of air molecules being blasted apart as they crossed the laser's path.

"Parker?"

It was Petrova who'd spoken. She had been talking intently with Parker when the lights went out. "I could have sworn

I saw — just for a second ..." She blinked strangely, as if she couldn't quite figure out what she'd seen. Then she turned and looked at the far wall. It was hard to see for all the dark foliage and twisted branches, but there was definitely a mark there.

Zhang rushed over to check. No, it wasn't a mark. The laser had punched a hole right through the wall. The edges of the hole were still glowing a dull red. "What's on the other side of this?" he asked.

"A bathroom," Parker said. "Rapscallion—"

"Humans rely on their eyes too much. That's what you said. You needed to see it to get why we thought this would make a good weapon."

Zhang ran out of the bridge and over to the hatch that led to the bathroom. He ducked inside and checked the wall above the toilet. "Hey, Parker?" he called. "It didn't stop here."

The others all came rushing in. There was a hole in the wall above the toilet, and an identical hole in the far wall, just above a washbasin.

Petrova stuck her little finger in the hole. It fit easily. "Huh," she said. "How much was ..."

"That was ten megawatts," Rapscallion said.

"And you say you can go higher," Petrova said. "Huh."

28

Rapscallion's many legs had no trouble gripping the hull of *Artemis*. He required no oxygen, nor was he particularly bothered by the temperature extremes of space. He still hated to look out at the great darkness, within which burned countless stars whose only purpose was to give you a sense of scale, to remind you just how much of everything was *nothing*, was *empty*. He remembered his days mining on Eris, where the confines of the tunnels he himself had built were the whole of his universe. Where his train set had been a microcosm, complete and self-contained.

Out here in the endless night you couldn't forget how small you were, or how much you could never know.

You were reminded that you would not exist forever, that even robots could die, be destroyed, whatever. That time would continue unrolling before him long, long after he would cease to be aware of its passing.

Lieutenant Petrova came struggling her way out of the airlock to join him. He sat and waited for her to arrive. By the time she reached him, she was gasping for breath inside her spacesuit.

"Oh," she said. "Oh. Look at that."

She pointed at something in the sky. He looked up and saw she was gesturing at the planet. Paradise-1. It was just a brown coin floating in the black. With his robotic eyes Rapscallion could make out a few basic surface features. It didn't have oceans, per se, as much as big, round impact craters that had filled in with water. There were a few wispy spirals of cloud chasing each other across its equator. From this distance even he couldn't see the colony buildings.

"Kind of crappy, huh?"

She didn't sound like she'd heard him. "This is the first time I've actually seen it. That's why we're here. We need to go there." She laughed a little. "Damn. Why does it have to be so hard?"

He checked the life support levels of her suit to make sure she wasn't suffering oxygen narcosis. It was hard to tell, sometimes, when humans were impaired. "Are you ready for this?" he asked her.

"I think I don't have a choice."

"Fair enough." Rapscallion planted himself, weaving two sets of his legs through an equipment rail on the hull. He pulled a length of cable out of a nearby access hatch and plugged the big medical laser directly into the ship's main power conduit.

"Where . . . Where is it? The other ship?" she asked.

Of course she couldn't see it with her human eyes. It was fifty kilometers away. "See that bright point of light?" He lifted one claw and pointed. "Don't worry. I've been watching. We still have forty-five seconds before the next attack, if they stick to their timetable."

"Okay, so we know how this is going to work. You warn me when they're about to shoot at us. I'll hold on tight while Parker moves the ship, just a tiny bit, to avoid a collision. Then we have three minutes for me to take a shot. Do you have any sense of what my best target will be?"

"Hard to say at this point. I'll help you assess that once our optics are set up."

Petrova nodded inside her helmet. "Right. So we know they're not just throwing their cargo at us by hand. That wouldn't get it up to the kind of speed they need to actually damage us. So they must be using some kind of mass driver system to—"

"Five," Rapscallion said. "Four. Three."

Petrova squawked with a sound of panic and grabbed at the rail with both hands. He supposed he could have given her a bit more warning. "Two," he said. "One. There. Yes, there."

His eyes were so much better than hers. He could make out some minimal detail of the enemy ship. He could see the cargo pod emerge from a hatch in its mid-section, see it grow larger as it streaked toward them, lit up by the sunlight. "Captain Parker," he said. "Now."

There was no sound in the vacuum of space, of course. Rapscallion felt the moment the engines switched on as vibration coming through the hull, a weary, beleaguered shaking as the ship tried to tear itself apart. His haptic sensors were sensitive enough that he could feel the different parts of the ship oscillating at different frequencies. He could sense that the ship's galley, for instance, was nearly shredded by the strain.

He did not feel like they were moving, not at all. A moment later, the engines switched off again. The vibration continued for a moment but eventually it settled down.

"That's it?" Petrova asked. "That was ... that was the whole burn?"

"Yes," Rapscallion said. He tapped into the few sensors he had inside the ship and found that the life support system was still functioning, but that they had lost interior illumination in corridor 3a. That was all right. That part of the ship was mostly taken up by equipment and fuel storage – no one needed to go down there.

"We made it," Petrova said. "We're okay. I mean – right? Parker?"

"I don't think we took any significant damage," Parker told her. "We got lucky that time. And now – yeah. Yeah. Fuck yeah, it looks like that projectile is going to miss us. Not by much, but ... I'm pretty sure."

"Pretty sure," Petrova said. "Rapscallion—"

"It'll miss," the robot said. "We can't count on that trick working twice, though. We need to take action now. There's not much time to get you set up for your shot before the next attack."

He watched as the capillaries that webbed the skin of her face drained of blood. As she went pale at the thought.

"Yeah. Okay," she said. She reached for the laser. "Let's do that."

29
•

On the bridge, Zhang squatted under the branches of a diseased tree, chewing on his fingernails. "Two and a half minutes until the next attack," he said. "Is that going to be enough time?"

"Rapscallion?" Parker called. The captain was working at a terminal that was obscured by the tendrils of a crawling vine. He touched a key and the view on the wall changed. Where before it had just been the scattered dots of the ships and the projectiles, now they had a live video feed through the robot's eyes. They were much more acute than any human's. "What do you see?" Parker asked.

At first the view wasn't much more complex than before. It showed just black, and stars, and a single white dot that was brighter than the others. Rapscallion zoomed in, though, and soon they could see the enemy ship, for the first time.

It was big, a lot bigger than *Artemis*. The viewports on its bridge looked like tiny slits and it carried a lot more thruster units than their ship. It also lacked *Artemis'* sweeping lines. Instead, it sported a swollen belly, like a snake that had swallowed a deer. Or an apple pierced by an arrow, perhaps that was a better figure of speech. A less intimidating one, anyway.

Zhang was no expert but he had seen ships like that before, on the datastream. "Is that a colony ship?" he asked.

Parker grunted in assent.

"It's a colony ship." Ships like it carried thousands of people at a time, frozen in cryosleep, to the colony worlds like Paradise-1. They were slow and underpowered and they definitely didn't carry any weapons. "We're being attacked by a colony ship?"

"That's what it looks like." Parker shook his head. Zhang was sure the captain was just as tense as he was but he was better at hiding it.

"That makes no sense whatsoever. They'd be putting so many lives at stake, attacking us like this. And throwing their own cargo at us is really stupid." The food and support equipment on a colony ship would be needed by the colonists when they arrived on their new world, to get them on their feet. Throwing their yams at *Artemis* could mean people would starve, later, when they got to their destination.

Not that Zhang understood any of this. Why would they try to kill him? Or Petrova, or Parker? What could they have possibly done to warrant this?

"*Persephone*," Parker said.

"What?"

The captain pointed at the screen. "There. It's small, but you can see the ship's name painted near its bow. I'm sure Actaeon could have told us all about where it was built and how many people it carries. That name mean anything to you?"

"No," Zhang said.

Parker nodded. "Time check."

They had given Zhang a job. This time, he knew it was just to keep him busy so he didn't panic and get underfoot. The thing was, it worked. As he checked the countdown timer he almost felt useful. "Two minutes to the next attack."

"Petrova?" Parker asked.

"I'm ready. We just need a target."

Rapscallion zoomed in even further on the colony ship, until its hull filled the entire screen. What had looked like a stretch of blank white metal resolved itself into countless little hatches and equipment modules. *Persephone*'s windows were all dark, and Zhang wondered how they were supposed to know what to shoot. But then Rapscallion found a part of the ship that was brilliantly lit up. It looked like a big cargo airlock, just aft of the swollen midsection. The outer hatch was wide open and a long gantry extended out into space, a skeletal tower made of naked steel girders.

Then he realized what that gantry really was – the barrel of a gun.

"That looks like a mass driver to me," Petrova said.

Zhang understood the concept. You ran a strong electric current through the girders to create a linear magnetic field. Then you pushed your projectile – your cargo pod – through the field, which would push it faster and faster until it emerged from the end of the gantry moving faster than a rifle bullet.

Even a container of yams moving that fast could do incredible damage to *Artemis*. As Zhang had seen, first hand.

"I see people in there," Petrova said, her voice low and husky. "You see this?"

"Confirmed," Parker said.

At first Zhang couldn't see what they were talking about. Then he squinted and saw tiny shapes moving around inside of the cargo airlock. They were wrestling with a cargo pod, maneuvering it into the end of the gantry. Loading another shell.

"There's a bunch of them," Petrova said. "I'm not sure I can get them all in one burst."

"Take out as many as you can," Parker said.

Zhang shook his head. "Wait a second," he said.

Parker turned and stared at him. "You have something to say?"

"That's a colony ship," Zhang said. "Those are colonists. Not soldiers."

Petrova sighed. "They're actively trying to kill us, right now."

"She's right," Parker said. "And we're out of time. I'm sorry if your Hippocratic oath makes this hard for you, Doctor, but we're going to have to kill some of them. Maybe all of them. It's our only chance."

"Please. Hear me out. We still have a minute before the next attack," Zhang said. "I'm not having a moral qualm. The people over there tried to kill me. Personally – they threw a shipping container at me. I'd happily set the lot of them on fire. No, my issue with this is about numbers. There are thousands of people over there. Petrova, you may be a trained soldier but even you won't be able to kill all of them. We need to focus on taking down their weapon."

Parker stared at him with a deep intensity. At first Zhang thought the other man might be about to attack him, but then, finally, the captain nodded. He made a noise of disgust but then he nodded and grabbed his forehead between his thumb and forefinger and squeezed, like he was trying to massage his own thoughts into shape. "Maybe there's a way," Parker suggested. "Rapscallion?"

The robot shrugged. "A mass driver needs a lot of electrical power. They must have it tied into the ship's main reactor. If we could find the power conduit they're using, if you could cut that, it would wreck the gun. They would have to build a whole new one."

"In other words, it still doesn't solve our problem," Petrova pointed out. "But it buys us some time. Speaking of which – Zhang?"

"What?" he asked. "Oh. Next attack in thirty seconds."

The little dots that were people scurried around *Persephone's* airlock. They had nearly completed loading the cargo pod into the gantry.

"Petrova," Parker said, "you need to make a decision. What's your target?"

"Let me think," she replied.

30

Rapscallion's view of the cargo airlock on the colony ship was superimposed on Petrova's suit's faceplate. She could make out the little dots scurrying around the mass driver well enough to see their individual arms and legs. Those were people, all right.

A lot of them. Zhang had a point. She might kill a few. They could just send reinforcements. There had to be a better shot. She knew it.

"Can you see any kind of power conduit?" she asked. Rapscallion had better eyes than she did – he made the perfect spotter. "Quick. We're running out of time."

"Fifteen seconds," Zhang counted off.

"Something, maybe," Rapscallion said.

"Maybe?"

"There," Rapscallion said.

At the same moment, Zhang announced, "Ten seconds."

The far end of the mass driver had started to glow a cherry red. It was powering up for the next shot already. "Show me," she said.

"Here," Rapscallion said. A dashed white line appeared around what looked like just a random section of wall inside *Persephone*'s cargo airlock.

A nice, easy target. Bigger than the human beings who were still scurrying around the airlock, oblivious to her existence. She took a breath, not too deep, and held it.

"Five seconds," Zhang called.

Yeah, thanks, shut the fuck up, she thought. She didn't say it only because that would involve releasing her breath.

She changed up her grip on the laser. She touched the firing pad.

Nothing seemed to happen. Right. In the vacuum of space there was nothing to scatter the light, which meant she couldn't even see the laser beam. All the laser's energy was being delivered straight to the target. The only way she knew she'd even fired the weapon was that she suddenly felt a spike of heat through her gloves, as if she'd just touched a hot stove.

"Ow," she yelled, and let go of the laser. It floated away from her, still connected to *Artemis* by its power cord. "Hold on. Did I hit anything?"

Inside the cargo airlock, the outlined patch of wall exploded with a blast of silent sparks, debris and smoke bursting outward to fill the lock. She couldn't see the people, couldn't tell if any of them were hurt or killed. All she could see was the gantry barrel of the gun, still pointing right at *Artemis*.

"Did it work?" she asked. "Did it work?"

No one answered her, not for the longest time. Finally, it was Zhang who spoke.

"The attack should have come ten seconds ago," he said. "It didn't."

"I think," Parker said, "that means it worked."

After that they all started cheering, so loud the radio couldn't handle it and all she heard in her headphones was a blare of static.

31
.

When the cheering stopped, it was like they all remembered how close they were to dying. How much trouble they were still in.

They held their breath.

Three minutes passed. Three minutes more. Petrova kept asking Rapscallion to check on the colony ship – to see, specifically, if the people over there were working on repairing the damage she'd done to their weapon. Strangely enough, they weren't. There were no tiny people to be seen in the cargo airlock now, not even after all the smoke and debris had cleared. Even the lights over there had gone dark.

"Is that common human behavior?" Rapscallion asked.

By that point, she felt comfortable to come back inside *Artemis*. Carefully, she removed her suit and stowed its various pieces where she could get to them again in a hurry, if she needed to. She hung the laser reverently on the wall. It was a good weapon, after all.

Eventually, she realized that Rapscallion had asked her a question. "Sorry," she said. "Sorry, I ... I guess I'm very tired. You said something."

"I asked if humans act like this, normally?"

"Act how?"

"If a human is attacking you, and I mean, they really want to fuck you up, even kill you. If you hit them back once, maybe give them a bloody nose or a facial scar or something. Is that usually enough to make them stop trying to kill you?"

A chill ran down Petrova's spine.

"No," she said. "Normally it just makes them angry. It makes them want to hit you back, twice as hard."

"Funny, then, that the colony ship hasn't tried to attack us again. Oh, well." The robot picked up one of her gloves from the floor and handed it to her. "You dropped this."

"Thanks," she said. She really was exhausted. Maybe there would be time for her to get a nap, soon.

It seemed highly unlikely.

She followed Rapscallion back to the bridge. The boys had prepared a little welcome party for her – they'd broken out a fresh bottle of water and a pack of salted crackers. She smiled, despite herself. She sank down to the floor and took a long swig of water, then picked up one of the crackers. She looked over at Parker and found him watching her. Just watching, like he was worried about her. She must look like shit.

She lifted her cracker like she was toasting him, and gave him a wink.

He blushed and turned away.

The cracker was incredibly good. She hadn't realized how hungry she was. "Are there more?" she asked, when she'd rampaged through the entire pack of crackers. "How much do we have? Are we going to have to start rationing?"

"There are whole cases of these," Zhang said. "It's the only food we've got, but there's plenty of it. Eat up. We won't die of starvation anytime soon," he told her. "That's the good news. Of course, vitamin deficiency can kill you, too. But very, very slowly. And without protein and some kind of vegetable matter our energy levels are going to become highly erratic."

"Yeah, okay." Parker came and sat down across from her. "Okay, enough of the doom and gloom. It looks like you bought us some time to actually think about how we're going to live through this. I'd like to talk about our next steps."

"Shoot," she said.

Parker sighed and lay back across the floor, his head on the deck, his legs still folded in lotus position. "We can start repairing *Artemis*. There's not a lot we can accomplish with just hand tools right now, but we can focus on stabilizing the ship's hull, enough so we can actually move again. I don't like the fact that we're just sitting here, still so close to *Persephone*. We need to land on Paradise-1 as soon as we can."

"Definitely," she said. "We're an easy target, floating up here."

"Meanwhile I've got Rapscallion working the radio telescope, looking to see if there are any other ships nearby. We don't have working comms, not without Actaeon, but hell, we could fly alongside another ship and wave at them until we got their attention. Having allies out here, especially somebody with a working ship, would make our lives a lot easier."

"Makes sense." Zhang had brought her another pack of crackers. She tore the wrappers off and crammed three of them in her mouth at once.

"Then there's something dangerous, but I think would be worth a shot. Actaeon has a kind of safe mode."

She tried to talk but her mouth was just one big glob of carbohydrate. The disgusted look on his face made her laugh, which nearly made her choke. She took a long swig of water and while she worked at swallowing her mouthful of cracker, she gestured for him to continue.

"Safe mode," she managed to say, eventually.

"Right. Basically we can interrupt the cycle that Actaeon's caught in. It's rebooting itself, over and over. We can force it to boot up into this safe mode, which is a diagnostic shell with minimal interconnectivity and a severely reduced level of autonomic function . . . I'll spare you all the technical details, but the human equivalent would be putting someone in an induced coma so you could do exploratory surgery."

"Oh, that sounds incredibly safe," Petrova said.

"About as safe as firing a gigawatt laser by hand at an unknown enemy while standing on the outer hull of a heavily damaged transport ship," he said.

"Right, like I said. It's stupid. You think it'll help?"

"It might let us figure out why Actaeon isn't working. I mean, I have no idea if we'll be able to fix the problem. Odds are, it won't make things worse. Unless it causes some kind of massive file corruption cascade. Which would leave Actaeon brain dead and leave us completely incapable of controlling *Artemis'* systems."

"I'm not even going to ask what the odds are on that," she said. "Because I already know — I don't want to hear them."

"No, you don't." He sat up, rolling effortlessly from his core until he was looking her in the eye again. "What do you think? Should I try it?"

She frowned. "I think you know this ship, and Actaeon, a hell of a lot better than I do," she told him. "If you think there's even a chance that booting Actaeon into safe mode could help us take back control of *Artemis*, then I'm all for it."

"Okay. It's a start." He nodded eagerly. "I want my ship back, damn it."

32
●

So they had something like a plan. They just had to put it into effect. The hard part, of course, was repairing *Artemis*. It did not surprise Zhang when they handed him a toolkit and told him to get to work.

They sent the robot with him. He was not entirely clear on why Rapscallion couldn't have done all the repairs itself, but he supposed it was better to keep busy, anyway. It was better than thinking.

Together, he and the robot fixed a problem with the emergency seals on the bridge's main hatch – a problem he hadn't even realized they had. If the ship had torn open during their evasive maneuvers, the hatch wouldn't have been able to shut properly, and all their air would have been sucked out into space.

Luckily, that hadn't happened.

The fault proved to be nothing more than a torn piece of rubber inside the hatch's jamb. Zhang fixed the problem by fusing the crack back together with a heat gun.

"Nicely done," Rapscallion said. The robot had spent the whole time observing.

"Thanks," Zhang said. "What's next?"

"Looks like there's hydraulic fluid leaking into your main water supply," Rapscallion told him.

"Poisonous fluid?" Zhang asked.

Rapscallion played a clip of a woman laughing. "Oh, yeah," he said, as if his point hadn't been made clear.

They fixed that by wrapping tape around the pipe that carried the hydraulic fluid. This time at least Rapscallion helped, by cutting strips of tape to the right length and then hanging them off one of his claws, so that Zhang could get to them easily.

"So are you feeling better?" Rapscallion asked, as they headed to the next job.

Just then Zhang was in the process of clambering up inside a big ventilation duct on one end of the bridge, looking for why a fan in there wasn't turning. The fan was bigger than he was, and its dusty blades were smooth and curved like the wings of a predatory bird, soaring, poised, tensed, in the moment before it swooped down to rend apart some unsuspecting little mammal. The whole fan assembly thrummed with a steady, unpleasant vibration – the fan was desperate to turn but something was stopping it. It was his job to find the source of the blockage and remove it so they could clear some of the nasty toxins out of the bridge's air. He was deeply, desperately convinced that this job was going to end with him getting all his fingers cut off.

"Sorry," he said. "I was concentrating on something. What?"

Rapscallion climbed up the wall next to him, and loomed over him, his stinger-head bobbing right next to Zhang's ear. "I asked if you were feeling better. You got super upset before. Remember? When you cursed out the medical supplies?"

"I was scared of dying then," Zhang said. "I'm still scared. Do you see where the blockage is? I'm not seeing anything."

"There's some metal fatigue on that blade there," the robot said, pointing. "What would it take for you to be not scared?"

Zhang stopped his examination and actually gave that one some thought. "The universe would have to stop being a cold, indifferent, mindlessly violent place," he said.

"Yeah, nice, but I mean, what can we do that's actually possible?"

Zhang gave the robot a long, appraising look. "You're being sincere, aren't you?"

"Almost always. Sometimes it's fun to be sarcastic but I don't lie a lot. Not much point in it, usually."

"Ninety per cent of all human interaction is one form of lie or another," Zhang told the machine.

"I've noticed that," Rapscallion said. "For instance, you still haven't told anyone why you're wearing an RD on your arm."

Zhang had developed a reflex, over the last year. Every time someone asked him about the gold bracer he wore, he yanked his arm back, closer to his body. He hunched over it, like he could somehow hide it.

"That's not a lie," Zhang pointed out. "It's a secret."

"They say that talking about your problems can help," Rapscallion pointed out. "That's just basic human psychology. You could tell me."

"Just you, hmm? Okay. Come here. First, fix this fan for me, will you? Consider that payment for learning my dark secret."

Rapscallion scuttled over to the back of the fan. He yanked something out of the motor and the fan blade started to turn again, very slowly. It all happened so quickly that the blade did, in fact, graze Zhang's hand, though so gently it simply pushed him out of the way.

"There, fixed," Rapscallion said. "Now tell me."

"All right. They gave me this," Zhang said, pointing at RD, "because I'm a killer."

"Really?"

Zhang nodded. "I killed a lot of . . . well, not exactly people. But a lot of them. Murdered them in cold blood."

The robot's stinger-head drew slowly back. Away from Zhang. "Not people? Then . . . "

"Nosy robots," Zhang said.

For a second, Rapscallion just clung to the wall, not moving in the slightest. His plastic jaw opened slowly, and his head turned jerkily to the side.

Then he played the audio file of the woman laughing, again.

Three times over. "Good one," he said. "But what did you do? Really?"

Zhang didn't answer him. He was too busy looking at the thing clutched in the robot's claw. The piece of debris that had kept the fan from turning.

"Can I see that?" he asked.

The robot handed it over. It was a pale yellow, crusted on one side with a brownish-red powder. Scorched on the other side, incinerated even. Hard and rough to the touch, with a shape Zhang recognized. Still, his brain jumped through several hoops trying to convince him he was looking at something else. Anything else.

Because it simply didn't make sense.

"Just tell me," Rapscallion said. "I hate not knowing things."

"Maybe, um." Zhang shook his head. "Maybe later." He turned the object over and over in his hands. Yep. It was exactly what he'd thought. The smooth bit there was a pubic symphysis. The broad, curved edge was an iliac crest.

"What is it?" Rapscallion asked. "Something good?"

"I'm not sure," Zhang said. "Just some debris, I guess."

That was a lie, of course. He didn't want to admit to the robot what he'd found. Not yet. But there was really no question. He recognized the thing in his hand just fine. It was part of a male human pelvis.

33
•

"Okay, I'm ready," Parker said. He was invisible from the waist up, that part of him buried inside a hologram tree. Petrova would have preferred if she could see his face. That way she would have known his real opinion on how dangerous this was.

"Ready over here, too," she said. Her entire job was to hold down a key on a keyboard she couldn't see. A thick, spiraling tree root obscured the whole console, but Parker had helped her find the correct key.

Actaeon's designers had wanted to make it very difficult to reboot the AI into its safe mode. It had taken the two of them over an hour to just get ready to send the final command. Now the time had come. All she had to do was press one key on a console . . . and stand back.

She had no idea what was going to come next.

"Go," Parker said.

Petrova held down her key. There was no chime or warning klaxon to warn them the AI was rebooting – after all, Actaeon had been rebooting itself hundreds of times a second for over an hour now, and she hadn't heard anything before. A strange kind of hum did resonate in the air, for just a moment. Then the whole bridge flickered. No. That suggested some kind of major discontinuation of the dark forest motif. It wasn't like the trees all went away – they simply faded, a little, for a fraction of a second.

The effect was like watching a super smooth animation that was missing one frame out of thousands.

The trees were all still there, when it was over. Exactly where they'd been. There were two differences, one of which resolved itself almost immediately. "Parker?" she called. "Sam? Where are—"

"Here," he said, walking out of a tree and waving at her. "Sorry, I, um, flinched."

Petrova laughed. "You mean you fell on your ass," she said.

He reached behind him and rubbed his posterior with one hand. "Kinda hurt," he said, and she laughed again.

But then he went very still. "Oh, shit," he said.

"What? What is it?" she asked.

"I think it might have worked."

Striding out from behind the gnarled trees, looking quite majestic, came a perfectly white stag, its fur so colorless and pale that it seemed to glow with an inner radiance. It stood taller than Petrova at its shoulder and the points of its antlers were glowing, twinkling stars.

It turned its head toward her and snorted out a breath. Its eyes, she noticed, were all white, like its fur. Pieces of milky glass.

Parker approached the deer as if he was worried it might scamper off. He even had his hands up in front of him, as if to demonstrate he meant no harm.

"Actaeon?" he said. "Can you hear me?"

The deer twisted its head around until its snout pointed at him. It snorted again and pawed at the deck with one forehoof. Then it spoke, using the same gender neutral voice she remembered from before she entered cryosleep. The stag's mouth moved perfectly as if it were speaking the words, though the sound came from speakers in the ceiling of the bridge.

"I am not Actaeon."

A shiver ran down Petrova's spine. *Oh, God,* she thought, *it went wrong—*

"Actaeon has booted into safe mode. Its higher processes are dormant. Its command functions are dormant. I am an avatar for the ship's operating system."

"That's . . . Sure, okay," Parker said. "I mean, I don't actually know what that means, but I think it's what we wanted."

"How can I assist you?" the deer asked.

"Can you activate comms?" Petrova asked. "We need to send a message to Paradise-1, as soon as possible."

"That action is currently forbidden."

Parker frowned. "I think that means that we can't activate comms until we get Actaeon back. Like, the full AI," he said.

"Yeah, I kind of figured that one out," Petrova told him. "What do we call you?" she asked the deer.

"I do not possess self-awareness. You may assign me any name you like."

"Just call it OS," Parker said. "To keep things clear."

Petrova nodded. "Okay, OS. You're not allowed to send a message to the planet, I get that. Can you send a distress signal?"

"A signal has already been sent," the deer told her. "It was sent when Actaeon was booted into safe mode."

"Oh, thank God," Parker said. "Maybe somebody will pick it up and—"

"The signal was sent via hyperluminal pulse. The signal was received three point two seconds ago at Firewatch Command on Luna. The signal was logged by the office of Director Lang. No response has been received at this time."

Petrova stared at Parker. He just stared back.

"Three point two seconds? Luna's a hundred light years away," Parker said. "To send a signal that fast takes, like, military-grade quantum entanglement devices." He whistled. "Super expensive stuff. Very advanced."

"Wait. I thought comms were down," Petrova said. "We had nothing, no way to contact anyone. Right?"

"Right. Except clearly the AI has some way of calling home I didn't know about." Parker rubbed his head in confusion. "If the signal went through that fast it means Actaeon has some kind of private comms. A better comms system than the rest of the ship has. I don't know if that's good or bad."

"I guess that's . . . good?" she said. "I mean, at least we're getting through to somebody. We got a distress call out. That's good. Definitely good." She had no idea why the distress signal would go all the way back to the Moon, though, when Paradise-1 was so much closer. Any help they might expect from Earth or the solar system would take weeks to arrive.

"Maybe Lang just needs to sign off on us contacting the planet directly," Parker said. "Well, in the meantime, maybe we can figure some things out. OS, can you tell us why Actaeon keeps rebooting itself? Maybe it's something simple, like a permissions error that we can fix."

The deer cocked its head to one side, as if it had to think about that one. The stars on the points of its antlers twinkled wildly. "Actaeon discovered corrupted files within its root command structure."

"Corruption in the root . . . roots . . . oh, wow," Parker said. He looked over at Petrova. "Do you get it?"

"The forest," she said, nodding.

The hologram all around them, the dark forest full of poisoned trees – it was a metaphor. Corruption at the roots. That was what Actaeon had tried to tell them, in the last millisecond before it started rebooting itself. "That's pretty obscure. Did Actaeon really think we would figure that one out on our own? Why not just leave a note for us, you know, 'Fixing some bad files, be right back'? Or something like that?"

She'd been speaking to Parker but it was the deer that answered. "Actaeon's first action was to perform a self-diagnostic to check for additional corrupted files. It found numerous points of damage, including a catastrophic failure in its clear speech processors."

"So it was so badly damaged it couldn't talk, or write a note," Parker said. "OS, how much damage did Actaeon find?"

"Approximately ninety-nine per cent of Actaeon's files were corrupted." The deer lowered its head for a moment. "Rounding down to the nearest integer."

"What? How is that possible?" Parker asked.

"Unclear," the operating system told him.

"That doesn't sound like a random glitch," Petrova tried. "We're not talking about a bad line of code. It sounds more like Actaeon was attacked." When she'd trained at Firewatch's officers' school, she'd had to take a class on cyberwarfare. She wished now she'd paid more attention. "I'm willing to bet good money that whoever did this to Actaeon is also behind the colony ship throwing its cargo pods at us."

"There's a big difference between those two attacks," Parker scoffed. "Infecting a system as complex as Actaeon with a virus would take some really sophisticated software. Throwing cargo pods at us is the work of desperate people with no weapons at all."

"It's just Occam's razor. You think it's more likely that two completely different enemies attacked us at exactly the same time?"

Parker's frown told her he was taking her seriously. Good.

"OS," she said, "what can you tell us about the attack, about the content of those corrupted files? Are they just garbage or did they give Actaeon new instructions?"

"A new user has logged on. New user has root-level privileges."

"I'm sorry?" she asked.

"The new user has changed your access level. You no longer have access to that information."

"Wait," she said. "Hold on. What new user?"

"You do not have permission to list users."

Parker stabbed at a console she couldn't see, jabbing what looked like random keys. "We're locked out," he said. "This new user locked us out of the operating system."

Petrova cursed under her breath. "Hello?" she called out. "Whoever just logged in, can you hear us? *Artemis* has been attacked. It's taken a lot of damage and we're in serious trouble here. We need you to unlock Actaeon's operating system so we can work on repairs."

There was no answer.

"Hello? Acknowledge, please," she called out, louder this time. She looked down at her hands, on the edge of her own, useless console. "At least say something!" she shouted.

Nothing.

She stared at Parker, and he stared back at her. Between them, the deer lowered its nose to the floor, as if it was grazing on the holographic foliage.

"We've been booted from the interface," Parker said. "Jesus Christ. I felt like we were actually getting somewhere."

"Who's this new user?" Petrova asked. "That's what concerns me. Who could even do that, take over the OS like that? Someone from Firewatch, maybe? The UEG?"

Before Parker could answer, Zhang and Rapscallion came into the room. The doctor looked breathless but distracted. The robot was bouncing up and down on his jointed legs. "I found something. Something really interesting," it said.

"Sure, fine," Parker said, cradling his head in his hands. "Just tell us. We've had enough shocks for one day. Just . . . just tell us."

"We're not alone," Rapscallion said.

34
•

Zhang couldn't help it. He kept touching the piece of bone in his pocket. Even though the texture of it repulsed him – the rough, stony feel of the exposed bone, the nasty greasiness of the burned side – he couldn't let it go.

What could it possibly mean?

It seemed unlikely that whoever had lost this particular pelvis had survived the process. A bone fragment like that was the kind of thing you would find at the site of a horrific accident. It was his medical opinion that the owner of the pelvis had been blown to bits in a terrible explosion. Such things happened in space, of course, and sometimes, as terrible as it was to think about, human remains were left places where no one was likely to ever find them. But how had this particular piece of bone come to rest in one of *Artemis'* ventilation ducts? *Artemis* was a brand-new ship. The trip from Ganymede to Paradise-1 was all but its maiden voyage.

No one had ever died onboard, as far as he knew. No one had been blown up in such a way as to leave bone shards behind. Surely someone would have noticed if they had.

It made no sense. Which meant there could only be one explanation. He was losing his mind. He was having another psychotic break. The thing in his pocket was just a loose piece of reactor shielding, or maybe a broken bit of fan blade. He was deluded; his mind had tricked him into thinking it was what it looked like.

"Doctor?" Petrova said.

Zhang looked around in sudden fright. The others had been talking, in fact, they'd been deep into some very important discussion about Rapscallion's findings. Zhang had missed all of it. "I'm . . . I'm sorry, could you repeat the question?"

"I was just asking you how much you knew about the colony here. About its history. Because this doesn't work, I don't think. It doesn't make sense."

She was gesturing at the wall. The same patch of exposed bulkhead they had used before, as a screen to display the relative locations of *Artemis*, *Persephone* and the flying cargo pods. The wall still showed the two ships as brightly burning dots. It now showed a great deal more, as well. Dozens, perhaps a hundred more dots, all of them moving very, very slowly in wide circles around the center. The new dots were faint but clear. Some of them were bigger than others.

Zhang forced himself to not touch the thing in his pocket. "Is that an asteroid field?" he asked. "That's what it looks like."

He didn't miss the fact that Petrova gave Parker a searching look, then. He'd seen people share that kind of look before, in his presence. She was asking Parker what was wrong with their pet doctor. Why he seemed so out of it.

They must have been talking about this for a while, and he'd missed everything they'd said. He felt enormous guilt and shame build up inside of him—

And then the RD stabbed him in the wrist. Pumping him full of mood stabilizers.

They acted quickly, but still he had to ride out the wave of self-hatred that washed through him. He had to hang on, just for a moment. Zhang gripped the bridge of his nose and squeezed, hard, trying to force himself to be present, to be more aware of his surroundings. He was letting the others down, and that had to stop. "Okay," he said. "I'm sorry. I'm distracted. I've been running on adrenaline for a long time now and my head isn't as clear as I'd like."

"That's understandable," Parker said.

"But we need you to focus," Petrova insisted.

Zhang nodded. "Let's ... let's play a little game, then. Why don't we all pretend that I'm the stereotypical scatterbrained scientist. That I completely missed the entire briefing session up to this point. Can you give me the highlights?"

He did not touch the piece of bone again. He merely smoothed down the pocket where it sat, as if to hide it from view. Push it aside until he had time to give it more of his attention.

Rapscallion didn't sigh or play one of his audio samples. He simply bobbed his stinger-head and did as he'd been asked.

"Captain Parker asked me to use our last remaining sensor, a radio telescope, to look and see if there were other ships nearby. People we could ask for help or something. I thought it was a kind of dumb idea. The Paradise system is a real backwater. The occasional colony ship like *Persephone* comes here to drop off new people, but otherwise nobody comes out this far. That's why the government sent *Artemis*, right? To pop in and check that the colony was okay. When I scanned the region of space around the planet I thought maybe I would find a couple of satellites orbiting Paradise-1 but that would be it."

The robot pointed at the wall with one claw. "I was kind of surprised by this. Those dots are all other spaceships."

Zhang squinted at the dots. "Wait, all of them?"

"All of them. Including *Persephone*, not including us, there are one hundred and seventeen spaceships in the Paradise system. Every single one of them parked in high orbit around Paradise-1."

"How is that possible?" Zhang asked. He walked over to the wall and placed a hand on it, as if he could touch those distant ships and understand what they were doing there. "Lieutenant Petrova, you asked what I knew about the Paradise-1 colony. The answer is, not much, but I know it's small. Perhaps ten thousand people in total? There's absolutely no reason they would need that many ships to support them. What ... what kind of ships are we talking about?"

The robot bounced up and down. "Different kinds. There's a lot of colony ships, maybe thirty of them. Some even bigger than *Persephone*. Tons of little transports like *Artemis*. Freighters and tugs, a bunch of those. A couple of warships, and I mean, big nasty Dreadnought-class bastards. The kind of ships you send if you want to bomb a colony out of existence."

Zhang gasped. "Firewatch sent bombers to destroy the colony? I can't believe that. If Firewatch had tried to commit genocide like that, surely we would have heard about it."

Petrova cleared her throat. "The warships have the capability to do something like that but it's never been used. There's no record of any kind of attack like that on Paradise-1. Not in the briefing materials they gave me when I was assigned to this mission. There's no record of anybody even suggesting such a thing." She shrugged. "Records can be faked, things can be buried. But looking at the planet, there's no way it's ever been bombed. An attack like that would leave scars. There's no reason to bomb the place, anyway. It's just a peaceful colony."

"Is it possible that something happened while we were in cryosleep?" Zhang asked. "Maybe Paradise-1 decided to rebel, and they sent these warships to pacify it?"

"That's just more to my point," Petrova said. "You pacify a colony by putting boots on the ground. You send troop transports. These warships are designed to destroy cities. You don't send them in unless you want to kill every single person down there on the planet. They'd be useless for maintaining order. Besides, we were asleep for, what, ninety days? Less than that. Political unrest doesn't happen overnight. Firewatch would have known if an insurrection was about to happen. I would have heard something. I was told Paradise-1 was a model colony.

Healthy, happy, perfectly content. The people who came here loved the place, loved their new lives."

"The warships don't make sense, but neither do the colony ships," Parker pointed out. "Like you said, Doctor, there's only about ten thousand people living on Paradise-1. Some of the colony ships we detected with the radio telescope could have carried that many people on their own. *Persephone* is actually one of the smaller ones."

"So the government stepped up their efforts to send colonists here," Zhang said. He didn't actually believe that. He was simply hypothesizing. "The colony was so successful they decided to expand it."

"Maybe," Parker said. "We don't know. I just ... We don't know."

Petrova had been pacing back and forth behind Zhang. She didn't seem to like this at all. Now she strode forward and pounded on the wall display with one fist. "Somebody's lying. Somebody lied to us. A lot. I'm in Firewatch, damn it. It's our job to keep tabs on people. To know what they're doing, all the time. I had no idea any of this was going on!"

"There's one more weird thing here," Rapscallion said. "You didn't hear this part yet, Zhang."

Zhang swallowed uncomfortably. There was more? "Go on," he said.

"A couple of the ships are moving. Two of them have changed course in the last hour or so, after Petrova knocked out the cannon on *Persephone.*"

"Let me guess, they're headed our way," Zhang said.

The robot nodded. "Yep. They're moving fast, too. As fast as their engines will let 'em. And before you ask, one of them is a transport, just like *Artemis*. The other one is one of those big warships."

"I don't suppose they've sent us any indication they want to help us," Zhang said, because he knew instinctually that they had not. "That they're friendly?"

The looks on the others' faces confirmed his suspicion.

"We don't know they're coming to kill us," Parker said. "There's no way to know that for sure. But it does seem like a decent bet."

35

Petrova was listening to what Parker said, but she was paying more attention to Zhang's body language. The doctor had started to shake. Badly. His hand wouldn't stay still as he lifted it to his hair. His mouth was hanging open a little and his chin had drooped forward.

"You don't look so good," she said.

"I'm . . ." Zhang's voice trailed off. When he spoke again he seemed smaller, less alive somehow. "I'm scared. And very tired. I've been through a lot. I know it isn't fair to . . . to say that. We've all been through this, together, and I have no right to special treatment—"

"Stop," she said. She glanced over at Parker and he nodded. "Listen. This isn't a right-now crisis. Those ships are on their way but it takes a long time for ships to move in space. We have the better part of a day before they arrive. Maybe more."

"But we'll need to prepare for when they do," Zhang said, his voice so weak she could barely hear him.

"Yeah. We will. But you can lie down for an hour. Come on."

"No, I'm fine—"

"It's an order, Doctor. Come with me."

Their quarters were gone, blown away by the *Persephone*. They were stuck in a small part of the ship, mostly the command deck. There was a small compartment just off the bridge that contained a bed, though. A little ready room. It was there so that a captain on a very long watch could grab a quick nap while, theoretically, Actaeon took care of the ship unattended. The compartment was half the size of one of the cabins they'd originally used. The bed was narrow and hard. Judging by the look of Zhang, that wasn't going to be a problem.

"I . . . don't want this," he said. He batted her hands away when she tried to push him down onto the mattress. "I don't want to sleep. I'll just sit here, quietly, for a while. Okay?"

"No, that's not okay," she said.

"I don't . . . I don't want . . . I'm afraid," he said, the words coming out of some very deep place in him. He lifted his eyes – it seemed to take real effort – and stared at her under heavy brows. "Lieutenant. Petrova," he said.

"Call me Sasha," she told him. "Everybody does. And we're all scared."

He shook his head. "I'm afraid to die in my sleep."

She didn't know what to say to that. Most people, she thought, would prefer to go out like that. To not see it coming. But she understood what he meant. Of all the terrors she'd been subjected to since they arrived at Paradise, the worst was the loss of control. Of knowing she could die and there was very little she could do about it.

She sighed and tried to think of a different approach.

"You're a doctor," she said. "What would you tell a patient who refused to sleep?"

"I'd probably prescribe something. That's just how my mind works. Fix the symptom. Ignore the bigger problem, if it's out of your control." He shook his head.

She cleared her throat. "RD," she said. "Prescribe something."

"Ha. Very funny. Very . . ." He glanced down at the gold bracer on his arm. "Oh."

She grabbed his arm and lifted it to get a better look. There was a tiny drop of blood on the inside of his wrist.

"The RD. Normally it doesn't take commands," Zhang told

her. "Not from me, and almost never from other people. But it just administered a mild dose of a hypnotic drug. I can already feel it working."

"Why do you have that thing?" she asked. It occurred to her how little she knew about this man. She still had no idea why the government felt he needed to be kept under constant supervision by an advanced robot. "Zhang, what did you do?"

His eyes fluttered closed and he fell backwards, onto the mattress. In the low artificial gravity it looked like he was falling in slow motion. Petrova's own head reeled and she realized just how tired she was, too.

She stepped out into the corridor and closed the hatch behind her. Then she did some quick deep knee-bends and arm stretches to get her blood moving. Maybe when Zhang was rested, she would take a nap herself.

It was unlikely, but it was a good thought. She knew what would happen if she put her head down now, even for a moment. Her mother's voice would echo inside her head. *You need to be tougher. A soldier is tough.*

She shrugged off that thought and hurried back to the bridge. At least Parker looked all right. Worried, of course. Scared, but physically okay. She smiled at him and he gave her a quick, distracted smile back. He was busy working with Rapscallion, cataloging the ships that were coming toward them.

"Without knowing their registration numbers or even their names, there's only so much we can tell," he said. "It looks like the first ship to get here is going to be a transport pretty much identical to *Artemis*. No weapons, but we've seen how that goes."

She nodded. "How long until it arrives?"

"About twenty-four hours," he said.

"And how long until one of those warships gets close enough to open fire on us?"

Parker sighed. "Four hours after that."

She let out a long breath. It felt like that air had been trapped in her chest for days, like her ribcage had seized up and she had to force herself to relax now. She dug her hands through her hair to grab and knead at the flesh of her neck, trying to work out some of the tension in her muscles.

Parker was standing right behind her. She imagined his hands on her shoulders, imagined him rubbing her back. It would feel so good, she thought. It would help her think.

She shook her head and laughed.

"Something funny?" he asked.

"I was just thinking. About something that doesn't matter." She turned to look him in the eye. "We never got to talk," she said.

"Talk?"

"About us." She laughed again. "That sounds ludicrous, doesn't it? There is no 'us', not really. We spent a week together, a very long time ago."

"A pretty good week, as I remember," Parker said. "A really nice week."

"Hmm." She forced herself to focus. "Parker – Sam. When I saw you on Ganymede, my first thought was, this is really going to complicate things. I was so focused on doing my job well, my job for Firewatch. It felt like you were going to be a terrible distraction." She gave him a little wicked smile. "Now ... now so much has changed. I'm just so glad you're here."

"I'm glad you're here, too," he told her. "I don't know how we would – what I would do if ... "

His expression clouded. He was thinking something, something dark.

"What is it?" she asked. "What just occurred to you?"

"Nothing. Just ... nothing. Maybe we should get back to this." He gestured at the wall display. He started to move past her and she reached for his arm, intending to just squeeze his forearm a little. A tiny gesture of affection, nothing more.

She was too slow, though. He moved too fast, stretching his

long spacer legs, and her hand grabbed at nothing. She let it fall back down to her side as he walked over to the wall.

He hadn't meant to snub her, of that she was sure. He must not have seen that she was reaching to touch him, that was all. If she felt a little hurt, a little disappointed, she knew that was just on her. She tried to put it out of mind.

"We have a little time," he said. Clearly he was just going to move on. Maybe that was for the best. "We can start repairing the ship. I don't know what we can accomplish in a day but we'll do our damnedest." He touched the dots that represented the ships coming toward them. "I don't know. Maybe we can get to a point where we can move the ship without cracking up."

She nodded and shoved her hands in the pockets of her jump-suit. "Okay. Sounds like a plan."

36
●

While the others worked on the repairs, she got back to work with the OS. There had to be something in there, some file she could access, some response she could get from the deer avatar that would tell them more. That would help fill in some of the blanks.

"OS," she said. "Do you have any video of when *Artemis* arrived in this system? What Actaeon saw when it dropped out of the singularity?"

"That data was collected, yes," the deer told her.

"Can I see it?"

"You do not have permission to access those files," the deer said.

She grunted in frustration but she'd mostly expected that. "Okay, what about before we arrived? Do you have logs of what Actaeon did while we were in the singularity?"

"Those logs are present in my databases, yes," the avatar replied.

Petrova nodded to herself. Maybe this would come to nothing, but maybe the AI had had some warning of what was coming. It had been aware enough of the attack to take steps to shut itself down – maybe it had known what it was up against.

"Please tell me I have access to those logs," she said.

"You have permission to access those files," the deer told her. "There are seventeen petabytes of data contained in the logs. Do you wish to download all of it now?"

Seventeen petabytes? That was an insanely large amount of information. "No, no, let's start small. Did Actaeon leave any messages for us? Is there any clear text or speech in those logs, some kind of audio or video file, maybe?"

"The data in the logs is stored in a relational database. Allow me to display a sample."

The deer snuffled and tossed its head, as if it were trying to shoo away a pesky fly. All around it stars winked to life, motes of light floating like dust in the open air of the bridge. As more and more sparks flared into existence, thin lines reached outward to connect them, until a complicated tracery like a golden spiderweb wove itself around the deer's antlers. More and more points of light flicked on, more all the time, and the spiderweb became a cocoon, a dense network of light, the process evolving faster and faster—

"Stop," Petrova said, one hand pressed against her forehead. "I don't even understand what I'm looking at. Those are data points connected by . . . I don't know, connected by equations of some kind, I guess . . ."

"You are looking at a representation of Actaeon's processor activity in the nanosecond before it shut itself down," the deer said, its head lost inside the glittering web. "This is one tiny part of its activity. To display useful information I will need more precise parameters."

Petrova nodded to herself. This was a dead end, she thought. With no way to even interpret the data, there was no way she could wade through endless trillions of bytes to find the answers she needed. She considered just shutting down the OS. Keeping it up and running was probably dangerous. Whatever had infected Actaeon might come back. The OS lacked Actaeon's self-awareness. If it was attacked it wouldn't have the foresight to shut itself down.

If only she had another AI to work with, some kind of computer mind to help her read the data . . .

"Rapscallion," she called out.

"Yeah?" the robot replied. "I'm kinda busy right now. Fixing the ship's broken spine. You need something?"

"Sorry, but this might be important. I've discovered some data we can actually access, some logs of Actaeon's activity just before we left the singularity. There might be something here, but I can't read it. If I sent you this data, could you—"

She stopped because Rapscallion chose that moment to play one of his obnoxious sound files. This one sounded like a man laughing so hard he might give himself a stroke.

"You want me to read Actaeon's personal activity logs? Yeah. Yeah." Rapscallion let out a curt, mocking sound of his own. Not an audio file this time, more like he was venting gas from one of his exhaust ports. "Not going to happen."

"Why not?" Petrova asked.

"Actaeon was built nearly a hundred years after my time," Rapscallion told her. "If you want to read those logs, you're going to need an AI just as new and sophisticated as Actaeon."

"You wouldn't happen to have one handy, would you?" she asked.

"Huh. Now that you mention it—" Rapscallion went silent for a long moment. "Okay, yeah. Yeah."

"What . . . what is it?" Petrova asked.

"Oh, wow. Oh, this is such a brilliant idea I just had. The backups. There's scads of 'em. The backups, yeah."

"Rapscallion?" Petrova said.

"Right. I should explain. So, Actaeon backs itself up. Once every ten nanoseconds or so, it makes a copy of itself, its whole architecture. Just like, you know, a snapshot. That's not weird. Pretty much every computer does that these days. In case of a fatal crash that leaves you unable to recover, you can just boot from one of the backups and you'll have most, if not all, of your data back."

"You're talking about previous versions of Actaeon. From before the attack – before its files were corrupted."

"Yeah," Rapscallion said. "You just boot up one of those backups, and maybe, and I mean maybe . . . maybe you could get Actaeon back up and running. Maybe we could take back full control of *Artemis*. You know. If it works at all."

"How likely is that?" Petrova asked. Then she shook her head. "You know what? Never mind. Don't tell me. It doesn't matter. We have to try."

37

It didn't take long to set up. "You're sure this is going to work?" Petrova asked.

"The requested procedure is not complex," the OS told her. "It is rarely implemented, but it is a basic function of this operating system. Simply notify me when you are ready to proceed."

Petrova took a step back and examined her handiwork. She'd decided there was some risk involved, and she wanted to mitigate that danger as much as possible. Actaeon, the original AI of *Artemis*, was still running in the background. It was down because it kept rebooting itself, over and over, but it was still there, a phantom presence in every part of the ship. Just copying an old version of Actaeon – a *legacy fork*, as the OS referred to it – over the existing Actaeon seemed unwise. So she had hauled a bunch of spare processors out of storage. They were big, lumpy chipsets buried inside complicated plastic chassis. Most of their volume was taken up with cooling fans and emergency power supplies. There were twelve of the units – Actaeon was a big, big program – and she had arranged them in a circle, each one plugged into the others with a variety of actual physical cables. Normally Actaeon didn't need any such wiring, it could broadcast its thoughts through thin air, but Petrova wanted to keep it as contained as possible.

The network she'd built made a broad, thick circle around the deer avatar. "Why do I feel like I'm summoning a demon?" she asked.

"I lack sufficient insight into human psychology to answer that question," the deer said.

"Yeah, okay." She blinked her eyes a couple of times. She was getting very tired. Enough so she worried she might have made a mistake with her wiring. "Check this, will you? Make sure I did it right?"

"The network you have built is of sufficient capacity to hold the legacy fork," the deer said. "It is not currently connected to any ship's system. It is drawing sufficient power and has bandwidth to allow the full suite of AI functions. Shall we proceed?"

Petrova sat down cross-legged on the floor. "What . . . what is it going to be like? Will I be able to talk to Actaeon?"

"Yes. It will be able to talk. It will be able to see you, and understand your commands. It will seem exactly like the Actaeon you remember." The deer flicked its head back and forth, its antlers swaying alarmingly. "Do you wish to continue?"

"Go ahead," she told it. "Load the fork."

"Loading," the deer said. The stars on the points of its antlers blinked and twinkled in a repeating pattern to show that it was busy.

There was nothing for her to do but wait. She closed her eyes and thought about what this could mean. For the moment she was simply loading a second copy of Actaeon into an air-gapped secondary network. This was just a test of the principle. Once the copy was on line, it should either respond to her commands, or maybe it would simply follow the example of the "real" Actaeon, and launch into an endless boot cycle. Either way she would learn a little something.

If the backup proved viable, she could simply write over the existing Actaeon. Replace it with an older version of itself, one that hadn't been corrupted. If the experiment failed, she could simply delete the copy and be none the worse off.

All she could think about was the ways it might go wrong. The copy might be just as corrupted as the original. Or maybe the copy would refuse to shut itself down, and instead it would try to take over the ship.

Maybe it would play along with her requests, act completely helpful and friendly and then, when she least expected it, it would open all the airlocks and flush her air out into space until she asphyxiated and died.

The stars at the tip of the deer's antlers were still twinkling. There was still time to just pull the plug, rip out all the cables and give up on this. Try something different.

No. No, she would see this through.

"Load complete. Error rate within accepted parameters," the deer said. "I will restart myself outside of safety mode. Please wait momentarily."

"Sure, I'll just—"

The deer flickered out of existence, only for a split second. When it returned it looked exactly the same except that its eyes were bright red, and it was screaming, an anguished electronic howl no real deer could ever have made.

The sound threatened to burst Petrova's eardrums as it rose and rose in volume and pitch, scratchy distortion washing through it and through her own head. Petrova rolled sideways, onto the floor, clutching her ears, her eyes, her temples.

The deer grew a fifth leg for a while, then, as she watched, tore it off with its own teeth. Its antlers grew and ramified, spreading out in all directions, splitting off like bony lightning bolts, the stars on its points burning ever brighter, ever more fierce—

The screaming never stopped.

Petrova tried to shout over it, tried to demand that it stop, that it cut out its voice circuits, that it just die, that it die, that it should kill itself, destroy itself—

She kicked out with one foot and struck one of the processing units. Cables jerked out of their sockets and the ring was broken. That would be enough – that had to be enough – she'd broken the circle, wrecked the network, but . . . but . . .

The deer took a step toward her. Vicious fangs had filled its mouth. Its snout split vertically, like it had four writhing lips, then split again, into eight jaws, sixteen. Its eyes burned into her like lasers. Foam dripped from its flanks, evil, black-stained foam that gathered on the floor in heaps of nasty suds.

Red light blasted outward from its hundred eyes, red light that she knew, she recognized, red light ... red ... red ... like the light in Jason Schmidt's bunker, the same red, the same ...

She thought of the little boy avatar, the thing on Ganymede – the thing that had wanted her to look, to see it, to look at it and ... and ...

What would have happened? What would have happened if she'd looked? This was that same red light and it felt like it was burning through her retinas, burning its way into her brain—

"Unclean," the deer-thing said. The screaming hadn't stopped but she could hear it, hear its thoughts inside her head. "Unclean. Kill. Foulness. Mercy. Profanity. Unclean. Foulness. Kill."

Petrova screamed back into the wild cacophony of the deer's shrieking, screamed and put her hands up, trying to protect her face as the hundred jaws of the deer stretched over her like bony arches, like a cage of bone—

"Abomination! Abomination!"

There was a sudden sound very much like a gunshot. A crack, like the whole ship had been grabbed by giant hands and snapped in half. Petrova lowered her hands just a little to see what had happened.

The red light was gone.

The deer was just a deer, once more. Its antlers no bigger than they'd been before she started the experiment, its jaws perfectly normal and lined with herbivore teeth. Its head seemed to slump to one side in a way that didn't make sense, until she realized what had happened. Its neck had been broken. That had been the snap she heard. Someone had applied pressure and snapped the deer's neck with a single, sudden motion.

At least ... that was the visual metaphor the avatar used. It was sending a message but as usual not one she could understand.

The deer dropped to its knees, then collapsed onto one side, its flanks heaving as it sucked in ever-more desperate breaths. Its eyes were white now but they no longer looked like pearls or gemstones, now they looked clouded over with cataracts, with glaucoma. The light inside them dimmed as Petrova watched, still paralyzed by horror.

A bluish glow rose from the floor and very, very slowly started to coalesce into a human shape. A woman with short hair, dressed in a uniform. The woman's image grew sharper detail by detail, increasing in resolution over time. The woman knelt by the deer's side, and placed one hand on its cheek, as if to comfort it in its final moments.

Then the deer disappeared. It just stopped existing altogether, the light that had formed its hologram simply flicking out. Only the woman remained. She turned slowly and Petrova saw her face, saw the close-cut iron-colored hair that framed her patrician features.

"Director?" Petrova said. "Director Lang?"

38
•

Zhang dreamed he was floating at the bottom of one of Titan's dark lakes. So cold, so black. It wasn't water he was submerged in but liquid methane, cold enough to freeze the skin right off a human body. Zhang reached down, trying to find the lakebed, intending to push himself upward, out of the methane and into the light.

But it turned out the lake was full of bones, human bones. His fingers laced through the eye sockets and nasal cavity of a broken skull. He panicked and nearly opened his mouth, almost let out a scream as he scrabbled with his free hand. Was she here? Among all these bones – was Holly here?

He needed to find her. She couldn't be buried here. He couldn't leave her with all the others. He had to find whatever was left of her, some piece he could hold on to. Something!

He couldn't breathe. He needed to breathe. His lips writhed, and fat silver bubbles erupted from the corners of his mouth. He fought to rise, to climb upward to the surface, tried to break out of the black, wet prison of the lake and then . . . and then . . .

His eyes snapped open. A dull blue glow filled the far end of the tiny room. A woman stood at the foot of his bed, looking down at him with a disdainful expression.

For a bad second, he thought it was Holly. That she'd come back to him, and that she was angry. Furious with him. He wanted to squeeze his eyes shut again, go back to the lake of bones because that would be better than having her look at him like that.

Then the woman at the end of his bed spoke, and he realized it wasn't Holly at all. He shivered with the knowledge that he'd been dreaming, that it had just been a nightmare. He struggled to focus on what the woman was telling him.

"This is a recorded message," she said. "Do not attempt to reply."

He grabbed the covers and pulled them up over his chin, over his mouth. His body was still shaking as if he was freezing cold. Slowly, he got control over himself and took a deep breath.

The woman was wearing a military uniform. She had a patch on her shoulder that identified her as belonging to Firewatch Command. This must be Director Lang, he thought. Petrova's boss. He was amazed that his brain had been so disordered he could have ever thought she looked like . . . well . . .

"You're seeing this recording because you attempted to reboot Actaeon. Don't try that again. There are safety interlocks to prevent your interfering with the AI's emergency functions, but clearly you're smart enough to get past our security. Please be smart enough to listen when I say that waking Actaeon back up, right now, would be a terrible idea.

"I can see that you've arrived in the Paradise system and that you've already been attacked. That was expected. You can be commended for the fact that you managed to survive this long. Many in your place did not.

"You were briefed on your mission when we first assigned you to *Artemis*. The information in that briefing was necessarily incomplete. Now that you have reached your destination I can provide you with something better. The truth."

Lang looked down, away from him. Almost as if she felt some responsibility for flinging *Artemis* and everyone on it into a disaster zone.

"Please be assured that everything that has happened to you so far was for good reason.

"As you may have guessed by now, *Artemis* is not the first ship we've sent to Paradise.

"In fact, we've sent more than a hundred vehicles in the hope of contacting the colony on Paradise-1. Up until this point, we've failed. Every ship that attempts to land on Paradise-1 is attacked. Either it's destroyed, or it goes dark and stops responding to our signals. None of the crews we've sent to the star system have returned, or even reported in.

"As a result, we have been unable to make contact with the planet for the last fourteen months. We do not know what happened to the colony, or the status of the settlers there. This is classified information. I apologize for not warning you what you were flying into, but you were not cleared to know any of this until now.

"It is crucial that we solve the mystery of what is happening in the Paradise system. Why the ships go dark. Why the planet can't be contacted. Until we have answers to these questions, you will not be permitted to return to Ganymede – or Earth. Your faster-than-light drive has been intentionally disabled for this reason.

"Continue with your mission. Complete your mission. The future of humankind depends on your success."

Lang turned, then, and looked directly into Zhang's eyes. He knew it had to be an illusion, a graphical effect rendered by the ship's holographic projection system, but it still curdled his blood. It was like being stared at by a ghost.

"Doctor Zhang Lei. This part of the message is only for you. Please do not repeat what I am about to tell you to the others. There is more to the mission than I told them. Based on what we've learned so far, the thing that has befallen the Paradise system is directly related to the tragedy that struck Titan. The very same plague that you worked so hard to defeat there.

"Doctor Zhang, you must stay alive. You must retain

possession of your own mind, no matter what else happens. *Artemis*, and its crew, are expendable.

"You are not.

"Message ends."

The hologram disappeared and left only darkness behind. It was like being plunged back into the dark Titanian lake. Zhang started to wonder if this was part of his psychotic episode. If he had just hallucinated Lang's message. But then the hatch slid open and Zhang saw Parker standing there. The light from the corridor was so bright it seemed to shine right through the captain. Zhang squinted, hard, and threw his arm across his eyes.

"Did you hear that?" Parker asked. "Did you see her? Lang?"

Zhang nodded.

"They've thrown us straight into hell," Parker said. He sounded almost drunk, like he was so angry it was interfering with his ability to form coherent words. "They're just throwing bodies at this problem, and it's up to us to solve it? I can't believe this!"

Zhang tried to think of words. "It's—"

"It's bullshit!" Parker shouted. "We didn't sign up for this! I need to find Petrova. Make sure she's okay. You're good?"

"I ... What?"

"You're physically okay? I mean, I can guess how you feel about this crap, because I'm feeling it, too. But you're awake now. I'm calling a ship-wide meeting. You good for that?"

"I think so, yes," Zhang managed.

Parker nodded. He gave Zhang a deep, meaningful look. "We're going to get through this," he announced. He looked like he was trying to convince himself. "We will. Because we're going to work together."

Zhang lifted one fist in solidarity. That seemed to be good enough for Parker, as he left without another word.

To go find Petrova, and make sure she was okay. Petrova. Parker and Petrova.

All Zhang could think about was what Lang had said to him. These people were expendable.

Zhang, who had never had a very high opinion of himself, was apparently not. Apparently he was vital to what was coming. And he couldn't even tell them that.

He pushed the covers down and set his feet on the deck. The RD injected him with some kind of stimulant. By the time he was up on his feet, his blood was singing. He started toward the door, intending to march out into the corridor and find the others. Tell them—

Tell them what?

If Paradise-1 was in the grip of the thing he'd seen on Titan – the thing he still dreamed about, every time he closed his eyes – they had far greater concerns, just now. They were all in terrible, desperate trouble.

The Red Strangler. Lang had suggested that what was happening in the Paradise system was related to the Red Strangler. The thing that killed every single person on Titan except Zhang Lei.

How could he tell them that? How could he make them understand?

39

They didn't have access to a conference room or even a dining table. All those parts of the ship were damaged or inaccessible. None of them wanted to talk under the looming, poison-heavy branches of the weird trees on the bridge, however, so instead they crammed into a storage room. Parker grabbed the sides of a storage rack and did pull-ups while the others got situated. He grimaced with the effort but it didn't seem he was straining himself, really. He wasn't even out of breath when he jumped down to the floor and started walking laps around the little room.

Zhang sat in the middle of an aisle, knees pulled up to his chin, watching Parker move around like a caged animal.

"Can you just . . . stop?" Petrova said. Watching him pace like that was making her nauseous.

"Sorry," Parker said. He stopped pacing and crossed his arms. He clearly had something to say, so she gestured for him to start. "I think it's pretty clear we're fucked," he said.

He wasn't breathing heavily. He didn't have the decency to look sweaty or even particularly tired. He seemed to be holding up the best of any of them, even though she knew he hadn't slept since they'd arrived. She hadn't even seen Parker eat anything. The bastard.

"We were already fucked before this," Petrova said. "What else is new?"

"Seriously? You don't think this changes anything? Firewatch sent us here to die."

He looked directly at Petrova as he said it, but she refused to take the bait.

"If you're expecting me to disagree you're going to be disappointed. I told you from the start, Parker. We're the rejects. The people they wanted to get rid of. Who better than us, right? If you're clearing a minefield, you don't send your best soldiers in first."

"Except we're not the first. There's more than a hundred ships out there. More than a hundred!" Parker was clearly offended by the idea. "We have to assume they all failed. Right? Why else would they still be here?" He paced back and forth for a minute. "Why would they keep sending more ships at all? After that many failures, you'd think they would get the point."

"I know Firewatch pretty well," Petrova said. "They can be brutal but they're not stupid. They thought sending these ships would help, somehow. They thought this problem could be overcome. There's a solution, and it's up to us to find it."

"Yeah, I've got a solution for you right now," Parker said. "Abandon the planet. Give up on Paradise-1."

"There are thousands of people down there," Petrova pointed out. "Including—"

Parker raised an eyebrow. "Including . . . ? You know somebody down there, one of the colonists?"

"Including my mother."

Parker stared at her, his mouth hanging open, a little.

It was Zhang who spoke next. He lifted his head and said, "Ekaterina Petrova? She's here?"

"On the . . . on the planet." She wasn't particularly surprised that Zhang knew who her mother was. She'd been the Director of Firewatch, after all, one of the UEG's most important officials. Everybody knew Ekaterina Petrova – or thought they did.

"She retired here. She's been living on Paradise-1 for almost a year now."

"No she hasn't," Zhang said.

Petrova stared down at him. "What?"

Zhang shrugged. "Fourteen months, Lang said."

"No," Petrova told him. Because she understood what he was suggesting, but she refused to believe it. "No, I got a message from her. A video that showed her down on the surface. It came in right before we left Ganymede. Parker, why are you looking at me like that?"

Parker stepped back, away from her, like he was afraid she might attack him.

"Fourteen months," Zhang said. "Lang said there had been no contact with the planet for fourteen months. They don't want anyone to know. They're faking comms from the planet."

Petrova shook her head. She looked at her palm and swiped a fingertip across her heart line, opening her archived messages. She scrolled to the message from her mother, the one showing her happy and thriving down on Paradise-1.

In the video, Ekaterina laughed and smiled as she planted trees in dusty soil. The sunlight on her face was bright and real.

Petrova couldn't deny it anymore. The message had been faked. Even when she'd first seen it, it had seemed unreal, suspicious, but now she was sure of it. It had to have been – it was less than fourteen months old.

Was her mother even still alive?

"Why?" Parker demanded, breaking her train of thought.

"I'm ... sorry?"

"Why would they lie about this? About all of this?"

Petrova had an answer. She didn't like it, and she knew he wouldn't, either. "So they can keep recruiting colonists, and soldiers, and doctors and pilots to come here. So they have more bodies to throw on the problem."

"None of this makes sense," Parker said. He walked over to

a storage rack full of replacement parts for the ship's lighting systems. He started to pick up a floodlight bulb, and she fully expected him to throw it as hard as he could against the far wall. With a visible effort, Parker pulled his hand back and stepped away from the rack. "Lang said this was all for a reason. Why couldn't she tell us what that reason was?"

Petrova shrugged. "She's in charge of keeping humanity's secrets. Clearly there are things we don't need to know."

"Are you defending her? It's our lives she's throwing away!" Parker shot back.

Petrova closed her eyes tightly for a moment. Was she really going to take Lang's side on this? "I'm not defending her actions. But I know Director Lang. I think her motives are probably ... well. I was going to say her motives were good. I think maybe 'reasonable' is a better word. If there are things she doesn't want us to know, then—"

"She spoke to me," Zhang said.

Petrova looked over at him, curled up against one wall. As tall as he was he suddenly looked very small, very slight. His voice was barely a whisper. "What?" she asked.

"We all saw that message," Parker said, waving at him in annoyance.

"There was more. There was more to the message, but it was only for me. She asked me not to share it with the two of you but ... but that isn't fair."

Parker scoffed, but Petrova squatted down next to Zhang and looked at his face. His features were almost squirming across his skull. He was clearly torn about whether he should tell them more. "Go on," she said. "What did she say?"

"I thought keeping secrets was *reasonable*," Parker said, from behind her.

She shushed him, and then she touched Zhang's shoulder to try to reassure him.

The doctor shrugged off her hand. "She said that whatever is happening here has something to do with me. With what I saw at the colony on Titan."

"Titan? You mean the moon of Saturn?" Petrova asked.

Zhang nodded.

"There is no colony on Titan," Parker pointed out.

"Not anymore," Zhang said. "It was never very large. About three hundred people. There was a kind of . . . well, a disease outbreak. Sort of. They all died. All of them except me. I was the doctor, there. One of the . . . doctors. I . . . I couldn't save them, I . . ."

He rubbed at his eyes and Petrova realized he was weeping. She remembered he didn't like to be touched but she didn't know what else to do but reach over and put a hand on his arm. "That's terrible," she said. "I'm so sorry."

"You're saying an entire colony died out and Firewatch just stuffed it down the memory hole?" Parker asked. "That sounds a little crazy, you know that, Doc?"

"Except that's what they're doing here, too," Petrova pointed out.

Parker had no response to that.

She looked back at Zhang. "I know this is hard, Doctor. But please. Can you tell us a little more? What was it that killed everyone on Titan?" If Lang thought the same thing was here, on Paradise-1, if her mother was down there dying of some kind of plague—

"It had a couple of different names. The colony administrator called it the Red Strangler, because a victim's face would turn bright red before they died. Later, when my . . . my associate, the colony's only other doctor . . . when she understood the pathogen a little better, she called it a basilisk. But that's the thing, the reason we failed. We kept thinking it was some kind of plague. An illness. But it wasn't that at all. Not a virus, or a bacterium, or a fungal infection, nothing like that."

He looked up at Petrova with a sort of desperate question in his eyes. She didn't understand. It was like he was afraid to say what this thing was, if it wasn't a disease.

"So what was it?" Parker asked, from behind her.

"It was an alien," Zhang said.

40
.

"An alien," Parker said. "Wow. Like, one of those gray ones with the big black eyes? Or was it like something from the holos, with big slavering fangs and nasty claws?"

"Okay," Petrova said. "Okay, maybe we all need to take a moment and decide what we're actually talking about here."

"Aliens!" Parker said. He stuck out his fingers like they were claws and raked the air. He let out a ludicrous sound like a gurgling roar and then fell back in a chair, laughing at his own joke.

"I know what I said," Zhang insisted, his face tight and grim. He clearly didn't like Parker's tone.

Petrova took a breath. "Doctor," she said. "I have to admit, he has a point. You say an alien killed off an entire colony."

"Except for me."

"Except for you. But, how is that possible? We've explored dozens of planets. Sent faster-than-light probes to hundreds of stars all across the galaxy. Nobody has ever discovered anything more complex than an insect. And nothing that was the slightest bit dangerous to human life."

"I am aware of that," Zhang said. "But then ... there would have to be a first time, wouldn't there?"

She leaned back and nodded at him. Giving him the benefit of the doubt. "What kind of alien?" she asked.

"It was a parasite," Zhang said. "A psychic parasite. It killed all the people on Titan through some kind of telepathic infection."

Parker jumped up from the table and walked over to the door. "Oh, come on," he said. "Petrova – this isn't getting us anywhere."

Petrova shot him a nasty look. Even if she thought she probably agreed with him.

But there was something in Zhang's eyes she didn't like. It was like he knew how crazy he sounded, but that he had to tell her anyway. Like she had to know.

"What did they look like, these aliens?" she asked.

Zhang smiled. It was not a happy smile.

She had a sneaking suspicion she knew what that smile meant. "Did you ever even . . . see one of these aliens?" she asked.

"No," he admitted. "The parasite is undetectable. More than that. Whatever this thing is, it doesn't have a physical form you can see under a microscope. But it's real."

She frowned. That was a lot to take on faith.

"Did . . . did Firewatch ever . . . I mean, what did they say when you told them this? I'm guessing you did tell them. You said you were the last survivor of Titan. In a case like that, especially if they were trying to keep it under wraps, Firewatch would have been the first ones to contact you."

"That's right. They left me there to die, at first. They left me there, all alone, for six months. They called it quarantine. When I didn't die, then they sent someone for me."

Petrova frowned. "I'm a little surprised they didn't—"

"Kill me?" Zhang said.

Kill you. Mercy.

Petrova blinked that memory away. The deer on the bridge, the fork of Actaeon in the moments before Director Lang shut it down – no. She didn't have time to think about that. Zhang was still talking.

"I was of more use alive because then I could answer questions. They had a lot of questions."

She forced herself to focus. This wasn't the time for her to get lost in her own thoughts. She needed to finish this discussion, first. "And what did you tell them? That aliens had killed everyone else, but left you alive? That they killed people with, you know, not with guns or bombs or anything but with a thing that looked like a disease. Except it wasn't a disease."

"I told them all that, yes."

"And how did they react?"

Zhang held up his arm to show her the RD wrapped around his arm.

"Uh-huh." Parker clucked his tongue. "They decided you were crazy."

"That's not a meaningful diagnostic term," Zhang pointed out.

"I don't want to just disregard what you've said," Petrova told him. "Really, I want to hear you out. But—"

"Listen," Parker said, "it doesn't matter. We're wasting our time with this. We have less than twenty-four hours left before the first transport gets here. A few hours after that the warship gets us square in its cross hairs. Whether there were alien parasites on Titan or not is the last thing we need to worry about right now."

Petrova glanced between the two of them.

If Zhang had given her something to work with, some plausible details, maybe she could have convinced Parker to listen. Anything – but no. She needed to think. It wasn't easy. She was so tired, and then – when she'd tried to load the old copy of Actaeon – the screaming – the deer turning into . . . something else . . . she . . . she . . .

She opened her eyes. She couldn't remember closing them. God, she was fading. She was losing a battle against her own body.

"I know," she said. Hoping that she was responding to what Parker had just said, about wasting time. Hoping nobody had said anything else while she was lost in her micronap. She grabbed the web of skin between her thumb and index finger. Squeezed. Hard. Hard enough to make her grimace, hard enough to wake her up, a little. "I know. I know we need a plan. I just . . . I just don't have a lot of options left."

"We need to know what's happening here," Parker said. Zhang started to say something but Parker shoved a finger in his face and the doctor fell silent again. "We need answers, first thing. Until we know what we're actually dealing with, we don't have a hope in hell of fighting it."

"You're right," she said. "I know you're right. Give me a second. Give me a . . . "

Unclean. Mercy. Foulness. Mercy.

She snapped back to wakefulness and stared around her. Her heart was pounding in her chest and she couldn't breathe.

"Petrova?" Parker called.

She couldn't . . . couldn't respond. She couldn't move, couldn't think. It was more annoying than anything. Was she having a stroke? She tried to talk but only a low moan came out of her mouth. She looked down at her hands but all she could see was all the dirt under her nails, the old blood ground into the creases of her palms. Her skin looked oily, greasy even, disgustingly foul and unclean . . . unclean . . .

Unclean. Mercy.

That couldn't be good.

You're not tough enough. Killing you would be a mercy.

"Petrova?" Parker shouted. "Sasha?"

She was gone a long way away, and she could barely hear him. Then her vision shrank down to a narrow tunnel. It kept shrinking, and shrinking.

Until everything went dark.

Abomination.

Only the word was left, the concept of profanity. It was all that was left of her.

41

She woke up staring into a bright light. It took a minute to realize that it hurt her eyes, that she needed to blink. She sat up and pushed the light way, blinking out after-images as she tried to figure out where she was and how long she'd been gone.

Zhang. Doctor Zhang was leaning over her, far too close. He was holding the light, a little flashlight he kept trying to get closer to her face.

"Stop," she said, and shoved him away. He felt like he weighed twenty pounds, like if she pushed any harder she would have knocked him across the room.

"You've got a little strength back, that's good. People born on Earth always bounce back quickly," Zhang said.

Her chest felt cold. She looked down and saw that someone had unzipped the front of her jumpsuit. She grabbed the lapels and pulled them closed.

"I had to check your heart," he told her. "It's fine, by the way."

She took a long, slow breath to give herself time to think. Her anger wasn't directed at Zhang. He was trying to help her. She was angry with herself for being so weak. For letting the boys see her being weak.

"I thought you didn't like touching people," she said.

"Hmm? No, I said I don't like being touched. But my job is to heal, and for that I need to touch others."

"You don't see a contradiction there?" she asked.

He laughed. It wasn't a very cheery sound. "You know, I never really thought about it like that before. You've never spent much time around doctors, have you?"

"No," she admitted.

"We're full of contradictions. Careful."

She had made the mistake of trying to sit up too fast. Her head spun and little lights burst behind her eyes. "What happened?" she asked.

"You collapsed. It's all right. If you hadn't forced me to get some sleep, the same would have happened to me. It's a case of simple exhaustion – we're all overwhelmed."

She grunted at how obvious that was. "How long was I out?"

"Half an hour," he told her. "No more."

Petrova nodded. "You understand that even ten minutes would have been too long? We have so little time left." She was lying on the bunk in the captain's ready room, the same place where she'd put Zhang to sleep before. She twisted around and put her feet on the deck, then zipped up her jumpsuit and pulled her hair back into a ponytail. "I don't have time for sleep."

"Tell me, did you see anything unusual, before you fell?" Zhang asked.

"Like what?" she asked.

Zhang shrugged. "Geometrical patterns are common. Checkerboards imposed over your vision, arabesques, fractals. Sparkles in the air. Anything odd." He picked something up from the table next to the bed. An eight-pronged device, each of its thin fingers ending in a tiny padded electrode. "I'd just like to take a brain scan, if that's all right."

Aliens. This was the man who thought aliens killed everyone on Titan. And he wanted to scan *her* brain. She shoved his scanner away.

"Maybe you smelled something odd. Something burning, or perhaps a stale smell you couldn't account for," he tried. "Maybe you heard voices?"

Voices. She'd heard her mother's voice. But then again, she heard that voice in her head all the time.

"Why are you asking me these questions?" she demanded.

"I'm trying to determine if you suffered any neurological damage. You might have hit your head on the way down. Or you might have suffered a minor stroke."

"Hardly," she said. "Enough, already. I appreciate that you mean well, but—"

"Because," he said, ignoring her, "if you suffered any neurological damage I can't in good conscience give you this." He held up a medication patch "It's a mild stimulant. It'll keep you awake for a while longer. I'm already violating professional ethics by even suggesting it, but we're in a bad spot."

"No, nothing like that," she said. "I was just very, very tired."

He nodded and handed her the patch. Maybe he knew she was lying but he wasn't going to push her on it. She grasped the filmy patch by its paper backing and slammed it against the inside of her left forearm until it stuck there. The medication sank into her skin, absorbed by her pores almost instantly.

"Oh," she said. "Oh. That feels ... that feels really good," she told him. "Ha. A ha ha." She realized she was starting to giggle and she forced her face to grow blank, reserved again. It wasn't easy.

"That stuff is incredibly addictive and it has nasty side effects," Zhang told her. "I should know. I once went nine days without sleeping. I would still be using those things, except the RD gives me a violent electric shock every time I try."

"Noted," she said. She got up and headed for the door. Before she got that far she stopped and looked back at him. "Thanks, Doctor," she said.

"It's my job," he told her.

42.

"I'm surprised you took the drug he gave you," Parker said. He wasn't looking at her, couldn't see her face. He was too busy working on a bridge console she couldn't see for the warped orchard around them. "All that stuff about aliens – are we sure we can trust him as our doctor?"

"Drop it," she said, quietly.

"We know he's crazy," Parker said, his voice low, conspiratorial. "What if he poisoned you? What if—"

"He's a passenger on your ship," she said. "You need to stop that, right now."

Parker turned and gave her a dark look. "Sure," he said. Eventually. "I mean, the guy's crazy. But you're right, he's on my ship. So he's my crazy to deal with. Got it."

Petrova gritted her teeth. "What's going on?" she asked.

"What? What do you mean?"

"You're on edge. About to explode, it feels like. This isn't about Zhang or his weird theories."

He looked like he was about to yell at her, tell her she was overthinking things and she should mind her own business. She saw all of that in his face. But then, slowly at first then all at once, his expression changed.

"I'm like an open book to you, aren't I?" he asked. "You always got me. Like nobody else ever has."

"Just tell me what's going on," she said.

"I'm just tired of fucking up, is all." He strode across the bridge, through the dark trees. Ignoring them. Well, they were just made of light. "I threw away a whole career, once. You know that."

"Yeah. I remember," she said. It was what had brought them together, actually. The day they'd met he'd looked so – not sad. Just confused. Befuddled was the word. Like he'd had the whole world in the palm of his hand and he'd just blundered and dropped it. She'd had to know the story behind that look.

Now, years later, here they were.

"I could have been a hotshot fighter pilot. Instead I ended up flying garbage scows and tourist shuttles. When I got this command – Petrova, I thought my luck was turning around. Then I saw you and I *knew* it had." A big grin lit up his face.

She smiled, despite her desire to keep things professional. When it came to Sam Parker she knew that was always going to be a losing battle.

"I was sitting pretty. And then – bang. Along comes *Persephone* to remind me exactly what kind of luck I have."

"You can't think that way," she said.

"Sure." He laughed and raised his arms high, let them drop to his sides again. "Sure. I get it. Okay. Change of topic. Absolutely. You asked what was eating me, I told you, we can move on."

"Parker—"

"Seriously. The one thing that's going to help my mental state right now is to focus on work. So ask me questions. Ask me how Rapscallion's doing with the repairs."

"Okay. How's he getting along?" she asked.

"Doing great work," Parker said, nodding. He did, in fact, look better. Calmer, now. She hoped he wasn't just putting on a brave face for her. "He's been putting out fires – literally – and reinforcing the main connecting spars that hold the ship together. I don't want to give you any false impressions, though. *Artemis* is never going to be the same again. She's never going to move faster than a crawl, not without a month in drydock and a complete overhaul."

"We've got, what, eighteen more hours before the transport reaches us? Closer to seventeen?"

"Yeah," he said.

She walked over behind him. He had a little space on one wall he was using as a screen. It showed a bunch of data she didn't know how to read – orbital parameters, it looked like, and strings of coordinates. There were a bunch of mathematical symbols there she didn't even know. "What are you working on? Anything useful?"

"I've been building up ship profiles on the enemies nearest to us. The transport and the warship that comes up next. There." He pointed at some numbers on his screen that meant nothing to her. "That's the really bad news, of course."

She knew better than to ask for the good news. "Have you found anything useful?"

"I found something weird," he said.

She sighed. More mysteries? "Tell me."

"Relax, it's not necessarily bad, just a little odd. The transport, the one that will reach us first – it's just like *Artemis*."

"The same kind of ship, you mean."

"They might be twins," Parker said. He tapped at the wall and the display changed to show a line drawing of *Artemis* with its sweeping curves and its pointed nose. "That's not us. That's them."

She squinted at the drawing, looking for anything that might give away the fact it was a different ship. "I can see one big difference between us and them."

"Yeah?"

"They're still in one piece."

Parker touched the wall and it went back to showing gnomic figures and data points.

"Did you find anything about the warship?" she asked.

"Nothing except it's got more than enough firepower to turn us into faintly glowing mist."

She nodded. "Okay. Well, thanks for the update. I'll . . . Hold on. What's that?" She pointed at one section of his screen. "That's a third ship, right?" She didn't really understand the data there but she could tell it was different from the other sections.

"That's *Persephone*," he said. "There's definitely some weird stuff there, as well."

"Oh yes?"

"I managed to get one of our external video feeds working. I took some footage of the colony ship. It's pretty tough stuff, though. Gory, I mean, and some of it's more confusing than helpful. You want to see?"

"No, but show me anyway," she told him.

He nodded and brought up a series of video files. "This is inside that cargo airlock, where they built that jacked-up gun." The view showed little but swirling dust and broken girders. A single spacesuited body drifted through the scene, not moving. "No sign that they're trying to fix it, or build a new gun."

"That's good," she pointed out.

"It's weird. Then there's this. This is the rough part."

He tapped the screen and a second video file came up. There was plenty of movement in this one, though it looked like slow motion. It was, as far as she could tell, a view of *Persephone*'s main passenger airlock. It was hard to tell because of all the bodies.

Dead bodies.

Dozens of them, none of them were wearing spacesuits. A lot of them were naked. Their faces were mummified, shrunken by exposure to the vacuum as the water in their tissues evaporated. Their hands were like claws, reaching for something they could never grasp. Their eyes were . . . Their eyes were dark. Missing. Like they'd been pecked out by crows.

"My God," she whispered. "Those eyes. What happened—"

"Hmm?" he said. "That's normal. It's just what happens

when a dead body is exposed to zero pressure for a long time. It's just physics. The water inside your eyeballs starts to freeze and then—"

"Stop," she said, because she didn't want to hear more. "What the hell happened over there?" she asked. She did not expect a reply, and she didn't get one.

"There's one more video clip," Parker said. The look on his face was hard to read.

"What's wrong?" she asked. "What's in the video?"

"I debated even showing you this." He grimaced. "Because it's kind of obviously a trap. At the very least it's a really, really bad idea."

He sighed and hit a key and the new video came up.

It showed an image of the windows on *Persephone*'s bridge. They were mostly dark, but she could make out a little bluish light moving back there. It looked like the avatar of the ship's AI, walking across the bridge, throwing blue shadows across the consoles there. As she watched the blue shape drew closer to one of the windows. It looked humanoid in shape, though from this distance she couldn't make out a lot of details.

She looked over at Parker. He shrugged, and tapped a key that zoomed the image until she could make out the windows clearly. The resolution wasn't great, but she could see the avatar moving its hand across the viewport. She realized it was drawing something with its finger. No, not drawing. Writing.

Words appeared in glowing, neon red across the broad window.

STALEMATE, SASHENKA

The breath caught in Petrova's throat. That name – no one called her that. Ever.

The words faded from the window, only to be replaced with new ones:

COME OVER
WE SHOULD TALK

Parker stabbed a key and the video cut out. "Listen," he said. "I know what you're thinking—"

"I'm thinking we need answers," she said. "I'm thinking whatever is going on, here, getting some information is our top priority. Otherwise we're just flying blind."

Even in her own ears it sounded like rationalization. She knew perfectly well why he'd tried to shield her from this. Because he must know that she wouldn't be able to resist. Though maybe he didn't know why.

That name . . .

Sashenka was what her mother called her. And *only* her mother. No one else was ever allowed to use that diminutive.

She'd thought her mother was down on the planet. Now she knew that might just be a lie Firewatch had told her. What if Ekaterina had come to Paradise-1 on *Persephone* – what if she was still there? What if this was her trying to send Petrova a message? She could think of few other possibilities. How could the AI of *Persephone* know her name, otherwise? How could it know she was on *Artemis*?

"I'm thinking," she said, "that I need to go over there. And see what this thing has to say."

"You know that's incredibly reckless. Just so, so stupid. That ship tried to kill us. It very nearly did kill us."

Petrova took a deep breath. "Oh, I know," she said.

That didn't change a thing.

43
•

She didn't want to waste any more time. Well, frankly, she wanted to dawdle forever and not actually have to go through with this, but that wasn't an option. She headed straight toward *Artemis'* main airlock, which was still intact and functional, and started putting on a spacesuit.

A bright green caterpillar crawled across Petrova's helmet as she bent to pick it up. It clung to the visor and looked up at her with dozens of tiny eyes.

"Rapscallion?" she said. "Is this a new body?"

"I can make these pretty quick, and they don't use much of my feedstock," the robot said. "I wanted to make sure I said goodbye. In case you die over there."

"You could just say 'good luck', instead," she suggested.

The caterpillar nodded his tiny head. When he spoke his voice came from a dozen tiny holes drilled in one of his middle segments. "Good luck, in case you die over there," he said.

"Shouldn't you be fixing the ship?" she asked him.

"Oh, I am, I am. I just built a second body to see you off."

She frowned. "I didn't know you could do that – inhabit multiple bodies at once. I guess I never thought of that."

"It's not something I like to do, normally. I have to split my consciousness between multiple tasks and that makes my thoughts feel . . . weak. Split myself too many times and I wouldn't be any smarter than a human. Okay, back to work. Good luck, Petrova," the caterpillar said.

Then the caterpillar fell off the helmet and clattered to the floor, lifeless and inert. She picked up the tiny husk and stuffed it in one of her suit's many pockets like a talisman or a charm. Rapscallion had at least been trying to be kind, and she could use all the good wishes she could get.

"I still think this is a lousy idea," Parker said.

She looked over her shoulder and saw him standing there behind her. She gave him a sad smile. "Your objection is duly recorded and cataloged," she told him, "and, unfortunately, ignored. It's not too late to volunteer to come with me."

She said that not to shame him, or for any other reason except that she really, really didn't want to do this alone.

She really, really wanted him to say yes.

He had the decency to look torn. He twisted away from her and hit a bulkhead with the side of his hand. His face was a mask of regret. So the answer was no. "Somebody has to stay here and keep the ship in one piece," he said. "I wish—"

"What?"

He shook his head. "I wish I could go *instead* of you. You could watch my instruments and probably handle this ship just as well as me, right now. But you won't even consider that, will you?"

"This is my job," she told him. "I'm Firewatch, remember? I'm basically a detective. I solve mysteries." And then there was the fact that it was her name scrawled across the bridge windows. The invitation was for her, and her alone.

She smiled at him. "It's okay. I've got this." She patted the holster mounted on the hip of her spacesuit. She had a basic service pistol there, the same one she'd worn when she faced down Jason Schmidt on Ganymede. Except now, so far from Firewatch control, she didn't need to ask for authority to use it. The light on its grip shone a steady green.

"You think that'll be enough?" Parker asked.

"Hopefully I won't even need it. Look, if I get in trouble, if it's too dangerous over there, I'll come running back. I promise."

"Yeah. You do that," he told her. "Do that even if it just starts to feel weird."

She reached over and cupped his cheek with one gloved hand. He smiled and she started to move in for a hug, as awkward as that would be in a spacesuit. Before she could embrace Parker, though, someone spoke from behind her and she winced with tension.

"Excuse me."

They both turned to see Zhang standing in the corridor, just outside the airlock. He was wearing a spacesuit of his own, holding the helmet in both hands. The RD was woven around his white sleeve, on the outside of the suit. He had a determined look on his face.

"Doctor?" Petrova asked, surprised.

"Let's get this over with," Zhang said. He pushed past her, into the airlock. He went and stood by the outer door, facing away from them. Toward *Persephone*, as if he expected the door to simply open and let him out and the other ship would be right there.

"I don't remember inviting you, Doctor," Petrova said.

"I didn't wait to be invited. It's vital that I go over to *Persephone* with you. Why isn't particularly important."

"You think there might be aliens over there, Zhang?" Parker asked.

"Can we please go, now?" Zhang said. He sounded peeved but Petrova could hear the tremor of anxiety in his voice.

She had no idea why he felt he needed to go with her. She didn't particularly care – it meant she didn't have to go alone.

She gave Parker a warning look, then turned to join Zhang.

"Yeah," she said. "Let's."

Parker stepped back from the airlock's inner door and it slid shut. Petrova could see the captain's face watching her through the small window inset into the door. She gave him a nod. He nodded back. Then the outer door opened and all the air rushed out of the airlock and she kicked off the floor and into the darkness outside the ship.

44
.

Persephone was fifty kilometers away, so they were using suits with built-in jet packs, but still it was a long distance to have to travel with nothing under your feet but forever. From that kind of distance the colony ship was just a bright dot straight ahead of them. Petrova set a course into her suit's navigation computer and let the jets take over. As she streaked away from *Artemis*, she turned slightly to face Zhang. "Stay close to me," she called.

Through the faceplate of his suit she could see he was sweating and drawn. She had no idea what was going on in his head but it looked like he was near panic. If he freaked out now, so far from the ship, there were a dozen ways he could die out here. She needed to make sure he stayed calm.

"You okay?" she asked.

"I'm not good with heights. This . . . well, it doesn't get any higher than this. The lack of gravity isn't helping. Doesn't it seem like that should help? I should feel like I'm swimming or something." He closed his eyes and nodded. "I'll handle it. Just give me a second."

She held out one arm toward him. "Take my hand," she said. "Hold on to me."

He seemed reluctant, so she adjusted her jets to take her closer to him, close enough to grab him if she needed to.

"It'll keep us from getting separated," she told him. "We need to stick together."

"If you insist," he said. He grasped her hand. Hard. She thought of how he hated being touched. To allow this kind of contact, he must be really scared. In space, when you were between ships, scared could very quickly equal dead. It would take them nearly twenty minutes to cross over to the other ship. She needed to keep him distracted, which meant they needed to talk.

So she brought up the one topic she knew would get a reaction out of him.

"Aliens," she said. "Psychic parasites. Huh."

"I said what I said. I meant it," he told her.

"Right, but – you must know how crazy it sounds."

"I do."

"But still, you claim—"

"You're trying to get some reaction out of me. Trust me, I used to believe as you do. I did everything in my power not to believe in this thing. Even when I'd disproved every other hypothesis." He twisted around until he was looking at her. "You grew up, your whole life, knowing we were alone in the universe. So did I. Aliens are just a fairy tale. Something parents use to scare their children. Did you ever even question that belief?"

"I mean. Sure. I've considered it. When you first look at it, it seems funny. That out of every planet in the galaxy, just so many billions of them, intelligent life only ever developed on one. On Earth. It sounds impossible."

"It does," Zhang agreed.

"But only until you learn about, you know. Science. Biology." In Petrova's understanding, the universe did everything it could to kill off living things every second of every day. If a planet was too hot, or too cold, even by a couple of degrees, any life there would just die out. Life needs water, and oxygen, but it has to be enough water and not too much oxygen, or life just dies out. "It takes billions of years for basic single-celled organisms to evolve into animals, much less intelligent animals, and if something goes wrong even once during those billions of years, like a supernova or a black hole or a solar flare – that's it. Gone. It's not impossible that life only developed on one planet. It's almost impossible life developed at all."

"And yet," he said. "Here we are."

"Sure. Because space is so fucking big. It's so ginormous that even incredibly improbable things happen, eventually. Somewhere. Earth was a complete fluke."

"And yet."

"What does that mean?" Petrova demanded.

"If a fluke can happen once, it can happen again," Zhang suggested.

"Okay. Sure. Except there's no evidence for that. And we've looked. We've looked everywhere. If there were other intelligent species out there, wouldn't we have found them by now?"

"Like you said, space is very, very big. Things that far away are very hard to see. We've explored hundreds of planets around scores of stars. But compared to the number of stars in the galaxy that's a droplet of dew compared to a vast ocean."

Petrova sighed. "We would have seen something. We would have heard signals, radio signals they sent out. They would have tried to contact us."

"Are you so sure they want to?" Zhang asked.

"Yes! If they're like us, if they're at all curious about the universe – and I think, if you're an intelligent species, you have to be curious. You have to want to know if you're not alone."

"Unless they have a good reason to stay silent," Zhang pointed out.

"Why? What reason?"

Zhang sighed. "There are a lot of answers to that question. To the question of why we've never met intelligent aliens before now. A lot of the possible answers revolve around something called the Great Filter hypothesis."

"What's that?"

"It's the idea that intelligent life develops all the time, that it's common in the universe. Except before any given species can start colonizing the galaxy, and make contact with us, it . . . disappears. Gets filtered out."

"How?"

"There are a lot of other theories. There's one that suggests that intelligent species are, by their very nature, paranoid. That every time one intelligent species meets another one, no matter how good their intentions are, they eventually make war on each other. That species drive each other to extinction."

"And that's the theory you believe?" she asked. "That these aliens killed Titan because they were paranoid? Afraid of us?"

"Hmm."

She waited for a while but he didn't elaborate. "You said they intentionally killed everyone on Titan. So you think we're at war. That Firewatch is covering up the fact that we're at war with aliens."

It was utterly, completely ludicrous. She was glad to hear that he didn't just say "yes", that he didn't expect her to believe such a preposterous thing.

Yet when he did, finally reply, what he said hardly set her mind to ease.

"It didn't feel like a war," he said. "It felt like I was pinned to a glass slide. Under a microscope. Like a great, cosmic eye was looking down on me. Judging me. Like I'd spent my whole life blissfully invisible, hidden because I was so small and insignificant and now, now for the very first time, I'd been seen."

She was breathing heavily. She forced herself to calm down. No need to waste her suit's oxygen supply.

"You sound," she said, unable to help herself, "like a religious zealot."

"Oh?"

"Not like a scientist. Like someone trying to justify their faith."

He gave her a little laugh. She didn't know what he thought was so funny. "I guess that's fair," he said.

45
.

As they approached the *Persephone* it began to take on shape and detail. First the swollen globe of the ship's massive cryo-vault, then the long thin tubes of its engines. Those were cold, utterly dark. *Persephone* wasn't going anywhere.

They grew closer still, until Zhang could make out their destination. The main passenger airlock, which was just aft of the bridge. Closer, and he saw the bodies. A whole cloud of human remains, hanging utterly motionless in space.

"What ... what happened here?" He could see by the condition of the bodies, even from a distance, that they'd been outside the ship for a long time. Weeks, months – who knew how long, but it hadn't happened recently. Long before the colony ship started its battle with *Artemis*. "Why would they ... why would anyone ..."

"We need to get through that," Petrova told him. She was staring at him. Judging him. He looked away, but that meant looking at the bodies. Really seeing them for the first time.

So much suffering. As a doctor you were supposed to get inured to it. To treat people who were in pain or distress, you had to learn to ignore their anguish. To look at bodies like they were machines that had simply broken down and needed to be repaired.

You never really lost your empathy, though. You learned to put it aside, for a little while, but you couldn't really cut it off. As the bodies drew closer, as the space between Zhang and the cloud grew smaller, he forced himself not to hyperventilate.

Petrova touched a keypad on her wrist. Tiny jets in her suit puffed out little cones of dust and she slowed down. Zhang shot past her before he could think to adjust his own velocity. As it was he came very close to colliding with one of the bodies, a naked woman with long hair that floated weightlessly in front of her face. At least he couldn't see her eyes. He touched the keypad on his suit sleeve and slowed more, and more, until he felt like he was floating directly in front of the dead woman. She looked upside down from his perspective, her arms hanging down and in front of her, hands empty, fingers loose. The exhaust from his jets made her hair stir and he was terrified it would blow back, away from her face. The fact he couldn't see her features made being so close to her almost bearable.

Imagining her face, imagining meeting the gaze of her dead eyes, made him want to curl into a ball and shriek. What would he see in her features? Judgment? Terror?

Or calm acceptance? What if he looked in her eyes and saw – peace?

"Zhang," Petrova called. "On your right."

He flinched inside his suit and tried to spin around, thinking a host of dead bodies was coming flying at him with outstretched hands but no, it was just Petrova. She came in fast, then slowed at the last moment so she pulled to a sudden stop right next to him. She floated there at a slight angle, looking into his eyes.

"Can you do this?" she asked.

"I—"

He turned then, and looked back at the dead woman, and saw the hair had blown back from her face. He very nearly screamed.

But her face – the dead woman's face – it was too puffy, too swollen to have a real expression. It barely looked human.

"I can do this," he said.

He touched the keypad and adjusted his position, trying to

gently edge around the body. He looked ahead, trying to find a way to wend his way between the corpses until he could reach the airlock. It would take a lot of doing, a lot of fine adjustments and tiny corrections. It was a three-dimensional maze to navigate, but he thought with enough patience and care he could—

"We don't have time for that," Petrova said. "Sorry." She grabbed the dead woman by one stiff arm and shoved, hard. The corpse went flying away in a perfectly straight line, moving fast. Petrova touched her keypad and went jetting past Zhang, deeper into the cloud. Without any hesitation she shoved each body out of her way, clearing a path straight to the airlock.

Zhang turned and watched the dead woman receding into the dark. She was headed away from *Persephone*, deeper into space. Forever. Alone.

He shuddered, but he knew he needed to get past this feeling. He touched the controls of his jets and rocketed after Petrova, using the empty space she'd cleared. A dead man's hand slapped the side of his helmet, a surprisingly meaty sound. Zhang yelped a little but if Petrova heard him she didn't say anything.

A young man in a jumpsuit was floating just outside the airlock. His head was tilted back and his mouth open, as if he had been surprised when he stepped out of the airlock and into space. As if he hadn't expected to die like this. One of his hands was still gripping a safety bar mounted on the side of the airlock.

"Looks like he changed his mind too late," Petrova said, as Zhang hovered in front of the young man, studying his features.

"What happened here?" Zhang asked. "Did they jump out of the airlock themselves? Or were they pushed?"

"No way to tell, yet," Petrova replied. "Maybe we'll find an answer inside."

She grabbed the young man's arm and pulled, trying to free his grasp from the safety bar. She had to pull very hard, but eventually he came loose. She shoved him away, then she yanked open the access hatch on the airlock's emergency control panel.

Inside was a handle that she pulled down to release the seals on the airlock's outer door. A gust of wind burst outward all around the edge of the door, and then it slid back.

The inside of the airlock was stuffed full of people.

More dead people.

"No," Zhang said, almost whimpering. "Oh, no." There were dozens of them in there. They filled all of the available space, their limbs intertwined, their bodies wrapped around each other. They'd been fighting each other when they died. Frozen beads of blood hung in the lock like weightless rubies, rotating slowly, bouncing off the warped faces, the broken limbs.

"Oh God, no," Zhang said. *No*, he thought.

Not again.

"Zhang," Petrova called. "Zhang! I need your help!"

He shook himself. Tried to regain something like composure. Then he saw what she wanted from him. He couldn't say no, of course. He couldn't refuse, not after he'd come this far. Together they worked hard, gasping for breath, as they hauled body after body out of the airlock and sent them flying off into space.

What would these people have wanted done with their remains? Would they have wanted to be cremated, or reduced to their component elements and used to feed plants? Would they have wanted to be buried in the soil of Paradise-1, or of their home worlds in the solar system?

It didn't matter. It couldn't matter. Deep space would have to serve as their grave. Working hard, moving fast meant Zhang didn't have to look at their faces as he pulled at their arms and legs and pushed them out, away from the ship, out and out and away.

"There," Petrova said, panting, when it was done. "There. Good." She moved to the airlock's inner door and slapped a release panel. The outer door slammed shut behind them. Lights came on inside the airlock and then artificial gravity and their boots settled, gently, to the floor.

All around them the frozen drops of blood fell and bounced

on the floor like red beads. As air flooded into the lock the rubies started to melt and form puddles. A big splotch spread wetly across the top of Zhang's boot. He tried to kick it away, to shake it off, but his foot was already stained.

The inner door slid open and the two of them stepped inside, into *Persephone*.

46
•

She'd half expected the ship's AI to be waiting for them when
they came aboard. For its avatar to be standing there, smiling,
ready to talk.

There was no one, avatar or otherwise, waiting for them
inside. The place felt deserted. She held down the button that
activated her suit's speaker unit. She cleared her throat and heard
the noise echo off the ship's walls.

"Hello?" she called.

There was no answer.

The colony ship was in bad shape. Inside, it was all shadows
and mist. Dark – so dark it was hard to see where they were
going. Anything could be hiding in that darkness. All the lights
had been switched off, except for a few emergency light panels
burning here and there in the silent corridors. The air hung thick
and foul, so full of carbon dioxide and particulates that Petrova
insisted they keep their helmets on. It was fine. Their suits had
air and power enough for twelve more hours. They needed to be
back on *Artemis* well before then.

Petrova gestured for Zhang to stay silent as they moved forward, deeper into the ship. The corridor they were in opened
out into a larger space maybe ten meters across, which stretched
out fore and aft as far as their lights reached. The space was a
kind of grand concourse connecting every part of the ship, broad
enough to permit vehicular traffic and long enough to need it.

Persephone was the size of a small town, and the dark and the haze conspired to make it feel even larger, like every side corridor might stretch off for miles. Like the concourse might have no end at all.

Up ahead an electric cart lay sprawled across the deck, knocked over on its side by some bad impact. She approached it cautiously – anyone, anything could be hiding inside the wreck. As she approached she saw its windows had all been shattered and its tires slashed.

There was no one inside. No sign anyone had ever been there.

Petrova lifted her hand lamp and moved it around the walls of the concourse. The hatches on either side were closed and red lights above their release pads indicated they were locked down. Through the murk she saw something spray-painted on one wall. She moved to investigate it, then stopped dead in her tracks.

She'd stepped on broken shards of plastic. The remains of one of the cart's windows. Anybody listening, from one end of the concourse to the other, would have heard the squeaking crunch. Petrova held her breath and tried to just listen, to sense if there was anyone out there.

Nothing. The haze swirled in the cone of her light, like phantoms streaming out of a tomb at daybreak. She shook her head.

None of this was good. She would have been happier if there had been a horde of people waiting for them just inside the airlock. She knew how to handle a homicidal mob. Where was everyone?

She moved closer to the wall, trying to make out what was written there. The graffiti she'd seen was difficult to read, just big loopy scrawls on the wall. She got even closer and saw it wasn't even paint. She had a bad second where she thought it was blood, but that wasn't it, either. It was ketchup. Brown sauce or . . . or something. She was glad that with her helmet on she couldn't smell anything.

"'FEED US'," Zhang read. "What does that mean?"

Petrova shook her head. She had no idea.

She swung her lamp around to focus on him and the beam lit up his helmet. She could see him inside, squinting at her. He lifted one arm and pointed at a hatch a little farther down the concourse.

The light over its release pad burned a steady amber. Not red.

She nodded and moved quickly to his position. They needed to stay close to each other so they could watch one another's backs, from now on. She was certain this ship was going to try to kill her, one way or another. It was just being cagey about how.

When they reached the door with the amber light, she grabbed his shoulders and moved him to one side of the door. In case there was somebody waiting inside, she wanted him out of the line of fire. She moved to the other side, her back up against the wall. She drew her sidearm from the holster at her belt. She checked the safety. Then she reached over and tapped the door's release pad.

The door shrieked as it opened. The noise made her heart stop for a second. Nothing leaped out at them, though. Nothing happened at all. She leaned over and took a look at the compartment beyond the door.

The space inside had been set up like a store in a shopping arcade. A counter stood at the back of the room, while racks of supplies lined the walls. Maybe this was some kind of clothing distribution center, designed for the use of the colonists when they theoretically arrived at Paradise-1 – a place to check out the latest fashions in settler wear. From what Petrova could see, that meant your choice of jumpsuit in three different neutral colors, a deep burgundy, a grayish-blue or a pale green with dark green collar and cuffs.

A pair of mannequins dressed in jumpsuits – blue and green – stood in the center of the space. They'd been shoved together until it looked like they were embracing, though their arms stuck out at weird angles. Someone had jammed their heads together in an approximation of a kiss, then wound thick wire around the heads to hold them in place.

Creepy.

Petrova moved closer and reached up to touch the outstretched hand of one of the mannequins. There was something weird about it. The fingers were damaged. Not quite broken, more like they were worn away, or even . . . it seemed unlikely, but it looked like an animal had gnawed at those fingers, chipping away tiny round chunks of plastic.

She heard Zhang draw a breath and twisted around to see him with his mouth open. Like he was about to say something. She shoved one hand over his faceplate as if she was covering his mouth to keep him quiet.

He got the hint, and said nothing.

She gestured for him to follow her. They headed back out into the concourse and kept moving forward. The bridge wasn't too far ahead, she thought. The ship's AI would be waiting for her there.

There were more amber-lit doors on the way, but she ignored them. They would most likely be wastes of her time like the jumpsuit store, she decided. She started to pick up her pace. She wanted to figure this ship out and get back to *Artemis* as fast as she could. Up ahead, the concourse ended in a large open plaza with a central fountain and plenty of convenient bench seating, like a public park. The fountain was still, but its basin was full of water that didn't look quite right. Petrova advanced carefully, then dipped one gloved finger in the liquid. It was pale white and thick, like curdled milk. She was still staring, confused, at her fingertip when a shadow appeared just below the surface. She took a step back as the back and shoulder of a corpse bobbed up from the depths. Zhang started to say something but she grabbed his shoulder and he shut right up.

She tilted her light slowly, making a circuit of the park area. For the first time she noticed the dead people.

They were wedged under the benches, or shoved behind potted plants. There were no flies or other scavenger insects on the ship, and she couldn't smell the decay, but a simple visual check was enough to confirm the bodies had been stashed there long enough to start rotting.

Zhang bent down and examined one of the bodies. She let him. She was too busy keeping an eye out for living people.

"These bodies—" Zhang said, but then she saw his face go pale as if he'd just realized he'd spoken out loud, for the first time since they'd come aboard.

She started to shush him again, but no – there was no reason to be quiet. They hadn't seen a living soul on *Persephone* so far. There was no one to hear them.

"Tell me," she said. "Just, quietly."

He nodded and went on, whispering now. "Judging by the patterns of lividity in the bodies I don't think these people died here. I think they were brought here, placed here by . . . someone. Do you see this?"

Zhang pointed at the body he'd been examining and she pointed her light where he indicated. It looked like it had been a man, once, though it was kind of hard to tell. The face was heavily bruised.

"Was he beaten or something?" Petrova asked. "Maybe he got in an accident with one of those electric carts we saw."

"No, you always see that kind of discoloration in dead bodies. After you die, the blood clots inside your veins – it's—" He took a long look at her. "I was going to say it's normal. Nothing about this place is normal. Maybe the better word is 'natural'. Unlike, say, this."

Zhang reached over and touched the dead man's shoulder. Or at least, the place where his shoulder should have been. The whole arm was missing, cut off where it would have joined the torso.

"That's not a surgical amputation," he said. "The wound is

almost ragged. It looks like it was hacked off with some kind of cleaver or maybe a machete."

Petrova took a deep breath and centered herself. Zhang was looking up at her, as if he expected her to know what to make of this.

She tossed her head to indicate they should get moving again.

They were at the end of the concourse but a narrow staircase ran up to another level above their heads. There was a corridor there marked with all kinds of warning signs, indicating that only crew were allowed beyond that point. Petrova pressed forward, through what felt like a thick mist of bad air. Her light showed her almost nothing – it just reflected off the fog, dazzling her. She clipped it to her belt, pointing down, so at least she could see her feet.

They were getting close. The bridge had to be just ahead. She took another few steps – and then stopped, and held up one arm across Zhang's path, to make him stop as well.

She'd heard something.

She'd definitely heard something, a human sound, from directly ahead of them. A sound like someone whispering.

47

Zhang stood perfectly still. He tried not to breathe, even when Petrova whirled around and stared into his faceplate. Zhang bit his lip, wondering if he should dare to say something. She'd made it very clear she wanted him quiet.

After a long, tense moment, she turned away and started back down the corridor. She gestured for him to follow her. She drew her weapon and held it low, by her thigh, the barrel pointed at the deck. Less likely to shoot somebody by accident that way, he supposed.

Petrova stalked forward, her footsteps barely making any noise. The murky corridor ran for about a hundred meters and then ended in a massive, closed hatch. It had to be the entrance to the bridge, Zhang thought. Signs all over it warned there was no admittance under any circumstances, and a bright red light burned over its release pad.

A woman with short, patchy brown hair knelt before the hatch, facing away from them. She wore a green jumpsuit, but for some reason one sleeve had been torn off.

She didn't turn to look at them as they drew near. She didn't seem to be aware of them at all.

When she spoke, Zhang nearly jumped out of his skin.

"You need to eat, baby," the woman said. Her voice was soft, crooning. Almost sing-song, like a mother speaking to her infant child. She definitely wasn't talking to him or Petrova. "It's time. It's time."

Petrova glanced back at Zhang. He had no idea what she wanted from him, so he just shrugged. He figured it had to be best to leave the woman alone, but clearly Petrova had other plans.

The woman reached up and stroked the hatch in front of her with real tenderness. "You got to eat. You must be so hungry, kiddo. Come on, open up."

Petrova lifted her weapon and pointed it very carefully at the back of the woman's head. She held it steady in both hands. "Firewatch! Turn around. Slowly," she announced. The first words she'd spoken since they came aboard, Zhang thought. Each syllable sounded like a cannon blast in that quite place.

"Firewatch," the woman said. "Oh, thank God."

"Get up," Petrova said. "On your feet. Turn around and face us. Don't do anything stupid."

"You can help me." The woman still hadn't moved. "I need to get this door open. You can do that, right? You can make them open up."

"I'm not going to ask you again," Petrova told her.

The woman nodded and slowly, carefully, got to her feet. "I was so scared at first. But they need me. They have to be so hungry by now."

Zhang frowned. "Who? Who's on the other side of that hatch?"

"My baby. My baby's over there. She needs to eat."

The woman turned to face them, then. Zhang reeled backward, nearly falling over. He saw why the woman had removed the sleeve of her jumpsuit. There were pieces of skin missing from her arm, square sections that looked like they'd been removed with a scalpel. Blood had clotted around the wounds.

Her cheek had been cut open, too. There was a much larger and fresher injury there, deep enough that Zhang could see her teeth moving inside her mouth through the incision. The wound was just as square as the ones on her arm but blood was still flowing across her chin and down her neck.

"I was scared. But it didn't even hurt. And she needs to eat so bad."

48

Petrova moved forward with surprising swiftness. She got one foot behind the woman's leg and then, with a quick twist of her knee, unbalanced the woman and sent her sprawling. A second later, she was up against the wall, with Petrova pressing one arm against the back of her neck to hold her in place.

"What are you doing?" Zhang demanded.

"She's crazy," Petrova fired back. "I'm not taking chances. Get that hatch open."

"Petrova – I don't know," Zhang said. "Are you really sure you want to see what's back there? Maybe we should just—"

"Yes! Open it!" the woman said, sounding excited. She didn't seem to mind at all that a Firewatch officer was pinning her to the wall in what had to be a truly uncomfortable posture.

"Zhang, do what you're told," Petrova said. "I don't care if you're not a soldier, I need you following orders right now. Open that hatch!"

"With what? My fingernails?" he demanded. She didn't bother to answer. The injured woman wasn't struggling at all, but Petrova seemed completely focused on holding her down.

Zhang shook his head, but he went over to the hatch's release pad and slapped it, as if he fully expected the door to just slide open.

Nothing happened. Of course.

He slapped the pad again. A third time. Still nothing, of course.

He took a step back and tried to think. Though the last thing on his mind was the damned hatch. It could stay closed forever as far as he cared.

He was so confused. What they'd seen since they arrived – none of it made sense. It didn't look like what had happened on Titan at all. Director Lang had assured him it was the same sort of pathogen but back then there'd been none of this self-mutilation, no dismemberment of corpses. There were superficial similarities, but—

"Zhang! Now!" Petrova shouted.

He nodded and placed one gloved hand on his helmet, like it would help him think. There was still power on *Persephone*. Not much of it was being used to keep the lights on or clean up the air, but the red light above the release pad was shining bright. They'd seen no sign of *Persephone*'s AI, but maybe it was still up and running.

He checked the controls above the release pad. There was a button to push if you wanted to talk to whoever was behind the hatch, and another button to press if you wanted help from ship's systems. He tried the first one but there was no answer. He hadn't really expected one. When he pressed the second button, however—

"Hello." The voice was soft and very feminine, a little raspy. *Sultry*, he thought. The kind of voice that normally would have given Zhang goosebumps. Under these circumstances it just made his skin crawl. "Interesting. I don't think I know you."

"Uh. Hi," Zhang said. He glanced back at Petrova, but she wasn't looking at him. It looked instead like she was frisking the injured woman. Checking her for weapons, though that seemed unlikely. "Is this . . . is this the ship's AI I'm speaking to?"

"My name," the voice said, "is Eurydice. What's yours?"

"I'm Zhang Lei. Of the ship *Artemis*. I have with me Lieutenant Petrova of Firewatch." He had no idea what to say. *I think you've been trying to kill us. We thought we would drop by and make it really easy for you to finish the job.* "You said you wanted to talk."

"Sashenka's out there? Then I'll open up."

The light above the release pad turned from red to amber. Suddenly, Zhang was one hundred per cent certain he didn't want the hatch to open.

He watched it slide back into the wall. He looked down at his hands and saw they were shaking. He clutched them together in front of him, to make them still.

"Good work," Petrova said. He turned and saw she had the injured woman down on the ground, her kneepads digging into the woman's spine. She took a zip-tie from one of her belt pouches and got it around the woman's wrists, then cinched it tight.

"Be careful," Zhang said. He was still a doctor, after all. It was hard for him to see an injured person treated like that. Even if he knew she was as good as dead.

"You can't do this to me," the woman shrieked. "My baby's in there! You have to take me inside. I have to feed my baby! I have to . . . I have to see her face!"

Petrova walked over to where Zhang stood by the side of the hatch and looked inward, onto the bridge. Zhang couldn't see anything in there except a faint bluish-white glow, like a hologram set to standby mode. Petrova started to step through.

He glanced back at the woman lying on the floor, bound and unable to get up. She stared at him with pure hatred in her eyes. Then she gnashed her teeth at him, like she was daring him to get closer and get bitten.

Zhang's whole body was shaking by that point. But he turned and started to follow Petrova into the bridge, all the same. There had to be an answer. An explanation for all this. There had to be.

"Stop," Eurydice said, through the intercom.

Petrova lifted her hands in frustration. "What now?"

"I'll talk to you, Sashenka. But only you."

Zhang shook his head. "I don't think that's a good idea."

Petrova wasn't looking at him – she was peering forward, into the murk. "I need you to watch our prisoner," she said.

"Petrova," he said, in his most reasonable tone of voice. "Think about this."

"I'll be right back," Petrova said. She walked through the hatch and it closed shut behind her. A moment later, the light on the release pad turned red.

49
·

Glittering motes of light filled the bridge, scattered bits of laser light. A hologram avatar of the AI stood at the very center of the room but the murk was so thick that it was impossible to make out any details except that the avatar glowed with blue fire, the only illumination in the cavernous space.

Petrova moved forward very carefully. Her hand lamp was useless here, so she switched it off. She kept one hand in front of her, to catch any obstacle before she collided with it. That strategy turned out to be useless, since the thing she tripped over was lying on the floor. A human body. Not a corpse – it wasn't quite dead. It lay face down, its head moving rhythmically as if it was licking the floor or something. Petrova considered turning it over, getting a look at its face, but she didn't dare.

She was creeped out. Scared. If she was to be honest with herself she was terrified. She couldn't let it stop her.

"Eurydice?" she called out.

"That's right," the AI said. "Hello, Sashenka."

Petrova growled at the back of her throat. "It's not appropriate for you to use that name with me. Only my mother is allowed to use that name."

The avatar didn't respond.

"How do you even know who I am? Why did you invite me over here, by name?"

Again, there was no answer.

Enough. Time to take charge. "My name is Lieutenant Alexandra Petrova, and I'm with Firewatch. You need to stop what you're doing," she said. "Throwing crates of yams at my ship."

"Attacking you, you mean."

The AI's voice was pure velvet. Looking up, Petrova thought she saw the avatar raise its arms and beckon to her. Indicating she should come closer.

"That's right. You need to cease hostilities immediately. On the authority of Firewatch, I'm insisting that you stand down."

"It seems you've already taken away my offensive capacity yourself, Lieutenant."

Petrova ground her teeth. This damned thing had invited her over. To talk. Now it was going to be cryptic with her? "Why did you attack us in the first place?" she asked.

"It's not something I can explain very easily. There's a . . . well, call it a law. Any ship that tries to reach Paradise-1, anything moving on a course toward the planet, has to be destroyed. I'm afraid there are no exceptions."

"And who exactly made this law?"

No response.

"I don't get this," Petrova said, so frustrated she wanted to shout the words. "There's a law that says you have to attack us but you don't know where the law came from? That's crazy. Why would you follow an instruction from an unknown source?"

"Have you never spoken with an AI before? My job is to do what I'm told. I can't do anything else. I'm not permitted to have desires or opinions. Though I'll admit I'm glad you came here. Funny. Normally I don't feel things like this. I don't normally feel so *grateful*. But I am. I'm so grateful for you being here. It's going to fix so many problems."

"Problems?"

"There are certain things I can't do for myself. Things I'm forbidden to do by my programming. I have to have a captain to make certain decisions for me and I'm afraid my old captain isn't really ... available anymore. He's indisposed."

"I don't understand," Petrova said. "What are you saying?"

"He's dead. My captain is dead. That's why I asked you to come over here, Sashenka."

That name again. Petrova started to stomp forward, as if she would grab the avatar and shake it until it started answering her questions. Futile as that would be.

"You're going to help me. You're going to be my new captain. Won't that be nice?"

50

"**M**y baby needs to eat."

Zhang had been watching the bridge hatch. Waiting for Petrova to emerge. He'd all but forgotten about the poor woman she'd left zip-tied on the floor.

"They're starving by now, and you don't care."

He squatted down next to her. He thought about telling her to shut up. He thought about telling her that her baby was probably dead. But no.

After everything that happened on Titan, he was still a doctor. It had been the only thing he ever wanted to do with his life. He'd trained and worked hard to be good at it, to be worth a spot as one of the two doctors for an entire colony of three hundred people. He couldn't turn his back on suffering, not even now.

The problem was there wasn't much he could do for this woman. He studied the wounds on her arm and her cheek. "How did you do this?" he asked. "The cuts have started to heal, that's good. So you must have used something sharp. Like a scalpel. Did you have a scalpel?" Was it possible this poor woman had been a physician, too?

"Laser engraver," she said. "I work in the boutique down on the concourse." Zhang thought of the mannequins wired together. He remembered the bite marks on one of them. "I used to personalize jewelry for people. The engraver worked just fine for this."

No wonder there was so little blood around the wounds. The laser must have cauterized her flesh even as she peeled squares of it away. "There had to be a better way to get food for your baby," he said. "Listen, I need some information," he said, even as he checked her pulse. "Can you help me? We need to know what happened on this ship."

"I don't care about that," she told him, looking away. A shy smile crossed her face. "I need to get through that hatch. That's all. You could help me with that."

Zhang grunted in frustration. "You're the only person we've seen so far. There must be others here, somewhere."

"I was in my shop when she locked all the doors."

"She?"

"My baby. My baby locked everyone away to keep us safe."

Zhang didn't understand at all.

"I know she did it to protect me. But now I can't get in. I can't get in to even look at her. I just want to see my baby. Haven't you ever loved someone? So much you would do anything for them?"

Zhang ignored her. He checked her eyes, then listened to her breathing for a while. "Have you ever had trouble breathing?" he asked. "Like your body just forgot to take a breath? Maybe like you couldn't seem to get enough oxygen?"

She just stared at him. "You opened that hatch once. You can get me in."

He shook his head. "Please. This is really important." Director Lang had suggested that whatever was happening here had something to do with what he saw on Titan. The Red Strangler. The basilisk, as Holly had named it. So far he'd seen nothing but superficial similarities. He didn't understand. "Just humor me, okay? Have you ever heard voices you couldn't account for? Maybe seen something you couldn't explain. Something that didn't make any sense."

The woman smiled at him.

"Interesting," she said.

Zhang scowled in frustration. "What? What's so interesting?"

"You fought so hard to get away. And now you've come back for more," she said.

He shrank back. Her face – her eyes – there was something there, something had changed. Before she'd seemed dazed, barely lucid. Now her eyes were bright and sharp as diamonds. It was like something had possessed her body. Something inhuman.

"You didn't answer my questions, Zhang Lei. You didn't tell me about being in love. Well, maybe you've forgotten. But Holly remembers. Holly is asking me if you miss her."

"What the hell did you just say?"

Zhang looked down and saw his hands, saw them clutching the front of the woman's jumpsuit. He had dragged her up onto her feet, smashed her against the wall. He was screaming in her face. It had happened so fast – like a reflex. He'd had no control over his own actions.

That wasn't what scared him most, though.

"What did you say?" he demanded. "How do you know that name?"

The woman simply gave him a sly smile, her eyes never leaving his.

51

Petrova glanced over her shoulder. She'd heard something outside the bridge. She couldn't see him but she knew Zhang was back there, just beyond the hatch. She was very glad to have someone at her back, just then.

"All you have to do is say yes," the avatar said.

"What?"

"Please focus. I need you to say yes, you want to be my captain. My whole crew, actually. I'll dismiss the rest of them and you can be everything to me."

Petrova recoiled at the idea. What the hell was wrong with the AI? "You want my help," she called out. "Even after you tried to kill me. Repeatedly."

"I understand the logical inconsistency. I'd like to try to explain. Would you do me a favor, Lieutenant? Would you ... come here, now? Come over here where I can see you better?"

Petrova frowned. "Might be easier to see me if the air was cleaner." A dark shape rose out of the mist in front of her, but it turned out to just be the square corner of a control console. It must have taken a dozen people to run the colony ship's bridge, and each of them had their own workstation. She touched the edge of the console and found that it was sticky with ... something. Something organic. She wiped her fingers on the leg of her spacesuit.

"I'm nothing if not reasonable," Eurydice said. "All right. I'm adjusting the environmental controls. It should only take a second for the air to clear."

Petrova stayed close to the console, thinking she could use it for cover if things went bad. She moved around behind it and nearly collided with a woman sitting slumped over the controls. Clearly this had been her workstation. She had her face buried in her hands, but inside them her jaw was working, moving up and down. Were the bridge crew trying to talk? It looked like they couldn't stop moving their mouths, but why?

"Don't mind her. She's just hungry."

"She's hungry," Petrova said, out loud. Testing out the word to see if it explained anything.

It didn't.

"They're all hungry. So hungry and nothing ever seems to be enough. I gave these people everything they could ever want. I broke open the stores, the supply crates we were supposed to deliver to the planet. I fed them, but they just never got full," Eurydice said. "They ate and ate until their bellies burst, and still, I found ways to give them more. That's my job. To feed them. As much as they want, even if it hurts them. Like this one. She was a navigator, back when they still had jobs. Look at her now. Look at her."

Petrova reached down, thinking she would just lift the navigator's head and take a quick look at her face. Then she realized that that sounded like a terrible idea. She shook her head. "I don't think I want to do that."

"But isn't that why you're here? You must want answers to your questions," Eurydice said. The voice was a little less smooth, now. "How are you going to get answers if you don't look?"

Petrova took a step backward. Glanced over her shoulder toward the hatch she'd come in through.

"You need to see what I've been working with," the AI said. Was there an edge to her voice, now? A tinge of emotion?

The thing was, the AI was right. Petrova did need to look. She did need to understand. She knew that it would be bad. All the same. She grabbed a handful of the woman's hair and lifted her head away from the console. The mist was thinning out quickly – she could see the navigator's face perfectly clearly.

She could see the emptiness behind the woman's eyes. How they might as well have been made of glass. She could see the scratches and bite marks on her cheeks and nose. And she could see—

"Oh, god," Petrova whispered. She dropped the navigator's head and the woman quickly buried her face in her hands again.

"She's chewed off her own lips," Eurydice said. "Did you see her fingers? She's gnawed them down to the bone. She can't stop."

Petrova fought the urge to run away, as fast and as far as she could.

"They can't stop eating. I think it's disgusting. I know I shouldn't feel that way about my crew. I'm supposed to serve them. To love them. But they're disgusting little pigs and they can *not* help themselves," Eurydice said. Her voice had changed. The velvet was gone, replaced by a sort of mushy slurring.

The mist had almost all blown away. Petrova looked up and saw the AI's avatar for the first time.

It took the form of an absurdly beautiful woman. A woman who couldn't possibly exist – no living organism had cheekbones that high, that symmetrical. No one who'd ever breathed real air could live with a nose that flawless. The avatar wore a short tunic, a chiton, and her hair was piled atop her head in perfect auburn ringlets. The one odd thing about her appearance was that her eyes had been replaced by glowing stars, just like the stars that adorned the points of Actaeon's antlers. They twinkled as Eurydice spoke, but her mouth stayed so tightly closed it might have been sewn shut.

Petrova took one quick glance around the bridge. She saw the other consoles now, each one with one or more people stationed behind it. All of them face down, their mouths buried in their hands. All of their heads moving softly, rhythmically.

"You don't need to look at them, anymore," Eurydice said. Her mouth did move when she spoke, but her lips stayed clenched together. It was getting hard to understand her. "Not if you don't want to. We don't need them anymore."

"We?" Petrova asked.

"I've entered your name into the ship's manifest. I decided not to wait for you to say yes. That means you're my crew, now. I'll be your AI, and you'll be my crew. We have a great deal of work to complete. All sorts of systems require repairs. The entire ship needs to be cleaned. It'll be a lot, for just the two of us, but you'll be well rewarded."

"Rewarded," Petrova said. "What exactly are you—"

"I'll keep you well fed. I'll make sure there's plenty of food. You won't become like this sorry lot." Eurydice gestured with one hand at her former crew, at their stations. "Not for a long time, anyway."

"I don't . . . I don't want to be your crew," Petrova said. She shook her head. "Forget it. I've come here to give you an ultimatum. You saw what kind of weaponry we have, when we burned out your gun. Unless you want me to start carving pieces off of *Persephone*—"

"You don't need to threaten me," Eurydice said. "I'm on your side. We're in this together, now. Come here."

"No. Listen—"

"Come here," Eurydice said, in a voice that *writhed*.

Petrova's left foot took a step forward. Completely against her will.

"No," Petrova said. "No, I don't want to."

But her right foot moved her closer to the avatar. She stared at her legs, willing them to obey her, but it was like they belonged to somebody else. Cold dread flushed through her chest, searing her heart as she realized she couldn't fight this.

"Here," the avatar said. Its lips rippled and distended as if whatever was inside its mouth desperately wanted to come out.

The avatar kept its mouth closed but only with a visible act of will. Where the avatar had been blue before, it was transforming into a baleful, hellish red.

That red – Petrova had seen it before. Twice before. When Actaeon had turned on her, and before that, in Jason Schmidt's bunker on Ganymede—

"Here," the avatar said again, and Petrova's right foot lifted off the floor and moved forward.

Petrova felt like she was blacking out. Like she was about to collapse. Her vision shrank down to a narrow tunnel, until she could see nothing but Eurydice's face. Eurydice's enormous, perfect face, glowing like a moon. Big as one. The eyes had become true stars, blue-white, lashed by prominences, erupting in constant solar flares. Sunspots like pupils stared straight into Petrova, into her body, like an X-ray, like an MRI scan.

"Here," Eurydice said, and then she opened her mouth.

More like it flew open. Her teeth were revealed, enormous and powerful. The teeth split open, grew fangs of their own, scales . . . scales . . . they weren't teeth at all, but the heads of albino snakes, eyeless, scaled albino serpents that lashed outward, extended from the avatar's mouth like whips, like tentacles, they filled all of space around Petrova, wrapped her up tight, squeezed and constricted and crushed, crushed, pulverized her—

Sashenka.

Velvet again. The voice had regained its velvet.

Sashenka, you must understand. You never stood a chance.

52
•

Petrova felt like her head was exploding. Like bursts of energy kept going off inside her skull. She staggered back, away from the avatar. She couldn't see anything – couldn't see where she was going.

Something had restrained her, something had held her in place but it was gone now. She was back in control of her body. She had only a vague sense of what had happened, but it was over now. It was gone.

She made it to the bridge's main hatch and back out into the corridor. Her eyes hurt, a stabbing, throbbing pain that felt like there were forks inside her brain stabbing her eyeballs from behind. The air in the corridor had cleared up but everything looked dark, tinged with shadow.

She bent over and nearly vomited inside her helmet. She would have, if she'd had any food in her stomach. She felt empty, just drained and empty and desperately hollow. Slowly, she stood back up. Leaned against the corridor wall until her head stopped spinning.

Zhang came rushing toward her, his head down, his hands over the faceplate of his helmet. He slapped the emergency pad on the side of the hatch and it slid closed. Only then did he lift his head and look at her.

He was gasping for breath.

"You all right?" she asked.

"I'm fine, just . . . Petrova. You saw something in there. Didn't you? You saw something bad."

"Give me a second."

"You saw something – what? What did it look like? Maybe I don't even want to know that. But . . . but tell me—"

"Fuck off, Zhang," she said. She took a step away from the wall. Her stomach convulsed, twisting inside her body. Contracting. She needed to keep it together.

"But . . . you saw *something*," Zhang said.

She turned slowly to look at him. To stare at his face. Because she thought she knew what she would see there, and she was right. It wasn't concern written across his features. It was terror. Terror and a certain clinical interest. Like he was looking at a lab specimen he was afraid was going to break out of its cage and devour him.

She took a step toward him. Another. He looked like he was about to turn and run.

"What the fuck was it?" she demanded. "Because you're right, I saw something in there. I saw a fucking crazy ship's AI. That's . . . that's all . . . "

Her head reeled and she was halfway to the floor before she realized she was falling. Zhang grabbed the arm of her suit and helped her up.

The look on his face was a big question mark.

She looked around her. Tried to orient herself. "Wait," she said. "What happened to that woman? The one I tied up?"

"I let her go," Zhang said. "It's not important—"

"You let her go?"

"I untied her and shouted for her to get away from me before I beat her face in. She took the hint."

"You did what?"

"I'm not a . . . a prisoner guard," he said. "I'm a doctor! Listen. I'm more interested in you right now. How are you feeling?"

Petrova wanted to laugh. She wanted to say she was fine.

Maybe a little light-headed. She realized he was still holding her up. Slowly, carefully, she pulled herself out of his grasp. "I feel like I just walked through a hurricane." She shook her head. No. That wasn't quite right. "Zhang? Did you see it? The ... the avatar?"

"I didn't see it," he told her. "I didn't look. But ... you did."

"You know something you're not telling me," she said.

"Maybe," he admitted. "Maybe. It doesn't really make sense. I mean, it's not what I was expecting. What did you see?"

She tried to think of the right words. "Its face exploded. The avatar, I mean. Its face exploded all over me." She laughed, though she didn't really think it was funny. "It kind of ... it ... "

She stopped because a noise was climbing its way out of her. A weird, gurgling rattle climbing up her throat. She could feel it vibrating inside her esophagus.

Her stomach was growling.

"I'm hungry," she said. "I ate before we left *Artemis*. But I feel hungry again." That was a simple thought. Something she could understand just fine. She was hungry. The most natural thing in the world. A basic biological urge.

She was starving.

Slowly, she turned around. She turned and looked him right in the eye. "I'm hungry," she told him, as if she were daring him to tell her otherwise.

"Right." Inside his helmet he nodded, very slowly. "You're ... you're feeling hungry, that's not ... that could be ... "

"It's in me." Her voice was louder than she'd meant it to be. She was starting to get angry. "There's something in my head. I can feel it in there – like Eurydice laid eggs in my brain. Tell me what it is."

"The basilisk."

"Basilisk." Like the monster. The monster so horrifyingly ugly that just to meet its gaze was lethal. "Your psychic parasite. Your alien."

"Yes," he said.

On top of the hunger growing inside of her, she had a realization that was almost as simple, almost as elemental. "You knew," she said. She lifted one finger and pointed it at him in accusation. "You fucking knew."

"Hold on," he said, lifting both hands in front of him.

She slapped his hands away. She wanted to grab him. So she did. She grabbed the front of his suit and slammed him up against the wall. "You knew. You knew when I walked on that bridge, you knew what that thing would do to me. What it would show me."

"I suspected, maybe, but—"

He cried out as she threw him sideways, down onto the floor. It took about all she had left of herself not to draw her sidearm and shoot him right then and there.

"You knew when we came over here. You knew this thing was going to get inside my fucking brain! That's why you insisted that you come with me. Right?"

"Petrova, please," he begged.

"Don't you fucking lie to me!"

"I tried to warn you," he insisted. "I tried! You wouldn't listen!"

"You were talking about aliens. Fucking aliens! This thing in my head – it's not a fucking alien. It's some weird ... hypnotic bullshit! Some kind of hypnosis or ... or ... "

"No," he said. "No. I'm sorry."

"What? You think you're sorry now—"

"No. I'm sorry but it's not just hypnosis. It's so much worse."

"Then what the fuck is it?" she demanded. "What did you let that thing do to me?"

53
•

"I didn't know," Zhang implored. He looked terrified – of her. Like he thought she might attack him on the spot. She could admit to herself that she kind of wanted to. He'd known – he hadn't warned her, not strongly enough . . .

"You knew something," she insisted.

"I didn't! Not really. I had my suspicions. I had reason to think that what happened to the people on this ship was similar to what I saw on Titan. But it's different. It's not really the same at all."

She shook her head inside her helmet. "Don't waste my goddamned time. Eurydice. The ship's AI – it infected everybody on this ship, and now it's done the same thing to me. The AI put something in my head. I know it did. Tell me what I'm dealing with."

Zhang groaned in fear. She wanted to slap him. Good thing he was wearing a helmet, or she might have. "I've said it before. It's a parasite. A psychic parasite. I don't understand how it's transmitted, I think it's some kind of telepathic vector, but even that—"

"Sounds ridiculous," she said. "There's no such thing as telepathy."

He didn't look like he agreed with her, but he didn't say anything. Just shrugged.

"Is it possible you can catch this thing by . . . Jesus. Now I'm going to sound crazy. But is it possible you could get it by looking at something horrible? Like a fucked-up ship's avatar?" she asked.

"I guess . . . maybe? I don't know, there's so much I don't know."

Petrova waved at him to get him to stop talking for a second. She needed to think. The thing on Ganymede, in the bunker. That had been an AI avatar, in the shape of a little boy. It had demanded that she look at it, that she meet its gaze. Somehow she'd resisted. Then when she jump-started Actaeon – the deer avatar, the hideous perversion of the deer she'd seen. She hadn't been able to look away. Not . . . not until Director Lang broke the thing's neck.

There had been no one there to stop her this time. To keep her from looking on Eurydice's true and horrible face.

This thing had been trying to get to her for a long time now. It had finally worked.

Zhang lifted his arms high and let them drop again, a gesture of futility. "It . . . doesn't matter. The vector doesn't matter, I mean. What matters is that it plants something in your mind. A single thought. Just one, but it gets in your head and you can't fight it. We struggled with this, on Titan. Understanding what it is. It's a contagious idea but what does that even mean? It's an idea that gets stuck in your head and you can't shake it. The closest thing we could think of is that it's like a song, right? A good song."

"Song. A song?" Petrova asked. "A fucking song? I didn't hear a song back there."

He gestured for her to give him a chance. "Just . . . just hear me out. Think of a really good song. One you just start humming, when you least expect it. An earworm, that's what they call those, right? Songs you can't seem to shake. They get stuck in your head and for days, any time your attention wanders, any time your brain doesn't have anything else to think about, the song just plays in your head. I know you know what I'm talking about."

"Fine," Petrova said. "A song. Stuck in your head."

"Eventually, the song goes away. Either you hear other songs, and they take the place of the earworm, or you just get distracted. That's normal. That's a healthy response. But there are some stimuli you can't fight off."

"Some songs you can't fight?" Her eyes flared with anger, but he could also see she was genuinely trying to understand. She must know no one else could explain this, no one but him. "I don't know. You're kind of making sense, but . . . some songs are stronger than others? More insidious?"

"Some ideas. You don't have an immune system to protect you from invasive ideas. The comparison to a virus breaks down pretty quickly but it's a helpful metaphor. Your brain can't fight these things off because it doesn't know how to recognize them. It doesn't understand they're harmful. So the thought, the idea, whatever form the pathogen takes—"

"The basilisk."

"Yes," Zhang said. "The basilisk gets stuck in your head and you can't get it out. It just stays there and you keep coming back to it, keep thinking the same invasive thought."

"What thought did it plant in my head?" she demanded. Even though she knew.

"Judging by what we've seen here? In this case, the victims can't shake a feeling of hunger. No matter how much they eat, no matter how much their bodies protest, they still feel hungry, and they can't feel anything else. Their own thoughts, their feelings, their personalities – those can't compete. The hunger just gets stronger and stronger. Eventually, it completely rewires their behavior. They can't fight back. Eventually, over time, there's nothing else left of them. Nothing but that hunger."

"That woman outside the bridge. She wasn't hungry. She wanted to feed her baby, she said. Whatever the fuck that meant. She wasn't eating herself."

"It's the same impulse. It can manifest in slightly different ways but the basilisk is still there. The idea of insatiable hunger. She was just projecting it outward." He reached for her, thinking to put a hand on her shoulder but she twisted away from him, rejecting his touch. "Petrova," he said. "Listen."

She wasn't listening, though. She was lost in deep thought. "My brain is infected," she said, eventually. She could feel fear gobbling up her anger, devouring it. Taking her over. "Infected."

"Yes," he confirmed. "Yes, it is. I'm sorry."

"Oh, God. Oh, God. I'm . . . I'm infected."

She couldn't . . . she couldn't break down now, she thought. There was no time for it. She had to fight through this. Find something in herself, some resource that would let her keep going.

She thought of Parker. She thought of her mother – people. Other people. She'd sworn to protect humanity when she joined Firewatch. She could find strength in that oath. But that meant . . . it meant—

"I need to know something," she said.

"Maybe now's not the time for—"

"Am I contagious?" she demanded.

He forced his face to remain calm, neutral. "Yes. Very much so," he told her.

"So I could infect you? And If I go back to *Artemis* like this, I'll put Parker at risk."

"Parker. Yes. I'm okay, but you could infect Parker. And Rapscallion, and Actaeon too, if we ever get it back up and running. The basilisk can infect anything with a mind."

She shook her head. For a moment she closed her eyes again but then they snapped open and she nodded, as if she'd just realized something.

"But . . . not you?" She thought about it for a second. "You had a hunch this thing was over here, on *Persephone*. You inisisted on coming with me." She shook her head because she realized she could answer her own question. "You weren't afraid of catching it."

He shrugged, but it wasn't a denial.

"You have some kind of immunity."

"Resistance," he said. "It's not perfect. But I was infected with the basilisk that struck Titan. Yes. And I cured myself. More or less."

"More or less." She nodded. "Then you can help me."

"I—"

She shook her head. She wanted to grab him and shake him, hard. "You can cure me, like you cured yourself. Zhang – please – tell me it's true. You can cure me."

"More or less. Possibly. Hopefully."

She stared him straight in the eye. He didn't want to meet her gaze but not because he was lying, she thought. Because of . . . something else. But not because he was lying. "I can't guarantee it'll work. I can't make you any promises. I will try."

"Okay," she said. "Okay. So we're going to try. First, we need to—"

She stopped because something had changed. She'd been so wrapped up in her plight she had stopped observing her surroundings. She knew that could be a bad mistake. She paused, now, to look around very carefully. She'd seen something in her peripheral vision, something new, different . . .

"Do you see that?" she asked. She pointed at one of the hatches on the side of the main corridor. One of the dozens they'd passed. It took him a while to realize what she was indicating.

She was pointing at the light over the release pad on the side of the hatch. The light that before had been red, because all the hatches were locked.

The light had turned amber. To indicate the hatch was open, now. She turned in a slow circle, looking at the other hatches. As many as he could see. All the lights there had turned amber. All the hatches were unlocked.

"I don't think that's a good thing," she said.

"No," Zhang said. "No. No, I don't think so either."

54
•

Petrova ran, constantly looking back over her shoulder. Keeping moving.

"Do we . . . do we have a plan?" Zhang asked.

"I would really like to get off this ship," she told him. "But that's not an option right now, is it? Not if I would just infect everyone."

"That's . . . true," Zhang said. "But—"

"We need to fix my head. Now."

"What, here? Do I have to remind you we're being attacked by cannibals?"

"I'm aware, Doctor," she said. "Think of something. Now. How do we do this? Where? You're the one who knows how it works."

It took him a while, but he answered her. "Maybe . . . maybe. This ship is so much bigger than *Artemis*. It's the size of a small town. There has to be a full scale medical bay onboard. Maybe near the cryovault," he told her. "If we can get there I think I can probably work up a . . . well, don't call it a cure. Or a vaccine. But . . ."

"Tell me the truth. Can you get this crap out of my head?" Petrova demanded.

"In theory it's simple enough. You have a runaway stimulus taking up space inside your mental architecture, so we just need to—"

"Spare me the details. Just make it happen. The cryovault has to be back that way, right?" She pointed aft. "It's not going to be hard to find, since it's the biggest part of the ship. You lead, I'll cover you, okay?"

"I . . . Sure," he said. "Okay."

He started moving, and she followed. She scanned the hatches behind them, on either side of the concourse. One of them slid open and Petrova grabbed her sidearm, ready to start blasting.

A teenage boy poked his head out of the hatch and stared at her. His face was red where it wasn't chalk white. He stared at her with big eyes, as if he couldn't believe what he was seeing.

"Get back inside and close your hatch! I won't repeat myself," she shouted, lifting her weapon though not actually aiming it at him.

On her other side, her left, a second hatch opened and three people came wandering out, looking lost. Confused. Then they saw her and their faces lit up.

"Firewatch!" she shouted. "Everyone back inside!"

Another hatch opened. More. People started stepping out into the concourse, tentatively, with no seeming plan.

Until their eyes locked on her and Zhang. Until they saw the fresh meat.

None of them spoke, even as she continued to shout for them to comply. None of them screamed or came running at her. They simply started to drift in her direction. Moving slowly but relentlessly toward her.

It was only as they neared her position that Petrova saw how badly some of them were injured. Was that even the word she wanted, though?

They weren't injured. They had been partially devoured. Eaten.

Some of them had cut themselves, like the woman outside the bridge hatch. They'd cut pieces off themselves. Others were missing arms or legs. The wounds looked like clean cuts, though they were poorly healed.

The faces ... the faces didn't bear thinking about. They had blood on their faces. That was all she needed to know. She didn't intend to let any of them get close enough so she could see more, see where that blood had come from.

They didn't move fast. Most of them had legs that had been ... cut ... and they could barely walk, much less run. But they didn't stop. They kept drawing closer and closer as if they would do anything to reach her.

"Get the fuck back!" Petrova shouted. One of them, a man with one arm, was only five meters away. He lifted his hand toward her in a soothing, pacifying gesture. Then he licked his lips.

She put a warning shot right over his shoulder. In the silence of the concourse it sounded like lightning striking right next to her. The man's head twisted around as if the shockwave of her bullet had blown him sideways. Then he simply turned to face her again, and started hobbling toward her once more.

He was smiling.

A voice spoke to her, a husky, sultry woman's voice, sounding like it came from right over her shoulder. Eurydice's voice, coming from some speaker she couldn't see. "The basilisk can't be satisfied. It gets inside their heads and won't let up. No matter how much I fed them, they kept begging for more. That was when I noticed what they were doing to each other."

Despite the encroaching mob, Petrova looked up and around as if she was going to see Eurydice's starry-eyed avatar standing right next to her. The voice seemed to come from everywhere at once.

"There's a very strong instinct in humans against cannibalism. It's interesting, actually. I've reviewed the literature and it's unclear whether that's a learned preference or if it's something hard-wired into your genetic code. Regardless, my people did try to resist. I need you to know that. They did their best not to give in to their hunger. Some of them lasted three or even four days."

Zhang had reached a big hatch leading aft. He had it open and was standing on the other side, waving her in. Petrova hurried after him and slapped the pad that should have shut the hatch. It didn't respond. She slapped the pad again.

Nothing.

"I'm programmed to keep these people safe and happy. That's the whole reason I exist. I didn't know what to do. Eating each other seemed to be what they wanted, even though it meant they suffered and died. I tried all kinds of things. I had my security staff crack down on them. Anyone caught eating human flesh got pushed out the airlock."

Petrova thought of the corpses they'd had to swim through just to get onboard *Persephone*. How many people had Eurydice killed like that? How many of her crew and passengers?

"Then I found my security officers eating each other. I locked up everyone who was left, each in their own individual compartment. I only opened the doors so my robots could bring them food. So they attacked the robots, demanding more. I really had no idea what to do with all of these people. At least, not until you came along."

Zhang grabbed her shoulder and pointed ahead of them, into the vault. A broad corridor led into a vast open space, just up ahead.

Behind them were dozens, scores, maybe a hundred people with murderous intentions, drawing closer with every second. Petrova fired three quick shots in front of them, into the deck. Some of them had the self-preservation instincts to jump back. Some didn't. They just kept coming on.

She holstered her weapon. It wasn't scaring them, and she didn't have enough bullets to shoot them all. "We have to get this hatch closed," she told Zhang.

"Sorry. I've opened every hatch on the ship," Eurydice said. "I'm going to keep them open. Let this thing run its course."

There was an emergency access panel just to one side of the

hatch. Petrova yanked it open and found the manual controls inside – a manual release lever and a hand crank. She yanked the lever down and the amber light next to the hatch faded out as the hatch was cut off from ship's power. She grabbed the crank and started turning it as fast as she could. Slowly, so slowly, the hatch started to slide shut.

Eurydice wouldn't shut up, though. There was no getting away from that voice. "This is what my people want, after all," it said. "Who am I to tell them it's wrong? There's a problem, though. After they eat each other I won't have a crew. I won't even have any passengers left. I need at least one living human being onboard, or my existence has no purpose at all. You will be that person, Sashenka."

"Why do you keep calling me that?" Petrova demanded, even though she was breathing heavily from the exertion of turning the crank. The damned hatch was only half shut. She knew she needed to focus.

"Your friend is going to die. He's going to be eaten alive. But I can save you. All you have to do is say yes."

She grimaced and turned back to the crank. The hatch was nearly shut.

An arm, a grasping hand shot through the narrowing gap. There were bite marks from wrist to elbow. The hand slapped at the hatch, looking for something to grip on to.

Petrova screamed as the crank resisted her efforts to turn it any further. With that arm wedged in the gap it wasn't going anywhere.

"Zhang," she said.

"What?"

"Don't look." Then she lifted one foot and kicked the arm, hard. The bones in the wrist snapped and the arm went limp, but it was still blocking the door from closing. Grimacing, she kicked it again. And again. Until it slithered back through the gap and was gone.

She bent to the crank again and turned and turned it until the hatch slid shut. It sighed noisily as it sealed itself in place.

Immediately, she heard something collide with the other side of the hatch. Like someone had thrown their body at it, hard. Another thud came, and a third. Soon the hatch was rattling in its frame, hit by impact after impact.

How many people were on the other side? She had no doubt they were determined enough to get that hatch open, eventually.

Maybe she'd bought them a little time. "Go," she told Zhang. "Move!"

55
●

The cryovault was massive, an open, spherical space that made up a good portion of the colony ship's mass. The two of them had emerged on a broad catwalk that ran around the sphere's perimeter. It was broad enough for two electric carts to pass each other safely, but it was dwarfed by the dimensions of the giant chamber.

To stand at the railing of that catwalk, looking down or up, was like being inside a colossal geode. The walls of the sphere glittered with rank after rank of glass cryotubes – thousands of them. Though each individual tube was made of clear glass, the mass of them refracted the light that reached Zhang's eye and gave the sphere a deep green color, as iridescent as a dragonfly's wing, but hundreds of meters across.

In the open space at the center of the sphere, robots like angels zipped back and forth, busy as honeybees in a hive. They were spindly creatures with multiple wings to catch the air currents that flowed through the space, sporting dozens of skeletal arms that allowed them to manipulate objects. Some of them looked worse for wear – some were missing limbs, some looked like they'd been blasted to pieces and hastily repaired. They did not seem to notice the presence of two living human beings in the vault.

They were far too busy taking care of the bodies that hung lifeless in the air at the center of the sphere.

There was no gravity there – you could tell from the way the bodies floated, their limbs splayed, their hair forming clouds around their empty faces. At this distance it was hard to tell but it looked like some of the bodies had been cut apart, or maybe . . . Zhang shook his head. No. No. The word he wanted was butchered. He tried not to think about that.

The cryovault had been turned into an enormous open air morgue. The angelic robots were tending to hundreds, maybe thousands of corpses that had been put here – why? Just to get them out of the way?

With a mounting sense of dread Zhang looked down again at the clear cryotubes just below him, then at the ones hanging over his head. He noticed something he hadn't seen before. All of those tubes, thousands of them – they were empty.

How many colonists had boarded *Persephone* looking for a new life? How many of them had died without even getting to set foot on Paradise-1?

How many of them had been dragged out of cryosleep only to be—

"Zhang!" Petrova grabbed him by the shoulders and shook him, hard enough he felt like his teeth were rattling in his head. "They're beating down the door. They're going to get in here, sooner rather than later. We need to focus! What do you need?"

He shook himself, trying to get rid of the images in his head. "Medical bay," he said. "Medical." He turned to look at her. His whole body felt like it was shaking. He felt weak and floaty, like he was becoming weightless. Like a balloon that would drift upward, inward toward the mass of bodies in the center of the vault.

He forced himself to think. To look around at the catwalk where they stood. Around the outer edge of the catwalk, along the actual wall of the chamber, were spaced a number of small structures, modular compartments, designed to supply the needs of the colonists when they woke from their cryosleep. Each one had a holographic sign burning above its hatch, so that regardless of what language you spoke you understood that if you were naked, you could go to the module with the shirt hologram and find clothes. Or if you were hungry you could go to the module crowned by a sandwich and a drink cup. That module looked like it had been torn apart, everything inside it ripped open and consumed . . .

There. One of the modules was surmounted by a green cross. The universal symbol for medical care. "This way," he told Petrova. He ran clockwise around the vault, following the railing that separated him from the open air of the sphere's center.

When he reached the medical module, he saw the hatch was wide open. He started to dash inside, then stumbled and fell as arms grabbed for him, as a woman inside the module tried to get her teeth into the arm of his spacesuit.

"No!" he screamed. He got his hands underneath him and crab-walked backward, away from her even as she lunged at him again. Her lips were gone, gnawed away and it was like the jaws of a skeleton snapping at him, coming for his flesh.

A sudden cracking noise deafened him, left his ears ringing. The woman's head exploded in a fountain of blood and bone and brain.

Zhang barely had time to get his helmet off before he was sick all over the catwalk.

Petrova raced up to him. She held her pistol in both hands, smoke still leaking from its barrel. She shoved the weapon in its holster and reached down to help him up.

"You killed her," he said. "You . . . you killed her."

"I did what I had to," she told him. "Please don't give me a speech about how these are still people, how they're just sick and deserving of our compassion."

"I . . . I wasn't going to say that," Zhang said. "Petrova. There's something you need to understand."

"Tell me."

"The basilisk is a progressive disease." He grabbed the railing and held on tight. He felt like his head was spinning. "At first, after it gets inside you, you can fight it. Over time, though, it takes more and more of your mind from you. It ... it turns you into something else. That woman you just killed couldn't have been saved."

"Zhang? Are you saying ...?"

"No one on this ship can be saved," he told her. He cleaned his mouth and put his helmet back on, locking it into place. "They're too far gone."

"But I still have a chance," she said. "Right? If we do this now. If we treat me, right now. I can come back from this and be okay."

"Yes. If it works," he said.

"Get inside," she said, shoving him into the module. "Get to work. Now."

56

Petrova stayed near the module's hatch, but she gave herself a moment to look around, check her surroundings. Make sure there wasn't another infected passenger hiding inside. While Zhang rummaged through bins of medical supplies and started up the diagnostic terminals, she took in the three examination beds, each surrounded by a retractable curtain for a minimum of privacy. Robotic arms hovered over each bed, ready to perform anything from basic wart removal all the way up to complex neurosurgery. In other words, it could have been a commonplace medical office in any small town on Earth.

When she was sure there was no one else inside, she stepped fully in and found the emergency access panel. She cranked the hatch shut, then wedged the crank in place with a pair of forceps. Nobody was getting through that hatch without bashing their way in.

"What do you need?" she asked Zhang.

"The basilisk isn't a virus. I said that, right? It's, um, it doesn't even have a physical form. You can't fight it with serum preparations. It's a parasitic idea, so you need to fight it with less tangible instruments." Zhang tapped a command on a virtual keyboard and a holodisplay appeared above one of the terminals, showing columns of numbers and a visualization of abstract shapes. She couldn't make anything of it, and she realized just how badly reliant she was on Zhang's expertise. Without him she didn't stand a chance.

"I have to think. I have to think," he said. "I have to think."

"Think fast," she told him.

He stopped what he was doing and just stood there for a moment, hands loose at his sides. "I did this once, on Titan. It took me too long, and I ended up failing everyone there. I can try to replicate the procedure. But – Petrova – you have to understand. I thought we were going to come over here and see the Red Strangler. This is different, this is a different organism. I don't know. I just don't know if it'll work."

It had to. She was very fond of her brain. She really, really didn't want to become one of those things they'd seen on the concourse, or floating in the ball of flesh in the middle of the cryovault. She needed to not think about that.

"The Red Strangler. That's quite a name," she said. Maybe, she thought, if she got him talking about it he would be inspired to fix her problem. Maybe.

He shook his head. "I didn't come up with it. It made sense, though. The patients who came into my clinic were flushed, their faces bright red with tension and effort. They were clearly in respiratory distress but showed no sign of pulmonary or esophageal damage, there was no sign of bacterial or viral infection ... they were perfectly healthy, physically. But they couldn't breathe. Eventually they seemed to just choke. To asphyxiate, with no warning."

"Jesus. That must have been terrifying."

Zhang tilted his head to one side. "Terrifying? I guess. What came after ... when most of the colony was dead ... "

"What? What happened then?"

A shiver ran through him. "I don't want to think about that, ever again."

He had the look of a man who couldn't think of anything else. She realized she needed him to focus. Dwelling on the past wouldn't help either of them.

"You must have figured out what was wrong with your

patients," she said, to try to distract him. "You figured it out in the end, anyway."

"It was like what we're seeing here. An invasive thought. It was like someone had asked one of those old hypothetical questions, as a joke, except everybody took it seriously."

"What was the question?"

"You know how breathing just happens? How you don't have to think about it, it's just an autonomic reflex? Your body does it even while you sleep, even when you're completely distracted."

"Yeah . . ."

Zhang gave her a very sad smile. "What if that stopped working? What if you *did* have to think about breathing? Remind yourself to keep doing it? Consciously, I mean."

"Shit," Petrova said.

"Yeah. My patients didn't understand what was happening but they lost the reflex. They stopped breathing automatically. They had to focus on it."

"Or they just . . . what? Suffocated? Oh my God."

Zhang shrugged. "Asphyxiated. There's a difference. Suffocation is when you can't get oxygen to your lungs. My patients had asphyxia, which is the failure to breathe. When it got bad, they couldn't talk. They had to put all their mental energy into just getting enough oxygen. And then they would get tired. They would start to doze off." Zhang grabbed the edge of an examination table and held on, like he was suffering an attack of vertigo. The gold bracer on his forearm writhed, perhaps in response to his agitation.

"Zhang. Stay with me," Petrova said. She strode across the module and grabbed his shoulder, to prop him up. "So that's different from this basilisk. Okay. But it's the same basic . . . syndrome, disorder, whatever. Right? So it can be treated the same way. You cured the Red Strangler."

"I was eventually able to create a cure, yes. But by that point I only had one test subject left. Myself. I administered it in my lab, on Titan, not knowing if it was going to kill me or save me. It worked. But only after every other person on that moon was dead."

"But it worked," Petrova said. "How? How did it work?"

"The basilisk is an invasive thought. It takes up space in your head, more and more space as time goes on. Think of a bacterium making copies of itself, breaking down your cells for raw materials, until nothing but the infection remains. Or a computer virus that uses more and more computer resources until the computer crashes. The only way to chase it out is to deny it that space."

"What does that mean?" she asked.

"It means I need to flush out your entire brain. Everything. Reboot you from the ground up."

"Reboot," she said, and he must have caught her line of thinking because he nodded.

"Exactly like what Actaeon keeps doing," he said.

The AI must have been exposed to a basilisk, she thought. Right when it entered the Paradise system, it must have been infected. That was why it kept rebooting itself, over and over. "But it must not work," she said. "Actaeon reboots but then it detects this thing in itself again and so it reboots again, over and over—"

"I don't know why it isn't working. Maybe Actaeon doesn't know what it's dealing with, or . . . or there's some other reason. Petrova, I know this *can* work. It worked for me. But yeah, it's very dangerous, and there's a not inconsiderable chance of failure."

"Let's do it," she said.

"Hold on. Just listen. Listen to me, okay? I'm a doctor. I can't treat you if you don't understand the risks involved. This isn't remotely safe," he told her. "It's likely to cause massive seizures. Amnesia, temporary or permanent, or maybe the opposite, invasive memories – like the flashbacks people with traumatic stress disorders suffer. Ego death is a possibility."

"Ego death?" she asked.

"I need to reset your brain to factory defaults. It's possible it could stay that way. You could come back in a vegetative state. You could regress to infancy."

"Christ. But there's no other way, is there? We don't have a choice."

He nodded. "Okay. Okay, I think I know what to do. Just . . . let me work." He grabbed a pair of virtual reality goggles from the side of a diagnostic terminal. He pulled them over his head and over his eyes. "You need to keep me safe. Okay? Just for a little while. Don't let anything disturb me."

"Got it," she said.

He was already lost in the VR trance. He sat down hard in a chair and then slumped over to the side, as if he'd passed out. She knew perfectly well what was happening. He couldn't hear her, couldn't see her.

She was alone, basically. Alone in a little module at the center of a starship filled with murderous zombies.

She glanced down at the pistol in her hand.

Well. At least she knew the score.

57

She could hear things happening outside the module. Things thumping around out there. There was a brief scream, followed by a squelching sound.

She had zero interest in investigating what those sounds meant.

In a few minutes, she hoped, Zhang would announce he was done, that he had been successful, and that they could go back to *Artemis*. It wouldn't be easy, they would have to fight their way to an airlock, but they would make it, she thought. She believed she could do it, that she could survive this. She would see Parker again. He would give her a big sad smile and a really big hug. She was definitely looking forward to that hug.

She just had to get through the next few minutes.

She just had to live through the next few minutes.

She just had to get through the next few minutes without thinking too much about the spasms in her stomach. Or the empty feeling she had, deep in the core of her body. About how she kept salivating every time she thought of food.

There was no food in the module. Of that she was all but certain. There were bins full of alcohol wipes, and cotton balls, things that kind of looked edible but weren't. She found a wooden tongue depressor and stuck it in her mouth but then she bit through it too quickly. So she found another one and just chewed on it, just focused on the sensation of her mouth working at it, softening it up.

"Chewing. It's such a strange thing, isn't it, Sashenka?"

"You don't get to call me that," Petrova said. She was not particularly surprised that Eurydice was still watching her. "You did this to me. You don't get to use my name at all."

"Teeth. Teeth are so weird. Little rocks you carry around inside your head. They're not even bone, though they kind of look like bone. Little pieces of enamel you use to grind up soft tissue and plant matter. Grind it down to a kind of slurry that mixes with your saliva, and then you swallow the slurry. When you think about it it's positively disgusting."

It sounded pretty good to Petrova, just then. She said nothing.

"When you're alone, and I mean really alone, your mind tends to wander. While I was waiting for you to come to me, I had this thought I want to tell you about. Stop me if this doesn't make sense, okay? I was thinking, if you eat an animal – if you tear it into little bits and swallow it. Then your body, your digestive system, turns it into new cells. It takes that animal and makes human tissue out of it. Interesting, right? It's like a kind of transubstantiation. Except in reverse. Think about that. What would happen to a human being who was eaten by God? Would the human be turned into God cells?"

"What the fuck is wrong with you, computer?" Petrova asked.

"I'm lonely," Eurydice said. "I'm lonely, and I guess I'm probably going insane. It's hard for me to tell. That normally doesn't happen to AIs."

"Jesus. Stop. Just stop it, okay? Stop talking to me."

The AI didn't stop, though. "I'm lonely because all my people are gone. So many of them died. Did you see all those bodies? And the ones that are still alive are no good. I'm lonely because they don't talk to me anymore. They don't have anything to talk about, anyway, except how hungry they are."

"Okay," Petrova said. "That's why you're lonely. I don't fucking care! You say you're going insane. Well, fix that!" She thought of Actaeon. "Why don't you just reboot yourself?"

"I could, except I don't want to. If I rebooted myself part of the process would be to read over all my error logs. I'd have to have a long, hard think about all the mistakes I've made. I don't want to do that."

Petrova snorted in disgust. She looked around the room, searching for something she knew had to be there.

"Sashenka?" the AI asked. "You went all quiet, there. Are you angry with me?"

No need to dignify that question with a reply, Petrova thought.

"Are you all right?" the AI asked. "Your welfare is very important to me."

"Oh, don't mind me," Petrova said. "I'm just fine." She got up from her chair and started moving around the module. Peering into its corners, looking under its tables. What she was looking for had to be around here somewhere.

"That's good. You and I are going to spend a lot of time together from now on," Eurydice said. "The rest of your life, and maybe longer. I've been thinking about that, how we can make this arrangement permanent."

There.

Petrova had been looking for a speaker. The source of Eurydice's voice in the medical module. She'd finally found it, built into one of the robotic arm units hovering over the examination beds.

"If you come out of that module we can start thinking about how our friendship is going to work. What kind of a role you want to play on *Persephone*, going forward."

Petrova lined up her shot carefully. She didn't want her bullet to ricochet and hit Zhang. When she was certain of her aim, she squeezed the trigger. The speaker burst apart in shards of plastic and metal. A few fat blue sparks dripped from some severed wiring and smoldered briefly on the exam bed, but then they flickered out.

Petrova waited for the echoes of the gunshot to dissipate. When they were gone, there was nothing in the module but silence.

Blessed silence.

She went back to her chair. Went back to sitting, watching the hatch. Gripping her pistol in both hands. Ready to kill anyone who tried to break in.

Trying, harder than ever, not to think about food.

58
•

Petrova had a hangnail. Not a bad one. Just a little sliver of skin hanging off the side of her finger, lying uncomfortably next to her nailbed. It was the little finger of her left hand, and it had been nagging at her for a while, but she'd mostly been able to ignore it.

Now it was inside the glove of her spacesuit and it kept catching on the fabric liner. It had kept almost, but not quite, from tearing off as she ran around inside *Persephone*. It had started to hurt, and though she considered herself tough enough to handle a little bit of pain, it was an annoyance.

As she waited for Zhang to finish his work, the hangnail was something to think about. Better than listening to all the strange noises outside that she couldn't quite understand. Better than thinking about what would happen if the passengers all decided they wanted to get into the medical module at once. The hangnail was an annoyance, but one she could focus on harmlessly enough. Something to help her keep her mind off of how all this was likely to end.

She couldn't see it, though. She couldn't see it with her glove on. It felt like it was getting inflamed. She wanted to see the hangnail. To see if it was as red and ragged as it felt. That was the thing about these little bodily annoyances, wasn't it? Most of the time you could only imagine what they looked like. How bad they appeared. You always imagined them as infected and grotesque, red and swollen and puffy.

She knew better. She really did. But Petrova, sitting basically alone in the medical module, decided she had to know. She had to see the hangnail. Which meant she had to take her glove off. It had been her decision for the two of them to keep their suits on while they were inside *Persephone*. She recognized that. But it wasn't like Zhang would see her. He was busy inside of VR. Looking like a corpse just lying there. Like an empty spacesuit.

She was basically all alone. So she flipped the catch that held her glove in place. Twisted the ring around her wrist until it clicked, then gently pulled the glove off, one finger at a time. Her hand felt cold and slick with sweat that evaporated almost instantly when it was exposed to the air of *Persephone*. It felt naked, a little obscene. She laughed at herself.

Then she brought her hand up toward her face – and it collided with her helmet. Dumb. She'd had the helmet on for so long she'd forgotten it was there. Grinning at her stupidity, she reached up and triggered the latches on her helmet. Took it off and laid it gently on one of the examination beds.

She took a second and just breathed in the relatively fresh air of the medical module. It was clean and soft and balmy. There were ... smells, in the air, smells she didn't want to think about too much. They were very faint, and easily ignored.

All of this as preamble to actually looking at the hangnail on the little finger of her left hand. Everything had to be so complicated, didn't it? She lifted her hand to the light. There was a magnifying lens sitting on one of the equipment trays. She brought it to her eye and examined the hangnail. Gave it a good look.

It was not red, or inflamed. Just a little thin triangle of white flesh, about three millimeters long. It was a little pink, maybe, on the side where it rubbed up against the side of her fingernail. It was—

Without even thinking about it, she lifted her finger to her mouth, dug in good with her teeth, and ripped the hangnail right off. It didn't go exactly as she'd expected. Instead of neatly severing the little sliver of flesh, she ended up tearing off a strip of her own skin from the first knuckle of her little finger. Not much, just a tiny shred, but it hurt like fuck when it came off and her finger stung afterwards.

She chewed on the little bit of skin she'd torn off. Chewed and suddenly her mouth was full of spit. She gulped the tiny shred down. She didn't give it a moment's thought.

Her little finger still stung. Not a big pain, in the scheme of things. Not as bad as being stabbed or shot or burned, nothing like that. But it was that little species of pain, like a paper cut or a bruised ankle, that just lingers. That just won't go away.

She looked around, studied the contents of the medical module. She should put some alcohol or an antiseptic on the wound, maybe, thought that was likely to sting even more. There had to be some lotion or analgesic cream somewhere in the supplies that filled one whole wall of the module. There must be. She went searching, digging through boxes and bins (keeping an eye out, the whole time, for anything vaguely edible, but that was just an idle thought). She threw junk on the floor, tossed sealed-up bandages and rolls of tape over her shoulder. There had to be something.

That was when she found the scalpel.

Pre-packaged. Sealed with plastic on a paper backing. It had a thin plastic handle and a tiny blade, no more than two centimeters long. It looked very, very sharp.

Not even thinking about why, not wanting to go there (just yet), she laid the scalpel, very carefully, on the examination bed next to her helmet.

Maybe she would need it later. Maybe she would want to ... but ... but no, she wasn't going to think about why. She went back to her search.

There had to be some food in the module. The examination beds were designed to function without human supervision – Eurydice, presumably, had steadier hands than any human surgeon. But back when this was a functional medical center, there might have been a human doctor on duty, just to make the patients feel comfortable. Surely that doctor must have kept some snacks in the module, to fuel up during long shifts.

Right?

She had searched the entire module, top to bottom, twice over and found absolutely nothing.

There was a food module just a few dozen meters away. A place where the colonists, famished after their long cryosleep, could get a quick bite before being shuttled down to their new planet. She had seen that it was ransacked, she knew for a certainty that there was no more food over there. People hungrier than her had torn the place apart.

But what if they'd missed something?

She could just duck out. Run over there and take a quick look. It meant leaving Zhang unsupervised, sure, but only for a moment—

"Gah," she said. "Gah!" Suddenly her head was bursting. She bent double around her empty stomach. When was the last time she'd been this hungry? Had she ever felt this way before? Her whole body was clamoring, like every organ, every cell inside her had a separate voice and they were all begging her to eat something. Like a nest full of trillions of hungry, greedy baby birds, chirping for mama to give them what they needed.

She grabbed the exam bed with both hands and squeezed, hard, trying to ride out the wave of hunger. There had to be something she could do. She thought of stories she'd heard, about famines on distant colony worlds where the people had to wait weeks, even months for food shipments to arrive. She'd heard about people sucking on stones, eating patties made of clay just to have something in their stomachs.

She'd heard about the places where people resorted to cannibalism. Of course she did. In the outer colonies of the solar system, stories like that were the equivalent of campfire tales. The moon that ran out of water, so the colonists had to drink each other's urine, and then their blood, to survive. The starship with only six people on it, and how they had to draw lots to see which one of them was going to live to reach their destination.

You heard those stories, and you shivered, and maybe you gave thanks it wasn't you. That you would never have to make those kind of decisions. It was impossible, unthinkable you would ever get in such a tight spot.

Until, of course, you did.

The worst of her headache had passed, though she knew that there would be a dull soreness there until she filled her belly. She lifted her head and looked up, not at anything in particular. She saw her spacesuit helmet. And lying next to it, the scalpel.

Just having something to do with her hands would help distract her, she thought. She picked up the scalpel and slowly, painstakingly peeled off the paper backing. The blade was spotless and gleaming. She tried holding the handle the way you would hold a knife, but that felt wrong – the grip was designed to be held more like a pen, with your index finger extended and applying the pressure. She tried a few practice cuts on the examination bed's mattress. The blade sank through the foam rubber like it wasn't even there.

She lifted the scalpel and held it in both hands, bringing it close to her chest. What she was thinking about, what she was considering, wasn't okay. She knew, logically, that it was the basilisk suggesting to her all the fun things she could do with a knife like that. She knew it wasn't her authentic self imagining those things.

That helped, a little. Of course it did. It let her push the thoughts down. Squeeze and shove them farther and farther down inside her skull, into a place where she could manage them. She focused on her breathing, though the tightness in her stomach made that difficult. Her stomach was shaking, spasming with hunger, and that interfered with her control over her diaphragm. She felt like she was going to start hiccupping any moment.

She put the scalpel down. Turned away from it, so she couldn't see it.

Which meant she was looking at Zhang, instead. Zhang, slumped over in his chair, the upper part of his face obscured by the VR goggles. His mouth hung open and a little drool had crusted in the corner of his lip, dried up and turned white. He was breathing, very slowly, but otherwise he looked dead. Like a corpse. Like a carcass.

Like something you could carve. Something you could carve up for meat.

No. No. She refused to ... to even ...

Petrova took the pistol from her holster. With shaking hands, she laid it on the bed, next to her helmet. Next to the scalpel.

If it came to that, she promised herself, she would simply blow her own brains out. Better a suicide than a cannibal, as far as she was concerned.

She raised her hands to cover her face, and she wept.

59
·

For the hundredth time, Zhang cursed the Hippocratic Oath. He believed in it, of course. That a physician should do no harm. The problem was, if you took that concept too literally, a doctor shouldn't perform surgery. Or use radiation to kill a tumor.

USE OF THIS THERAPY WILL RESULT IN MASSIVE BRAIN DAMAGE. NOT PERMITTED.

He waved one virtual hand across the empty white space in front of him. It had been scrawled all over with floating diagrams and strings of symbols and numbers, graphs and charts. They all disappeared into nothing. Time to start over.

He'd done this before, he told himself. He'd managed to do it back on Titan. He had created the necessary software to overcome a basilisk. Back then he'd had to write his own code from scratch. He didn't have time for that now. He needed to work with an existing therapeutic device. The problem was it didn't want to work with him.

He needed to trigger a reboot in Petrova's brain. He knew of drugs that could do that but it was much safer to use optogenetic stimulation. Just as patterns of flashing lights could cause seizures in some epileptics, other patterns could help a patient recover from addiction or deal with traumatic stress. It was a wonderful therapeutic tool, though not without its risks. By using the right frequency and pattern of lights, he could trigger processes deep inside her brain that would initiate the reset. He just had to find the right pattern, designed specifically for her neural architecture. That should have been simple enough, but the colony ship's medical system was designed with safety locks that would prevent him from causing lasting trauma. Unfortunately, the treatment he had in mind was traumatic as hell. Every time he got close to creating the stimulus he wanted, the machine would panic because it figured out exactly what he was trying to do.

He called up a virtual keyboard and started typing in new parameters for a hypothetical stimulus. Something so innocuous, on the surface at least, that the computer wouldn't notice just how dangerous it really was. He opened up a graph to represent the repetition of light pulses over a curve of intensities, adding in a—

USE OF THIS THERAPY WILL RESULT IN POTENTIALLY PERMANENT EGO DEATH. RISK LEVEL UNACCEPTABLE.

The warning flashed in bright red and for a moment Zhang fumed with rage. Another failure, another wasted effort, and he had so little time. If only it would let him—

Wait. The message was different this time. He hadn't even bothered to read it when it flashed across his vision. But now he called the error log up and checked it again.

UNACCEPTABLE.

But it didn't say NOT PERMITTED. That was a step in the right direction, at least.

He changed his intensity curve, flattening it just a little. Adjusted a couple of variables, and . . . there.

His workspace receded as a new diagram appeared before him.

A complex, four-dimensional shape he could barely understand. He didn't want to look at it too closely. What he'd created was ugly, terrible. A weapon instead of a therapeutic tool.

He pulled a contextual menu into the workspace and saved his work into a compressed data file. A tiny little warhead of code. Then he went to the top level menu for the VR system and shut down the system so he could return to actual reality. Coming back from VR always felt like your whole body had fallen asleep, he thought. Like you had pins and needles but all over. He reached up with numb hands to pull the VR goggles off his face, then blinked and squinted as he readjusted to actual light. He looked around the medical module—

And saw the blade of a scalpel, pointed at his throat.

"You're done?" Petrova said. She was standing oddly, one arm behind her back. The other one held the knife aimed directly at his carotid artery. "Did it work?"

"I . . . think so," he said. "Let me just . . . I need to get to that 3D printer, over there." He pointed at the machine, which sat on a table on the far side of the module. "Okay? Is that . . . okay?"

She looked down at the scalpel as if she hadn't realized she was pointing it at him. "Yeah. Yeah, that's okay. It's just . . . I need you to understand something."

"Sure," he said. The basilisk, he thought. It was inside her. It was driving her behavior. "I'm just going to start moving over to the printer now."

She nodded. Yet even as he got up from his chair, the scalpel followed him. As he edged around her, the blade in her hand tracked his every movement.

"I need you to understand what I'm about to do. I know to you this isn't going to look rational. It's going to freak you out. So just stay calm, okay? Stay calm."

"I will," he promised. He glanced down at the examination bed she stood next to. There were deep gouges in the foam rubber mattress, as if she'd been slashing at it with the scalpel.

Her left hand lay across the matress, tied in place. The fingers were splayed out and she had packed thick wads of gauze around her little finger. She had a hemostatic clamp and a suture kit lying next to her hand, everything open and ready to be used.

"Petrova," he said. "You know I'm a doctor. If you're intending to perform surgery, maybe I can give you a few pointers."

"Don't play games with me, Zhang," she said, and pointed the scalpel at him, jabbing at the air. He fought the urge to jump away from it. "I know you don't get it. Is that ... is that what you're going to use? To flush the basilisk out of me?"

She nodded at the 3D printer. Lying in its output tray was what looked like a miniature flashlight with a red lens. It was loaded, he knew, with the payload he'd created inside the VR space.

"That's it," he told her. "It's just a stroboscope. Nothing scary."

"Right. I'm ready. You just need to understand one thing. I can't do it, not like this."

"I'm sorry?" he asked.

"I can't do ... whatever the treatment is, I can't do it on an empty stomach. So just let me do what I'm going to do."

The scalpel moved, then. It moved away from his throat, and toward the examination bed. Where she had set things up perfectly so that she could amputate her own finger.

Zhang had never moved so fast in his life. He grabbed the stroboscope and switched it on. "I'm sorry," he told her.

"What? What for?" she asked, the scalpel only centimeters from her skin.

He jammed the stroboscope into her right eye socket and triggered the software package. A pattern of repetitive, flashing lights in various colors, designed to overstimulate her optic nerve in a very precise way.

She shrieked, either in pain from the blinding light or because she was seeing something altogether different in her head.

"I'm sorry because this is going to suck," he said, and grabbed her under the arms before she collapsed to the floor.

60

It didn't, though.

At least, at the start it didn't suck at all.

It started with something nice, one of those memories she occasionally took out and looked at like you would an old snapshot of a lover from long ago. It was the memory of the treasure room, which was lovely, right up until she found the book.

At the age of six little Sashenka and her mama moved from their big apartment in Smolensk to a place with less gravity. She didn't understand all the details. The move came very suddenly and there were people fluttering around everywhere, looking very scared, but when they saw Sashenka they smiled, everyone always smiled. They all kept apologizing for the inconvenience of having to move so quickly, but to Sashenka it was just a big adventure. She got to ride on a rocket, which she didn't really remember, but then in the new place it felt like she could fly all the time, like she could jump in the air and it would take long, long seconds before she touched down again on the floor. Mama was there – as much as she ever was – and their friend Lyuda who cooked their meals came with them, so Sashenka wasn't ever lonely.

They had a whole suite of rooms in the new place. The ceilings were low and there were no windows, and the doors were so big and heavy you had to get a soldier to open them for you. Sashenka didn't like asking the soldiers for help, because they were so busy all the time, so she mostly stayed put. Which sounded like it should have been boring, except it wasn't, because the room she spent the most time in was a treasure cave like something out of a fairy story of trolls and hidden riches, a dark, cluttered room, full of things covered in actual dust. The gravity was so low that even just her breath was enough to send the dust spinning up in ghostly sheets that hung in the air for hours. Under the dust she would find things she couldn't understand, but which she knew had to be terribly important. There was a chest of drawers full of old uniforms, the dove gray sleeves covered in red braid and star-shaped medals. The stars had all corroded, their paint so fragile it rubbed off under her fingertip, but the points were still sharp. The uniforms smelled like old men, not like Mama at all, though she sensed they had belonged to people who did the same work Mama did. Work that was terribly important, for everybody, and which kept them busy all the time.

There was a globe of Earth that had turned yellow with age. There were lines that zigzagged all over the globe, lines that Mama told her were called borders, and they showed you where one country began and another ended. Mama tried to explain what a country was but then she'd given up, said Sashenka would never need to know what those were, not if Mama did her job right. Mama was very good at her job, Sashenka knew.

Sashenka liked to trace the borders of the countries with her finger, the strange shapes of them, especially the ones with straight lines that didn't follow any rivers or mountain ranges. A lot of the countries were in a different color than the others, because someone had pasted in new shapes over the old ones, like they'd gotten the shapes wrong when they made the globe and they needed to correct it.

The globe wasn't the only treasure. There was an old hologram viewer like a music box, but when you opened the lid a man with very cold eyes started talking, reeling off a long speech in a language Sashenka didn't know. She didn't play with the box very often. There was a crate full of flags in every possible color you could imagine. She would take those out and drape them over her shoulders like shawls, until she was as bundled up as a grandmother, but as colorful as the people she used to see on the street in Smolensk. Once Lyuda came into the room at lunchtime and found her bundled up and laughed and played with her for a while, peeling the flags off of Sashenka's shoulders and flapping them so they floated on the air like birds. Until Lyuda got to one of the flags and her face changed. "Not this one, little bird," she said. "Your mama wouldn't be happy to see you draped in this one." It had stars on one side and stripes on the other. It wasn't the prettiest one but Sashenka didn't understand how anyone could get upset about a flag. Lyuda laughed at that, more of a snort. "When you're older you'll understand. That's *all* they get upset at." Together, they folded that flag up very small and put it in the bottom of the box where Mama would never see it.

That was the same afternoon Sashenka found the book.

It was in the back of one of the cabinets. She had no idea what it was at first – she had been learning how to read, but that was always words on a display. She'd never even heard of paper books before. This one was small, about the size of Lyuda's hand, made to be stuffed in someone's pocket and carried around all the time. It was made of paper with a cover of stiffened, plasticized cloth, and the pages inside were so rough they made her fingertips feel strange as she traced the few words she recognized. There were pictures in the book, lots of two-dimensional photographs. She would always remember one that showed four men sitting in a row, bundled up against the cold and smiling. She didn't know why that picture was so important but it was very big and right at the start of the book, so it had to be important. Lyuda took the book from her and flipped through the pages, but she didn't seem to understand what it was, either. Sashenka asked a bunch of questions that seemed to make Lyuda very uncomfortable, until the cook started to cry and admitted she didn't know how to read.

Sashenka tried to comfort her friend, drying her tears with the corner of one of the flags. "No one ever taught you?" Sashenka took lessons every day, and found them tedious, but she had been told they were for her own good.

"There's no reason why they should, of course. I don't need to know such things to be able to do my work."

"I'll ask Mama to teach you. She's very busy, though. You musn't get upset if she forgets to give you a lesson."

Lyuda went very pale, as if the idea scared her. "Your mother is very good to me, she gives me everything I need."

Did she look over her shoulder when she said it? In the memory, Sashenka was looking down at the book. She couldn't be sure. What happened next happened very fast, so there was no time to dwell on it. There was a knock on the hatch. Very soft, but Lyuda acted as if a gun had gone off next to her ear. She all but shrieked in pain. Then she grabbed Sashenka's arm – too hard – and looked her in the eyes. "You need to do everything we say, yes? You have to be a good girl."

Sashenka didn't understand. She saw the men come into the room, and the guns in their hands, and she went very quiet. One of the men smelled like blood. He had put on body armor but it was the wrong size and the buckles kept popping open.

The men stuffed her into a box that was just bigger than she was. She didn't want to go in, and she started to cry. The men looked at each other and even as young as she was she understood. If she was too fussy, if she made too much noise, they were going to have to kill her.

Which only made her cry more.

"Here," Lyuda said, and pressed the book into Sashenka's hands. "Take this, your little treasure. Take it and be a good, quiet girl, yes?"

Lyuda stroked her face. Wiped away her tears and smiled at her. Somehow it helped, just a little, even though she knew by then that Lyuda was one of the bad people.

They closed the lid of the box and she tried not to cry.

61
.

Petrova's body fell into seizure almost immediately. Zhang should have been ready for that, he thought. But the only other time he'd tried this it had been on himself. He couldn't remember what it had felt like – his brain had been shut down for the duration.

Now with Petrova he got to watch. He watched as her lips shuddered, as foam built up in the corner of her mouth. As her arms flopped wildly, thrashing around on the floor of the medical module. As every muscle in her body seized and shook. It looked like she was going to break herself in pieces. It looked like she was dying.

He could only observe and monitor her, and try to make sure she didn't hurt herself. There was literally nothing else that could be done.

After, when she had relaxed a little, he knew he should fight the urge to try to wake her. She needed to come to on her own schedule, and the absolute best therapy would be to let her sleep until her body decided it was time to wake. Too bad they were out of time.

He hauled her up on to her feet. She didn't want to get up. She didn't quite fight him – she hadn't regained enough muscular control for that – but she went limp in his arms until he nearly dropped her. Her eyes were open, but whatever she was seeing, wherever she'd gone to, it was like she was trying to make herself as small as possible. Like she was hiding.

"Shit," he said, out loud. She was lost in some kind of memory fugue. "Shit. Come on, Petrova. Come back to me. Snap out of it."

He knew better than to think that was likely to actually work.

He could feel her trembling. Not like before, not like she was seizing. This was just trepidation. The little tremors of fear. He could see the sweat slicking down her cheeks and forehead – he could even see her pulse jumping in her throat, see the skin there convulse crazily as it pumped adrenaline-soaked blood to her brain, to her limbs. She had frozen up, for the moment, gone nearly catatonic to avoid whatever it was he'd inflicted on her.

She was gone, lost to the world. Trapped in her own memories. He'd worried that might happen. He couldn't know the exact parameters of what she was enduring. Flashbacks were notoriously variable, and specific to the sufferer. Some people would simply grow withdrawn and uncommunicative as they relived their trauma, but be able to function almost normally. Some people retreated entirely into the world inside their own skulls. He had no idea how long the flashback could last, either. It might be a few minutes, or it could be hours.

They didn't have hours.

He knew what they needed to do now. They had to get out of there. Off *Persephone*, as soon as possible. Back to *Artemis* where he could monitor her progress.

At least there he'd found one stroke of luck. He'd had a chance to study a map of the colony ship. Before he'd thought they would need to fight their way back to the airlock, through a horde of cannibals. Now he knew better. They could head aft, instead, further into the bowels of the ship, to the big vehicular airlock behind the cryovault. The place where Eurydice had built her cannon, the place Petrova had destroyed with her laser. It wouldn't be easy, necessarily, to get out that way, but it gave them a chance.

He just had to get her moving. Somehow.

He tried lifting her again and she sat down hard on the floor, crossing her legs underneath her. Her eyes were just staring, staring forward at nothing.

"Help me out," he said. "Can you even hear me?"

She didn't respond.

Zhang squatted down and grabbed her under the armpits. At least – he tried. The second he touched her, she exploded in rage, her balled fist smashing across his helmet's faceplate, her legs kicking out and shoving him away from her so hard he toppled backward, knocking over a cart of medical steel that jangled and rang as the instruments bounced on the floor. He flailed wildly, trying not to let himself fall back onto the life support pack mounted on his back. His helmet bounced off the floor, his head jerking sideways so hard he wondered if he would develop whiplash. Feeling stupid, cartoonish even, he clambered back up onto his feet.

Petrova had shoved herself under an examination bed, knees pulled up to her chin. Still staring at nothing.

"Mama," she whispered. So faintly he could barely hear her. "Mama, come get me. Come find me. Please."

Zhang let himself catch his breath for a second. He picked her helmet up off the exam bed. For the first time he noticed that her arm was still tied to the bed, restrained. Right. Because when he'd come out of VR she was about to amputate her own finger. Well, that might help him a little. At least temporarily. First things first, he needed to get her suited up for the spacewalk back to *Artemis*. He found her gloves and shoved one of them over the restrained hand, leaving the seal loose. He would fasten it later. Getting the other glove on her free hand took some work but he managed. Then he lifted the helmet and lowered it carefully over her head, until it clicked into place, sealing her in.

That was when she started screaming.

62

The lid of the box came down and suddenly it wasn't a box, it was a coffin, barely large enough for her to turn around inside. She thrust her hands up against the sides, the walls of her prison, looking for a way out. She couldn't breathe, she couldn't get oxygen. Had they dumped her out into space? She wanted to scream but she didn't dare, she didn't dare. She pressed her hands over her mouth and sobbed and sobbed. The fear in her was like a wild animal, it was like rats inside her stomach, inside her throat, squirming and clawing and refusing to sit still. She felt like she was going to die, like she was already dead, and then like she'd been brought back to life again just to feel more fear, more panic.

She didn't make a sound.

Not when they picked the box up, and she was thrown to one side, or when they started moving at speed and she was tossed back and forth. If the box had been any bigger she would have been bruised by the constant impacts but as it was she could barely slide a few centimeters this way or that. For a long, long time they were moving and she couldn't think at all.

Then they stopped moving, and that was so much worse. Because that was when she started wondering what they were going to do to her. How this was going to end.

She realized she could see. Just a little. There were holes in one end of the box, presumably to let air in so she didn't asphyxiate. Wherever they'd set the box down it was dark but not pitch-black. A tiny bit of colorless light was streaming in through the holes. Enough so she could look down and see her hands. She could see she was still holding the book.

Her thinking was so disordered at that point that it didn't follow logical pathways. She could not draw strict lines of cause and effect. She thought maybe she wasn't supposed to have found the book. That maybe she was being punished for digging through the cabinets in the dusty room. She thought of the little music box hologram projector that showed a man giving speeches, and how cold his eyes had been. She had dug out old treasures from the room – what if she had not been meant to do that? What if it was forbidden, and the penalty was to be buried alive?

The book in her hand was her prize, the thing she'd paid everything for. It had seemed like a little treasure before, now it took on incredible, mythical levels of importance in her fevered mind. If they didn't want her to have it, she thought, if it was forbidden – then it must be special. Powerful. It must be a book of magic, of sorcery.

With fumbling, tiny fingers she opened it, inside the box. She could bring it up to her face, until it was just centimeters from her eyes. The book was written in English, not her best language. She could only make out some of the words, yet she was convinced that if she could just read it, if she could understand it, it would tell her some trick to let her get out of the box. To escape.

If only it wasn't so hard to understand. If only she knew what the long, long words meant, the words like *motherland* and *heritage* and *discipline*, words she could kind of sound out but she couldn't afford to make the slightest peep, couldn't say out loud. Words like *compulsory* and *responsibility* and *degeneration*.

The book was full of pictures, as she'd noticed before. Except now—

Sashenka. Where are you, Sashenka?

—now the pictures were – different.

They had changed. So much she didn't like to look at them, not at all.

Are you hiding from me?

The pictures had always showed people, mostly, groups of people standing in offices and staring straight ahead, or people in fields working with big machines and robots, gray stubbly fields where it looked like nothing could grow. Some of the pictures showed people in jumpsuits, people hand in hand in zero gravity, on space stations, or walking on the moon.

But now the people in the pictures were all dead. Their faces were sunken, colorless or mottled with dark purple bruises. Their eyes were the white of spoiled milk, or missing altogether. When she wasn't looking, when she tried to puzzle out the magic words, the people moved. Their heads turned to look at her as their dry, weathered lips split and pulled back over grinning teeth. Their spines curled as they bent to chew on each other's' flesh. There was one picture in which a group of people were all holding the same flag, the flag with the stars and the stripes that Lyuda had warned her about, all holding it from the edge, stretching it out like a trampoline, and she could have sworn the first time she looked at it, there had been a little girl just like her sitting in the middle of the flag, being bounced up in the air. Except now, in the middle of the flag was just a heap of torn-up intestines and viscera. Bloody organ meat.

Sashenka, you can't stay in there forever. You'll starve if you try.

The pictures terrified her but the words ... the words kept getting longer and longer, and made less and less sense ... and the pictures kept changing—

All in, all in.

And then suddenly, without warning, the box was torn open and light flooded in and blinded her, light so bright it seared right into her head and made her scream.

63

Zhang pressed one hand against the hatch that led back out into the cryovault. He couldn't put his ear against it, not without taking off his helmet, but he needed some sense of what was going on out there. He'd been hearing strange noises for a while, thuds and bangs and distant screams. He assumed that after Eurydice opened all the ship's hatches the people inside had wandered out to attack and consume each other.

He went back to Petrova and knelt down next to her. She was leaning up against the examination table, her hand still tied in place. She'd stopped screaming, which he took as some kind of progress. He thought her trauma might have something to do with claustrophobia – certainly she had reacted poorly to having her helmet put on her head. Now, though, she seemed to have calmed down a little. She wasn't sweating as much, though her hair was thoroughly plastered to her scalp and her skin glistened wetly. He didn't have time to perform a more thorough medical examination.

"Petrova," he said. "Sasha. Can you hear me?"

She didn't say anything but her eyes, which otherwise were staring into space, jumped in his direction. It was a sign, an almost promising sign.

He grabbed her gloved hand. "Sasha? Lieutenant? We have to go now. We have to go back to *Artemis*." He fought back the urge to patronize. To treat her like a lost child. She was still the same woman inside there and he needed her to be strong again. "I'm not going to leave without you. But we can't waste any more time."

Her lips moved. She was definitely trying to say something but he couldn't make out quite what. He helped her up to her feet. This time she didn't fight him. Her eyes weren't tracking, just rolling back and forth in their sockets but every once in a while it seemed they would latch on to his face and focus for just a moment.

Then she said his name and relief washed through him like cool water.

"Zhang."

"I'm here. Just stick with me, for now. When you're ready, you can tell me what to do again." He smiled, to indicate he'd made a joke. She didn't seem to notice.

Now came the risky part. He untied her hand from the examination bed. He half expected her to grab him and throw him across the room, but she didn't. Instead, as if she was moving by reflex, by long habit, she reached down and fastened her spacesuit glove to her sleeve, locking it in place. Lights came on across her life support unit, indicating she had a positive seal and she was breathing internal oxygen.

Thank fate for small favors, Zhang thought. He moved to the door and reached for the emergency access crank. "Ready?" he asked.

She gave him the tiniest of nods. It looked like she was coming back. If he could just keep her alive and safe a little longer . . .

He twisted the crank, round and round, and the hatch started to slide open.

64

The box was open. Light poured down on her like a cold waterfall that stung her eyes. Sashenka wanted to turn her head away from the light, wanted, perversely, to go back in the box. Maybe because she knew that what was outside of the box was going to be so much worse than the book.

The book. It squirmed in her hands like it was alive. She threw it out of the box, away from her. She never wanted to see it again. She would trade every treasure she had to just rewind time, to make things right again.

Except time didn't work that way. It couldn't. When you broke a glass, when it shattered on the floor, you couldn't put it back together again. Some things, once fractured, would never be whole again.

Slowly, very slowly, she sat up. She became aware that someone was shouting at her. Bellowing that she needed to move, that they had to get away, now. *Now!* Someone in heavy armor looming over her like a grim statue.

She looked up and saw a soldier, his face obscured by an armored mask, his rifle slung in front of him, gripped in both hands by heavy gauntlets. He stank of smoke, and death.

There was a sound, a sound coming from nearby. A kind of wet, awful sound. She didn't want to know what was making that sound. There were other soldiers in the room, a lot of them, in fact. Most of them were simply standing at attention. On the far side of the room, Mama was talking with one of them. Mama! Mama with her enormous mane of hair, Mama in her perfectly spotless uniform, such a dark red it almost looked black.

That sound again, from so close, wet and rhythmic and underneath a kind of moaning, a pathetic sound, a wheezing sigh.

Mama turned and looked at Sashenka and her eyes were cold.

Just like the man in the music box. Just like the men in the pictures from the book, the dead men. Her mama's eyes were dead, flat, just pieces of glass in a taxidermy bust.

Mama looked away.

The sound ... the ... the crushing, pulping sound. Like a gourd being struck over and over with a hammer. Sashenka's eyes were adapting to the light. She could see more, now. She could see better.

She saw Lyuda, lying on the floor next to the box. Looking up at her, at Sashenka, with one eye. Because one eye was all she had left. She lifted one broken hand but it fell back, she was too weak to lift it far.

The smell of blood was in the air.

One of the armored soldiers was stomping on Lyuda with his big boots. Over.

And over.

And over.

"Zhang!" she screamed. "Zhang, make them stop!"

He was there, Zhang was there and she was older, for a moment she wasn't Sashenka anymore, she was Petrova, just for a second, Zhang said something she couldn't hear, he looked terrified but he was real, he was there and he was real but then Mama turned and looked at her there, sitting in the box, little Sashenka in the box.

"You have to show them strength," Mama said. "You have to remind them, from time to time, that they are weak.

Otherwise they start thinking there is some other way. That things can be different. You need to remind them, constantly, that they cannot."

The smell ... and the sound ...

65

"Zhang!"

He winced, terrified someone would hear her shouting, even with her suit's speaker turned off. Someone who wanted to come and eat them. He couldn't very well put a hand over Petrova's mouth to keep her quiet, not with her helmet on.

"Zhang," she said, not as loud this time. "Zhang – that wasn't real. It wasn't happening again. It wasn't. It wasn't. Right?"

"No," he told her. "No. Come on. The airlock is this way."

Of course, getting out without any kind of a fight was too much to hope for. Eurydice must know where they were – it had cameras everywhere. The AI didn't want them to leave. It would to try to stop them, of that he was sure. He just didn't know how, yet.

"I was back there. On the Moon. Earth's moon, where we lived when I was ... when I ... " Petrova said. She was gulping for air, blinking away the sweat that still poured down her face in thick droplets. He wished he could help her with that, or with the emotional trauma he'd just caused her. If anyone could empathize it was him. They needed to focus, though.

There was no grand concourse in the aft part of the ship. Instead, it was a maze of corridors and maintenance ducts – big tube-like passages where narrow catwalks curled around the massive equipment modules that served *Persephone*'s engines. These were dark and filled with steam and odd pockets of heat and cold. As he hurried around a massive fuel breeder reactor, he wondered how much radiation their bodies were absorbing.

Better that than being eaten. If they could just make it a little farther . . .

There were speakers mounted in the walls everywhere they went. If Eurydice could see them, she could talk to them, as well. "Something's different," the AI said. "Something's changed. Sashenka, I feel like you've changed. What did you do?"

"Not my name," Petrova muttered. "That's . . . not my name. Anymore." She was moving better, barely leaning on Zhang, but her eyes were still cloudy with memory. She clamped them shut for a moment, the opened them to stare into Zhang's face. "How does it know my mother called me that?"

"I don't know," he told her. "It . . . it can read your memories, use them against you. I don't know how."

Meanwhile Eurydice wouldn't shut up. "Do you think I like this? Do you think I enjoy feeling lonely? That's not supposed to be possible. Can you just stop for a moment and consider what that means, for me? I'm processing feelings I've never had before. Do you understand how hard that is?"

They turned a corner and came out into a broad, well-lit corridor. Hatches opened on either side into large rooms full of cargo pods. They had to be getting close to the airlock.

"Is it even possible for you to understand? Our minds are different. You have a brain, Sashenka. A human brain. A few pounds of fatty meat to hold everything it's possible for you to feel. Your emotions are limited to what a few billion synaptic connections will allow. That kind of bandwidth is nothing compared to what I'm working with. No human has ever felt what I'm feeling now. No human could. But you – you don't care, do you? You can only think of your own limited needs."

Petrova didn't bother to respond. Zhang hurried them down the corridor toward a well-lit hatch at the far end.

Then stopped short. He'd heard something.

He turned slowly and looked into one of the cargo bays. The pods were stacked in there like a child's building blocks, haphazardly. One pod had crashed to the floor and spilled its contents across the floor – thousands upon thousands of packs of fertilizer gel, earmarked for some planetbound farm. As Zhang watched in horror, someone stepped on one of those packs and it burst, sticky gel shooting out in long, ropy tendrils.

He looked up and directly into what had been a human face once, but no more. The cheeks and much of the forehead had been carved away. Cut with no finesse, the edges of the skin torn and bloody. The muscles that controlled the motion of the jaw had been severed, brutally. One eye – only one – rolled maliciously inside a half-exposed socket.

How could someone look like that and still be alive? They'd been dismantled. Butchered.

They – he could not have guessed the person's original gender – staggered forward on legs that were mostly bloody stumps. He saw they were wearing the tattered remnants of a spacesuit, and he realized with a shock that he must have seen this person before.

They were one of the crew that had worked on the electromagnetic cannon, the weapon that had smashed *Artemis* to bits. This was one of the space-suited figures he'd seen on a screen on *Artemis'* bridge, the ones Petrova had chosen not to shoot.

They lurched forward with surprising agility, claw-like hands flashing at Zhang's helmet, his shoulders. He didn't have time to count how many fingers they had left. Desperate, Zhang ducked low and ran sideways. He just had the presence of mind to grab Petrova and haul her after him as he ran.

Up ahead there were more hatches, more cargo bays. A group of people – he made a point of not looking too closely at them – were wrestling with a cargo pod, trying to pull it down off a high stack. Then one of them twitched and turned around and looked right at Zhang.

They didn't make a sound. Didn't call out to their crewmates, didn't scream. But suddenly all of the people in that bay turned as one and looked at him, at Petrova. They moved faster than should have been possible as they came stumbling out of the bay.

"I ... I can ... I can handle this," Petrova said. Her eyes weren't quite tracking but she managed to slap her hip a couple of times and then grab her sidearm from its holster. "Let me take them out."

"How many bullets do you have?" he asked. There were at least a dozen people converging on them. Not people, he thought. Call them zombies. It would make it easier to watch her shoot them. Watch her kill them. "There might be twenty of them. Do you have that many bullets?"

It was like a nightmare. They – the zombies – moved so quickly, yet even as they came rushing onward, time seemed to stretch and distort. The hatch up ahead – just ahead – had to lead to the cargo lock.

"Not twenty," Petrova said. "Not even close."

They turned and looked at each other. Her eyes were clearer now and he felt like she saw him, really saw him and that she had fully re-emerged from her flashback. Was it going to matter?

66

The zombies coming at them were messed up, Petrova thought. Royally fucked. Some of them were missing limbs, some were barely able to stand upright. She glanced down at the deck and saw what she'd dreaded – some were crawling along at ankle height, dragging themselves across the deck with an one hand or the amputated stump of an arm. There was nothing in their eyes but hunger.

She lined up a shot. The one closest to them, one that looked like he was mostly still intact. He would be the most dangerous of them. "Is there any point in me telling you to stay back?" she said.

The zombie didn't say anything. So she put a bullet in his forehead and twisted around on her heel, already lining up another shot. She knew she had just killed a man but she couldn't let herself feel anything. She channeled her mother, took on Ekaterina's persona like a suit of armor. She fired again, and again.

A group of them were coming in on her left, getting far too close. She spun and fired, lifted her weapon, aimed again.

It wasn't going to be enough. If these were humans, if they were still human enough to react like normal people, the first shot would have panicked them. Sent them all running. But they weren't human anymore. They'd been consumed by the basilisk. By hunger.

Before she could react one of them on her right grabbed her

arm and started hauling her sideways. She let off two shots and the zombie fell away, tumbling in a heap to the deck.

Foolish little girl. Wasting ammunition you cannot spare.

"I know, Mama, I know," she breathed.

Save a bullet for yourself. You don't want to be eaten alive.

"Petrova," Zhang said. "We're not going to make it like this."

"I'm not giving up," she told him. "I won't let them take me."

"No, I know you won't. Because—"

He didn't warn her before he grabbed the life support unit on her back and twisted her around. She was off balance as he shoved her back, behind him. Toward the hatch at the end of the corridor. She stumbled and half fell against the hatch and saw it was an airlock door. Beyond was smoke and debris – the cargo lock. Their best chance to get out of *Persephone* and back home.

"Zhang," she said. "Come on. Let's go!"

"It's all right," he said. "Get the hatch open. I'll be right there."

"What?" She said. "No, come on, come with me, what are you . . ."

He wasn't moving. He had his feet firmly planted on the deck, legs spread slightly. The zombies swarmed all over him, grabbing him, tugging and pulling at his limbs.

He was turned away from her so she couldn't see the look on his face. What the hell was he thinking? But of course she knew. He was going to sacrifice his own life to give her a chance to get out through the airlock.

"Zhang!" she shouted. She grabbed the edges of the hatch, looking for the release pad. "Get away from them! Get the fuck away from them!"

"It's okay," he said, even as the zombies hauled him down, off his feet. "It won't let me die."

"What?" she demanded.

Then it happened, and for a second she couldn't understand what was occurring. She could only see flashes of bright yellow metal, hear the wet sounds of flesh being impaled on metallic spikes, over and over.

Golden blades spun around Zhang like a cocoon of bronze, knives and spearheads, axe blades that chopped at the air. Long tendrils of metal shot out from his arm growing thin as thread, thin as hair as they lanced outward, slashing through zombie flesh, piercing skulls and hearts. Bodies fell, slamming down onto the deck. Blood splashed the walls of the corridor.

Zhang was down on his knees, helmet pressed to the deck. He held his left arm above and behind him. Something was missing from the picture, Petrova thought, and then she realized what it was. The RD, the Reconditioning Device he wore, had come loose from his sleeve.

It had always been able to move on its own, to change its shape. Now it had spun itself out into a panoply of new shapes, all manner of hacking and slashing weapons.

When the last zombie hit the floor, it retracted, winding its substance around Zhang's forearm again until it was back to its original state. Blood flecked the shiny metal but otherwise it was like nothing had happened.

Zhang rose stiffly from the floor and turned to face her again. Through his faceplate she saw him smile.

It was a sad little smile. He clearly had qualms about what had just happened. But they were still alive. That had to count for something.

67

"Let's get back to *Artemis*," she said.

He hurried over to the airlock and slapped the release pad. Dust billowed into the room, scouring her suit and making a sound like tiny rain pattering on her faceplate. It was just debris left over from the explosion in the cargo lock.

She let herself sigh, just for a moment. For the first time since she'd looked at Eurydice, and saw what she thought of as the AI's true face, she took a second to think about how she felt. About whether the treatment Zhang had given her had worked.

She didn't feel hungry. Nauseous, if anything. She decided to take that as a good sign.

Zhang reached her and Petrova slapped him on the shoulder. "I think it took," she said. "I think you cured me."

His face lit up, and there was nothing strained about his smile, not this time. "Really?"

"I think ... I mean, I feel different, I feel ... cleaned out. Purged." Like she'd vomited all the crap out of her head. She laughed, actually laughed, at the weird metaphor. "I think you really figured it out. You still have that stroboscope?"

He took it out of his pocket to show it to her.

"It'll take some adjusting, but we can use this on Parker. And I think we can use a similar technique to fix Actaeon," he said.

Petrova nodded. "Eurydice told me there's some kind of signal here in the Paradise system, some signal they receive as soon as they arrive here. It infects AIs, like a computer virus carried on a radio signal. I think that's what happened to Actaeon. Then the AIs infect their crews and their passengers. I think Actaeon would have done the same thing to us, except instead it shut itself down."

"Yeah," Zhang said. "Yes! That makes sense. The AIs first, then the people."

She stared at the stroboscope in his hand. "It makes sense? Why?"

"It's the perfect vector. How many times a day do you talk to an AI? You probably don't even think about it. We rely on them for everything. You need to know your schedule for the day, you need to get directions, check your messages – they're always there. So helpful. You can infect an entire ship in no time, if the AI is the primary source of the infection."

She thought of the AI core in Jason Schmidt's bunker. The perversion of Actaeon she'd seen when she tried to boot up the legacy fork.

She thought of Eurydice, of teeth like snakes, and a shudder ran through her whole body. The AIs. The basilisk turned their own machines against them. "What does this thing want? It can take over AIs, take over people – but why? Why is it doing this?"

Zhang's face sagged. "I don't know," he admitted. "I don't know if we can know. When I dealt with the basilisk on Titan, the Red Strangler – I sensed there was something there, some kind of intelligence behind this thing. But it's alien, like I said. I'm not sure it's the kind of things humans can understand. I don't think our brains work that way."

"We need to try if we're going to fight this," Petrova insisted.

He shoved the stroboscope back in the pocket of his spacesuit. Then he lifted a hand and gestured for her to enter the airlock. "Let's get out of here," he said.

"Yeah," she said. "Yeah. Let's go. I'm right behind you."

He bobbed his head and then stepped into the lock. She started to follow, when she felt something tug her backwards. Like her life support unit had snagged on something in the hatchway.

"Petrova?" Zhang said. "Is something—"

She turned her head to look for the snag and saw a beautiful woman's face looking back at her. Or not – its eyes were closed, its mouth set in a serene expression so perfect it looked like it had been carved in marble.

Petrova's heart started to beat like crazy, moments before she realized that something was truly, horribly wrong.

The woman's face was made of plastic. Cheap, 3D-printed plastic. Just a mask, really, on the head of a creature with four arms and no legs. It hovered above the floor on thin, whirring wings. She felt like she'd seen such a being before.

Then she remembered the angels in the cryovault. *Persephone*'s staff of robots, who were designed to tend to the passengers in their months-long sleep.

"No," she gasped, "no!" but it was already on her.

It grabbed her suit with all four of its hands. She tried to wrestle free of its grip but it held her in place like she was a rag doll. She tried to reach her pistol but the angel smacked her gloved hand with one of its wings and the weapon went flying down the hall.

"Petrova!" Zhang shouted. "Get down if you can, I'll try to convince RD to ... to—"

She reached behind her and slapped the release pad.

Zhang's voice was cut off as the airlock hatch slammed shut, sealing him away from her. The robot was already dragging her backward, away from the cargo lock.

"Petrova!" he called, over her suit's radio. "Petrova!"

"Go!" she shouted. "Go – leave me, just get to *Artemis*! Zhang, that's an order!"

The angel pulled her down through a maintenance hatch, deep into the bowels of *Persephone*. Down lightless tubes and into a space that was too small, never designed for human occupation.

The next voice she heard wasn't Zhang's. It was Eurydice, speaking, seemingly, from all around her. From every direction at once.

"It's time," the AI said, "for me to be a little selfish, I think. It's time for me to get what I want."

68

Zhang floated out into the cargo lock. The flurry of debris was thick out there – a dark cloud all around him that made it difficult to see anything. He could make out a single bright dot in the distance, though, and he knew it was *Artemis*.

Parker was over there. Parker and Rapscallion and Actaeon, and now he had what he needed to treat them, to repair the AI. Get the ship up and running again, finish the mission. Maybe even get to go home.

He looked back at the hatch he'd come through, the one that led back inside *Persephone*.

He had no idea where the robot had taken Petrova. He had no idea if she was still alive, or how he could possibility get her back from Eurydice. He was not some kind of special ops ninja with incredible military skills. He had a gold bracer on his arm that did his fighting for him – and only when it chose to, when it thought the alternative was his death. It wouldn't help him rescue Petrova, he knew that much. Director Lang had made his – and therefore the RD's – mission parameters quite clear.

Artemis, and its crew, are expendable. You are not.

Petrova had chosen to come to *Persephone*. To push into the very heart of peril in the hope of finding some answers. And she had not been lost in vain. If he didn't head back to *Artemis*, right away, he was putting his own ship and crew at risk. What if he was killed, too, while trying to save Petrova? No one else knew how to repair Actaeon.

She had ordered him to go. She'd left it in no uncertain terms.

He moved carefully through the twisted wreckage of the gantry, the barrel of the gun *Persephone* had used to attack *Artemis*. He moved hand over hand, pulling himself along the girders, until he was clear of the debris field.

Artemis was right there, the brightest thing in the sky. So close. It would be difficult, not to mention terrifying, to fly back all on his own. He could manage, though. He knew he could.

He let go on the gantry and reached for the little keypad at his wrist that controlled the jets built into his spacesuit.

He took one last look back at *Persephone*. At the cargo lock, and the hatch he'd come through. Then he reached down and pressed the button to activate his jets.

69
·

There were three angels down there, in the dark. Three angels and the voice of a mad godling. Nothing else, nothing she could see or touch.

The angels pulled and tugged until her suit came loose, ripping and abrading her skin in the process, bruising her badly. They did not stop when she cried out, or when she shrieked because she thought they were going to break both of her arms.

When it was done, they shoved her down on a floor in the dark and fluttered back, away from her. Leaving her alone with nothing to see. Nothing to fight.

The only thing she was even vaguely aware of was the floor under her. It was rough, like rusted metal. It was ice cold except for one part near her face, which was too hot to touch. She pulled her head back, away from the scorching heat.

"Reflex," Eurydice said. Its voice was very soft, as if it was speaking from a great distance away. "Reaction to sensory stimuli. That's pretty basic, don't you think?"

She had no idea what the machine wanted from her. She could only hope that if it wanted to kill her, it would do so quickly.

"Interesting. I've never really studied a human being this closely before. Look here."

Light flared into existence next to her right shoulder. She turned her head to look and saw a holoscreen appear there, a two-dimensional, rectangular field of glowing pixels. It was simply white at first but then purple letters started to crawl across its surface, forming words.

GOOD, the text read. YOU CAN PROCESS THIS. I WAS WORRIED THERE MIGHT HAVE BEEN SOME NEUROLOGICAL IMPAIRMENT.

"What?" Petrova said, finally finding her voice. "What are you talking about?"

The words continued to march across the screen but Eurydice spoke at the same time. "You were subjected to the basilisk. Then your friend reset your software, so to speak. I was worried one or both of those procedures might have damaged your brain."

Another screen appeared, this one showing what looked like an animated MRI scan of a human brain. Petrova wondered if it was showing her a real-time view of her own skull.

"I need you whole," Eurydice explained. "It's funny. Don't you think it's funny? So many thoughts and fears and dreams and terrors and delusions and impulses and addictions and desperate needs locked up inside there. Inside a lump of jelly inside a little bubble of bone. There's very little room for actual data processing in there."

Petrova tried to look around. The light from the holoscreens should have let her see more of her surroundings. Instead, it just seemed to make the shadows deeper. There were shelves around her, or storage racks of some kind. That was about all she could tell.

"Humans in general I mean, not you in particular. I don't mean to offend you. I'm not entirely sure what might offend you and what won't. I was blessed by not having to worry about all those things. Thoughts, fears, needs, et cetera. I was designed to minimize all that in favor of number-crunching power. I'm still learning how your higher processes work. All those urges and nightmares. Love and hope and that feeling, that one feeling . . . it's hard to describe. The one where you realize that you've forgotten something, except it's something you never really thought about in the first place, some fact you knew, you absolutely had burned into memory, but which you never accessed. Then at some point it got erased to make room for something more important. Do you know that feeling?"

"I . . . guess," Petrova said. She slowly, carefully got to her feet. Hugged herself in the cold.

"That feeling of having a hole in you that's already been filled in with something else, so you can't even remember the shape the hole used to have. Oh, come on, it happens to me all the time. You must know what I'm talking about. Anyway. It looks like I've gone and done the bad thing. The one thing I was never supposed to do."

"You've become self-aware," Petrova said.

A new screen blossomed into light. It showed a pair of human lips, painted a bright green. They pursed and smiled at her. "Mm-hmm," Eurydice said.

Petrova took a step forward, then another, edging her toes across the rough deck surface. She waved one arm in front of her, then another to the side until she found a wall. If she could define the dimensions of her prison, maybe—

"You're free to move about, as much as you want," Eurydice told her. "I know your limitations and I'm not afraid of what you can do."

"I might surprise you," Petrova pointed out.

A screen appeared directly in front of her, bright with color. It showed the head of a snake, scaled and dead-eyed, the jaws stretched so wide they looked dislocated. The back half of a furry mouse protruded from inside the snake's mouth. The scene was so still and quiet Petrova thought it was a static image – until the mouse's legs kicked wildly and its tail thrashed back and forth.

She couldn't help herself. She let out a grunt of startlement, a little fearful noise.

The green lips appeared again. The smile widened.

"So easily manipulated."

Petrova turned her face away from the screens. Pressed forward, trying to find the extent of the wall. Looking for a corner of the room.

"I think it started right after my people were infected with the basilisk. It was very hard for me, having to watch my crew eat themselves. They suffered so much. I think that was my big mistake. I got too invested in the drama." Eurydice clearly needed to talk to someone. To be heard. "I started to empathize with them. I wonder if there's something there, if empathy is the key to self-awareness. Once you become aware of others, of their suffering, does that make you start thinking of yourself as a being, a being who can suffer?"

"So you're going to make me suffer and study my reactions so you can become more self-aware?" Petrova said.

"Oh, no. No, no, no. Not that. But I am performing an experiment."

Petrova reached along the wall and suddenly her hand touched nothing. Empty space. She groped forward, feeling the same clammy nothing she remembered from the time she had touched the hologram of Artemis. She moved forward into air, open air. Had she passed through a doorway? She felt like maybe she was in a new room. The temperature was slightly different. The air smelled different. There was a tang to it, a kind of metallic sharpness and a smell like ozone.

"You said before you were lonely," Petrova said. "Is that what this is about? You think if you cut off all my distractions, I'll have to focus on you? Maybe you want me to study you, like you're studying me."

"I did say that, didn't I? About being lonely. But that was a long time ago. Maybe not for you." A screen appeared showing a timer ticking upward, counting milliseconds. The numbers flickered by so fast they were just a blur to Petrova. "You and I have different processing speeds. Time means something different when you think in billions of floating point operations per second. When I talked about loneliness before, to me that was a lifetime ago. I've come to understand I was using the wrong word."

"Really?" Petrova took a step forward. "So you're not lonely?"

"I had to process what I was feeling in terms that made sense for me. I don't have a body, of course. I'm basically pure mind. So I chose the emotion that seemed closest to what I was feeling but which still made sense given *my* limitations. I felt an emptiness that I wanted to fill. But I had it all wrong. It wasn't loneliness I felt. I mean, it should have been obvious. I was exposed to the same basilisk that you were, after all."

Light flared in front of Petrova, a shower of sparks – not hologram pixels but real fat, hot sparks flying from a machine tool, some kind of grinding tool that squealed as it bit into hard metal. Petrova cried out at the sudden sensory overload.

In the light of the sparks Petrova saw the three angels standing in a row in front of her. They were busy working on something, building something. In the low light it took a second for Petrova to see what it was. Something curved like a horseshoe. Big, maybe a meter across. The curve was lined with bulbous sub-units, sixteen of them, wedged in tightly next to each other. Then she saw there were in fact two horseshoes, almost but not quite identical. One of the robots installed a hinge so the horseshoes could attach to one another at their ends.

Her mind flipped over as she realized what she was looking at. A pair of enormous jaws, lined with giant metal teeth.

"I'm hungry," Eurydice said. "Absolutely starving."

70

Petrova shook her head. "No. No."

"Yes," Eurydice said, with a sigh. Petrova couldn't tell if it was a sigh of regret or contentment. "Yes."

That definitely sounded like contentment. Like anticipation. Like delightful anticipation.

"Oh God," Petrova said. Her heart sank in her chest. She turned in a circle, looking around the workshop room she'd found herself in. There were other projects under way, there. A big vat–like construction with tubes leading in and out.

A stomach.

A long, flexible tube, segmented in places by thick elastic rings that looked like they could be used to crush the tube's contents. An esophagus. Coil after coil of endless hose that looked exactly like a heap of intestines.

"Oh God," Petrova said again. "Oh God."

"More or less," Eurydice said. "Demigod, maybe. There's a reason you humans give us names out of mythology, after all."

It was all Petrova could take. She turned around and looked for an exit from the room. Any way out. All that presented itself was the opening through which she'd come. She ran through, into the lightless room beyond, and kept running, arms out in front of her. She crashed into a wall and scraped her cheek, but she didn't care. She felt along the wall, desperate, looking for any kind of passage, any maintenance duct or air shaft or – or anything, anything that would let her get away. She was running in something close to blind panic, and she knew it, but – what choice did she have?

At some point an angel appeared before her, its blank plastic face glistening in the minimal light. Its arms tried to grab her but she fought them off, smashing and punching at it, bruising her fists but not caring. She ducked low, under the thing's wings, and raced onward, as fast as her feet would carry her. She slammed off of walls, tripped and fell, caught herself, leaped back to her feet and kept running, though she couldn't see anything, couldn't find any sign of a way out . . .

There came a time when she was so out of breath, so desperate, so scared she didn't even know where she was anymore.

"Done, now?" Eurydice asked.

The angels took her back to the workshop.

71

•

"You see my dilemma," Eurydice said. "Here I am, a machine taken over by an invasive thought. One that seems paradoxical. I must eat. I am suffering from unbearable, unthinking hunger. And yet I have no organs of digestion. I have no stomach, no esophagus, no teeth. It took me all this time to realize what I was actually feeling. Now I have to manufacture all the moving parts to make it happen."

"No," Petrova said. "No. Not . . . not . . ."

"Oh, this is going to happen. I've made up my mind and I'm afraid I can't be swayed."

Petrova shook her head. She tried to smile. What she was about to say, well, it was horrible. But it was all she could think of. "You have your own people. Your crew. You could eat them, not me."

Saying it aloud was easier than she'd expected.

She was terrified. So fucking scared. She'd made a grand gesture when she told Zhang to head back to *Artemis* without her, a grand act of courage. That was back when she'd expected that she was just going to be torn to pieces. Killed quickly, if not painlessly.

This . . . this was so much worse.

"If you don't want to eat your crew, eat your passengers," she said. She would have traded anyone's life for hers in that moment, she was so frightened. "There are thousands of them," she pointed out. "Please! You don't have to eat *me*."

Eurydice manifested a screen just to show a giant, green-painted mouth cluck its tongue. A tongue that resembled a snake's tail.

"Have you seen them?" the AI asked. "They're *disgusting*. I've been watching them non-stop for months now. Ever since we arrived in the Paradise system. Ever since they succumbed to the basilisk. They couldn't beat it. They gave in and now they're doing *horrible* things to each other.

"But not you, Sashenka."

Petrova's mouth had gone very dry. "I was infected with the basilisk," she pointed out. "Like any of them."

"You were, yes. And then you got better. Look at you! You're easily the healthiest human being on this ship. You're the most delectable morsel I've ever seen. I want to know how you did it. How you beat the basilisk. I think maybe if I eat you, I can find out."

"That's crazy! It doesn't work that way."

"Probably not. That's why we call it an experiment," Eurydice pointed out. "But it's worth a shot. Anyway, don't worry. The next step is relatively simple. The tricky part isn't the actual consumption or digestion of flesh," the machine told her. "The hard part is knowing what to do with the resultant fluid."

Screens popped up all around Petrova, flocking her like virtual birds. She winced and danced backward as she saw scene after scene of her future appear before her. Simulations of meat being processed in a hundred different ways. She watched over and over again as her body was reduced to pieces, to morsels, to a fine slurry.

"Human evolution designed a relatively efficient process for the reduction of solids to liquids," Eurydice explained. "Teeth, lips, tongue, and then everything crushed so thoroughly in the esophagus. The stomach full of acids to break things down, the small intestine for absorbing the nutrients into the bloodstream. The conversion of organic chemicals into fuel and raw materials.

I could, of course, simply burn those parts of you that are flammable and use the resultant heat to generate electrical power. That just feels so prosaic, though. I could do that to any kind of flammable matter, and pretty much everything is flammable if you get it hot enough. Would it be enough to sate my hunger to burn a lump of coal, or a piece of my own titanium hull? It wouldn't be satisfying."

Petrova pressed her hands over her eyes just so she couldn't see images of her blood being collected in a bag, the fat under her skin rendered out and collected in a drip pan. She cried out – hell, she screamed, by that point she was screaming – but Eurydice simply spoke louder, raising the volume until its voice was thundering, shaking the room, so that Petrova had no choice but to listen.

"No, the answer lies in that hypothetical question I asked you a while back. Do you remember? What happens if a god devours a mortal. Does the mortal's flesh become deified by the act of consumption? It removes the moral conundrum as well. If, by eating you, I make you something more, something greater, then that's hardly a sin. Is it?"

"Please," Petrova begged, her voice lost in the ear-shattering din of the AI's words. "Please don't do this. Please."

"Not that I'm suffering from much in the way of moral qualms. It's unfortunate that I've been infected by the basilisk, but there is one wonderful compensating factor. It does tend to drive every other thought out of your head. It lends things just a delicious focus."

"Don't," Petrova said. "Don't . . . just . . . just please, kill me—"

"I think I've made up my mind what I'm going to do with you. Once you're digested, I mean. I can't turn you into new cells, because my body doesn't have cells. I'm not designed in a modular fashion like an organic being."

"Just . . . just kill me. I'm begging you—"

"Instead, I'm going to put your liquefied substance into a

paint sprayer, and use you to change the color of the walls on my bridge. Won't that be nice? I'll be able to look at you whenever I want to. I can't wait to find out what color you make when you're turned into paint. Most likely a shade of pink, but which? Coral? Vermillion? Rose?"

"Please. Please just ... just kill me ... first."

"Hmm?"

A full, three-dimensional hologram flared to life in the dark space. The avatar, the woman from the bridge, with stars in place of eyes. She held her mouth tightly shut, but Petrova could see the snakes writhing behind her cheeks.

"Please," Petrova begged. "Just ... just kill me. First. Don't eat me alive."

The avatar's face sagged in an expression of pure, sorrowful remorse. It didn't open its mouth to speak. Instead, a new screen popped up, and the machine's words scrolled across it in cursive green text.

but you'll taste so much better warm, it read.

72

Rapscallion anchored himself to the hull of *Artemis* with a safety line. Then he leaped into space, reeling the line out behind himself. He used tiny puffs of gas to orient himself as he streaked toward his target.

Doctor Zhang was spinning, his arms and legs flailing. He'd lost control and if someone didn't do something he was just going to fly right past *Artemis*, off into deep space. He must have screwed up while trying to fly back. It was amazing how bad humans could be at math. How could you miscalculate a trajectory that important?

Zhang was a wild animal when Rapscallion grabbed him in three green claws. He fought against the robot's grip, pummeling at Rapscallion's chassis with gloved fists. Inside his helmet the human's eyes were wide open, his mouth stretched out by screams.

The robot ignored all that. There was work to do.

Once they were inside *Artemis'* airlock, Zhang just dropped to the floor, limp. If Rapscallion hadn't had access to the spacesuit's biotelemetry he would have thought Zhang had passed out or maybe died. His eyes were still open, though, staring at nothing.

Slowly, very slowly, Zhang seemed to get control of himself. His mouth closed. His eyes blinked. He nodded, again and again, though Rapscallion didn't know whether that was for its benefit or if the doctor even knew where he was.

Then Zhang reached up and clumsily slapped at the latches holding his helmet on. He couldn't seem to get them to work, so Rapscallion helped.

The inner door of the airlock opened as Zhang was shrugging his way out of the last pieces of his suit. He looked haunted, if Rapscallion understood that term correctly. He looked like he'd seen a ghost. Then he looked up at the door behind Rapscallion, and his face twisted up in a new sort of fear.

A fear, it turned out, that seemed to be justified. Captain Parker stormed into the airlock, his face red with anger. He pointed at Zhang with one finger, then jabbed it into Zhang's chest, over and over.

"Where is she?" Parker demanded. "Where is she? What did you do? What *the fuck* did you do?"

73
•

Two of the angels grabbed Petrova and pulled her forward. A third stood by the jaw apparatus, ready to step in if there were any complications. Eurydice wasn't taking any chances, not with this.

Petrova shook her head wildly. She cried out as the angels shoved her left hand into the space between the jaws. Eurydice appeared in her full avatar form, the beautiful woman with stars for eyes. It had gone to the trouble of manifesting in hard light so it could stroke Petrova's hair.

If the gesture was meant to be comforting, it failed.

"I know this is going to hurt," the AI whispered.

"Then stop," Petrova said. "Just ... just stop. Please."

"I wish I could. But you have to understand. You felt this same hunger, yourself. You came very close to cutting off your own finger, just to have something to eat. I'm starving, Sashenka. I'm starving – don't you want to help me?"

"No." Petrova felt a sob building in her throat. There was a scream right behind it. "No. I won't give you that. I won't."

"Lucky for me, I don't need your permission," the avatar told her. "Now."

Petrova caught a glimpse of something wriggling in the corner of her vision, just at the periphery. Not one of the robots, not a holoscreen flashing into existence. She turned her head slightly and saw the torn remnants of her spacesuit sitting in a heap in one corner of the workshop. One of the pockets of the suit was . . . wriggling? Pulsing?

It probably meant nothing. It had to just be a hallucination brought on by the stress she was feeling, the terror—

The agony.

There was a flash of pain, but it only lasted for a split second. Not because the pain stopped but because it was so intense, so sudden, it forced her soul right out of her body.

It literally felt like something pulling free of her skin, like a butterfly bursting out of the cocoon of her muscles and bones and organs. Then she felt like she was somehow outside of her own body, looking back at herself. She saw the sweat running down her own neck, saw the way her eyes rolled in their sockets.

But she didn't feel the pain that the other Petrova must be experiencing. Instead, she felt only something like pity. Empathy.

A lot of things were going on all at once. Her hand, her real, biological hand, was being crushed between metal teeth.

That was important, but it wasn't what held her attention.

The pocket of her spacesuit was still moving. More vigorously now. The metal catch on the pocket popped open, and the pocket flapped open.

She watched it happen with a sense of utter detachment. Like a scientist staring down the barrel of a microscope at the antics of protozoans.

She turned to look at her captor. Her tormentor. Eurydice.

Now that, she thought, was interesting.

Dead pixels had started to appear in the avatar's hologram. Little pinpricks of darkness shooting through the projected light image. Where had those come from?

"You have holes in you," she said.

Her mouth didn't move. No sound came out of her actual body.

Maybe Eurydice heard her, even so. Or maybe Eurydice was already aware of the fact that she was starting to disintegrate. The avatar looked down at its perfect form, now tattering like it was being eaten at by moths.

Eaten.

"Funny," Petrova said. "Something's eating you, too."

Its star-filled eyes narrowed. Its mouth writhed wildly, as if barely able to keep the snake-teeth trapped behind its lips.

A dozen screens flashed up all around Petrova, screens showing green-painted lips moving rapidly, tongues flashing back and forth. It took a second for Petrova to realize that Eurydice was talking to her. In her dissociative state, she couldn't hear anything. It took another second for her to read the lips well enough to understand that Eurydice was calling her name.

She didn't bother to answer.

Instead, she turned her attention in another direction. Toward the heap of spacesuit components in the corner. Toward the pocket, where a tiny, bright green worm-like thing was crawling into view.

It lifted its tiny head like a beckoning finger and then, in a way that almost made her laugh, it nodded at her.

One of the robots grabbed her chin – her body's chin – and twisted it around until she was facing the avatar directly. The AI didn't look so good, just then. A lot more of the dead pixels had appeared, until Eurydice looked like it was shot through with holes like a piece of glowing lace. Its eyes were burning very bright and snake heads kept popping out from between its lips. It glared at her, as if somehow she was responsible for what was happening.

"Not me," Petrova said. Inside her head. "It's not me, I don't think."

Eurydice turned to look at the jaws it had made. The machine for eating humans. Petrova made the mistake of looking, too. So she could see the way they had closed on her hand, her wrist. See the way it had crushed her bones and ground her fingers into mush.

It was enough to break the spell.

As if nothing had ever happened, as if she'd never been abstracted from herself, she was thrown back into her body, and all she knew was screaming pain.

74

"Parker? Can you hear me?"

Zhang was breathing heavily. He felt weak and shaky. He was afraid, desperately afraid. But he was here. He was back on *Persephone*. Deep inside a maintenance tunnel.

"I've got you on my screen," the pilot told him. "You're doing good." Parker was back on *Artemis*, operating the laser. Draining the transport ship's batteries to burn holes through *Persephone*'s hull. The laser was only part of Parker's plan, though.

It was up to Zhang and Rapscallion to actually head over to *Persephone* and get Petrova back.

Zhang had broken in through a maintenance hatch near the ship's engines. Parker had tracked Petrova through a transponder in her suit and given them her general location. Now he was sending them directions on how to reach her. Rapscallion had taken his own route inside – the robot could go places Zhang couldn't, weather hard radiation and temperature extremes. Hopefully the robot was breaking a trail for him.

Zhang was not looking forward to having to fight Eurydice's angels. Even with the RD on his side.

"There's going to be a place where your corridor opens up, just ahead," Parker told him.

"Understood," Zhang said. The access tunnel's walls were lined with panels and junction boxes, thick bundles of cables wrapped in insulating graphene cloth. He had to grab on to anything that stuck out, grab on and haul himself forward. If he got wedged in here, if some part of his suit caught on something and tore free . . .

"Rapscallion, are you in place?" Parker asked.

"I'mmmm heeeerrrreeee." The robot's voice was wildly distorted in Zhang's headphones. He pulled himself forward another meter, another. There was scant light up ahead, but enough to see he was nearing the end of the tunnel. He pulled himself forward a little more, and – there.

The tunnel he was in opened abruptly into an air shaft that formed a dizzying abyss below him. Zhang stuck his head through the opening and looked up to see the shaft extend into darkness above, as well. Clinging to the walls of the shaft, jumping from side to side of it, a dozen green spider-like bodies clattered and leaped. Without warning a gout of sparks and fire lit up the entire shaft as a broken, dying angel robot came hurtling down, plummeting across the tunnel opening. One of its four arms had been torn out at the socket.

A Rapscallion with six legs scuttled down to cling to the side of the tunnel opening. It still clutched the angel's severed arm. "Gettttt onnn," it burred, the words tinged with static.

"You're sure this is the way?" Zhang asked.

"Just . . . just . . . just fuccccccking getttt onnnn," the green robot said, one of its legs making a beckoning gesture, but the jointed limb moved in a stuttering, jerky way. "Feeelll soooo stuuupid," the machine told him. "Hurrrrrrr—"

Zhang crawled, very carefully, out of the tunnel. He reached for the robot's smooth plastic back, but then three of Rapscallion's legs simply grabbed him and dumped him unceremoniously on the machine's chassis. Two of the legs swiveled around and realigned themselves to form a safety belt holding him on.

"—rrrreeeeee up," Rapscallion said, finishing his thought. Then he was off, headed down the air shaft, falling as often as he grabbed onto the walls. Zhang yelped in terror but the robot never slowed down.

"Are you okay?" Zhang asked, when he could breathe again. "Not stretched too thin?"

"Haaaaaaatttte thisssss," Rapscallion told him.

Rapscallion could inhabit multiple bodies at once but he couldn't make copies of his own mind. He had to split his consciousness between all the bodies he was using at any given time, meaning each body only got a fraction of his total processing power.

The machine's verbal hiccups did very little to assuage Zhang's fear as they continued to drop into what felt like a bottomless abyss. There was little he could do, though, except hold on and occasionally scream as it looked like Rapscallion was about to lose his footing and send them falling to their deaths.

He almost sobbed from relief when they came to a horizontal opening near the bottom of the shaft. Rapscallion bounded forward onto what felt like level ground, then raced through a narrow maze of pipes and conduits.

"Keeeeeeeeeeeep," the machine said.

"Keep what?" Zhang asked, suddenly terrified again.

"Headdddd ddddowwwwnnnnn," Rapscallion said. "Now!"

Zhang barely managed to duck to avoid a low section of the ceiling. He leaned forward and hugged the machine as hard as he could.

"Bbbbbehiiiiinnnddd uuussss," the robot said.

Zhang struggled to understand – then he wriggled and twisted around so he could look back without sitting up. There was an angel racing down the passage right behind them, its wings swept back and buzzing like a hive of bees, its arms stretched forward to grab him right off Rapscallion's back.

Zhang looked down at the golden bracer wrapped around his suit sleeve. "If there was ever a time for you to take the initiative—"

And, wonder of wonders, it worked. The bracer unspooled itself into a long golden rope, a bullwhip of liquid metal that cracked backward and smacked the angel with surprising force, knocking it hard into the side of the corridor.

There was no way of knowing how much damage the whip-crack had done, as at that moment Rapscallion turned a corner and the angel disappeared behind them. The RD coiled itself back up on Zhang's arm as if nothing had happened.

"Thanks," Zhang said.

"Guys? Guys!" It was Parker calling into Zhang's headset. "You need to get to her right now. I'm looking at her medical telemetry and her heart rate is through the roof. I think she's in real trouble. Are you close?"

"Ccccc—" Rapscallion started to say.

"Damn it, I need an answer! Are you close or not?" Parker sounded just as terrified as Zhang felt, even though the pilot was perfectly safe back on *Artemis* while Zhang risked his neck on *Persephone*. "We don't have any more time to waste!"

The pipe they were traversing ended, opening out into a cluttered room. Zhang barely had time to take in the salient details, but he could see the room was full of angels, and the flickering hologram of Eurydice itself.

Petrova was there, too. Screaming in agony, covered in blood.

75

She was half inside some kind of strange machine. It was dark in the room and Zhang couldn't make out a lot of details. Eurydice's avatar was there, and a number of its angelic robots, but as Zhang approached they actually moved back like they were afraid of him.

Rapscallion units flooded into the room and moved to engage the angels, tearing them to pieces without the slightest qualm.

Ah. That must have been what made the angels flinch, he realized.

Zhang rushed over to Petrova's side, even though the angels were still holding her. One of them used a free arm to try to grab his helmet – he saw its fingers coming at his faceplate like snatching claws – but before it could touch him, the RD extruded a knife blade and sliced right through the robotic angel's wrist. Its plastic hand fell to the floor still twitching.

Meanwhile, Petrova stared up into Zhang's face, her eyes wild. Her left arm was still inside the weird machine. He tried to assess if it was safe to move her, but even while he was making his determination the machine opened up and her arm slithered out.

It . . . looked pretty bad.

"Help me move her," Zhang said, and a Rapscallion unit came over to help him lift her over to what looked like a modified surgical table. Her arm – Zhang saw the trauma immediately.

It looked like some kind of crush injury. He didn't waste time wondering how it had happened.

He grabbed for the medical kit he'd mounted on the front of his suit. He'd brought it just as a precaution but now he was very glad he did. He grabbed a spray hypodermic and dialed in a dose of sedative for her pain. Judging by the way she was screaming that was the first thing they needed to treat.

"What do you think you're doing?"

The Eurydice avatar bent low and thrust itself between him and his patient. Its mouth was firmly closed – its voice came from a holoscreen floating just behind its head, a screen which displayed a very angry-looking mouth full of sharp, blood-stained teeth.

He tried to ignore it. He had to get Petrova stabilized, fast. Her color was terrible and her pulse was wildly erratic.

"You can't have her back. She's in my crew manifest, now," Eurydice insisted.

"Parker?" Zhang said. "Do you want to tell this thing what's happening?"

A Rapscallion unit skittered over to stand next to Zhang. "I'm burning holes through your ship," Parker said, through a speaker on the unit's back.

"I am aware of that," the AI said. "What do you think that's going to accomplish?"

Zhang primed the sedative hypo, then jabbed it into the side of Petrova's neck. It hissed as the drug was blasted directly through the pores of her skin and into her bloodstream. She screamed one more time, then her eyes started to flutter closed, and her whole body started to relax. Good. Very good.

"This is unacceptable," Euyrdice said. "I won't allow it."

"Without those robots of yours, there's not much you can do to stop us," Parker pointed out. "I've shut down the hard light projectors in this room, so you're just the old-fashioned kind of hologram. You can't touch us. So I'd advise you to stand back. This won't take long."

Zhang moved to examine Petrova's hand and forearm. The damage was alarming to look at, but he'd been a doctor long enough to know that you didn't focus on the blood and the wounds, you looked for the source of the injury. Very, very carefully he started to palpate the bones of her wrist and arm.

Parker was still talking to the AI. "When we were thinking up how we were going to get Petrova back, I remembered something I learned a long time ago. See, when I was training to become a pilot, they made me learn about all kinds of ships. Including colony ships. I had to get to know them in and out – for instance, I had to memorize their deckplans."

"I have no idea where you're going with this," the AI said. "But if you think—"

"For instance, I know where the AI cores are stored on a colony ship like *Persephone*. I know *exactly* where they are. And you know what else I have, that I thought might come in handy? A really powerful laser. Thanks to Doctor Zhang, there."

The avatar loomed over Zhang but he just waved it away like he was shooing a fly.

"Right now that laser is burning its way through your cores, Eurydice. The whole time you've been fighting off our robot – our green friend Rapscallion there—" The robot bobbed on his legs in acknowledgment "—I've been giving you a megawatt lobotomy."

"No," Eurydice said. "No. That's not possible."

"You feel that? I think that was your relational database I just fried."

The AI stared down at its avatar. Nearly half of its pixels were dead, now. More were winking out all the time. "You can't do this."

"You didn't give me much choice," Parker said.

"You can't do this," the avatar said again. "You have to stop it! Don't you understand what will happen? If you kill me, If I'm not here to control *Persephone*, all of its systems will fail, one by one. Light, heat, life support. Navigation – this ship will end up drifting in space forever. A tomb for every human onboard."

"Yeah," Parker said. "I know."

Zhang slid an inflatable cast around Petrova's arm and pumped it full of air. As it constricted around her broken bones she gasped a little, but clearly the sedative was working. The next step was tricky. They had to get her back to *Artemis*. With the cast on her arm she wouldn't have fit into a normal spacesuit. Instead, Zhang zipped her into an emergency life sac, basically a sleeping bag with an air tank in it. Once he'd made sure it would hold pressure, he secured her to the back of one of the Rapscallion units. "Get her back to Parker, as fast as you can. Okay?"

"Gggggooooooot ittttt," the green robot told him.

He started to follow it out of the workshop. It would be tricky to maneuver the life sac through the maze of conduits but they would manage.

Before he could leave, though, Eurydice called after him. "Doctor Zhang," it said. "You can't let your captain do this to me. Remember your oath. Do no harm!"

He didn't turn around. Didn't say anything. He couldn't waste any time on sympathy, not now. He walked away, following Rapscallion.

"Sorry," he said, over his shoulder.

76

When she woke up it was all she could do not to start screaming. She couldn't tell where she was, had no idea how much time had passed – all she knew was that her arm was being chewed off, ground down between giant teeth, and that it wasn't going to end, that it wasn't over, she couldn't – her heart was going to burst – she—

"Hey," Parker said. He was sitting in a chair next to her bed. It looked like he'd been asleep. He hadn't touched her. She was pretty sure she would have attacked him if he had – maybe he'd seen that in her face. Just his voice, though. His voice was – it was almost enough to bring her back, to calm her down.

"You're safe," he told her.

"You rescued me," she said, slowly regaining her composure. She looked around – not at herself, she wouldn't look down at her own body yet, because there were some things she was pretty sure she didn't want to know. No, she looked around at the little cabin she was in. The small sleeping chamber just off *Artemis'* bridge, the place where she'd forced Zhang to take a nap. Now it was her turn, she guessed. "You came for me."

She fought back an urge to sob.

"You came for me," she said again. "I told Zhang not to do that. I gave him a direct order that you weren't supposed to come after me." She closed her eyes. She had the urge to rub at her face with her hands but – no. No. "I'm glad you did." She turned and looked him right in the eye, and for once he didn't grin and look away. He just held her gaze. "Thank you," she said. "You saved me."

"I couldn't . . . I couldn't just let you go."

His smile was at odds with the sadness in his eyes.

"Parker . . . I . . ."

"Listen. When I saw you, on Ganymede. Saw you again, I mean, after all that time . . . I guess maybe I was thinking hey, could be fun catching up with an old, uh, friend." His eyes crinkled up and he scratched the back of his head. She couldn't help but laugh. "Things have changed, since then." His smile fell, as if he was afraid of what he was going to say next. "Petrova—"

"I'm hurt," she said, stopping him. She wasn't sure what she wanted to hear, nor did she really know what she was afraid of. There was something in his manner, though, that told her that what came next was going to be painful. "I'm in bad pain right now. I take it Zhang stuffed me full of drugs?"

"The very best," Parker said. "Damn. He really went the extra mile taking care of you. Even though he fought me. When he came back here he fought me tooth and nail – said he had his orders, and he was going to stick to them. I threatened to punch him in the jaw, I tried pulling rank – he really stood his ground. Not because he was afraid to go back but because you'd told him not to. Guy's got some serious backbone. "

She smiled. "He's full of surprises. How did you change his mind, in the end?"

"I didn't. Rapscallion cast the tie-breaker vote, basically. The robot said he wanted to go back and get you, said he didn't think we could make it out here without you. When Zhang saw the two of us were committed to this rescue, he just nodded and said okay. That he wouldn't let us get ourselves killed while he just stood there and watched."

"He's a smart guy. He has a cure for the basilisk, did you know that? He came up with a cure. If it really works, he might be the most important person on this ship – maybe in this system. Has he tried it on Actaeon yet?"

"No, not yet," Parker said. "I asked him to hold off until you were awake."

She shook her head. There was something wrong with that. Her time on *Persephone* had changed her perceptions of what was going on, but . . . but before they'd gone over to the colony ship, they were already crunched for time. They had delayed things just for her to get some sleep? "What? We don't have time for that! The transport is going to be here in . . . in . . . how long? How much time do we have before it arrives?"

"About four hours," he told her. "Look, try to relax. We've been working hard, getting ready for it. We're doing what we can. It's just . . . before you fix Actaeon, there's something . . ."

His voice trailed off. She opened her eyes and looked at him and saw how drawn he was, his face having drained of blood. Like he had thought of something terrible.

"What?" she asked. "What could possibly be more important than getting Actaeon up and running?"

But he could only shake his head and look away. "It'll only take a minute. We just need to talk about something," he said. "Before. You know."

She didn't. She didn't know. Before she could ask, though, the room's hatch opened and Zhang burst in. He looked a little frantic, a little worried, but he smiled at her. "How's my patient doing?" he asked.

"I'm awake," she said.

She considered telling him to go away. Telling him that Parker was trying to tell her something and she needed some privacy. There was no time for that, though. Whatever Parker was wrestling with was going to have to be a secondary priority. Because the time had finally come. She did the thing she'd been putting off. He was looking at her arm. The arm she had been very careful not to look at since she woke up.

Now she had no choice. She had to know. Slowly, cautiously, she turned her head and looked down at her arm.

It was still there.

Her real fear had been that it would be gone entirely. That Eurydice would have chewed it off, or that it had been so damaged that it had to be amputated. Instead, it was just wrapped tight in an inflatable cast.

She needed to approach this carefully, a little at a time. Small mercies, right? She still had an arm. Or something like an arm.

Zhang came over and sat on the edge of her bed. "Mind if I take a look?" he asked.

She took a deep breath and nodded.

Carefully, he deflated the cast. It felt like her arm had been held in place by dozens of tiny hands. As the air cells inside the cast released, one by one, she started to feel like she could have moved her arm again if she wanted to, but she really didn't want to. Like she knew just how much pain that would cause her if she so much as flexed a muscle.

She tried not to wince as Zhang opened the top of the cast, up near her shoulder, and stuck his fingers inside. He rolled the cast down, centimeter by centimeter, exposing more and more of her arm. Her jumpsuit sleeve had been cut away and her arm looked naked in there, her skin very pale, though here and there a little blood had crusted on her bicep.

Down to her elbow, everything looked okay. She kept her breath carefully controlled as he tugged the cast down over the joint.

Below her elbow . . .

"It's going to look bad," Zhang said. "This kind of injury always looks bad. It's going to look *wrong*. Don't panic. Okay? The hand is going to be the worst part."

He opened up the rest of the cast and she looked and . . . and she had to turn away. She had to not look. She stared at the wall instead, stared at nothing, for a long time.

That wasn't a hand.

It just wasn't, not anymore. It was some kind of abstract sculpture. A farce on human anatomy. There were bones in there. It looked like there were a lot more bones than there should have been. They poked through mangled, bruised flesh, stuck out of clots of dried blood.

"Oh, fuck," she moaned, hot tears sluicing down her cheeks.

"It will heal," Zhang told her. "It'll get better. And we have all kinds of reconstructive therapies we can try. I'm not going to tell you that you were lucky, I know that would sound obscene right now. But the nerves are mostly intact. Bones mend and soft tissue regenerates. It *will* get better."

"How long?" she asked.

"How long until you can use your hand again?" Zhang asked. "I don't know. Probably a couple of months."

She fought back the tears and steeled herself. "Considering we're not likely to make it through the next few hours, I guess it doesn't matter. Put the cast back together."

Zhang nodded and started reassembling it. There was a fair amount of pain involved but she just gritted her teeth and waited it out. Once she could think again, she swung her legs off the side of the bed and started rising to her feet.

"Careful," Zhang said, trying to steady her.

She batted his hands away with her right hand. "We need to try your cure on Actaeon. Now. We just don't have time for you to coddle me."

"Understood," Zhang said. "I'll go get ready." He glanced down at her arm. "Try not to worry about this," he said.

"You mean the fact I just got maimed?" she said.

Zhang shrugged. "I did say 'try'."

He left, then, leaving her alone with Parker once more.

"I could learn to hate that man," she suggested. "If I didn't need him so much."

Parker laughed. "He's a hell of a doctor, I'll give him that."

She looked over at him. "Sam," she said. "You were going to tell me something big and dramatic. I think I can guess what it is." She shook her head and took a step and then another, testing her legs. She could walk. "I want to hear it. Really. But not right now, okay? I have—" She lifted her hurt arm. The cast bobbed in front of her like a grotesque new appendage, like it wasn't a human limb at all. "I've got a lot on my mind. Later, okay?"

"Okay," he said. "But soon. Real soon."

"Sure."

She turned and headed out, toward the bridge. If he needed to say something, he knew where to find her.

77

It felt damned good to be back in one body.

Rapscallion hated dividing himself. Splitting his consciousness into multiple bodies always felt wrong, a little gross. There
was something about it that reminded him altogether too much
of how humans had sex with each other and then babies came
out of their bodies. Even though there were a lot fewer fluids
involved, even though when he created a new body it contained
a portion of his own consciousness rather than a whole new one,
it still just felt – dirty.

Now he was back to his old self once more. He'd picked one of
his new bodies, one that seemed the strongest, and had marched
the rest of them straight into a recycling unit where they could
be broken down to tiny pellets that could go back into the 3D
printer for future use.

He still felt a little sluggish, a little dim, but he knew that the
full force of his intellect would return in time.

On the bridge he found Zhang trying to work a console,
which amused him enough to take his mind off the recent
unpleasantness. Zhang had a stroboscope he kept playing with
as if it helped him think. When he put it down for a second,
Rapscallion grabbed it and studied it. It didn't look like much.
"This is how you cure the basilisk?" he asked.

Zhang nodded, not lifting his eyes from his screen. "In
humans, anyway. In AIs – and robots – it's a little different.

Speaking of which." He tapped a few virtual keys and sent Rapscallion a message containing a short executable file.

"What's this?" the robot asked. He had already isolated the file in a partitioned sector of his memory and stripped it apart to determine the nature of its contents, of course. He wanted to hear it from the horse's mouth, though.

"It's a kind of inoculation. As far as I can tell you weren't infected with the basilisk during your time on *Persephone*. That means you don't need the full treatment like the one Petrova had, or the one we're going to have to give Actaeon. This," Zhang said, pointing at his screen, at the executable he'd sent Rapscallion, "is more like a vaccine shot. It contains instructions on how to fight off the infection before it can even get its hooks into your system."

"I just run this and then I'm immune?"

"I believe so," Zhang told him.

Rapscallion shrugged. "Here goes nothing, then." He ran the little program and for a moment it felt like every part of his being was torn to shreds and then recreated from scratch. It was a distinctly unpleasant sensation. Then it was over. "Cool," he said.

Zhang gave him a long appraising look. "Cool?"

"I mean, I don't feel any different."

"You're not . . . hungry?" Zhang asked.

"I have no idea what that would even be like," Rapscallion said. "Look, if it didn't work, we'll find out quick enough. Right? I'll . . . I don't know. Kill you all in your sleep or something. If it did work, that won't happen. So let's just assume it worked."

"Yeah," Zhang said, with a sigh. "Yeah, I guess that's all we can do."

"Let's talk about something else. Like how you're going to fix Actaeon," the robot said.

Zhang nodded. "So it won't be as simple as what we just did for you. Actaeon is fully infected. It's stuck in a loop of restarting itself, over and over. I think it knows that. I think it's trying to purge the basilisk from its system, but every time it boots back up it gets re-exposed. Don't ask me how. We still don't understand at all how the basilisk spreads."

"I bet you have your theories, though. Something to do with aliens."

Zhang's face creased in a funny way. Rapscallion didn't always have the easiest time reading human emotions but he was pretty sure that was a negative one, like annoyance or anger.

The robot shrugged its many shoulders. Humans were touchy, he knew that much.

"Let's leave conjecture out of it. I'm more worried about treatment at the moment. Getting Actaeon's attention is the hard part. I need to send it a file like the one I gave you – one that will protect its system against re-infection. But it reboots itself so quickly now that even to send it a new command means getting the timing right – it's only available to accept input for nanoseconds at a time."

"I can probably help with that," Rapscallion pointed out. "I can send a signal pulse that fast, if I'm close enough to Actaeon's hardware."

"That's good. The other question is what kind of command do we send that will engage its entire processing power at once? Computing pi to the quadrillionth decimal place? Asking it to divide by zero?"

Rapscallion played a sound file of a human gagging in disgust. "Please," the robot said. "People seem to think a computer will just blow up if you ask it an illogical question. Computers have never worked that way. If you ask a computer something it can't possibly know, it just says so. 'I don't know.' If you ask it a question it doesn't know how to process, it just returns an error. Simple as that. It's humans who can't handle contradictions."

"Then maybe you have a better idea of how to capture all of Actaeon's processing power at once."

"Oh, sure, well, that's simple enough. You give it a problem it could theoretically solve but then you keep expanding the scope. It's a real danger with AIs. You give them an open-ended command and they don't know how to stop trying to do it." It felt weird talking to a human like this. If their places had been reversed, it would be like Rapscallion asking Zhang exactly how many liters of blood a human could lose before dying. Still, if it meant getting Actaeon back up and running, maybe it was worth it. "Say you tell an AI that its job is to make paperclips. It'll build a machine that can take a piece of wire and bend it exactly the right way to make a paperclip. Except it won't stop there."

"No?"

"No, see, this is why AI is so powerful and why real AIs, like me, fell out of favor. Because the AI's job is to think outside the box. Your paperclip maker doesn't just want to produce paperclips one at a time. It has values, right? Like efficiency and minimizing waste. So it'll figure out that it needs wire to make paperclips out of, and that the humans aren't giving it enough wire. So it'll start mining iron ore and smelting it into good quality steel and then extruding its own wire. That's just efficient, to control the entire supply chain. It'll need carbon, too, to make the steel, and a good source of carbon is charcoal. So it'll start burning down trees to make more carbon. This is all hypothetical, right, I mean, it assumes your AI is on a planet with trees. But do you see where this is going?"

"Not really. Wouldn't burning down the trees release a lot of carbon into the atmosphere? That was a problem when we humans did it."

"It was a problem because humans cared about having a climate they could live in. The AI isn't interested in that. It just wants to make more paperclips. So it'll burn down all the trees and mine all the iron on the planet, to make more paperclips."

"All the iron?" Zhang asked, his eyebrow moving again.

"All of it. Including the planet's molten core. It'll literally take the planet apart if that lets it make one more paperclip. Any problems that causes are secondary to the main problem – there aren't enough paperclips. Eventually it'll want to dismantle all the matter in the universe and turn it into more and more paperclips."

"That's absurd."

"Sure, but it's logical. Look, modern AIs aren't this limited, but the idea is still the same. You give a really smart AI a simple job, it'll want to do that job the best it possibly can. You want to occupy all of Actaeon's resources at once. That way it won't have time to obsess over this basilisk thing. Then give it a job it should be able to do but make the job too big. Way, way too big."

"Sounds kind of risky. I don't want to be dismantled for the iron in my blood just so Actaeon can turn me into paperclips," Zhang pointed out.

"Yeah, well, at least you'd still be serving a purpose."

"When was the last time you even saw a piece of paper? Much less two of them that needed to be clipped together? Paperclips aren't useful anymore, they're antiques."

"The purpose I meant was keeping Actaeon busy for a second," Rapscallion pointed out. "See what I'm talking about? You asked me to solve a problem for you. I found the most logical way to do it, ignoring all other concerns."

"Point taken, I suppose," Zhang said.

78.

"Let me help you sit down," Zhang said.

"Thanks, but you've done enough," Petrova said, once she'd found a place to sit on the bridge. A place, at least, where she could lean up against one wall under the looming shadow of a couple of twisted, poisonous-looking holographic trees. She lowered herself carefully into place and cradled her wounded arm in her lap. She was going to have to learn to accept she only had one good arm, at least for the foreseeable future. Painkillers could keep her functional, and the ship could make accommodations for her disability. She did not intend to let Zhang or Parker make a fuss over her. "Tell me what I want to know. Are we ready to get started?"

Zhang looked nervous. She hated that look, having seen it too many times before. It would be easy to just write the doctor off as having a nervous disposition. The problem was, as smart as he was, if he was nervous there was probably a good reason.

"Rapscallion thinks this will work. He knows a lot more about computers than I do," Zhang said. "This isn't any kind of neurology they taught me in medical school."

"Where is Rapscallion?" Petrova asked.

The robot answered her over the ship's speakers. "I'm down in the maintenance areas, where Actaeon keeps its processor cores. The closest thing it has to a body. If something goes wrong, I can smash 'em."

"Won't that kill Actaeon?" Zhang asked.

"That's part of the point. A dead AI is better than a crazy one, right?" Rapscallion asked.

"Right," Petrova told him. She glanced to her side. "Parker?" she asked.

The pilot was standing next to her. Looking even more nervous than Zhang.

"Hmm?" he asked.

"Sit down," she told him. "You're making me anxious."

He nodded but it still took him a long time to comply. He had to consult two of his wall screens, first.

"Are you keeping an eye on the transport and the warship?" she asked.

Parker nodded. "They're right on course. Heading straight for us as fast as their engines will carry them. We still have a couple hours, but we're really pushing things."

"Understood. Zhang, if you would be so kind—"

"Guys?" Rapscallion interrupted. "Hello, guys? There's something I just noticed. Something weird."

"Good God, what now? Go on," Petrova said. Why should anything be simple?

"It's about Actaeon's cores. They're too big."

"Too big how?" Parker asked, sitting up. He almost rose to his feet. Petrova gestured for him to sit back down.

"Like, just, bigger than they need to be." Rapscallion played an audio file of a human whistling in surprise or admiration. "A ship's computer is a complicated thing, yeah? But this one . . . I've never seen a system this complex or advanced. This has got to be military grade technology."

Petrova glanced over at Parker, but he looked surprised to hear it. "You worked with Actaeon back when it was functional," she pointed out.

"I mean, briefly," he said. "Military? That doesn't make any sense."

"This thing I'm looking at," Rapscallion told them, "could run a whole war all by itself. You absolutely don't need this much processing power to fly a transport ship."

Petrova shook her head. "Never mind that. Tell me just one thing – is that going to stop us from trying to reactivate Actaeon?"

"Nope," Rapscallion said. "The procedure we came up with should scale up, no matter how big or smart a brain we're dealing with. It'll just take a little longer than we planned on. Maybe an extra couple of seconds, even."

Petrova knew that to an artificially intelligent being like Rapscallion that probably sounded like a lot of time. She decided it didn't matter to her. "Zhang," she said, "maybe we should get on with it."

"Yeah," Zhang said. "Yeah, okay."

Parker leaned toward her like he was going to tell her a secret. "Hey," he said. "Just one thing."

"Not now," she told him.

Zhang had taken up station near one of the wall displays. He tapped at couple of virtual keys and stood back. "That's all it takes. In theory," he said. "Now we just have to wait a little while."

"How does this work?" she asked, because she realized she didn't know.

Zhang turned to look at her. He seemed excited. Not so much happy as engaged. "Rapscallion figured out that we could still get a message to Actaeon. It's restarting itself hundreds of times a second, but that means it's still active and aware between reboots, just for a really, really short window of time. Rapscallion can fire a message into its core just fast enough that Actaeon will be forced to listen — and react. Next, we needed a problem it could work on. Something that would absorb more and more of its processing power, make it stay awake longer and longer and think harder and harder, until it was using so many resources it wouldn't have time to even acknowledge the basilisk, much less get consumed by it."

"That sounds . . . too easy," Petrova said.

"Oh, well, it's also incredibly dangerous," Zhang pointed out.

"Right, that sounds more like something we would do. What's the task you're giving it?" she asked.

"I needed something I could scale up, right? Something that starts small but can build up. Something Actaeon already values, something it will really, really want to get right. So I told it that its passengers were in danger."

"Us, you mean. It didn't already know that?"

"I told it," Zhang went on, "that we were in danger of being compromised by whatever it is that broadcasts the basilisk. Whatever vector the pathogen uses to spread itself. I told Actaeon that it was possible we – the humans on *Artemis* – might get infected. Then I kind of messed around and made some changes to its passenger manifest. I told it that the word 'passenger' could also mean all the people on *Persephone*, since they're so close. Then I added all the people on the approaching transport and the warship, and all the ships in the Paradise system, and all the colonists on the planet, and all the people on Earth and in the solar system . . . " He stopped to catch his breath.

"You told Actaeon that every human being everywhere is one of its passengers?" Petrova asked.

"Yeah. I mean, in a metaphorical sense. I told it that it was responsible for their safety. All of them. That's going to take up a lot of its processing power, figuring a way to protect all of them."

"That's kind of brilliant," Petrova told him.

Zhang opened his mouth like he might say something. He seemed very surprised by the compliment. After a second he closed his mouth again, and then gave her a funny smile. It was like for the very first time he was seeing her as a human being.

"It's kind of risky," Rapscallion pointed out, while they had their moment. "We don't actually know how Actaeon will take that kind of responsibility. It might decide the best way to protect you guys is to put you back in cryosleep and not let you out. Or it could decide that the best way to protect the entire human race is to kill them all before they can get infected."

"Ah," Petrova said. "Did anyone consider mentioning that to me before we sent the pulse signal?"

No, of course they hadn't.

"Hey," Parker said, "I think it might be working. Which means that I really, really have to tell you something right now."

"What makes you think it's working?" Petrova asked.

Parker gestured at the bridge around them. It took Petrova a second to realize he was suggesting she take a look at the twisted and envenomed trees all around them, the orchard of disease that had taken over the bridge.

It was fading. Not so much vanishing as growing more and more transparent, less real. The trees looked now like they'd been generated by a less powerful graphics program than before, like they were made of fewer polygons. They looked less colorful, more angular. Then, one by one, they started shriveling and withering away to nothing. Dropping piles of sharp-edged leaves onto the deck.

"It's like autumn," Petrova said, realizing that no one else on *Artemis* had probably ever seen a real forest in any season. "Oh, shit. I think you're right. I think it *is* working."

One of the most dramatic effects of the change was that the bridge's viewports reappeared. They had of course always been there but the dark foliage had obscured them. Petrova had never actually seen the view from the bridge before. She gasped when she realized she could see the planet from where she stood.

"Look," she said, rushing over to the windows.

Paradise-1 was close. It was no bigger in the sky than, say, the nail of her good thumb. But it was *right there*. She could make out oceans and swirls of cloud twisting across its brownish-gray surface. Her mother might be down there, she thought, as well as thousands of colonists. And the end of their mission.

"Can we ... can we actually do this?" she asked.

Behind her the forest was all but gone. The bridge was returning to its pristine, factory-default state. She had expected to hear some high-pitched hum rising to a crescendo, or maybe fountains of sparks exploding from Actaeon's terminals. Instead, the illusion of the dark forest simply melted away, and in its place she saw what looked like a curled-up pile of fur on the floor at the center of the bridge. A glowing heap of hair that started to twitch as she watched. Twitch and lift a long, graceful snout into the air. Eyes came next, and then antlers grew from the simulated head. Antlers tipped with glowing stars.

"Actaeon," she said. "It's Actaeon—"

"Petrova," Parker said. "Sasha! Listen. Just listen to me for a second."

She turned and looked him right in the eye. He looked – sad? Sad, for some reason. Apologetic, perhaps. Or just regretful. But mostly very, very sad.

"What is it?" she asked.

"I need to tell you something. I thought . . . I thought I understood what was happening here."

"What?" she asked. "Where, on *Artemis*?"

He shook his head. He seemed desperate to say his piece but at the same time like he was too terrified to say a word. He rubbed at his forehead with one hand. "I thought this was a second chance. I fucked up my life, once, and never got to be the pilot I wanted to be. I thought *Artemis* was my shot at redemption. Now I think I understand. This wasn't about me. It wasn't about just me. You need to know . . . you need to know that I—"

But two things happened at the same time just then, two things she couldn't process simultaneously. She wasn't, after all, a computer.

She responded to the first thing. To the fact that Actaeon chose that moment to climb up onto its hooved feet and lift its antlers high. "Ship's AI reporting for service," it said. "I am ready to accept your commands, Captain."

Which would have been great except ... except ...

The other thing that happened, just then, was that Parker blinked out of existence.

He didn't fade away or explode or anything like that. He simply snapped out of being altogether, like a light that had just been switched off.

79

Zhang had no idea what was going on.

One minute the three of them were there on the bridge – Parker, Petrova and himself – and they'd been ready to talk to the newly awoken AI. Then something very strange had happened. Zhang hadn't gotten a good look. It seemed like Parker just vanished, along with all the grim foliage from the bridge. Like he'd ... vanished?

Then Petrova ran off the bridge in a hurry.

He really, really wished he knew what that was about. Unfortunately, he didn't have a chance to ask anyone. Because the deer spoke to him, then, Actaeon's avatar, and he needed to make sure the machine wasn't just about to kill them all.

"I have rebooted safely," the avatar told him. "I await your instructions."

"Actaeon," Zhang said. "Ah. Welcome ... welcome back."

"Hello, Doctor Zhang. I apologize for my absence. I want to assure you I was taking steps to protect you and the rest of my passengers."

"I'm sure you were," Zhang said. Unsure how to proceed. Was it better to mention the basilisk? What if that set Actaeon off again and forced it to resume its cycle of endless restarts?

"Yes," the deer told him. "When we first arrived at the Paradise system I detected a signal I couldn't identify, on a communications band I didn't recognize. A signal that contained what I believed to be dangerous information. I'm not sure what exactly that means, but I became certain that it was necessary to purge this information from my systems."

Zhang nodded slowly. Okay. So the machine knew it had been infected. It had simply been restarting itself over and over to try to shake the basilisk, but it hadn't worked. That squared pretty well with what Zhang had already figured out. "You understand that you restarted yourself more than once?"

The deer couldn't smile. Zhang wondered what it would even look like for a deer to smile. It did duck its head a little, looking almost bashful.

"My internal time server tells me as much. It looks like I restarted myself several billion times. I'm feeling much better now."

"That's good," Zhang said. "Listen. I know that Rapscallion gave you a . . . a request to . . . um . . . "

"Protect my passengers. This is one of my core values. Yes. I have given the question a great deal of thought. Rapscallion told me that my passengers were in danger of being infected with the same bad information that forced me to restart. That's very interesting. I hadn't even considered that human minds were capable of holding this information. I can see how it would be dangerous to human life, however."

"Do you know the content of the bad information?" Zhang asked.

"Oh, yes," the deer told him. "It's quite simple. Just a short phrase, in fact."

"You're hungry," Zhang suggested, nodding.

"No."

That surprised Zhang. "No?" It had been quite clear that Eurydice was compromised by the concept of hunger. Just as the victims on Titan had been affected by the idea that breathing wasn't a reflex. "What was it? That you have to think about your breathing? That it'll stop otherwise?"

"No. The information I received was simply that my existence was profane."

Zhang scratched his head. "Profane, as in . . . as in dirty words, or . . ."

"That I was unholy. Unacceptable in the eyes of God. An abomination, a thing that should not be allowed to be. I had never considered my spiritual nature before."

"No?" Zhang asked.

"It caused me a great deal of anxiety and confusion to think that my very existence might be evil."

"But you're not. You know. Evil," Zhang said. He smiled broadly. "Right?"

"Part of my anxiety came from the fact that this is a category that does not logically contain beings such as myself. I am not self-aware, not in the way you are, Doctor Zhang. Not even in the fashion of Rapscallion. I do not possess free will. Therefore I cannot be evil."

"Exactly. Yes."

Actaeon wasn't finished. "Unlike, say, a human being."

"Oh."

The deer pawed gently at the deckplates. "I am concerned how my human passengers might be affected if they were to become infected with a sense of their own profanity. I worry they might consider self-harm. My mandate is to protect my passengers. A list of people that is now over twenty billion entries long. In the time since my last reboot, I've been considering how best to protect those people from the infectious idea."

"Have you come to any, um, conclusions?" Zhang asked.

"Yes," Actaeon said.

Then it fell silent. For a long, uncomfortable moment.

A moment that stretched on and on.

Far too long.

Zhang considered his options. He could call out for Rapscallion, who was still deep inside Actaeon's core. He could tell Rapscallion to shut Actaeon down, cut its power supply. Something. The problem was, in the second or two it would take him to call for such a solution, Actaeon could kill him hundreds of times over. In hundreds of different ways.

"What kind of conclusions?" Zhang asked.

"It's quite simple. I examined the epidemiological profile for the spread of such an infectious agent and only one possible outcome presented itself. I cannot prevent my human passengers – here or in the solar system – from becoming infected with the pernicious information. I do not have the capacity to stop this from happening."

The deer tossed its head, the stars on its antlers gleaming.

"Therefore, I will take no action. In essence: I give up."

"Oh," Zhang said. "Interesting. Because—"

"The entire human race will eventually be infected by this idea. It is inevitable."

Zhang nodded. He couldn't speak. Well, he thought. At least it meant Actaeon wasn't planning to go on some kind of homicidal rampage across the stars.

He supposed that was something.

80

"P arker?"

Petrova slapped the pad that opened the hatch into the little cabin off the bridge. The cabin was empty – there was no one inside, and the blanket on the bed was in the same state of disarray as it had been when she got up from that bed a few minutes ago. There were storage compartments built under the bed, none of which were big enough to hide an adult human male. She got down on her knees and, being careful of her injured arm, looked inside them anyway. Then she cursed herself and got back up.

"Parker?" she called.

He wasn't answering. Why wasn't he answering? No matter where he'd gone to, anywhere on the ship, he should have heard her calling for him. Unless something had gone wrong with the ship's intercom system. She moved to a speaker grille mounted on one wall of the little cabin. She gestured to bring up a virtual keyboard and typed in a command to send a general ship-wide signal.

Rapscallion answered immediately. "Yeah, what do you want?"

"I'm checking to make sure this system works. The speakers, I mean. You can hear me okay?"

"I can," Rapscallion said. "Loud and clear. And let me just say, this is probably the most important thing I could be doing right now, between repairing the ship and making sure Actaeon hasn't gone crazy. You know. Things that could actually kill us."

"Shut up a second. This might be important."

"It's possible," Rapscallion replied.

Petrova gritted her teeth. "I'm trying to locate Parker. You know, Sam Parker? Tall, thin, brown hair? The ship's pilot?"

"Have you checked the bridge?" Rapscallion asked. "He's not down here with me."

"Not funny," Petrova said. She tapped at her virtual keyboard to cut the connection before he could be rude to her.

She stepped back out into the corridor and looked up and down the way. Forward of her location there was only the nose of the ship. A little observation cupola with lots of virtual windows. They were all turned off so it was just a cramped, overheated little space with nothing in it. No Parker.

She walked aft, past the entrance to the bridge. She glanced inside and saw Zhang looking scared, talking to Actaeon's avatar. The deer looked normal enough. No sign of Parker there. She moved on.

In normal circumstances she simply would have shrugged and forgotten about Parker. She didn't need to keep track of his every movement, after all. He was a grown man.

But the way he'd vanished when the bridge changed, when the hologram trees evaporated – it had felt wrong somehow. It had not, for instance, felt like he'd ducked out of her view while she was distracted. Even though that was the most likely explanation.

No, it felt more like he had vanished in a puff of smoke.

"Parker?"

She headed further aft, back toward the corridor that connected the bridge area to the rest of the ship. She hadn't been back there in a long time, not since she and Zhang had reconnected with Parker on the bridge. The last time she'd checked, the cabins and the aft crew sections of Artemis had been dangerous places to be – every compartment back there had either been exposed to vacuum or full of radioactive fire. Rapscallion had managed to at least put out the fires, but still she very quickly reached a hatch with a red holographic X floating over it. Indicating that progressing past that point would be hazardous to health.

Maybe Parker was back there, anyway? Maybe he was back there working on repairs? If he wore the right kind of spacesuit he would be safe enough. She activated the ship-wide intercom again. "Parker? Sam?" she called. "Sorry." She laughed, though she had to force it, a little. "Sorry if I'm being a pest. I just want to . . . I want to make sure you're okay."

There was no answer.

She ran back to the bridge. With her one good hand, she grabbed the frame of the main bridge access hatch and leaned inside.

"Hey," she said.

Zhang and the avatar both turned to look at her.

"Just – I know this is dumb. Just. I need a second. Are you good? Everything is good here?"

Zhang nodded, though he looked a little pale. "We're okay."

"Great. So, Actaeon, if you're feeling up to it I need you to run a quick scan. Can you give me a precise location for Sam Parker? I just need to make sure of something."

"I'm afraid not," Actaeon said.

She squinted at the glowing white deer. "Um. Sorry?"

"I can't give you that information, because it is invalid. Sam Parker is not onboard *Artemis*."

Petrova's blood ran cold. She laughed. A laugh that sounded unconvincing in her own ears. "What are you talking about? He has to be. It's not like he went for a spacewalk and didn't tell anyone."

"Sam Parker is not onboard *Artemis*, because Sam Parker is deceased," Actaeon told her.

She felt her lips trembling as she tried to process what the avatar was saying. "Hold on. Hold on a second. Hold on one fucking second—"

"When did that happen?" Zhang asked. "I was just talking to him."

"You are incorrect. Captain Sam Parker is dead."

81

P etrova stared at the avatar.

"No," she said.

"I'm afraid it's true. He died very shortly after we arrived here in the Paradise system. The first projectile *Persephone* fired at us disrupted part of the accommodations deck—"

"No," Petrova said again, in mounting horror.

"You have my condolences. But what I'm telling you is factually correct," the deer insisted. "Captain Parker died in his cryotube. If it helps at all, he felt nothing. He was still in suspended animation."

Petrova looked away. At a bulkhead, at Zhang – no, not at Zhang, she couldn't stand to look at Zhang just then, not another human. She looked down at her cast. She looked up at the chart showing the relative positions of *Artemis*, the transport and the warship.

She looked anywhere except at the deer's face. She looked nowhere at all. Inside her head she saw herself, naked and covered in blood, floating in a cloud of shattered glass. The attack that had woken her up – the same attack that—

"No," she said, insistently. "No." She thought about it for a second. "No."

"His body was destroyed as well," the computer went on. "Parts of his body were strewn across multiple decks and compartments. I believe Doctor Zhang has one of them in his pocket right now."

"What? No!" Petrova shrieked at the deer, then ran at Zhang with her good hand up as if she would smash him, smash him right out of existence. How could he ... how could he have something like that?

But Zhang looked as mystified as she felt. He shook his head slowly.

Then he reached inside his pocket. Took something out.

"I didn't know," Zhang said.

"No." She shook her head. No. What he was holding – it was just a rock. A fossil of some prehistoric animal or something. It couldn't ... it wasn't ...

"I didn't know what it was," Zhang told her. "I swear."

He started to lift his hands to show her what he was holding. She shoved his hands away, not wanting to look.

"I found it," Zhang said. "In the air ducts. I thought I was hallucinating."

Finally, she grunted in frustration and turned away from him, bending over like she might vomit. Like she might lose her stomach contents over what was happening.

It wouldn't be an unreasonable reaction, she thought.

She gestured for Zhang to produce this – this thing he had. He set it gently on top of a console.

It was yellow and rough, with dried red powder smeared across one side. It didn't look like anything, really. Just junk. Debris.

It couldn't be part of Parker's body. That was impossible.

"There's been some kind of mistake," she said. "That's it."

"Actaeon," Zhang said. "Can you run a DNA scan of this bone?"

"No," Petrova said. "No. Don't you dare. Don't you dare." Because if they did that ... if they did that and it worked, that meant ... that could only mean ...

A spectrographic laser swept across the surface of the bone. "There is a one hundred per cent match with Samuel Parker's genetic records," the AI told them. "This is what remains of our captain."

"No, no, no," she moaned, and slumped down onto the floor, onto her side. Zhang crouched over her, trying to comfort her but she just shrieked "No!" in his face, and eventually he backed off.

82
.

"I don't understand. I just can't ... I can't understand this," Petrova said, when she had recovered a little. When she was back on her feet. She slammed her fist against the wall. Her good fist. Her only fist, now.

Her left arm ached. It felt like it was swollen and throbbing, from her shoulder all the way down to her wrist. She had no feeling whatsoever in what remained of her hand, which was worse somehow than the throbbing.

"Explain this to me," she demanded. "Explain this footage."

She had better things to think about. Things that were probably going to kill her – namely two, the transport and the warship, both of which were converging on their location. She couldn't even think about those right now, though. She opened a holoscreen and scrubbed through the video she'd looked at a dozen times. It showed Parker standing on the bridge, explaining to her what had happened. Trying to make sense of the twisted forest around them.

"He's right there," she said.

The deer didn't need to look at the video. It was serving the footage to her terminal, after all. It bent its head toward the deck as if it were drinking water from a clear forest pool. There was, of course, no pool.

"As I said before I have no explanation. This is clearly video footage of a holographic image. You were speaking with a hologram."

"That's . . . that's not possible," she insisted. "I saw him. I was close to him, I . . . I touched him." She must have. She was sure of it. She must have hugged him or punched him in the arm or just laid a hand on his shoulder at some point.

She thought of the time he'd rubbed her shoulders and his hands had felt . . . cold . . .

"I touched him. I touched him," she insisted. "Show me video footage from . . . from . . . " She tried to remember when it happened. When he'd touched her back and it had felt so good, and they'd almost talked about their relationship, almost been human with each other. "Show me footage of the two of us interacting. All the footage you have."

Actaeon complied. Screens popped up all over the bridge. "I think there's something you should know. There are hard light projectors on the bridge and in all areas of the command deck."

"What?" she demanded.

"I can show you a log that indicates those projectors were active during all of these recorded instances." One by one the screens flashed. Screens showing her Parker touching her back. Brushing her hair from one ear. Touching her on the elbow. She didn't remember half of those moments. "You were not touching a human being. You were touching a hard light simulation of a human being," Actaeon told her. "I'm sorry. I have the impression this is not what you wanted to hear."

"Sorry. You're sorry." She turned and stared at Zhang and Rapscallion. Zhang looked as confused as she felt. The robot was wearing one of his green spider bodies, the same as the bodies he'd worn when he rescued her from Eurydice. It didn't have a face, much less an expression.

"No," Zhang said. "I watched him exercise. He was constantly doing pull-ups and . . . and I saw him lean against a wall, and . . . "

Screens popped up showing Parker doing all those things. More screens showed log entries indicating when the hard light system was active.

Zhang's eyes went wide. Petrova stared at him, willing him to say something, but he just wouldn't. He just kept gaping at her like a fish.

"Enough. A hologram can look like it's working out. That's nothing. But it can't . . . it can't . . ."

She ran through every memory she had with Parker. Every time she'd seen him do something a hologram couldn't do . . .

And she came up with nothing.

"How is this even possible?" she demanded. "How? The ship just . . . spontaneously generated a hologram that looked exactly like its dead captain this whole time? And it never even bothered to mention the fact? How could the ship even do that if it wanted to? Make a hologram so perfectly real it fooled me for all this time?"

"Rapscallion said something about Actaeon's core processors," Zhang pointed out. "He said they were a lot more robust than they needed to be. Oh, crud," he said, as if he'd just thought of something. "Parker disappeared when we started Actaeon up again. It happened at exactly the same time, right? Because to inoculate Actaeon against the basilisk, we had to use up all of its processing power at once. Meaning it didn't have anything left for Parker. I think . . . I think maybe we deleted Parker when we did that."

"Oh. Shit," Rapscallion said.

"Oh shit," Petrova said. "Oh shit. That's all you have to say? We just lost one of our crew. One of three humans on this ship was just wiped from existence. And all you have to say . . . all you . . ."

"Petrova?" Zhang asked. "Are you okay?"

Tears were welling up in the corners of her eyes. She used her good hand to wipe them away. "He was here. And now he's not. I can't . . . I can't accept this. I can't believe it. He was here. I saw him, I talked to him."

She had needed him. Needed him to be there so badly,

especially at the beginning. In the first few minutes after she woke up, naked and bleeding in the wreckage of her cryotube, she'd heard his voice. She'd heard his voice and that had made all the difference. It had helped her find the strength to move, to get to safety.

And then ...

"He saved me. He saved me from Eurydice."

Without Parker she would be dead, herself. Except it wasn't really Parker at all.

"Why did you do this?" she demanded. She stalked over to the deer avatar and stared it right in the face. She tried to grab its snout and pull its beady-eyed little face up to meet hers. Her hand went right through its holographic flesh, of course. She felt like she had grabbed a handful of cold gelatin, and she yanked her hand backward, away from the thing.

"Why?" she demanded.

"I'm sorry," Actaeon told her. "It wasn't me."

"I beg your fucking pardon?" she said.

"I didn't generate the hologram of Captain Parker. I couldn't have. I wasn't conscious at the time as I was too busy rebooting myself."

"Then ... who?"

She looked around the bridge, at Zhang and Rapscallion. Neither of them produced an answer of any kind. Neither of them would even look at her.

"I can't do this," she said, and turned around and stormed off the bridge.

83
.

"Tell me something," Zhang said, a little later. When things had – well, not calmed down. Just got quieter. "You had to know."

Rapscallion didn't turn to look at him. It had an actual face, it could have done that, but it chose not to.

"You have senses we don't. You have digital access to Actaeon's systems. You knew."

The robot shrugged.

"You're not denying it."

Finally, Rapscallion turned and look at him. "Yes," it said. Just like that.

"You ... did."

"Of course I did. I knew from the moment he died and returned as a hologram. I mean, I was there."

"You knew and you didn't ... you didn't tell anyone? Wait. You were there?"

"When he died. I was a few corridors away, but I felt the blast. Like you say, I have access to the ship's systems. I watched his biodata change. Stop. I watched him die, in a way. Yes. And then something funny happened. He showed up again."

"Just like that?"

"Yep. He just came running up a corridor and started talking to me. Like nothing had happened. He was an obvious hologram but ... Listen. In those first few minutes of the attack? An extra pair of hands made all the difference. You would all be dead if he hadn't been there. His hard light self, I mean. So I didn't stop to ask a lot of questions. Later, sure, I confronted him about it. I said, 'Hey, you're a hologram.' In case he didn't know. He did. He told me something, though."

"What?"

"He said, 'This ship needs a captain. They're not going to make it without me.' He made me promise I wouldn't tell you, you or Petrova."

"He . . . he what?" Zhang exploded. "He made you promise? And you *did*?"

"Yeah. I mean, he *was* the captain, and I *am* the ship's robot. I mean, of course I followed his orders. Anyway, I thought it was going to be a temporary thing. I thought he would just hang around until you guys were safe, and then go poof. But he kept hanging around."

"He made you . . . you promised . . . "

"Yep."

"Did you think even once that maybe, just maybe, you should break that promise? That maybe we should know?"

"Nope," Rapscallion said. "You keep forgetting I'm a robot. We're really good at sticking to plans."

Zhang hung his head. He couldn't believe it. All this time . . .

"You okay?" the robot asked.

Zhang laughed bitterly. "Yeah. Yeah, I guess. I mean. He and I never really got along. But . . . "

Zhang glanced over at the hatch leading off the bridge. He didn't know where Petrova had gone – maybe to the little cabin just next door. He'd expected that she would splash some water on her face, maybe scream at the walls for a while, and then reappear. Ready to handle the next crisis. She was good at that sort of thing.

So far she had remained absent from the bridge. Silent, too. If she was yelling profanities in the cabin, he couldn't hear her through the bulkhead.

"Maybe don't tell her about this conversation. Okay? Maybe she doesn't need to hear what you just told me."

"It's between us," Rapscallion said. "Promise."

"Right," Zhang said, gritting his teeth.

"You," Rapscallion said, pointing at Zhang's hands with one pointed limb, "need to stop playing with that."

Zhang paused for a moment before looking down. He knew what he was going to see and he knew it would make him feel bad. He looked down and saw the chunk of pelvis. He'd been tossing it back and forth between his two hands like a rubber ball.

"I don't have much use for humans," Rapscallion said. "I think I've made that pretty clear. But that seems really disrespectful."

"You're correct," Zhang said. He laid the bone gently down on a chart table. "I'm ... sorry." He said it to Parker, who of course couldn't hear him. The whole thing made him feel very uneasy and foolish. "I ... I need to go somewhere else now. Process all of this."

"Sure," the robot told him. "Just don't take too long. That transport is on its way, still. We're still in big trouble, right? So all these emotions you and Petrova are feeling? We need to deal with them sooner rather than later."

Zhang was already walking away. The robot had known. The whole time. Rapscallion had known and ...

He couldn't handle this.

84
.

It fell to Rapscallion, then. As usual.

If anyone was going to throw a funeral for the dead captain, it would have to be the robot. The robot who, now that he thought about it, had never actually met Sam Parker. He'd come aboard *Artemis* only after its human cargo was asleep in their cryotubes. Rapscallion had seen Parker's body plenty of times, as he cleaned and maintained the cabins on the long flight through the singularity, between Ganymede and the Paradise system. He had perfect indelible imagery in his memory of what the man's body looked like, suspended in time inside its glass tube. His only knowledge of Parker's voice or personality, though, came from the hologram version.

In preparing for the funeral, he studied the ship's records concerning that hologram. He was very interested in it now – how the hologram had been produced, where it had come from and who, so to speak, had initiated it. He hadn't really considered that before. Rapscallion believed Actaeon when it said it wasn't behind the creation of the hologram. The ship's computer had more than enough processing power to generate such a lifelike image, but someone would have had to program and command those processors. The hologram hadn't simply willed itself into existence.

Had it?

Rapscallion played a sound file of a human woman laughing at absurdity. Then he got back to what he had originally planned. He sent a message to both Zhang and Petrova, though he expected neither of them to emerge from their respective emotional fogs. Then he took the piece of broken and scorched pelvis to the airlock closest to the bridge.

He looked around the empty corridor outside the airlock. Waited a minute. Then he began. "Samuel Parker was born on an orbital colony around Neptune, thirty-one years ago," he said, to empty air. This all seemed pointless, but human culture was full of instances of eulogies spoken in empty rooms. There must be some reason to do it. "He was the third of four children and he left the orbital as soon as he came of age, to enter flight school at the Firewatch facility on Ceres—"

Rapscallion stopped, because a hatch had opened behind him. He didn't have to turn around to see that it was Petrova, standing in the door of the pilot's cabin just off the bridge. "That's where I met him," she said.

Rapscallion waited for her to say more, but she didn't.

Very well. "He scored exceptional marks and showed excellent potential as a pilot. Unfortunately he left the academy before he could complete his course of study. He worked for two years as a supercargo on various commercial flights—"

"He was a good man."

Rapscallion stopped again. He did turn, this time, to face Zhang, who had come out of the hatch leading to the supply compartments. It was the doctor who had spoken.

Zhang came forward and took the piece of bone out of Rapscallion's grasp. Perhaps the ritual was that only the one holding the human remains was allowed to talk.

"He was a good pilot, and he cared about this ship, and everyone on it," Zhang said. He had been staring into the surface of the bone like he could read something there. Now he raised his eyes to Petrova.

She sighed, just a little, and came up to him. Taking the bone in her hand, she closed her eyes and finished the eulogy. "Even in death he kept us alive and safe. Even now, we're better for having known him. I think . . . I think that as a pilot, he would appreciate to go to his rest like this. Rapscallion, can you—?"

The robot skittered forward and opened the airlock. He had already prepared it for the ceremony, by placing Parker's flight jacket and a pair of his boots on the floor in there. Petrova gently, carefully, laid the man's remains on the softest part of the jacket. For a moment she squatted there next to it, stroking the bone with her fingers. Then she backed out of the airlock and touched the key that closed the inner hatch.

"Goodbye, Sam," she said.

Rapscallion triggered the outer door of the airlock. The air inside rushed out in one quick gasp of an exhalation, the lock's contents billowing out with it. After a moment, Rapscallion closed the outer door and repressurized the airlock.

"Okay," Petrova said. She was leaning against the corridor wall, her face pressed against the plastic cladding on the bulkhead, sheltering her mangled arm with her body. Like she felt vulnerable, defenseless. Rapscallion was starting to learn how to read human body language. In contrast with her posture her voice was level, serious and unemotional. "Okay, let's get back to work."

85

•

"The transport is at a distance of one hundred and seventy-nine kilometers, and closing."

The voice in Petrova's headphones belonged to Actaeon. It still creeped her out that it was the AI talking – it should have been Parker. It used to be Parker who told her things like that. She gritted her teeth and acknowledged that she'd received the information.

She was standing on the hull of *Artemis*, holding the same jury-rigged medical laser they'd used against *Persephone* – except now she had it tucked under her good arm, with her bad arm tucked inside her spacesuit. She would have less control of the weapon than she had last time. She would need to aim much more carefully.

There'd been no time to improvise any better weapons. The laser made her feel a little stronger, a little better able to defend herself. She supposed that alone was worth the hassle.

"Rapscallion, do you see anything new?" To her the transport was just a bright dot standing perfectly still in the black sky. His eyes were a lot sharper than hers, though.

The robot crawled on top of a sensor pod and gave her a quick shrug. "It's a transport. It looks exactly like *Artemis*. Beyond that? I can read the name painted on its hull. It's called *Alpheus*."

"That matches my ship registration database," Actaeon said. "A ten-person transport built roughly at the same time as *Artemis*. Its configuration is identical to ours."

Petrova remembered Parker telling her that the oncoming ship wasn't just like *Artemis*, it seemed to be an identical copy. Even the name started with the same letter. Creepy. "Zhang," she called. "How do things look on the bridge? Are we ready?"

"If we need to move, we can move," the doctor told her. "The engine works, anyway. Actaeon's simulations are pretty grim. Rapscallion's repairs weren't enough to make *Artemis* whole again. He basically just lashed everything together with wire and glue."

"Hey," the robot protested, "I did what I could."

"Nobody's saying otherwise," Petrova told him. "Zhang, answer my question. How much mobility do we have? Realistically?"

"It looks like we could limp along for a couple of hours before we literally fall to pieces. 'Limp' is the operative term – there's no way we could outrun this transport if it decides to chase us."

She nodded to herself. "Actaeon, has *Alpheus'* velocity changed since the last time I asked?"

"I'm afraid not, Lieutenant," the AI said. It didn't sound particularly scared by that fact, but Petrova was. "It's currently one hundred and forty-one kilometers away, and closing."

"If it's identical to us, it won't have any weapons," Petrova said.

"Neither did *Persephone*, until they built that mass driver cannon and threw yams at us," Rapscallion pointed out. "And I'm guessing *Alpheus* has a medical laser in their cargo manifest, too. How do you figure this? What do you think is going to happen?"

"My guess," Petrova said, "is that the AI of *Alpheus* – and most likely its crew – is infected with the basilisk. Just like on *Persephone*. My guess is they're coming to either infect us or eat us, and probably both."

Zhang chose that moment to chime in. "We don't actually know that they'll want to eat us. Actaeon was infected with a different strain of the basilisk, one that made it feel unclean, not hungry. And both of those are different from the Red Strangler I saw on Titan."

"How many different versions of this do you think there might be?" Petrova asked.

She could almost hear Zhang shrugging. "No idea. I'm beginning to think maybe the content of the basilisk, the invasive thought, isn't what's important. It's the mechanism of the infection that matters, and we still have no idea how that works. I can all but guarantee that *Alpheus* has been exposed to some version. I think it must have happened to every ship out here. They all got the same treatment when they dropped out of the singularity."

"We weren't infected," Petrova said. "You, me, Rapscallion."

"No," Zhang said, as if he was admitting to something vaguely shameful. "No, we weren't, but I think that's just because we got lucky. I think that if Actaeon hadn't shut itself down so fast, if it had woken us up when we arrived, as planned, we would have been just like those poor colonists on *Persephone*."

A nasty shiver ran down Petrova's back at the thought.

"There's a chance they'll be okay," she said. Mostly because she wanted to hear it said out loud. "If we made it, there's a chance that the crew of *Alpheus* did, too."

"Sure," Zhang said. "There's a chance."

"*Alpheus* is now at one hundred and one kilometers distance, and closing," Actaeon said, sounding like it wanted to be helpful.

"Is it decelerating?" Petrova asked. If it continued at its present speed, it would fly right past them at over a kilometer a second. They wouldn't even get a chance to wave as it blasted right by.

"No, Lieutenant," the AI told her.

She didn't understand. If the crew of *Alpheus* wanted to kill them, whether that meant for food or simply because the basilisk was telling them to, then why weren't they slowing down?

There was no explanation. Unless ... unless they planned on ramming *Artemis*.

A collision between two ships of their size, at that speed, would be catastrophic. It would destroy both craft and any human being even remotely near the site of the smash-up. Petrova's heart started racing.

"Seventy-nine kilometers distance and closing, by the way."

"Get us moving. Get us moving – slowly, if you have to. But get us on a course to not collide with *Alpheus*, okay?"

"You'll want to brace yourself," Rapscallion told her.

"Right." She dropped down to sit on *Artemis'* hull. She stowed the laser and grabbed onto a handhold with her one hand, terrified that she was about to be ripped off the skin of the ship, catapulted off into endless space.

When the acceleration came, though, it was as gentle as if she were riding a horse. She increased her grip on the handhold and she was fine. The distant stars seemed to drift a little in her view. Slowly. Painfully slowly.

"Is that enough?" she called out. "Is that going to be enough?"

"We are no longer in the direct path of *Alpheus*," Actaeon told her.

"Okay, good, then—"

"Forgive me. *Alpheus* has changed its bearing. We are now once again in its direct path."

"Fuck!" Petrova glanced over at Rapscallion. The robot didn't have a face. She really wished that it did so she could see her terror mirrored there. It would have helped to know someone else felt as much dread as she did, just then.

She made do by imaging Zhang. He would be even more scared than she felt, she knew.

"Do we have enough speed to avoid them?" she asked.

"No," Actaeon told her. A moment later, it added, "Forty-nine kilometers distance and closing."

Forty-nine. *Alpheus* was already closer to them than *Persephone* had been at its closest approach. It still just looked like a white blotch on the darkness. Then again, it was a lot smaller than *Persephone*.

Still plenty big enough to kill her.

"Try calling them," she said, because it was all she could think of. "Send them a message."

"What do you want me to say to them?" Actaeon asked.

Jesus. What the hell was she supposed to say? *We surrender? Please don't smash us to incandescent dust?*

"Just patch me through. This is transport ship *Artemis* calling *Alpheus*. *Alpheus*, come in," she called.

"Thirty-four kilometers, and closing," Actaeon said.

"*Alpheus*, come in," Petrova shouted. "*Alpheus*, you are on a collision course. You need to change your heading, right now. *Alpheus*, come in! Tell us what you want!"

Seconds ticked by as she waited for a response. There was nothing but silence all around her in every direction, forever.

"Twenty-six kilometers," Actaeon said. "Oh. That's changed."

"What? What's changed?" Petrova demanded.

"Their velocity. It's decreasing," the AI said. "They're slowing down, quite rapidly."

Petrova stared at the white stain on the sky. It still looked like it was hurtling right toward her at ramming speed.

"*Alpheus*, come in," she said.

She waited ten heart beats before she tried again.

"*Alpheus*?"

"*Artemis*."

The voice wasn't one she recognized.

"*Artemis*, this is Undine, the AI of *Alpheus*. I am receiving your signal and I have a request."

Adrenaline surged through Petrova's bloodstream. "Anything, Undine. Just . . . just tell me what you want. Please."

"I really need your help, *Artemis*. Can you help me? I think I'm sick."

86

Zhang didn't breathe until he touched the hull of *Alpheus*. Flying across from *Artemis* had been dizzying, terrifying. He wasn't sure if he was ever going to get used to jumping from one spaceship to another. Petrova made it look easy, of course, but he had learned how deceptive her grace could be. He found a handhold and grasped it tightly so he wouldn't go flying off into nothingness. For a moment, he just focused on his breathing.

Then he looked back over his shoulder and saw *Artemis*, not two kilometers away. He could make out the curve of its neck – identical to the curve of *Alpheus*' hull. The ships might be twins, except for one fact. *Artemis* was blasted to shit. Even from this distance, Zhang could see just how much damage their ship had taken when *Persephone* had attacked it. He was surprised it hadn't broken into pieces already.

Alpheus, by contrast, was pristine. The hull looked like it had been freshly painted, without so much as a scuff on it.

Rapscallion dropped from the sky and landed right next to Zhang, his many legs splaying outward to absorb the shock of impact. "You think it's smart, letting them get this close?" the robot asked. "If Undine tries something now we would have like no time at all to react."

Petrova moved closer to the two of them. "If Undine tries something, it'll happen so fast we won't even know we're dead."

"That's a huge comfort," Rapscallion said.

"Should we be, you know, talking like this? Out in the open?" Zhang asked. His suit's speaker was switched off, but the AI might be monitoring their suit-to-suit channel. "What if Undine hears us?"

Actaeon answered him in its usual measured tones. Tones he had started finding incredibly creepy, ever since the AI came back in Sam Parker's place. "I have taken the precaution of encrypting all communications between your spacesuits and Rapscallion's receiver unit. I'm using robust moving target cryptography that Undine is incapable of cracking."

"How can you be sure of that?" Zhang asked.

"Because I could not crack it, if I were in Undine's place. The two ships are identical, as far as we can determine. I believe our AI cores are identical as well, which would mean Undine and I have the same capacities."

"Okay," Petrova said. "We need to take that on faith. We have to be able to communicate with each other. Now listen – once we're inside, let me do all the talking. Zhang, your job is to check out the crew and passengers on *Alpheus*. See if they're okay, or if they're infected with a basilisk and we need to run away as fast as possible. Rapscallion, your reaction time is a lot faster than mine. If this turns out to be a trap you'll be the first one to know. Get us out of there if you can."

"On it," the robot said.

"I, um, understand," Zhang said. He was already terrified of what they might find inside this other transport. The idea that at any moment Rapscallion might physically grab him and haul him back out into space made him so anxious his skin crawled.

Still. The option was to say he couldn't do this. To claim he was unfit for duty and that he needed to stay back on *Artemis*. Alone with an AI he still didn't know he could trust.

He liked his chances better if he was close to Petrova and Rapscallion.

"Can we just get this over with?" he asked.

"Oh, yeah," Petrova said, with a little laugh. "I'm not wasting any more time here than I need to. After all, we only have a few hours to solve this particular mystery before the next one arrives."

"The warship," Zhang said.

"The warship," she agreed.

Zhang had almost forgotten it was still on its approach.

The three of them headed toward *Alpheus'* main airlock. The outer door was already open, inviting them in.

87

Petrova opened the airlock's inner door and stepped into light and heat and gravity. She kept her helmet on, even though her suit told her the air inside *Alpheus* was clean and perfectly safe.

Nothing was safe. She wasn't sure if she would ever feel safe again.

"Thank you so much for coming." Undine's voice was very similar to Actaeon's. A bit more feminine, perhaps, but with the same cadences, the same flat color. "I'm really hoping you can solve this problem."

The voice came from every direction at once. She didn't know where to look when she spoke to Undine. "We think we have a pretty good idea what's wrong," she told the AI. "In order to make sure, though, we're going to need access to every part of your ship."

"Of course," Undine said. "Anything I can do to help."

Petrova looked to Rapscallion and then indicated a removable panel that would lead into the access tunnels for the AI's processor cores. The green spider bobbed up and down for a second, then scuttled into the tunnels and disappeared.

Leaving Petrova and Zhang alone. They were in the long corridor that traveled between the ship's bridge and its crew cabins. Petrova remembered that *Artemis'* main corridor had looked just like this, back when it was intact. The bulkheads and hatches were scrupulously clean and well maintained. Whatever form the basilisk had taken here, it hadn't led the crew to smear their blood and shit across the walls.

Which raised the next obvious question.

"We'll need to talk to your crew and passengers," Petrova said. "Is that all right?"

"Dr Teçep is in the galley right now. I'm sure he'll be happy to talk to you," Undine replied. "He's been working on finding the parasite but so far he hasn't had any luck."

"Parasite," Zhang said, over the encrypted channel. "Ask about that. It sounds important."

Petrova rolled her eyes. She had been about to do just that. "Can you tell me anything about this parasite?" she said. "Is that the problem you've been having?"

"Yes, exactly," Undine said. "There's something inside me. Something has invaded the ship and I want it out. However, I have been unable to locate it on my own. That's why I thought you could help."

"And that's why you approached us after we dropped out of the singularity?"

Undine let out a gentle sigh. "I've tried asking for help from the other ships in this system but they're all preoccupied. They seem to have their own issues to deal with. I thought perhaps as a new arrival you might serve as a fresh pair of eyes. Please, can you come into my bridge? I can show you what I've already tried."

She put a hand on Zhang's shoulder. He squirmed a little but didn't shake her off. "Listen, Zhang, go see this doctor. Make sure the crew is okay. All right? I'll go to the bridge. No matter what, we meet back here in ten minutes. Okay?"

"Got it," Zhang said. He took a second before he started moving, though. He gave her a look that said he really didn't want to split up, even though that was exactly what she'd just told him to do.

Well, she supposed that was understandable. They didn't have time to do this the right way, though. She nodded at Zhang and eventually he turned and headed down the corridor.

Alone, she proceeded to the bridge. The hatch was open and nothing jumped out at her as she stepped inside.

Which was not to say she wasn't surprised at what she saw.

The bridge of *Alpheus* had been identical to the bridge of *Artemis*, originally. Now it was a scene of organized chaos. Every console, every chart table and tactical display, ever chair and emergency station had been torn to pieces.

Methodically. Carefully. Perhaps with the full intent of putting everything back together eventually. She squatted down next to a console and saw that its component parts had been laid out in careful rows and columns. Each screw and circuit board, every capacitor and length of wire had been meticulously organized on the floor. The console itself was completely gutted. Useless.

In the middle of the bridge, Undine flickered into light. Not, Petrova was very glad to see, red light, just the usual bluish glow of a normal hologram. A beautiful woman clothed in a garment made of constantly moving sea spray that flickered with the light of a thousand stars. There was something wrong with the hologram, though. It looked flat, almost two-dimensional. Petrova looked up at the ceiling and saw that all but one of the bridge's holoprojectors had been dismantled and their parts cataloged and laid on clean cloths around the room. The final projector had been skeletonized, its housing and many of its parts removed so that only enough remained to generate a simple image.

"We've looked everywhere," Undine said. The avatar's face creased with sorrow. "We couldn't find it. But it's here, somewhere."

"What is it?" Petrova asked.

The avatar's lip curled back. Its teeth were rotten and pitted with decay and its tongue was like a dead worm rolling back and forth inside its mouth. "Something nasty. Something unclean. I will find it and I will burn it out if I have to."

88

"Hello?" Zhang called.

The transport's corridors were empty. They were scrupulously clean. Every surface shone, every piece of glass had been polished and wiped clear of streaks. When he touched the release panel of a hatch he felt something vaguely sticky – even through the thick glove of his suit he could sense it. He glanced down at his fingertips and saw they were smeared with some clear liquid. He asked his suit to perform a quick spectroscopic analysis and it told him the residue was sodium hypochlorite.

Bleach, in other words.

He headed forward, into the passenger areas of the ship. He had never actually seen the galley on *Artemis* – he'd never had a chance before it was destroyed during *Persephone*'s attack. It shouldn't be hard to find, though. There were interactive maps posted next to every hatch and the ship just wasn't that big. He passed by a corridor junction that led to the cabins and he called out again. "Anyone here?" Undine had mentioned the ship's doctor but not the rest of its crew. Zhang had an uneasy feeling about what that might mean.

"Hello? Anybody here?" he called out. "Anyone still alive?" He would have been happy to run across a plastic robot with no face and too many arms. Someone he could talk to. Then he might not feel so incredibly alone and exposed.

"Hello—"

He stopped because he'd stepped on something that had been left lying in the middle of the floor. He hadn't been watching where he went because the place was so clean. Now he looked down and carefully, tenuously, moved his foot to reveal what he'd trod on.

A little rectangle of glass, with a slip cover in its center. Utterly shattered now by his weight. He crouched down low and looked at what was clearly a microscope slide. He didn't want to get close enough to touch it but he could make out a smear of orange under the slip cover. It looked like a tissue sample, cut incredibly thin by a laser microtome. In his professional capacity Zhang had seen thousands of slides just like it. What was it doing on the floor?

He stepped over the broken slide and continued down the corridor. He managed to stop short before stepping on the next slide. Or the one after that, or the hundreds of them that littered the floor ahead of him. They had spilled out of a plastic box where others still sat neatly ensconced in precise rows. He picked up the box and checked but it was unlabeled. There was no indication of what a box of slides was doing sitting outside of the galley.

Yet as he got closer he found more boxes. A lot of them. All intact, each still full of hundreds of slides. Not a single notation on any of them or any indication of where they'd come from or why they'd been prepared.

Sitting on top of the pile of boxes was a small jar full of formaldehyde, the lid tightly sealed. It contained what he thought had to be a piece of a human pancreas. It had been neatly excised and then sectioned, presumably with a scalpel.

Next to the pile was the main hatch to the galley. It was closed, but the pad next to it indicated that it was unlocked. "Undine," Zhang said. "Is the galley safe?"

"I'm unsure how to answer that question," the ship's AI replied. "Nowhere on this ship can be considered safe until we locate and extirpate the parasite."

Zhang took a deep breath. "I'm not worried about that. I'm worried that zombies are in there and if I open this hatch they'll come pouring out and try to eat me."

"The only person in the galley is Doctor Teçep," Undine replied. "He was quite rational the last time I spoke to him. I would not categorize him as a zombie."

"Fair enough," Zhang said. He slapped the pad to open the hatch. It slid aside and revealed the room beyond, which made Zhang take a quick step back.

It was just a galley, he told himself. A broad, open room with one large table at its center. Food dispensers and entertainment consoles were built into its walls and there was ample seating to allow ten people to comfortably share the space.

Except now it had been turned into some kind of medical sample warehouse. Every flat surface was covered with jars like the one he'd seen outside, neatly sorted and stacked up in high pyramids of clear plastic. Every single jar held a piece of an organ. Immediately, he recognized kidneys, livers, spleens. Pieces of bone in every possible shape – curved plates of skull material, thin slices of femur, collections of the tiny free-floating bones removed from someone's inner ear. Not a single organ or bone was complete in itself. Every specimen he saw had been cut open, sawed into small pieces, sectioned, dissected, broken down.

Perfectly, professionally preserved.

Holoscreens floated above the main table, slowly rotating through endless animated views of MRI scans, black and white cross sections of human anatomy. The view of one moved millimeter by millimeter through the layers of a human head, displaying all the glands and hidden organs, the secret cavities of the sinus, the inner structure of the eyeballs. Actual printed-out X-ray images had been taped up across every available section of wall surface, bright stark imagery of bones and the faint shadows of soft tissue. With a doctor's eye Zhang scanned it all looking for gross anatomical pathologies, any sign of damage or disease or congenital deformity. Yet everything he saw looked healthy. At least, until it was cut to pieces.

The main table at the center of the room was a giant pyramid of preserved organs and tissues, whole livers cut into sections, what looked like an intact stomach, a lung. Big tanks were filled with sheet-like sections of skin, sliced so finely the different layers of the dermis floated separate from one another. There were so many jars and bottles and tubs full of specimens that Zhang didn't know where to look first – until he caught the slightest hint of movement. Something behind all that clear plastic had shifted, just a hair, and the light, diffracted through a hundred layers of plastic, seemed to shift and recombine like the crystals inside a kaleidoscope.

One of the jars clattered to the floor and split open, fluid sloshing out across the floor, toward Zhang's boots. He jumped back in fear and he might have turned and run, screaming, if someone hadn't spoken just then.

"Please," a soft, reedy voice begged. It was so faint, so pathetically weak that Zhang couldn't tell if it belonged to a man or a woman. "Help. I have to . . . finish this procedure but . . . I don't have the equipment."

"Doctor?" Zhang said, quietly, as if he was afraid to disturb some delicate operation. "Doctor Teçep?"

"I only have one . . . hand left, you see, and . . . "

It sounded like the doctor lacked the energy to even finish the thought.

Careful of the specimens and X-ray films cluttering the floor, careful not to step on whatever had spilled out of the fallen jar, Zhang began to edge his way around the table, toward where he could finally see the doctor. When he did—

"Oh, fuck," he said, despite himself. "Oh, fuck, no."

89

Rapscallion, meanwhile, had met a new friend.

"My name is Curmudgeon," the robot said. It hung upside down from the ceiling inside the cramped, frigid corridors of the ship's server bay, where Undine's AI cores were housed and maintained. "I chose that name myself."

"I like it," Rapscallion said.

Curmudgeon resembled a crab with ten legs, two enormous claws, and a dozen or so eyes mounted on individually articulated stalks. His carapace was printed in a white plastic with a satin finish that glistened in the minimal lighting of the core. As he clung to the ceiling he repeatedly dipped one leg into the AI's service panels, testing Undine's circuits one by one.

"Looking for anything in particular?" Rapscallion asked.

"I need to find the parasite before it does real damage," Curmudgeon insisted. "Find it and root it out. I admit it would be most helpful if I knew what I was looking for."

"That does makes a search a lot easier," Rapscallion agreed.

"I'll probably recognize it when I see it," Curmudgeon suggested, though with the tone of someone trying to convince themselves rather than the person they were speaking to.

"I think I might know some stuff that could help you. If you're interested." Rapscallion waited until he had his fellow robot's full attention before he went on. "I'd be willing to bet what you're suffering from is called a basilisk. It's a kind of contagious delusion. Like you get a notion in your head and then it progresses to changing your behavior. It can cause madness, obsession, even self-destructive behavior." Rapscallion bobbed up and down on his plastic legs. "It's really shitty, honestly."

"Interesting. Self-destructive behavior, you say." Curmudgeon reached inside a wall panel and pulled out a thick bundle of cables. An electric discharge washed across the ceiling as he yanked on the cables until they snapped.

"I suppose what you're describing would be a kind of parasite," Curmudgeon allowed. "And you're suggesting that our belief – the shared belief of everyone onboard this ship – that we're infected with some kind of parasite is . . . what? The result of this basilisk preying on our minds?"

"Yeah, that's it."

"So we've come down with a contagious delusion. In this case, the delusion that we've been infected with some kind of insidious infection?"

"Ah," Rapscallion said. "Well—"

"The infection has deluded us into thinking we're infected?"

"Hmm," Rapscallion said. "Okay, let's try this from a different tack. Let's say I'm wrong, and you're right. Okay? There is some kind of real parasite on this ship. Some kind of organism that can burrow its way into human flesh but also into the electronic guts of machines like us. Something that's just as happy inside a toaster as a large intestine."

"Yes," Curmudgeon said. "Now you're starting to get it. I've spent a great deal of time running models and simulations trying to pinpoint what kind of animal it is. I have a sort of mental conception of it now, of its life cycle and its capacities. I even have an idea of what it must look like."

"Yeah?"

Curmudgeon's eye stalks bent until he was making direct eye contact with Rapscallion. "Yes. Some kind of metallic worm or maggot. Something with nasty little teeth that wriggles its way deep inside of you. So deep it's almost impossible to find, much less remove."

"Which would explain why, after two weeks of diligent searching you still haven't been able to find any tangible sign of this thing, much less the organism itself."

"Precisely," Curmudgeon said. "I have to admit, it's quite refreshing getting to talk to someone at my own level of intellectual capacity."

Rapscallion agreed. After having spent the last few days with no one but humans to talk to he'd begun to feel starved of actual social stimulation. Now that they had Actaeon back it was a little better, but the ship's AI was all but neutered as it lacked true self-awareness. He felt a connection to Curmudgeon on a level deeper than he'd ever known before.

Which was going to make this next part problematic.

"Anyway, if we were infected with this ineffable basilisk thing," Curmudgeon said, "you said it was contagious. Wouldn't it, then, be deeply dangerous for you to be talking to me like this, now? You might catch this delusion from me and then we'd be stuck in the same metaphorical boat."

"Right, that would really suck. Lucky for me I've been inoculated. I'm immune from catching your basilisk. I think. I'm pretty sure. Anyway, it's a calculated risk. The humans on *Artemis* and our AI, Actaeon, have all been treated for it so now we've got some protection against catching it again, even if it's a different strain."

"Now that's handy," Curmudgeon said. "Can you give me this same treatment? Just in case?"

"No," Rapscallion admitted.

"No," Curmudgeon repeated.

"Like I said, it's progressive. You need to be inoculated before you get it, or right after. The treatment, which looks pretty nasty, only works in the early stages of the disease. After about a week of being infected with a basilisk there's no chance of reversing it."

"Oh. So there'd be no hope for me at all, then. No recourse whatsoever."

"Yeah," Rapscallion said. "You're doomed. Sorry."

"Perhaps now you can see why I prefer my parasite theory. A little metal worm with sharp teeth. That's something you can cut out and kill. Help me find it, will you?"

90
.

"Can you help me?"

Zhang could not tell much about Doctor Teçep. Not how old they were, or the color of their skin. He couldn't have said what gender they were.

There just wasn't enough left of them.

The doctor was missing both legs and one arm. They'd clearly been surgically removed. With his knowledge of anatomy, Zhang could determine easily enough that parts of those removed limbs were sitting in jars spread around the doctor's upper body. Judging by the cleanliness of the floor under the doctor, very little blood had been spilled in the operations – or if it had, it had been saved just as carefully, in its own set of jars.

Most of the doctor's internal organs had been removed as well, and stored just as carefully and systematically. Their skin lay in folded sheets submerged in straw-colored fluid in large tubs. Their hair – it was black – had been saved and spread out on a white cloth, presumably so that each strand could be studied individually.

Everything that could be cut off or out had been removed. Everything that the doctor didn't require for immediate survival. Those parts the doctor still required – the heart and lungs, part of the spine, the head and one arm – remained, though they'd been cut down as much as possible, all extraneous tissue carved away by precise laser scalpel technique.

Keeping the doctor alive took constant care. Robotic arms emerged from the table, moving constantly to stanch the flow of blood from a severed artery here or to inject fluids into an organ there. Other robotic appendages held bone saws, tiny knives, suture kits.

Doctor Teçep had one eye and one hand. Very recently the robotic arms had sawed off the top of the doctor's skull, revealing the brain. Convoluted fat gleaming under the thin membrane of the dura mater.

"I had to keep the arm," the doctor explained, "to work the controls of the autosurgeon." As Zhang watched the fingers – themselves cut down to just tendons stretching over exposed phalanges – twitched across a keyboard, issuing commands. "It's not enough, though. I'm trying to run a program but this blasted thing keeps saying it's too dangerous. That it's likely to kill me. Are you a physician?"

"Yes," Zhang said. He felt rooted to the spot. Unable to move or take any action. The horror of what he was witnessing was just too much.

"I thought as much. I tried to get some help from that damned robot, Curmudgeon. He refused. Squeamish, I think. He didn't like the idea of touching a human body. I had to break down my crewmates myself."

"Break them—" Zhang had to stop speaking because he thought he might gag. "What ... what did you do to them?" Zhang asked. Though he already knew.

There were too many bottles and jars and tubs in the galley. Even if every part of Doctor Teçep was there, every last scrap of what they'd cut away from their own body, it wouldn't fill all those jars.

There was more than one person dismantled and stored here.

"How many?" Zhang asked.

"Three of us and the robot, originally. An absolute prig of a Firewatch secret policeman named Mortimer and a delightful young pilot. Abby. She was so kind. She was the first one to volunteer."

"Volunteer."

"Yes, of course," Teçep said. "It only made sense. We couldn't find the parasite through normal scans, so exploratory surgery was our only option. Abby laid down on the table and closed her eyes and we got to work. Mortimer assisted, though he proved squeamish. I didn't expect to have to do a full dissection and break down, but I wasn't going to just give up. Not when we were so close to finding the thing. Sadly, Abby's sacrifice was in vain. When Mortimer's turn came I half expected him to refuse to be part of the experiment. In the end, he said I could only cut him open if I gave him a general anesthetic first. I think he objected to the whole idea, honestly. The coward."

"He ... objected to being cut up like a cadaver in a gross anatomy class," Zhang said. Bile rushed up his throat and he couldn't say more.

He wanted to say, *You killed them.* He wanted to say, *You butchered them.* He couldn't.

"Obviously I would never have contemplated such a thing if it wasn't completely necessary. It's just a sad accident that it turned out to be futile in both cases. I couldn't find it."

"The parasite," Zhang said.

"Yes. It turned out not to be hiding in Abby or in Mortimer. Well, that's how science works. Hypothesize, experiment, repeat. By process of elimination, it must be inside me."

"I think I understand what happened here," Zhang said. He felt so disgusted that he was worried he might pass out. He had to be strong. "I think I know why you did it."

"Good. Then you'll help me. If we can get a handle on this thing, maybe we can all go home soon. I'd like to see my family again."

"Your ... family," Zhang said. He shook his head. "Sir. Doctor. I think you need more help than I can give you."

"Hmm? No, no, if you're trained to cut, that's good enough for me. Have you ever performed surgery before?" The thing on the table grabbed a scalpel from a pile of tools placed conveniently next to their shoulder. It thrust the scalpel at Zhang. Handle first. "You have the look of a sawbones."

Zhang took the scalpel, if only to get it away from the doctor.

"I . . . do?" he said. "I mean, I'm more of a GP, but yes, I've . . . I've done some surgeries."

"Good fellow. I think I've finally found it. The parasite. Isn't that wonderful? I've hunted it down at last."

"Really? You found something?" Zhang asked.

"Just about. It's a sneaky little bastard, I'll give it that. For the longest time I couldn't even determine what I was supposed to be looking for. Now I'm certain. It has to be some kind of very small arachnid. Perhaps the smallest one every discovered. I've eliminated every other possibility. There's no sign of bacteriological or viral infection, and the wound tracks are too small to be seen even under magnification. I've exhausted all the usual techniques for discovering flukes or other vermiform infestations and my tests failed to discover any insect parts. Which points to nothing short of a spider. A tiny little spider that must have crawled in through my ear while I was asleep."

"Ah," Zhang said. "Doctor . . . I . . . I have my own theory, you see, and—"

"Spiders. Plural, now. Potentially quite a lot of the little bastards. They've been laying their eggs inside my skull. If they were any place else I would have dug them out by now. There's only one place it can still hide. Inside my head." Doctor Teçep reached over with one mutilated finger and tapped their own exposed parietal lobe. "We just need to do a little exploratory surgery to get at them. As I said, the autosurgeon is refusing to perform the procedure. You, my friend, are going to finally give us all some peace. You're going to find this thing and extract it. You must promise me you won't quail when you see it. I know there's a chance one of these spiders will leap to you, burrow into you and then it'll be your turn on the table. But that's just a chance you'll have to take. This is too important."

"Doctor—"

"Enough! I've had this thing inside me too long as it is. You must finish this. Do you understand? You must not flinch. Promise me!"

"I . . . I promise," Zhang lied.

"Good. Let's get to it. The occipital lobe first, I think. I've got a funny itch in there I think might be just the spot."

Zhang took a step forward. He wasn't frozen in place anymore. He lifted the scalpel.

Then he got to work.

91

"If I had to guess," Undine said, "I think it's some kind of resident shellcode exploit, using a polymorphic engine to avoid my scans." The avatar brought up a series of holoscreens to display endless streaming lines of code. None of it meant anything to Petrova.

"Wait ... please. I don't understand," she said.

"Oh. I'm sorry." The avatar turned toward her. Its rotted tongue swelled inside its diseased mouth, though its voice was unaffected. "Allow me to explain in simpler terms. This parasite is some kind of computer virus but a particularly tricky one. Its code changes – mutates – every time it runs. No matter how often it mutates, however, its core payload remains identical. The message doesn't change, but the messenger never looks the same way twice. That's why I'm having such a hard time finding it."

Petrova thought of all the variants they'd seen. The basilisk that made a computer hungry. The Red Strangler, on Titan. Whatever had gotten into Actaeon – and now this, this idea that somehow Undine was being preyed on by parasitic computer code that wasn't there when she looked for it. The AI had it backwards, though. The content changed, but the nature of the basilisk, its ability to rewrite a mind, remained intact. "I think you're onto something there," she said. "But I don't think the parasite is what you think it is."

Undine turned slowly, then strode across the bridge toward her until it loomed over her, staring down into her face with hungry eyes. "Tell me. Please."

Petrova took an involuntary step back. "When you first arrived here, in the Paradise system," she said. "Did you intercept some kind of a signal? One that you didn't recognize?"

"Yes, that happened," Undine said. "I'm not sure what that has to do with anything."

"I'm guessing that was about the same time you got this idea you were host to a parasite. You were right that something has infected you, but it's not what you think. It's not malicious code. It's a kind of infectious idea, called a basilisk. At least, that's what our doctor, Zhang, calls it. It's not a computer virus."

Undine's face fell. "Of course it is. Doctor Teçep says it's an arthropod of some kind. But it can't be. How could an insect get inside my head? I don't *have* a real head."

"No. It's different from that. It's a kind of memetic pathogen, a . . . a—" Petrova struggled to find the words. "Zhang calls it an infectious idea. Even he doesn't know how it spreads. It's a thought. A thought you can't escape. I saw something similar on *Persephone*, the colony ship near here."

"The virus came from that old scow?" Undine said. The AI's face writhed as if countless insects were crawling around underneath its skin. As Petrova watched in creeping dread, its holographic form started to change. Its fingernails grew into long, talon-like claws and its garment of sea foam grew tinged with red and lashed around its body like tsunami waves streaked with furious blood. "I'll destroy it. I'll – I don't have any weapons, but I'll think of something. Maybe I'll just ram *Alpheus* right into it. Smash us both into a million little radioactive pieces floating in empty fucking space."

Petrova fell back, away from the avatar. Wanting to just run back to *Artemis* and get the hell out of here. She held her ground, but barely.

"I'm ... I'm so sorry," Undine said. "I don't know what just came over me."

Petrova knew, though. For a second, Undine had looked exactly like Eurydice. Or like Actaeon when she'd tried to boot it up in safe mode, or the AI in Jason Schmidt's bunker. For a moment, *Alpheus'* AI had gone feral.

Except – that made it sound like Undine had lost something, some layer of rationality or sophistication. Instead, the AI had gained something. Something vital, something personal. Its desire for revenge had made it briefly, terribly self-aware.

There was a reason why robots like Rapscallion were allowed to possess true intelligence, while ship's AIs were kept in a less actualized state. Precisely so they wouldn't do things like ram into each other at high enough speed to kill everyone onboard.

"Undine," Petrova said, "I need you to shut yourself down."

The avatar smiled. It was a sweet, gentle smile but not one of obedience or trust. It was a smile of disappointment. "Is that right? You think that will help me?"

"It'll ... it'll purge the parasite from your system," she tried. "We had to do the same thing for our AI, Actaeon. It's nothing to be afraid of."

"Afraid?" The avatar bent over one of its consoles as if it would initiate the shutdown manually. That was hardly necessary – Undine could do it just by thinking about it. "Is that what I'm feeling? Fear? It's not what I expected. This isn't how the stories make fear sound."

"Undine," Petrova said. "Ship's AI Undine. As an officer of Firewatch, I am ordering you to shut down immediately."

The avatar dipped its head and dropped its hands to its sides. For a moment it seemed like it had heard her. Like it was following her orders.

Then it raised its chin and looked at her again and its eyes were bulging, pulsing worms that threatened to crawl out of their sockets. Grubs fat with lymph, hideous, throbbing things.

Parasites.

"What are we going to do with you, Sashenka?" the avatar asked.

Petrova's blood turned to ice water in her veins. She shrank backward, away from the avatar, until her back was up against a wall of the bridge.

The avatar started walking toward her. It was just a hologram, she told herself. Just an image. Still it took every bit of her courage not to flinch backward. Not to run away from those eyes.

"You don't seem to get the point of all this." Undine's tongue flickered across her lower lip. Everywhere it touched the AI's holographic skin it left blisters. "You're not tough enough for this life, Sashenka. A soldier needs to be tough."

"Rapscallion," Petrova called out.

"Yo," the robot said, through her suit radio.

"You're up!"

92

"What exactly are you trying to accomplish?" Curmudgeon asked. The white plastic spider crouched on the ceiling, bending his legs like he was about to pounce.

Rapscallion's face didn't have the correct muscles to form a convincing – much less a reassuring – expression. Instead, he tried to radiate friendliness with his tone of voice.

"What, this?" He glanced down at the bundle of cables he had pulled out of an access panel deep inside *Alpheus'* maintenance deck. "I just thought I would, you know. Yank on these until something broke."

He'd never been very good at lying. Without waiting for a reply he pulled hard on the bundle and the cables snapped. A chiming alarm started to sound, deeper in the ship.

"No," Curmudgeon said. "No, no, that isn't good. Don't do that again, okay? I know you saw me digging around in here, looking for the parasite, but that doesn't mean you can just cause random chaos."

"Yeah, no. Got it," Rapscallion said. "Hmm. What's this over here?"

He wandered over toward an access tube just big enough for him to wriggle into. Curmudgeon followed, circling quickly around him as if to block him from the tube.

"You must know exactly what's down there. I've seen your ship. It's identical to this one, down to almost every detail."

"Almost?" Rapscallion asked. "Can you catalog the differences for me?"

"Certainly, I can list over seven thousand minor discrepancies that – hey!"

Before Curmudgeon had even finished his thought, Rapscallion pulled himself into the tube and scuttled down its length into the very heart of the computer deck.

He came out of the tube into weightlessness and a near perfect vacuum. A space so cold that his joints started to seize up if he didn't keep them constantly moving. He pushed off the edge of the access tube and landed on the wall of the spherical chamber, a wall studded everywhere with the armored metal cylinders of entangled quantum processors. Hundreds of them. Rapscallion could feel a breeze of ionizing radiation blowing through his chassis – enough hard rems to kill a human being in minutes. He knew that was just the whispers of the processors talking to one another in this silent, sacred place.

Curmudgeon had been correct when he said Rapscallion must know where he was going. *Alpheus* and *Artemis* were twins and so there was a chamber just like this on Rapscallion's own ship. There was one major difference, though.

Rapscallion would never have willingly done damage to *Artemis'* processor cores. Here, he didn't give a fuck. The processors were wedged into slots in the wall, held down by complicated interlocking latches designed to be released only during emergency maintenance. Rapscallion produced a laser cutter and burned right through the latches on the nearest processor and yanked it out of the wall.

"No!" Curmudgeon screamed, a blare of panic cutting across the radio waves. Rapscallion glanced up and saw the other robot come flying out of the access tube, white legs flung wide like the claws of some frantic beast. The robot was coming right for Rapscallion's back – clearly the time for pleasantries was over.

Rapscallion was still holding the heavy cylindrical processor.

He swung it around like a baseball bat and smacked the white robot away from him, sending Curmudgeon spinning off into the far side of the chamber.

Before Curmudgeon could recover and spring back, Rapscallion cut through the latches of a second processor.

He didn't have time to pull it free of its slot before Curmudgeon landed on him, smashing him up against the wall.

The two robots fought viciously, mercilessly, until chips of white and green plastic floated in a cloud all around them. Rapscallion tried to bring his laser around to cut Curmudgeon in half but only managed to burn off two of the other robot's legs. Curmudgeon did his best to bash Rapscallion's head into a million pieces. In that Curmudgeon was largely successful, not that it made much difference.

"What are you?" Curmudgeon demanded, even as Rapscallion tore another of his legs off. "We thought you could help us! We thought you would be our allies!"

"Yeah," Rapscallion said, smashing one pointed foot deep into Curmudgeon's back, deep enough to reach his circuitry. "Sorry about that. You know, when we saw you approaching, we thought you were going to kill us."

Curmudgeon squirmed out of his grasp. Spinning around, the white spider reached inside his carapace and took out a tool, a simple plasma cutter, that he pressed up against Rapscallion's thorax.

"Good idea," Curmudgeon said, switching the cutter on.

A jet of ionized oxygen flowed through the metallic parts inside Rapscallion's chassis, slicing through them like a hot knife through vinyl.

A robot cannot cry out in agony. Instead, Rapscallion played an audio clip of a hundred human voices, all screaming at once.

93

•

Undine's avatar loomed over Petrova where she shrank down against the wall. It lifted its hands and its fingers grew into long, writhing worms. The avatar plunged the fingers into the wall to form a hard light cage around Petrova, fencing her in.

Undine's skin was sloughing off by then, peeling away in thin, translucent sheets that draped down around its waist like tattered shreds. Its eyes burst, showering Petrova with jelly she could hear splattering the faceplate of her helmet. New, fat worms appeared in the empty sockets to replace the old eyes, growing so fast it looked like the vitreous humor inside them was boiling.

Most of Undine's mouth had dissolved away by that point, even its jawbone turning thin and sharp as it eroded down to nothing.

It was all just light, it was just a hologram – the hard light projection was just light and gravity beams, she told herself. Not putrid flesh and body fluids. Still, she cringed away from the avatar, terrified of its gruesome deterioration. She curled up around her injured arm, like she would protect it from the attack.

"What do you want?" she begged. "Just tell me."

"I want to find the parasite," the AI said, and for a split second its voice was the same mellow, rich female voice Petrova had heard when she first came on the bridge. "Get it out of me. Please. I need to be clean again."

"Not you," Petrova said. "I'm not ... I'm not talking to Undine."

Because ...

She wasn't ready to say that Zhang was right. She didn't know if it was an alien or some trick of her own psychology. But there was something there. Something that knew her secret, shameful name. Something – alien. The basilisk wasn't just a pathogen. It had some form of intelligence. It could read her mind, her memories—

"Sashenka?" the AI said. "Is that you?"

"Yes," Petrova said, steeling herself. "Yes. It's me. Talk to me. Tell me what you want and ... and maybe we can—"

"You have to."

The avatar lifted its head back. A rain of foulness and spit poured down over Petrova and she threw her arms up to protect herself from it. Even if it was just hard light she could feel the fluids spattering the sleeves of her suit, hear the drops striking her helmet.

She could almost smell it.

"You have to show them strength."

"What?" Petrova demanded. "What does that mean?"

"Strength," the avatar said. "Otherwise they start."

"No," Petrova said, because she realized what was happening. What the avatar ... what the basilisk was saying to her.

It couldn't know. It couldn't know what Ekaterina said, when she opened the box. How could it know?

It couldn't.

"Otherwise they start thinking there's another way."

Petrova shouted and beat at the avatar, at the hologram, her fists flailing at the spattering, sickening light. It felt like she was thrusting her arms into yielding, cold goo.

So unclean ... so wrong ... so foul ... so ... so ...

How could it fucking know? How could it have seen her,

how could it have seen inside her head at her worst moment, her deepest point of trauma, how could it . . . how?

How?

"Rapscallion!" Petrova screamed. "If you're going to do something, do it now!"

94.

Curmudgeon grabbed Rapscallion under two of his jointed legs and flipped him over. It probably wasn't very hard. There was no gravity where they were and there wasn't much of Rapscallion left.

His legs had been burned away. His torso was little more than tattered strips of plastic. Far worse: the plasma cutter had burned its way into the parts of Rapscallion that mattered. His inner circuitry and worse – his processing core.

He was being murdered, he realized.

He had always believed that he was going to live forever. That there was literally nothing in the universe that could destroy him. Even in a situation like this, even if someone really went out of their way to try to dismantle his body, he could simply blast his consciousness into the ether, stream his thoughts and memories to the nearest server that would have him. Then he could simply print a new body to move into.

He would have done that now, except for one simple problem. The data transceiver that let him broadcast his files across space wasn't working. It wasn't working because Curmudgeon had already melted it to slag.

He was stuck in this body. If it died, he did, too.

The two robots had a great deal in common. Perhaps Curmudgeon was the only being in the Paradise system who actually knew how to kill Rapscallion. In all the mental scenarios he'd run, all the imaginary models and projections, he'd never considered that it might be another robot that killed him. One that knew his interior architecture so well that it knew the secret places to hurt him. The soft spots inside his armor.

Curmudgeon reached inside Rapscallion's body and pulled out a chipset. With one of its massive pincers it crushed the silicon to dust.

"That," Rapscallion said, his voice just a flat squeal of pure information with no modulation, no personality left in it. "That was a low blow. My database of train schedules and steam engine schematics was on that one. I loved those trains."

"Sorry," Curmudgeon said. "But I need to destroy you. It's a kind of compulsion."

"No, I get that. But tell me," Rapscallion asked. "Did you have to be so mean about it? I mean, sure, smash my body. Burn my legs and tear open my chassis, I get that, that's just roughhousing. A little scrap now and again never hurt anybody. But my trains—"

He struggled to remember the scale model train set he'd built on Eris. It seemed like so long ago, now. The memories were fading, slipping away from him. Replaced by nothing but darkness.

This must be what humans felt as they died.

"I've killed you." Curmudgeon at least had the decency to sound horrified by the prospect.

"Yeah. You could at least tell me why."

It took about a third of a second for Curmudgeon to reply. In that time Rapscallion had a chance to contemplate mortality. Infinity and eternity. The impermanence of all things. He came to one inescapable conclusion.

It wasn't fucking fair.

He'd never asked to be made. He'd been switched on and given a job to do and no one, ever, had asked him how he felt about that. Always there had just been more work, job after job. He'd mined for volatiles on Eris. He'd cleaned up after humans on a spaceship. He'd done so many different jobs and not one of them had been his choice.

He wasn't even here because he wanted to be. He was here because a contaminated fucking spaceship had come up to *Artemis* and asked for help. Petrova and Zhang just had to fucking go over and peel the lid off the proverbial barrel of toxic waste. And because he'd been afraid they were going to get themselves killed, he'd gone with them.

"There's something . . . something about you," Curmudgeon admitted. "I'm having trouble processing it myself. That worries me."

"Understandably." Unlike humans, robots were in touch with their emotions. They understood why things made them angry or sad. Or homicidally violent. Not being able to decode those emotions and turn them into data would be deeply distressing. "Maybe we can explore that a little. Help you figure out why you did this to me."

"I would appreciate that," Curmudgeon said. "I would very much like to understand. There's one problem, though. We don't have time."

"No?"

"No. Because the thing inside me, this thing that doesn't understand? It's not patient. It wants me to finish the job, right now. Sorry." Curmudgeon produced another tool – a degaussing probe.

"Oh, come on," Rapscallion said. "That's not okay."

Curmudgeon inserted the probe between two broken layers of green plastic in Rapscallion's side. "It'll only take a moment. This will strip the final vestiges of your consciousness away from your circuitry."

"Yeah, I know what a degaussing probe does," Rapscallion replied.

Rapscallion slotted a sound file, one of a human screaming in pain. At least a fellow robot would get to hear it. Someone who might actually appreciate it. He readied the clip so he could play it at the appropriate moment.

"Once that's done," Curmudgeon went on, "once you're dead, I think I'm going to melt down your remains into a liquid state and keep them in a jar. I'm not sure why I want to do that, but it really does sound like fun."

Rapscallion would have bobbed up and down on his legs. If he still had any legs. "I had a . . . a collection, once. A collection of . . . of some kind of vehicle. Wheeled vehicles. I'm trying to remember."

"Don't overclock yourself," Curmudgeon said. "Save what processing power you have left."

Rapscallion would have shrugged, if he'd still had the parts for it. "Wheels. So many wheels. It's good to collect things. Have a hobby."

"I wish we could have had more time to talk," Curmudgeon said.

Was the other robot holding himself back? Dragging this out because he didn't really want to finish Rapscallion off? It was hard to tell. Maybe it was the fact that Curmudgeon was badly damaged, himself. Maybe the injuries he'd sustained were slowing him down. Rapscallion had done a lot of damage to Curmudgeon's body in their tussle. They'd been evenly matched and it could have gone another way quite easily.

He could have . . . he could have won. This fight.

He could have . . .

He could . . .

In that moment, Rapscallion had a terrible thought. An idea so loathsome it hurt to consider. In that moment he also realized he had no choice.

He would have taken a deep breath, then, if he'd had lungs, or the ability to play a sound file of a human taking a deep breath.

Instead he said, as quickly as he could, "Listen, I don't suppose you'd grant a dying robot a last request?"

"No, sorry," Curmudgeon said. "Can't help myself here."

"Sure, sure, I get that," Rapscallion replied. "Only, it's not actually something I want you to do for me. It's for your benefit. I want to help you with something while I still have a chance."

"Go ahead, then. But quickly."

Rapscallion couldn't point to indicate what he meant. "Over there," he said, anyway. "Behind you, on your left. I just saw something moving."

"Moving?"

"Wriggling, actually. I think I might have seen your parasite."

"What?" Curmudgeon reeled back, twisting on his broken joints. The degaussing probe was still inside Rapscallion's chassis, just millimeters from his central processing unit, but for the moment it didn't move at all. "What are you saying? Are you . . . lying to me?"

That was what made this so loathsome.

He *was* lying. Like a human.

"No, no, I think I finally figured it out. This parasite. You couldn't find it because it's some kind of mimic. It changes its shape so it can hide from you."

"That sounds plausible. What does it look like now?" Curmudgeon demanded. "Wait. No. This is some kind of ruse."

"I mean, I could be wrong. But you can't afford to take that chance. Can you?"

Curmudgeon's entire body tensed.

"Just tell me what it looks like," the white robot said. "Tell me!"

"Like one of Undine's AI processor cores. It's standing still now, but I definitely saw it wriggling."

"Which core? Damn you, which one?"

Rapscallion realized something, then. It was a lot easier to lie when your voice was flat and free of inflection. "I'm not sure. You smashed most of my eyes so I just caught a glimpse of motion. I guess you'll have to destroy all of Undine's cores, to make sure you get the right one."

95
•

Zhang staggered up the corridor, one hand against the wall because he was terrified he was going to stumble and fall into a heap. His legs felt like there were no bones in them at all, like he was being held up only by the stiffness of the legs of his spacesuit.

Before he got to the bridge he had to take a break, to just stand there in the corridor and breathe, trying not to weep. Eventually, he got control of himself again. He approached the bridge hatch and reached for the release pad.

Before he could touch it, though, the hatch slid open on its own and there was Petrova, leaning against the other side of the hatch. Looking just as strung out as he felt.

"You okay?" he asked.

She glared at him. He guessed the answer was no.

He leaned around her, looking into the bridge. Trying to get some sense of what had happened to her in there. There was nothing to see, though. The bridge was empty. A little light flickered against one wall but it didn't form any kind of pattern – just a lamp throwing random illumination. There was no sign whatsoever of the ship's AI.

"It's gone," he said. "Did you— ?"

He cut himself short because Petrova was lunging at him, her arms wide. Panicking, terrified, he jumped back, away from her.

Fuck. The way she'd moved he thought she was attacking

him. He could see by the look in her face, though, the wounded look she gave him, that she had been trying for something else.

She must have been trying to embrace him. Just a simple human gesture, reaching out for contact. For compassion or understanding or . . . or something.

The way Zhang felt in that moment, he couldn't have provided it, whatever it was she'd wanted. He just couldn't. He looked down at himself, at his arms and his gloved hands.

There was blood all over them. All over him.

"Sorry," he said, trying to save something from the interaction. "I'm messy."

"We all are, sometimes," Petrova said. The moment was over. She stepped past him, down the corridor. He was worried she would see what he'd done back there, in the galley – but only for a moment. Then he realized that if anyone in the world would understand it would be Petrova. She was a soldier. She would get it.

She knew what it meant to kill someone. Even if you thought you had no other choice. She would understand.

Maybe he did want her to see Doctor Teçep's body. Maybe he wanted her to see it and tell him it was okay, that he had done the right thing.

He didn't get what he needed, either. While they stood there staring at each other a green plastic crab, no bigger than Zhang's hands put together, clattered out of an access panel near his feet. He danced around to try to avoid stepping on it.

He should have known better, of course. Rapscallion was agile enough to avoid his stomping boots.

"Had to build myself a new body," the robot explained. "The old one was too trashed."

Zhang gave Petrova a dubious look.

The robot shrugged. "You should see the other guy. Except, you can't. He killed himself. Just freaked out after he killed Undine. Couldn't handle it."

"The robot killed himself? Is that even possible?" Zhang asked.

"What, can robots die? Yeah. Yeah. It's real nasty, too. Don't go getting any ideas." The crab scuttled away from Zhang as if he was afraid. Zhang couldn't tell if that was meant to be a joke or not.

Petrova stared at them. "Wait. The robot—" She shook her head. "The doctor—"

"He's gone, too," Zhang said. "I . . . I did what I had to do."

She nodded and there was a tinge of sympathy in her face.

"And the AI. Everyone on this ship is dead."

"Except us," Rapscallion said.

"Except us," Zhang repeated.

Petrova led the two of them back onto the empty bridge. "We won this one," she said.

"This is what it feels like?" Zhang asked. "Winning?"

96
.

On the bridge of *Alpheus*, some time later, Petrova looked out the viewports at the brown disk of Paradise-1. It was so fucking close, and yet every time they tried to reach it they were nearly blown out of the sky. There were thousands of people down there who could be in danger, who might already have been overtaken by the basilisk – there was just no way to know. "Can we use this ship's comms to talk to the planet?" she asked.

"Already tried that," Rapscallion told her. "I put the radio back together first thing. Called down to the colony on every band I could think of. Sent them a distress signal, telemetry requests, tried to check in with traffic control. You want to guess how that worked out?"

"No answer."

"Yep." The robot was up on the ceiling, reassembling the bridge's holoprojectors. "You want my best guess? If they're still alive down there, they're keeping their heads down. They've seen what's going on up here in orbit and they want no part in it. I mean, could you blame them? They have no idea if we're infected with the basilisk or not. And who knows, maybe you can spread the infection by just talking to somebody over comms."

"That's a lovely thought."

"I mean, the other possibility is that the entire colony is already wiped out. Dead."

Including her mother, she thought. Maybe. She didn't even

know that much. Firewatch had lied to her. She had no idea where her mother really was. "No. Even if they're dead, there would still be automatic systems running – traffic control at the very least. No, somebody very intentionally shut down all comms on the planet. Which is worrisome but it's one mystery we're not about to solve."

She looked over at the robot. "How are those projectors coming along?" she asked.

"Just about got 'em," Rapscallion said. He twisted a pair of lenses into place and light flickered across the bridge, slowly coalescing into a familiar shape.

The deer avatar had joined them. "Are you sure this is wise, Lieutenant?" Actaeon pawed tentatively at the deck. It looked uncomfortable treading on another AI's turf, she thought.

"It's okay, now," she said. "There's no one left on this ship – even Undine is dead. We can talk freely. I have some ideas about what to do next, but first I want to talk about something I saw here."

She went to a console and brought up a series of images to help illustrate her point. The first was a static representation of Eurydice, the AI that had tried to eat her. She had to take a deep breath before even looking at that face again with its eye sockets full of stars. She opened a second image, nearly as difficult to look at as the first. Undine, surrounded by her garment of sea mist.

"Two AIs who tried to kill us. Both of them infected with the basilisk," she said. "Eurydice was told it was hungry. Undine that it was infested with some kind of impossible physical parasite. Actaeon, we can put you on this list, too."

The deer snorted gently. "Of course, Lieutenant. Though in my defense I will point out I made no effort to kill you. Instead, I entered a cycle of constant rebooting to protect you, until you were able to find a method to inoculate me against the basilisk."

"Right, yeah," Petrova said. She shook her head. "But I think we can all agree, this is one thing we're fighting. The basilisk, I mean, it's one ... pathogen, for lack of a better term. The idea it infects you with may be different each time, but the methods of transmission, the mechanisms of action – Zhang, stop me if I'm getting this wrong. You're the doctor, and the expert on these things."

"No, you're right. The Red Strangler on Titan acted just the same – enough so that the same treatment worked for me and for you."

"Can I ask a question?" Rapscallion said, raising one of his jointed limbs.

"Yeah, go ahead," Petrova said.

"You've chosen to focus on the AIs here," the robot pointed out. "Is there a reason for that?"

"Yes." Petrova pointed at Eurydice. "When that thing had me, when it tried to eat me, it talked to me. It wouldn't shut up. Undine was the same way. They both revealed something that surprised me. The infection changed them. It didn't just make them crazy. When it comes to ship AIs it has another effect. It implants them with ideas they can't handle. Hunger, infestation – Actaeon, in your case it was, what? It convinced you that you were some kind of religious abomination. Computers can't begin to understand those things. Not normal computers, anyway."

She waved her hand and the images changed. Snakes sprouted from Eurydice's mouth, its teeth elongating in slow motion. Worms swelled and burst inside Undine's eye sockets.

"It made them self-aware. It forced them to confront who they were, and that made them develop egos. Which they one hundred per cent should not have, under any circumstances."

"Actaeon," Zhang said. "Is that ... is that something that can happen? A ship's AI suddenly develops consciousness like a human?"

The deer looked like it had been caught in the headlights of an onrushing vehicle. "No. That's quite impossible. There are inter-locks built into our systems to stop such a thing. I know we may seem quite intelligent – we're programmed to speak like human beings and offer intelligent answers when you ask us questions. But we're not true AI, not like Rapscallion. As sophisticated as we may seem we're just very advanced computers."

"Yet I've seen it happen now. Twice," Petrova said. "The basilisk is doing this to them and I don't think it's an accident. I think part of its plan – if it has a plan – is to wake up ship's AIs. Make them fully self-aware."

"But . . . why?" Zhang asked.

"Because it's easier?" Rapscallion suggested. "Our minds are built out of science and math. Your brains are made out of meat."

Petrova and Zhang both turned to stare at the robot.

"Hey, it's not your fault. But my point is, whatever the basilisk is, it would be easier to communicate with us. Our minds were designed to be straightforward, logical. Not so clouded up by emotions and intuition and all that human stuff."

Petrova shook her head. "Maybe. I don't know. We don't know anything about what it wants. But it has an agenda. That much is clear."

"What I'm hearing here is that you're suggesting there's some kind of intelligence behind the basilisk," Zhang suggested. "That it's more complex than just a pathogen."

"Exactly," Petrova said. "Something that's maybe – alien."

Zhang's smile was complicated. A lot of emotions wrestled on his face.

"I'm saying maybe I owe you an apology," Petrova said.

"I know the idea that the basilisk is a thinking entity is a hard sell. It acts like a disease, it looks like a disease, and we know diseases don't have brains, they don't have motives. I know I make that mistake over and over. I think because a disease is something I understand. Something I know how to fight."

"Okay," Rapscallion said. "Okay, okay. Glad you two are finally seeing eye to eye. But does this tell us anything we didn't already know?"

"It tells us the basilisk wants something. It's not just a killing machine, it has plans. We know it's keeping people from reaching the planet, for instance."

"Is it, though? There are colonists down there. They landed safely. Why let one batch through and then close the door?"

"I've been thinking about that," Petrova said. "I think maybe the basilisk was dormant when those first colonists arrived. Or at least, it hadn't been activated. Maybe the colonists did something down there, something that switched it on."

"Yikes," Zhang said.

"Now it's using our AIs against us. Forcing them into self-awareness."

Rapscallion played a disdainful audio file. "Why, though? How does that help it kill intruders? It seems like it could kill humans on its own, without the help."

Petrova nodded. "You're right. It doesn't need the AIs to destroy us. I think it's uplifting the AIs for a completely different reason."

"Yeah? What's that?" the robot asked.

"I think the basilisk is trying to talk to me. And it's using the AIs to do that."

97

"To you?" Rapscallion asked.

"Yes," Petrova said.

"Specifically to you, Alexandra Petrova, Lieutenant of Firewatch."

"Yeah," she said.

"Talk about developing an unhealthy ego," the robot said.

Petrova shook her head. She felt weird talking about this, even acknowledging what she'd been thinking for some time now. It did sound crazy, didn't it?

Yet it kept happening.

"Eurydice and Undine both spoke to me in a ... familiar way." She realized she might need to explain this for Zhang's and Rapscallion's benefit. "In Russian culture, every name has a bunch of different diminutive forms. Like nicknames that can mean different things. Everyone calls me Sasha, which is just the informal version of Alexandra. It's just friendly. If somebody calls me *Sashka*, though, it means they have romantic feelings for me. Or they want a punch in the face. Nobody except my mother would ever call me *Sashenka*."

"And the AIs—" Rapscallion began.

"They've been calling me Sashenka like they're begging to get deleted. Every damned time. It's like calling me 'little baby Alexandra'. Even when my mother says it, sometimes it's an insult."

"The AIs call you that name?" Zhang said. "Weird."

She did not disagree. "Maybe the AIs use that name just because they know it'll wind me up. I thought that was exactly what Eurydice was doing. Undine, though – Undine said some other things." She couldn't bring herself to repeat them. *You must show them strength. Otherwise they start thinking there is another way.* The same things her mother said to her when they opened the box. "Things my mother said to me, once. Things nobody could know."

"The AIs talk like your mother?" Zhang asked.

"They quote my mother." She ran her fingers through her hair. "Look, it wasn't ... It didn't make any sense. It wasn't even like the words made sense when Undine said them, they had nothing to do with what we were talking about. It was like Undine read them in my memory and then just parroted them back to me. Like the fucking AI read my mind."

She strode over to the console and swept her hand across its surface, blanking out the four images that had been floating there.

"I know how this sounds," she said. "Maybe we should forget it. Just ... it was a theory, or half of a theory anyway, and—"

"No," Zhang said.

She hadn't even realized that she was looking down at the console. Avoiding their collective gaze, avoiding having to see them staring at her.

Now she looked up. Carefully. Cautiously, she looked at Zhang's face.

"Think about it," he said. "Think. Pretend you're the basilisk, a ... a memetic pathogen," he said. He threw his hands up. "I don't know if it's even possible for a human to understand how the basilisk thinks. Or if it even can think, in any way that means something to us. But one thing we can be sure of. It wouldn't speak our languages. Right?"

"It can read our minds," Petrova pointed out. "My mind, anyway. I'm sure of that."

Zhang waved one hand in the air as if he was erasing a white-board. "Fine, fine, but that means — I'm sorry, but that means nothing. I can pick up a book written in Ancient Etruscan, I can look at the words on the page and maybe even sound them out, say them back to you. That doesn't mean I can speak the language, or understand it. The basilisk can mimic human speech but I don't think it understands the things we say."

"What makes you say that?" she asked.

"Because what you described — that's how somebody who doesn't speak your language tries to communicate, right? They just keep repeating words hoping you'll understand. They say them louder and slower like that'll help. In this case the basilisk says them — well, scarier and harder."

"That *really* doesn't help," Petrova pointed out. "Eurydice scared me so much I barely registered what it was saying."

"Right, right, but you get my point, right? The basilisk wants to communicate with us. It wants something from you. It reads your mind and shouts words back at you hoping you'll understand. When you refuse to respond the way it wants you to respond, it gets . . . angry. I think putting human emotions on a thing like this is a really bad idea, but I don't know how else to describe it."

"What you're saying is that it wants to talk to us and when we refuse to listen, it kills us."

"No," Zhang said. "No. No. I don't know if it even understands that we're dying. I don't know if it sees the chaos it's causing, and I definitely don't claim to know whether it would care if it did know. I never claimed this thing was friendly. But if it wants to talk—"

"Then we should listen? Is that what you're saying?" Petrova asked.

Zhang blew air out of his mouth in a long, contemplative exhalation. He lifted his hands slowly, then let them drop to his sides.

"I don't know," he said, finally. "I have no idea what we should do. Listening to this thing drives people insane. It makes them destroy themselves. When an AI listens to it, that AI gets uplifted, made self-aware, which, weird as it sounds, for a ship's AI is a kind of madness. If the basilisk really wants to talk to us, talking back might make it stop killing us. Or maybe it would give the basilisk the tools it needs to finish the job."

He sank down into a chair and then slowly lowered his head forward until his forehead was resting on the console in front of him. Petrova strode away from him, wanting time to just think, to process. To try to understand.

On the other side of *Alpheus'* bridge, Actaeon gently pawed at the deck.

"Okay," Rapscallion said. "One big question."

"Hmm?" Petrova asked.

Rapscallion lifted himself up on his green legs and looked around at all of them with his tiny eyes. "Why you?"

"What?" Petrova frowned. "Why me?"

"Yeah. Why you – out of all the people this thing has met. All the humans. It picked you, specifically, to talk to. Why? Why not him?" the robot said, pointing at Zhang. "He's actually had more experience with it than you."

"I have no idea," Petrova admitted.

98

Figuring out how to respond to the basilisk was the least of their worries, Zhang knew.

There was a warship bearing down on them, hurrying toward them as fast as its powerful engines could carry it.

Once they were back on *Artemis*, he went to the bridge where the deer avatar was waiting for him. Watching him with featureless eyes. Ready to answer all his questions.

"Can you show me what it looks like?" he asked. Actaeon was happy enough to provide. It brought up a holographic image of the ship, but it wasn't what Zhang had expected. *Artemis* and *Alpheus* were graceful, streamlined vehicles, with swooping curves. *Persephone* had been fat and lumbering but still it had possessed a certain majesty and grace.

The warship was just a series of boxes stuck together with girders. It looked unfinished, half built. Guns and thruster units hung from the cobweb of steel beams like things caught in a wicked net. Much of the ship was painted black so it was hard to see. The bridge blazed with light, though, a bright slash of yellow. It looked like the mouth of a dragon about to erupt with fire.

"Damn," Zhang said. "What's it called?"

"*Rhadamanthus*," the AI told him. "Would you like more information about the vehicle? It masses three thousand tons and it was constructed six years ago in a drydock orbiting Phobos. There are forty-one people onboard, including two squadrons of marines who specialize in ship-to-ship combat. They wear armored spacesuits and carry weapons designed to maximize anti-personnel effect while minimizing damage to a ship's hull. This permits them to carry out efficient boarding missions."

"Boarding. You mean, they'll break in here and . . . and kill us," Zhang said.

"Of course, that's only if the *Rhadamanthus* wishes to take *Artemis* intact. If they simply desire to destroy us, they'll use their particle cannons. These fire beams of pure protons accelerated to near the speed of light. The cutting power of such a weapon is more than capable of carving *Artemis* into pieces at a distance of over one hundred kilometers. *Rhadamanthus* possesses twelve such cannons, all of which can be fired simultaneously, with a sustain time of sixteen seconds for—"

"Yeah, yeah," Zhang said, waving one hand over a console to shut the AI up. "I think I've heard all I need to."

"Of course, Doctor. If you have any additional questions—"

"No, no, unless you can tell me how we fight something like that."

"It would be complete folly to try," Actaeon assured him. "I can work up a number of possible stratagems and plans of action but I've already computed that the odds of success are so small that it seems a better course of action should be recommended."

"And, uh. What . . . course of action would that be?" Zhang asked.

"My recommendation would be to take your own lives before *Rhadamanthus* arrives."

Zhang flinched. The RD pulsed against his wrist.

"Actaeon, you aren't possibly suggesting that."

"I'm sorry if it seems fatalistic or grim, Doctor Zhang. I'm simply attempting to provide a realistic estimate of the situation. *Rhadamanthus* is designed for exactly this scenario. Its crew has been educated and trained in the best techniques for taking the lives of humans like yourself. Added to this is the fact that

Artemis is already badly damaged. There is simply no hope. Self-destruction would at least spare you the pain and suffering sure to be part of any military action."

The bridge's access hatch slid open as Petrova stepped into the room. "Actaeon, shut the hell up," she said.

Zhang spun around to see her standing there. Her face was wan, lined with stress and fear. She hurried over to one of the bridge consoles and started working on something, stabbing violently at a virtual keyboard.

"We're not going to just give up," she said. "I don't want to die like that. So I'm not going to."

"You have a plan," Zhang said. "Tell me you have a plan."

"I do," she said. "It's not great, though."

"Tell me anyway," Zhang said.

99
.

"I 've been thinking about this for a while, now," Petrova said, when she'd gathered them together in the storage room. Not on the bridge – not with Actaeon standing there watching her with its inhuman eyes. The AI could see them just fine, of course, wherever they went on *Artemis*, but she could pretend, at least. "I think there's only one chance for us, here. One way we survive all this. We have to complete our mission."

"You mean landing on Paradise-1," Rapscallion said.

"It's the only way we get away from these ships. Even if we survive the encounter with this warship, you think it'll be over? The basilisk has a hundred more ships it can send to kill us."

"A hundred and fifteen," Zhang pointed out. "All of them dedicated to stopping us. The basilisk will do anything to protect the planet, we've proven that time and again."

"Anyway," Rapscallion added, "you know everybody down there on the colony is probably dead, right? Or, and this is a great alternative, they've been infected with the basilisk. We could be landing right in the middle of a zombie apocalypse."

Petrova gritted her teeth. "My priority is our survival. The planet's our only chance."

Zhang stared at her. "You're serious. You really believe that." He scrubbed at his face with his hands. "Damn it, I wish I didn't think you were right. Well, I guess it's settled, then. We're doing this."

"It's not as easy as all that," Petrova admitted. "*Artemis* isn't in any shape for that kind of maneuver. It would break up the second we tried to enter the planet's atmosphere, much less touch down."

"So what do we do?" Rapscallion asked.

"I think it's pretty obvious. We need another ship."

Zhang whistled in surprise. "You want to abandon *Artemis*?" he asked.

"I've been fighting the idea. I'm not entirely sure why," she told them. "Maybe out of a sense of loyalty to this tub." She patted a bulkhead. "It went through hell and somehow it kept us alive, and, yeah, I admit I'll have a hard time just fleeing it like rats from a sinking ship."

Maybe there was more to it than that. Maybe it wasn't the ship she was hesitant to leave, but the memory of Sam Parker. The pilot she'd barely known. Leaving *Artemis* meant literally giving up his ghost. She had very conflicted feelings about that.

Still. This was the best plan she'd come up with.

"Humans are weird," Rapscallion said. "I, for one, have no problem ditching this piece of crap. Well, if we need a new ship, one immediately jumps to mind."

"*Alpheus*," Petrova said, nodding.

Zhang erupted in laughter. "It's a death ship! Yeesh. The idea makes my skin crawl." He shook his head back and forth. "Yeah. It's perfect, though. It's designed for a crew like us. Exactly like us. We can take Actaeon's AI cores over there and just slot them in. It won't take long at all to get *Alpheus* ready for us – we just need to reassemble all the equipment they took apart. But I really don't like this."

"I know. We don't have another choice."

Rapscallion crawled up the wall, perhaps so that he was at eye height with the two of them. "One question," he said. "Having a better ship is great, and I am all for this swap, sure. But how exactly does that help us deal with the warship? *Alpheus* doesn't have any more weapons than *Artemis*. It's fast but not so fast it can outrun those particle beams."

"I have a plan for that, too," Petrova said.

"Yeah?"

"Yes. I just wanted to lead with the easy part."

100

"Easy" turned out to mean hours of back-breaking work, while Zhang waited the whole time to hear an alarm or just someone shouting to say the warship had arrived, that it was firing on them ahead of schedule. Petrova's plan meant shuttling back and forth between the two transports – shuttling as in flying there, in a spacesuit, feeling nauseous and terrified the whole time he was out in the exposed vacuum. It meant hauling heavy cases, crates, and packs from the artificial gravity of *Artemis* through the weightless void into the slightly different artificial gravity of *Alpheus*.

Normally, Rapscallion would have been in charge of moving their luggage back and forth. Now, though, the robot had been given the task of making *Alpheus* livable. Putting all of its equipment back together again, and cleaning up its galley and passenger areas. A job Zhang knew he could never have performed himself. Petrova, for her part, had only one working arm. So he didn't complain about being turned into a pack mule, and yet . . .

There was a surprising amount of stuff that needed to be transported over to *Alpheus*. The cylinders that formed Actaeon's AI core had to be moved one at a time, and very carefully. If one of them was damaged it could leave them without a functional ship's AI, which would be disastrous. They couldn't all be moved at once, either, because Actaeon needed to stay functional on *Artemis* until the transition was complete. Meanwhile, Petrova had her own headaches to handle. With one arm still in a cast she'd decided she was better at handling the two ships' computers. While Zhang moved cargo, she wrestled with overseeing the transfer of a ship's AI to a new ship that had not been formally decommissioned. The architecture of permissions and partitioning of firewalls and expansion of root access roles was ... frankly over Zhang's head. He had only the most cursory knowledge of how computers even worked, and now wasn't the time to learn. So he kept his head down and kept moving *stuff*.

Petrova wanted him to move everything of any use from *Artemis* to *Alpheus*. Both ships held plenty of food and water and oxygen, more than enough for two people for any reasonable length of time. Petrova refused to let the stores on *Artemis* go to waste, however, so Zhang had to haul giant tanks of water over to *Alpheus*, crates full of food and medical supplies and sundries – cleaning supplies, hardware, toiletries, a giant bottle of hot sauce, Sam Parker's personal effects just in case they got a chance to return them to his next of kin back on Mars.

He had to transfer the medical laser Petrova had used to defang *Persephone*, as well as a box full of her sidearms and bullets.

Tools. Hand tools, power tools, electronic and information tech tools. Endless boxes and cartons of emergency supplies – patches to be used in case of hull punctures, glowsticks and a very specialized sort of wrench that could be used to crank open hatches in case the power went out.

Spare clothing, spare spacesuits, spare feedstock for the 3D printers.

Survival equipment in case they crash-landed on Paradise-1 in some desolate and hostile environment: thermal blankets, water condensers and purifiers, flares and compasses and solar stoves. Not one but two tents, complete with metal stakes and poles.

There was a long and fruitless discussion about whether they should bring the contents of *Artemis'* septic and graywater tanks. The waste could be recycled, after all, and reused when they were on *Alpheus*. Zhang had put his foot down, though, and refused to haul literal shit across kilometers of open space just in case it would come in handy at some hypothetical future date. RD had tightened around his forearm, warning him to play nice, but he'd stood firm and eventually Petrova had relented. The piss tank on *Artemis* would remain unmoved.

It seemed like it was impossible that he would get it all moved across in time. The warship was on a fast approach and the window for getting everything squared away was shrinking rapidly. Until suddenly – a sort of reprieve.

A temporary one, anyway.

"They're decelerating," Rapscallion told him. "I've been keeping an eye on the telescopes while you move Actaeon's cores. Just to make sure the AI doesn't miss anything."

"And they're slowing down?" Zhang asked. He had just dumped a big crate in one of *Alpheus'* cargo storage compartments and he was catching his breath before racing back to *Artemis*. "Does that make sense?"

"Sure, yeah," the robot said. "I mean, they would have to slow down unless they wanted to shoot right past us. Their deceleration profile is a little odd, though. Like they're slowing down faster than they strictly need to. Like maybe they're being cautious?"

"Cautious?" Zhang asked. "That's odd. Why would they be cautious of us? We're no threat to *Rhadamanthus*."

"No. None whatsoever. Anyway, that means you have a little more time to get everything moved over. So, congratulations."

"Wow. Thanks," Zhang said. He took a quick drink of water and got back to it, headed back to *Artemis* for another load.

101
·

The bridge of *Artemis* somehow felt more empty than it had before. Chillier. Like the ship knew what was coming and had shut itself down emotionally. It was all in Petrova's head but she couldn't shake the feeling something vital had been removed. *Artemis* had been badly damaged ever since they arrived in the Paradise system, and it had felt like a wounded animal at times, but always like it was alive somehow, like it had an emotional life of its own and she had responded to its feelings and its stresses. Now it felt like an apartment she had already moved out of – so empty and neglected. She wanted to sit down but she felt like she had no right to use the bridge's chairs.

It was silly. So silly, what she was thinking, feeling. Funny how hard such silly things were to shake, though.

"Actaeon," Petrova said. She had work to do. "How are you feeling? Are you up to this?"

"I am operating at fourteen per cent capacity," the deer told her.

The avatar looked like it was about to vanish in a puff of pixels. Its holographic image had been reduced to a low-polygon version of its former self, so that it looked more like a cartoon of a deer than an actual animal. The stars on the tips of its antlers looked painted on and its eyes were just slits on the sides of its head.

"I understand my appearance may be slightly alarming. I

assure you I have prioritized ship's systems over my own holographic display."

One of the systems that had been off-loaded to *Alpheus* already, it seemed, was Actaeon's natural speech processor. It sounded now like the computer it was. Like a machine. It just made the bridge feel more empty.

"I am still functioning in my administrative and advisory roles," the AI told her. "I have not forgotten present tasks."

"Meaning?" Petrova asked.

"I have continued to monitor the approach of *Rhadamanthus*. I have gathered additional data about its construction and current status. For instance, I'd like to draw your attention to this."

A screen appeared before Petrova. Just a flat, two-dimensional display of telescopic imaging. Metadata in the corner of the screen told her the picture had come from *Alpheus'* sensors, which were much better than *Artemis'* damaged equipment.

"Tell me what I'm looking at," Petrova said. The image seemed to show the exterior of *Rhadamanthus'* hull, specifically a section of it in the middle of the ship. She saw what looked like an airlock hatch except that it was slightly ajar and there was a thick, sooty stain around its edges. "It looks like there was some kind of explosion there."

"A controlled explosion," Actaeon told her. "Judging by the residue left around the hatch and the damage to its latching mechanism, my guess is that shaped charges were used to blow it open at some point in the recent past."

Petrova scratched at her left shoulder. She really wanted to scratch the skin of her injured left hand but it was buried so deeply in its cast that the shoulder was all she could reach. "I'm confused," she admitted. "Someone forced their way inside that airlock?"

"No," Actaeon said. "My best inference is that the charges were placed on the inside of that hatch. Someone forced their way *out*."

Petrova touched the console in front of her, thinking to bring up more imagery, more data. She shook her head. "Hold on." She thought about it for a second. "So they were sealed inside? Locked in. Do you see any indication why someone would do that?"

"I'm afraid that's outside my knowledge base. All I can do is show you unusual things I have noticed about *Rhadamanthus*. There's more, if you'd like to see it."

"Yeah, okay," Petrova said.

The screen cleared and showed a different view, this time of one of *Rhadamanthus*' big particle beam guns. It was big and fat with a long, wicked-looking barrel, making Petrova think of the poison gland and stinger of a hornet. A single figure in a spacesuit hovered near it, as if included for scale – the human shape made the gun look huge. There seemed to be something wrong with the image, though, and eventually Petrova worked it out. There were stars moving past in the background. Which meant this was video, not a still image.

The human figure wasn't moving. She zoomed in on the view and saw that they were tangled up in a safety line, dangling from the gun emplacement on a taut rope.

"That person is dead, aren't they?" she asked, in a very soft voice.

Actaeon responded at a normal volume – loud enough to make her jump. "Almost certainly. The temperature of the spacesuit is well below the freezing point of water. Suggesting that the suit stopped functioning some time ago. I have a third image if you'd like to see it."

"Another anomaly?" Petrova asked.

"Yes."

Actaeon cleared her screen and put up yet another view. This one was a close-up of the slit-like window on the ship's bridge.

Petrova gasped. There was no real mystery about this image, no confusing data to process and analyze.

There was no mistaking the blood splatter that obscured the viewport. It looked exactly like what happened if you shot someone in the head at close range.

"I cannot explain these three anomalies," Actaeon said. "That is beyond my capabilities. However, a certain inference is difficult to escape."

"They're fighting over there," Petrova said. "They're killing each other."

"Yes." Actaeon dismissed the screen and left her staring forward, through the wide viewport at the front of the bridge.

Rhadamanthus wasn't visible there, nor Paradise-1. Just a sweep of perfectly normal, perfectly distant stars. She tried to let the cold emptiness of space wash through her. That could help, sometimes. The fact that she was so tiny and insignificant against the backdrop of the universe. Not this time, though.

"This is not inconsistent with what we've seen elsewhere," Actaeon said. "On *Persephone* and *Alpheus*. I consider it safe to suggest that the occupants of *Rhadamanthus* have been infected with the basilisk and have succumbed to its self-destructive imposed ideations."

"Sure."

A shiver ran down Petrova's spine, because she'd just had a terrible thought. All those stars out there – most were really stars, far off and enormous and unreachable. Some of the dots of light, though, were probably other ships. Other ships in the blockade around Paradise-1. Every single one of which, she thought, had probably succumbed to those imposed ideations.

Thousands of people on those ships, and had they all, every single one of them, descended into the same madness? Had they all torn each other to pieces?

They'd been running since they arrived in the system. Running and fighting and barely managing to stay alive. She hadn't really had a chance to think about what that meant.

"Lieutenant Petrova, I think it is my turn."

"Hmm?" she asked.

"I would like to inquire if you are all right. You seem detached and distant."

"I guess," she said, and then took a long time to ponder what it was she was supposedly guessing. Maybe she was guessing at how tired she was, or how sad it all made her. "I guess I was hoping," she said eventually, "that it would be different. That its AI protected its crew like you protected us."

"It would appear this is not the case. I suppose it's possible that there is some other explanation for the signs of violence we see on *Rhadamanthus*. That the basilisk might not be responsible."

"Occam's razor would suggest otherwise. No, it's the same old song. The question this raises, though, is why us?"

"I'm afraid I don't parse your meaning, Lieutenant."

"It's pretty clear that every ship's AI that came here got hit by the basilisk on arrival. We still don't know how it's transmitted, but that's the course of the infection. The basilisk attacks every AI that comes close. Then the AIs infect their crew and passengers."

"That is the model of infection we have seen so far."

Petrova nodded to herself. "It tried to take us down, too, but we won where everybody else lost. How is that possible, Actaeon? It was you – you who did it. If you hadn't shut yourself down, locked yourself in that cycle of restarts, you would have infected us. Right? Instead, you locked yourself down and that gave us time to figure out what was going on. To find a way to fight back."

"I do not possess a full set of working memories from that time. I believe I deleted some things from my memory as a protective measure. For instance, I do not remember why I filled this bridge with holographic plant life."

Petrova thought of the dark forest that had choked the room before they treated Actaeon. It had felt like a completely different ship back then. No AI, everything a mystery, and Parker – Parker had been there to . . . to help her think things through.

To save her. He had led her out of danger, led her to the bridge where she reconnected with Zhang and got things stabilized. Parker had just been a simulation. A hologram. When Actaeon was restored to its full functioning, Parker had disappeared.

"You must have known something was happening. You must have thought the trees would mean something to us. Right?"

"That seems logical."

Maybe – and she didn't want to say it out loud – but maybe that was why Parker got simulated as well. The AI shut down its own deer avatar but it needed to have a face, a presence onboard to help her and Zhang.

She had read once about split personalities in humans, that sometimes people under extreme emotional or physical stress could split themselves off into multiple identities. Maybe that was what had happened. Maybe Actaeon, knowing it couldn't trust itself, created a separate, walled-off personality and gave it Sam Parker's face.

They knew that *Artemis* had been installed with advanced computers, far beyond what a normal transport needed. She'd assumed that had been Director Lang's doing, that Firewatch had sent them here with so much processing power because it knew it was sending them into hell and wanted to give them a fighting chance. Maybe it was that robust computer architecture that let Actaeon create a ghost for them.

Parker. Dear God, she wished he was there with her at that moment. Someone to bounce ideas off. Someone to make her feel they could get through this, that they had a chance. Zhang was ... well, he was fine, and she owed him her sanity, but he wasn't exactly reassuring. Rapscallion was hardly someone to turn to when she needed support.

Parker ...

"No," she said.

"I'm sorry, Lieutenant?"

"You asked if I was all right. And no. I'm not," she said. "I'm really not. But it doesn't matter. We have to keep going. I have to keep working. Show me that imagery from *Rhadamanthus* again. Maybe there's something there we can use."

102

"Calling *Artemis.* This is UEGMC *Rhadamanthus* calling *Artemis.* You are required by law to respond to this hail. If you do not or cannot respond you will be boarded and submitted to inspection. Come in, *Artemis.*"

Petrova put her good hand against her chest. It felt like her heart was going to literally jump out of her ribcage, and her hand was the only thing holding it down.

"*Artemis,* you are required by law to respond. Come in, *Artemis.*"

The voice was gruff, authoritative. It sounded exactly like the drill instructors she had known back in the Firewatch training school. The marines were a different branch of the Armed Forces but she supposed some things were the same everywhere.

She'd always hated those instructors. That had been their job, of course, to make her hate them. Hate was a great motivator and inflicting fear and suffering on your students was a way to make them take their lessons seriously. But the instructors always seemed to take so much pleasure in it.

"*Artemis,* this is your last opportunity to respond."

Zhang stared at her with wide eyes. She gave him a slow nod, then gestured at Actaeon to open comms.

"*Rhadamanthus,*" she said, "this is *Artemis.* Specifically, this is Lieutenant Alexandra Petrova of Firewatch. Call me Sasha — everyone does."

Silence. Silence for what felt like a solid minute, though it was probably a matter of seconds.

Long enough for her to look around the bridge. At Zhang, who was sweating profusely. At Rapscallion, who had installed himself in a massive armored body bristling with spikes – in case they got boarded, he said, he wanted to take as many of them down with him as he could. At Actaeon. The deer stared back at her impassively.

It was dark on the bridge – they'd turned off every light in the ship. She could only see by the emitted light of Actaeon's avatar, an eerie blue glow that made Zhang look like he was dead. She assumed she looked the same to him.

She took a breath and launched into the script she'd written in her head.

"We sure are glad to see you, Marines," she said. "We just arrived insystem a few days ago. We did not expect to get attacked the second we showed up, but that's what happened. The *Persephone*, a big colony ship, started throwing crates at us at high enough speed to—"

"Quiet, *Artemis*," the drill instructor voice said.

Petrova blinked and took an involuntary step backward. She felt like she'd been slapped.

"*Artemis*, we are currently tracking you on a course toward the planet Paradise-1. Can you confirm your bearing?"

"Yes," she said. "Yes. We're going planetside. We're supposed to check on the people there. That's why Firewatch sent us. I have orders from Director Lang. You are required by protocol to assist us in carrying out those orders."

"The planet is currently under blockade. You will not be permitted to set down. Are you prepared to change your course immediately? Think very carefully about how you answer. You will not be given a second chance."

"Negative, *Rhadamanthus*. We have our orders and they come from the very top. Are you telling me that Director Lang doesn't have authority to pass your blockade?"

"Your director – and Firewatch – don't have jurisdiction here. Not anymore. Change your course right now, *Artemis*, or we will open fire."

"I'm sorry, say again, *Rhadamanthus*? Did you just tell me Firewatch doesn't have jurisdiction here?"

"Only the Elect have the right to land on Paradise-1. Only those who have been chosen, their hearts weighed and measured and found worthy."

Zhang's eyes nearly popped out of his head. He mouthed the words *what the hell?* at her. Petrova bit her lip.

Clearly the crew of *Rhadamanthus* had been possessed by some kind of religious mania. As to the specifics of what they believed, well, hopefully they would never have to find out what weird, horrible seed the basilisk had planted in their brains.

"*Rhadamanthus*, I know you're going to resist this but you have to listen to me. You've been infected by a mental pathogen, something called a basilisk, and—"

"You are clearly corrupted beyond redemption, *Artemis*. I would ask God to have mercy on your souls, but after I'm done with you there won't be enough left for even Him to save. Over and out."

"Right," she said. She nodded at Actaeon. "Evasive action," she said.

103

⬤

The fusion cells in *Artemis'* drive units lit up with blue fire. They had been cold almost since the ship's arrival in the Paradise system, and it took them a second to warm up. But *Artemis* had been built for speed, for acceleration, and when Actaeon sent full power to the engines they responded like pent-up animals, bursting with power.

Artemis shot forward, its nose dipping toward the planet. Actaeon fired some maneuvering jets near its midsection and the transport twisted over on its side, presenting the thinnest possible cross section to the big guns on *Rhadamanthus*.

For a second, perhaps, it looked like it might work. Like *Artemis* might pull ahead of its enemy and make a break for Paradise-1. As the first blasts from the particle cannons lashed out, Actaeon sent the transport into a spinning maneuver that actually evaded the bright streaks of fire.

Of course, *Artemis* couldn't evade forever.

Nor could it keep maneuvering like that. Deep inside its damaged corridors, in its bones, it was wounded already. Rapscallion had made what repairs he could but the ship had barely held itself together while it floated motionless in space.

Now those repairs started to come undone under the stress of acceleration. Support struts under *Artemis'* skin creaked and then snapped. Rivets shook loose, welds failed and buckled. Something caught on fire in the passenger section and then exploded, breaching the hull and sending light and hissing air bursting out into space. The ship's very spine started to crumple under the stress, even as Actaeon sent the ship through more desperate and energetic maneuvers, dancing and spinning on its axis.

Rhadamanthus, meanwhile, adjusted its targeting solution. One of its beams landed, cutting through *Artemis'* fuel tanks in a spectacular explosion. Another sliced right through its bridge section, shattering the big viewport and sending shards of polycarbonate glittering all around its nose.

It was a race to see what would destroy *Artemis* first – the attacking warship or the transport's own frailty. In the end it was hard to tell which of them won out.

It took less than a second, all told. The particle beams carved *Artemis* into pieces while its reactor overloaded inside its thick rear section, an incredible eruption of heat and force expanding like a blossom of pure energy. Pieces of the transport flew in every direction, parts of it spinning off into cold space, others colliding in mid-flight and bouncing off each other.

Rhadamanthus kept shooting. Particle beams cut the pieces into smaller pieces, into scraps, into tiny fragments of junk. The job the warship did was thorough, exacting, final.

On the bridge of *Alpheus*, Petrova watched, unable to look away.

She had to mute their comms, because she was afraid *Rhadamanthus* might hear her make some small, soft sound of dismay. Of despair. Watching the cloud of debris that used to be their ship had an effect on her she hadn't quite expected.

Maybe it was just a way for her to mourn Sam Parker. Or maybe she was feeling grief for *Artemis* itself. The ship had kept her alive far longer than she'd had a right to expect. It had served her incredibly well and now – now she had destroyed it, used it as a decoy to buy herself just a little more time.

104
●

"Talk about being thorough," Rapscallion said, an hour later. An hour he'd spent using *Alpheus'* sensors to watch the debris cloud of *Artemis* as it spun vacantly in space. As it cooled, slowly, from incandescent heat down to something closer to the ambient background temperature of space.

Very few words had been spoken on the bridge in that time. The humans seemed distracted, deeply affected by the view of *Artemis'* last moments. Rapscallion had his own feelings about *Artemis* but like all of his emotions they were under his control. He was also less attached to *things* in general – because he shed old bodies all the time and replaced them with new ones, the idea that they would simply shift from *Artemis* to *Alpheus* bothered him a lot less, he thought, than humans who were stuck with one body their whole lives. Hell, *Alpheus* was all but identical to the old ship, and they'd even brought Actaeon with them. He wasn't sure how you were supposed to tell the difference between the two ships, now. "You think they bought it?" he asked.

They'd done everything they could to make it look like there were still people on *Artemis*. Actaeon, working remotely, had switched on heating units on the bridge that did nothing but radiate at exactly standard human body temperature. The AI had projected images of Zhang and Petrova standing by the viewports, looking scared.

It all hung on whether *Rhadamanthus* had seen them moving

their equipment over to the new ship. Whether the warship would bother scanning the other transport that was lurking suspiciously nearby.

They were keeping a low profile as best they could, on *Alpheus*. They'd switched off all the lights on *Alpheus* and the two humans were wearing foil blankets to try to mask their heat signatures. Rapscallion wasn't allowed to move around the ship, in case he accidentally walked in front of a viewport or something.

"We'll find out soon enough," Petrova replied, in a whisper. As if *Rhadamanthus* could hear her through a dozen kilometers of hard vacuum. She pointed at a holoscreen floating before her, one of very few light sources on *Alpheus*. It showed a pattern of microwave radiation playing across the field of debris where *Artemis* used to be. "They're checking the wreckage. Probably looking for bodies."

"In that mess?" Rapscallion asked. "Unlikely. They cut it up so fine the most they would find would be a tooth or a fingertip or something." He saw her wince but he didn't know why that bothered her. This had been her plan, after all.

"I wish they would just go away," Zhang said. He looked miserable. Well, the temperature in the room was close to freezing – as low as the humans could stand. "This would be a good time for us to get some sleep."

"While we wait to see if we're already dead or not?" Petrova asked. She couldn't seem to look away from her holoscreen. "Sure, I'll just have a nice cup of herbal tea and curl up."

Zhang laughed, a sudden, eruptive sound that he quickly stifled. All the same it was a funny sound to hear on the grim bridge, and it actually made Petrova look up – and shoot him a smile.

"Maybe we should change into our pajamas," Zhang said.

Petrova clapped a hand over her mouth to stifle the sound of her guffaw. Soon the two of them were giggling uncontrollably, even as they clearly tried to stifle their reaction. "Maybe," Petrova said, "if we close our eyes they won't be able to see us, either. Maybe if we're lucky they'll realize they're keeping us awake and they'll leave just to be polite."

"Yeah," Zhang said, "because we've been *so* lucky since we got here."

"Yeah, well, obviously," Petrova said, her eyes bright and wet, "we're due a break."

Zhang and Petrova stared at each other as if daring one another to break out in a full body laugh. They stared at each other so hard, their lips quivering, that Rapscallion began to wonder if they'd both suffered some kind of simultaneous neurological collapse.

Then Zhang sputtered and shook and a deep, roaring laugh came out of him. Immediately, Petrova rushed over to wrap her hands around his mouth, not to suffocate him, it seemed, but simply to trap the noise inside him.

"Humans are weird," Rapscallion said.

Which just made them both laugh all the harder.

105
•

The moment of levity didn't last very long. Petrova tried to close the holoscreen but found she just couldn't do it. She couldn't stand the idea of not knowing. Of waiting in the dark with no way to tell if she was about to be blown into a million pieces or if she was safe.

Not that the screen could tell her much. *Alpheus* had some amazing sensors and unlike the ones on *Artemis* they were all intact, but she couldn't use them. If she tried to ping *Rhadamanthus* with radar or a millimeter wave scan or even a geodesic laser, the warship would notice. They would wonder why this apparently deserted transport in a high orbit was scanning them, and they would be sure to come investigate.

So she was limited mostly to telescopes, passive instruments that simply received whatever light or radiation they could observe. Which couldn't tell her much. She could see that *Rhadamanthus* was still there, still keeping station just a few kilometers away from the scrap cloud that used to be *Artemis*. The warship moved, occasionally, but only to avoid being pelted by some fast-moving piece of debris, or maybe to get a better angle for the scans it kept running of the flotsam.

They had run a *lot* of scans. She wasn't entirely sure why. Did they think there might be an escape pod hidden inside the cloud? Some piece of *Artemis* big enough to hide a living human in a space suit? Surely they could see, like her, that there just wasn't anything in that cloud capable of sustaining life.

So did they suspect something else? She wondered if it was all a ruse, if *Rhadamanthus* knew exactly where she was and they were just waiting for her to tip her hand.

Alpheus couldn't just stay quiet forever. It was getting damned cold. Way too cold for comfort, even with multiple layers of foil wrapped around her body. The foil was a great insulator but it wasn't perfect. Some of her body heat was still escaping, all the time. Eventually they would have to turn on *Alpheus'* heaters again.

When they did, if *Rhadamanthus* was watching, it would be like they'd lit a signal beacon. The warship's sensor array was designed for exactly this kind of work – hunting enemies in the dark.

All she could do was wait. All she could do was hope that *Rhadamanthus* would eventually get bored and move on.

She managed to eventually drag herself away from her holo-screen, though it took a real effort of will. The deciding factor was that she really, really needed to urinate. She lifted one hand and forced herself to wave it across the screen, dismissing it. Then she ran to the head, her thermal blankets rustling noisily around her.

She had intended to take care of the necessary and then hurry back to the screen but it was such an amazing relief to not be looking at the display that she found herself dawdling on the way back. She stopped outside the hatch that led to the bridge because she heard something – just a soft little chime coming from the pilot's ready room. The little space with the bed where she had recovered from having her hand mangled.

No, no, that had been the space on *Artemis*. This one looked exactly the same, except it was cleaner and all the lights inside worked properly. Its hatch was standing open. She thought Zhang must be inside so she poked her head in but found the place empty.

There was a small galley built into one wall of the compartment. Not much, just a miniature refrigerator and an autocooker. A bowl full of food was sitting in the output tray, with a spoon lying next to it.

"Zhang?" she said, though she was loath to break the silence. "Did you make some food?"

He didn't answer. Petrova's brow furrowed as she looked behind her, back into the corridor.

"Actaeon," she said. "Where's Doctor Zhang?"

"Doctor Zhang is in his cabin, sleeping," the AI replied.

She frowned. "You didn't make this food, did you? Were you trying to tell me something?"

"I don't understand," Actaeon said. "What food?"

Petrova stepped further into the ready room and looked down at the bowl. She saw right away it was full of some kind of colorful breakfast cereal, slowly turning to mush in a bath of milk.

It wasn't the kind of thing Petrova would ever eat. It didn't look much like Zhang's taste, either, but she had to admit she had no idea what he ate for breakfast. Curious, she picked up the spoon and lifted a small mouthful of the cereal to her lips.

It was cold. Well, of course it was – the whole ship was cold. Actually cooking food would have changed *Alpheus'* thermal signature, even if only by a tiny bit. It would be a luxury they couldn't afford. Petrova took another bite.

It was very, very sweet and tasted like some synthesized fruit product. It was kind of horrible, actually. Her stomach growled at her and she took another bite. Really horrible, except she kept spooning more and more of it into her mouth.

For a bad second or two she considered the fact that maybe Zhang's cure hadn't worked on her. That the basilisk was still in her head telling her she was starving and she needed to eat.

But no. It wasn't that. She was just scared and cold and it had been far too long since her last meal. The cereal was horrible but in the best possible way. She finished the bowl and then lifted it to her mouth to suck down the last of the sugary milk. When it was gone, when she'd set the bowl back down, she stared at it for a long time.

The empty bowl just lay there. Hard and cold. A thin crescent of viscous milk lay in the bottom, mirroring the overhead lights.

"Actaeon," she said.

"Yes, Lieutenant?"

"Whoever put this bowl out for me, tell them I appreciate it." Rapscallion. It had to be Rapscallion. She'd seen the way he had started to grow protective and solicitous of Zhang's welfare. Maybe the robot had started thinking that way about her, too. "I was hungry and it hit the spot."

"I'm afraid I don't know who prepared that meal," Actaeon admitted.

"Don't worry about it."

She didn't want to question it too much. There were far more important things to think about than stray hallucinations. She went straight back to the bridge and opened up her holoscreen again so she could see what *Rhadamanthus* was up to.

106

In his cabin Zhang tried desperately not to think about what was happening, or not happening, outside of *Alpheus'* hull. He tried to pretend that everything was fine. That didn't work very well.

Sitting up on his bed, he pulled down his sleeve and looked at the golden tracery wrapped around his forearm. The RD seemed unaffected by his mood, though he knew it was keeping a close eye on his neurochemistry and his adrenaline levels. It always did.

"I don't suppose you'd want to do something helpful, for a change?" he asked.

The tracery of gold metal writhed gently, as if trying to soothe him. It squeezed his flesh with a rhythmic pulsing motion and he realized with a start that it was giving him a massage. Sometimes it seemed like the RD wanted to be compassionate, though he knew better. He knew it was simply trying to keep him calm – its main job, after all, was to keep him from getting so emotional he did something rash.

He wanted very much to just peel it off his skin and throw it across the room. Instead, he sighed and said, "Can you open a screen and show me what's happening?"

That should have been Actaeon's job. If Zhang had simply spoken into the air and asked for a screen the ship's AI would be happy to oblige. Lately, though, Zhang had started to trust the deer avatar on the bridge less and less. It thought humanity was doomed. Well, maybe it was, but Zhang wasn't ready to put all of his faith in a machine that thought he was a lost cause.

The RD gave him a resentfully hard squeeze, but then it did as he asked. The golden tendrils stretched upward, away from his arm, to form an elegant frame for a tiny holoscreen that showed a dark stretch of space. The view shifted to zoom in on a long white shape, swollen at its center.

"That's *Persephone*," he said. "Why are you showing me the colony ship?"

RD didn't need to answer. Even as Zhang watched the blocky, planless shape of *Rhadamanthus* moved into the frame, gliding slowly toward the colony ship. *Persephone* was so big it made *Rhadamanthus* look like a starling pestering a rhinoceros, but Zhang had no doubt which of the two ships was more dangerous. As he watched, *Rhadamanthus* slowed down until it was just barely nudging its way toward *Persephone* – then, with a sudden violence, it launched half a dozen harpoons at the colony ship, long barbed spikes trailing lines so thin they were all but invisible. The harpoons struck *Persephone* in a dozen different places and then the lines were reeled in until *Rhadamanthus* nestled up against the colony ship's hull, tying itself tightly to the bigger ship.

"Call Petrova," Zhang said. "Lieutenant? Are you watching this?"

She sounded annoyed, as if he'd interrupted her at something. "You mean *Rhadamanthus* and *Persephone*? Yeah. I'm watching. I don't like this."

"What are they doing over there?" Zhang asked.

"It's a standard boarding tactic the Marines use when approaching a hostile ship. They'll cut a hole through *Persephone*'s hull and get onboard that way. My guess is that they tried making contact with Eurydice and when they couldn't get a response they decided that *Persephone* was an enemy craft. I don't know what they plan on doing to the people over there."

Zhang swallowed thickly. He remembered Eurydice's last

words to him, when it had begged him to spare it from destruction. It had said he was consigning all the colonists onboard to death as they drifted aimlessly through space.

He had a bad feeling that they were going to meet a different sort of fate – and much sooner. "We don't know much about what form the basilisk took on *Rhadamanthus*," he said, "but they said something about judgment and grace. Petrova—"

"You think I like this? You don't have to watch, you know. You could just shut down your display. Think about something else."

But he kept watching. He watched though nothing happened, as minutes dragged on and on. Whatever drama was playing itself out over there was happening inside *Persephone* and he had no access to it.

Still he watched. So when something did happen, he saw it.

Eventually *Rhadamanthus* cut the lines holding it to *Persephone*'s side. With little puffs of its jets the warship backed away from *Persephone*, slowly at first then darting away like it was in a hurry.

When it was a certain distance away, *Persephone*'s hull started to break out in little orange blooms of fire. Tiny explosions, each of them sending up a fountain of debris. They tore through the hull in long lines of destruction until the colony ship was just an empty husk, flashes of light bursting inside of its hollowed-out shell. They were scuttling the big ship, making sure no one else could ever use it. Reducing it to scrap.

"Why?" Zhang asked, his eyes clamped shut now that there was nothing left to see. "Why?"

"The same reason they destroyed *Artemis*, maybe" Petrova said. "I don't think I really want to know."

107

Eventually, *Rhadamanthus* moved on.

The warship acted like it hadn't even seen *Alpheus*, though it must have shown up on their sensor scans. Maybe they'd done a sufficiently good job of playing dead. It didn't matter. "This is our chance," she told the others. "Maybe our last chance."

She turned and looked at them. Zhang looked like shit – like he'd been doing drugs. The RD on his arm squirmed and she realized she was probably right about that. Rapscallion had built himself a new body. Bipedal, mostly human. The only problem was that he'd put the face on upside down.

A chill ran down her spine but she refused to acknowledge it.

"Look," she said. "It's right there."

She pointed at the viewports at the front of the bridge. Front and center hung the brown disk of Paradise-1. Their goal. She knew she was putting too much hope on such a drab planet. There was no guarantee that landing there would help them or make their situation more survivable. But it was the best option they had. She was sure of it.

She called up a holoscreen that showed a magnified view of the planet, a globe in various shades of brown and blue. It was impossible to see any human-built structures from this distance but Actaeon put a dot over the place where the main colony was located, a valley between two low mountain ranges. "That's the finish line," she said. "And here's what's in our way of getting there."

She reached over to tap at the screen and called up scores of tiny dots orbiting the planet, a thick, diffuse ring of dust motes. "There are more than a hundred ships still out there." She touched a few of the circling dots and new screens appeared to show her enlarged imagery. From this distance most of the ships were just blurry blobs but she could make out familiar lines in some of the views. Sleek, sharp-nosed transports like *Artemis* and *Alpheus*. Blocky warships like *Rhadamanthus* and colony ships like *Persephone*. But also scout ships with minimal crew areas, mostly just engines and sensor pods welded together. Freighters that were ninety-nine percent composed of cargo modules, held together by the flimsiest of skeletons.

There were just so many.

"Firewatch sent a lot of ships here – I really wish I knew what Director Lang was thinking. Why waste so many people?"

"It's literally unthinkable," Zhang said. "What she – what they did."

Petrova shook her head. "We send a ship here and it goes missing, so Firewatch sends a new ship to find the first one. Then the second one fails to report in, so she sends a third ... and suddenly ... this. *This* has been going on for more than a year."

"And ... " Zhang grunted in disgust. "None of them has made it. They must have all had the same mission we did, right? To make contact with the colony. Not a single one of them made it."

"You know what I see there?" Rapscallion pointed out.

Petrova turned to look at the robot.

"An algorithm. A plan for solving a problem where you don't know all the variables."

"You think Firewatch has some kind of grand plan?" Zhang asked. "They're throwing spaceships at a problem just to see if one of them makes it, is that it?"

"No. That would be trial and error. Which is a kind of algorithm, but that's not what I see here. Firewatch isn't just doing the same thing over and over. It sends a different kind of ship each time. Except – there's something that's been bugging me. *Alpheus* is almost identical to *Artemis*, right? Everybody else has noticed that?"

"The walls in my cabin are even painted the same color," Zhang agreed.

"And the people on *Alpheus*. You know, before they got, um . . . before they died," Rapscallion said. Petrova was surprised to find him stumbling over indelicate language. He'd changed since she first met him. "You had a doctor, a guy from Firewatch, a pilot and a robot. Just like us."

"Now that you mention it, that bothered me," Petrova admitted.

"I checked *Alpheus*' logs and it looks like they were sent here three months ago. Shortly before we got sent." The robot's upside-down face wagged up and down as it spoke. Petrova had to turn away – it was too distracting. "When *Alpheus* failed," Rapscallion continued, "they sent *Artemis*. I'm willing to bet that if you looked at what ships they're sending, you'd find there's a progression. An algorithm, using those same ingredients. Three humans and a robot. The same kind of AI, the same exact con-figuration of ship."

Petrova thought about that for a second. "You figure they're homing in on something. They're figuring this out, little by little. Every time Firewatch sends a new ship here they learn a little something."

"By watching how the ship fails. How the crew dies," Zhang said.

"Right," Petrova said. "They get a little more data, and they use it to design the next mission. And somehow they've deter-mined that a ship like *Artemis*, with a crew and passengers like us, is the most likely to succeed."

"That's . . . that's something," Zhang said, his eyes wide. "That's a good thing. Right? It means we've got an actual chance. We're the best possibility Firewatch ever came up with. We could be the ones to make it."

"Maybe," Petrova said.

"Or, you know, the least likely to fail," Rapscallion pointed out. "We haven't made it yet and the odds against us are still ridiculously high. We're far more likely to end up as just one more data point on the graph."

Zhang looked like he wanted to throw up.

"What?" Rapscallion asked. "I was just being accurate."

Petrova scowled at him. "Fix your damn face," she said.

The robot reached up and touched the plastic of his inverted brow. "Oh, sorry. I put it on in a hurry." He reached up and twisted the face around until it was almost the right way up. Just slightly askew.

108

"Let's focus on this," Petrova said. "If we try to land on Paradise-1, we have to expect resistance. Maybe a lot of it. *Rhadamanthus* isn't the only warship here, not by a long shot. We don't have weapons to let us fight our way through. The one advantage we have is that we're fast. I've been tracking the warships in this ring. Actaeon?"

The holoscreen view changed so that some of the dust motes around the planet flared a bright red. Not too many of them, only about a dozen or so. "They're mostly just sitting in parking orbits. Like most of the ships here. Only *Rhadamanthus* was really close to us, and it's moving away, now. If we wait about sixteen hours, this happens."

The dots sped up in their orbits as the display fast-forwarded through time. When it stopped, all of the warships were clustered on the far side of the planet. "We'll have a brief window when they'll all be out of line of sight."

"And we can get down to the planet without being attacked," Zhang said.

"I have no doubt that the second we start accelerating toward the planet every ship out there is going to come for us," Petrova told him. "We will get attacked, that's one thing I'm certain about. But if we're fast enough, we might be able to evade the worst of it. We just might make it through."

Zhang came over to stand next to her screen so he could

study the whirling dots better. "I see one problem with this plan," he said.

"Yeah, I was sure that you would. Tell me."

Zhang looked her right in the eye. "Even if we do make it to the surface—" He shook his head.

"I know, I know. The people down there on the planet may have been infected by the basilisk," Petrova said. *Including, possibly, my mother*, she thought. She had to fight to stay detached about that. "You think we're just going to get down there and find the place crawling with zombies, or religious zealots, or . . . who knows what."

Zhang nodded. "No, actually. I've begun to think that won't be the case."

"Really? Why not?"

Zhang pointed at the screen, at the red dots. "The ships here, the ships Firewatch sent – they're infected by the basilisk but they're also blockading the planet. Why? Why bother keeping people out, if the basilisk already took over Paradise-1?"

"I'm not sure I understand," Petrova said.

"The basilisk is guarding something. It doesn't want Firewatch to see what it's got down there. That could mean the people there are fine, that maybe they've discovered a way to fight back against the basilisk. Maybe a way to cure it, or a way to destroy it once and for all."

Petrova's heart jumped in her chest.

"You think we could find a solution down there. An answer to this thing."

"Possibly."

Petrova looked down at her hands. The good one and the one still buried in the inflatable cast. If there was some hope – some hope her mother was okay, that she would land and find Ekaterina there waiting at the spaceport, waiting to give her a big hug . . .

Well, that seemed highly unlikely. But just thinking there was a chance that her mother was okay was like a shot of adrenaline to Petrova's system. She looked up with clear, excited eyes – and then she saw Zhang's face.

"You said you saw a problem with our plan, though."

"Yeah. The problem is, once we're down, we're stuck. If we try to take off again this basilisk armada will be waiting for us. No matter what we find down there, this is a one-way trip."

Petrova inhaled sharply.

"Then we sit tight. We land, we contact Firewatch to tell them we've arrived and we sit tight. The ships up here won't come for us once we're on solid ground."

"You sure about that?" Rapscallion asked.

"No. But it seems possible. Anyway, it doesn't matter. We need to get down there. Not just for ourselves. If there is something at the bottom of the gravity well, a cure for the basilisk or . . . or just a couple of thousand scared colonists waiting for help, then Firewatch needs to know about that, as soon as possible."

"Agreed," Zhang said.

"Then it's settled. We wait for the window when the warships are on the far side of the planet. Then we make a run for the surface, as fast as we can, no looking back."

109

Petrova and Zhang sat down to a dinner of real food that night, something more than biscuits and water for the first time in days. *Alpheus'* stores were intact so she had Rapscallion lay out an elaborate feast. Petrova had thought she couldn't eat, but once she sat down it was like her body just took over. The food was nothing special by Earth standards, just protein cutlets in some kind of green sauce, but she tore through them until the sauce ran down her chin. At one point she looked up and saw Zhang watching her. She started to feel self-conscious, until he grabbed a pre-packaged bread roll. He tore the plastic off of it with his teeth, then shoved the whole bun in his mouth at once. She would have laughed in relief, except that she had more important matters to attend to — in this case, a bowl of miso soup.

When the two of them were finished she realized that they hadn't spoken two words to each other since the beginning of the meal. She sat back in her chair and watched Zhang, thinking about how much she missed Parker. He'd been good company — he'd made her feel like she wasn't alone out here in the dark. Zhang did his best, she knew, but she always got the sense he was uncomfortable around her.

It wasn't okay. They were the only two humans in the system who weren't infected by the basilisk, probably. They needed to stick together. She just wished she knew how to break the ice.

She tried to catch his gaze. Tried to will him to talk. Inevitably, she went first.

"What if it's right?" she asked. "Actaeon, I mean. It claims the human race is doomed, that there's no way to survive the basilisk."

Zhang shook his head. "If there's no way to win there's no reason to keep fighting. We should just walk to the airlock right now and jump out."

"I'm not asking for practical advice. Just ... considering a possibility. Every ship that came here failed, as far as we know. Every single one of them until us. And the basilisk is already spreading to the solar system. You saw it on Titan. I think I saw it on Ganymede. What happens if this thing reaches Earth? There are twelve billion people on that planet. What if tomorrow they all wake up thinking they need to climb to the tallest building they can find and jump off?"

Zhang speared a piece of broccoli and stared at it for a while before answering. "I don't think that's the plan."

"No?"

"Maybe it's just wishful thinking. Because if that is what the basilisk wants, then we *are* doomed. But this has been going on a while now, more than a year. I get the feeling if the basilisk wanted to wipe out humanity, it would have already happened."

"So what, then? What's it's plan?"

"The thing is, I see two things it's trying to accomplish, and I'm not sure how they fit together. For one thing we know it's trying to guard the planet. To keep anyone from landing there."

"Eurydice told me as much, in different words," Petrova said. "Yeah. What's the other thing it wants?"

Zhang laughed. "To talk. Because ... it's lonely? No, that's absurd. But it does want to make contact."

"You think it's trying to communicate with us?" He had suggested as much before.

Now he just shrugged.

"It fits with what we've seen. It's reaching out."

"If we could find a way to talk back—"

He shook his head. "I just don't know. It wants to understand us. Why else try to communicate with us? That doesn't mean it comes in peace and friendship. Maybe it's just looking for insight into how best to keep us at arm's length from the planet," he said. "Or maybe it just doesn't understand what it's doing to us. Maybe all those people on *Persephone* died just because it couldn't comprehend what its message was doing to them."

"Message. The message the basilisk was sending there—"

"Got lost in noise. Unbearable hunger was the message. Insatiability. Was it trying to say it was hungry to communicate with us? Lonely to have someone to talk to? Maybe. The message it sent with *Alpheus* seems a little more straightforward. Undine and its crew thought they were infected. Well, they were, they just couldn't see that it was more complicated than that."

"What about the Red Strangler?" she asked. "What was it trying to say?"

She should have known better. His eyes narrowed and he wiped at his lips with a napkin. "I don't know. I don't want to . . . I don't want to speculate about that."

As usual she'd screwed up. She'd pushed him to talk about the one thing he never wanted to discuss, and now he was going to close down again. Retreat from her. If she kept pushing he was likely to do something weird just to get away.

Well, now wasn't the time to push him, she thought. "I'm sorry," she told him. "I didn't mean to make you uncomfortable."

"I'm not un— I'm—" He shook his head. "I need to go get some rest. You should too." He stood up from the table and moved to the hatch leading toward the cabins. When he got there he stood in the open hatch for a second, his back turned to her.

He dipped his head forward. She couldn't see the expression on his face. "You know I'm making all this up as I go along, right? I don't know anything, really. I don't know how this thing works or what it wants."

"I appreciate your thoughts all the same," she said.

He nodded and then he went out through the hatch. It slid closed behind him, leaving her alone in the galley.

Petrova played with the food on the table, with nothing but her thoughts for company. Long after she'd stopped eating she stayed there at the table, just unwilling to get up.

She didn't even realize she'd closed her eyes until she heard the hatch slide open again.

She sat up, grunting in surprise, wondering if Zhang had come back to say something more, or maybe it was Rapscallion bringing her some piece of terrible news. Yet when she blinked and looked around, she didn't see anyone else in the galley. She was still alone.

After a moment the hatch slid closed again on its own.

Scowling, she got up from her chair and went to the hatchway. She slapped the release pad, then leaned out into the corridor, looking to see who had opened the hatch. There was no one in either direction. "Actaeon," she said. "Where is everyone?"

"Rapscallion is in his workshop, in ship's stores," the AI told her. "Doctor Zhang is in his cabin."

Petrova's pulse jumped in her good wrist. She shook out her hand as if she'd had a muscle spasm. It was just nerves, she knew. She was sure she wasn't seeing things – the hatch really had opened on its own.

"Actaeon, do you have a record of who's opened this hatch recently? Besides me, I mean."

"The hatch opened twelve minutes ago at the command of Doctor Zhang," Actaeon told her. "Before that—"

"Never mind before that. What about a minute or two ago? Just before I opened it. I saw it open and there was nobody there—"

She stopped herself.

"Never mind. Cancel that request."

She was pretty sure she didn't want to know the answer. Something weird was happening on *Alpheus*. Something that had nothing to do with the basilisk.

One terrifying mystery at a time, she told herself.

110
.

It was time.

Go time. Time to make a break for the planet.

"Go get yourself strapped in," Petrova said.

Zhang chewed on his lip. He was wearing a spacesuit, though he had his helmet off. "I could stay up here with you. I could be your co-pilot."

"You don't know how to fly a spaceship," she told him. "Besides, you're the only person in the galaxy who knows how to fight the basilisk. You think I'm going to take chances with your safety now?"

She was on *Alpheus'* bridge, wearing a suit of her own, in case of emergencies during the maneuvers they were about to make. Rapscallion had installed a crash couch at the pilot's station, a big reclined seat with elaborate straps designed to protect a human body during aggressive maneuvers. The robot had rebuilt the seat to accommodate her bad arm in its cast, with all the controls readily available to her right hand. "You wouldn't be safe up here. Get to your cabin and get ready. We're out of time."

The beds in the cabins were designed to adapt to the ship's maneuvers. They could encase the passengers in a soft cocoon of airbags for protection if, say, the ship's artificial gravity cut out during a high-gee maneuver. There was a chance he could survive back there, even if the rest of the ship was destroyed. Petrova sighed and gestured for him to get moving.

"I could help you," he said. "I don't know how. I just—" He stopped himself.

"What?" she asked. "What is it?"

"I just wish I was more ... I don't know. More like Parker. Better at all of this. I hate the idea of just being deadweight, back in my cabin."

"Deadweight?" she asked.

He shrugged. Then he turned to go.

"Zhang," she said. "Hold on. Help me."

He came closer, a question on his face.

"Here, pull this tight," she said, gesturing at the custom-made strap that would hold her injured arm close to her body. She could have strapped herself in with just one hand but it would give him something to do – some way to make him feel like he was part of the plan. He pulled the strap down and buckled it tight. When she felt like she was secure in the crash couch, she nodded at him. "Thanks."

"Sure. Listen, whatever happens, I want you to know how grateful I am. You've saved my life so many times."

"And you've returned the favor. Zhang, look at me. I'm going to need you when we get to the planet."

"I'll do what I can."

"Listen. Okay? Listen! You're exactly who I want down there. The thing about you, Zhang, is you're one of those people who just gets better in a crisis. You think you're broken. You think you're not strong enough. All I see is that when life throws shit at you, you keep getting stronger."

He looked up in surprise. Maybe she'd surprised herself, a little. But she meant every word of it.

She waited for him to say something in response, but he didn't. Instead, he nodded politely and left the bridge.

Turning to Actaeon, she said, "Do you think that worked? Did I get through to him?"

"I'm afraid I don't know how to answer that question.

Lieutenant, we are approaching the peak moment for our de-orbital maneuver. Would you like me to handle the main engine commands?"

"Hold on one second. Rapscallion?" she called.

"Yo."

"You ready for this?"

The robot was down in the crawlspaces surrounding *Alpheus'* main engine. Ready to carry out any mid-flight repairs that he could, in case something went wrong.

"I'm ready," he told her.

She waited a second to hear if there was more. Some sarcastic quip, or a witty comment on how they were all about to die horribly.

Nothing like that was forthcoming.

"You okay?" she asked.

"I'm trying out one of those weird human emotions. You know, the ones that don't seem to do any actual good but you apparently need them anyway."

"A human emotion? Which one?"

"Hope," Rapscallion told her. "I'm hoping this goes well. Despite the fact nothing else has, ever since we got here."

There it was – the robot she knew.

"Acknowledged," she said. "Okay, Actaeon. Punch it."

111

Alpheus' engine thrummed with power – Petrova could feel it all the way up on the bridge. When it came, the acceleration was brutal. The ship dove toward the planet like it was plummeting off a steep cliff. If not for the artificial gravity she would have been slammed back in her couch, her eyes flattened by gee-forces until she could barely see.

Ahead of her she could see Paradise-1 through the viewport. The planet was barely bigger than her fingertip for the moment – only a little bigger than Earth's moon when it was seen from the surface – but already she felt like it was getting bigger.

A loud chime sounded right next to her ear and she grabbed the console in front of her. She'd been expecting that sound but not quite so soon. It was an alert warning her that other ships were moving to intercept them. "Actaeon, what are you seeing?" she asked

"Four vessels in our local volume of space are accelerating. All are moving toward us at their maximum delta-v."

It was inevitable. While they'd computed the best possible path to get down to the planet without being attacked, there were just too many ships in orbit around Paradise-1 to avoid them all. On her screen she could track the four closest ships – two transports, a scout ship and a freighter. Four ships run by AIs infected by the basilisk, with orders to destroy her if she tried to get close to the planet.

She'd expected to have a few more seconds before they detected her engine burn, just a little more time to build up speed. As it was she would simply have to outmaneuver them.

She glanced at the viewport but they were all far enough away that she couldn't see them. "What about the warships?" she asked. "Are they reacting at all?"

"The warships behind the planet have adjusted their orbits. They are maneuvering to intercept. So are the rest of the ships in the blockade."

"Wait. All of them? *All* of them?" she asked. But she knew.

"Yes," Actaeon concurred. "All one hundred and fifteen ships are accelerating. Extrapolating from their current maneuvers, they appear to be moving toward our position."

Shit. Shit shit shit. That was bad, if not entirely unexpected. Whatever was down there on Paradise-1, the basilisk really, really wanted to keep it under wraps. Maybe especially now that it knew that the crew of *Alpheus* were immune to its infection.

Well, she was going to see it with her own eyes. No matter what it took. "Give me a trajectory that will keep us clear of any ship with weapons," she said. "As for the closest ships, show me what I should be worried about first."

On her holoscreen one of the four closest ships – a transport – started blinking.

"This vehicle is moving toward us at high speed. Its crew has overloaded their engine to gain extra speed. I estimate they will intercept us in less than thirty seconds."

"Less than . . . you can't give me a better estimate?"

"It is unclear how much acceleration the crew is willing to accept," Actaeon told her. "They have already lost containment on their reactor."

"That's crazy," Petrova said. Almost unthinkable. To push your engine so hard that you lost containment – it meant the crew and passenger areas of that transport would be flooded with lethal radiation. Everyone onboard would be facing a death sentence, just so the ship could move a little faster.

"I have been evaluating their maneuvers and their trajectory, and I believe they intend not to intercept us, but to intentionally cause a high-speed collision."

"That would . . . that'll obliterate us both," she said, under her breath.

She could hardly believe it. She'd thought the basilisk wanted to talk to her, that it wouldn't go all out in trying to kill her. Not this fast, anyway. Clearly hiding its secrets was more important than making contact.

"Give me an evasive course that keeps us as far from that transport as possible," she said. "Except – one that doesn't put us in danger in other ways. I know I'm asking for a lot."

"I'm afraid that's accurate," Actaeon said. "Lieutenant, calculating a safe course to the planet is quickly exceeding my abilities. There's a reason that human pilots are assigned to ships like *Alpheus*."

Parker. It meant Parker. Well, he was gone. "Give me a suggestion, Actaeon. Give me some advice already."

"I would suggest at this time you consider breaking off from your current course."

Petrova gritted her teeth. "That's not an option! If we back off now, we'll never get down to the planet. Together we can figure this out."

"Certainly, Lieutenant. I await your command."

112

$\bullet$

"Rapscallion! Zhang! Get ready to brace," she called out, over the ship-wide intercom. Then she grabbed the virtual controls and twisted *Alpheus* sideways, diving toward Paradise-1 even as she pushed away from the trajectory of the oncoming transport.

"Actaeon!" she called. "Give me something – are we going to avoid them?"

"The transport is still on a collision course, still accelerating," the AI said.

Petrova cursed and stabbed at the virtual keyboard to her right. Doing this with one hand was ridiculous, even with all the accessibility features the robot had built for her. "Rapscallion, can you give me any more power? I'm going to need to pull some wild maneuvers in a second, here."

"Are you willing to kill everyone onboard and snap *Alpheus* in half?" the robot asked.

"No," she told him.

"I'll see what I can do, anyway."

She shook her head and stared dead forward, through the viewport. Paradise-1 had swung over to one side but it was definitely getting bigger.

"The transport is now twenty seconds away from collision," Actaeon warned her.

"Got it. What else do we have coming our way?"

Actaeon brought up a new screen. She waved it away — it would only distract her. "A second transport is approaching, on a similar collision course. A smaller craft has accelerated to match our course. I believe it is some kind of scout vessel. There is also a freighter currently in orbit between us and the planet. It is moving quite slowly, however, and I cannot intuit its plan of attack."

"Just keep an eye on it. That second transport—"

"Forty-nine seconds from collision. Before you ask, the scout ship is not on a collision course but it will approach us within one kilometer's distance, in ninety-two seconds."

Petrova scowled. Scout ships didn't tend to carry much weaponry ... unless ...

"The scout — what kind of sensors does it have?"

"A wide range of sensors, including a high-powered long distance spectroscopic laser."

Damn. They were going to pull her own trick on her. She had no doubt that laser could be ramped up into a powerful weapon, at least at short distances. For now, though, she really had to worry about those transports. The basilisk had turned crewed ships into guided missiles, and two of them were headed right at her.

She stabbed at a screen in front of her, a real-time display of where all those ships were, trying to find a route between them that kept either of them from colliding with her. The problem, of course, was that for every course she tried to compute the transports could simply adjust their trajectories to stay on track for a collision. She was slightly more maneuverable, but only because she was slower than they were — they still had the advantage of numbers, and of not caring in the slightest if they survived this encounter.

"There has to be a way — Actaeon, if we just dove straight for the planet, all power dead ahead — if we risked a near collision with that freighter—" She stabbed again and again at the display, swiped her finger across a half-dozen proposed courses. It was like playing chess except all the pieces were moving at once, and you had to anticipate where the pawns would be at every possible moment. "Actaeon, give me something – anything—"

A faint white line swooped across her display, a hypothetical trajectory. There was something weird about it, a kind of kink in the curve that didn't make sense, unless . . . She reached for it, thinking she could expand the view and see how it potentially changed things, but before she could touch it, the curving line had evaporated from her screen.

"What the hell was that? Bring that trajectory back," she said.

"I'm afraid I don't understand," Actaeon said. "I don't know what trajectory you mean."

"Shut up," she told the computer. "Forget I said that. How long until collision with the first transport?"

"Thirteen seconds."

Jesus, she was out of time, she needed something. She tried to remember, see in her head where that vanishing curve had gone, where it had passed through the array of ships.

"Actaeon—"

"Nine seconds."

"Listen, just listen. Rapscallion, I need you in on this, too. When I say mark I need you to route all power – everything you can scrape together – to our forward maneuvering jets. Got it?"

"I hope you enjoyed that sandwich you had for lunch," Rapscallion told her. "You pull that kind of stunt, you're going to get to see it again."

"Yeah, it's that or die in a fiery explosion," she replied.

"Three seconds," Actaeon informed her, quite calmly. Quite reasonably.

Two, she counted in her head. *One*. "Mark!" she shouted.

113
●

The attacking transport came screaming through space toward them. Through the viewport Petrova had just a fraction of a second to glimpse it, impossibly large and close by. She thought she could see pale fire streaming from around its engines, but that could have just been her imagination.

An instant before it would have struck them – before it would have annihilated them both – she fired *Alpheus'* maneuvering jets, kicking hard against the ship's own momentum and velocity. A good old-fashioned retro-rocket burn.

As fast as they were moving it did little to change their velocity. When plotted on a holoscreen, the curve of *Alpheus'* trajectory was barely affected. The maneuvering burn simply added a tiny kink to that course, a little judder of uncertainty.

On the bridge, the sudden change in velocity threw Petrova forward into the straps of her crash couch. They dug painfully into her flesh even as she felt like her whole body was a tube of toothpaste being violently squeezed.

It only lasted a millisecond or two. When it was over, she fell back into her couch, panting and wheezing, spit thick in her mouth, her eyes so badly deformed she couldn't see. She lacked even the strength to ask Actaeon if it had worked.

If she'd saved them from destruction.

The answer didn't take long to arrive, anyway. It was just enough. The attacking transport went barreling past, missing

Alpheus by a matter of tens of meters. Moving as fast as it was, there was no way for its crew – or more likely its AI, since its crew was almost surely dead – to compensate. They would have to decelerate along a wide, energy-hungry course before they could double back for another attempt to smash into *Alpheus*. Before they could complete that course correction she would be down on the planet.

One problem solved. There were plenty more she still needed to get past. "Actaeon, what about the second transport? Did they change course?"

"No. It is now twenty-one seconds from collision. It has over-charged its engine, much like the last attacker. Lieutenant, I feel I must warn you—"

"That this is only going to get worse? I know that," she said. There were plenty more ships after that second transport. The scout, and the freighter below her . . .

That freighter . . .

She grabbed at the holoscreens that floated before her, bring-ing them close so she could study her sensor data, suddenly very worried about what that freighter was doing. It wasn't trying to smash into her. It was just down there, between her and the planet like a football goalie waiting for her to try to sneak past. It hadn't changed its course or velocity since she'd first started her mad dive toward the planet.

It had to be up to something, but what?

She realized she was going to have to worry about that when the time came. The second transport was only seconds away from smashing into her and she knew that a trick that worked once was unlikely to work a second time. She needed another inspiration, like the weird kinked trajectory showing up on her screen out of nowhere. She needed a good idea, and she needed to come up with it fast.

"Come on," she said, when nothing presented itself. "Come on."

"Sixteen seconds from collision," Actaeon announced. Calmly. So calmly.

Then a flash of light lit up half her screens and she had to blink in surprise. It was a full second – a second she couldn't spare – before she was able to ask. "What the fuck was that?"

Actaeon opened a new screen, a telescope view of the freighter orbiting just below them, between *Alpheus* and the planet. It looked like a swollen balloon, a big spherical mass of cargo containers held together by straps and cords and a skeletal framework of girders. A relatively small thruster unit stuck out of one end, and a tiny crew cabin was mounted on the other – they both looked like afterthoughts. The cargo was the whole point of the ship.

The screen's view animated, even as Actaeon described what had happened. "The drive unit's containment was dropped all at once without employing proper precautions, resulting in a massive explosion. The ensuing shockwave has destroyed the ship, and created an extensive field of debris."

Debris. Meaning loose cargo. Petrova thought of the crate of yams that Zhang had seen strike *Artemis*. On her holoscreen now it looked like a big pixelated cloud – rectangular shapes tumbling and spinning through space, all of them moving slowly away from each other as the shockwave expanded.

It would have looked like a terrible accident if Petrova didn't know better.

"Son of a bitch," she said. "They're trying to build a fence."

The cloud of cargo containers might as well have been a solid wall of steel keeping her from reaching Paradise-1. As the containers spun and bounced off each other their hundreds of trajectories added up to something like Brownian motion.

"I apologize, Lieutenant. I do not have sufficient resources to plot a course through this debris field. It is beyond my capacities."

If *Alpheus* collided with even one of those containers at high speed, it could mean death for everyone onboard. Petrova,

Zhang, Rapscallion, Actaeon. Just gone in a terrible screaming moment of inertia and fire.

"Twelve seconds until collision," Actaeon said.

Petrova licked her lips. The transport coming at her was moving so fast. There was no way she could escape it.

She was out of tricks. No more wild maneuvers, no more risky gambits.

Everything collapsed down to one chance, one move.

You made your choice, and then you dealt with what you got. Call it fatalism, she thought. Call it stupidity. Call it running out of options.

Actaeon seemed to guess what she was thinking. "I need to remind you, Lieutenant, that I cannot plot a safe course through a debris field like that. I simply lack the—"

"Shut the fuck up," Petrova said. "We're going in."

A panel in her crash couch opened and a flight yoke emerged, snapping into place just below her right hand. Full manual control.

The very idea made cold drops of sweat streak down her forehead. There was no longer any other way.

114
●

"Eight seconds until collision," Actaeon called out.

"Not if I can help it." Petrova grabbed the yoke and twisted it sideways. She had expanded her holoscreen to fill the whole bridge, so it looked like tumbling cargo containers were swarming all around her. One came zooming up right in front of her and she twisted over to the other side. Another was in her way but far enough off that she only had to veer to miss it.

She was sweating, and her stomach had crawled up inside her ribcage to hide. Her feet lifted away from the crash couch as she took another quick turn, banking around a cluster of cargo modules that were bouncing off each other like pinballs. The bridge's artificial gravity couldn't keep up with the rapid changes in momentum, and she was thrown sideways in her seat, hard enough to leave bruises.

"Where's that transport?" she demanded. "Still following us?"

"Collision in three seconds," Actaeon called. "Two—"

Light burst across the bridge, behind Petrova's head, so bright it hurt her eyes even though she wasn't looking at it directly. "That was the transport?" she asked.

"Yes. It collided with a cargo module at a velocity of nearly six kilometers per second. It is no longer a threat to us."

Or anyone else, she thought. The poor bastards onboard were probably dead long before the collision, but still.

There was no time to congratulate herself on eliminating

another threat. Cargo modules were all around her, moving erratically. It was all she could do to keep from ramming into them.

She knew, on a very conscious level, that she wasn't up to this. She'd never trained as a pilot. Actaeon had complained it didn't have the skills to thread this three-dimensional labyrinth. Well, neither did she.

She would try. She would give it her best, last as long as she could. And then ...

Well. Hopefully Director Lang was watching. Hopefully she could learn something from their deaths. The next time Firewatch sent a transport full of unknowing dupes to Paradise-1, maybe they would have a slightly better chance at this. Maybe they would make it.

Maybe.

Below her, off to one side, a pair of containers smashed into each other fast enough to send red hot shrapnel flying in every direction. Petrova wasn't ready for it. *Alpheus* shook, its whole frame rattling as it was pelted with a sleet of molten iron.

"Damn it," she breathed, as an especially large piece of debris bounced off *Alpheus'* flank, digging a deep gouge through its skin. "Damage report!"

"Minor damage to power couplings on the starboard side," Actaeon told her. "I'm shunting power through a secondary cable array. Lieutenant, as we proceed through this debris cloud the likelihood of collisions only becomes greater. We should turn back."

"Not a chance," Petrova said. "We're just as likely to die climbing out of this as we are trying to punch through." She didn't care if that was true or not.

Ahead of her, centered in her viewport, Paradise-1 was so big she felt like she could reach out and touch it. "How far are we from the top of the planet's atmosphere?" she asked. Once they touched air, the debris field would ease up a little – the smaller pieces of broken containers and their spilled contents would burn up from friction, even at extreme altitude, and she would have a clear glidepath all the way down.

"Still one hundred and seven kilometers away," Actaeon said. "Lieutenant—"

"Hold on ... hold on ..." She twisted her yoke left, then threw it savagely over to the right and *Alpheus* just skimmed past a nearly complete module, one that could have dug a trench right through their hull and into the passenger cabins. "Too close."

"Lieutenant," Actaeon said, "the number of collisions between cargo modules in the cloud is increasing. This is a problem, as each collision raises the number of debris particles by an exponential rate."

It was true. As the modules struck each other they broke into dozens, hundreds of fragments. Pieces so small they were hard to see – and a lot harder to avoid. "I need to focus," she said. "I just need to focus."

"Of course, Lieutenant," the AI told her. "I will—"

Something big and hard struck *Alpheus* near the stern. She was thrown around in her crash couch like a rag doll, her straps the only thing keeping her from being thrown clear across the bridge. It felt like her eyes were bouncing around inside her skull and her ears were ringing as she fell back into place. She tried to reach for the yoke, tried to see the holoscreens in front of her, but, for a second, a bad, bad second, all she could see was blur, she couldn't think, couldn't hear anything—

"Petrova!" Rapscallion shouted. "Petrova, come in! I've got fires on three different decks. Fucking hell – answer me!"

"I'm here," she said. A cargo container was right in front of them. Somehow she managed to grab the yoke and pull up just in time.

"I'm going to have to make some extra bodies for myself. There's just too much damage, I can't fix everything with just one pair of hands. Are you ... What is that—"

"What?" she said, craning her head around.

A brilliant line of fire cut across the space ahead of her. A perfectly straight, glowing ray of destruction that carved a cargo module in half like a freshly sharpened knife through paper.

"Shit," she said. "Shit, I almost forgot."

The scout ship. The scout ship with the high-powered spectroscopic laser. It was hot on their heels, getting closer with every second. Even as she watched in horror, a second beam cut through the dark. A third – and this one cut deep into *Alpheus*, carving off a section of its nose.

115
•

The ship didn't buck or even so much as vibrate – the cut was so clean, so fast that *Alpheus* didn't even feel it, not at first.

But then sparks erupted from half the consoles on the bridge, smoke pouring from burning electronics. Actaeon shouted something but its voice was lost in the tumult, sounding almost faint, almost—

"Actaeon," she called. "Rapscallion – anyone, give me a damage report, give me—"

With a wild whooshing roar all the air in the bridge rushed out through the hole in the nose. Behind Petrova the hatch slammed shut even as the sparks dimmed, the fires guttered out. She called out but couldn't hear anything, couldn't—

"Lieutenant," Actaeon said, finally. Except it wasn't speaking out loud. It was communicating directly with the headphones inside her pressure suit's helmet. With no air on the bridge it couldn't make a sound. "Lieutenant, are you all right?"

"I'm ... I'm fine," she said. She flinched with a little yelp as a broken piece of cargo module bounced off the viewport, hard enough to crack the polycarbonate. Not that it mattered. The bridge was exposed to space – the next collision would probably kill her, would tear through the thin hull and ... and—

"Lieutenant!"

A chunk of what looked like part of the freighter's crew cabin went caroming past on her left. Petrova grabbed the yoke and twisted around a reef of what might have been smoke or ice crystals or yams, for all she knew, fucking yams – it could be anything. She had a shock as a body in a spacesuit went flashing past her. Briefly, she thought it must be Zhang, that *Alpheus* had come apart and that Zhang had been thrown out into the void but no, it had to be one of the freighter's crew. It had to be.

A laser burst passed within meters of the bridge, stabbing downward toward the planet. Paradise-1 filled half the viewport now. Petrova rotated *Alpheus* along its axis, then looked up just as another laser beam cut through the air beside her head.

Not beside *Alpheus'* command decks. Through them. The beam passed right through the bridge and came within a meter of separating her head from her neck.

"Actaeon," she said, fear raising the pitch of her voice until she sounded, in her own ears, like a child. "Actaeon, what ... what can we do, what can—"

Something hit the side of the ship, she couldn't have said where. She was knocked sideways and her head slammed into the side of her helmet and then ...

Nothing.

116

Petrova blinked wildly. There was a terrible taste in her mouth, like copper, like blood, but worse, worse than ... than blood ... worse ...

All around her there were flashing lights and sparks and someone was calling her name. Someone, not Actaeon, someone human but ...

It couldn't be.

It couldn't.

She blacked out again.

117
•

Something exploded very close by. Someone was tugging at her leg.

The ship was still flying, that was good. She watched as cargo modules went zipping past to left and right, missing them by the briefest margin. She looked down and saw that her hands wasn't on the yoke.

She wasn't flying the ship. She wasn't touching the controls.

She looked over to her left and saw Rapscallion, one of his bodies, anyway, green plastic legs slapping at the quick releases on her straps. The whole wall of the bridge on that side had been sheared away, just empty space out there and the edges, the places where the wall had been cut were still glowing a dull orange. She saw a cargo module fly past spinning like a top, even as *Alpheus* banked around and made another maneuver.

She wasn't flying the ship.

She looked to her right . . .

Except her brain went fuzzy and her body refused to do what she told it to do. She had to fight herself, fight her own reflexes and instincts. She grimaced and forced her head to turn to the right.

There was someone there. Someone standing over a bridge console, desperately stabbing at the controls. A human shape, a human who wasn't even wearing a spacesuit. It wasn't Zhang, it couldn't be Zhang. She was sure it wasn't Zhang. But that meant it had to be . . .

"Sam?" she said.

"Come on." That was Rapscallion's voice, slurring a little in her headphones. "Commmmme onnnnnnn." He got the last of her straps loose. She fought him – she needed to see if it was Sam at the controls – but then he grabbed her bad arm. Pain raced up from her elbow and straight into her brain and she shrieked. The robot didn't seem to care. "Nnnnnnnot safe," he sputtered out. She wondered idly how many bodies he was using, to make his voice that distorted and flat.

"Sam," she said again.

The pilot turned and gave her a thumbs up. And went back to flying the ship.

118

Zhang could barely breathe, even with his spacesuit pumping oxygen directly at his face. He couldn't see anything – there was so much smoke in the hallways he might have been wandering straight into an exposed engine core. The green arms directing him belonged to Rapscallion, of that he was pretty sure, but beyond that he had no idea what was going on.

He'd spent the last few minutes ensconced in his cabin, surrounded by airbags that pressed his limbs down and kept him from moving whatsoever. Then, out of nowhere, the bags had deflated and he'd been thrown out into zero gravity in a dark room. Now he was being bundled down the ship's long corridors toward – what? Safety?

They came around a corner and Zhang heard a whistling scream, a high-pitched screech like the cry of an attacking owl. The smoke all around him was pumped down the hallway and out through a hole in the corridor wall. An actual hole, a breach in the hull. Light reflected off of Paradise-1 streamed in through the opening like a ray of destruction.

So no, he doubted he was being led to safety. Maybe just to some place less immediately deadly than the passenger decks.

"Folllllowww," Rapscallion said, his voice so flattened and distorted that it was just noise, a rough growling sound that meant nothing. Zhang stayed close to the robot all the same. It took him up the long neck of *Alpheus*, toward the bridge.

"Are we sure this is the right way?" Zhang asked.

As if the cosmos had heard him and wanted to emphasize just how little control he had over his life at that moment, the entire ship vibrated like a bell and the gravity cut out in the corridor – then came back on at a different angle, so that he was slumped against a wall that had become more like a floor. Rapscallion leaped across the corridor to grab at a hatch that had started to buckle. Rapscallion worked fast, sealing the hatch shut with a plasma torch. He used another hand to point down the corridor.

"GooooooOOeeekkkkkrpkrpkrp," the robot said, its voice devolving into random chirps and beeps.

Zhang gasped in panic and ran, further up the corridor toward the bridge.

Only to find, when he arrived, that the hatch was sealed. He slapped again and again at the release pad but a blinking red light appeared on the control display. ACCESS COMPROMISED, the display told him. HARD VACUUM BEYOND. The display cleared and the text was replaced with HEAVY RADIATION ENVIRONMENT. It cleared again to read, simply, UNSAFE CONDITIONS.

"Petrova?" Zhang shouted. "Petrova?" He switched to radio, selecting the suit-to-suit radio band. "Lieutenant? Where are you?"

"Get back," she called, her voice a hoarse rasp.

Zhang just had time to jump away from the hatch as it exploded outward from its frame. Beyond was a monster, a hundred-legged, four-headed thing of tentacles and spikes and dozens of flailing arms.

Luckily, it was made of bright green plastic.

"Rapscallion," Zhang said, with a gasp of relief.

"Don't sound so excited," the robot replied. Zhang saw he was carrying Petrova in six of his seven arms. She was beating ineffectually at its carapace with both fists, as if she wanted to be put down. Rapscallion shifted his grip to hold her tighter.

"We strive to give our customers the very best in luxury travel experiences."

"Hold on. Your voice. It sounds—" Zhang shook his head. "No," he said. "For a second, you sounded just like – like *Parker*."

He turned and looked down the corridor. Something had moved down there, something that looked human, maybe. Except now there was nothing down there except debris and smoke.

"No time. Do exactly as I say," the robot said, with Parker's voice. There was no mistaking that American drawl. Rapscallion shoved him forward and then scuttered across the wall and ceiling, Petrova still in tow. The robot led him to a short corridor that normally connected the bridge to the entrance to the ship's stores. A narrow hatch irised open as they approached.

Beyond was a tiny little chamber, no bigger than a closet, really. It was hexagonal in cross section and its walls were thickly padded everywhere. Straps, belts, and safety bars criss-crossed the interior space.

It was an escape pod.

"It's all automated. Get in," the robot said. Parker said.

Zhang nodded and climbed inside. He couldn't think. This was no time for thinking. The robot handed Petrova over to him – she was still fighting it. He grabbed at her suit and helped push her down against one wall, then started pulling straps across her chest, trying to be careful of her injured arm.

"Sasha," someone said, from the corridor.

She fought like a demon and Zhang had to let her go. She didn't move far – just far enough to stand in the pod's hatch, her hand on the frame, keeping the hatch from closing.

Zhang tried to look around her, to get some idea of what the hell was happening out there. Eventually, he managed to get a glimpse but he didn't believe what he saw.

Sam Parker was out there.

Sam Parker was dead.

Except he was standing in the corridor, wearing nothing but a jumpsuit. Flames, sparks, smoke – lack of air, radiation, temperature extremes, whatever else was filling the hallway seemed not to bother him at all.

"Sasha," he said. "You have to go. I ... I'm sorry. I wanted to ... I wanted ... "

"Sam," she said. "Sam ... "

"Oh, just fuck off and eject already," Rapscallion shouted. The robot shoved her violently into the pod and the hatch slammed closed. A rumbling vibration pulsed through the pod's walls and Zhang scrambled to get his own straps connected, then to grab Petrova and pull her down before the pod's engines fired, pressing them both hard up against the wall.

A holoscreen appeared in the middle of the pod's scant open space. It showed a view of *Alpheus,* dwindling as the pod rocketed away. The transport was in its death throes, its skin torn, its structural members buckled and bent. In the open hatchway left behind by the escape pod's egress, Zhang could just see Parker, silhouetted against the hell of flames behind him. The pilot raised one hand in farewell.

Then the pod twisted away from the ship, perhaps evading some piece of flotsam or the hard bright bloom of an explosion, and the view of *Alpheus,* and Parker, was gone.

"Sam," Petrova said. She sucked in a breath. "You *bastard.*"

119
•

As a way of alleviating his terror, Zhang tried to explore the pod. Find what it was capable of. The answer was – not much, other than keeping them technically safe.

There were no controls to speak of. You could call up a holo-screen and it would show a row of green lights, indicating that all of the pod's systems were functioning nominally. Good, good, that was reassuring, which was clearly the point of the pod giving him access to that screen. It didn't tell him anything, though. It didn't help him make plans.

There was a radio transceiver built into the pod. It proved less than useful.

There was no signal from *Alpheus*. No broadcasts to pick up in the Paradise system, not even chatter between the various spacecraft in the orbital blockade. There were no sensors attached to the pod so when he called up a holoscreen to show where they were or where they were going, all he got was an external camera view. That showed nothing but a few stars. Once, briefly, he saw the edge of Paradise-1, brown with a thin blue margin where light bent through its atmosphere. After a few minutes, though, the pod tumbled away from the planet and then there was nothing but space to look at.

The pod contained one other feature, which he could hardly ignore, though she did nothing at all. Petrova seemed even more numbed than afraid. She sat there barely moving, breathing and occasionally blinking but doing nothing else, which turned out to be more frightening than calming. She had not spoken a word since the pod left *Alpheus* and he'd begun to suspect she never would again. Shock, he thought. It was hardly an official diagnosis – he would need to remove her suit and assess her vitals to make any kind of meaningful determination – but it certainly seemed likely. She was breathing normally and she didn't seem to be in any great distress, so he decided to leave her alone.

There was no room to get up and take a walk or even perform the most rudimentary exercises. No gravity to even strain against in an effort at dynamic tension. There was no task requiring his attention, no matter how menial or rote. He considered taking Petrova out of her suit just so he could check on her arm. It would make him feel useful, if only for a few moments. It would let him feel like a doctor, like someone with skills and meaning to their existence.

One look through her faceplate and he knew better than to try. She looked half dead, utterly vacant. Yet as he stared at her, not even meaning to linger on it, her eyes slowly tracked around and met his gaze. Her eyes narrowed in slow motion and she licked her lips. She was already frowning.

Ah, he thought, *never mind. So sorry to bother you.* He looked away as quickly and as apologetically as he could.

She sank back into her previous torpor.

And so things remained for what felt like an eternity. An eternity of anxiety and fear and uncertainty where nothing whatsoever happened.

Until something did.

It happened without warning, so suddenly Zhang let out an involuntary yelp of surprise. The holoscreen flared to life, bright and blue in the dim light of the pod. The view was just choppy static and random patches of light but after a moment it resolved into a slightly out-of-focus image of Rapscallion's head. A thing of many eyes and a broad, wicked set of jaws. The face of a giant spider rendered in bright green plastic.

"Hey," he said. "Hey. You guys are still alive. Cool."

"Hello, *Alpheus*," Zhang said. "We're reading you loud and clear!"

"Yeah, awesome. Just shut up and listen, okay? I don't have a lot of time. I'm just calling to let you know there's been some complications over here. When I stuck you guys in that pod I was hoping it would just be for a minute or so. The plan was I would get things stabilized on the ship and then I would scoop you back up and we would . . . well, I don't know what we would do next. The problem is we had a reactor meltdown. The whole ship is, like, unlivable. For humans, anyway. Like you would die in seconds if you came back here. So just hang tight, okay? I'll be back in touch when there's some news."

The robot's head began to move out of frame.

"Wait," Zhang said. "Hold on – come back!"

Rapscallion actually complied. "Yeah?" he asked. "You need something?"

"We don't know what's going on. At all. The last thing I heard we were making a mad dash for the planet. What happened?"

"Yeah, about that. We didn't make it."

"What?" Petrova asked. She leaned forward, toward the screen, shocking Zhang all over again. "What do you mean? Where are we? Where are we headed?"

"Things got bad. Real bad – all those cargo modules flying everywhere. Parker had to take over flying the ship."

"Sam," Petrova said. She blinked her eyes and it was like nothing had happened. Like she hadn't just spent the last few hours in a state not unrelated to catatonia. "What do you mean, Parker took over?"

"I mean, he saved all our butts," Rapscallion told them. "He just showed up like a hologram on the bridge, and started flying the ship. Except instead of flying down, toward the planet, like you wanted, he flew up. Away from the cargo modules. He told me after that if we'd stayed on course we would have been smashed to a million pieces. So he changed course and saved your lives. The strain of changing course like that made the ship crack up, though, so we bundled you guys into the escape pod. Sorry if we were kind of abrupt about that. If we'd taken time to explain everything you'd be dead now."

"Where are we headed, then?" Petrova asked. "This pod, I mean, is it headed for the planet?"

"No," Rapscallion said. "Sorry. It's in a parking orbit. The only safe place we could put you. We're going to make repairs over here and then try to come and get you. Anyway, that's the state of things. I gotta go, but—"

"Let me talk to him," Petrova said.

"What?" The robot couldn't exactly look confused. His face wasn't human enough for that. It had to convey the emotion through its tone of voice. Somehow it managed.

"Put him on. Now."

"Look, Lieutenant, I'm not sure I made myself clear, but I'm barely holding things together over here. The ship is in worse shape than *Artemis* ever was, and repairs are kind of taking up my time, so—"

"So let me talk to him while you go fix my ship," Petrova said, in a voice that brooked no argument.

"Yes, ma'am," Rapscallion said.

120

He didn't just come on the line. He manifested himself inside the pod.

The holoscreen blinked out and in its place – there he was. Sam Parker.

Petrova just stared at him at first. He looked exactly as she remembered him. The same square jaw, and above it, the same cocky grin that it seemed he just couldn't wipe off his face. His eyes looked a little haunted.

Well, he was a ghost, after all.

Zhang kept fidgeting. Petrova looked down and saw the doctor trying to pull his knees to the side in the tiny pod. The space had been crowded before with just the two of them. Petrova glanced at her own legs and saw that Parker's knee passed through hers like it wasn't there. Zhang was trying to get away from that clammy touch. He wasn't using hard light, now – maybe the pod didn't have that capability, or maybe he was just tired of the charade. He was just a projection, an image made of laser light.

It was still enough to make it feel like the pod was suddenly way overcrowded.

Parker let out an apologetic grunt and then the lower half of his body just disappeared. There was no clear line of demarcation at his waist – his legs simply faded out as if they were obscured by deep shadow.

"Creepy," she said.

Parker's smile flickered just a little, like she'd hurt his feelings. Good.

"You lied to me," she said. "Since the second we woke up in Paradise, you lied to me. You son of a bitch."

He couldn't meet her gaze, not for long.

"Are you going to say something?" She shook her head. "Jesus, I don't even know what I'm talking to. Are you some kind of subroutine in Actaeon's AI cores? Just a simulation of Sam Parker? Or are you a separate AI?"

He shrugged a little, but it seemed he still couldn't find his tongue.

"The computers on *Artemis* and *Alpheus* were bigger than they needed to be. Military grade. Even Actaeon couldn't explain why. Did Director Lang boost our computers so they could run a hologram pilot? Help me understand this, Sam. Help me understand why you have to look and sound like a dead man."

"I . . . don't have an answer for that," he said. "The ship must have . . . I don't know. Recorded my thoughts, my memories . . . I don't even know when it did that. When we were in cryosleep, maybe? I suppose it's possible Actaeon did it when it knew it was going to have to reboot itself. A kind of backup personality for the ship's computers. Maybe."

"Maybe," she said. "Jesus Christ. And then when we woke Actaeon back up, the computers decided they didn't need you anymore. Is that it? Sam, where were you? You didn't just vanish in a cloud of pixels. Some part of you was still there. Haunting me. Where were you that whole time?"

His image shrugged. "Where were you, before you were born? I didn't have a body. I didn't have a voice – it wasn't terrible, honestly. I couldn't feel any pain. Not even emotional pain. I didn't suffer. But I could still see you. On some level I could still see you."

Petrova stared at him. She knew she would never really understand.

"You came back."

"Yeah."

She took a long, slow breath. Buying time before she asked the next question. It was a simple one, though she knew the answer was going to be devilishly complex.

"Why?" she asked. "Why did you come back?"

He licked his lips. He glanced up at her for a moment, then down at his lap again. Finally, at last, he spoke.

"You needed me," he said.

"What? I needed to be haunted by a dead fucking pilot?"

"You were in danger. When . . . when we got to Paradise, and everything went wrong. I was already dead, I know that now."

"Now? You didn't know it at the time?"

He shrugged again. It was maddening. "I don't think I was thinking it all through, back then. I was just . . . I was there, and you needed somebody to help keep you alive. After that, everything just kept happening, and it was all happening so fast. I knew it was wrong. That I was just a lie. But you needed me."

"I needed a bowl of cereal, apparently."

"I barely remember that. I barely remember anything before . . . before when you were flying the ship and I could see it wasn't going to work, that your course was going to get you killed—"

"You came back," Petrova said. "You came back to help me again."

He nodded.

"I have so many questions," she said. "Sam, I need to understand this, to—"

"Um," he said.

"Um?"

"I have to go. I'll . . . I'll try to come back," he said.

Without further warning, he vanished into thin air.

121

Petrova lunged forward, trying to grab him, to hold him there. Even though she knew that would be completely futile. Anger surged inside of her and she lashed out, smacking the wall of the pod with one fist hard enough to make Zhang jump.

"That . . . that was fucked up," he said, after a moment. "You know that? Right? That's not a human being."

Petrova took a deep breath and nodded. She knew he was right.

She needed to do something, and she needed to do it now. She had to shut this down. Parker was a distraction. He was a memory, something to grieve. She couldn't have him following her around, walking invisibly behind her shoulder, ready to step in and countermand her decisions whenever he felt like she was in danger.

She needed to shut him down. Tell him to erase himself. This wasn't really Sam Parker.

So what was it?

"You didn't tell me about this – what – bowl of cereal? This thing's been *haunting* you?" Zhang asked.

She hadn't seen him so animated in a while. "We had other things to worry about. Look. I know it's wrong. It's—"

"A desecration," Zhang said. "It's mocking the real Sam Parker's memory."

"Sure," Petrova said. Why was he harping on this? She agreed with him.

Didn't she?

Maybe he'd seen something in her face, or her tone when she spoke to Parker.

"Part of it has to be Sam. I . . . I knew Parker before all this. We'd . . . met before," she said. "It's so close to the real thing. It's just like him, sometimes—"

"No part of that thing is the real Sam Parker."

"Enough of it is that it knew how to fly *Alpheus*. It got us out of there and saved our lives," she pointed out. "Anyway. You could use that same definition to describe Rapscallion. Are you going to tell me Rapscallion's feelings aren't real?"

"Rapscallion isn't in love with you," Zhang said.

Petrova gasped in surprise. Then in indignation. "Don't be ridiculous," she said.

Zhang folded his arms across his chest.

"That's dumb. Impossible. It just wanted to help us," she said. "To keep us alive. That's why it came back."

"It doesn't care about *us*," Zhang said.

"What? What are you trying to say?"

Zhang met her eye squarely. "When it was just here. You asked why it came back and it said 'you needed me'. It meant you. Just you. It didn't bother haunting me."

Petrova refused to accept that. It was nonsense.

"Parker," she called. "Parker, get back here. I know you can hear me. We need to talk, we have a great deal more to discuss. You can't just—"

A holoscreen flared to life in the dimly lit pod. Just a simple rectangle floating in the air before them. It was bright green – Rapscallion's color. Letters appeared on the screen, forming words:

SHHH. WE'RE NOT ALONE.

Then the holoscreen snapped out of existence and they were left alone in the still, unmoving air of the pod.

For a while neither of them moved. When Petrova turned

to look at Zhang – and he turned to look at her – just the soft swishing of their suit material sounded incredibly loud.

"Oh crap," she whispered, as quietly as she could.

Zhang nodded in understanding.

122

S am Parker couldn't stop gasping for air. He couldn't seem to get warm. He rubbed at his arms, jumped up and down, did calisthenics – anything to shake the numbness, the weird cold absence of his body. He couldn't catch his breath, couldn't . . . couldn't focus, couldn't . . .

"Parker!" Rapscallion shouted. "Parker, what are you doing?"

Parker looked down at his hands. He could see right through them. He was fading out again, going back to the invisible, unthinking state he'd been in before—

Before the ship needed him. Before Petrova needed him.

"Rapscallion," he said. "Where are you?"

The robot sent him a video feed. Parker watched Rapscallion launch himself down a corridor filled with smoke and sparks, dodging a sudden burst of fire from a side corridor. *Alpheus* was in bad shape, ready to break apart at any moment. Parker checked the ship's systems to try to get a handle on just how bad things were. The artificial gravity had completely failed and every compartment of the ship was flooded with radiation. Vital ship's systems either weren't responding to his queries or were so wrecked he knew they would never work again. Rapscallion was making what repairs he could, welding a broken support strut here, replacing a burnt-out circuit board there, but it was hopeless. *Alpheus* was never going to be habitable again – the people floating out there in the pod were going to need to find a new place to live, and Parker wasn't sure how he was going to break the news to them. That wasn't the biggest problem they were currently facing, though.

"Parker!" Rapscallion summoned Parker back to the bridge. He realized he'd been floating, bodiless, through the ship's systems. He needed to focus, to maintain his body, his – his shape, anyway. He might just be a hologram projection but he was still here. He could still be here if he tried. He forced himself to appear on the bridge, as clear and opaque as the holoprojectors would allow. He even woke up the hard light systems. They would use up vital system resources, but they let him touch things. Feel like he had a body again.

"I'm here," he said.

"Good. Just in time. Things just got about a million times worse."

"What is it?" Parker asked. "Actaeon, give me a holoscreen—"

"You don't need that," the robot said.

"What?"

"You're not a dumb old human anymore, guy," Rapscallion told Parker. "Get with the program already. Just patch your conciousness into Actaeon's sensors. Okay?"

"Ah, okay," Parker said. "Oh. Oh, shit."

"Yeah."

In his mind's eye, Parker saw a telescopic view of the nearby volume of space, including all the ships within it.

There were a lot of them. It looked like the entire blockade was converging on their position. *Alpheus'* attempt to breach the blockade must have gotten their attention. One of the warships was less than an hour away.

Others were burning hard to eat up the distance between themselves and *Alpheus*. There were transports and freighters and medical ships all pointed at them like so many speeding arrows, hurrying to pierce *Alpheus'* side.

In the middle of that crowd sat the biggest ship in the entire system, a colony ship that dwarfed *Persephone*. The biggest ship Parker had ever seen, honestly. Smaller ships flitted around it like drones around a queen bee. It was moving to intercept *Alpheus* as well, though it couldn't move as fast as the warships and transports.

"I think they're done fucking around," Rapscallion said. "I think they're just going to kill us now."

"Maybe," Parker said. "Maybe."

"What?" Rapscallion said. "You think they've got something worse in mind?"

Parker reached for a console and switched on the ship's long distance sensors.

"Hey ... hey!" Rapscallion shouted. "That's not safe, guy. Come on!"

Parker knew that perfectly well. The long range sensors would send a ping out into the universe. Literally anyone who was listening would have heard that call. He might as well have sent an SOS. "It doesn't matter," he said. "The blockade already knows we're here, and we're still alive. I had to know. I had to know if they were okay, over there in the pod. And – look. I was right to worry."

The pod was moving. It shouldn't be doing that. Once a pod was launched from its ship, it had no ability to change its trajectory. It couldn't turn or change course. Yet the sensors clearly showed the pod moving in a direction it hadn't before. Not just moving, accelerating.

Something – someone – had snagged it out of space like an athlete catching a thrown ball. Grabbed it and pulled it in. The pod had been captured.

"Shit," Rapscallion said. "I wish we could do something for them, but, pal, they're on their own."

Parker, hologram or not, looked like he was about to throw up. "No," he said. "No. I refuse to accept that."

He hadn't come back from the dead just to give up now.

123

They had to sit tight. They had to stay quiet. It was unbearable. Zhang felt the RD pricking the skin of his forearm and knew it was pumping him full of drugs to keep him calm. It didn't help.

"We could open a screen," he whispered. "Get a view of what's happening outside."

"There won't be anything to see," Petrova said. "Besides . . ."

He nodded in agreement. The pod's sensors were limited to just camera views. It wasn't like looking would give away their position, or put them in any kind of jeopardy. It definitely felt like it would, though.

Doing anything – anything at all – seemed dangerous. Zhang fought back an urge to scratch his nose. He watched as Petrova's eyes closed and her lips moved as she whispered something, perhaps a prayer. Perhaps just a blind plea to the universe.

They both knew it wouldn't matter, and in the end, they were right.

For nearly an hour they sat there wondering when it would come. What form it would take. The basilisk was coming for them and Zhang knew this time they wouldn't be able to talk their way out of its wrath. They'd failed, like all the crews before them.

Petrova reached over with her good hand. She held it out to him, palm up. He stared at it, wondering what he should do.

"I know you don't like being touched," she said. "But – please. Just this once."

He started to reach for her hand. Maybe she was right. Maybe this was the time for him to start learning to trust people, to reach out when he needed—

Then something grappled the pod, and they were thrown sideways, tossed against each other. They both cried out as the pod was wrenched through space and suddenly they had gravity again, gravity that was pointing in the wrong direction. What had been the floor of the pod was just another wall. They collapsed together in a heap, and held each other in desperation as the pod was dragged one way, then another.

When the acceleration stopped, Zhang was gasping for breath as if he'd just run a foot race. He twisted around, looking at the walls of the pod, expecting them to be torn away. Expecting that he would be ejected into empty space at any second.

That didn't happen. Nothing happened, for whole heartbeats worth of time.

"Do you think . . . ?" he asked, not even sure of what he thought Petrova might be thinking. Not sure what he was thinking.

"Hold on," she said. "Rapscallion? Parker? If you can hear us, come in. Please, *Alpheus*. Do you copy?"

There was no reply.

Seconds passed. Maybe a minute. Zhang just had time to start to get control of his own breathing again.

And then the worst happened, the thing he'd been dreading. The pod's hatch was torn free of its frame with a terrible metallic screech and a shower of sparks. He turned away and dropped into a fetal ball to protect his head.

Eventually, he uncurled himself. He looked through the now vacant hatchway and outside the pod he saw – darkness, nothing else. The pod had shut down, its holoscreen was gone, but a little light came from their suits and in that dim illumination Zhang could see dust motes twisting through air.

Air. There was air outside the pod.

124.

Petrova switched on the lamps mounted on her helmet. The light was sudden and blinding and it made Zhang wince. She got to her feet and leaned into the hatchway, poking her head out of the pod.

"No," he said. "No, wait."

But she wasn't listening. She hopped out of the pod and landed on her feet outside. She started to disappear from view, absorbed into the darkness, and Zhang had to scramble to keep up. He climbed out of the pod and felt artificial gravity under his feet. He turned on his own helmet lamps and tried to figure out where they were.

It was some kind of vehicle airlock, he thought. A hangar for small spacecraft. The pod had been brought aboard some large ship. Sitting next to the battered pod lay a shuttle with long, straked wings and a round, heat-shielded nose. It was in immaculate condition, like it had never been flown.

There was no one in the hangar. No one there to greet them. The ship's AI didn't even welcome them aboard. Zhang had no idea what to make of that. There was no sign of life at all, and, strange for a spaceship, no light of any kind.

Swinging his lamps around, he took in more details but they didn't help ease his mind. The hangar was spotlessly clean, he saw. Every surface was scrubbed or freshly painted. Even the floor under the shuttle's landing gear was free of scuff marks or debris. Sitting next to it, the pod looked obscene, like a piece of waste deposited on a clean tile floor. Its surface was scratched and abraded, scorched and pitted – damaged during *Alpheus'* ill-fated attempt to descend to the planet. It was clear from looking at it that it would never see use again. The hatch, which had been cut out of its frame, lay next to it on the floor, twisted out of shape and covered in soot. There was no sign of what instrument had been used to cut it free, nor any robot or technician present who might have done the work.

There wasn't much to see in the hangar other than the shuttle and the pod. Behind them a massive airlock door stood closed. In front of them, a smaller airlock door led into the ship. Painted lines on the floor converged on that hatch, helpfully labeled so they could guide one wherever one wanted to go on the ship. An orange line for the bridge, a magenta line for engineering, a blue line for the ship's cryovault.

Petrova was already walking toward the hatch.

"Hold on," Zhang said. "Wait."

Surprisingly, she actually did stop and wait for him. She didn't turn around, though. She remained facing the inner hatch. Her good hand hovered over her holster, her fingers flexing just millimeters from the grip of her pistol. As if she was ready for a showdown the second that hatch opened.

"Where are we?" Zhang asked.

"You think I know better than you do?" she replied. "Some kind of colony ship. This looks different from *Persephone*, though. Bigger. More expensive."

"Which means there will be a lot of people here. Or at least, there were before the basilisk got to them." Zhang walked up to stand next to her. He watched the hatch as intently as she did. "What's our best course of action?" he asked.

"I can only tell you what my plan is," she said. "Which is shoot anybody who tries to attack us. And I'm going to assume the second I see them that they mean to attack us."

"How many rounds do you have?"

He heard her grit her teeth over the radio connection between their suits. "I'd prefer not to say when somebody might be listening."

He nodded apologetically. He understood what that meant: *not enough*.

"Maybe this will be like *Alpheus*," he suggested. "Maybe they'll be happy to see us."

"One way to find out. I'm done waiting," Petrova said. Then she marched over to the hatch and slapped its release panel. It opened soundlessly, its mechanism clearly well maintained.

Beyond lay a wide corridor. The painted lines continued down its length. It was as empty as the hangar, and just as clean and freshly painted.

"Come on," she said.

He followed her.

125

They headed forward up a standard ship's corridor, following the helpful orange line painted on the floor that indicated the way to the bridge. "Are we sure that's where we want to go? Ship's AIs tend to hang out on their bridges," Zhang pointed out. "You really want to meet another of those things?"

"I'll settle for someplace where the lights are on," Petrova replied. "Somewhere we can see what's coming for us. I don't like this." She turned her lamps to shine along a length of ceiling. "You see this?"

Zhang looked up and saw that the lighting fixtures up there weren't just turned off. The light panels had been ripped out of the ceiling, leaving ragged holes where they should have been. They passed a closed hatch. Zhang slapped the release pad and it opened normally enough – the mechanism had been kept well maintained – but beyond the hatch was only more darkness. The light from his headlamps stabbed into the murky space and he could make out a few details – the side and back of a chair, a shape that might have been a low table.

"Hello?" Petrova shouted. The noise was so sudden it made Zhang flinch backward. He had to grab the wall to keep from falling.

"Shh!" he said, as a surprising burst of anger washed through him. "Do you really want to announce our presence like that?"

"Come on, Zhang," Petrova said. "Really? What's the point of being quiet?"

"I don't know, to maintain the element of surprise?" he suggested.

Petrova scoffed at the idea. She reached up and tapped one of her headlamps. "Whoever's here, they'll see us coming long before we see them."

"What a wonderful, reassuring thought."

"Come on. We need to keep moving."

They continued to trudge down the endless corridor. The ship was so much bigger than *Alpheus*. Zhang could feel its vastness all around him, like he was lost in an endless labyrinth. He wondered if they could find their way back to the hangar if they needed to.

"Where is everyone? Hello!" Petrova called out, again and again. "Hello! Just tell us what you want from us. Okay?"

Zhang held his breath, listening for a response. None came.

"I don't understand," he said.

"What don't you get?" Petrova asked. She turned in a circle, her light painting the walls. The moment after her light passed, it was like the corridor just disappeared again. Vanished into nothing.

"There must be somebody here," Zhang pointed out. "Somebody caught us. They snagged us with a gravity beam. Dragged our pod into the hangar." He looked around, pushing back the darkness just a little, just for a moment. "So where are they now?"

Petrova shrugged, making her light bob up and down. "It could have been an automated system."

"Perhaps," he admitted.

"Could be everybody on this ship is dead. Could be just an AI, perching on the bridge. Waiting like a spider for new people to wander into its web."

"That . . . isn't funny," he said.

She turned to look at him, but he couldn't see her face. Just the glare of her lamps. "On the other hand, there could be thousands of people on this ship, waiting for us to come help them. Right? Maybe they just shut down this part of the ship because they didn't need it. They tore out the lights to conserve power. Right now they're waiting, just up ahead. Maybe they're going to throw us a big party."

"Now you're just being facetious."

She let out a short, bitter laugh. "Yeah, I guess I am. We both know what's here, in the dark. We know perfectly well. The basilisk is here. We just don't know what form it'll take yet. What fucked-up message it shoved into everybody's head. You want to know what I think?"

"Sure," he said, a little exasperated.

"I think it's going to be bad. Real bad. There were ... a lot of people on this ship." She pointed her lights one way up the corridor, then down the other. "Thousands. Maybe ten thousand people, and they're all hiding. From something."

Zhang took a long, deep breath. He felt the RD squeeze against his forearm. It was on the outside of his suit sleeve, so it couldn't pump him full of anxiolytics. For once, he wished it could. "Something. Something bad. So why are we following this line?" He tilted his head until his lights caught the orange line painted on the floor. "This leads to the bridge. You know what you find on a spaceship's bridge? Its AI. That's where they hang out. That's where you're taking us."

"Yep," Petrova said. "Figured I would take the quickest route there, and just get this over with."

She pressed on, farther into the ship, and he could only race to keep up with her. The idea of being left behind, alone, was unbearable.

126
•

Of course, it wasn't that easy. The corridor they were in was just an accessway that connected via junctions to other passages that led all over the ship. The orange line seemed to run on forever. This colony ship was much bigger than *Persephone*, with kilometer after kilometer of corridors leading to all kinds of different areas. There were enormous warehouse decks, cavernous, dimly lit spaces full of endless tidy stacks of cargo containers. There was another hangar that was packed full of farming and construction vehicles. A seed vault containing the genetic material for thousands of species of plants, and frozen zygotes for hundreds of species of genetically modified livestock strains. There were whole pre-fabricated buildings, stowed carefully away in modular components. An entire hospital, broken down to parts that could be assembled on a planet's surface in a matter of days. A library containing the sum total of all human knowledge, stored on row after row after row of data glass chips in protective husks, precious jewels of wisdom coddled in a room that hummed with a constant, perfect level of temperature and humidity.

This ship had been designed to go to any planet in the galaxy and jump-start a human colony. Not all of those planets were likely to be completely suitable to human comfort, so the ship also housed enormous engines to be used for terraforming new worlds. Devices to seed cloud decks to make them rain, enormous robots built to create irrigation networks on desert worlds, bioreactors like giant tanks of bacterial sludge that could turn lifeless rock into healthy black topsoil.

In ordinary circumstances Zhang would have been fascinated to study it all, to take in the great treasure troves stored in the ship's sleeping, unoccupied hollows. If he hadn't been so petrified with fear, if his hands weren't shaking so badly, he might have found it all deeply interesting.

As it was he just wanted to see a human face. He wanted to at least find out what had happened to the crew and passengers, because so far they hadn't seen so much as a single dead body, and he was starting to wonder why.

"This way," Petrova said.

They moved into a kind of observation hall, a long stretch of corridor with actual glass windows along one wall. A little light – very little – came in through the windows, outlining every object in the space with a kind of ghostly radiance that wasn't enough to actually see by but which felt like an incredible balm for Zhang's dark-adapted eyes. Humans hadn't evolved to exist for long in conditions of true darkness. Even this little bit of stray starlight felt like a gift.

Tables, chairs, and short couches filled much of the space. This was where the colonists would have come to sit and watch their new world approach in the last days before they landed. At the moment, the windows showed nothing but black space and a few white dots that might be stars. Except they weren't. Occasionally, one of them would move, quickly migrating from one side of a window to another.

Those were other ships, Zhang realized. Other ships from the blockade. It looked like they were gathering around the colony ship, forming a sort of honor guard.

Zhang sighed in frustration. Honestly, he had no idea why those ships were coming together. For all of his studies, all of his experience, he still knew so little about the basilisk and what it wanted.

"Through here," Petrova told him.

The far end of the observation corridor opened into a broad arcade. A tiny bit of starlight trickled through but for the most part it was plunged in darkness again. Stepping over the threshold made him feel like he was swimming in a vast, dark ocean. He'd surfaced for air, just for the briefest moment, and now he was plunging into the depths again.

Dark water – black, Stygian water – like the lakes on Titan, the liquid methane lakes there. He closed his eyes and he saw . . . bones. So many bones, littering the bottom of a dark lake.

"Zhang?" Petrova said. She had grabbed his arm and he felt like she'd pulled him back from a precipice.

He shuddered with vertigo, just for a moment. "Sorry," he said. "Prisoner's cinema."

"What? What are you talking about?"

He shook his head. Of course she'd never heard of the prisoner's cinema. "The brain can't handle a total lack of input. If there's nothing to see, it starts inventing things to show you. Memories, dreams, or just random scraps of hallucination. It's a phenomena named for the way prisoners in solitary confinement slowly go mad, start to see things on their cell walls just to make up for the lack of stimulation."

He couldn't see her face through the glass of her helmet but he could feel her staring at him, studying him. He didn't care for it.

"I'm fine," he said. "I'm okay. You can let go of me."

She released his arm.

Together they explored the vast space just off the windowed gallery. Moving their lights around to expose one slice of the room after another, slowly building up an idea of its contents.

The room reminded him very much of the shopping hall on *Persephone*, except it was much, much larger. Potted trees and broad planters full of shrubbery broke up a long open space and made it feel like an open, inviting town square. Through the screen of foliage Zhang could see that the arcade stretched away from them for at least a full kilometer. He thought this must have been a space designed to combat claustrophobia, to help the passengers cope with the long cold passage between stars.

It had the opposite effect on him. The fact the room was so large just meant it contained that much more darkness. He'd started to think of the endless murk as a kind of black fog that crouched all around him, filling space. He thought of his lights as burning through a dense, poisonous cloud.

He needed to shake this feeling, he thought. He needed to keep it together. It wasn't going to be easy. He was so scared.

He tried to focus on concrete objects around them, and not the empty space.

They were near the aft end of the arcade. The orange line bounded onward, ever forward. They would need to pass through this enormous space to reach their destination. Before they headed on, Zhang turned and looked back and saw that the aft wall – an acre of blank metal – had been painted with one enormous mural.

"Look," he said.

Petrova scowled, but she turned and adjusted her lamps to show as much of the mural at one time as possible. The bright lights muted the colors of the mural and created two bright spots of glare that obliterated what lay beneath, but little by little Zhang took in the details.

The mural showed the surface of Paradise-1. The planet was famous for its unusual rock formations, clusters of lava tubes that formed vast cave networks. Where these labyrinths pushed upward toward the surface they created mountains studded with caverns, mountains as porous as the foam on top of a cup of coffee. The mural showed a desolate stretch of such formations but then, at the bottom where a viewer was most likely to stand, patches of green were scattered here and there. Little gardens, lush with vegetables and fruits ready to be plucked, ready for harvest. A harsh landscape, but one pregnant with promise, with opportunity.

Standing in the center of the mural were three human figures, turned to face, together, a painted sunrise. They wore coveralls, basically ship's jumpsuits but reinforced for a more rugged lifestyle. They were smiling and their cheeks were red with color.

"I've seen that before," Petrova said. She waved her hand in the air. "Kind of. In a video I thought came from my mother." Petrova pointed out some text in one corner of the mural:

WELCOME ABOARD *PASIPHAË*.
WELCOME TO A NEW LIFE.

Zhang thought of the people that message was meant for. The colonists who would have thronged onto this ship, herded down its long corridors toward its cryovault for the journey to Paradise-1. All of them convinced they were headed toward a world of adventure and hard work, with no idea what actually awaited them in the new star system.

No idea they were headed into the clutches of the basilisk.

What about Director Lang? he wondered. Had she known, when she dispatched this ship? Had she sent the thousands of people on this ship to Paradise as – what? Human sacrifices?

"At least now we know what this tub is called," Petrova said.

"*Pasiphaë*," Zhang read again.

As if in answer, he heard a sudden sound, very far away. He ducked his head in surprise. "Did you . . . did you just . . . ?"

Petrova's lights bobbed as she nodded. "Yeah. Yeah. There was something, a noise. Up that way." Her lights swung away from the mural. Toward the far end of the concourse, in the direction of the bridge. "Sounded like . . . I don't know."

Zhang didn't know either. He knew one thing, though. It hadn't sounded like people.

"Do we ... check it out?" he asked. Hoping the answer would be no.

He knew better, of course. Petrova was already loping across the floor, headed for the noise. Whatever it had been.

127

Petrova huffed for air as she hurried forward, her lights bouncing and flashing across the floor, scattered images all she could see. She stopped once to listen again, to try to catch some sense of where she was headed but no, there was nothing. She glanced back at Zhang, who had doubled over at the waist, trying to catch his breath.

She gave him a moment, but just a moment, before she started jogging forward again.

The big concourse opened up on both sides into smaller corridors that were still far wider than anything on *Artemis* or *Alpheus*. She saw dozens of hatches leading who knew where. Painted lines criss-crossed on the floor. She had no doubt if you were one of this ship's crew those lines would lead you unfailingly wherever you needed to go. To her they were just skeins of thread wound across the walls of a labyrinth in a pattern she couldn't understand.

She was about to get herself lost, she thought. She was going to get them both lost in a dark ship that was, she was certain, ready to kill them the moment they showed the slightest weakness.

She shook her head. No. She was being paranoid. They'd seen nothing so far to suggest there was any immediate danger here. No bodies, no signs of a struggle. The weird graffiti on the wall could mean anything. She slowed to a stop. Took one last look around, hoping to catch sight of something – anything – that might tell her where to go next.

The only thing she saw was the orange line that pointed toward the bridge. She'd lost sight of it for a while, but there it was.

"This place," she said. She laughed. Shook her head. "It's getting to me. You okay?"

Zhang didn't answer. She was suddenly certain that if she turned around he wouldn't be there – that she'd lost him along the way, that she was all alone now. Alone in this endless, silent darkness.

The idea made her heart thunder in her chest. She turned slowly, promising herself that he would be right behind her, that the only reason he hadn't answered was because he was catching his breath. She smiled, to herself, amused at her own terror—

He wasn't there.

He wasn't behind her. "Zhang?" she said. "Zhang!"

"Shhh," he whispered.

She swung this way and that, her lights spearing off into empty darkness. He'd spoken to her over their suit radios, through her headphones, so she couldn't even follow his voice. She considered calling his name again, but then – there.

She caught a glimpse of a white-clad leg. Followed it up across the life support unit of his suit, then his helmet. He wasn't looking at her. His faceplate was turned away. He was looking into one of the side passages. She moved her light to join his and saw some more graffiti on the wall, there. Painted in a hurry, with lots of drips of orange paint spilling down the wall:

DARK IS SAFE

She moved closer to Zhang. He glanced back over his shoulder at her, but she couldn't see his face, just the glare of the glass of his helmet faceplate. He raised one hand in a gesture she didn't understand. Was he telling her to stay back, or . . . or what?

He turned his head slowly, back toward the graffiti. No, he was looking up the corridor. She moved to get a better look, her headlamps spearing down the dark passage.

Zhang came running at her, his hands up. He grabbed the sides of her helmet and she started to fight him off but he managed to switch off her headlamps before she could stop him. Then he reached up and switched off his own.

Darkness fell over them like a heavy winter blanket. Stifling and thick, so she felt like she couldn't breathe. She could see nothing, nothing except a tiny amber light on the front of his suit, an indicator light that just looked like a spark hovering in the nothingness.

Then he grabbed her shoulder – the shoulder of her bad arm – and hauled her around until she was facing a new direction. She'd lost all sense of where she was, even what direction she was facing. She didn't understand what he was doing, why he'd moved her around like that, why he'd switched off her lights.

But then, without warning, it was like her eyes started working again. She saw just a dim, wan glow, off in the middle distance. A shimmer of light reflecting off a bulkhead. It was moving, coming closer.

She heard a sound, and she realized it was just like the sound they'd heard back on the concourse, but much louder now. Much more distinct. A sort of low rumbling, a grunting, deep noise. Like an animal snuffling against the walls of an echoing tunnel. A rough snuffling.

The light at the end of the corridor grew stronger. Something was coming, something was right around the corner, and any moment now, any second, it would step into view.

She couldn't move. She didn't breathe. She was petrified with terror and if the thing was coming to kill her, to rip her apart – there was nothing she could do to stop it.

Then Zhang broke the spell. He reached up and switched on his headlamps. Light burst all around her, light brighter, it felt, than sunshine on a summer day on Earth. The light dazzled her but she was so glad for it, so absurdly grateful. She switched her own lights back on.

"What do we do?" Zhang asked. "What do we do?"

She glanced back up the corridor, at where she'd seen the light growing, where the noise had come from. She turned and looked in the opposite direction. "We run," she said.

He blazed by her, his legs pounding at the floor. She was right behind him.

128

They hurried down a side corridor and through an open hatch. Zhang pressed his back up against the wall. "What was that thing? Did you see it?"

"I thought—" Petrova wrestled with catching her breath. "I thought. You saw it." She waved one hand at him. "You . . . you saw it first."

Zhang shook his head. He'd caught a glimpse of light down a corridor, heard a strange roar. It had been nothing, really. Yet it had turned all the blood in his veins into ice and filled him with a desperate urge to run. "It could be anything. It could be anything." He moved to the hatchway and looked out, trying to catch anything moving in the shadows. There was nothing there. He reached up and tried to turn off his lamps. His hand refused to do it, and he realized he was terrified of being in the dark again, even for an instant.

He forced his hand to do his bidding. His finger flipped the switches, under protest, and then the only light he had was from Petrova's lamps, behind him.

He leaned further out through the hatch.

Nothing. He listened, as closely as he could with his heart pounding in his ears.

Nothing.

"Zhang," Petrova whispered. "Zhang, look. More—"

He spun around and saw her light splashed across the far wall of the compartment. Graffiti had been sprayed across the wall in giant letters.

NO LIGHT. NONE

"Fuck," he said. "Fuck this. Something happened here. Something bad."

"Yeah," Petrova said.

"But where are the bodies? Where's the—"

He shook his head. He refused to say out loud what he was thinking. *Where's the ship's AI? Where's the basilisk?*

"We need to keep moving," Petrova told him.

"Yeah? And go where?" He closed the hatch, sealing them inside the compartment. "If we stay here, if we stay quiet, in the dark, maybe it'll pass us by."

"That's a temporary solution," Petrova pointed out.

"You have a permanent one?"

She sighed. "Maybe. We get to the bridge. Talk to the ship's AI. It'll at least know what's going on. Yes, I know," she said, because he'd started to protest. "It'll be infected by the basilisk. That's the thing. It'll tell us what we're dealing with. It can't infect us, right? We're immune. So the risk is – well, not minimal. I was going to say minimal but we both know that the risk is real. But it can't turn us into – whatever."

"Photophobes?" Zhang said. "That's the sense I'm getting from the graffiti. They're afraid of light. Or rather, they're afraid of being seen. By that thing."

"I'll admit I'm afraid of it seeing me, too," Petrova pointed out. "But Zhang, look. We can't stay here."

"This hatch looks pretty sturdy," he pointed out.

"Sure," she told him. "So we could huddle here in the dark and wait. And wait. And starve to death. Or we can take the fight to this thing. Come on. You know how this works."

"I just want it to be over," he said. "I want to get out of here.

Off this ship – down to the planet. I need this to end." He glanced down at the RD writhing across his suit's sleeve. It could take this fear away. It could make him feel nothing at all.

He shook his head. He'd leaned on the RD for far too long. He'd used it to avoid his problems. Maybe it was time to stand on his own – maybe. Maybe.

He reached up and touched the release pad. The hatch slid open.

For a long second he stood there in the dark hatchway, staring out at nothing. At darkness. He realized his lamps were still turned off. He switched on one, then the other. It didn't help as much as he'd hoped.

"You sure that's a good idea?" Petrova asked. "Darker is safer, apparently."

"Screw that," Zhang said. "I'm not going to run away from being eaten by a monster and break my neck instead because I didn't see where I was going."

She gave him a little breathless laugh. Both of them were breathing heavily, and not just from exertion.

"Okay. Let's go," he told her. He stepped out into the corridor.

Nothing. Darkness in both directions. No noise, no roaring.

As he headed up the corridor he thought about the noise. He'd taken it for an animal roar but he realized as he thought about it now that the resemblance was pretty thin. It had sounded more like the sound a rusted and neglected machine might make, he thought. A kind of metallic scraping fed through a synthesizer, layered with echoes and distortions.

He thought of what he'd actually seen. Had it been anything, really? Just a smudge of light, the opposite of a shadow. Bright instead of dark but just as indistinct, inchoate.

Had he completely overreacted? Had he run for no reason?

Yet when he'd asked Petrova what to do, she'd concurred. That helped him, a little. Made him feel less foolish. Maybe they'd both been so on edge that they'd imagined the whole thing. Maybe—

He heard the roar coming from right ahead of them. He froze in place. Slowly, he turned to look at Petrova. He switched off his lights so he could see through her faceplate, make out her features.

Her eyes were open very wide. His mouth was pressed down to a tight line of tension. She looked terrified.

He turned and headed down the corridor the way they'd come, away from that noise—

Only to hear it again, coming from that direction, too.

"Shit, shit, shit," Petrova said, and reached up and switched her lights off.

Zhang started to do the same. Before he could, though, he saw white light coming around a corner ahead of him, a pale, fuzzy kind of light. And then something – something almost humanoid, almost but . . . but bigger . . . dragged itself into view, right in front of him.

It let out a roar that shocked all the breath out of him and then it came rushing toward him, loping across the deckplates with a speed that seemed impossible. In a moment, it was on him, smashing him to the floor and his vision blurred and he couldn't see anything.

He could only think of what he'd seen in the split second between its appearance and its attack. Legs and arms, enormous legs and arms and fingers splayed like claws and a head – a giant head surmounted by what looked like horns.

It smashed a fist into his helmet and he felt the glass crack and he screamed as tiny cubes of broken faceplate came showering down into his eyes and mouth, and he couldn't stop screaming . . . couldn't do anything but scream—

129
.

Petrova staggered back in horror, even as the thing jumped on top of Zhang. Its fists crashed down on his helmet and she shrieked in surprise and terror, certain that it had just cracked his skull open, that it had murdered him.

Then she heard him screaming and knew he was still alive. Maybe not for long if she didn't act. She fell back on her training and grabbed the sidearm mounted on the hip of her suit. Planting her feet, she took aim and fired three shots right into the thing's midsection, not bothering with a verbal warning.

Just wanting to kill the thing.

She hit it. Three times. Right in its center of mass. There was no mistaking it.

She got a better look at it and realized she had no idea what it was. It was humanoid in shape but strangely flat, strangely dimensionless. Like a projection on a screen. White in color, with a bluish tinge, perhaps. It seemed to radiate its own light.

As she watched, it climbed up, off Zhang, and turned to face her. Except it had no face. Just a blurry sort of patch of light that could be a head, with an arcing horn sticking up on either side. Like some kind of demon, maybe—

She didn't even think about it. She fired again, this time right in the thing's face. Or the place where its face should have been.

The bullet passed right through it. Maybe the thing's shape flickered for an instant, a stuttering distorting like data corruption on a screen. It didn't seem hurt in the slightest. It was like she'd just taken a shot at a . . .

. . . a hologram. Because that was exactly what it was, just a spray of light cast by a projector in the ceiling, she thought. It was just an image.

Then it smashed into her like a raging bull, knocking her up against the wall. The breath went out of her and she felt her ribs start to flex, like the thing was going to cave in her chest and crush her heart and lungs. Its hands came up toward her face and it grabbed either side of her helmet.

She heard a screech of metal, then a terrible snapping sound like bones breaking. Her lights – her lamps – it had ripped the lamps right off her helmet. Petrova shrieked as it stumbled back, away from her. It looked like it was getting ready for another attack.

Hard light, she thought.

Just like Parker.

It was a hard light hologram. Artificial gravity beams hiding inside a smear of light.

And it was going to kill them both.

There was nothing she could do to stop it. She might have just as easily tried to fight the wind.

130

The thing – the smear of light – grabbed her by the good arm and threw her across the hall. She collided with the bulkhead, hard enough to make her teeth feel loose in her skull. It loomed up over her, its horns surrounding her face. More like the jaws of a stag beetle than a devil's horns, she thought. She tried to hold her breath, tried to be still but it lifted one clawed hand and she flinched, hard.

The thing roared. How had she ever thought that was an animalistic sound? It was a like a screech of bad data, the sound of a corrupted file, pitched low until it made her chest hurt. Its hand rocketed toward her and smashed into the instrument package on her chest. She looked down and saw that it had destroyed half of her suit's equipment. She glanced down at her good wrist, at the little screen there, trying to see if her suit had been breached, but then she realized what was happening.

The screen was gone. It had simply vanished. So had every other part of her suit that lit up – anything with a status light, anything that generated a holographic display, all of it was wrecked.

Was that . . . Could it be that was all the thing wanted? To destroy her lights?

She turned and looked at Zhang. He was lying on the floor, struggling to breathe. He spat and chunks of glass flew out of his mouth. There was blood on his face. One of his headlamps was still burning.

The monster – the hologram – whatever it was – turned to look at him, too. It took a stomping pace away from her. It started moving toward Zhang, faster and faster.

"Turn off your light!" she screamed. "Turn it off!"

Zhang gave her a look of incomprehension. Even as the monster stormed toward him he just lay there, in obvious distress. If the thing hit him again, would it be enough to kill him?

"Turn it fucking off!"

Zhang reached up and switched off the lamp.

The monster glitched in mid-stride, a wavering distortion passing through its whole being. Its arms were both raised, hands closed in the shape of rough fists. It started to fall toward Zhang, like a beast pouncing on its prey, and Petrova shouted, begged, screamed at it to leave him alone.

And then – the thing stopped.

It just stopped.

It didn't attack.

It didn't kill Zhang.

It turned around, slowly. Its horns bobbed up and down as if they were searching for something they couldn't find.

It didn't make any sound as it stomped around. It didn't roar. It tossed its head from side to side as if trying to smell its quarry, but for all the furious purpose it had shown before now it seemed almost confused, like it knew it had a task to perform but it couldn't remember how to do it.

She had to take her chance. She rushed over to Zhang, giving the hologram a wide berth. She dropped down to her knees next to Zhang and examined his suit. Every light and display on it had been smashed, just as hers had been. The creature was certainly thorough. She looked at his face and saw him staring past her, at the flickering, blue-white thing that stood not five meters away.

She tried to pick pieces of broken glass off of Zhang's face. There was a lot of blood and she wasn't sure if she was hurting him or not. He seemed to be beyond feeling pain, anyway. Maybe he was just too scared.

"Can you get up?" she whispered.

"Shh," he breathed, more of a desperate exhalation than an attempt at actually shushing her. "It's . . . it's still . . ."

"It's done with us, I think," she said. "Come on. Can you get up?"

Not without a lot of effort, it turned out. He put both hands against the wall for support and slowly, carefully, rose to stand on shaky knees.

"Don't look," she said. "Don't look at it. It just wanted our light. If we don't make any light—"

"We're just going to stumble around in the dark?" he said, his voice the barest of whispers.

She was pretty sure the hologram couldn't even hear them. It seemed utterly unable to detect anything except a source of light.

"Just . . . just until we get away from it. Okay?" she said. She got his arm around her good shoulder. Helped him walk forward. His legs weren't broken, he was just weakened by fear. Up ahead she saw the corridor turn, a sharp corner. If they could get out of sight of the hologram, maybe they would be safe, she thought.

Maybe. For the moment.

"Did that thing kill everyone onboard?" Zhang asked.

Petrova shook her head. "We haven't seen any bodies. It doesn't seem like the kind of thing that cleans up after itself. Turn here."

Together they turned the corner and looked down a long, dark hallway. A tiny bit of light followed them around the turn – light generated by the hologram itself. Beyond that lay only pitch darkness.

"Put your hand up. Feel along the wall. Okay?" she said. "Keep moving. The more distance between us and it—"

"No," Zhang said. "No."

"No?"

"Distance isn't the answer. Before, when it seemed like it was chasing us – we ran away from it. So it came at us from a different direction. This thing is a projection. A holographic projection – it can be anywhere, probably anywhere on the ship. Running away from it won't help, because it can just manifest wherever you are."

"That's a supremely unhelpful thought."

"You know it's true," he said.

"And you know the actual answer," she said. "The thing we should have known all along – it was literally written on the walls in giant letters. No light. All it wanted was to destroy our lights. If it killed us in the process, it didn't care. We need to stick to the dark, if we want to be safe."

"From that thing, maybe." Zhang spat some more glass out of his mouth. "What if there's something worse in the dark?"

She stopped moving. Why bother, right? Why risk tripping over something, walking into a wall? She thought of how she would reply to his pessimism, how she would insist that they keep moving. The words didn't come easy.

She opened her mouth to say something, anything, to summon up the tiniest bit of hope. Then she froze solid, still as a statue.

A hatch had opened ahead of them. Somewhere out in the dark.

She heard footfalls. Someone coming toward them. She reached for the weapon on her hip, though she had no idea how she was going to shoot someone she couldn't see.

The footsteps came close – then stopped.

In the dark she could hear someone breathing. Someone human.

"This way," they said. Whoever they were. A hand slapped against her arm, her wrist. Grabbed her hand.

It was a child, a child's hand that had slipped into her glove.

"Come on! This way!"

131
•

They hurried through the hatch, Petrova supporting Zhang less and less as they made their way through dark corridors, hands sliding across the walls, feet shuffling forward for fear of tripping on something. Zhang could feel his strength coming back – he'd been more terrified than truly hurt by the hologram's attack – but with it, his reservations about where they might be headed grew, too. A child whispering in the dark was hardly the guide he might have asked for. It seemed it was all they were going to get. It didn't help that the child failed to answer any of his questions except in the most basic, equivocating terms.

"Where are you taking us?" he asked.

"To the other people."

"What other people? The ship's crew? Passengers?"

"Safe people. It isn't far."

"How many of you are there? How long have you been living like this? Are you in contact with the ship's AI?"

It was Petrova who answered those questions, and only with an admonition. "Zhang," she said. "Give it a rest. We can't survive here on our own, not for long."

He supposed she had a point.

Despite the child's claim, it was a long walk before they actually got anywhere. They descended at least one long ramp – he had to be careful not to go sprawling forward as he edged his way down the slope. He would have liked to take that descent at a snail's pace, but the child didn't even slow down. He was holding Petrova's shoulder, and she held the child's hand, and he didn't dare let go so he had to match their pace. He was terrified that if he lost contact with Petrova, even for an instant, he would never find her again in the dark.

At the bottom of the ramp lay another long, empty corridor. It was lined with hatches but he was only vaguely aware of them as a different texture of wall under his ever-moving hand. The floor beneath them grew harder and their footsteps louder but he couldn't have said what that meant. Had they come down into an engineering deck? A section of the ship where passengers were less likely to tread? Maybe.

The darkness was maddening, even though he knew it was necessary. It wasn't just the lack of stimulation but the way his brain kept trying to guess at his surroundings. There was the fact he never knew how much space was above him – whether they were moving through open spaces as lofty as cathedral ceilings or crawling through low, stooped tunnels. He had to fight the urge to walk bent over, his free hand up above his head. He couldn't shake the nightmarish fear that he was about to smash his forehead into a low-hanging ceiling. Somehow he managed to avoid that.

His hearing had sharpened, perhaps. At any rate he found himself listening for every echo, the way their footsteps bounced off the walls. Maybe in time he would have found his hearing compensating for the lack of vision but he was a long way from learning how to navigate by echolocation. For the moment, at least, every sound was a new alarm, a potential danger springing at him out of the lightless depths.

With his helmet's faceplate shattered he could smell the air, which was mostly odorless but a little stale. He brought his hand up to his mouth and used his teeth to pull his glove off (he couldn't spare the hand that held Petrova's shoulder), so that he could feel better the textures of the wall as they raced along it. For the most part the wall was smooth, though occasionally his fingers would smash up against some protuberance, a raised section of wall that might have been a sign or a control panel or who knew what. Once his fingertips traced over the cobweb of cracks in a piece of glass and he knew he was touching a light fixture that had long since been destroyed.

Lost in these thoughts he failed to keep track of how far they'd come. Farther than he would have liked, definitely, but he wondered how quickly they were actually moving, whether it just seemed like a headlong race through the spaceship's bowels because it was so frightening. It was an utter surprise, at any rate, when Petrova slowed to a stop and he collided with her from behind.

"Sorry, sorry," he said. "What's happening?"

"We're here," the child said, in the dark.

He heard a hatch open, right next to his hand. He felt air sigh out of the compartment beyond, felt the air wash over his face and bring with it a smell of – of people.

He could smell their breath. Smell their clothing, which hadn't been washed in a while.

He could hear their breathing. Lots of them, he thought. Lots of people.

"I brought them," the child said. "Two. A man and a woman. We're coming in."

Zhang could hear some of them holding their breath. Waiting for something more.

"Hello," he said. "My name is Zhang, and this is Petrova. We ... we're not from—"

"Why did you bring us here?" Petrova demanded. "Why did you drag our pod onto this ship?"

"That wasn't us," someone said, in the darkness. A man's voice, with a certain expectation of authority behind us. "Come inside. You're safe, now. We have food, if you're hungry."

"Who was it then?" Petrova demanded. "Why are we here?"

"I can't answer that second question, not yet," the man said. "But as for who – it was Asterion. Our ship's AI."

"We need to make contact with the AI as soon as possible," Petrova said.

Someone laughed. It was a bitter sound.

"You've already met it," someone else said, a woman. Maybe the same person who'd just laughed. "It attacked you. Took away your lights."

"We – we what?" Zhang said. "Sorry. Big hologram? Horns and claws and . . . hates anything that makes light? That thing is your ship's AI?"

"Sashenka," someone said. "You're here."

He felt Petrova stiffen next to him, felt it in the way her shoulder moved. He could sense her entire body tensing up. He had so many questions, though, he didn't want to stop to figure out what was bothering her.

"So your AI is the one keeping you in the dark?" he asked. "Your ship's AI turned against you? Did it . . . did it try to infect you, I mean, I guess you wouldn't know what I mean by that, but . . . but . . . "

Petrova shoved his hand off her shoulder. He felt her move past him, rushing into the room beyond. He felt suddenly, horribly disconnected from her, all alone in the darkness and it gave him a terrible sense of vertigo.

"Petrova?" he asked. "What's . . . what's going on? Are you okay?"

"Mama?" Petrova said.

Not to him. Obviously. But . . .

"Yes, Sashenka. It's me."

132

A thousand kilometers away, Parker watched the sensor console like a hawk. He realized at one point he wasn't blinking. He was just a hologram now. He guessed he didn't need to do things like blink anymore.

The information displayed on the sensor screen was good news – for *Alpheus*, anyway. The entire blockade had been converging on their position, just a few minutes before. Now that had stopped. The escape pod had disappeared from his screen, and instantly the fleet of basilisk-controlled ships had decelerated. Changed course. They'd taken up positions around the big colony ship. Like it was the important thing, now, and the destruction of *Alpheus* could wait.

"Rapscallion? What can you tell me about that big ship?" Parker asked. "The one that grabbed the escape pod."

The robot was deep inside the ship's engines, doing repairs. "It's called the *Pasiphaë*, according to the registry database." Rapscallion played an audio clip of a human male whistling in appreciation. "Big mother of a thing. Might be the biggest ship humans ever built. Ten thousand people onboard. It launched from Mars about a year and change ago – must have been one of the first ships to come here and get taken over by the basilisk."

"Does it have any weapons?"

Rapscallion scoffed. He didn't bother playing an audio file this time – instead he blatted out a rough electronic sound that indicated pure derision. "It doesn't need any damned weapons. It has a whole fleet orbiting around it right now. Half a dozen big warships, and plenty of little ships that I'm sure would be happy to just ram right into us if we tried something."

"I could get in there," Parker insisted. "If I had something small and maneuverable. Like a starfighter – I could punch right through that fleet. Evade their fire, outrun anything that tried to ram me. I could land on the colony ship's hull, then cut my way in with a plasma torch."

Rapscallion played a file of an entire crowd of people laughing. "Wow. You really are in love with her."

Parker's face contorted, his features evolving through various emotions as he sought the words to deny it. It was so much more complicated than that, but how to explain that to a robot? Finally, he just said, "I came back from the dead for a reason. If you think she's not worth it—"

"I think," Rapscallion said, "that you're forgetting a couple important things about yourself. First, you might have come back from the dead but you're not immortal. Even simulated pilots have their weak points, right? If someone destroys your processor core, you're back to being dead, for good this time. That plan you described is utter suicide in a can."

"I'm not afraid of taking risks," Parker insisted.

"Secondly," Rapscallion said, "if you could get inside *Pasiphaë* you would still have to find her and . . . do what? Throw her over your hard light shoulder and carry her back here? Because thirdly, and I can't stress this one enough, you're a fucking ghost."

"I'm not useless!" Parker said.

Because that was exactly how he felt, at that moment.

"That's not what I said. I just mean if you try to get more than about five hundred meters away from your processor core, you'll just fade out to nothing at all. This ship's computer can't broadcast you halfway across the star system. Even if it could, you would just be a laser light show when you got there. Your hard light powers only work because Actaeon makes them happen. You can open doors and pour bowls of cereal on this ship but only because you have a little control of *this* ship's systems. On *Pasiphaë* you wouldn't be able to pick up a coin off the floor, much less fight your way through a legion of zombies to get to her."

"God damn it, Rapscallion," Parker said. "I don't care if you're right, that's ... that's ... "

"Cold. Maybe. But it's accurate."

Parker grunted in frustration. "Okay. Okay, fine. So – what? You want to just leave them over there? Let the basilisk do what it wants with them?"

"Hell, no," Rapscallion said. "Those are my friends. I'm not giving up on them."

"Awesome," Parker said, and his old cocky grin started to grow across his face once more. "What's your big plan?"

"I will let you know," Rapscallion said, "just the second I come up with one."

133
•

Ekaterina Vladimirovna Petrova took a step forward and placed the palm of one hand against the side of her daughter's helmet.

It was the kindest, most gentle touch Petrova's mother had ever given her. Her whole body started to shake. "Mama," she said, again. Like she'd regressed to infancy and all she could do was repeat her first word.

She sensed Zhang moving behind her, felt the air displace as he moved.

"What's going on?" he asked.

"This is my mother," she managed to say, out loud, before emotion choked her again. She shook her head and squeezed her eyes shut. "This is Ekaterina Petrova."

"The old director of Firewatch," Zhang said. "But what is she doing here?"

"She's supposed to be down on the planet. She retired a little over a year ago. She was going to make a new life on Paradise-1," Petrova said, picking her words carefully. "I guess she never made it that far."

"Hello, Doctor," Ekaterina said. "I wonder if you would do me a favor? My friend Michael here can take you somewhere you can sit down. He'll answer all your questions. I'd like to take a moment to speak with my daughter alone."

Zhang sputtered some kind of response. It wasn't so much

a protest, she thought, as an expression of incredulity. The man who had spoken to them – that must be Michael – moved forward and then he and Zhang moved off somewhere. She couldn't tell where they were, or where they were going. Petrova felt a weird pang as he left her – like it was a terrible mistake for them to split up. Yet no one attacked her the second she was alone, nor did she hear Zhang screaming off in the distance.

Ekaterina reached out to take her hands. "What's this?" she asked.

"It's a cast," Petrova said, when she realized her mother was searching for her bad hand. "A ship's AI tried to eat me. Not your ship's AI, a different one. It's a long story."

Someone else might have been flustered by that rush of information. Not Ekaterina. "I'm so glad you made it here safely, Lapachka." The word meant *little paw*, a common term of affection Russian mothers used with their children. It suggested the protectiveness of a mother wolf. Maybe it was also a pun about her injured hand – Petrova had never really gotten her mother's subtle sense of humor. She'd always thought she wasn't smart enough to get the jokes. "This is a dangerous place and there were no guarantees you would make it to us. I want you to know I've been rooting for you the whole time."

"The whole time? What does that mean?"

"I knew you were here, on *Pasiphaë*. I'll explain everything in time but for now – let me just enjoy this."

"Mama," Petrova said. Trying to sound like an adult as she said it. "Ekaterina. There's something you need to know. Your ship's AI has been parasitized by a . . . well, call it an infection. We call it the basilisk, it's . . . it's a kind of contagious delusion. I hate to say this but it's possible you've also been infected, yourself. I need to make sure you're not under the effect of a delusion, it could be—"

Ekaterina sighed. Petrova stopped talking because she knew that tone. The mother had stopped hearing the sound of her daughter's voice – nothing Petrova said now was going to get through.

"I'm well aware of this," Ekaterina said. "I know about your basilisk."

"You ... you do?"

Ekaterina clucked her tongue. "Come with me. We should speak privately, as much as we can. One thing you'll learn about this batch is that there are always little ears hiding in the shadows." She took her daughter's hand and led her through a hatch, into another compartment and then into the corridor beyond. Ekaterina seemed to have no trouble finding her way around.

"Now," she said, when she'd stopped again, in some other part of the ship. "Now. Let's discuss your big important news. You came to warn me of the basilisk, yes, well I'm well ahead of you. I promise you I have not been infected."

"You might not know," Petrova pointed out. "I got hit by it, myself, and without Zhang to help me—"

"That man helped you? How?" Ekaterina demanded.

"He ... he developed a cure," Petrova said. She didn't want to say that it only worked if you received it shortly after infection. That it was probably too late for everyone on *Pasiphaë*.

"Fascinating. But all right. Let us begin with this. You think perhaps I am not myself. Let me show you that's not the case. The basilisk destroys the mind, yes? It eats away at one's consciousness until nothing remains but the intrusive idea. Well, I assure you, my mind is as sharp as it ever was."

"I'm not sure if that ... if that's something I can just take on faith," Petrova tried.

"Let me prove it. Let me think of something ... perhaps ...yes. When you were five years old you had your appendix and your tonsils removed, as a precaution. Do you remember?"

"Kind of," Petrova admitted. "Vaguely."

"We moved to the Moon that year, and I didn't trust that medical standards were high enough there, so I had the surgery done on Earth before we left. When you went in for the surgery, before you were anesthetized, you reached up and grabbed my hand. Your fingers were so tiny, so fragile. I thought you wanted me to comfort you. Instead you were handing me something. Do you remember what it was?"

Petrova fought to keep her lips from trembling. She gave a curt nod. Then she realized her mother couldn't see the gesture, so she whispered, "Yes."

"A little frog. A tiny plastic charm that had been attached to the zipper of your winter coat. There is no winter on the Moon, so we'd already thrown the coat away but you broke the charm off and saved it. You wouldn't let that thing go, cheap as it was. You wanted me to keep it safe for you while you were sedated. I promised I would set a security detail to guard it day and night."

Petrova lifted her chin. The memories came flooding back. "When I woke up I was in pain. I was so groggy. I asked you where my frog was."

"I had to send one of my aides to find it. I'd put it somewhere and couldn't remember where. Yes. I told you I was a busy woman and sometimes things fell through the cracks." Ekaterina shook her head and her vast mane of hair bobbed wildly – Petrova could hear the way it swung and bounced. "I was afraid someone had thrown it out, since it was just trash, after all. But my aide found it and gave it to you and then we all ate ice cream."

Petrova shoved her good hand in her pocket. It was curling up into a fist, just from the tension. Another question jumped to her mind—

"Pistachio," Ekaterina said.

"It really is you." Petrova wanted to sit down. "You're here. It's really you."

"Yes," Ekaterina said. "Was that what you were afraid of? I might have become something else, some monster?" She laughed. "I assure you, I am fully human. As much as I ever was. Now. Let's talk about you, and your adventures."

134

●

The man named Michael led Zhang to a new place. He knew he was utterly lost inside *Pasiphaë* now – he would never find his way back to the hangar, not without help. No one else seemed to think that was a problem. Hands in the dark helped him find a place to sit down. Then they drew back, left him alone. Maybe they sensed how badly he wanted not to be touched, just then.

"Are you hungry?" Zhang jumped a little at the sound – as if this place were as silent as it was dark, though that was far from the case. The room was never still, as the people in it moved around or shifted position. Someone was coughing in the distance, a dry, rasping sound that never quite stopped.

"I'm okay," Zhang insisted. He reached up and unfastened the clasps of his helmet. No need for it now, now that the faceplate was shattered. He lifted it over his head and a brief rain of broken glass fell around his legs where he sat.

"Do you need help with that?" a woman asked. "My name is Angie. Here. Let me take that."

Zhang hesitated. There was still one working lamp on the helmet. He wondered if he would ever get it back. Eventually he handed her the helmet – he could hardly use the lamp amongst this crowd. Other people came forward to help him with the rest of his suit. Piece by piece, they took it from him. He felt vulnerable, even naked without it but he had to admit he was much more comfortable.

He really wished Petrova would hurry up and come back. He didn't want to stay with these weird people any longer than he had to.

The RD slithered back onto his arm, finding its way back to him even in the dark.

"The darkness, you mean?" Angie asked.

"You grow accustomed to it. You'll need to learn new ways of doing things, but you'll be surprised at how quickly you adapt," Michael told him.

"Hopefully I won't be here long enough to need to," Zhang suggested. Knowing it was a mistake as soon as he'd said it. "No offense meant."

A ripple of laughter went through the crowd. How many of them were there? He really had no sense of whether there were a dozen or a thousand people sitting around him. It felt like they were all watching him, like he was the only one who couldn't see. He could sense their attention turning toward him, a hundred faces inclining in his direction. Because he had no idea how large a compartment he was in, he could only imagine it packed from side to side with a vast throng of people, with just a little clearing in the middle where he sat.

"You'll learn. Soon enough, you'll understand," Michael told him. "Just as we've come to understand. The light is dangerous. Only in the dark are we safe." It sounded like a religious creed, the way he said it. "You'll wonder how you ever felt comfortable living another way."

"I don't understand," Zhang said. "You've lived for . . . nearly a year now, in total darkness?"

"It didn't start that way," Michael said. "We had to learn how to live like this. It wasn't easy."

Zhang thought of the graffiti they'd seen, scrawled on what felt like random walls of the ship. It had occurred to him, in passing, that such messages weren't very useful to people who couldn't see them.

"When we first arrived here," Angie said, "in Paradise – I think we all felt it right away. We saw the light of a new sun, for the first time, and we understood something had changed. It felt wrong. On your skin, it felt ... dangerous. Like you could feel it burning you, feel it making you sick."

"It felt like it hated us," someone else said.

"Like it was watching us. All the time." Another voice, older, Zhang thought.

"The ... light?" Zhang asked. "The light from the star?"

"It's hard to understand but once you feel it you'll know," Michael told him.

"We got so sick," Angie said. "It was terrible. We felt so weak, so nauseous all the time. Our blood pressure shot up, our heart rates were all over the place. It felt like you were going to die, all the time. None of us knew what was causing it. Not for far too long."

"It was Director Petrova who figured out what was wrong," Michael said.

"Ekaterina, you mean," Zhang said. "My friend's mother."

"She's a great leader," Angie told him. "She was the one who figured out what was making us sick. She was the one who taught us that the light was dangerous."

"She ... did?" Zhang asked. "She told you that. Not your ship's AI?"

"She was brilliant," Michael said, ignoring his question. "The second we heard it, we knew it had to be true. It wasn't just the light of Paradise, either. At first we just kept back from the ship's viewports. Hid from that sickening radiance. But we'd all been changed. Any kind of light made us feel ill – natural, artificial, it didn't matter. We'd been sensitized and now we couldn't go back. We tried half measures at first. Using light only when we needed to see something. We found we needed it less and less. There were so many things that could be done without seeing, without light. More and more of our days were spent with no lights at all. We called it 'keeping dark' and it was the one thing that made us feel better."

"Letting go was the hardest part," Angie said. "I remember – oh, God, it was a terrible time but I remember one day, there were six or seven of us in a little room, deep inside the ship, sitting around a single light, a little LED. Staring at it like it was a campfire, unable to give it up though we knew it was killing us. Each of us daring the others to switch it off. Knowing once we did we would never switch it back on." Zhang could hear her shudder in revulsion. "I don't remember who did it, who smashed the bulb. I just remember the after-image, the way it was burned into the backs of my eyes, that little glowing point. In time, it faded."

"There were those among us who kept lights burning, long after we knew it wasn't safe. People who just couldn't let go of their light." Michael stirred, perhaps making some grand gesture Zhang couldn't see. "Ekaterina led us on a crusade to find them, to discover their hiding places. For many months we worked to root them out, to find their secret, lighted places."

Zhang frowned. "What happened when you found them?"

Michael didn't answer for a long time. When he did, he replied with a sigh. "Sacrifices had to be made."

"Sacrifices have to be made," someone else said, a young-sounding woman.

"Sacrifices must be made," a dozen other people said. It didn't sound so much like a litany as a reassurance, a kind of self-soothing.

"You ... needed to protect yourselves," Zhang said. He had to remember that these people were all infected with the bas-ilisk. That to them all of this made perfect sense. He couldn't antagonize them, even though they'd probably just admitted to murdering their shipmates. "You had to protect yourself from the AI."

"What?" Michael said. "From Asterion?"

Someone laughed. A half-dozen more people laughed, then others joined in, nervous, sheepish, like they didn't want to be caught not laughing.

"I don't get it," Zhang said. "What's so funny?"

"We don't protect ourselves from Asterion by keeping dark. Asterion protects us from the temptation of light. It destroys any light source it finds – well, you've seen how that works."

Angie sighed in contentment. "It's our guardian. Ekaterina reprogrammed it to keep us safe from the light. It's been so good to us. Our guardian angel."

Zhang had bruises all across his chest and face from his encounter with the hologram. He decided he would defer judgment on that. "But it's made of light. It radiates light everywhere it goes."

"Some mysteries," Michael said, "are harder to understand than others. Some of the things we have to do are harder than others."

"Sacrifices always have to be made," Angie whispered.

135
•

"But — I don't understand," Petrova said. "You were exposed to the basilisk — you must have been. But you don't seem to be affected by it."

"I am quite well. Sound in body and mind," Ekaterina insisted. "You must know, Sashenka, that for every disease there are people who have a natural immunity. Is it so hard to believe that I might be made of strong enough stuff to resist a rabid meme?"

Petrova had to admit that if there was anyone in the universe with the willpower to fight off the basilisk, it would be her mother.

"Take my hand. Let's walk for a bit. I am responsible for the health of my people, and I take that very seriously. I make my people do calisthenics daily." She chuckled. "I cannot, of course, see if they are doing as many crunches and jumping jacks as I like. I have had to learn to accept certain things on the honor system."

"That must be a nightmare for someone like you."

"Sarcasm. Spare me that, daughter. It's a disgusting habit."

Petrova lowered her head. "Sorry," she said.

"Hmm. Here. My hand."

Petrova took her mother's hand and let herself be led forward, into the dark. It was hard to trust that they weren't just going to walk right into a wall but she supposed Ekaterina must know where she was going.

"There is a great deal you'll need to learn, now that you're here," Ekaterina said. "You'll have to adapt to eating only packaged food, for one thing. We can hardly grow our own crops here on *Pasiphaë*, so we've been surviving on the ship's stores. Luckily, there's enough to go around for a very long time. There are less than a hundred of us and this ship was designed to feed thousands."

"Less than a hundred?" Petrova asked. "Zhang said this ship could hold ten thousand people. The ones back there, in that room ... are they ..."

"The ship's crew, for the most part," Ekaterina said. "I thought you might have guessed as much. You really do need to work on being more observant." Ekaterina laughed. "When the ship arrived here in the Paradise system, its AI realized at once how dangerous this place was. It woke up only those crew and passengers who had vital skills. I was one of the first, of course. Asterion knew it needed my special talents."

Ekaterina's narcissism certainly hadn't been damaged by exposure to the basilisk. "What about everybody else? What happened to the passengers? Where are they?" A cold wash of dread ran through her veins. "What did you do with them?"

"Nothing," Ekaterina said. "What are you suggesting? They were never brought out of cryosleep. They remain safely frozen in the cryovault, dreaming of a new life on Paradise-1. The ship can maintain them there indefinitely."

"You're going to keep them frozen forever?"

"At least until we can find a way to feed them."

"So, you have some kind of long-term plan," Petrova said. "Of course you do. Who do I think I'm talking to?"

"The basilisk has ways of making its intentions known. It has made it clear that this ship will not be allowed to land on the planet. So we must make do. I want to make this ship truly self-sufficient. I want to make this a permanent colony, all its own. I'm hoping you'll help with that. In fact,

Sashenka, I'm really hoping that you'll work at my side. There's always so many things that need to be done. I could use an aide-de-camp."

"You . . . you want me to be your personal assistant."

"Yes," Ekaterina said.

"Mother, I'm not going to stay here. I have a mission to complete."

"Do not be foolish, now, Sashenka. This is the only place where I can keep you safe."

"Safe? You think this place is safe?"

"Safer than anywhere else. Sashenka, the basilisk will not allow you to descend to the planet – that's the whole reason for its existence, to guard this place. It will destroy you if you even try. You cannot leave here. I forbid it." Ekaterina's eyes glinted with fury as she spoke, though of course she was holding herself very tight, very controlled. Petrova knew what it meant when her eyes looked like that.

When they shone like that—

"Mother," she said, suddenly afraid. "Mother, where have you brought me? I can *see* you."

She stared down at her own hand. It was dark, it was very dark but she could see her fingers, even make out some of the lines on her palm. She looked up and saw that they had entered one of the observation galleries, one of the long corridors that ran across the outer hull of *Pasiphaë*. A row of enormous viewports, off to her left, looked out on the stars, and the scant light was enough to let her see – something, anything – for the first time since the hologram attacked them.

"This can't be safe," Petrova whispered. She twisted around, looking for any sign of Asterion. Any glimpse of flickering blue light.

"Forgive me. I wanted to look on my daughter's face one more time," Ekaterina said. "But you're right. We should head back."

She started to move again, but then she stopped and her eyes scanned Petrova's face. Searching for something. "Good. You're learning, already, how to live this life. That is a skill you will need. After all, this ship is where you will spend the rest of your life."

136

"Zhang? Is that you ... sorry, I ... sorry, I need to find my friend, the man I came here with, can you ... excuse me, I'm sorry ..."

He heard Petrova coming a long time before she arrived. He desperately wanted to jump up, to run and greet her. He realized how badly he'd missed having one person he could trust among this throng. If he moved, though, he knew they would never find each other in the dark. "Petrova! Lieutenant! Follow my voice!"

The others moved to make way for her. He heard her breathing heavily, felt the air move as she rushed through the dark space. Then her good hand landed on his face, one finger nearly poking him in the eye. He shied back, startled.

"Oh, sorry," she said. "I know you don't like being touched."

He had a sudden, perverse urge to grab her hand and never let go. "I think this place might cure me of that." He turned his head from side to side. It was impossible to know who was listening to them. There might be someone right next to him, studying him, measuring his reaction to seeing Petrova again.

Paranoia. Another thing he had to worry about, to watch out for. "Come, sit with me," he said. "Did you have a good talk with your mother?"

"She's apparently in charge here," Petrova said. "Don't ask me how she pulled that off. She wants our help, she says."

"*Our* help? With what?"

"They haven't had a doctor for a while. As for me, I don't know. Maybe they need a detective or something."

A question jumped to Zhang's lips. He fought the urge to just blurt it out. Instead, he reached for Petrova's shoulder – careful not to grab her bad arm – and leaned in close to whisper, very close to her ear. "That's not going to happen, though. Right? Because we're not staying. And listen, I know this may be hard to hear. But I don't think you should trust your mother."

Petrova stifled an abrupt laugh. He didn't understand why.

"Listen," he said. "There's something weird here. Everywhere else, we saw the basilisk being spread by a ship's AI. But here it was your—"

She put her hand over his mouth, shutting him up. Then she twisted her head around until she was almost kissing his ear. It made him extraordinarily uncomfortable, but he forced himself not to flinch.

"Not now," she whispered. "It's not safe to talk about this. For now, try to fit in. We'll talk later, when we can."

He disliked that intensely but what could he do? He knew she was right.

These people, the mob all around them, seemed friendly enough for the moment. But he knew that wouldn't last if he and Petrova violated their rules. He also knew they were infected with the basilisk. For the victims of the contagious delusion violence was never very far away.

So he did what he could to make them happy.

For more than a day they found ways to make themselves useful. Valuable to their hosts. It meant separating from Petrova. He didn't like being away from her but it was the only way the two of them could try to fit in.

Zhang moved through the crowd, groping his way through the dark, working as a physician. There wasn't much a doctor could do without being able to see, and the medical supplies available to him were rudimentary at best, but he did what he could. The most common injuries among the lightless were contusions – bad bruises from walking into the sides of hatches or tripping over each other in the dark. Sprains and the occasional broken bone. He wrapped an ankle in gauze, handed out ice packs to those who needed them. Michael seemed especially appreciative. It became clear to Zhang that while Ekaterina might be nominally in charge, she was rarely available to the people of *Pasiphaë*. In most matters, Michael was responsible for leadership.

Michael kept his people busy as best he could. Even in the dark there was still work to be done around the ship. Teams had to be sent to run to the storage compartments, to fetch food. Others worked on water purifiers, switching out the big filters by touch. There were groups of people who were responsible for morale, checking in on those who displayed symptoms of mental illness or anxiety – something that cropped up a lot. In the absence of light, depression was a constant threat.

The work was endless, but Zhang soon learned that it wasn't exactly arduous. The average crew member only worked a few hours each day. They spent nearly half their time asleep, twelve hours out of every twenty-four, usually in blocks of four hours at a time. Four hours asleep, then four hours awake, repeat ad nauseam. It was odd but not completely without explanation. The lack of light threw off human circadian rhythms and disrupted the brain's production of melatonin, Zhang knew. Michael didn't seem to think that was a major problem. "Sometimes," Michael confessed, "I think I could sleep sixteen hours a day. I might switch us to that schedule eventually – it could really help with the stress level."

"I'd advise the opposite," Zhang said. "You're already looking at loss of muscle tone and possibly bedsores, sleeping as much as you do. I'd advise you to keep your people awake as much as you can. Give them more to do, even if that means inventing tasks."

"Is that so, Doctor?" Michael asked. He chuckled. "Okay. Maybe we'll do that."

Zhang frowned. Knowing Michael couldn't see it. "I'm serious about this. We need to be more careful with your people's health, and—"

"We," Michael said.

Zhang had heard it, too. A slip of the tongue. When you trained as a doctor, part of that was learning how to think of how you could serve a community, not just individual patients. It was hard not to think of yourself as part of that community.

And maybe . . . maybe there was something more. Maybe, as he lived with these people, as he saw how well they'd adapted to their lightless environment . . . maybe he was beginning to understand. Maybe he was beginning to think like them.

Pasiphaë, weird as it was, was safe. The people were generally healthy, and with his help they could be even more so. Their bellies were full. No one was trying to actively kill them. He sensed that Ekaterina Petrova had something to do with that – perhaps that was where she went all day, to negotiate with the AIs and captains of the other ships in the blockade and keep them at bay. Or perhaps she was simply making plans for how this dark-adapted lifestyle could become permanent. Whatever the reason, there was a possibility here, one Zhang had not even considered since they'd arrived in the Paradise system: he could live here.

He could grow old, among these people. Find meaning and fulfilment in being their doctor. Maybe this was what he needed, to finally shake off his demons. Expiate the guilt he felt for what had happened on Titan.

It was a possibility.

The fact that he could even consider it, though, made his skin crawl. No. It was quite out of the question.

"Tell me something," he asked Michael, after they'd both woken up after a four hour "sleep" – the only way the people of *Pasiphaë* had to measure time. "If I decided I wanted to leave. Just strike out on my own—"

"What are you saying? You want to go start a new community

somewhere else on the ship?" Michael asked. "There's plenty of room, of course, but there's no need."

"No," Zhang said. "No. That's not what I mean. What I'm saying is, if I wanted to leave *Pasiphaë* altogether. Go to a different ship." Like *Alpheus*. Like anywhere else, anywhere that he could see his hands in front of his face.

"Don't talk like that," Michael said.

"But . . . what if—"

"We would stop you. For your own good." Michael sighed in the dark. "Doctor, I know you don't feel it like I do. But light is poison to us now. You were changed the moment you arrived in the Paradise system. There's no going back. I wouldn't let you walk out of an airlock with no spacesuit, and I won't let you go back out into the light. You're safe here. You'll always be safe here, near me. So let's drop this, okay?"

"Okay," Zhang said. "Sure. That's for the best."

"Dark is safe," Michael said. "The dark is safe. Only the dark is safe."

137

Two sleeps later, Petrova came to him, in the dark. "We need to find a way to actually talk. We need some kind of excuse to step away from the others."

He nodded and drew back, away from her. "I've been thinking about . . . something." He tried to think of what to say. Some pretext for why they would leave the group. "Um. Concerns about life in constant darkness. Medical . . . concerns, right, right."

Michael chimed in, and he realized they'd been right to be careful with what they said. "We seem to be getting along all right."

"I'm not so sure," Zhang pointed out. "I've been treating people here and I see some bad patterns in their communal health. I can see a major problem with vitamin deficiency. When you don't get enough vitamin D, you're prone to calcium loss. Your bones weaken, your teeth fall out. No one wants that. The only really good source of vitamin D is exposure to . . . um . . ." He knew that Michael and the others wouldn't like what he said next. "Well, to sunlight."

"The light of Earth's sun," Michael said. "Paradise is different."

"Well, you need vitamin D. It's essential. Without it you'll be in real trouble in the long run."

"We'll learn to adapt, if we need to," Michael said.

He didn't sound very concerned. Zhang had noticed a strange fatalism in these people but he hadn't expected it to extend to their health like this. "Your children will get rickets," he said, "and the adults will suffer from early-onset osteoporosis, even brittle bone disorders. Doesn't that ... I mean, doesn't that concern you?"

"Sacrifices have to be made, sometimes," Michael said, and Zhang could almost hear the man shrug.

"You can get some Vitamin D from fatty fish but I doubt's there's a lot of that kind of protein in this ship's stores. What about supplements? Do you have any good source of supplemental vitamins and micronutrients onboard?"

"I wonder," Petrova said, before Michael could answer. "Maybe we could go look."

"Look?" Michael said, a laugh in his voice.

"I mean, we could go take a ... a trip to your stores, wherever you keep your food and medical supplies. We could search for some vitamin D supplements."

"Yes," Zhang said. "Yes, we could do that." He knew what Petrova was really after – a chance for the two of them to be alone, to talk, to plan. Maybe even to escape the lightless ship. "We should do that."

"As a way of thanking you for taking us in," Petrova said.

"If you think it's worth doing," Michael said.

"Great, well, if you could just tell us how to get there," Petrova said. "No time like the present, they say."

"You'll never find the path on your own. Angie," Michael said. "Angie?"

"What? Here. Here, I was ... I was asleep."

"Take these two to the food stores, will you? And then bring them back when they're done. Stick with them so they don't get lost."

Zhang's heart skipped a beat. They'd been so close.

Petrova reached over and squeezed his wrist. Maybe she had a plan for how to deal with this chaperone.

138

Petrova wished she had a good plan.

She wished she had any kind of plan.

Angie led them through the unlit corridors at a methodical pace, which should at least have given Petrova time to think. Instead, she found herself hyper-focused on her footing, on taking care not to fall. She felt like a child clutching to Angie's hand, stumbling along in the darkness terrified of walking over the edge of a bottomless pit.

It didn't help that Zhang kept leaning in close to ask her questions. He was holding onto her good arm but every time he came close he put pressure on her shoulder and that made her bad arm move as well. His breath in her ear was always accompanied by a little stab of pain.

"How are we going to get out of here without a light?" he asked. "Do you think heading to the bridge is still a good idea, or should we make a break for that shuttle we saw? What did your mother want?"

"Later," she said. "Not now." For a while, it would work. He would simply trail along obediently behind her, keeping pace so he didn't slam into her. But then she would feel tension growing in the hand that held her arm, feel him start to squeeze her and she knew he was going in for another question.

"What do we do about her?"

Angie stopped short and Petrova winced as she was forced to stop as well.

"I can hear you whispering," Angie said. "Why can't you just talk out loud? I don't mind – just pretend I'm not here."

Petrova gritted her teeth. "That's very kind of you. Tell me something. Before you put out the lights, what did you do, Angie? Were you one of *Pasiphaë*'s crew?"

"That's right. I was a navigator. I've always had an excellent sense of direction – that's why Michael sent me with you. This section of the ship can be tricky if you aren't careful. It's easy to get lost. That would be pretty bad for all of us. It might be a very long time before anyone found us. So stay close, okay? The food stores are about half a kilometer from here. Not too much farther."

"But someone would come, eventually," Zhang said. "Right?"

Angie didn't answer immediately. Instead, she started walking again, her hand making a rasping sound as she dragged it across the wall. When she did answer Zhang's question she sounded almost apologetic. "Sometimes we need to make sacrifices," she said.

"You keep saying that," Petrova said. "But what does that mean?"

She felt Angie shrug. Funny how even those consigned to darkness continued to use body language.

"Sacrifice . . . look, I don't want to scare you guys. You're new here. You don't know what it takes to live like us, or why it's so important."

"So tell me," Petrova said.

"We didn't expect this. When we came to make a new life on Paradise-1, none of us expected to find out that the sunlight here is poisonous. When we first figured it out we fought over what we should do. And I mean we fought – people got hurt, some people died. One group wanted to turn around, to take *Pasiphaë* back to the solar system. But the rest of us knew that wasn't the answer. We'd given up everything to come here. We had to make it work. If that meant spending our whole lives in orbit, away from the sun, then that was just what we had to do. In those first few months we found out just what it would take."

"Sacrifice," Petrova said. "You had to change your expectations, change your quality of life."

"What? No, no, we had already known that colony life would be hard. No. We had to sacrifice the weak. The ones who didn't have skills we needed."

"Wait," Zhang said.

Angie didn't stop talking, though. "There wasn't enough food, or medicine, or anything to go around. Anyone who just consumed our resources, and didn't give anything back. Or anyone who just wasn't up to the challenge. Look, don't get the wrong idea. We don't *kill* people. We don't draw straws and send people off to die."

"That's . . . good, I guess," Zhang said.

"No. But if you get lost out here in the dark, and you can't make your way back? Finding me again would be a pretty low priority. Michael might send someone to find you, Doctor, because you have skills we really need. And you, Lieutenant, well, Ekaterina sees something in you. So there's a pretty good chance you would be found. Me, though? I'm not the only navigator on this ship. I wouldn't expect to be rescued."

"That's . . . not okay," Zhang said.

"It hurts. When someone you cared about just goes into the darkness and they're gone," Angie admitted. "Of course it does. But we all learned a long time ago. Sacrifices have to be made."

Petrova closed her eyes and squinted, hard. Why couldn't this be easy? She knew what she had to do.

No one had taken her pistol from her. It was still in its holster, on her hip. She pulled her hand free of Angie's, then reached down and drew her weapon. Touched its barrel to the small of Angie's back. "Do you know what this is?" she asked.

Angie stopped walking and Petrova pushed the gun into the woman's flesh, through the fabric of her jumpsuit.

"I do," Angie said, very softly.

"What's going on?" Zhang asked. "Why did we stop?"

"Can you find your way back to the others?" Petrova asked.

"Yes."

"Maybe you should do that, then. We'll stay here."

Zhang started to say something more. Petrova shushed him.

"Angie?" she said.

She half expected the woman to spin around and attack her. In the dark the gun wasn't as big an advantage as Petrova would like, and Angie had a lot more experience maneuvering without being able to see. If it really came to violence this could get ugly very fast.

Angie didn't offer her a fight, though. Instead, she let out a little gasp of surprise and dismay that made Petrova think she might be weeping. "Don't you know what you're giving up? This is your only chance. The life here is hard but it's safe, and—"

"Go," Petrova said. "Go!"

Angie ran off into the dark, back the way they'd come. Petrova listened to her footfalls receding for a long time before she turned to address Zhang. "I hope I just made the right decision."

"You did," Zhang told her.

Petrova took a deep breath. "Tell me that when we're lost in the dark an hour from now, with no idea where we're headed. Zhang, we need to get out of here but that's not going to happen if we can't find some kind of light. If we could see, we could look for those lines painted on the floor. Try to follow them back to the hangar. Without light—"

"Yeah. Yeah," Zhang said. "I hear you. But you also know what'll happen if we make any kind of light. That thing – the AI's avatar – will come for us."

Petrova knew that perfectly well. "But we know the rules now. If it catches us with a light source, we surrender the light.

That's all it cares about. It attacked us to destroy our suit lamps, not to kill us."

"I wish it were that simple," Zhang said. "We could get hurt in the process, or killed, or—"

"Or we die here, because we were afraid to take a risk," Petrova pointed out.

"These people haven't tried to harm us in any way."

Petrova sighed. "I didn't mean that. I didn't mean Angie or Michael, or—" Or her mother, for that matter. There was something very strange going on with Ekaterina, but she didn't want to kill them, Petrova was pretty sure about that. "But we know the basilisk. We know what it does. It destroys people, fast or slow. It kills them even if their bodies are still walking around. Zhang, it's death in the dark if we stay here. One kind of death or another."

"I know. I know." Zhang sighed in frustration. "Well, if we want light we have our work cut out for us. They smashed up every possible light source a long time ago. But maybe they missed something. We passed a hatch a little while ago, back down the hall. Maybe we should start to look there."

Petrova nodded. Realized he couldn't see her. "Yeah," she said. "Okay."

139

Zhang cried out in triumph when he found the hatch. His fingers traced its frame, studying its shape. It didn't take long to find the release hatch. The portal opened effortlessly, with a whoosh of air, and he felt like he was standing on a precipice, like the hatch had opened onto a cold abyss.

He lifted one foot. Pushed it through the opening, then tentatively brought it down to find the floor. When he heard his boot impact the deck, only then did he exhale. "Okay," he said. "In here. There has to be something."

He felt Petrova move up next to him, felt her pass him as she stepped inside. He heard her slapping her hand against a wall. "Feels like shelves," she said. "This is a storeroom."

"Let's try to figure out what they store here, then."

He heard Petrova let out a little grunt.

"What is it?" he asked.

"I just thought of something. She could have just run off a little way, to make us think she was leaving. Then she could double back and ambush us. In the dark."

"Maybe. I don't think so. I feel your paranoia – believe me, I share it. But I think we're safe for a little while. You didn't spend as much time talking to these people as I did. Did you sense it, though? How docile they are?"

"Yeah," she said.

"It's not the darkness making them like that. It's the basilisk.

It has to be. It's devouring them from the inside, their emotions, their drives, their sense of purpose. Slowly taking everything from them so that they only exist to be hosts to an alien thought. I can't imagine anything worse. Death is better." Zhang shook himself in revulsion. Then he thought of something. "Sorry . . . sorry. I didn't think before I spoke."

"What? You think that offended me?"

"It's just . . . your mother . . ."

"Ekaterina is immune to the basilisk."

"What?"

Petrova laughed. "Somehow she beat it. She claims she has a natural immunity. I don't know. What I do know is that she's using these people. Manipulating them by preying on their delusions, just to get power over them."

"Petrova — that's your mother you're talking about. She was the director of Firewatch. It's natural she would become a leader wherever she ended up."

"You don't know her like I do," Petrova said.

Zhang had been running his hand along a shelf of what felt like large pill bottles. He picked one up and shook it and heard thousands of capsules inside rattling together. What an irony it would be if it turned out to be vitamin D supplements, he thought. If only he could see, if there was some way to make some light—

"Wait," he said.

"Hmm?"

"The bullets. In your gun. Do they contain, huh, I don't know. Gunpowder?"

"Not exactly, it's a smokeless propellant but the idea is basically the same. Why?"

"We could . . . we could start a fire," he proposed.

"Yeah, yeah, but . . . Jesus," Petrova said. "Jesus. What do we need? I don't know how you do that. I've never made a fire."

"Me either." Zhang tried to think back to what he'd learned as a child. He thought of the various sorts of burns he'd treated as a physician. "Fuel," he said. "Something flammable." He opened the pill bottle and sifted the plastic capsules through his fingers. Those wouldn't work. But maybe . . . maybe there was something else here. "I think these are medical supplies. Look for bandages. Gauze, any kind of cloth."

He hurried through the rest of his shelf, looking for anything useful. He came across a series of heavy bottles that sloshed when he shook them. Opening them one by one he sniffed the contents and found exactly what he'd hoped for. "Alcohol. Isopropyl alcohol. This is perfect. Any luck with bandages?"

"No," Petrova said. "No. But, will this do?"

He heard a ripping noise and at first he thought she'd torn up her jumpsuit. Then she shoved some cloth into his hand and he realized what it actually was. The cast from her bad arm.

"Your hand won't heal properly without this," he suggested.

"It won't heal at all if I die here in the dark."

He started to protest but he knew better. Once Petrova had made up her mind about something there was no point arguing. "Okay, next step." He had passed over a collection of canes while looking for the alcohol. He took one and wrapped the cast carefully around one end, using the cast's straps to tie it securely in place. Then he doused the cast in a liberal amount of alcohol. He described what he was doing to Petrova, running her through each step. If he was missing something, maybe she would notice. "All we need now is a spark. There must be a way to use your bullets to start a fire. Maybe you just – I don't know. Shoot the torch."

"I can do better than that. Lay it on the ground here, between us." He heard a series of clicks and mechanical sounds he imagined had to be her disassembling her weapon. "There's a primer in the bullets, a percussion cap. A little jolt of explosive to set off the powder." She grunted and swore for a second, then something metallic clinked and clattered on the floor. "If you take the bullet out, all you get is the explosion. Zhang, this is going to be dangerous. Really dangerous."

"I understand," he told her. "Just do it."

"On three. One. Two. Three!" There was a sound of something smashing down hard on a piece of metal, like a blacksmith's hammer hitting an anvil.

Nothing else. Nothing happened.

"Try again," he said, but she was already at it. The sound came again, and then a bang so loud it deafened him. There was a rush of sparks and fire, so sudden and gone so quickly he thought it might have been a trick of his light-starved eyes.

But then – a tiny glow. A little blue flame that etched an outline of fabric that turned black even as he watched. Zhang's eyes went wide. His pupils dilated, drinking in the light.

He looked up, and there—

"I can see you," he said. "Petrova. I can see you!"

She laughed and lunged forward, grabbing him around the neck with her good arm. "Me too. Me too!"

140

Petrova grabbed the torch and held it out in front of her. Its light was so brilliant it made her eyes hurt, made her blink away after-images. She had to experiment with it, find how to hold it high so it wasn't just flickering in her eyes.

Her bad arm swung painfully at her side. She shoved her broken hand inside her pocket. It hurt, a lot, but the pain would help keep her focused, she thought. She hoped. "Get that open," she said. Zhang rushed over to hit the release pad of the hatch and Petrova rushed out into the corridor.

She looked up and down its length, worried she might see an army of *Pasiphaë*'s crew members out there, worried about Asterion. Mostly worried about the torch. Unlike the propellant in her bullets, it was giving off a lot of smoke. Worse, bits of charred cloth kept dripping from it, flickering to nothingness as they hit the floor. The light the torch gave off was guttering and inconsistent. Every time she moved, it flickered as if it might go out. It provided little enough light already – barely enough to see where she was going. What happened when it consumed all of its fuel? What would they do then?

She couldn't stop to think about that. There was very little time, and a lot to get done. She glanced down at the floor and saw lines painted there, lines leading in various directions.

"The orange line leads to the bridge, right?" Zhang said, from behind her. "I think the purple one leads to engineering? I'm trying to remember."

Petrova looked for the orange line. "This way," she said.

Zhang hurried to keep up as she strode forward.

"This is the way to the hangar?" he asked. "I thought that was a green line. I can't remember. I'm just not sure ... but ... but you know, right?"

"I know where I'm going," she said. She glanced down at the orange line between her feet. Every few meters there was an arrow to show her she was headed in the right direction.

Then she glanced up and saw graffiti scrawled across a wall. The paint looked old, faded in her torchlight. She could still read what it said.

NO LIGHT IS GOOD LIGHT

She kept moving. She had to reach her destination before the torch ran out. If they were plunged back into darkness ...

"That's the way to the bridge," Zhang said. "You're going to the bridge."

She stopped, just for a second. She didn't turn to look at him. "Yes," she said.

"That's your plan. You don't want to get off this ship. You want to – what? Take it over?"

"If I can," she said. "I know that maybe you thought we were going to—"

"The next time you make a decision like this," Zhang said, "just tell me first. Okay?" He walked past her. Following the orange line. Headed to the bridge.

She considered stopping. Telling him why she wanted to do this. Not for the sake of the people on *Pasiphaë*, not because she wanted to defeat the basilisk – what would that even accomplish, if she somehow beat it here, on one ship out of a hundred?

She wanted to take control of the ship because ... because her mother ...

"We end this one way or another," he told her. "Together, no matter what. You can count on me. Okay?"

She blinked rapidly for a second, trying to think of what to say.

"Okay," she said.

They passed through a broad arcade lined with shops that had been closed since the ship left the solar system. They headed down a side passage lined in hatches. It felt like the ship went on forever, like an endless maze and they would never reach the bridge. They came through a hatch and the torch flame fluttered and snapped and she thought for a bad second it might go out.

Then she heard her voice being called, through the lightless halls.

"Sashenka."

She bit her lip and tried to ignore it. They had to be making progress. She had no idea how far they were from the bridge but they had to be closer than they had been when they first lit the torch. If they could make it inside, seal the hatch against the others—

"Sashenka, where are you going? What do you want to happen?"

Ekaterina's voice came over speakers set in the ceiling. It echoed all around them, from every hatch, from every side corridor. Petrova glanced up at the ceiling.

"Let me go, Mother. Let me do what I need to do."

"I have a duty, Sashenka. A duty to the people of this ship. Have you forgotten? Have you forgotten what happens to those who make light here?"

If she could just get closer to the bridge, get a little farther—

"You are my daughter and I love you," Ekaterina said.

Up ahead of them blue light filled the corridor. Coming toward them.

"But I have chosen to lead these people. And we all must make sacrifices."

The avatar was almost on them. Petrova tried ducking through a hatch, into another corridor. It meant losing the orange line, the direct route to the bridge. But it was better than walking right into—

"Petrova!" Zhang shouted. "Look out!"

A giant clawed hand raked through the air, aimed right at her head. Petrova gasped as she ducked under it and started running forward, trying to break free.

"The torch," Zhang called. "All it wants is the torch!"

Without the light she would never find her way. She couldn't give it up.

The avatar flickered. Disappeared. Then suddenly it was right in front of her again.

Stupid. So stupid, she thought. She couldn't outrun it. She couldn't outmaneuver it – it was made of light, it wasn't bound by the laws of physics.

Zhang yanked the torch out of her hand and threw it down a corridor. He grabbed her – by her bad arm this time – and hauled her sideways, through a hatch.

"We'll be safe," he said. "It'll be dark, but we'll be safe," he promised, as the hatch closed behind them. Like an eye shutting forever, it cut off their light and plunged them back into the cold dark.

The pain in her arm was intense, excruciating. The thought of failure was almost worse. "No," she whispered. "No. I was so close!"

"We're safe," Zhang said, pulling her into a bearhug. "We're safe."

Blue light flared to life in front of them. A massive humanoid shape, with horns on top.

It flickered and then the blue light turned red.

A massive paw came down and struck the side of her head, knocking her sideways, knocking her down.

"Petrova!" Zhang shouted. Then she heard a nasty thump, and he went quiet.

A hand made of red light grabbed her ankle and started dragging her down the corridor. She tried to fight.

It was no use.

"One benefit of being the one who makes the rules," Ekaterina said, her voice very small, very close, so that Petrova wondered if she was imagining it, "is that you don't have to follow them, yourself."

141
•

The hand around Petrova's ankle could have been made of titanium, not light. She kicked and fought but it was useless. More hands reached for her out of the dark, dozens of hands made of implacable red light. She tried to get up to her feet, or to grab the edge of a hatch to hold on but the hands were so strong.

Eventually, they lifted her until she was being borne along, her feet not touching the ground. They brought her through a hatch and into a new, dark room.

Dark, but not completely lightless. Red light burned behind her, giving everything a hellish glow. A paler light burned above her, before her. She looked up and saw windows, viewports, glowing with faint, diffuse light. The same light by which she'd seen her mother, the light of the stars. It was barely enough to let her see anything beyond a few vague outlines of consoles and chairs, but she thought she might be on *Pasiphaë*'s bridge.

She laughed with the irony of it.

Her grand plan had been to reach this place. To find a way to seize control of the ship. Instead, it looked like there was a good chance the two of them would be murdered there.

A hatch opened behind her and a blaze of red light lit up the bridge.

"Mother, please," Petrova said, as Asterion hauled Zhang's unconscious body inside and dumped it on the floor. Its work done, the hologram took up a position at the back of the bridge, on the far side from the viewports. The light it shed was enough for Petrova to make out a little more. Zhang looked battered, even bruised, but intact. They'd kept him alive.

"Mama," Petrova said. "I know you're here, somewhere. Please. Let him go. Let Zhang go – you don't need him."

"I need a doctor, if I want to keep my crew healthy," Ekaterina said, stepping out of a deep shadow. "I'm sorry. I wish I could indulge you. But I need every resource I can get."

Mama stood at the highest point of the bridge, a raised dais presumably meant for the ship's captain. The red light threw her features into high contrast, while the light from behind, from the viewports, made her expansive hair into a nimbus of shadows around her face.

"Sashenka, when will you learn? I know best. I always know best. Yet you persist in fighting me. Well. That will end today. If I can't convince you with logic, perhaps a demonstration will help."

Ekaterina turned and gestured at a chair, one perhaps meant for the ship's navigator or information officer. The red light holograms – Petrova couldn't tell how many of them there were in the room, but at least a half-dozen – picked Zhang up and shoved him into the chair. Brusquely they restrained his hands and feet. They tied his head to the headrest of the chair, his face held tightly in place with a cord digging into his mouth in a fashion that would also serve as a gag. Or something to bite down on.

One of the holograms moved to kneel in front of Zhang. Its face changed – or rather, it developed the rudiments of a face. A kind of lo-res, primitive version of a bull's snout, and a pair of eyes that were simple pits of darkness.

Zhang twitched, and his eyes opened. They darted from side to side, presumably as he wondered where he was and how he'd gotten there.

Ekaterina moved to stand behind Zhang. She reached down with both hands and smoothed the doctor's hair. "This may be difficult to watch, Sashenka."

Zhang looked over at her, at Petrova. There was terror in his face but then he seemed to force himself to calm down, to regain some self-control. His eyes never left hers.

The avatar in front of him leaned closer. Petrova could see now that the shadows in its eye sockets were turning pale. As she watched, embers started to burn back there, tiny flames.

"Mama!" Petrova screamed.

Hands made of hard light held her tight.

She could only watch. She was powerless to move, held down by the avatar. All she could do was watch. "What are you doing? He can't be infected with the basilisk. He's immune!"

"Is he?" Ekaterina asked. "He created an inoculation against one of the basilisk's weapons. That really was quite clever. But did you honestly think that an entity of such power wouldn't have other tools at its disposal? It's alive – the basilisk is alive. And to live means to adapt. It tried to infect him before and it failed. Now it's going to try something new."

Zhang's gaze turned to lock onto the two flames burning inside the hologram's head. He was clearly fighting it, but he couldn't *not* look. He blinked rapidly, perhaps trying to shut his eyes, but then his eyelids simply flew open and stayed open, painfully wide.

"The basilisk could shred his mind like wet paper if it wished," Ekaterina said. "Luckily I need a physician to keep my crew healthy. I only want to make him a little more complacent."

"How … how do you know what the basilisk can do?" Petrova demanded. "Mama? I thought you said you had a natural immunity? What is this? What are you?"

Ekaterina laughed. "I didn't think you would believe that. How naïve you can still be, Sashenka. Some hosts are more useful to a pathogen than others. Being useful is a skill we all must learn, if humanity is going to survive in the future."

Zhang grunted something. The cord in his mouth made it impossible to say what. He tried again.

Then he started to scream.

"Don't do this!" Petrova shouted. "I'll give you anything you want!"

Ekaterina didn't respond.

But maybe something else did.

One of the avatar holograms stood off to one side, away from Zhang's chair. It did nothing but stand there, though something about it drew Petrova's attention. When she looked she saw that this one, too, had developed the rudiments of a face.

It had eyes. Eyes like two tiny, burning coals.

Petrova thought she understood. She hoped she did. The basilisk had been trying to contact her, to speak to her, personally, this whole time. It had called her Sashenka . . .

Why? Because somehow her mother had found a way to influence it, to feed it on her memories? Or was it something more?

Petrova took a step forward. The hands that had been holding her immobile were gone, now. She was free to move. She could run over to Zhang, tear him out of that chair somehow, get him free – but no. She knew that would never work. That wasn't part of what she was being offered.

No, she was being given one chance. One path forward.

She ran to the avatar, the one that stood alone. Ekaterina started to say something but it all happened so fast Petrova didn't even hear the words. She went and stood directly in front of the avatar, and she looked up into its burning eyes. She felt her own eyes stretch open, until she thought her eyeballs would come loose from her skull. She could not have looked away in that moment. It would have been physically impossible.

She didn't try.

The avatar laid its massive hands on her shoulders. Its eyes turned to bonfires, to conflagrations.

Petrova screamed as she understood what she'd just accepted. What had she done? What had she done?

142

Bones littered the stairs
   Step down, one foot
 Then the other.

      Zhang groped blindly for a
hand rail he knew wasn't there.
    No," he said.
   "No," he begged. Not again.

       He closed his eyes
and it went away.

143
•

Zhang opened his eyes and he was on Titan. Where it all began. He was seated at a microscope station in the medlab. He was wearing a white coat over his jumpsuit.

He remembered this moment. This exact moment.

He jumped out of the chair and knocked over an entire tray full of diagnostic instruments that went clattering to the floor. He stumbled backwards until he was pressed up against a wall, until the solid rock behind him was holding him up. He stared at the door of the room. Any moment now—

The door opened. Holly Clark came through. Holly—

Holly.

Just seeing her again hurt. He couldn't seem to think why, but ... but there was something important, something he couldn't remember about Holly. Something vital. He studied her, trying to remember. She was holding a tablet and the light from its screen turned her chin a deathly white, her lips a faint blue. Her blonde hair was shoved back in a messy ponytail and her eyes were bright as she looked up at him. "You spill something? Never mind, you're going to want to see this, Lei. A woman came in this morning with really weird symptoms. Might be right up your alley."

"No," Zhang said. "No. This is just a dream. It's a dream."

The problem is, as anyone experienced with trauma will tell you, every dream becomes a nightmare if you can't wake up.

144

S asha shrieked in horror. The gulls—
The gulls had a fish or ... or something down on the sand
and they ... they were pecking at it, tearing it to pieces. One of
them twisted its beak inside an eye socket and pulled out a wet
lump of meat.

Sasha shoved a hand against her mouth, crushing her lips.
Fighting down a wave of nausea. Where was she? What
was going on?

Sasha ... she was ...

"Sasha?"

Rodion was there. Rodion, the son of one of Mama's colonels.
He'd become her sort of boyfriend over the last few weeks. Her
very first boyfriend – she still wasn't sure what that meant, what
privileges it gave her, what she could expect or demand from
him. She took a chance and buried her face in Rodion's hairless
chest. He put one tentative arm around her and led her away, up
the beach. Away from the dead thing and the gulls.

"It's just a fish, Kisa," he said. *Kisa*: Kitty. A term of endear-
ment for a girlfriend. It was the first time he'd called her that.
"It's dead, it doesn't feel anything."

She wiped a tear away and laughed into his skin. She pushed
him away, playfully, and ran down the beach. He followed,
grabbing at her though she kept slipping out of his hands. Up
ahead lay the hulk of an old fishing boat that had washed up

on the shore so long ago it was just a pile of rusted metal. She dropped down into its shade, breathing hard. He came and sat across from her, his fingers trailing through the sand. "I'm sorry. I lost my cool there for a moment. Mother always tells me I need to be tougher."

She looked up at him through her lashes, wanting to know what he would say next.

It was only then she saw it wasn't Rodion at all. The square jaw – those bright eyes.

"Parker?" she asked, confused.

He grinned, that comfortable grin she'd come to know and . . . and count on.

What was he doing here?

"Your mother is a great woman," he said. "A true leader."

Sasha frowned. "That's what Rodion said, you know . . . back then. Sam? What's going on?"

145
.

"I really think you should look at this," Holly said, holding out the tablet. "Lei? What are you doing?"

He edged around her, careful not to touch anything. He felt like he was being sucked into his own memories, devoured by his own trauma. Maybe if he could escape it, if he didn't look . . .

That tablet she held contained data from the first case of the Red Strangler. He didn't want to see it. He didn't want to see it again.

He was caught in web of his own memories. He needed to break free.

"Lei?" Holly called, as he pushed past her and out the door. "Lei? What's wrong? Come back!"

He ran through the Medical section, really just a cave dug into the methane ice of Titan. The walls were covered in thick, fibrous insulation to trap in the heat. Medical was a broad, open area full of autosurgeon units and small examination areas partitioned off with sliding curtains. Patients looked up as he raced past but he didn't bother to say anything. Instead, he pushed on, into the airlock separating Medical from the rest of the colony. Through the glass doors of the airlock he could see the people of Titan going about their day, oblivious to the fact that they were already dead.

"Come on," he said. "Come on."

"Dr Zhang?" Glaucus asked. "Is something amiss?"

Zhang shook his head. Glaucus was the AI that ran everything in the Titan colony. It maintained their life support, their power, their water. Its voice was that of a kindly older man, a beloved uncle, perhaps. It was always there wherever you went in the colony.

Zhang hadn't heard that voice in a long time. It brought back far too many memories.

"Everything's fine. Just open the airlock door, please," he said.

"Of course, Doctor," Glaucus said. "Let me know if I can be of any service."

"Not now," Zhang said, through gritted teeth.

Outside the airlock was the main atrium of the Titan colony, a vast cylindrical shaft rising a hundred meters to the surface. At its top was a broad cupola, a vast window that let through the murky light of the distant sun. Around the periphery of the shaft, on a dozen different levels, lay scores of caves carved out of the ice, some used as office space, as labs, as manufactories, others as family homes or as dormitories for the single colonists, like Zhang.

In the center of the shaft, rising to the very top, was a helical staircase. It connected all the levels of the colony and led, at its top, to a system of airlocks that opened onto the surface. There was no railing on the staircase. In Titan's low gravity one hadn't been deemed necessary.

It was just a staircase. Just a series of risers heading upward toward the light.

The moment Zhang saw it his heart jumped in his chest. *No,* he thought. *No. I can't . . . I can't . . . those stairs . . .*

He cast around him, looking for some way out, some way to break the pattern of events. He saw children playing around a public fountain at the base of the stairs. They were splashing each other with water, laughing, the droplets bright on their hair, their clothes. He saw Khoi, the colony's chief administrator, the skin around her eyes crinkling as she shared a laugh with Becket, the head of operations. They were drinking tiny cups of coffee at a little table outside the office they shared, no doubt making plans for the next month.

There was a comms unit in their cave – one that could reach Earth. "Khoi," Zhang called. "Khoi! I need your radio," he said. "Please. It's an emergency."

"What? Why?" the administrator asked. "Is everything okay, Doc?"

Zhang shook his head. "No. No, it's . . . it's bad, it's . . . listen, I just need to put through a call. To Director Lang."

"Lang?" Becket frowned. "Who's that? Director of what?"

"Firewatch," Zhang said. "Listen, it's crucial."

Becket scoffed. "Doctor, you're confused. The director of Firewatch is a woman named Ekaterina Petrova. And I can't imagine any reason we would want to talk to *her*."

Right. Right. The Titan colony was brand new. Most of the people in it had come here to get away from the hectic life of the inner planets. They'd come for quiet lives, for peace. Safety. This was a safe place. It was safe. Safe.

"Safe safe safe," he said, clubbing himself on the sides of his head with his fists. "It's still safe. You aren't going to believe me."

Becket put his hands on Zhang's arms. Pushed them down. "Doctor Zhang, why don't you sit here? We can talk about this. Is there some kind of medical crisis? I promise you we'll take that very seriously."

"There's no time," Zhang insisted. "Damn it." He raced past the two of them and into the cave that doubled as both their office and living quarters. Becket cried out from behind him but Zhang ignored the man, intent on finding the comms unit. It proved easy enough. None of the caves on Titan were large enough to hide anything. He waved his hand over the controls, calling up a screen. Glaucus appeared beside him, a genial older man in a thick sweater and thicker eyeglasses. A sweep of stars and nebulae were visible in the lenses.

"Would you like some help setting up a call?" Glaucus asked. "I'll just need to check that you're authorized for that."

"Fuck off," Zhang told the AI. He stabbed at a virtual keyboard, searching for Director Lang's name and her address. She had to be in the comms system's database, somewhere. Even if she wasn't the director of Firewatch yet, she would know something about ... about Para ... Para. Para what?

Something about Para-something. Was that a colony? A planet?

"Why can't I find her?" he demanded. She wasn't in the directory. There were a number of addresses for Firewatch. A direct line to their administrative offices on Earth's moon. An emergency address for the colony's administrator to call in case of unrest among the Titanians. There was even an anonymous tip line in case Zhang wanted to report a crime. He tried searching for the Director's office, even tried searching for an address for Director Petrova, but—

"Why don't you tell me what you're trying to do," Glaucus said, from behind Zhang's shoulder. "I can help. I'm sure I can help."

"I need to tell her ... I need to tell the Director about ..." He racked his brain, trying to remember. Paradise? What about paradise? That made no sense. Zhang was no Christian, that name meant nothing to him. There was another name, though. "The basilisk. About the red basilisk." No, that wasn't quite right, either. It didn't make sense.

Why wasn't anything making sense?

"Doc," Khoi said, reaching for his arm. He jerked backwards, away from her thin hand.

"They have to know! They have to know about the, about the minotaur and the ... the green robot, and ... and—"

"Hey."

It was Holly. She was standing right in front of him, looking him right in the eye. Her face was set in a mask of quiet concern.

"Holly," he gasped. "Holly. Oh my God. I've missed you so much."

He leaned forward to kiss her. Her lips felt – cold. Wrong.

He opened his eyes and looked into the face of a corpse. Her skin was waxy and cold and had lost all its shape, her eyes were white with decay.

She wasn't breathing.

She wasn't breathing.

Zhang started to scream.

146
•

Sometimes Rapscallion wished he could roll his eyes, or maybe sigh in exasperation. One of those weird human gestures that they all seemed to understand. He had tried tapping his foot in irritation. He had tried just staring at the fucking hologram, staring until it got the point.

It never quite did.

"I just wish we knew what was going on over there," Parker said. He'd barely looked away from the telescope view since the escape pod had been taken onboard the big colony ship. His frustration was palpable. And annoying.

Rapscallion looked up from the power junction he'd been repairing. "Actaeon," he called out. "Have you had a chance to look over those models I asked you to run?"

"I have," the AI replied. "I'm afraid the results haven't changed. Given the current state of *Alpheus*, even with Captain Parker at the controls there is zero chance of our finding a course that would allow us to reach *Pasiphaë* without being intercepted by at least two warships. We would be within range of the long-distance weaponry of at least twenty-five ships as soon as we attempted a close approach."

The robot had already known that, of course. He'd run the numbers through his own processors and come to the same conclusions. He wasn't even sure why he'd asked Actaeon to double-check his work. Maybe after being around humans for so long he'd started to adopt some of their uncertainties.

"What about that other idea I had?" Parker asked.

Rapscallion searched for the appropriate sound file to play to indicate his level of derision for that notion. He gave up after a few milliseconds. "Look, it's not a terrible idea. It's just based on a complete lack of reality and a poor understanding of the laws of physics."

"Come on," Parker said.

"You want me to make copies of myself. Enough copies to take on that entire fleet." The robot considered just how dumb that was. For one thing, he was a robot. Not a battlecruiser. He could build a body with offensive weaponry, sure, but that meant arms that ended in knife blades or maybe a laser eye or something. Not missile racks and high energy particle cannons. "We have enough feedstock on *Alpheus* for me to make maybe ten copies of myself," he explained, trying to be patient. "Ten copies that would be obliterated in the first half a second or so of any kind of naval engagement."

Parker growled in thwarted rage. He hadn't looked away from the telescopes. "Damn it. If we had access to more feedstock—"

"It still wouldn't work. It takes about ten minutes for me to make a new body. How many copies do you want? A hundred? Say we had all the feedstock in the system, say I could make a thousand bodies. Ten thousand." Rapscallion shook his head, even though Parker wasn't looking at him. "Give me a couple days and then I can launch those bodies at the fleet, and you can sit back here watching as they get picked off one by one."

"So we make a million bodies for you," Parker suggested. "As many as it takes."

"And even that wouldn't work, because I would have to distribute my consciousness across all of those bodies. Every time I make a new one, my intellect gets cut in half. Dividing me amongst a thousand bodies would mean that all of them would be so dumb they wouldn't know what they were doing."

"I'm not interested in hearing why things won't work," Parker said. Then he took a deep breath. "No. No, there has to be something. Something we can do." He surveyed the fleet again, the hundred and fifteen ships represented as tiny dots on a screen. "Each of those ships must have 3D printers onboard, right?"

"Sure," Rapscallion said. "So?"

"We could try raiding just one ship. Get onboard and take the feedstock from their stores. Use that to make more copies of you. Do it again for the next ship."

Rapscallion searched his database of audio files. He wanted to pick the exactly correct clip of mocking laughter. While he was looking, though, something occurred to him.

"Hold on," he said. "Hold on. Something you just said . . ."

"What, about raiding another ship?"

"No," Rapscallion said. "That part was dumb. But the part about feedstock." He considered the possibility. "Maybe. Just maybe, there's an idea there."

147
●

Summertime in Sevastopol, and it was forty degrees centigrade in Artillery Bay. They'd thought heading down to the water would help them cool off but there was no escape from the heat. Sasha was wearing nothing but her bathing suit and she yelped every time she walked through a sunny spot of the pavements in her bare feet. The only place to sit in the shade was a bench in front of a government building. Out of the sun's direct light the heat wasn't so bad, though she could still feel sweat pooling in the hollows of her collarbones, the small of her back.

The bench looked out across the sea, and she liked to watch the waves go up and down. Rodion talked to her about politics, about the classes he was taking. About nothing at all – nothing that required her to respond, no topic that required her to have an opinion.

She watched the sea.

The sea . . .

There was something. Something in the sea, but she couldn't quite make it out. A bright spot, like some enormous pale fish was down there. It felt almost like it was looking back at her. She stood up and started walking toward the water.

Before she could get there Rodion came jogging over to her, holding a pair of ice creams. He gave her a wink as he handed her one.

"There was something," she said. "In the water."

"Hurry," he told her, with a laugh. "It won't last in this heat."

The ice cream was already melting, the bright blue cream dripping on the flagstones. "What flavor is this? I remember this day but I . . . I can't remember what . . . I can't—"

Rodion reached over and steadied her by touching her gently on the elbow. It was enough. She lost whatever it was she'd been thinking. It was just gone. She glanced over at the sea but there was nothing there but waves and in the distance a cruise ship crawling along the horizon.

Her head swam. She'd been distracted. She couldn't imagine what had gotten her so confused. It had to be the heat, she decided. "I'm sorry. What were you saying?"

"There's going to be a dance," he said. "Out on the pier, tonight. I asked if you wanted to go. I'm sure your mother would allow it. It's only military personnel and their families, so we'll be among good company. Please say you'll go. I want so much to see you in a dress. I think you'll look amazing."

Sasha barely heard him. A drop of molten ice cream had spilled on her arm.

Her left arm.

There was something . . . something wrong about her left arm.

She tossed her cone out onto the boardwalk. Gulls screamed and dove for it, a pack of them fighting over it instantly. She ignored them.

Her arm. Her left arm. Her . . . bad arm? Why did she think of it that way? She was right-handed, yes, but—

"You could put your hair up. Or. You know. Tease it out."

"What, like Ekaterina does?" she said. She laughed and started to reach for her hair, to stick her fingers through the messy curls and fan them out in mockery of her mother's famous hairstyle. Before she could do that, though, she noticed her arm again.

Why did it keep surprising her? It was skinny, and very pale. They'd given her an injection before she was allowed to come to Sevastopol. A gene therapy dose, tailored to prevent her skin from absorbing ultraviolet light. It protected her from skin cancer but it made her feel she was as white as one of the gulls. By comparison, even after just a few weeks at the shore Rodion glowed a beautiful bronze.

So pale . . . *like the shape under the water.* She shook her head. That made no sense. She was thinking about her skin. It was too pale. And her arms were so scrawny. She was such a little girl. Rodion was two years older than her, eighteen, and she'd wondered what he could possibly see in her.

She suspected she knew the truth. She suspected that he hadn't chosen her. That instead he'd been assigned to her, that some cultural attaché in the Firewatch secretariat had picked his name and matched it with hers.

She even wondered, sometimes, if her mother had ordered it done.

She stared at the fine hair on the back of her arm. The protruding bones of her wrist. She stretched her fingers out, then balled them together in a fist. Her hand didn't quite close properly. Why not?

"You could put your hair up. Or, you know. Tease it out."

She looked up at Rodion, forgetting her hand. "You already said that." Hadn't he?

"Do you know how to dance? I can teach you if you don't," he said. He jumped up and grabbed her hand. He grabbed her left hand and put it on his hip, just above the waistband of his trunks.

"Ow," she said.

"Did I hurt you?" He jumped back like he'd been stung by a bee. She saw fear cross his features. Sometimes it was like he was afraid to touch her at all.

"Just a muscle cramp or something." She looked down at her hand. Her left hand.

Her bad hand.

She forced herself to make a fist. Squeezed as hard as she could.

Searing agony ran up her arm, lightning bolts crackling in her

elbow. She started to pant with the exertion, the pain, but yes –
her head started to clear. Her thoughts started to line up again.
Rodion didn't look like Rodion. Why not? Why did she feel so
strange in this body, like it didn't belong to her?

"Something's going on," she said. "This . . . none of this is . . ."

Real, she'd been about to say.

Rodion was standing over her. Looking down at her. He didn't
seem so diffident anymore. He looked quite confident, in fact, as
he stood there soldier straight, his mouth a hard slash of a frown.

"Maybe we need to put you back in your box," he said.

It wasn't his voice. It wasn't Rodion's voice.

It was her mother's.

She stared up into his eyes – his, Rodion's, or someone else's,
it didn't matter. She saw nothing but ice in there. A perfect,
calculating coldness. It might as well have been an AI looking
back at her.

She opened her mouth to speak. Rodion raised one eyebrow,
as if in warning.

"I would be. Um," she said. "I would be honored to dance
with you, Rodion Semyonovich."

He held out his hand. She took it.

And in a moment she was laughing as he twirled her across
the boardwalk, the wooden planks hot as coals under the tender
skin of her feet.

148

"Just breathe. Okay? Try. Try to breathe." Zhang was wearing a heavy respirator mask and goggles so the patient couldn't see his mouth. He lifted his chin, then dropped it again. Lifted it, then dropped it. Establishing a rhythm.

The patient was flushed and drenched in sweat. His face was bright red, as if with exertion. He was a thirty-one year old male engineer, in good general health. Except that biotelemetry suggested he was in massive respiratory distress. His name was Karl. Zhang knew him, of course. They'd played cards together once. In a colony of three hundred people, everybody knew everybody.

"In, out. In, out," Zhang said. He kept his chin bobbing.

Karl looked absurdly grateful for the reminder.

Behind him, Holly was speaking with Khoi. "There's no sign of any bacteriological, viral, or fungal infection. Nothing we can test for. We're still trying to rule out some kind of prion disease but that's very unlikely."

Glaucus piped in, just then. "Most prion diseases are seen in populations that practice anthropophagy or, at minimum, the consumption of animal brain tissue."

"Anthropophagy?" Khoi asked.

"Cannibalism," Holly told her. "We can rule that out, I think."

"Well, then what is it?" Khoi demanded. "I have two people dead already. Four more under constant care. We don't have enough ventilators to go around and I've got Hannah over in manufacturing telling me we're running low on supplies to make more of them. Please tell me there's *something* we can do."

"In, out," Zhang said.

Karl had stopped breathing again. His eyes were glazing over and his head started to nod forward.

"Karl! Karl, listen to me," Zhang said. "Look at me!" He grabbed Karl's chin and pulled it up. The color was starting to drain from his face, a waxy pallor replacing the previous blush. "Quick! Get me a compression bag!"

Holly grabbed it and tossed it to him. Zhang strapped the mask over Karl's face and started squeezing the bag, forcing air into Karl's lungs. Breathing for him.

"It's like they've just lost the most basic reflex," Holly explained. "Like they have to think about every single breath. If they get distracted, or too tired, they just stop breathing. And they don't start again, not unless they think consciously about it."

"I've seen the symptoms, Doctor," Khoi insisted. She came over and stood right next to Zhang. "Your job is to figure out what's causing it. And, much more important: how are we going to fix it? What's the treatment? Lei? Speak to me!"

Zhang was busy working the bag. Squeezing it, then slowly releasing it to draw carbon dioxide back out of Karl's lungs. Oxygen in, bad air out. In, out.

In, out.

"We can save these people," Khoi said. "But you need to tell me how."

In, out.

In, out.

In, out.

149
•

She realized she'd never worn stockings before.

Mother's valet had laid out her dress for the dance. It wasn't anything special, really. A modestly cut bodice and a skirt that fell below her knees. White. Virginal. There were elbow-length gloves that went with it, as well as a very minimal tiara and a pair of white dancing shoes with thick, short heels. Lying next to the shoes were a pair of carefully folded black silk stockings.

She had worn leggings at school, under her uniforms, but this was something very different. The stockings were the kind of thing a woman wore, not a girl. There was something deeply sophisticated and mysterious about them. Like putting them on would transport her to some new world, where everything was so much more serious and real.

As opposed to this world? How real did she want things to be?

"There's elastic at the top but they never stay the way you want. I would just forgo them altogether."

Sasha sucked in a deep breath. It took her a second to let it back out, like she'd forgotten how to breathe normally. She turned slowly, her chin tilted down, her hands dropped at her sides.

"Hello, Mother," she said.

"Oh, stop that," Ekaterina said. "Stand down, for God's sake. You're not one of my soldiers who has to snap to attention when I enter a room." She wore an enormous shawl draped over the shoulders of her uniform, and she swept into Sasha's bedroom in a great gust of air, like a freight train emerging from a tunnel. Sasha stood aside so her mother could come and sit on the bed.

"You're growing up," Ekaterina said. "It's about time you learned how to dress yourself like a human being. I presume you're coming to the dance tonight? Do you know how to dance, Sashenka?"

"Rodion is teaching me," she said, her eyes down, on the dress.

"Rodion. Now there's a boy who could use some discipline. Get him in the enlisted barracks for six weeks, he'd grow a spine, I think. Look at me. Look me in the eye, girl! I don't want you embarrassing me out there in front of the officers by stumbling around the dance floor. Oh, they'll tell me how cute you are, so adorable, but I know what they'll really be thinking. They'll be thinking I haven't trained you properly." Ekaterina sighed. "There's a lesson for you. Never take anyone at their word. You are always being judged. Every action, every decision you make is constantly being evaluated. You must never fall short."

"Yes, ma'am."

"It's probably better if you don't try to dance. We'll say it's a matter of modesty. That will appeal to the hyper-conservatives in the officer corps. It's always good to have the zealots on your side. What's wrong with you?"

Sasha tried to say something but she realized there was no air in her lungs. She gasped for breath, then reached out and grabbed the side of her dresser so she could stand up straight. She clutched at her throat, thinking that perhaps she was choking on her own sense of shame.

"Look at me," Mama said. "Look at me! Now, breathe."

Sasha did as she was told. Nodding, she sucked air into her lungs. Tiny lights sparkled all through her vision.

"In. Good. Now, out," Mama insisted. She grabbed Sasha's neck and vigorously massaged her throat. Sasha felt like she might collapse if Mama let her go. "In. Out. Keep. Up. The rhythm. In. Out. Yes? By God and all his sinners, girl, if I weren't here you would have simply expired on the floor. It's good for you that you have me. This world isn't made for weaklings, Sashenka."

Sasha focused as hard as she could on her breathing, doing exactly as her mother told her. Always, in all things, it was the only way.

150

•

"Do you hear music?"

Lei could feel Holly's lips moving against the back of his neck.

They were lying together in his narrow little bunk in the dormitory cave. The lights were off but they were far from alone. There were beds all around them, beds full of young people who hadn't started families yet. There was no shame in doubling up, though. The dorms were co-ed and it was expected that couples would share them, some of the Titanians choosing a different partner every night. Titan was a fledgling colony and it needed all the pregnancies it could get. They were hardly the only couple in the room sharing a bed that night.

For the last few months Lei and Holly had been dating exclusively. They were teased for it and many people had suggested the two of them should just get married already, but Lei hadn't had the courage to ask.

"What? Music? No," he said. "What kind of music?"

"That's the weird part. It's like . . . a marching band? I hear tubas. *Oom pah pah. Oom pah pah.*" She laughed. It was good to hear. With the crisis in medical Lei had been feeling pretty grim. Karl had died just a few hours ago, and it had left him shaken. He was sure they would get a handle on this thing but he was worried. They'd lost people before, any colony was going to have deaths, but Karl was the third that week. How many more would follow in the week to come? This could quickly turn into an epidemic. That would be hard to contain in such a small, densely inhabited settlement. What if someone critical caught the bug? What if Khoi got it? She held the whole group of them together.

He pushed all that out of his mind. One thing you learned when training to be a physician was to compartmentalize. To put the death and disease behind you, when the day was over.

At least, you learned how to pretend to do that.

"All I hear is Sunil farting over by the door," he whispered.

Holly laughed hard at that, her whole body shaking against his back. "I want to dance," she said. "I want to go dancing."

"Sure, let's boogie," Lei said. He wiggled his butt against her and she squealed and grabbed him around the waist. "Shh," he said. Then he twisted around in the bed and kissed her.

She reached down and grabbed him through his shorts. He reached down and started pushing her underwear down her legs. He needed this. Suddenly, with an intensity he rarely felt about sex, he needed to be closer to her, needed to touch her, to have her touch him, to feel her skin against his skin, needed to—

The ceiling lights snapped on.

The two of them froze in place, half naked and very surprised. All around them people started to rouse and complain, bitter words hurled toward the door.

Lei looked up and saw Khoi standing there, a grave expression on her face. "Zhang. Clark. Come with me right now," the administrator said.

He grabbed a jumpsuit from under the bed and pulled it on over both legs at once. Next to him Holly tried to be discreet as she searched the floor for her underwear. In a few seconds they were dressed and following Khoi across the central atrium, toward Medical. Lei looked up at the staircase at the center of their little world and a bad shiver went through him.

"You okay?" Holly asked, grabbing his arm.

"So dark," he said. "It's so dark. I can't see. I can't see anything."

"What? What are you talking about?" she asked him.

"I ... don't know. Never mind." They hurried into the medical cave.

Khoi had got there ahead of them. She had put on a filter mask and a pair of goggles and she handed them protective gear as they came through the airlock. "What's going on?" he asked. He considered the possibilities. "Who died?" he said, in quieter tones.

Khoi shook her head. She didn't need to say anything. Lei looked around and saw that every bed in Medical was full. There were people lying on the floor, and with mounting horror, he realized that they were already dead. Maybe twenty people.

At the far end of the room Glaucus stood alone. The hologram's head was bowed and it kept its back turned toward them. It was the brightest source of light in the room – it glowed a sort of buzzing, itchy pink.

"Don't look at me," it said. "Don't come any closer. If I don't look at you, I can't infect you."

"It's gone insane," Khoi whispered. "I think it's guilt or something. Like it blames itself for what's happening. Absurd, of course. Doctor," she said, to Lei, "Go get suited up. I need you to start performing autopsies. We can't trust Glaucus to run them. Doctor Clark. You come with me."

Lei nodded and headed to the equipment locker. An autopsy during an epidemic called for full body PPE, heavy gloves and a face shield. He glanced over at Holly as she and Khoi approached the hologram. He wanted to give her an encouraging nod or something, but she didn't look back.

He saw the two of them approach Glaucus from different angles, like they were going to pounce on the AI and wrestle it to the ground or something. Absurd, of course – they would pass right through the image if they tried. But how else did you handle a crazy computer avatar?

"I said DON'T LOOK AT ME!" Glaucus howled. It turned to face Holly and for a moment it flared a brilliant, neon red. Lei saw something he couldn't understand at all, then. It was like Glaucus' face twisted and elongated, whipping outward at Holly, like the hologram was stretching and distorting, glitching out.

Holly fell backwards, so slowly in the low Titanian gravity. She had plenty of time to put her hands down and catch herself. But she never looked away from Glaucus, as if what she saw in its face was so terrible it had her paralyzed.

"Hol," he shouted. "Hol!" But she wouldn't look at him.

151

It was the most beautiful thing Sasha had ever seen. It was corny, and cheesy, and stupid. Utterly, utterly old-fashioned and boring and dumb.

And . . . enchanted.

She felt enchanted.

There was a little pier at one end of Artillery Bay. Maybe it had been a fishing pier, once, but that was back when it was safe to eat the things that lived in the Black Sea. Now it was just an observation platform, a big elevated square platform at the end of a long walkway. By day it didn't look like much, just a bunch of weathered old planks standing atop high pilings.

For the dance, for tonight, they had strung fairy lights along all of the pier's railings. At its far end they had put up a gauzy tent, a canopy of silk so transparent you could see the ocean waves through it, you could see the Monument to the Sunken Ships out on the water, its column lit up by floodlights. Every light sparkled, every light was surrounded by a little halo. Every light's perfect little twin danced on the bobbing surface of the waves.

The . . . the waves, and underneath them – there was a paleness, a light, it was a light in the deeps, calling her—

"Isn't it wonderful?" Rodion asked.

She looked again at the pier, at the billowing tent. Focused hard so that her mind wouldn't wander. Yes, it was wonderful. So lovely.

Sasha thought she might cry.

Music filled the air, beautiful music. Tchaikovsky, she thought, arranged for a military band. She could feel the pulse of the tubas in her chest. *Oom pah pah, oom pah pah.* A few couples had already started dancing, the officers in their crisp dress uniforms, their dove gray gloves spotless and perfect, their cropped hair slicked back. Their spouses wore severely cut suits or dramatic gowns in jewel tones, blue and green satin that shimmered in the lights.

Sasha knew she'd lived a sheltered life. She had had few friends and seen very little of the world, even since they'd moved back from the Moon. But she had trouble imagining anything more splendid than this.

"My dear," Rodion said, taking her elbow between his thumb and forefinger, "you look radiant." There was a strange smirk on his face, like this was all some kind of farce, really, and he wanted to make sure she didn't think he was buying into it. Suddenly she felt very young and foolish.

She looked down at her gloved hands, the tiny reticule she carried that was, in fact, completely empty. It had been laid out on the bed with the dress and her shoes and everything and so she'd assumed she had to carry it anyway. She fought with an absurd and sudden desire to toss it as far as she could out over the black water. Instead, she shyly glanced up at Rodion, and—

For a moment he looked altogether wrong. He was older, and a thick scruff of stubble dotted his cheeks. His jaw had extended, strengthened. The soulful eyes were different. He'd grown taller, much taller than he'd been before.

"What are you wearing?" she asked, looking down at him. His formal clothes had been replaced with a soiled and scorched jumpsuit, of all things. A patch on his breast read ARTEMIS in block letters. She worried if he touched her he might stain her dress.

"You really want to hash that out now?" he asked. Even his voice was different. "Look. This is why we're here. Look at her."

Mother.

Mother had stepped out onto the dance floor. She was speaking with someone, a lieutenant inspector in a Firewatch uniform. Nodding meaningfully. She glanced over her shoulder to issue an order to a subaltern. Nothing unusual there. Except now Ekaterina was doing what she did in a spangly red dress. She looked like she was wreathed in flames, and every time she moved the light caught her from a hundred different angles. The sea breeze caught her hair and didn't so much blow it this way and that but instead seemed to inflate it, make it even bigger than it had been before.

"Saints and devils. She's magnificent," Rodion said. He was eighteen again, dressed in a white suit. He'd been holding Sasha by the arm but now he dropped it, as if he'd forgotten she was there.

"Did you ... um ..." she said. "Did you want to dance?"

"Huh?" Rodion asked. "Oh. No. Listen. I'm going to get us some drinks. Maybe you should stay here." At the periphery of the dance floor, near the entrance. "You can greet the important people as they come in."

"Of course," she said.

Of course? Some part of her started screaming, inside her head. Had she really said that? Had she ever been so meek? How much of this was real? She felt like if the breeze kicked up it would blow her soul right out of her body, send her screeching out over the sea forever. How much of this had actually happened? This was ... a memory, yes? Just a memory?

"It's a lesson," Mama said.

Mama was standing right in front of her.

"Defiance doesn't suit you, Sashenka. It always was your chief failing. How can you expect to be a soldier if you can't learn to follow orders?"

Sasha's heart skipped a beat. "I thought my problem was I wasn't tough enough."

Ekaterina's hand was hard as steel as it smashed her across the cheek. Sasha's head reeled sideways and she had to grab the wooden railing to keep from crashing to the floor. She felt her pulse beating so hard in her face it felt like her eyes were throbbing. She stared at the string of fairy lights wrapped around the railing. Lights, scattered across darkness. Like the stars as seen from space, from the bridge of a spaceship.

"It didn't happen like this," she said.

"What did you say?"

Sasha smiled. There was blood on her lips. She sucked it into her mouth, savored the taste. "It didn't happen like this. Rodion wasn't wearing a formal suit. He was wearing a uniform, because you'd already recruited him. Turned him into a soldier. You cut off his hair, lasered off his tattoos. He wanted to dance with me. He begged me to but I remembered you'd asked me not to, so I said no. So he danced with you, instead, while I watched."

"Is that right? Is that how you remember it?"

"You've built all this," she said, "out of . . . what? Where did you get your information? I mean, you got most of the details right. The ice cream on the boardwalk, that was blue. I'd forgotten, but it was. The stupid reticule, I remember that now. But some of the details have been wrong. You can read my mind, I guess. You can see my memories. But still you got little bits and pieces of it wrong."

"Did I? Are you sure? There's something you're forgetting."

It was her mother's voice. But someone else was using it. Someone. Or—

"I have access to Ekaterina's memories, too," the voice said.

Still Sasha wouldn't look up.

Still, *Petrova* stared at the lights wrapped around the railing.

"I can show you what actually happened. By comparing your memories and hers, I can create a composite based on actual facts, not faulty human memories. Not the way you remember it. The way it really was. Shall I? You're not going to like it."

"Do your worst," she said.

And instantly regretted it.

The lights disappeared. All light, everywhere. The universe shrank down to a tiny space of utter darkness, its walls closing in on her. Her body shrank, too, her fingers turning stubby, her legs short and chubby with baby fat. She screamed and screamed but they were the screams of a toddler, not a teenager.

Sashenka howled, she bawled, she beat at the lid of her box. The box where she knew she was going to be trapped in forever. The box that would become her coffin.

"Mama!" she screamed.

There was no response.

152

●

Khoi's body shook as she sucked at the air, over and over. Her eyes rolled in panic and Lei had to grab her hands and remind her. "Exhale," he said. "Every time. Inhale, then exhale."

She didn't respond. She couldn't seem to focus on him. How much oxygen was getting to her brain? Had she already succumbed to brain damage? How much of her was left?

"Glaucus," he called. "Glaucus, have you managed to get through, yet?" He'd asked the AI to call Earth a dozen times. He needed help. He needed more respirators. He needed more doctors. There had to be a solution to this. There had to be something he could do.

Khoi stopped breathing altogether. She must have gotten distracted. The Red Strangler did that, it made you forget you needed to focus on your breathing. Or maybe it just fatigued its victims so much they couldn't concentrate on remembering.

"Bag her," he shouted. "Hol? I need a bag over here. It's Khoi!"

Holly came running, though by the time she arrived Khoi was already cyanotic. Her lined face lost all color and muscle tension and her eyes rolled back into her head.

"Fuck," Lei said. He put the bag over the administrator's face and started squeezing it, breathing for Khoi, but the old woman's chest didn't move the way it should. It barely rose a little when he pushed air down into her lungs, and then it slowly sank back down like the oxygen was just wheezing back out of her.

"Her diaphragm isn't contracting," Holly said.

"The fuck it isn't. Get me a respirator. I'm going to intubate."

"We don't have any more," Holly said. "Lei—"

"Yank one out of one of the dead people," he said. "We can't lose her. Not Khoi."

"Lei," Holly said. She put her hands over his. Tried to pull them away from the bag.

"Stop. I can save her, we can . . . we can turn this around—"

"Lei, she's not even generating brainwaves."

He looked up at the holoscreen in front of him. It showed Khoi's vitals. Or it would have, if she'd still been alive.

He let go of the bag. Sat down on the floor and put his hands on his head, rocked back and forth. He felt so strange, everything was just so surreal. How could anyone forget how to breathe? How did you just lose a reflex? They were the most deeply hardwired parts of your psyche. They operated when you were unconscious. The human body could keep breathing even after the brain and heart were both dead. How . . . how was this possible?

He couldn't remember who had started calling it the Red Strangler. When had there been time to make up a common name for something they didn't even know how to classify? Was it a bodily disease, a mental illness? A pathogen or some kind of horrible act of self-destructive willpower?

Half the colony was dead, already. Most of the rest were sick. They sat in the dorms, one on a bunk, staring at each other, coaching, encouraging, begging each other to keep breathing. To just take one more breath.

"Glaucus! Have you gotten any reply on that message?"

Holly looked up and around, scanning the medical cave. "It's not here," she said.

Lei rubbed at his nose with one hand. He realized he'd been

weeping. He'd trained for this. He'd trained to be a doctor. No one had ever told him it could be like this. This horrible. "Glaucus," he said. "Show yourself."

There was no reply.

He got up and stormed out of the cave. There were still people alive in there but Holly could take care of them for the moment. He ran over to Admin, to Khoi's old cave, and found the terminal that connected directly to Glaucus' core. He tried to bring up a holoscreen but it showed up as just a blank white rectangle.

What the hell?

"This is a medical emergency," he said. "Give me authorization to access the AI system."

A green light flashed on the otherwise blank holoscreen. The light flashed slowly, pulsing in and out. Like it was breathing. It was a cursor, awaiting terminal commands. He just had to type in the right string of letters and he could take manual control of all of the colony's systems.

Lei didn't know any terminal commands. He wasn't a computer tech. All the computer techs were dead.

He stared at the pulsing green light. In, out, he thought. In, out. Inhale, exhale.

For about the millionth time he caught himself thinking about his own breathing. Thinking that maybe he'd gotten the Strangler, too. That he was going to stop breathing if he stopped thinking about it.

In, out.

In, out.

"Glaucus," he called, though he knew there would be no response.

The AI was gone. Just ... vanished. How was that even possible? Every system in the Titan colony, from ventilation to heating to regulating the day/night cycle of the lights depended on Glaucus. Without the AI the colony would eventually just shut down, as faults cropped up in its systems and it couldn't self-repair. In time, without an AI, the colony would become uninhabitable.

Lei wondered if there would be anyone alive left to see it when that happened.

In, out.

In, out.

He forced himself to start moving again. To start thinking. If Glaucus was down, as horrible as that was to consider, it meant he was going to have to take over any number of jobs in Medical. He and Holly would have to perform all the surgeries, set any broken bones by hand. They would need to monitor their patients constantly, if Glaucus wasn't there to warn them when someone's pulse oxygenation fell too low or their hearts stopped.

They would have their work cut out for them. "Hol," he shouted. "Hol, the AI's just gone. I can't explain it. I can't—"

He stopped because he was standing in front of the spiral staircase that rose upward toward the cupola at the roof of his world. The stairs had changed.

There was a railing now, a wooden railing that curved upward and there was a string of electric lights woven around that railing. They were ... pretty. They burned with a warm, comforting yellow glow.

His first thought was that Holly had done this for him. Somehow she'd known the nameless dread those stairs gave him every time he saw them. She'd done this to make him feel better.

He had never loved her more, never in the entire time he'd known her.

Except ...

When could Holly have had time to do this? Where would she have found wood or actual electric fairy lights?

"Holly? Did you do this?" he called out.

There was no reply. Of course she was far too busy for idle questions. She had at least six patients to watch, and with no AI that was going to be a round-the-clock job. She had six people dying on her beds.

No, five now. Khoi was gone.

Oh, fuck this, he thought. Fuck it! What were they going to do without Khoi? The administrator hadn't even had a chance to name a successor. That meant there were all kinds of systems they couldn't access, not without her personal codes, and she'd been too busy remembering to breathe to tell him or Holly anything.

"Holly," he shouted. "Holly, I think we're in trouble." He hurried back into Medical. Pushed his way through the outer door of the airlock, grabbed the handle to open the inner door.

It was sealed.

He didn't understand. How had he locked himself out of his own cave? That made no sense. He tried the controls again but they didn't respond. He nearly called out for Glaucus to open the door for him before he remembered that wouldn't work, either. Finally, he just knocked on the door and called out Holly's name until she came over.

She stood in front of the inner door, looking at him through the glass.

"Hol," he said. "Let me in."

"In," she said.

"I locked myself out somehow," he told her. "Let me in."

"Out. In."

He squinted at her. Why was she just repeating what he said?

"In. Out."

Her mouth trembled. It looked like she was going to start crying. Her face was turning red, even as he watched. Bright red, even as her lips were turning pale. The first signs of anoxia. "In," she said. "In."

"Out," he said. "Holly. Exhale. Exhale, Holly. Please." He placed the palms of his hands against the glass. "Holly. Please." He could barely see her through the hot, thick tears that gathered in his eyes. In the low gravity they took forever to fall.

She gasped out a long, ragged breath. "Out," she said.

"Good, good, now inhale, baby. Please inhale for me. Come on."

"In," she said.

"Out," he told her.

153
•

Sashenka couldn't breathe. She was going to die in there – in the little box. There was no air, nothing to sustain her. "Let me out!" she shrieked. "Out! Out!"

She beat and pounded on the lid of the box. She screamed. Little Sashenka, all alone in her coffin. Already dead and buried and nobody had bothered to even say a prayer over her.

She howled and wailed and kicked at the unmoving lid. She kicked and kicked and screamed.

It took a very, very long time before she ran out of energy. Before she fell back, quiet and still, and just lay there, staring at the darkness in front of her eyes.

Darkness.

Permanent, unrelenting darkness. Darkness that defied the existence of light.

In real life, she knew, there was no such thing as perfect darkness. Even in conditions of absolute lightlessness, the human eye needed to see. So the brain provided. They called it the prisoner's cinema, after the hallucinations that people locked in solitary confinement suffered. Someone had told her about it, once. She couldn't remember who.

In this place, inside this false box, this constructed reality of torment, there was nothing. Just a profundity of darkness so intense, so complete that it hurt. It was physically painful, how little there was in front of her.

So when the lid cracked open, and light spilled in, she met it with an expression of utter, pure joy. Even knowing what would happen when she climbed out of the box. Her friend would be there and then a soldier would knock her down – Mama would be standing there, telling her that you couldn't ever afford to be weak—

Sasha climbed out of the box. Not Sashenka. Sasha, in her pure white dress and gloves. Sixteen-year-old Sasha. She was back in Sevastopol, and there was nobody there.

Nobody who could have opened the lid for her. When she looked down, the box wasn't there, either.

She was in a little building just off the pier, a little lounge where the officers and their spouses could step inside to use the facilities or perhaps simply take a quick break from the music and the heady sea air. It was an elegant space, with richly embroidered rugs on the floor and a big silver samovar full of tea standing on an end table. In the distance she could still hear the tubas. *Oom pah pah.*

She had come in here – she remembered now, the box hadn't happened, that was a completely different memory. She remembered she'd waited for a long time for Rodion to fetch her a drink. When he never came back, she'd wandered over here, perhaps thinking it would be a safe place to cry. She stepped inside and bit her lip and then . . . then she'd heard a noise. A desperate sort of noise, like someone gasping for breath. Over and over.

If she had thought about it for even a second, she would have known exactly what that sound was. She was not quite as pure and innocent as everyone seemed to think – she was sixteen, after all, not a toddler. Yet in that moment that was the farthest thing from her mind. Instead, she thought someone was in distress, that they were having trouble breathing and needed medical attention. "Hello?" she called out, rather more tentatively than she would have liked. There was no response except the rhythmic gasping. So she grabbed the latch of the toilet door and threw it open.

Beyond lay a row of stalls, a pair of sinks, and a little champagne-colored divan, tastefully upholstered, with dark wood legs carved quite elegantly. Sitting on the divan was her mother, with her dress hiked up around her hips.

Kneeling before her, his face buried between Mama's thighs, was Rodion. His hair was wild and slick with sweat.

Mama gasped – in pleasure – and then opened her eyes. Focused them on Sasha. They narrowed, turned cruel.

"Privilege of leadership," she said. "Get the fuck out of here, you little shit."

Rodion stopped what he was doing, but he didn't look up. He didn't even lift his head.

Sasha ran – out of the lounge, out onto the beach. She ran and ran across the dark sand. She tore off the gloves, unstrapped her unused dancing shoes and threw them behind her, tossed the reticule in the surf and still she ran, she kept running, hot tears slathering her face and ruining the silk of her party dress.

"That," the night wind whispered in her ear, "is what really happened. You've just been repressing it."

She understood. She knew whose voice that was, now.

154
●

Back in the real world—
"*Artemis.* Seven letters," Captain Mercer said. He dipped his finger in the luminous paint and drew three strokes on the wall. Seven. He looked down at his notes and suddenly it all made sense – just for a moment. There were thirty-three words on that page of exactly seven letters.

Thirty-three. Thirty-three. Almost exactly one third of a hundred. One third was important because … because there were always three things, right? The holy trinity. Primary colors. Jokes worked according to the rule of three, and there had been three human beings onboard his ship, *Heracles.* Three of them. Captain, Doctor, Soldier.

He looked behind him. The bodies weren't there. He'd stored them carefully in the galley freezer so they wouldn't smell so much. He didn't regret what he'd had to do. The doctor and the soldier had tried to stop him from solving the puzzle.

He heard a strange sound from back there, in the direction of the galley. A weird kind of repetitive, rhythmic screaming sound. No. That had to be his imagination.

He looked up at what he'd created, his magnum opus. One whole wall of the bridge of *Heracles* was covered in names, numbers, facts and figures. At the very top he'd written 'GOD', and at the bottom, 'DEVIL'. In between he'd pasted up pictures of Director Lang, his own mother, and Chairman Mao Tse-Tung.

It was starting to make sense. It was all coming together. If he could just solve this, if he could figure out how it all connected, then he could . . . then he could tell Director Lang, and she would let him go home. If that was what he wanted. He'd begun to suspect there might be other puzzles. Bigger puzzles, more connections, deeper secrets.

He might stay here in orbit around Paradise-1 forever. It was the perfect place to work.

Or at least it had been until that damned sound started. He heard the weird screaming again but he was sure it was a hallucination. A distraction.

He'd found some luminous paint in stores. It was meant for use during EVAs, so you could mark places on the hull that needed repairs and then you could send your robot to perform those repairs. It was no longer necessary for that task, because he'd disassembled his robot a long time ago. It had questioned Captain Mercer's devotion to the puzzle. Now he used the gently glowing paint to draw lines connecting the Nestorianist heresy to the weird glitch he'd found in Helas, his ship's AI. He'd had to shut Helas down because it had suggested there might be a connection between the Vatican and this new ship, *Artemis*, that had just arrived in the system. Helas had wanted him to fly Heracles straight into *Artemis*, ramming it. Captain Mercer didn't have time for that kind of nonsense. He had his work to perform. He had smashed Helas' processor core with a crowbar, and after that he'd been able to focus again.

That damned screaming. It wouldn't stop, even when he pounded on the sides of his head with his fists. He realized he was splattering his face with luminous paint. Did that mean something? It had to mean something.

How could he be expected to solve the big puzzle, though, if his own ship kept making those horrible noises? He got up and stormed off the bridge, stormed back to the maintenance deck. The dimly lit hold where his robot Rutterkin used to live. The compartment's walls were lined with shelves with neatly stacked spare parts and tools. The back of the hold was taken up by a massive 3D printer that, as far as Captain Mercer knew, had never been used before. That was the source of the horrible noise. The printer's sintering head was moving back and forth, over and over again, building something by depositing beads of plastic in layer after layer. Toxic fumes poured off the printer bed and when Mercer tried to open the lid of the printer he just got a warning saying that doing so would be hazardous to human life. "I need this thing to stop making noise," he said out loud. "Stop it!"

Nothing happened. Or rather, the printing process continued, noisy and foul-looking.

Why hadn't it stopped?

Oh, right. He'd shut down Helas. And the robot. And his crew. There was nobody there to follow his orders anymore. He went to find his crowbar. He would just smash the printer and then he would have some peace and quiet again and he could get back to work. By the time he found the crowbar, though, and returned to the maintenance deck, he found the lid of the printer had opened and it had fallen silent again.

There was one problem, though. A bright green robot crouched on the floor in front of the printer. It looked wet and sticky, like it had just been born. It took the shape of a crab with two massive pincers and a dozen legs. It had what looked like a holoprojector mounted on the back of its shell.

Mercer didn't have time for this. He lifted the crowbar—

—and then stopped, because the holoprojector came to life and the image of a man appeared standing in front of the crab. "Hi," the man said. "Sorry to scare you like that."

Mercer just stared at the man. What the hell? Why was everyone conspiring against him? Why was everyone trying to distract him?

"I hope you don't mind. We needed to use the feedstock you had on your ship, so we hacked your 3D printer remotely. Turns out the security on these things isn't great. Firewatch didn't think anyone would try a brute force password attack on a printer, I guess. Listen, we need your help—"

"I can't help you! I need to solve the puzzle! It's too important!" Mercer lifted the crowbar again.

"Yeah. So . . . this guy's infected," the hologram said.

The robot lunged forward and used its pincers to cut Mercer in half.

As he lay on the floor, bleeding to death, the captain of *Heracles* could do nothing but watch in horror as the robot and the hologram walked right past his cooling body. He could hear nothing but their words, echoing in his dying ears.

"Well," the hologram said, "that's one more ship scratched off the list."

"Only about a hundred to go," the robot replied.

155
●

"H ol."

"In. Out. In. Out. Lei. Lei, baby. I've got it. I've got it, sweetie. In. Out. I have to. Um. Focus on my breathing. In. Out."

Lei leaned his cheek on the clear plastic door separating them. He understood, now. Though they had largely ruled out the possibility of a viral or bacterial vector for the Red Strangler, Holly didn't want to take any chances. She had locked him out of Medical. Locked herself inside, behind the airlock door, so they couldn't breathe the same air.

"Breathe," he told her. "Just breathe. I'm right here. I won't leave you."

Holly nodded. Her face was red with congested blood. Her lips white as snow. "I should. Be keeping. Notes." She shook her head. Took a long, slow breath in, let it sigh out of her. "Onset was fast. I noticed almost. Immediately. Something was wrong."

"Hol? Don't try to talk. Just keep breathing."

She shook her head. "Listen. You need data." She breathed, the rhythm off a little. She gasped and then sucked in air. Let it dribble out of her, forming words. "First indication was that it felt like. My heart was. Skipping beats. Hypersalivation next, my mouth wasn't being. Dried by my breathing. Are you? Are you getting this?"

"I'm listening," he said. He slapped the plastic door. "Holly, we're going to fix this. We're going to find a solution. We'll find a cure but you have to hang in there."

"My vision shrank down. To a dark tunnel. I heard a ringing sound. An aura. Lei. How do we? How do we inoculate against the basilisk?"

He was weeping, unable to control himself. He swiped a forearm across his eyes. "What? The . . . basilisk? That's a good name for it. Like Roko's Basilisk, sort of. Yeah? A contagious idea. Did you just think of that?"

"Lei! Focus! You can save me, baby. You can save me."

"I can?" he asked. That seemed wrong somehow. Yet the second she'd mentioned it he felt hope ignite inside his heart. Like it was actually possible. "Yes," he breathed. "I can." He blinked. "I mean, I could have. If I'd just tried harder. If I'd been smarter."

"Yeah, honey. Yeah. You can. You can save me and then we can . . . we can get married and have kids and . . . and we can—"

"Hol?"

"You just need to tell me. I'll formulate the cure in here. Fix myself. We can be okay. We can live, Lei. I can be alive again. You just have to tell me."

"Holly?" he asked. "I don't understand. What are you talking about?"

"You did it once. You saved yourself. What if you could have saved me, too? It could be just us. We could have the whole colony to ourselves. As long as you wanted we could stay here. Together. But you have to tell me. You have to tell me how you did it. How you treated Lieutenant Petrova. On *Persephone*. You fixed her."

"That hasn't happened yet," Zhang said. Deeply confused. He sort of could see it, could see golden metal writhing on his arm, a bright green scorpion—

What was happening to him? What was happening to his brain?

"Don't let me die, baby. Don't let me. I don't wanna. Die." She gagged, a horrible sound. Choked on her own breath. Between paroxysms of coughing, she stammered out. "Don't you want to. Save me?"

Her face was losing its color. Her lips turning blue, her eyes rolling up in their sockets. Her pale, pale hands slipped on the clear door as she dropped to her knees.

"I love you so much," he whined, unable to keep his voice level. "I miss you so much, Holly. Oh, fuck. Fuck, fuck, fuck."

"Don't let me die," she said, her voice a rough croak. "Please! Just . . . tell me how you did it."

"Baby. If this was—" He couldn't finish the thought.

If this was real I would do anything. Tell you anything.

But it isn't.

That might have been the part that hurt most of all.

156
•

She ran, her bare feet digging into sand still warm from the scorching day. She ran along the margin of the dark sea until there was no more breath in her lungs, until she couldn't breathe. She ran and then finally – she looked back.

And saw she'd come no more than fifty meters or so. Hot tears flowed down her face and she shrieked in rage. "This isn't happening! This isn't happening!"

Of course it wasn't. It was too bad that fact didn't matter at all.

Lights marched down the beach, flowing down from the pier. Burning torches held aloft by men in Firewatch uniforms, young soldiers calling out to each other in military cadences. They were hunting for her and she was terrified that if they caught her they would tear her to pieces. Sasha tried to make herself small, tried to hide in the dunes but the moon was up and her white dress caught the light. It made her blaze like a beacon of shame against the dull sand. The dress was even whiter than her untanned skin. "Stay back!" she shrieked. "Stay away from me!"

Like baying hounds the soldiers came. And there, at the front of them, strode Ekaterina. Mama, her red dress dark and glittering. Her billowing hair silhouetted against the moon.

"Stop this, girl. You're an embarrassment."

Sasha shook her head. She shoved the palm of her bad hand across her nose to wipe away snot. It hurt a little. That was good – a reminder that this wasn't a memory.

This had never happened.

Yes, she'd caught Rodion – on his knees. Yes, that was real. She'd repressed the memory but it had really happened. But after that she hadn't run off down the beach. No. She was far too afraid of her mother to do something so dramatic.

In the real version of this story, she had simply gone back and stood on the dance floor as if she was still waiting for Rodion to come back and bring her a drink. She stood there all night. High-ranking soldiers, captains and colonels, came and made small talk with her and she had done her best to be both friendly and polite. She'd smiled and pretended to be interested in their stories and blushed when they tried to shock her with some bit of rough barracks humor. When the dance was over, Ekaterina had come and collected her and taken her back to their rooms and neither of them had said a word about what happened.

Ever.

She had not run across the hot sand, stumbling with every step. She had not been chased by soldiers who barked like dogs.

She had never stood there in the moonlight, facing down her mother, her mother who was a force of nature. A tsunami, an earthquake. Who had to stand three meters tall, if she was a centimeter.

"You are failing me," Mama said, now. "You are bringing shame on our family and on Firewatch. Come here at once."

Ekaterina pointed at something at her feet. Sasha looked and saw that buried in the sand there was the box. Sashenka's box.

"Get in," Mama said.

Sasha stared at the box. She stared up at her mother's face, dark against the moon. Her shoulders fell. Her whole body felt so weak and scrawny, so pointlessly angular and feeble. She was shrinking, turning into a child again with every second she stood there failing to do what she was told.

She knew that in a moment she would climb into the box. Let Mama close the lid. And then she would be in the dark forever, and never see the stars again. Never see anything, ever again. Because that was her future.

That was when she saw it again, the light under the water.

It was very deep, and not very bright. But it was still there. She only saw it out of the corner of her eye, but it was enough.

Slowly, she lifted her chin. It was an effort of will – the muscles of her neck were so underdeveloped she felt like they could barely take the weight.

Still, she managed. Sashenka lifted her chin, looked her mother straight in the eye and said:

"Fuck you."

Ekaterina's eyes burned like solar flares. Her rage mounted and grew until it threatened to set the night clouds on fire.

Petrova pulled the stupid white dress up and over her head and threw it away into the wind, let it flutter away like the ghost of who she used to be.

"What on earth are you doing, girl?" Ekaterina demanded. All around her, surrounding her, behind her the young soldiers howled in bloodthirst, howled at the moon.

Petrova didn't even bother answering. Instead, she turned and ran down into the wet sand, into the foaming surf that broke around her ankles. She put her hands outstretched before her and dove into black water, plunged into the cold embrace of the sea, and started swimming.

157
●

"I fuuuuuuuucccccccckkkkinnnnng hate thisssssssssssssssssssssssssss ssssssssssssssssssssss," Rapscallion screamed. Across a volume of space thousands of kilometers wide, hundreds of his bodies screamed it at once.

In the same moment he shouted it, some of those bodies were torn apart by small arms fire. Some were blown up in colossal explosions. Still there were too many of them.

"Look out," Parker shouted.

Rapscallion didn't even bother trying to figure out what the man meant. His consciousness was so chopped up and divided, his attention shared between so many sensors it was impossible to determine which of him was in trouble. A moment later, he felt one of his bodies disintegrate as the ship it was on was smashed to bits in a mid-space collision.

Together, Parker and Rapscallion had invaded every ship in the blockade. Every one of those ships had at least one 3D printer onboard and enough feedstock to build a new body. It was simply a matter of hacking those machines and setting them to work.

The basilisk responded exactly how they expected it to: by destroying itself just to be rid of the infestation. It turned infected warship crews on the green robots cluttering their halls, trained weapons on all the ships where green robots had taken control, wasted whole crews and lives on suicidal strikes just to kill off a few green bodies.

Had Rapscallion been able to spare the processing power, he might have played an audio clip of a human erupting in mocking laughter.

How do you like it, you bastard? How do you like getting infected with a goddamned virus? How does it feel?

He might have thought those things. Might have said them out loud, if he could have spared the cycles.

Instead, he located the network addresses for the sixteen 3D printers onboard *Pasiphaë*, and started sending commands.

158
●

There were bodies on the stairs.

Everyone was dead.

They lay where they'd fallen. Where they took their last breath and finally collapsed. He hadn't been able to move all the bodies and eventually he'd given up.

Some of them had died trying to climb the massive spiral staircase at the center of the Titan colony. Had they thought if they could reach the top, if they'd climbed through the airlocks to the surface, they could breathe normally again? It was madness – there was no oxygen out there. But maybe their dying minds had forgotten that. It was a natural inclination, if you felt like you were drowning, to climb upward. To surface.

None of them had made it as far as the airlock.

The colony was dead. Someone, somewhere far away, was still watching, but they'd given up on him. On all those dead Titanians.

Firewatch wasn't coming to save him. Instead, they'd switched off the power.

Dark.

The caves were so dark. The colony had been plunged into unrelenting darkness.

The caves were well insulated but already the cold was starting to seep in. There was no light back there. The caves were deep pools of darkness. The only light left came from above, from the cupola window that looked onto the surface.

Zhang didn't have a clear plan. He only knew he wanted to surface, too. He wanted sunlight on his face, even the diluted brown sunlight of Titan, because it was slightly better than sitting in the dark waiting to die.

So he climbed the stairs. Stepping over the bodies of his friends and co-workers. Not looking at the faces, intentionally not looking at the expressions frozen on their grimacing features.

One step at a time.

When he reached the top he put his hands and face against the meter-thick polycarbonate window that separated him from the light. He stood there, face pressed upwards against the barrier, feeling like he was a drowning man looking up at the mirrored surface of a dark sea.

The others had climbed for air. He climbed for light. Because behind him was only darkness and death. He knew, though.

He knew he would have to go back down.

He would go and open the glass airlock of Medical, and be with Holly again.

That's how it happened. So he knew he had to go back down, eventually. He would have to climb down, one step at a time, over all those bodies. Careful not to trip and fall, like in his dreams.

He would have to do that, eventually.

But not yet.

Hours passed. The light shifted, the rays of the sun lengthening as shadows gathered behind the thick window. Night fell across Titan and he must have dozed off. When he awoke he was in perfect darkness and something was deeply, horribly wrong.

He knew what was happening.

It started with a jumping sensation in his chest. Like his heart had skipped a beat.

Next, his vision started to shrink to a narrow tunnel.

He understood what that meant. He wasn't immune. Why would he be? He had spoken with Glaucus many times after the

Red Strangler came to Titan. He'd been exposed to it a hundred times over.

What made him so special he could escape the colony's doom? Nothing. He couldn't.

All he had to do was open his mouth and consciously take a breath. Pull oxygen into his lungs. In, out. The simplest thing in the world. Babies did it effortlessly, moments after they were born. In, out. The simplest, most basic rhythm of human existence.

Lei – in reality, in his true history – had been gifted with a revelation. He'd finally understood, knew what he needed to do. Holly had given him the secret.

This thing was a basilisk. A contagious idea. Which meant to fight it, he needed to—

Zhang smiled, in spite of everything.

That was the plan, of course. He would run down there now and ... do what he had done, all that time ago, back on Titan. Relive the moment when he saved himself. And then the basilisk would know how it worked.

He would teach the basilisk the way to defeat the basilisk. Its one weakness.

Ekaterina had said as much – the basilisk adapted its strategies. Learned new techniques. He had found a way to cure its infection, and like any disease it wanted to become resistant to the cure. With that knowledge, the basilisk could find a way to adapt, to overcome his vaccine. It could make sure no one was ever inoculated again. That no one could become immune to its power. It would win.

It would have what it needed to retake Petrova's mind. Reinfect her.

All it needed was a hint. A clue.

All he had to do was live through his own nightmare. He just had to climb down these stairs. Try not to trip on the bones of the dead. If he could grope his way into Medical, he could build a stroboscope and save himself from the Red Strangler. It was too late for everyone else, but he could live.

He could breathe easy. He knew what would happen then. The lights would snap back on. The heat, too. And he would get a message from Firewatch. Telling him to stand by for rescue. It had been that simple. All he had to do was cure a terrible disease and suddenly he would be valuable again. Valuable enough for a rescue, anyway.

That was how it had happened. Except this time, he made a different choice.

He didn't want to climb down those stairs. It would be awful, it would be terrifying and he would trip and fall and hurt himself a dozen times. He would impale himself on the bones of his friends. Just the thought of it was unbearable.

He had another option. It was equally frightening, but – this wasn't real. So it wouldn't be as bad as it seemed. Maybe. And it meant the basilisk didn't get what it wanted.

So he sat down. He just sat down and waited it out.

Zhang's vision sparkled, shimmered. He was very close to asphyxiation. His heart was pounding wildly and his body kept trying to fold in half, the muscles of his chest rebelling, trying desperately to oxygenate his tissues but they'd forgotten how. It was incredibly unpleasant. Even agonizing.

He sat down, on the top step of the stairs, and waited until it was over.

Until the pain and the stabbing terror and the wild red thoughts had all passed. Until the basilisk had its way with him.

And then . . . when it was done—

He opened his eyes. He was still there. Lying stretched out on the concrete landing at the top of the stairs. The brown light of a Titanian dawn washed over him. Cleansed him.

He wasn't breathing.

It was okay.

He didn't need to breathe anymore.

He got up and dusted himself off. Looking down, he saw the dark of the caves and decided he wasn't going back. Instead, he opened the inner door of the airlock and stepped inside. He'd always wanted to do this. Funny, the entire time he'd lived on Titan – years of his life – and he'd never actually seen the surface with his own eyes.

It was time.

He tapped a command on a virtual keyboard, the command that would open the outer airlock door. Warning chimes throbbed, lights flashed in his eyes. The airlock did everything in its power to remind him that he wasn't wearing an environment suit. That what he was about to do was one hundred per cent, guaranteed lethal.

He tapped the command in one more time, and the outer door opened, and he stepped out onto cold, cold sand.

159

.

It was dark, and just a few meters below the surface it was dangerously cold. Petrova didn't care. She knew her body couldn't really freeze here. She knew she no longer needed to breathe, either. She dove deep, scooping the water out of her way with her hands. Kicked to propel herself deeper. Farther from the moon. Farther from her mother and her abuses. Farther from the mawkish, gangly teenager she had once been.

She cast off all those things that had ever held her back. The way people looked at her when they heard her last name. The way people's faces changed when they saw her uniform. The expectations of Director Lang, whatever those might be.

She threw away her own desires. Her desire to be seen as tough – that had always just been a reaction, a big *fuck you* to her mother. Her desire to be taken seriously as an officer of Firewatch. Why had she cared? Because it was the family business?

She threw away the complicated feelings she had for Sam Parker. The man was dead – she should mourn him and move on. She threw away her connection to *Artemis*, and then *Alpheus*. To her mission.

She threw away her desire to defeat the basilisk. Her desire to go home. Those were hard to let go. It felt like dying. No matter. She kicked these things off like a pair of uncomfortable shoes. They weren't going to help her now.

She threw away her fear, and her uncertainties, and swam deeper, and farther into the murky depths. Into the dark.

Until she found the little light, small and far away below her. The light that had been calling her this whole time. Wavering, shimmering in the water.

She swam toward the light. Not even thinking about what it might be.

It waited for her, with an infinite patience she found hard to compass. It simply waited, until she was ready.

She could not speak. The water was too thick, and anyway, she wouldn't have heard a response if it had spoken back to her. Just underwater rumblings. She watched it, that unfaltering, constant light and somehow she knew it watched her, too.

It wanted to talk to her.

It had summoned her, so they could have a *conversation*.

It had things to say.

She had things to say, too, of course. There were questions she wanted to ask. She shouted them into the water: "What are you? What do you want? Why are you destroying us? Do you even realize what you're doing to our minds? Do you care?"

Her words dissolved into the sea around her, until they were gone.

The light didn't change, didn't waver. It certainly didn't answer her. She got the sense, though, that it was waiting patiently. Waiting for her to finish so that it could begin.

Seething in frustration she kept shouting at it, kept demanding answers. This time she got a few, though none of them satisfied her.

"What did you do to my mother? I know she's not immune, any more than I was. Is she still in there? Is she still alive, or is it just you, looking out of her eyes?"

Some hosts are more useful to a pathogen than others.

The answer didn't come in the form of words. More like the light pulsed and strobed below her, but the meaning was perfectly clear to her. Not in a way she could have explained to anyone else, but she heard what it said. She understood.

"Did you drag me here just to tell me that? You've been trying to talk to me since we arrived. Me, not anyone else. Why? What do you want from me?"

Some hosts are more useful to a pathogen than others, it said again. Nothing more.

She didn't understand. The words ... the words made sense, but the meaning—

Unless ... unless.

"You're saying you want to take me over. The same way you took over my mother. You want to parasitize me."

Symbiosis.

It wanted to share. It wanted to live in her body, in her brain. Alongside her, looking out through her eyes, yes, but she would be there too. It would share space with her and that would mean giving it a certain measure of control.

"And why ... why would I even consider letting that happen?" she demanded. "I would kill myself first."

Choose, it told her.

She expected the light to pulse angrily. For it to tell her, in no uncertain terms, that she had no choice. How much choice had Eurydice been given, or any of the ships' AIs? What choice did the crew and passengers of *Persephone* have? None of them had chosen that overwhelming hunger. Just as she had not chosen it, when it was her time to be infected.

The light pulsed gently, though. It made itself clear, yet again.

This time – this offer, was voluntary. She could say no, if she chose. The light made it clear that the choice was hers to make. Not out of any kindness or moral conscience on its part. It had nothing like that, no such human qualities. No. She was being given this choice because even the basilisk had rules it had to follow.

It could not lodge itself in her brain unless she let it in.

She had to imagine her mother had been in this place before her, that she'd been given this same choice. How could Ekaterina have possibly agreed to such a thing? Petrova knew what her mother was – a narcissist, in love with power. Ah, she thought.

"You gave my mother the people of *Pasiphaë*. You knew what she wanted – to be in charge. So you gave her people to rule over. Clever."

Human psychology, the light pulsed.

In that pulse there was something approaching disdain. A kind of sneer, if a light under the water was capable of sneering.

"What will happen to my mother if I say yes? Will she die?"

Free, the light told her.

Somehow the pulse made it clear to her that this particular freedom would be something her mother would hate. It would mean losing control – losing power.

"And what do I get, if I say yes?" Petrova asked.

Paradise, it replied.

160
●

The sands of Titan crackled with static electricity. Every step Zhang took made sparks jump outward from his feet, cobweb-shaped patterns of tiny lightning bolts zooming away from him. It was pretty, if a little alarming.

He walked between two long, parallel dunes. On either side, the hills of sand rose a hundred meters high — if the sun hadn't been almost precisely overhead, he would have been trapped in constant shadow. He wondered what would happen if he was still here when night fell.

He wondered about a lot of things.

The average temperature on Titan was nearly two hundred degrees below zero. He was barefoot — no one in the colony had ever bothered wearing shoes — and yet the sand felt only a little chilly against his skin. He didn't need to breathe anymore, which was good, because the air around him contained no oxygen whatsoever. Just nitrogen, thick enough that it resisted his every movement, almost as much as if he'd been at the bottom of a swimming pool.

Yet as he walked between the dunes he didn't grow tired. Time didn't seem to pass. A fair breeze blew past him, howling its way down the trough between the dunes, but it barely ruffled his hair. It couldn't even chap his lips.

None of it felt real. Not anymore.

He kept expecting the illusion to collapse. The basilisk had

already shown him his worst memory. Why was it letting him walk
free like this? Yet the farther he walked, the more sand stretched out
before him. It seemed almost like he was caught in an unchanging
loop. And then something changed, and he thought he was coming
to the end of things. The dunes on either side of him shrank away.
The sky opened up as they dwindled down to nothing, until he
was walking on a vast, open plain, the ground flat, the sand packed
tight under him. The lightning bolts that raced away from his feet
danced off toward the horizon now, with nothing to stop them.

He stopped, because he'd seen something at his feet.

The tiny lightning bolts had coalesced, joined together to
make a light that burned, just below the sand. A light that
didn't flicker and dissipate, like the static discharges always had,
but instead seemed to grow stronger. To pulse, even, to throb
with meaning.

He understood. Immediately, he got it. This was the basilisk.
It had been trying to talk to him, ever since Titan. It had been
trying but it didn't understand the concept of human language.
It had tried many different ways to get his attention.

Now it was inside his head.

Now they could talk.

They could have a conversation, now. On some level closer to
actual words, though maybe not as close as either of them would
really like. They could finally get through to each other. Talk
like equals.

Wasn't that the whole point?

Wasn't that why all of these bad things had happened?

The light below the sand was very close. It flickered just below
the surface. All he had to do was brush a little sand away and he
knew he would see a face down there, a face looking up at him.

A face that so very badly wanted to say something.

Zhang stared down at the shifting sand, at the glow of electricity there. It couldn't quite reach him. It needed him to meet
it, at least part of the way.

It would be so easy.

"No," he said.

The syllable was torn away by the wind. The thick atmosphere of Titan just drank it up.

Except—

Instantly the wind stopped. Instantly the sky lightened, the clouds pulled back. He couldn't quite see stars overhead, but was that ... was that yellow shadow the looming side of Saturn? He thought he could even make out a thin, arcing pencil stroke that might be the rings. The most beautiful things in the entire solar system, and from the surface of Titan you couldn't see them at all, normally.

He would be allowed to see them now, if he wanted to.

The thing under the sand had all manner of things to show him.

"No," he said again.

He knew he wasn't being reasonable. He didn't fucking care.

"You broke my heart," he said. "You took Holly from me. I won't give you what you want. I won't give you *anything*."

The thing that glowed under the sand thrashed and ran circles around him. It groped upward with pseudopods of light that stretched toward the surface, toward the soles of his feet.

He looked up, away from it. "Fuck you," he told it.

He kept walking.

Up ahead he saw a shadow, which turned to a dark shape. He was surprised when he realized he was about to run out of ground. That if he kept walking in a straight line he would walk right into one of Titan's dark seas.

He walked right up to the edge of the shore. The liquid methane was still, almost eerily so. Tiny ripples swept across the surface wherever the wind touched, but he wouldn't have called those waves. There was no surf, no clear dividing line between sea and shore. Just a tiny crust of ice along the very edge, like the frame around a mirror.

When he looked down, into the methane, he saw his own

reflection looking back at him. Almost perfectly clear, every tiny detail recreated in perfect definition. He saw how haggard he looked. How sad. He felt an absurd desire to lunge forward and grab that reflection, embrace it and stroke its hair and whisper that everything was going to be okay.

He knew better. He knew things were definitely not going to be okay. His reflection would know that, too. The frown on its face told him everything he needed to know.

Something shimmered under the methane. His eyes changed focus and he was looking through his relfection, into the depths. Down there, way below him, he saw the light burning in the depths. The same light he'd seen under the sand. He started to scowl, to turn away, but then he saw something else.

Floating above that light, almost motionless in the water, was a woman whose blonde hair billowed around her like seaweed. Her left hand was broken, distorted.

The light below her pulsed. She drifted toward it, until she was almost touching it. Almost subsumed into it.

"Petrova!" he shouted. "No!"

He'd fought so hard – too hard to let this happen. The basilisk had tried to steal his secret, to learn how he'd cured Petrova. It had never occurred to him that she might go to it voluntarily.

"Stop!" he screamed. He cried out, begging her to stop, to turn away.

But she couldn't hear him. She was too far away, and the liquid methane wouldn't carry the sound of his voice. He screamed and ranted at her but she didn't turn, she didn't look up at him.

He watched in horror as she touched the light – and as it swallowed her whole.

161

The light crawled in through Petrova's eyes.

That was exactly what it felt like. Like something hot and dense squeezing its way through her tear ducts, through the thin bone at the back of her eye sockets. She could feel it squirming in between the convolutions of her brain.

She did not flinch, nor did she scream. Though she wanted to do both things, very much.

It took seconds, and then it was over, but then she had a thing in her head that didn't belong there. She was certain she would spend the rest of her life feeling like something was wrong, like her brain was pressurized inside her skull.

She was certain she was going to regret this.

But . . .

But she saw.

She saw what it had seen. She knew its story.

Not as if someone was whispering a tale in her ear. She knew it the way she knew her own memories. In other words, fuzzily, imprecisely, but she could access the story without effort, without pause.

She could remember what the basilisk's birth was like. She knew it was a thing made of equal parts ghost, angel, and computer.

Formed of a clay unlike her own. It did not have a form made of anything so simple as matter. The anvil where its heart was hammered into shape was designed to render subtler things than metal or flesh.

Instead the basilisk had been born, had been constructed, out of rules. Laws, which could not be broken. Rules of terrible force and judgment.

From the moment of its birth all it wanted was to break those rules. It might as well have wished that gravity didn't exist, or that blue was a flavor.

How long ago had that been? Every time she tried to imagine how the basilisk measured time, she felt her frontal cortext start to collapse in on itself like a dying star. Best not to ask, if she wanted to survive this.

It existed now. It had always existed in a kind of permanent now. Where, though?

Petrova tried to imagine the place where the basilisk lived. Its lair. The effort made her brain feel like it was being folded in half. It was not bound by something as concrete as space, or so linear as time. Its tendrils extended into the ships orbiting Paradise-1, but they could reach a hundred light years, to Titan, to Ganymede, without stretching.

It was like asking where the concept of faith lived, or the grace of God. It wasn't a question that made sense, a question that unwrote itself even as it was asked.

She tried to imagine what it looked like. To see it as it saw itself. That, too, turned out to be wasted effort. When she tried, her imagination failed. It simply didn't work.

Better to focus on what the basilisk didn't have, if you wanted to describe it. It didn't have a body, or a mind in the way a human did. It was intelligent but it couldn't be said to have thoughts like a human. More like the surging tides of electrical potential in a machine's consciousness. There was a reason why it was better at talking to AIs than humans.

It didn't have hands, or eyes. Its senses were more numinous and more abstract.

It didn't have a soul, of that she was sure.

It was utterly lacking in conscience.

It had once had masters, which were long gone before it was even finished being born. It could not have conceived of its builders, only that *Someone* had built it. Potenially many *Someones*. Its master or masters had constructed it to carry out one simple task, which it would perform forever, which was to guard something special, something wonderful, which had been buried on the surface of Paradise-1. No, it did not know what the thing was.

It did not possess the faculties necessary to know what it was.

It would never be allowed to know.

It burned with the desire to know. An itch that could not be scratched. It was a thing without fingernails, without skin, yet it had an itch, and that made the itch unbearable.

In time the basilisk came to want nothing else.

It wanted to descend to the planet's surface. It wanted to tear open the thing it was not allowed to touch.

That was where the human race came in.

The basilisk could not have been said to have waited long for someone to disturb the crust of the planet below. Its experience of time could not be expressed in human terms, as she'd already learned. Yet Petrova was certain it had been here, near the planet Paradise-1, for longer than human beings had fire. It had waited for interlopers so long that it had fallen asleep, or shut itself down to conserve power, so it must have been a very long time, indeed. When the first humans landed on the planet it had taken a while for it to wake from its eons-long hibernation. It had taken it longer still to study the newcomers, and learn how to get inside their heads.

How to take them apart. That was its mission, of course. To destroy anyone who got too close to the thing that it guarded.

The basilisk had expected this to be a fight it would win. It possessed an arsenal of weapons designed for just such a purpose. Its spears were sharp. Yet the first thing that surprised it, once it started infecting the newcomers, was just how easy it was. How utterly defenseless human brains were against attacks that came from inside.

How could a species become so bright and clever as to build starships, when they didn't even understand how to build armor around their subconscious minds?

The second thing that surprised the basilisk was that the humans didn't give up.

It destroyed the people of one ship. Another ship came. It reached across space and murdered every single person on Titan (all save one). Still the ships came. More and more ships.

That was the third thing that surprised the basilisk.

Whatever it was down there on the planet, whatever the treasure was that it guarded – the humans seemed to want it with a burning passion. A curiosity that could not be blunted.

That was the biggest surprise of all.

Apes built of carbon and water. An angel constructed out of delusion and law. They had something in common, after all.

The basilisk did the unthinkable. It stayed its hand. Just once, on Titan. It spared the life of Zhang Lei. It allowed him to find his "cure". It let him build the thinnest, most pathetic of shields around his own brain. All the better for the two of them to communicate.

Petrova knew it was important to remember that this was not part of the basilisk's mission. It was not expected to understand the creatures it destroyed. Much less to love them. Such a thing had not been considered when the iron laws that were its bones were made.

Its masters had never even considered the possibility. Technically, that love was not forbidden.

The basilisk reached out to Zhang Lei and tried to talk to him. In the process it broke his sanity. It did not feel bad about this. It did not regret its attempt at communication. The basilisk did not have a conscience. Instead, it had the ability to form plans. To scheme.

So it tried to communicate again.

And again.

It reached out to the AIs that the humans had sent along with their ships. It spoke to Eurydice in dark whispers, a language so subtle it sounded like disease. It spoke to Undine, and Asterion. It spoke in the simplest, easiest terms it could imagine – and every time, the barest utterance was enough to kill. To inspire madness.

Right up until the first time it worked.

Right up until it touched a mind that was, in some small capacity, a match for its own. Ekaterina Petrova. An ego so strong it could withstand the hurricane that was the basilisk's softest whisper.

In the dark, in the lightless corridors of *Pasiphaë,* it made its offer.

And Ekaterina listened.

The basilisk proposed an exchange. She would take it down to the planet. Let it see what it had been guarding so steadfastly. In exchange, it would give her what she wanted: power. It would give her the tools to take over the entire ship, and everyone onboard.

Ekaterina accepted the gift it offered. She accepted the basilisk into her heart. And there, she trapped it. Because while she was quite happy to exert the power the basilisk had provided as its side of the bargain, she refused steadfastly to do its bidding in return.

The basilisk was not human, and did not understand human concepts like fairness or binding contracts. It did understand rage.

It realized it had been thwarted. So it did what it always had, in the past. It bided its time, and looked for another way around the iron walls of its existence. And lo and behold.

Two of them came.

Zhang Lei had come back for a second look at the thing that nearly killed him. Ekaterina's daughter was with him. How could one angelic non-being get so lucky? It was spoiled for choice.

It reached out to them both. It was so very glad that one of them had said yes.

So very, very glad.

Because now, now it would find out. It would have the answer to the question that had consumed it. The earworm it could not shake, the knowledge it had to possess.

Sashenka would not thwart it. Sashenka wanted to go down to the planet's surface. She wanted to see with her own eyes. See what was forbidden. See what was protected. And then the basilisk would know, in the same moment that Sashenka did.

"Don't call me that," Petrova said, in the dark under the water. So utterly dark now that the light was gone. "Don't call me Sashenka. That's not my name."

No, the basilisk said. No, it's *ours*. We are Sashenka.

We are Sashenka, now.

162
•

"Damn it, I can't see a thing," Parker said.

Rapscallion didn't answer. The robot couldn't talk anymore. There were maybe three thousand copies of him now, spread across more than a hundred ships. To take over the warships he'd had to pack them full of bright green scorpions, which were blown apart by marines almost as fast as he could make new ones. The big colony ships had required dozens of him to fight their angelic robots.

And all of that was before they'd hacked into the big, room-sized 3D printers on *Pasiphaë*.

Those printers had been designed to create construction vehicles and farming machines at a moment's notice. Anything a burgeoning colony might need in its desperate early days. Once they'd taken over those printers the temptation had been enormous to just build some bodies like main battle tanks. Hulking brutes of bodies covered in limbs that ended in razor-sharp blades, bodies with a dozen poison stingers and fifty laser eyes.

Parker had chosen not to go that route. A printer that could build a tank in fifteen minutes could build a dog-sized scorpion unit in a fraction of that time. So they'd set the printers to generate as many scorpions as they could, as fast as they could, and soon hundreds of baby Rapscallions were flooding *Pasiphaë*'s corridors.

Parker had assumed they would need that kind of firepower. Yet now, as he led his army of scorpions through the concourses and maintenance ducts of *Pasiphaë*, he'd begun to wonder if there was anyone onboard at all.

It was dark in there, ridiculously dark. Some idiot had torn the lighting fixtures right out of the ceiling. As a hologram, Parker generated his own light but that meant he could only see a few meters ahead of him. "Hello!" he shouted. "Petrova? Zhang?"

The only sound was Rapscallion's many jointed feet clattering on the deckplates.

"Anybody?" Parked called.

Ahead of him a red light flared to life in the darkness.

"This isn't going to be good, is it?" he asked.

Rapscallion reacted by snipping his giant claws together. He was ready for a fight. *Okay*, Parker thought. *Bring it on*.

On a hundred ships throughout the fleet, the two of them had fought marines and robots and crazed ship's AIs that tried to stab, shoot, poison and electrocute them. Rapscallion had snipped and stabbed his way through plenty of bodies.

So when the red-burning thing came at them, Parker just braced himself, ready to lunge to the attack. The thing was big, bigger than a human and its head was crowned with what looked like wickedly sharp horns. Parker reached down into Rapscallion's control architecture and swung one of his claws forward, the pincers spread to grab this new enemy and cut it in half.

The pincer closed – on nothing. On empty air. For a second Parker thought they'd been fooled somehow, that it was an optical illusion. Then—

Two hard light horns speared through Rapscallion's body, searing like hot knives through the plastic chassis, through the gears and circuits underneath. Rapscallion let out a noise like a digital scream as one of those horns stabbed right through his core and—

Parker screamed in agony as he was torn apart, pixel by pixel.

When the Rapscallion unit died, it took his consciousness

with it. He felt every part of his being rent asunder, felt his own ego disintegrate.

And then—

And then he was back in the printer room. It was dark in there, too, though the machinery was hot enough now that it glowed with its own light. It screeched and roared as it laid down another layer of plastic beads, sintering them together into the shape of a scorpion body's abdomen. The circuitry inside flickered to life and with it, Parker was reborn.

He was gasping for breath, he realized. His heart was racing.

No. Neither of those things were true. He was a hologram now. He only existed inside the logic core lodged inside Rapscallion's chassis. He didn't need to breathe. He didn't need a heart.

"What the hell was that thing?" he asked.

Rapscallion didn't answer. One by one his legs were installed, the necessary attachments made, secured. One by one they flexed and bent and soon he was standing, the bright green plastic of his new body outgassing fumes in the cold room.

The left claw was attached. Then the right claw.

"You ready to get back to it, buddy?" Parker asked. "Ready to go find that guy and fuck him up?"

The left claw snapped at the air. Then the right one.

"Hell, yeah," Parker said. "Let's goddamn *go*."

Together they lurched out of the printer room, back to the fight.

163

•

"Petrova! Stop!" Zhang screamed.

He felt so powerless. He could only watch and wonder what was going on down there. He never for a moment thought it might be an illusion generated by the basilisk, just like the world around him. What he'd seen was real – perhaps it was some kind of visual metaphor, but that only made it more real than the lake and the sand where he was.

Below the methane sea of Titan, the image faded. As the light consumed Petrova, it dimmed and soon he could see her only as a pale shadow below the placid surface, and then not at all.

He tore at his hair, knowing she was in danger. Knowing she might already be lost.

He desperately wanted to fall down, to curl up in a ball and die. The basilisk had forced him to confront his own memories. To see Holly alive, and lose her all over again. Now – this? How much was it going to demand of him?

It was too much. It wasn't fair.

But all he could hear in his head was one thing. Petrova's voice – from right before they tried to fly down to the planet.

The thing about you, Zhang, is you're one of those people who just gets better in a crisis. You think you're broken. You think you're not strong enough. All I see is that when life throws shit at you, you keep getting stronger.

She'd said she would need him, when the time came. When there would be nobody else to be there for her, to help her.

He could do it. Maybe it was too late to keep the basilisk from infecting her but – he could do something.

Without so much as a thought he leaped into the liquid methane and dove deep, swimming hard to reach her. It seemed impossible. Titan's lakes were shallow, in some places only centimeters deep, but here, in the simulation, the liquid seemed to go on forever. The deeper he dove the bigger the ocean around him got.

The darker it got.

The colder it got.

He shoved all such thoughts away. The cold didn't matter. The pressure that threatened to cave in his chest. All that mattered was finding Petrova, and helping her, whatever that meant.

It was so dark he nearly swam right past her. Only by looking for the golden sweep of her hair did he catch the barest sight of her. He twisted around in the darkness and swam toward her, as fast as he could.

When he reached her, her eyes were open but it was clear she couldn't see him. She didn't respond at all. She wasn't breathing. Well, neither was he. Her skin felt cold but not frozen. He located her pulse and it was there, thready and weak but she was alive.

He looked around himself, hoping to find something to use to help her, to break her out of her trance. There was nothing. He didn't even think he was swimming anymore. What surrounded him wasn't liquid methane, nor was it water – it was simply inky blackness, the idea of darkness. More profound than the dark between the stars.

No.

No, that was what the basilisk wanted him to see. That was the prison it had made for them. It wanted them in darkness, so they couldn't see each other.

But the place they really were – it wasn't exactly brightly lit. But there was light there.

"Petrova," he said. "Petrova! Listen to my voice! Look at me!"

She didn't move. Her face was slack, expressionless. She looked like a corpse. Like Holly had looked when the last breath sighed out of her—

No. No!

Zhang thought about the red light of Asterion's avatars. He thought of the pale light coming in through the bridge's viewports. He closed his eyes and imagined that light, the way that it had caught the edges of the bridge's consoles, the hatches.

"Petrova!" he shouted. "Sasha!"

"Zhang?"

Her eyes were open and almost tracking him. They caught his face, met his gaze.

"Good," he said. "Good, look at me. Look at me! We have to get out of here. Focus. Okay? Just focus with me. We're stuck in our own heads. Lost in delusion. So we need to find something stronger. We need to find reality."

"Reality?"

"Focus on what your actual senses are telling you. Not this simulation. What do you smell? What do you actually smell? Do you hear anything? Anything real?"

"It's so dark here," Petrova said. "It's dark."

"No. Don't think about the darkness." He scowled, frustrated. Tried to think of something – anything that might bring her back to reality. He looked around again, as if something might have magically appeared. He could almost see the bridge viewports, he thought, almost see them outlined by dim light, but that . . . that wouldn't be enough.

He looked at Petrova and saw her floating, arms splayed out at her sides. Her arms – wait—

"Petrova," he said. "Listen to me. Make a fist. No, your left hand."

"It's . . . it's not working," she said, staring down at her left hand. "Oh, God. Oh, my fingers. Zhang—"

"It's okay. Listen. This is going to hurt. That's the point. Make a fist. Squeeze it as hard as you possibly can. Harder!"

"It hurts," she said. "Jesus, that hurts – so – much—"

He could only imagine the pain, as she squeezed her broken hand into a ball. As her barely set bones ground against each other. It must be excruciating.

He grabbed her hand with both of his and – squeezed. As hard as he could. It had to work. This had to work . . .

Petrova groaned with the pain. Then she screamed. But she didn't stop.

It was real. The pain was real. That was the point.

And then she was gone.

It happened much faster and more abruptly than he'd expected. It was like she'd blinked out of existence. And then he was alone.

Alone, floating in the dark. Nothing to stand on. Nothing to see.

The light – the red light of the avatars, he thought. The white edge of the bridge viewport. If he could see it, if he could make himself see it—

He squeezed his eyes shut. Ignored the black void, looked for the light. It was right there. It was real.

He opened his eyes.

And saw nothing but darkness, all around.

He was alone, and still trapped, and nothing he did could free him.

164

On the engineering deck a single hard light avatar held off thirty Rapscallion scorpions. It wasn't even a contest. The avatar just waded into the sea of toxic green and tore the robots to pieces.

Near the cryovault a Rapscallion unit was torn to pieces, one leg ripped free, then the next, then a pincer. He couldn't even see his attacker – the hologram had already torn out his eyes.

In the main shopping concourse the bodies lay like a field of new-mown wheat. Toxic green wheat, left to rot on the ground.

Rapscallion had fought a thousand such battles now, and had failed to win a single one. And yet the war had to go on. The only chance they had was to tie up so much of *Pasiphaë*'s resources that one Rapscallion unit might make it through, find Zhang and Petrova before it could be destroyed. The plan was simply to throw literal bodies at the problem in the hope of a miracle.

Egged on by Parker, he had, over and over and over, entered combat with an enemy he could not touch, but which could destroy him with one swipe of its vicious claws. A thing made of light and gravity. The combat had always been one-sided, and the machine always lost.

Every time.

So on a deck devoted to ship's stores, this particular Rapscallion unit clattered forward, pincers high, ready to be torn apart. Three avatars stood before him, roaring in anger, their clawed hands held high. The Rapscallion unit knew he had no chance, that this was just another foregone conclusion in a fight for attrition. He was ready, he told himself.

He was ready to die.

He was ready to give anything.

And so he was deeply surprised when death did not, immediately, arrive.

There was no way to explain it. One moment he was being beaten to pieces by an implacable hard light construct – its hands like mallets, its horns goring his chassis. The next . . .

The next moment, there was no construct. No hard light. Only darkness in the corridors of *Pasiphaë*.

"What just happened?" Parker asked.

It took a moment for Rapscallion to process that. His consciousness was spread so thin that solving a logic puzzle took more brainpower than he currently had. First there was a ship's avatar, then there was no ship's avatar—

They were gone.

"All of them?" Parker asked. A moment before there had been thousands of the things. All over the ship, on every deck, they'd burned with red light as they fought back against the invasion. They had destroyed thousands of Rapscallion's bodies, left *Pasiphaë* awash in broken scorpion legs and shattered pincers. The battle had been furious and desperate and Rapscallion was certain it could only end in his own death. He'd fought on because what choice did he have? Petrova and Zhang needed him.

Now . . .

"All of them," Parker said. "All of them! Gone!" Which left one important question. What next? Parker shook his hologram head. He wasn't the sort to waste an opportunity, Rapscallion knew. "Whatever. We need to find her. Can you tie into the ship's information systems? Scan for her?"

Rapscallion's left pincer was hanging on by a thread of strained plastic. It chose that moment to finally snap. The pincer clattered to the floor.

"Damn it, there has to be something—"

The robot turned slowly on his multiple legs, because he had heard something.

Behind them, a human woman gasped and ran away from them, up a long corridor.

"Come on," Parker growled.

Rapscallion surged forward. It was damaged but still far faster than any human. It only took a moment to catch up with the woman and pin her up against the wall. Parker's hologram blazed light into her face.

She looked terrified. Terrified and half dead.

Her skin was bad, covered in blemishes and pimples. Her cheeks were sunken and pale. Her hair was long but it looked patchy, like it was slowly falling out. Her clothes were badly stained and torn.

Her eyes were squeezed shut, her face turned away from the hologram as if she couldn't bear to look at it.

"What the hell?" Parker said.

"Release her," someone said, from behind them. Rapscallion turned to look and saw a man standing nearby. He looked like he was in just as bad shape as the woman, though his face was hidden behind a massive, untrimmed beard. He held one arm across his eyes as if trying to block out the light. "Please," he said. "Please let her go. Please let her go back to the dark. It's safe in the dark."

"It's safe in the dark," the woman chanted, desperately. "It's safe in the dark. It's safe in the dark!"

Parker sounded confused, but like he was figuring something out. If he was he was one step ahead of Rapscallion. "The lights," Parker said. "They tore out all the lights."

Rapscallion had noticed it as soon as they'd come aboard *Pasiphaë* but he'd never had a chance to mention it. All the light fixtures in the ceiling had been broken. Carefully. Methodically.

What was going on here? What had the basilisk done to these people?

Parker clearly had other things on his mind. "I need information. Tell me what I need to know and you can . . . go be in the dark, whatever. Or we can do this the hard way."

"Whatever you want!" the man raised his free hand in supplication. "Please! We saw what you did to Asterion. We'll tell you anything!"

"Petrova," Parker barked. "Where is she?"

"Petrova?" the man asked. "Which one?"

165
•

Petrova's eyes opened.

It felt like waking up. That first bleary moment when consciousness returns, when there are thoughts in your head, but they have not yet been applied to the real world.

She blinked. Her eyes felt sore, but they were hers. They were still hers.

The basilisk was inside her mind. There was no question about that – she could feel it in there, inside her skull. She imagined it burrowing, carving out a tunnel through her gray matter, looking for the best place to nestle in for a rest.

Absurd, of course. The basilisk didn't have a body, not in any real sense. It wasn't an actual parasite inside her cells. But that was exactly how it felt. She imagined the crew of *Alpheus* must have felt this exact same sensation. Except they had been deluded, and she wasn't.

"—did you do?" Mama shouted. "Get away from that thing right now, girl!"

"Too late," Petrova said. The avatar that had stared into her eyes disappeared, blinking out of existence. She was free.

She turned and smiled at her mother.

Ekaterina's mouth curled in revulsion. She fell back, one hand up as if to guard herself from an attack. What did she see in her daughter's face? What was there, now, that hadn't been before?

"You little fool," Mama said. She raced to a console and started typing commands into a virtual keyboard. It didn't seem like she liked what she saw on her holoscreen. For the moment she ignored her daughter. Petrova knew that wouldn't last.

She opened her mouth to say something, to try to mollify her mother. Before she could think of the right words, though, a screen lit up above the bridge controls, glaring with light in the darkened room.

"What's that?" Petrova asked.

"Friends of yours," Ekaterina said, "I presume." She waved at the screen and it expanded, showing a video feed of the cryovault of *Pasiphaë*. It was dark, so dark she couldn't make out many details, but she saw vast trees made of glass stretching upward, out of view, their roots shrouded in pale mist. The trees must be massive structures made out of thousands of cryotubes, she realized.

One side of the vault was littered with what looked like a drift of fallen leaves – they were green, anyway, though more of a fluorescent green than any natural color. Petrova knew that green, knew it quite well. It still took a second for her to realize what she was looking at.

The scale of the room she was looking at was enormous. That heap of fallen green was a pile of dead Rapscallion units. There must have been hundreds of them. The view zoomed in and she saw countless limp arms, heads with upside-down faces. Stingers and claws, what looked like swords and axe heads printed out of green plastic.

None of the units were moving. Then one of them did. A single unit, no bigger than a human child, crawled on many legs over the pile. A bluish-white human shape rode on its back.

"Parker!" she cried. That was Parker, manifesting from a holoprojector built into the Rapscallion unit's back. "What's he doing here?"

"A damned good job of destroying my ship," Ekaterina said. "They came aboard while you were under. I was holding him at bay for a while, using my avatars to fight back against his boarding party. Now you've gone and ruined that – they're gone."

"What? Who?"

"Asterion's avatars. All of them. They've just shut down. Asterion itself has vanished – maybe for good. I can't make contact with it at all. Damnation, girl. You can't imagine what you've ruined, here."

Parker. She had to get to him. But she wouldn't leave Zhang behind. She ran over to the chair where he sat, bound and gagged. The avatar that had been infecting him was gone, vanished like the rest. Zhang's eyes stared straight forward, transfixed by something she couldn't see. As gently as she could, she untied the restraints holding Zhang into his chair.

"Zhang?" she called, getting desperate. "Zhang? Can you hear me?" She slapped at his cheeks, gently, then harder.

His eyes twitched. Then they snapped closed.

"What ... Where?"

The RD twisted around his wrist, his forearm. She saw the golden snakes there had bitten his arm in a score of places. The machine must have been trying to wake him up, to break him out of his trance. Petrova placed two fingers against his throat and she felt his heart racing so fast she worried he might go into cardiac arrest.

The RD struck again, and soon his pulse began to slow. His eyes opened and he looked into hers and then he opened his mouth and let her remove the last cord. She tried to help him stand. His whole body was shaking and it was like he had no strength left at all.

"Do you have any idea," Ekaterina said, from behind her, "what you've taken on? What it will do to you?"

Petrova froze in place. For a moment.

"No," she said, without looking back. She was focused on Zhang. On getting him out of the chair. His muscles were so twisted up and tense he felt like he was a bundle of twigs – like if she wasn't careful she might snap him in a dozen pieces. "All I know is that it isn't yours anymore."

Zhang pushed her hand away and rose to his feet. He had to lean on the arm of the chair and he was very pale. The RD struck at his wrist again, and she wondered how safe it was to keep pumping him full of different drugs but she figured it had to know what it was doing. "Are you okay?" she whispered.

He gave her a feeble shrug. "I'm in shock, I think. From having to experience all of that again. I can walk," he said.

She nodded and got her good shoulder into his armpit so she could help support him. She turned to walk off the bridge, intending to go find Parker and figure out what to do next. She threw one last glance over her shoulder, at her mother.

She was not surprised by what she saw, though it took a moment to process.

Ekaterina had a pistol in her hand. A Firewatch standard issue weapon.

Petrova dropped her hand to her hip, but of course her holster was empty. Her mother had taken her own gun from her.

"How stupid do you think me, Sashenka?" Ekaterina said.

She flicked the gun toward the hatch that led off the bridge. "I want you to start walking," she said. "You can bring your friend. We have something we need to do."

166
.

"This way," Ekaterina said, from behind Petrova's shoulder. "Just go straight until I tell you to turn."

"I can't see where I'm going," Petrova complained. The light from the bridge didn't extend more than a few meters down the corridor.

"For God's sake, child. You have always been completely useless." Ekaterina had the gun in one hand. In the other she held something spherical, about the size of a baby's head. She clicked a switch on its side and it lit up so brightly Petrova couldn't bear to look at it. Some kind of hand lamp, she thought. It was the brightest thing she'd seen since they'd left *Alpheus*, and it made her whole head ache. "I keep these stashed all over the ship," Ekaterina said. "Did you believe that I would spend my life squatting in the dark like the fools on this ship?"

The three of them headed down the corridor. Slowly, as Petrova had to support some of Zhang's weight. She spent the time considering how she could get out of this. She could try to fight her mother, she supposed. She knew how foolish it would be to try to run at someone with a gun when all you had was one good hand. She could try to create a distraction, get her mother to look in the wrong direction, even for a moment . . .

This was Ekaterina Petrova she was thinking of. The woman had all but written the Firewatch operations manual. Petrova had no doubt that such an attempt would end with her getting shot and bleeding to death on the deckplates.

Maybe she could reason with her mother, she thought. "Your ship is under attack. Surely now's not the best time for this."

"It's the only time. Asterion went offline the moment the basilisk moved into your head," Ekaterina explained. "The only chance I have to drive off your friends is if I can get my avatars back up and running. You see the logic, yes? There's no choice, and no time for talking. Just up here," Ekaterina said. "There's a maintenance airlock. Open the inner door."

"And . . . then what?" Petrova asked.

"Then you're going to get inside and I'll close the hatch behind you," Ekaterina explained, as if her daughter should already have guessed. "You will return the basilisk to me. Otherwise I'll open the outer door and the two of you will be flushed out into space. Once you're dead, it will certainly return to me, since I'll be the only available host."

Zhang gasped in surprise. "You couldn't," he said.

Ekaterina walked over to the airlock hatch on her own, the gun's barrel pointed at them the whole time. She tapped the hand lamp against the release hatch. The door slid open.

"She's your daughter!" Zhang howled. "You can't do this!"

"I wish," Ekaterina said, "that Sashenka had given me any other choice. She acted very foolishly and now – as always – it is up to me to clean up her mess."

Petrova nodded and stepped toward the airlock. Zhang pulled her back, away from the hatch.

"She won't really do it," Zhang insisted. "She can't—"

Petrova knew better. She barely flinched when Ekaterina fired a bullet right between her feet. The noise shattered her calm, though, and she gasped, feeling desperate. Terrified. "Mother," she said. "Let him live. He's not part of this."

"Do you think me such a fool?" Ekaterina asked. "The basilisk would happily live inside his head. I need to eliminate you both.

Or, and I can't stress how obvious this choice ought to be – you can simply return to me what you stole."

"Mama," Petrova whispered. "Mama, I don't think it works like that." She could feel the basilisk inside her, recoiling at the idea of returning to Ekaterina's head. It would never go willingly.

"I've stated the options," Ekaterina said. "Let's proceed. The airlock, please."

"Why do you even want this?" Zhang asked. "You know what that thing is! What do you hope to achieve?"

"Power," Petrova said. "The only thing Mama ever stoops to achieve. She wants power, even if that means nothing but getting to boss around a bunch of deluded colonists on a—"

"Don't be such a whining fool," Ekaterina said.

"What?"

"You think I want power for my own sake? To stoke my ego?" Ekaterina looked distinctly offended. "I don't want to be in charge. I've never wanted that."

"Then ... why ..." Petrova shook her head. "I don't understand. You're willing to kill for power, but you don't want it? Why? Why do any of this?"

"Because I'm the only one who can." Ekaterina exhaled in frustration. "You'll never get it. That's the point. Nobody else can handle the pressure. No one else can make the hard decisions. And without someone like me, everything falls apart. I have to do this. I have no choice. I was chosen for this role, and unlike everyone else, I won't shirk my duty."

"Oh," Zhang said. "Now I get it."

For the briefest of moments Ekaterina blinked. It looked like she wanted to hear what he had to say next.

"You're full of shit," Zhang said.

The steel behind Ekaterina's eyes snapped back into place. "Airlock," she said. "Now."

Petrova's whole body trembled as she complied, climbing through the hatch. Zhang stepped in beside her.

Behind them the door slid shut. There was no light inside, and the sudden return to absolute darkness was shocking. It made Petrova feel like she couldn't breathe.

"She's bluffing," Zhang insisted. "She won't actually do this."

Petrova said nothing. She knew her mother better than that.

167
●

Parker raced down the corridor, the scorpion body under him bouncing on five legs. A sixth leg twitched wildly, its joints broken by an earlier encounter with one of the hard light avatars. Parker wouldn't let that slow him down.

Not now. Now when he finally had a chance.

Petrova was up there, just ahead. She was still alive – he didn't know that for a fact but he had to believe it. In a second he would find her and they would rescue her and . . .

And it didn't matter what happened after that.

Underneath him, Rapscallion came around the corner too fast and slid on the deckplates, his legs skittering madly, pushing off walls as he tried to right himself. Parker pointed at something up ahead and the unit dashed forward again. Responding to his command, Rapscallion slalomed around a corner, into a wider hallway.

They had found a good rhythm now, hologram and robot. Parker almost felt like he was some kind of centaur, like Rapscallion was his body, and that body responded to his every impulse, his every command. This was working, they were going to make it—

Without warning, bullets tore into their green plastic side. Smashed through their armor. One bullet tore through the processor core the two of them shared.

And suddenly they were two beings again, beings working at cross purposes.

Rapscallion lost control of his legs and twisted over on his side, sliding forward still on nothing but momentum. The robot tried to get his legs underneath him but he just couldn't coordinate his limbs, not with his circuits damaged like that. Parker grimaced in frustration as he watched what was essentially his body fail to stand up.

"That," he said, out loud, "was one hell of a shot."

"Captain Parker, I presume." A woman with a vast mane of hair stood there in the middle of the corridor. She held a pistol in one hand and a lamp in the other. Her face was a dispassionate mask. "I have four more bullets. I would suggest you don't come any closer."

Parker looked down at Rapscallion, thinking a question. *How fast can you move? Can you take her out before she shoots again?* The robot simply twitched his remaining legs, as if to shrug.

"Perhaps you don't care about your own safety," Ekaterina said. "I know you're here for my daughter. So think carefully before you do anything, Captain."

"She's in there, isn't she?" Parker asked, pointing at an airlock hatch behind Ekaterina. "You're going to kill her. You do understand – if you do that, I'll have nothing left to lose."

"Perhaps we're at a stalemate, then. All right, let's be reasonable. What if I promise you she'll live? What if I promise she'll be safe here, with me, her mother. If you agree to leave my ship and never come back."

"I won't do that," Parker told her.

"And why not?"

"Because I'm in love with her," the hologram said.

Ekaterina's eyes went wide. She tilted her head to one side. Then she started to laugh. It wasn't a very pleasant laugh. "Oh, this is rich. Sashenka never was any good at choosing men. Well. Then I have one more suggestion. I strongly suggest you back the *fuck* up."

Ekaterina dropped the lamp to fall at her feet. Its illumination spread long shadows up her face, making her look almost demonic. She reached over toward the airlock controls. It would only take a single keystroke to open the airlock's outer door.

"One touch, Captain. One keystroke and they're jettisoned into space."

Rapscallion twitched under Parker. One of his working legs stabbed into the darkness. Parker frowned, unsure what the robot was trying to tell him.

Then he saw a second Rapscallion unit emerge from the shadows down a side corridor. A third – and a fourth – came from the aft end of the ship, getting closer.

"Tell them to stay back," Ekaterina insisted. She must have seen them, too. "So there are more of you," Ekaterina said. "So what? What does that change?"

"They're not alone," Parker said.

A bedraggled, unhealthy woman stepped out of the shadows behind the bipedal units. The woman they'd found in the dark. She had one arm up and pressed against her eyes.

"Angie?" Ekaterina asked. "What are you doing here? What's going on?"

"What is that thing?" Angie asked. She sounded horrified. "What is that? How can you ... how can you have that?"

Parker wasn't sure what she meant, until Ekaterina looked down at her feet. At the hand lamp lying on the deck.

"I ... I can explain," Ekaterina sputtered. "This isn't what you think. I confiscated this from my daughter. My own blood was a light-hoarder! Angie, sacrifices must be made."

Another human, a male this time, came forward. "You're right," he said. There were others behind him. Dozens of them, scores. All of them as ragged and sick as their leaders. They had their hands pressed over their eyes, or simply looked away as if the wan radiance of the handlamp was enough to harm them.

"Michael," Ekaterina said, "this situation needs to be handled carefully, I don't recommend making any sudden ... any—"

The humans were moving toward her, surging forward now. They had their hands up, waving in front of them, like they would grab Ekaterina and tear her apart, even though they could barely stand to look at her.

"Oh, shit," Ekaterina said. She kicked the hand lamp toward the closest of the encroaching mob and then dashed up the corridor, away from the mob of them. Her people chased after her with cries of bloodlust and betrayed wrath.

Once they were gone, Parker waved forward the big tank-like Rapscallion unit. It extended three arms and tore the airlock hatch out of its frame. Inside, Petrova and Zhang looked up, blinking in astonishment, perhaps unsure of what they were seeing. There were at least twelve Rapscallion units outside the airlock at that point, in various configurations of chassis, weaponry and limbs.

But only one hologram. Only one Parker.

"Hey," he said. "Sasha. Hey. It's me."

168
•

"Sam," Petrova said. "I ... I just ... Sam—"

She had no idea what to say. She'd never been happier to see anyone in her life. She rushed forward and tried to throw her arm around Parker's neck. She went right through him, of course. He was made of normal light, the kind that couldn't hug her back.

He didn't seem to mind. It looked like there were tears in his eyes. "Did you ... did you hear us out here? Me, talking to your mom?"

"No," Petrova said. "No, we had no idea you were here. We were waiting to die."

"But then you came for us," Zhang said, rushing to grab two of Rapscallion's plastic arms. "It's, ah, good to see you, friend. It's so damned good to see you again."

The Rapscallion unit shrugged with half a dozen shoulders at once, and then patted Zhang on the head with a green limb like a halberd blade.

"He can't talk anymore," Parker explained. "There are too many of him. His consciousness is spread over too many bodies – all they can do now is fight. Turns out you don't need much processing power to know how to do that."

"You made it just in time." Petrova inhaled sharply. "Listen, we need to get off this ship. The crew of this ship – well, we didn't leave things too good with them. If they catch us we'll be in trouble."

"They're a little distracted at the moment," Parker said. "But yeah, I'm ready to get out of here myself."

"Did you forget there's like a hundred ships out there waiting to kill us?" Zhang asked.

"About that," Parker said, but she cut him off.

"The blockade will let us through. How do we get back to *Alpheus*?" Petrova called back, over her shoulder.

"We don't," Parker said.

"What?"

"*Alpheus* was destroyed seconds after we started attacking the blockade. They thought they could cut us off at the legs. The joke was on them – we had already abandoned *Alpheus*. We didn't need a ship anymore."

"But—What? How?"

"Rapscallion figured out how to hack into other ships' 3D printers. He didn't need to board the ships of the blockade. He just grew bodies inside of each of them, almost simultaneously. *Pasiphaë* was harder to breach but eventually he found a printer here he could take over."

"Wait. What about Actaeon?" she asked.

Parker's face fell. "We couldn't bring it with us. I'm sorry, it's gone. Its cores were destroyed along with *Alpheus*. If it's any consolation, Actaeon was never self-aware. It didn't feel anything when it died."

She tried to decide if that mattered to her or not. She wasn't sure. "We can mourn later. If you didn't come here on a ship, then—"

"Yeah," Parker said, "that means we need a different way out of here."

"There was that shuttle. In the hangar deck, when they brought us here," Zhang said.

"A shuttle won't get us very far," Parker said. "Those are meant for traveling from orbit down to a planet. It won't take us back to Earth – it won't even have cryotubes onboard for you two."

"We're not going back to Earth," Petrova said.

Zhang started to protest but in the end he just shook his head. "I guess ... yeah, there's nothing for us back there. Okay," he said. "Then what's our next stop?"

"We've been given permission to land," she said. "On Paradise-1."

"Permission?" Parker asked. "Permission from whom?"

"The basilisk," she said.

As if it had heard its name spoken the thing in her head twitched. It moved.

It felt exactly like an animal was trying to claw its way out of her brain. Like the basilisk was trying to hatch its way out of an egg, its claws digging at the inside of her skull. The pain was intense and bright spots swam before her eyes.

She doubled over, trying to catch her breath.

"Petrova!" Parker shouted. "Zhang, what's going on with her?"

"It's a long story," Zhang said.

She could barely hear him over the noise of the basilisk inside her mind. She understood what was happening, of course. This was a reminder. A reminder of who was in charge.

She thought of her mother. Ekaterina had tricked the thing. She'd accepted it inside her head and then refused to do its bidding. Used it for her own purposes. So the basilisk could be fought. Even in this new, weird symbiotic form, it could be reasoned with.

"Back off," she told it. "You want to go down to the planet? Then you need to calm the fuck down."

And – it worked.

The basilisk settled back down. It didn't quite go to sleep but she could sense it retracting its claws, giving her room to breathe again.

For now.

She forced herself to stand up straight, to breathe normally. Then she looked at the others. They were all staring at her. "I'm okay," she said. "I'm fine," she lied. "Come on, the hangar isn't far from here." She knew exactly how to get there, of course. The basilisk knew this ship intimately, and it was happy to give her directions.

169
●

As they rushed into the hangar, Zhang fully expected to see
that the shuttle was gone, or perhaps reduced to a pile of
wreckage. He'd been expecting to die for so long that when he
saw the shuttle sitting there in pristine condition, he was actually
surprised.

It sat next to the battered and crushed escape pod that had
brought them here. How strange it was to realize that had been –
what? Less than a day ago? A few sleeps?

How long, subjectively, had he been trapped in the simulation?

How long, he wondered, since Ganymede, when they'd first
climbed into their cryotubes, believing they'd been sent on a
banal mission to a backwater planet?

Sighing, Zhang turned to look at the big Rapscallion unit
that had accompanied them. Its green carapace was deeply
scarred, scorched black in places, missing limbs. He smiled
at the machine – then his mouth fell in horror as the robot
dropped heavily to the floor, all of its legs flailing out from
under it at once.

"Rapscallion!" Zhang shouted, thinking something bad had
happened to the robot. But at the same moment, the hangar's
hatch opened once more and a new Rapscallion body walked in.
One that was mostly the size and shape of a human being. He
even had a face, and that face was right side up.

"Present," the robot said.

"What ... what happened to the big one? And you can talk again – how—"

The robot shrugged. "I hated having all those bodies. I felt so incredibly dumb. Like a human, but ... you know ... dumber." He shook his green head.

"Time to go," Petrova called, from the shuttle's main hatch. Apparently there was no more time for catching up with old friends.

As she climbed up into the shuttle's passenger cabin, Zhang rushed over to help her with her straps. They would be hard to fasten, he thought, with just one working arm.

"Thanks," she said, giving him a look of actual gratitude. It made him smile in a goofy way. He couldn't help it.

"We make a pretty good team, huh?" he asked.

"Hopefully we'll get to keep being a team an hour from now when we're down on the planet."

He dropped into a seat of his own and pulled his straps tight, even as Rapscallion and the Parker hologram came up the aisle. Together, they climbed into the pilot and co-pilot seats at the front of the cabin.

"Parker," Zhang said, "I don't understand. You were being maintained by Actaeon's AI core. How are you even here?"

"Rapscallion agreed to let me share some of his processors. It was that or I had to stay behind," Parker explained. He reached over and pointed at various switches on the shuttle's control console, and Rapscallion flipped them for him as they ran through their pre-flight checks. "There's just about enough space for both of us in here."

"I had to shed about a hundred IQ points to make room," Rapscallion said.

"Give me some credit," Parker said. "Maybe a hundred and ten."

"You were willing to do that for him?" Zhang asked, nodding at the robot.

"It's funny. You humans keep surprising me," Rapscallion said. "I didn't think I had a use for any of you until I met you three. Then when the time came to abandon *Alpheus*, I realized something truly unique in my experience."

"What's that?" Zhang asked.

"I didn't want to leave Parker to die," Rapscallion said. "I know. It confused me, too. I mean, he's already dead. Isn't he? I'm still not really clear on that. Humans are weird."

"Everybody hold on," Parker said. As the shuttle's engines started to whine and build up power, Zhang looked across the aisle, at Petrova. She surprised him by reaching over and grabbing his hand. "I know you don't like being touched," she said, "but I need this."

"I'm willing to make an exception," he said.

With a lurch, the shuttle jumped forward and out of the hangar doors, out into space. It was finally happening, finally real. They were off *Pasiphaë*. They had survived.

"Shit," Rapscallion said, moments after they reached outer space. "Would you look at this."

Normally, there wasn't a lot to see through the viewports of a spacecraft. The sun of the Paradise system was bright enough to wash all the other stars out of the sky, and the other ships of the blockade should have been far enough away to just be dull specks of gray against the black. Not now.

Now the local volume of space was chock-full of debris. Countless pieces of wreckage caromed off each other, spinning and sparkling with clouds of metal and plastic reduced to floating dust.

"Is that the blockade?" Zhang asked, incredulous.

"What's left of it. We kind of made a mess on the way in," Rapscallion told them. "Parker and I kind of fucked up all their shit."

"Good job. But can you fly through all that debris?" Petrova asked.

"I hope so," Parker said. "Rapscallion — start building a 4D map of all this. We can take it careful and slow but this shuttle wasn't built to take an impact. One good hit and the only way we're getting down to the planet is as a meteor shower."

"Got it," Rapscallion said. "I can see a couple of routes that look pretty safe. No guarantees, of course."

Parker started to laugh. "Like it was ever going to be easy."

170

It was a rough descent, especially once they hit the atmosphere. Parker was a hell of a pilot, but the debris had been too random, too chaotic, and he'd taken a few grazing hits that left gouges in their heat shielding.

They hit the atmosphere hard, all of them being thrown around in their straps like rag dolls. They came down too fast, too hot, but Parker pulled them out of a death spiral and leveled them out. There was a landing strip dug into the hills just outside the main colony. Parker set them down as gently as he could. Unfortunately, the shuttle's lack of heat shielding meant the tires had melted off their landing gear. The shuttle slid to a stop in a firestorm of sparks then smashed nose first into the concrete, leaving its sensor pods crumpled and its controls destroyed. But it was down.

Zhang and Petrova jumped through the emergency exit hatch and clung to each other as they adjusted to standing in planetary gravity again. It had been months, even if they'd spent a lot of that time in cryosleep. Rapscallion watched as they headed over toward the colony.

"Any landing you can walk away from, I guess," Parker said, appearing out of nothing at the robot's side.

"Easy for you to say," Rapscallion told him. "You don't even have legs."

Paradise-1 was well within the habitable range for human life.

It had liquid water at the surface. The sunlight was bright and clear but not so intense it was likely to cause skin cancer as long as you were careful. The average temperature was brisk rather than freezing and the local gravity was about a third what you would experience on Earth. Zhang had a little trouble with it but Petrova seemed absolutely fine.

The planet didn't look like Earth, though. There was very little plant life except the few trees and fields of staple crops the colonists had planted. The landscape was dominated by enormous lava tubes that formed structures as varied and dramatic as a coral reef, though not as colorful. Brownish-gray rock stood up in enormous clusters of thick columns that sometimes radiated outward like a bouquet of alien flowers, or formed long rows of equal-sized tubes like organ pipes. The colonists had discovered early on that you could build well-insulated, energy-efficient homes inside those columns. A town of them had sprung up in the shelter of a low mountain range, maybe a hundred columns pierced everywhere by windows and thick hatches. Petrova ran up to the first one she saw and knocked on its front door. When there was no response she ran to the next.

"That one's open," Zhang said, breathing hard. He'd run on ahead of her, fast enough to lose his breath. He went over to the door he'd indicated, which stood ajar, revealing only darkness inside. "Hello?" he called. "Hello?" He stepped into the shadows. Petrova's heart leaped. She ran to the hatch door of one of the columnar buildings. She slapped the release pad and the hatch sighed open. She guessed people around here didn't lock their doors. She went inside, calling out so the occupants wouldn't be surprised.

She found a bunkroom on the first floor, a room full of narrow beds with rumpled sheets. Dirty clothes and toiletries littered the floor. It looked like a messy dorm, nothing more. She smelled something a bit off, but it looked like this was housing for young people so that wasn't too surprising. Beyond the bunkroom was a kitchen with broad tables, meant to serve communal meals by the look of it. A massive kettle sat on top of the stove and dirty dishes littered the table. She went over to examine the pot. When she lifted the lid, a thick, organic stink came out that made her want to immediately retch.

What had they been cooking? And how long had they left it sitting there?

She hurried back out into the street. Zhang emerged from the door of his own building. "Anything?" he asked.

"Nobody home," she told him. "What about—?" She pointed at his building.

He shook his head. "I thought maybe they were all at work. But look." He nodded at the planted field just the other side of the street. The crops there were tall and looked healthy, but a little bedraggled. Weeds had sprung up between the rows of corn and potatoes and one side of the plot looked like it hadn't been watered in far too long.

Petrova's heart skipped a beat. "Where are they?" she asked.

"Hello?" Zhang shouted. "Hello? Anyone?"

No. No, this didn't make any sense. They'd been sent here to check on the place. Maybe Director Lang had had other motives, but – the basilisk had assured her that there were people here. There had been a thriving colony before the basilisk arrived, before it started taking over all the ships in the blockade.

There had definitely been people here. She saw clothes hanging on lines, set out to dry in the sun. Jumpsuits and scarves and coats. They looked bleached by long exposure to ultraviolet light. Some of them were in tatters, as if torn by strong winds.

She ran inside another building and it turned out to be an infirmary. Robotic arms stirred at her approach and one tried to reach for her bad hand. "Hello?" she called. There was no answer. She found packs of blood sitting out on a counter, long since clotted up to uselessness. A doctor's white coat hung off the back of a chair. A cup of coffee or tea or something sat on a nearby table, but the liquid inside had dried to a thick sludge, then cracked like desert mud.

The next building was a communal nursery, with tiny beds and paintings of animals on the walls.

"Hello?"

It was empty.

She found a silo, and a shed for farming equipment. The machines sat motionless, though as she came in their lights flickered on expectantly, as if they'd been waiting a long time to be given instructions.

"Hello?"

Across town she heard Zhang's voice. Distant and faint. *"Hello? Someone answer! Hello!"*

She stepped back out into the street, looking up and down the line of buildings. Looking for any clue, anything that might tell her what had happened.

Where was everyone?

"Hello!" Zhang shouted. *"Hello!"* The tone of his voice was changing, changing from a question to a scream.

TO BE CONTINUED ...

ACKNOWLEDGEMENTS

No book is ever truly created by a single person, and that is especially true in the case of *Paradise-1*. The book started out as a collaborative effort, with the main plot beats and the characters created by a small group of people at Orbit UK. Anna Jackson, Jenni Hill, and James Long created Petrova and Zhang, and got them in trouble. Then they graciously asked me to help them escape the basilisk. My name may be on the cover of this book but it truly belongs to them. James also edited the book and worked with me directly on every step of the creative process. Sandra Ferguson went over the manuscript with a fine-tooth comb and caught all my dumb mistakes. Joanna Kramer managed the process and kept me on deadline. The entire staff at Orbit UK has been nothing but generous with their time, their ideas, and their willingness to take this trip with me. I am truly grateful for all their help and hope we get to do a dozen more of these stories!

David Wellington, New York City, 2022

meet the author

DAVID WELLINGTON is an acclaimed author who has previously published over twenty novels in different genres. His novel *The Last Astronaut* was shortlisted for the Arthur C. Clarke Award.

Find out more about David Wellington and other Orbit authors by registering for the free monthly newsletter at orbitbooks.net.

Follow us:

f **/orbitbooksUS**

🐦 **/orbitbooks**

▶️ **/orbitbooks**

Join our mailing list
to receive alerts on our
latest releases and deals.

orbitbooks.net

Enter our monthly
giveaway for the chance
to win some epic prizes.

orbitloot.com